'A work whose joys are so many and so varied ... displays how flexible and original the Irish tradition is'

Erica Wagner, *The Times*

'A new and refreshing attempt to map out the shape of contemporary Irish fiction'

Bill Maxwell, *Irish Independent*

'Impressively comprehensive and even-handed, a very satis-fying volume. I remain very impressed with the scope and sweep of the book ... presenting what has been happening on the cutting edge of Irish fiction over the past quarter century'

Noeleen Dowling, *Irish Evening Press*

'For any readers who think short stories in pastoral terms of yon green hills and country folk, the anthology is a revelation. Indeed, it revels in diversity of subject and approach. To be sure, that Ireland of yesterday can be found in William Trevor's poignant "The Ballroom of Romance", in which a 39-year-old spinster who looks after her crippled father and a small farm finally puts away thoughts of love. But it's a gritty, urban Ireland that encompasses the characters in an excerpt from Roddy Doyle's vibrant "The Snapper"'

Nancy Pate, *The Orlando Sentinel*

Born in Dublin in 1959, Dermot Bolger has been at the heart of the new wave of Irish writing, both as an award-winning novelist and playwright and also, for the fifteen years of its existence, as founder, publisher and editor of the Raven Arts Press – and more recently as co-founder and executive editor of New Island Books.

He has published seven novels, *Night Shift*, *The Woman's Daughter*, *The Journey Home*, *Emily's Shoes* and *A Second Life* (all with Penguin) and *Father's Music* and *The Temptation* (both Flamingo). He also edited and co-wrote the collaborative novel *Finbar's Hotel* and edited its sequel, *Ladies Night at Finbar's Hotel*.

His eight plays include *The Lament for Arthur Cleary*, *In High Germany*, *The Holy Ground*, *Blinded by the Light* and *The Passion of Jerome* (all published by Methuen) and *April Bright* and *One Last White Horse*.

The author of six volumes of poetry (more recently, *Taking My Letters Back – New & Selected Poems*), he has received, among others, The Samuel Beckett Award, The A. E. Memorial Prize, The Stewart Parker BBC Prize, two Edinburgh Fringe First Awards and The Macaulay Fellowship.

He lives and works in Dublin.

THE NEW PICADOR BOOK OF

Contemporary
Irish Fiction

Edited by Dermot Bolger

PICADOR

First published 1993 by Picador as
The Picador Book of Contemporary Irish Fiction

This expanded edition published 2000 as
The New Picador Book of Contemporary Irish Fiction by Picador
an imprint of Macmillan Publishers Ltd
25 Eccleston Place, London SW1W 9NF
Basingstoke and Oxford
Associated companies throughout the world
www.macmillan.co.uk

ISBN 0 330 37216 5

1 3 5 7 9 8 6 4 2

A CIP catalogue record for this book is available from
the British Library.

Typeset by SetSystems Ltd, Saffron Walden, Essex
Printed and bound in Great Britain by
Mackays of Chatham plc, Chatham, Kent

Contents

Introduction – xi

Editor's Note to this Expanded Edition – xxxii

PART ONE

Samuel Beckett – *For to End Yet Again* – 3

PART TWO

Tom Mac Intyre – *The Man-Keeper* – 9

Sean O'Faolain – *The Talking Trees* – 14

Mary Leland – from *The Killeen* – 29

Desmond Hogan – from *A Curious Street* – 36

Francis Stuart – from *Black List, Section H* – 44

Jennifer Johnston – from *The Christmas Tree* – 57

PART THREE

John McGahern – *High Ground* – 67

Bridget O'Connor – *Postcards* – 79

Bryan MacMahon – *A Woman's Hair* – 83

Aidan Higgins – from *Balcony of Europe* – 91

Mary Lavin – *Happiness* – 95

Contents

Éilís Ní Dhuibhne – *Blood and Water* – 113

Shane Connaughton – *Ojus* – 126

Patrick McCabe – from *The Butcher Boy* – 142

Clare Boylan – *Villa Marta* – 152

Glenn Patterson – from *Burning Your Own* – 161

Eugene McCabe – *Cancer* – 171

PART FOUR

William Trevor – *The Ballroom of Romance* – 187

Molly Keane – from *Good Behaviour* – 209

Neil Jordan – *Last Rites* – 216

Bernard MacLaverty – *Between Two Shores* – 226

Mary Beckett – *Heaven* – 240

Val Mulkerns – *Memory and Desire* – 250

Mary Dorcey – *The Husband* – 265

Edna O'Brien – *What a Sky* – 282

PART FIVE

Roddy Doyle – from *The Snapper* – 295

David Park – *Oranges from Spain* – 303

Eoin McNamee – *If Angels had Wings* – 319

Benedict Kiely – from *Proxopera* – 325

Maeve Kelly – *Orange Horses* – 334

Dermot Bolger – from *The Journey Home* – 348

Colm Tóibín – from *The Heather Blazing* – 357

Joseph O'Connor – *Mothers Were All the Same* – 373

Sara Berkeley – *The Sky's Gone Out* – 387

Contents

Robert McLiam Wilson – from *Ripley Bogle* – 398

Hugo Hamilton – from *Surrogate City* – 405

Michael O'Loughlin – *A Rock-'n'-Roll Death* – 418

Deirdre Madden – from *Remembering Light and Stone* – 425

Sebastian Barry – from *The Engine of Owl-Light* – 432

Brian Moore – *The Sight* – 442

Aidan Mathews – *Incident on the El Camino Real* – 463

PART SIX

Anne Enright – *Men and Angels* – 481

Gerardine Meaney – *Counterpoints* – 490

Leland Bardwell – *The Hairdresser* – 496

John Banville – from *Mefisto* – 504

PART SEVEN

Dermot Healy – *The Death of Matti Bonner* – 511

John MacKenna – *Absent Children* – 520

Mary Morrissy – *Divided Attention* – 524

Colum McCann – *Through the Field* – 534

PART EIGHT

Antonia Logue – from *Shadow Box* – 549

Seamus Deane – from *Reading in the Dark* – 563

Philip Casey – from *The Water Star* – 570

Blánaid McKinney – *The Outfielder, the Indian-Giver* – 580

Mike McCormack – *Thomas Crumlesh 1960–1992: A Retrospective* – 627

Contents

Ronan Bennett – from *The Catastrophist* – 635

Frank Ronan – from *Lovely* – 644

Emma Donoghue – from *Hood* – 656

Keith Ridgway – from *The Long Falling* – 666

Micheál Ó Conghaile – *Father* – 676
(translated by Frank Sewell)

Anne Haverty – from *One Day as a Tiger* – 685

Maeve Brennan – *The Springs of Affection* – 698

Eamonn Sweeney – from *Waiting for the Healer* – 742

Claire Keegan – *The Ginger Rogers Sermon* – 752

Niall Williams – from *Four Letters of Love* – 767

Biographical Notes – 777

Acknowledgements – 788

Introduction (1994)

OVER THE past two and a half decades an extraordinary
explosion of contemporary Irish writing has forced its way
on to the centre stage of the English language. This new awareness of Irish writing is constantly growing, with débuts of new
Irish writers a perpetual occurrence in Ireland, England and
elsewhere. This anthology focuses on the huge range of fiction
written in this period, which has appeared simultaneously with
the poetry of Seamus Heaney, Derek Mahon, Medbh Mc-
Guckian, Anthony Cronin, Paul Durcan and Michael Hartnett
in English, and Nuala Ní Dhomhnaill and Michael Davitt in
Irish, the richly innovative Irish language fiction of writers like
Séamus Mac Annaigh in novels such as *Cuaifeach moo Londubh
Buí*, and the plays of Tom Murphy and Brian Friel. Indeed one
of the most interesting features of the younger generation of
writers included here is the breaking down of barriers before
forms – six of those born after 1955 began their careers as poets
and five are also playwrights.

The scope and achievement of this fiction is remarkable
if you take into consideration that the combined population
of Ireland – North and South – is approximately half that of
London. It is even more remarkable when viewed in the overall
context of Irish literature produced within this century. Dublin,
for example, a city roughly the size of Bologna, has produced
three Nobel Prize winners in literature with Yeats, Shaw and
Beckett, in addition to Joyce (probably the most important
prose writer of the century), J. M. Synge and Oscar Wilde, as
well as housing – and inspiring for all his working life – that
wondrous multi-layered mind which singularly comprised the

Unholy Trinity of Flann O'Brien, Brian O'Nolan and Myles na Gopaleen.

Possessing such immediate and famous ancestors can be both beneficial and problematic. The benefits include inheriting a sense of self-confidence and (through Joyce and Beckett) a sense of belonging within the mainstream of European literature. The problems would include the fact that if, as Joyce said, history was a nightmare from which we were trying to awaken, then frequently Joyce and others are shadows that newer Irish writers are trying to avoid being pushed under. It is not just a case that we are presumed to share a city or country with Joyce, but those themes which obsessed him and his generation – Catholicism and Nationalism and the role of the artist – are somehow supposed to be central to our own work, so that at times our work can be judged on how we handle subjects which are, in fact, absent from them. In my early childhood even if *Ulysses* was not actually banned it still had the reputation of being difficult to acquire. A walk through the streets of Dublin today would tell you how Ireland has changed. Any public house which is not currently named after Joyce or one of his characters is likely to be so rechristened should you turn your back. Inside them badly executed pen sketches of Joyce, Yeats, Beckett, Flann O'Brien and Patrick Kavanagh line the walls like photofit portraits of criminals in a police station. Contemporary politicians invoke Joyce and other writers in all kinds of unlikely contexts with a fervour only equalled by that with which clerics once denounced them. If all this lip-service can frequently add up to a sense of claustrophobia for a young Irish writer, it is also the reflection of a society where the printed word is still of prime importance, where writers are still read by a far wider cross-section of the public than elsewhere and – by the nature of the size of the country – where the success of writers can at times be watched, shared or argued about with great intensity.

Yet Ireland is also a society which has changed, in some respects, more rapidly in the past quarter of a century than many European countries. Independence for the South was followed by several decades of adjustment that were characterized by an inward-looking stagnation, and this sense of isolation was reinforced by Ireland's neutrality in the Second World War – far more understandable when one remembers that it was just seventeen years since we had finally and forcibly persuaded a foreign army, whom we would have had to invite back in, to end a seven-hundred-year occupation. All this, plus a stringent censorship and mass emigration, kept the post-war changes sweeping through Europe at bay. It was only in the 1960s, when this anthology begins, that Ireland began to emerge from this stagnation.

In many instances since then, sections of the country have taken to the twentieth century like Hollywood Indians to whiskey. From being an essentially drug-free culture some years previously, by the mid-eighties Dublin had become the heroin capital of Europe. Where many European countries have a declining population, almost half the Irish population is now under twenty-five. For the past quarter of a century the most extraordinary violence has been an everyday reality in Northern Ireland. And the more intense the Northern violence has become, the greater the distance has grown between the two states on the island. Although some commentators still speak simply about two cultures existing in Ireland – a Catholic/Nationalist and Protestant/Unionist one, the response of the largely untouched South to the frequent barbarism of both sides in the North has been such that recent statistical analysis has shown the citizens of the Irish Republic to feel now that they have more in common with the Scottish, Welsh and English than with any section of the population in the North.

The introduction in 1968, the year the work in this anthology begins, of free second-level education in the Republic of Ireland obviously had a profound effect (as did the British Education Act when belatedly introduced in Northern Ireland) in producing new writers and readers. Although many writers who stayed in Ireland in the 1940s and 50s fought against cultural stagnation – O'Faolain and Peadar O'Donnell being examples – there were others who while at once disgusted by the attitudes of the young state were also, as has been pointed out, the middle-class inheritors of that state – the chosen people who were going to be the judges, broadcasters and senior civil servants. Often these writers chose to keep the realities of their country at bay in their work, to create either an aesthetic or a hackneyed version of Ireland (loved by foreign literary editors) to hide behind, while the rest of us were simply washed away by emigration. But by 1968 emigration had stopped briefly, a young educated generation were coming up who were not going to be shunted abroad or walk into safe living-death jobs, a generation of writers and readers who had nothing to lose by taking apart that state to examine how it worked inside. The intense fury surrounding John McGahern's *The Dark* (which was banned in 1966), the vehement rejection by the Abbey Theatre of Tom Murphy's raw and violent study of an immigrant family, *A Whistle in the Dark* (1961), on the grounds that such people did not exist in Ireland, the controversy surrounding Eugene McCabe's stage début with *King of the Castle* in 1964, and the end of Edna O' Brien's *Girls in Their Married Bliss* in 1964, mark four good starting points in the history of the struggle by contemporary Irish writers to write in their own way and to have that work recognized on its own merit – both inside and outside Ireland.

This struggle has continued for the past quarter of a century. One vital breakthrough has been the development of a vibrant, indigenous Irish publishing industry. Eleven of the pieces included here were first published in book-form by Irish publishers, others like John McGahern's 'High Ground' or Clare Boylan's 'Villa Marta' or my own extract, first appeared in the *Irish Press* and the *Irish Times* and the *Sunday Tribune*, while yet another twenty-one of the writers have had other books published in Ireland.

As a young publisher I remember trying to interest a London publisher in co-imprinting the work of an Irish poet. 'This work is marvellous,' the publisher replied, 'but when I want to read about urban blight I read a poet from Hull and when I want to read about the countryside I read a poet from Ireland.' Rather like the EC milk-quota scheme, the idea existed that we were some sort of minor tributary of British literature with our allotted role to play there. The ridiculous phrase 'Anglo–Irish literature' has helped to reinforce this academic crippling notion of what constituted Irish literature, so that the literature of a young nation undergoing such rapid change was still supposed to be denominated either exclusively by the Northern Troubles or by icons like the Catholic Church, an inbred peasant hunger for land, red-haired girls on the bog or navvies lusting after pints of porter. Looking through American or British publishers' catalogues it was hard to find an anthology of Irish writing without its cover photo of broken Celtic crosses or donkeys who gave the impression of being stuffed and moved from location to location in the photographer's boot. European cover designers have been more inclined to the geographically bizarre notion that British tanks cause most of the potholes in the roads of Dublin.

All the above issues may still have their place within the themes of Irish literature, even if that place is now generally tiny. Indeed Eugene McCabe's recent *Death and Nightingales* (1992), set in 1883, has reclaimed and reinvented a great deal of this traditional raw material, only now approached with savage honesty. And there is no doubting the major and continuing importance of the Northern Troubles. As writers like Benedict Kiely, David Park, Eoin McNamee, Glenn Patterson and Eugene McCabe have shown here (in addition to poets like Ciaran Carson and Padraig Fiacc and playwrights like Graham Reid), this terrible slaughter is something which Irish writers have confronted – frequently with great humanity, outrage, insight and success. It has unfortunately also, especially in the 1970s and early 1980s, exercised the minds of an extraordinarily large number of second-rate, non-Irish novelists who flooded bookshops with stunningly ill-informed and ill-conceived novels centring on what is called 'The Troubles'.

All this – along with various anthologies of poetry and prose – helped for a period to reinforce the notion that the North was central to all Irish writing, so that, as a writer from the Republic of Ireland – which is three times the size of the North – one frequently felt that you were writing about a society which had been rendered invisible. The genuine changes and struggles and the separate reality of people's lives in the South seemed to count as nothing for academics, editors and critics with their own agendas. One was confronted by a constant set of double standards. While anthologies of Northern writing or documentaries and studies of it frequently appeared, any anthology of writing solely from the Irish Republic would have been condemned.

Even Patrick Kavanagh, Ireland's most important poet after Yeats, was attacked by one influential critic, for being 'a Free State poet' and for not dealing with themes like colonization (which would not have existed to any major extent in the society he knew around him) rather than for reflecting the reality of his own country.

Certainly there are strong overlaps and shared understandings, but in terms of education, background and social experience this anthology contains the work of two very distinct societies. The sense of entrapment in a duality between being Irish and British is something which seems to have genuinely exercised and troubled the minds of many Northern writers, and which is a very real and fundamental issue for them. It is an issue which has produced great individual works of literature from both sides, like the poetry of Heaney and others and the plays of Brian Friel, and from some older Southern-born writers like the playwright Thomas Kilroy and the novelist William Trevor. Yet it is no more possible for critics to impose these writers' valid sense of 'colonialism' or 'post-colonialism' on the rest of the island than it is for me, as a young Southern writer (from a society more interested in a contemporary and very different – if equally challenging and potentially diverse – relationship with Europe), not to acknowledge that their dilemma genuinely exists.

Almost three-quarters of a century has passed since the Irish Republic, under different guises, attained its independence. Of the thirty-two writers born in the South, only four were born before the British army was expelled in 1922. While fully respecting any struggle with identity that they, or others born in the early years of the state, may – or indeed may not – have, it is simply not possible to allow a phrase like 'postcolonial literature' still to wander about like a decomposing chicken in search of its head, and to have it foisted upon the backs of younger writers.

The inherent suggestion behind it is of a society somehow obsessed with its relationship with a former colonial power – something which might certainly have been true in the pre-European Community society of a quarter of a century ago, but on which the work in this volume speaks for itself. Certainly I have never felt myself to be either a post-colonial writer or engaged in anything as marginal as Anglo-Irish literature (summed up, perhaps a tad excessively, by Joseph O'Connor as 'anybody who owned a castle and scribbled'), and I doubt if any of the young Southern writers included here would feel otherwise.

What is certain is that over the past quarter of a century Irish society, North and South, has undergone intense changes. This anthology sets out to attempt to throw off both the supposed shadow of previous Irish writers and predecimal notions of what is still supposed to dominate Irish writing. It tries instead to capture the true scale and achievement of a new, vibrant literature perfectly capable of standing by itself. By using only fiction published in the last quarter of a century, loosely arranged in the chronological order of the period in which it is set, the book moves from the traditional to the iconoclastic and futuristic to capture the contemporary Irish experience, as much in America, Britain and Europe as in the Republic of Ireland and Northern Ireland themselves. This covers the late triumphs of Samuel Beckett, Sean O'Faolain, Mary Lavin and Francis Stuart, the generation of John McGahern, Edna O'Brien, John Banville and Jennifer Johnston, and moves right down to rapidly emerging figures like Patrick McCabe, Colm Tóibín, Anne Enright and Glenn Patterson.

Although anthologies of Irish fiction are not uncommon, most still in print are out of date by a decade and almost all have focused exclusively on the tradition of the Irish short story. These give us a view of modern Irish literature going back to Daniel Corkery's *The Hidden Ireland*, and continuing with Frank

O'Connor, Liam O'Flaherty and all those who worked in the tradition of 'the lonely voice'.

The myth of the short story as Ireland's national art form has had a good innings. In the past it was, perhaps at least domestically, more easily understandable and even, in cases, politically desirable. The short story was certainly going to shine brighter in an environment where novels by almost every major Irish writer were being banned. Yet even today in *The Granta Book of the American Short Story* (1992), editor Richard Ford has no hesitation in declaring the short story to be Ireland's national art form. Likewise, Ben Forkner, in his introduction to *Modern Irish Short Stories* (1981), speaks of a writer like Aidan Higgins, with his short story 'Killachter Meadow', making a brilliant contribution to 'one of the triumphant achievements of a national art form in modern times'.

While Forkner is most certainly correct in praising 'Killachter Meadow', the ironic point he misses is that Aidan Higgins was not content with that achievement, and – perhaps in a metaphor for the way Irish prose has changed – went on to develop 'Killachter Meadow' into his far more significant 1966 novel, *Langrishe, Go Down* – described by the *Irish Times* at the time as 'clearly the best novel by an Irish writer since *At Swim Two Birds* and the novels of Beckett'. That refusal to be content to work within any supposed tradition has been a hallmark of much Irish writing since. John Banville's début, *Long Lankin* (1970), was his only brush with the short-story form and never approaches the power which he immediately brought to bear on the novel form. John McGahern's three books of stories are superb achievements in themselves but never, for me, quite match the savage black intensity of his novels like *The Barracks* (1963), *The Dark* (1965) or his recent *Amongst Women* (1990).

Looking back at the achievements with the short-story form of Frank O'Connor and Sean O'Faolain – who both did try novels like *The Saint and Mary Kate* (1932) or *Bird Alone* (1936) – it is hard to know how much the problems of censorship in their own country influenced their bent towards short fiction (there is a thirty-nine-year gap between novels for O'Faolain), or how much the society they existed in lent itself more readily towards the short story. One of them once joked that as the entire population went to weekly confession a writer only had seven days to develop a plot and bring it to a conclusion. Certainly, as Colm Tóibín has pointed out, Irish writers of the period discovered that by swapping Joyce's legacy of novels for the let-out at the end of his story, 'The Dead', 'if you wrote short stories you didn't have to mention sex, you could end in the bedroom with the spurned husband contemplating the snow'. Short stories occur in a limited place and time. Within that form, Tóibín claimed, 'we need not deal with the bitterness of the past, the confusion of the present or the hopelessness of the future'. In such a society where censorship and mass emigration were rampant 'the writing of short stories is a suitable solution to the writer's dilemma'.

I am not in any way attempting to put down the shortstory form – 'The Talking Trees' (1971) and 'Happiness' (1969), both included here, are classic examples (from a huge legacy) of what it can achieve, while the more recent stories of Anne Enright and Aidan Mathews show just how alive and reinvented the form is today. But the belated acknowledgement has to be made that *Ulysses* and *Finnegans Wake*, along with Beckett's trilogy and *At Swim Two Birds*, among others, make the novel as much, if not far more, a national art form than the short story ever was. And certainly, in a society where confession is no longer the social highlight of the week, where censorship of fiction has essentially long ceased and – perhaps just as important – where the equally dangerous (and potentially far more self-crippling) censorship of political correctness has not taken a stranglehold, the major achievements of contemporary Irish fiction in recent years have been most frequently in the novel form. In this situation it seems to me no longer possible to produce a volume that is representative of an overview of Irish fiction comprising only short stories, which is why there are seventeen extracts from novels included here.

In attempting to reflect the cutting (and changing) edge of contemporary Irish literature in this book I have decided, as previously stated, to focus purely on fiction which has been published since 1968. Although this brings in many major figures like Mary Lavin, Samuel Beckett, Sean O'Faolain and Francis Stuart who were born in the early years of the century, it presents their later work within the context of the younger writers working around them.

With fifty writers included there are many different forces, perspectives and generations working within this book. As against simply arranging the authors by age, I have been anxious to throw them together, occasionally spark unlikely combinations off each other and observe both the differences and similarities between how different generations approach certain themes and periods. Essentially the work is presented in a loose chronology based on the period, and occasionally place, in which it is actually set.

This is not to suggest, in any way, that the work should be read purely as an historical journey through a society. Part of the liberation of these writers is that few see themselves as social commentators. Each has been concerned with creating his or her own fictional universe, and it is within the contexts of these private worlds that they should be judged. None of these stories or extracts were chosen for the period in which they are set and no work was excluded for the same reason. But the one thing that unites so many of these authors (and characterizes much contemporary Irish, and indeed American, fiction) is the sense of being engaged with understanding both their own and their parents' past. As I began to collate my selections from each author's work the general order of this book began to fall naturally into place.

Yet what excites me most about the writers in this anthology is not the things that unite their work, but the extraordinary diversity of themes and styles displayed here. One writer I have obviously left outside of any time-frame is Samuel Beckett (b. 1906) – an increasingly central figure, I suspect, to many new writers here. Other pieces like Tom Mac Intyre's (b. 1931) marvellous 'The Man-Keeper' (which hones down all the simplicity, vividness and freedom of folklore) simply and joyously refuse definition, while a story like Bryan MacMahon's (b. 1909) tender exploration of an instinctive bond between two women, which crosses the barriers of age and class, is essentially timeless. Rather than proving any central point, many of the pieces put side by side frequently contradict and jostle with each other. Their themes, styles, ambitions and conclusions are often light years apart and yet, at times, they do, unintentionally, cast light or darkness upon each other.

Chronologically the book moves from pre-war Ireland to the undated and undatable future. Thus the first chronological section starts with the pre-war child's-eye perspective of Sean O'Faolain's (b. 1900) Cork boy on the verge of a lost innocence, and filters that same city through the extreme right-wing characters of Mary Leland's (b. 1941) *The Killeen* (1985) who are anticipating both the secret illegitimate birth of a revolutionary's child and the forthcoming war in Europe. It examines neutral Ireland during that war through Desmond Hogan's (b. 1951) *A Curious Street* (1985); encounters the confusion and destruction (and possible ambiguity of Ireland's position) in Europe in the immediate aftermath of war through Francis Stuart's (b. 1902) semi-autobiographical account of his arrest, imprisonment and eventual release without charge in *Black List, Section H* (1971); and closes at the start of the 1950s with the father of Jennifer Johnston's (b. 1930) heroine explaining, in *The Christmas Tree* (1981), why, as an Irishman, he fought in the British army to keep Ireland out of that war.

The next section opens with John McGahern's (b. 1935) 'High Ground', where his insight into the workings of the Irish political system, although set firmly in the Leitrim of the 1950s, rings true in a contemporary context (and was most certainly read – correctly or not – as being written in response to current political events when first published in an Irish newspaper in the 1980s). That same countryside – distorted (possibly by a second-generation telling) into an almost surreal landscape as though now being used against itself – is the setting for the English-born, second-generation Irish writer Bridget O'Connor's (b. 1961) 'Postcards'. This fresh perspective, mingling Irish phrases like 'over there' (for abroad) with foreign terms like 'exam grades', creates a child's trapped world which could be Kashuba or Connemara. It is used again, but now with the harshness of winter set against an extraordinarily instinctive feminine bond in Bryan MacMahon's 'A Woman's Hair'.

Set in Spain in the winter of 1962, *Polnische Juden* in Aidan Higgin's (b. 1927) novel, *Balcony of Europe* (1972), is where Desmond Hogan's old man frogmarching through Athlone with the toothbrush moustache in 1943, or Benedict Kiely's figure clutching an unopened *Mein Kampf* under his oxter, cease to be comic local colour, and the personalized musings of H in *Black List* and the wishes of the family in *The Killeen* collide with the reality of our century.

Mary Lavin's (b. 1912) 'Happiness' takes us back to Ireland and can only be termed a short-story masterpiece in its depiction of the relationship between a mother and her daughters.

A different relationship between female generations and between the crossover of families from rural to urban life is at the heart of Éilís Ní Dhuibhne's (b. 1954) 'Blood and Water'. Although the older suburbs date from more than a century ago and Dublin's great modern satellite towns date from immediately after the war (the estates of Cabra being rushed up in the aftermath of Germany's bombing of the North Strand) this aspect of Irish life, despite being an everyday reality for an increasingly large percentage of the population, was almost totally absent from Irish writing until recently. Even Brendan Behan, who lived most of his life on the Corporation estate in Crumlin, kept his day-to-day surroundings at bay in his work, focusing instead on the slums of his childhood. It is only in the post-1968 generation that the confidence to remain true to the ordinary modern urban experiences around them finally begins to be displayed by writers like Ní Dhuibhne, Paula Meehan, Michael O'Loughlin, Paul Mercier and others.

In the midst of the profusion of very different forms of Irish writing produced at the end of the 1980s, Shane Connaughton (b. 1946) in 'Ojus' – from his book *A Border Station* (1989) – breathes an impressive quality of life into the traditional images of the Irish childhood in what may perhaps be a formidable swansong for that particular genre of Irish short story. This is especially true after Patrick McCabe (b. 1955) takes most of the traditional ingredients of the Irish small town childhood and gleefully bludgeons them to death in a richly black comic *tour de force* excursion into a deranged mind wandering about during the Cuban Missile Crisis in *The Butcher Boy* (1992).

Like Aidan Higgins before her, Clare Boylan (b. 1948) moves her characters out into Europe in 'Villa Marta'. But this time, by the end of the sixties, it is not to encounter the ghosts of the extermination camps, but to entice the sailors of the American fleet with the dreams of New World luxury they embody.

Back in Ireland, the North is about to shatter apart, as seen from the perspective of a young Protestant boy at a bonfire in Glenn Patterson's (b. 1961) *Burning Your Own* (1988) and through Eugene McCabe's (b. 1930) elderly Catholic brothers on the border in 1969 in 'Cancer' (1978).

Were it not for the date in the opening paragraph, it would be hard for us to conceive of William Trevor's (b. 1928) 'Ballroom of Romance' (1972) as set in the year of its publication, but he powerfully captures a part of Ireland where nothing seems to have changed (except, maybe, for a few whitewashed signs of *No EEC* on the walls) and a people who are from areas of Ireland which are escaping (or feel like they are escaping) from the profound changes that are sweeping across it.

One small and ever-shrinking class who were certainly feeling the winds of change were the Anglo–Irish, reduced from the opulence of their pre-independence lives to, in Molly Keane's (b. 1905) *Good Behaviour* (1981), concocting chicken from rabbit which 'has been forced through a fine sieve and whizzed for ten minutes through a Moulinex blender'.

Under the pseudonym 'M. J. Farrell', Molly Keane produced eleven successful novels between 1928 and 1956. One of them, *Two Days in Aragon* (1941), includes a description of a local 'big house' being set ablaze. In an ironic twist – and example of not only how power has shifted in Ireland, but also of how the centre has shifted in Irish writing – Colm Tóibín's *The Heather Blazing* (1992) includes a reference to the same house being burnt. Only

Tóibín's viewpoint is from that of the burners, our emerging fathers looking in through the gates, who saw not only the ordered sweep of majestic boughs along the avenue, but also, in the words of Michael Hartnett:

> *. . . black figures dancing on the lawn,*
> *Eviction, Droit de Seigneur, Broken Bones:*
> *And heard the crack of ligaments being torn*
> *And smelled the clinging blood upon the stones.*

In *Good Behaviour*, the aristocratic St Charles family have left their mansion behind for the world of reduced circumstances, and Molly Keane, after decades of silence, produces a wickedly powerful black comedy of manners.

Two writers, whose careers were to cross very strongly into film, made their débuts with short-story collections within a year of each other in the mid-seventies. Both those first books of Neil Jordan (b. 1951) – who later directed *Company of Wolves* and *Mona Lisa* – and Bernard MacLaverty (b. 1942) – who wrote the screenplays of his novels *Lamb* (1980) and *Cal* (1983), as well as the television drama *Hostages* – contain powerful descriptions of the world of Irish emigration to London in the 1970s in 'Last Rites' and 'Between Two Shores'.

If this period marked the débuts for Jordan and MacLaverty, it marked a return to writing and very belated collection débuts for another pair of very different writers. Both Mary Beckett (b. 1926) and Val Mulkerns (b. 1925) released first collections after a long silence. Although the BBC had begun to broadcast her stories at twenty-three when she was teaching in her native Belfast, Mary Beckett had abandoned writing for twenty years after moving south while she raised her children, and it was not until 1980 that her début, *A Belfast Woman*, appeared. Likewise, Val Mulkerns, who had been assistant editor of *The Bell* from 1952–4 and had produced novels in 1951 and 1954, underwent a similar (if not as total) silence while rearing her family until her return with a powerful short-story début, *Antiquities*, in 1978. With Mulkerns' early novels long forgotten, it was very much a case of two very talented writers having to relaunch their careers at fifty-three and fifty-four years of age respectively. Although this would not be true for all the women of their generation – Edna O'Brien made her début at twenty-eight and has continued to produce a book every two to three years since – the role of women in Irish family life in the past has to be a factor in the relatively late débuts of writers like Mary Leland (44), Jennifer Johnston (42) or Maeve Kelly (46). It is an interesting reflection on both Irish writing and society to contrast this with Sara Berkeley (26), Anne Enright (28) and Éilís Ní Dhuibhne (34).

But, the notion that the female voice is only now being heard for the first time in Irish writing is one which often annoys many older female writers like Mulkerns and Jennifer Johnston, who feel it greatly demeans the achievements of the likes of Elizabeth Bowen, Kate O'Brien, Mary Lavin and others. It is the sheer impressive quality of women's writing, despite their difficulties, over this period which explains women's genuine anger at being more or less written out of some recent anthologies, like sections of that massive and laudable undertaking *The Field Day Anthology of Irish Literature* – which the general editor, to his credit, has offered to make amends for, or Thomas Kinsella's *Oxford Book of Irish Verse* (without a single woman), which the editor has not.

Perhaps mindful also of the conservative American university audience which the anthology seems – in part – geared towards, *Field Day* is coy about gay literature – describing Forrest Reid, for example, whose work is published by the Gay Man's Press as 'interested in relationships between young men'. Val Mulkerns' description of a repressed gay businessman who has never allowed himself to be himself leads into Mary Dorcey's (b. 1950) 'The Husband' (1989), a powerful study of a wife leaving her husband for another woman. Dorcey's story is all the more effective for being presented through the hurt perspective of a husband who is incapable of fully comprehending the situation.

Edna O'Brien (b. 1932) – no matter what she has since

produced – seems condemned to be known as the author of *The Country Girls* (1960). As a novel it has all the classic symptoms of the Irish traditional novel/short story, from the claustrophobic rural religious upbringing, through the betrayal of innocence, and down to the conventional ending of the heroine/hero fleeing Ireland on the deck of the cattle boat. But *The Country Girls* is only the first part of a trilogy which in its time moved into new and more important areas of the Irish experience. If the country girls in their summer dresses glimmered like icons trapped in a vanished past, then, as has been mentioned, the closing section of *Girls in Their Married Bliss* (1964), where Kate – the trilogy's heroine – has herself sterilized in an expensive London clinic, was a far greater landmark and years ahead of its time in Irish writing. 'Such a Sky', from her 1990 collection, *Lantern Slides*, has one of O'Brien's female characters returning from London to confront both the nature of her own sick father and of herself.

Few recent Irish writers can have caused more controversy in Ireland than Roddy Doyle (b. 1958) who, firstly in theatre along with playwright Paul Mercier, and then in a series of ever-contrasting novels, has created a new and vibrant genre in Irish literature. The primary aim of any writer of quality is to create his or her own fictional universe and in Barrystown (where his initial trilogy of novels was set) Doyle created his own distinctive, true and original set of characters who have added vitality and humour to Irish fiction.

With simplicity, directness and economy, David Park's (b. 1953) 'Oranges from Spain' effectively captures the sheer random horror of the past twenty years in Northern Ireland, as Eoin McNamee (b. 1961) – from a far grimmer perspective – equally succeeds in his short story, 'If Angels Had Wings' (1988), which – again in a sign of change – was later turned into a novel, *The Last of Deeds* (1989). However, in the words of the *Irish Times*, Benedict Kiely's *Proxopera* (1979) 'may well turn out to be the best book yet on the tragedy of the North'. The story of a man who is given the choice of driving a bomb to one of two places in his native town which he loves and where he is respected, while his family is held hostage by masked gunmen, is a deeply powerful and outraged novel.

Maeve Kelly's (b. 1930) 'Orange Horses' (1990) is where the 'tinkers' of Bryan MacMahon's 'A Woman's Hair' collide with 'the knackers camped near the Ward' in *The Journey Home* (1990), my own (b. 1959) novel which links back into the Senator's world in McGahern's 'High Ground'. Making sense of the constitution of that land is Colm Tóibín's (b. 1955) Southern judge in *The Heather Blazing* (1992). His abstract legal arguments in relation to the rights of women take on a new physical reality in Joseph O'Connor's (b. 1963) 'Mothers Were All the Same' (1991) – where, a decade later, the image of the Irish emigrant in London – complete with university degree and plane ticket – has changed from Jordan's labourer bearing only his brute pain.

In his 1980 introduction to *The Bodley Head Book of Irish Short Stories*, David Marcus (who has since edited a more undated selection in the recent *State of the Art*), states: 'One rule, however, I felt, could not but be observed: every story had to have an Irish context.' Even perhaps in 1980, 'an Irish context' could still be taken to refer to work set in Ireland or in some way concerned with the Northern political situation. However, at the present juncture, and from here on in this anthology, what constitutes 'an Irish context' (by which I mean whatever embraces the Irish experience) becomes increasingly difficult to define. Indeed, with Ireland's utter failure to sustain a society with a role for the bulk of its young people, even what constitutes an Irish writer seems likely to become increasingly difficult to define. Four of the eight writers here born in the 1960s live outside Ireland, along with six or so of those born in the 1950s. (Although it is as interesting to note the number of those born in the 1950s who were able to make the deliberate decision to stay.) And not only have we begun again to export our writers (after the false spring that my own generation was born into) but a huge section of their native contemporary readership now also live as Irish people outside the island. To try and take the traditional themes which are supposed to obsess Irish writers and tie them to writers like Sara Berkeley or Anne Enright is as absurd as to try and brand them as 'postcolonial' writers. Sara Berkeley's (b. 1967) characters effortlessly cross frontiers and are equally at home in Europe or America as Ireland. Similarly, the startlingly articulate tramp sleeping rough in London, in Belfastman Robert McLiam Wilson's (b. 1964) début, *Ripley Bogle* (1989), bears little resemblance to the archetypal down-and-out Irishman.

The European experience of Hugo Hamilton (b. 1953) in Berlin in his novel, *Surrogate City*, and Michael O'Loughlin's (b. 1958) Irish journalist and rock star in Amsterdam in 'A Rock-'n'-Roll Death' (1989), and Deirdre Madden's Irish woman in Italy in *Remembering Light and Stone* (1992), add a new scope and direction to Irish writing, as does the American world of Sebastian Barry (b. 1955) in his experimental novel, *The Engine of Owl-Light* (1988), and Aidan Mathews (b. 1956) with his grey, anonymous lecturer receiving a hand-job driving to work in 'Incident on the El Camino Real'. Sandwiched between them is the Belfast writer, Brian Moore b. 1921), who observes the effect of a superstitious elderly Irishwoman on a successful, secular American suddenly confronting his own mortality.

The sixth section deals with work which might best be termed as belonging to the future – be it the curious crystal brilliance of Anne Enright's (b. 1962) triptych in 'Men and Angels' (1990), or the angry, raw world of the abandoned outer suburbs in Leland Bardwell's (b. 1928) futuristic 'The Hairdresser' (1987). The forgotten tongue in 'Counterpoints' (1988) by Gerardine Meaney (b. 1962) – the only writer in the anthology not to have published a book yet – may perhaps be Irish, but it equally could be any extinct or invented tongue in a future place.

The quality of the language in *Mefisto* (1986), (where John Banville's (b. 1945) narrator, recovering from a horrific accident, is soothed and borne in and out of consciousness by painkilling drugs) speaks for itself. Turning the big house genre on its head with *Birchwood*, and exploring both the inner world and historical times of European figures like Copernicus and Kepler (and indirectly Newton) in his fiction, over the period of this anthology, Banville has been at the forefront of change and innovation in Irish writing.

Introduction

I have felt it important for this anthology to remain a strong and contemporary selection for many years after publication. Because of this I have taken the liberty of extending the original selection of forty-six writers to fifty by including work published since the hardback (or about to be published) by Mary Morrissy, John MacKenna, Dermot Healy and Colum McCann, to form a seventh section which obviously does not follow the same loose chronological pattern as the rest of the book.

The Death of Matti Bonner is a self-contained chapter from *A Goat's Song* (1994), a novel by Dermot Healy (b. 1947) – the publication of which was held up for legal reasons at the time of my initial selection. The extract describes the girlhood of Catherine, a Northern Protestant and daughter of a policeman, who discovers the body of a Catholic neighbour who has hanged himself midway between the two churches in her native place. A respected playwright and poet, Healy, in his collection of stories, *Banished Misfortunes* (1982), and his novel, *Fighting with Shadows* (1984), has already uniquely captured the borderland and small-town landscape which he shares with Patrick McCabe. Sweeping north and south of the border with equal accuracy and insight, *A Goat's Song* is a major and powerful novel.

A different death and landscape inform John MacKenna's (b. 1952) story 'Absent Children', where a man visiting the mother of a recently killed child is drawn back into the childhood memory of witnessing a playmate die. This is just one of three separate but linked stories, all bearing the same title, in the author's début, *The Fallen*. Collectively, as the links fall into place, they grow and add to each other in impact and depth to form an astonishingly effective triptych of absence and grief.

In *The Fallen* MacKenna, with great deliberation and skill, set about investing the relatively anonymous landscape of his native Kildare with an extraordinary resonance. It is a measure of his skill and confidence that he creates an equal resonance in the rural landscape of eighteenth-century Northamptonshire in his début novel, *Clare* – an intimate and lyrical exploration of the life of the poet John Clare.

Introduction

If the worlds of Healy and MacKenna can be firmly rooted in a definite landscape, then the anonymous suburban scape of *Divided Attention* and many other stories in Mary Morrissy's (b. 1957) superb début, *A Lazy Eye* (1993), could be any modern city. The resonances she creates rely on the slowly unfurled insights which characterize these stories and which have led John Banville to describe her as 'one of the subtlest and most penetrating of the latest generation of Irish writers'.

In the title story of his début, *Fishing the Sloe-Black River* (1994), Colum McCann (b. 1965) describes the surreal and imaginary riverbank of a small Irish town where elderly parents cast rods into the water, fishing in vain for their emigrant children – even though they knew how futile it was 'when the river looked not a bit like the Thames or the Darling or the Hudson or the Loire or even the Rhine itself . . .' McCann, who was born in Dublin, lived in America and now works in Japan, seems a classic example of the diaspora he describes above.

His stories are the work of a most vivid imagination. *Through the Field* (which I have included here) is an evocation of the landscape and mind of Texas. It seems a highly appropriate way to finish this book. More than ever it is clear that future editors will not just be turning to the banks of the Liffey, the Lee and the Lagan, but to McCann's 'the Thames or the Darling or the Hudson or the Loire or even the Rhine itself' to search out the new heart of Irish writing.

For such a small country, and paring it down to just a quarter of a century of writing, one might think that an anthology of fifty writers would be fairly comprehensive. In reality, although the vast majority of these writers automatically picked themselves, I am well aware that there are quite a number of cases where another writer from a particular generation or genre would have been equally representative as the one chosen here. Every editor has a prejudice. Mine, in this case, has been to attempt the – perhaps impossible – task of photographing a moving object, of trying to present for the first time together, and in the context of their immediate and still active predecessors, a generation which is still in the process of forming itself;

an anthology of writers, at least more than half of whom can have genuine reason to expect that their best work is ahead of them; a new wave of younger Irish writers whose most remarkable characteristic is to share almost nothing in common except originality; a body of writers who are all working from equally valid, equally true and yet equally different viewpoints and visions.

Even between writing this revised introduction and the anthology appearing I know that there will be a dozen more débuts or sequels to débuts, each an equally valid voice clamouring to be heard. And I am well (and, at times, painfully) aware that, in focusing so much on the future of Irish writing, I have been forced at times only to sketch in the full achievement of other generations working during this period. Time may well show that I have overlooked older writers whose achievements to date will far outshine the final spectrum of work by some of the lesser-known names here. In my defence I can only point out that many more traditional anthologies of Irish writing are readily available – and well worth reading.

I have refused to place these writers in any tradition of Irish writing – beyond the obvious one of generally using the English language far better than anybody else. A tradition – and therefore definition – by its nature can restrict a writer within a narrow focus. This is not to ignore the vast weight of superb Irish writing in whose wake they are creating their own paths, but to say that – with equal cognizance of the Becketts and Joyces, the O'Connors and O'Flahertys, the Bowens and Kate O'Briens, and also of the wider European and world literature around them – their work, along with that of the older writers here, reveals a remarkably confident and yet challenging and dissenting young European literature in the act of redefining itself and the world around it.

DERMOT BOLGER

Dublin, July, 1992
Revised December, 1993

Editor's Note to this
Expanded Edition (2000)

Londonn, 17 March 1993 and the first edition of this anthology is published amid the standard publicity and controversy, queues for book-signings and public debates that such an undertaking generates. The book shoots to number one in the Irish bestsellers. In the UK the first edition is sold out before publication date. A new generation of writers stand before the cameras. Irish writing is suddenly fashionable in places where it was previously unheard of.

I wonder where Maeve Brennan was on that same St Patrick's Day? Probably, if not enduring one of her frequent bouts of hospitalization, she was frightening visitors to the *New Yorker* building where she had taken up semi-permanent residence in the ladies' toilet as a psychotic and sometimes violent baglady. Within months, Maeve Brennan, one of the finest of the fifteen additional writers included here, had died in poverty, at the age of seventy-six, unknown and unmourned in her native country.

So who was she? It is interesting to ask the question, on the precipice of a new millennium, when Irish writing is suddenly attracting huge attention amid the perpetual search for the next great white hope.

Maeve Brennan was born in Dublin in 1916, the year when her father, the Irish revolutionary Robert Brennan, was sentenced to death for taking over Wexford with several hundred men during the week-long Easter Rising against British rule. After fourteen other leaders were executed, his sentence was commuted to penal servitude, but a year later he was back on the streets, paying fleeting visits to his daughter as he helped organize the underground government which gained freedom for the South of Ireland after the War of Independence.

Independence led to its ritual share-out of jobs and by the mid-1930s he had become Ireland's first envoy to Washington. But when her family returned to Ireland after the war Maeve Brennan opted to remain in America. She joined the staff of the *New Yorker*, where, between 1953 and 1973, her extraordinarily rich and biting stories of the intricacies of Irish family life were published.

As a daughter of the revolution, every door in Irish society would have been open to her had she returned. But it is interesting that, as a woman writer, she deliberately chose exile, while never leaving Ireland in her work, thereby freeing herself from the restraints which that country – shaped by her father's own comrades – placed on women of her generation.

Given the difficulties, until recently, in finding work by Mary Lavin or Kate O'Brien in print, it is not surprising that such a woman writing in America was ignored in her own land. Although partly explained by the status then afforded in Irish literary quarters to women, it had at least as much to do with the status given in our national consciousness to emigrants. Out of sight, out of mind was always Ireland's motto with that part of every generation culled into exile.

Not that Maeve Brennan's exile was complete. Unlike Joyce or Beckett, she did return once in later life, staying in the new Dublin suburbs in the 1970s with her first cousin, whose young son remembers their visitor with affection, even if her behaviour, even then, was sufficiently erratic to attract attention when she suddenly left and was found wandering the streets. Ireland being Ireland, the son in question was Roddy Doyle, whose *A Star Called Henry* is among the most important Irish novels published since the first edition of this anthology appeared.

Editor's Note to this Expanded Edition

It may seem strange, in introducing an extended selection to this anthology – intended to focus on figures likely to emerge as central to Irish writing in the first decade of a new millennium – to include a writer who ceased writing two decades before the first edition was published. But writers have exits as well as débuts and, sixty years from now, who knows which writers, included or omitted from these pages, will await rediscovery to complete a picture of the Ireland of their day. Literature is fickle. Today's sensation can be quickly forgotten. It may be worth asking where Irish writing is going just now and if it is being led by a boundless wellspring of talent or by marketing demand for fresh faces and sales angles in the publishing industry.

Thirty years ago Irish publishing was so much in its infancy that when the radical New Writers Press, then just starting out, published a collection by the gifted poet Brian Lynch, they called it *No Die Cast*, because this was the longest title they could construct from the eleven letterpress letters they had purchased to print the title of their last book, *Dedications*, and they lacked the resources to obtain any more lead type of the same font and pointsize.

When I was founding Raven Arts Press in 1977, the Irish Writers Co-op had just started to break the near silence then pertaining in Irish fiction, especially in the Irish Republic, which, for foreign editors and journalists, lacked the deadly glamour of war. On their first attempt to rep their books in London, the Co-op managed to sell just one copy of their initial débuts, by Neil Jordan and Desmond Hogan.

Today, when doors are immediately open to any new Irish writer, it is as hard to imagine the hostility and indifference which once existed to Irish writing, as it is to guess at the number of previous Irish writers of genuine potential who lacked that opportunity to see their first work in print and develop their voices from there.

It is equally hard to guess at how Irish writing will stand when the new writers here attain the age that Maeve Brennan died at. Yet even if the case of Brennan (like Gerard Manly

Hopkins, who died, unknown, in a room in Dublin that is now, ironically, also a public toilet) shows the impossibility of trying to photograph the moving object that is a contemporary literature, I still firmly believe that many of the additional voices included here will be celebrated in fifty years time.

Even in the seven years since the first edition, relatively unknown writers whom I was sometimes initially criticized for including, like Eoin McNamee or Colum McCann, have emerged as central figures in contemporary Irish writing. This additional selection could easily focus on many established writers whose continuing achievements since 1993 have shown that their omission, due to pressure of space, from my original selection was perhaps unwarranted. But their success speaks for itself and I have been keen to keep with the spirit of this enterprise by focusing mainly on writers who have made their débuts (or in some cases are, at the time of writing, on the verge of doing so) since the softback edition was published in 1994.

The only exceptions (along with Brennan, whose work was finally published in Europe in 1999) are Frank Ronan and Ronan Bennett who have opened Irish writing up to new areas of experience in recent books like *Lovely* and *The Catastrophist*. Also included is Micheál Ó Conghaile, one of the Irish language's foremost contemporary prose writers, but who has yet to publish a début in English.

A valid criticism of my initial selection was the absence of any Irish language novelist, though in my defence it could be said that too little of this work has been available in English. For too long it was absurd that many of our finest Irish language writers were deliberately (sometimes as a political act) not translated into English. Their work has been inaccessible not only to readers abroad but also to the vast majority of their fellow citizens. Things have improved greatly since the controversy surrounding the first major dual language anthology of contemporary Gaelic poetry, *The Bright Wave: An Tonn Gheal* (Raven Arts Press), which I edited in 1985, and Ó Conghaile is just one of four Irish language prose writers (along with Pádraic Breathnach, Dara Ó Conaola and Alan Titley) showcased in *Fourfront* (Cló Iar-Chonnachta, 1998), while English translations of novels by writers like Padraig Standun are often bestsellers.

But Irish writers no longer feel corralled by any received notion of Irishness in the scope of their ambition, as is evidenced by Antonia Logue's (b. 1972) début *Shadow Box* (1999), written in the voices of the English modernist poet, Mina Loy, and the two men who competed for her affections, Jack Johnston, the first black heavyweight world champion, and Arthur Cravan, the Dadaist provocateur. The extract here is in Johnston's voice.

Seamus Deane's (b. 1940) *Reading in the Dark* (1996) has been one of the most long-awaited and celebrated débuts of recent years. Dealing in minute and crystal detail with the author's childhood in Derry, it is part of a process of the deliberate blurring of lines between fiction and autobiography which has become prevalent in Irish writing, so that while around three-quarters of this début could conceivably be also classified as autobiography, parts of Dermot Healy's autobiography, *The Bend for Home*, published in the same year, could equally and deliberately be termed as fiction.

In the same year as Deane's mother was sensing ghosts on the stairs in Derry, England was starting the process of rebuilding its shattered capital. Born there to Irish parents, Philip Casey (b. 1950) was fortunate in being one of the few Irish at that time whose parents were eventually able to return to their native Wexford where he grew up. But his *The Water Star* (1999) is a brilliant evocation of post-war London in all its diversity, wounds and rebirth, capturing both the British and German experience of the aftermath of war, as well as the experience of the migrant Irish flocking to find rebuilding work. The torched buildings of Hamburg in RAF raids are as real as the improvised mountain slopes of Wexford that its main protagonists, Hugh and his widowed father, leave behind. Hugh shares lodgings with Karl, a German haunted by the horrors he endured in Hamburg where his family were killed. In this extract, in a cratered bombsite at night, Karl relives something of that horror.

As I write, Blánaid McKinney (b. 1961) has yet to publish her first book, but such is the confidence and mother-wit evident in her story 'The Outfielder, The Indian Giver' (1998) – set on a journey across America – that it is hard to believe it to be the work of a writer just starting her career.

Mike McCormack's (b. 1965) writing has always verged on the deliberately macabre, injecting a uniquely black humour into his sparse and yet Gothic prose. 'Thomas Crumlesh 1960–1992: A Retrospective' is from his début collection of stories, *Getting It in the Head* (1996).

Set in the Congo in 1959/60, at a pivotal moment in its history, Ronan Bennett (b. 1956) in his fine novel *The Catastrophist* (1998) uses the story of a writer obsessed by a woman, Ines, to explore a colonial world slipping out of control and a new African order violently being born.

It has not been my intention to hone in on gay writing in Ireland, but it is more than a coincidence that four writers, who automatically picked themselves by the strength of their work, should explore that facet of human experience in their books. There is a new found confidence here and a lack of the deliberate (and sometimes necessary for survival) repression that sometimes clouded the work of previous Irish gay writers. This is not to say that there was no Irish gay writing until recently, but that, even when openly done by respected writers, Irish society managed to marginalize and discreetly ignore it, whereas now it has moved without fuss or pyrotechnics into the mainstream.

If *Lovely* (1996), Frank Ronan's (b. 1963) superb evocation of a drug and rave culture in overdrive, is geographically far removed from Ireland in characters and location, then Emma Donoghue (b. 1963) deliberately makes her lesbian couple and their situation as humdrum and normal as possible in *Hood* (1995). In this extract the narrator, a teacher in a middle-class Dublin school, arrives at the church with the quiet father of her lover, Cara, who has been killed in a car crash.

In equally radical fashion, Keith Ridgway (b. 1965) gives us a deliberately unsympathetic gay central character, Martin, to whom his mother, Grace, flees after killing his brutish thug of a father in *The Long Falling* (1998). Even though Martin has been forced to leave the Irish countryside by the violent prejudice of his father, and has a new, open life with a gay lover in Dublin, we slowly learn that inside he is still a son made in his father's image. In this extract, the timid Grace, awaiting arrest and betrayal, intrudes upon an intimacy between her son and his lover.

A very different relationship between father and son is evident in Micheál Ó Conghaile's (b. 1962) 'Father' (1997), translated here from the author's Irish by Frank Sewell. Set in the heart of the Irish Gaelteach and steeped in detail of a small farm, it concerns a son coming out to his elderly father.

That countryside is evoked both accurately and bizarrely in Anne Haverty's (b. 1959) début *One Day as a Tiger* (1997), which marries a perfect ear for the nuances of rural life with the tragicomic relationship between a man and a pitiful sheep who has been genetically 'improved' in an experiment with human genes.

Too often an attempt is made to divide Irish life neatly between country and city, whereas there is a whole different urban experience in small towns beyond the pale like Wexford and Sligo, where the inhabitants ('townies') feel themselves equally estranged from the inhabitants of local farms as from the population of Dublin.

If Joyce brilliantly captured every nuance of Dublin life in 'The Dead', then Maeve Brennan (1916–1993) does equal justice to the cramped back lanes of small-town Ireland in 'The Springs of Affection' (*New Yorker*, 1972, published Europe, 1999). In the black humour and sharp pain of her portrait of Min, a bitter old woman ensnared by a life-long cocktail of prejudice, inferiority and pride, Maeve Brennan created one of the most masterful Irish short stories of this century.

Just how small-town life has utterly changed in a quarter

of a century is seen in *Waiting for the Healer* (1997), Eamon Sweeney's (b. 1968) searingly violent study of a man reluctantly returning from England for the funeral of his brother who was murdered in what is evidently Sligo town.

Meanwhile Claire Keegan (b. 1968) superbly captures present-day life and budding sexuality in 'The Ginger Rogers Sermon' (1997) in the same Wexford countryside from which Min had once considered it almost as terrible for her brother to have married a non-townie stranger than if he had married a foreigner.

Finally Niall Williams (b. 1958) invests both city and countryside with a unique Irish magic realism in his début novel *Four Letters of Love* (1997). This is an Irish novel not afraid to be 'unrealistic', creating its own reality in a universe where miracles and everyday life co-exist. In this extract, Isabel Gore – whose life fills half of this slowly merging narrative – leaves her island home for school on the mainland.

This anthology does not aim to act as a social history of modern Ireland, yet I suspect that part of the dynamic which produced so much fine writing in this period arises from the authors being part of a society in such total flux that – seven years on – the Ireland which I contextualized in my original introduction is radically different in many respects from the Ireland pertaining today.

In the North intransigence and mistrust between both sides often obscures the genuine miracle that an uneasy ceasefire has, in the main, held for so long, with tortuous but genuine progress, compared to the bloodshed common in 1993.

In the South chronic emigration has been reversed by the fastest growing economy in Europe, with companies begging graduates once forced abroad to return home. While Irish politicians once stressed the case for leniency and green cards for illegal Irish emigrants filtering into America, now they cope with a weekly influx of refugees arriving as stowaways on lorries and ships. A constant succession of court cases and tribunals expose the past abuses of a Church in disarray and the culture of 1980s political corruption.

Editor's Note to this Expanded Edition

Once again in trying to cover these last seven years my problem as an editor has not been what to put in, but to justify leaving so many other writers out. When Robert Brennan marched off to take on the might of the British empire, he could never have imagined that, seventy-six years later, his infant offspring would die as a virtual baglady in a foreign land. We are seeing the birth of many careers here, yet another wave of confident, original and highly talented Irish writers on the cusp of a new millennium. We too can only guess ahead at the strange journeys of their offspring and at the future of the land that they sprang from.

DERMOT BOLGER

Dublin, summer 1999

PART ONE

Samuel Beckett

For to End Yet Again

For to end yet again skull alone in a dark place pent bowed on a board to begin. Long thus to begin till the place fades followed by the board long after. For to end yet again skull alone in the dark the void no neck no face just the box last place of all in the dark the void. Place of remains where once used to gleam in the dark on and off used to glimmer a remain. Remains of the days of the light of day never light so faint as theirs so pale. Thus then the skull makes to glimmer again in lieu of going out. There in the end all at once or by degrees there dawns and magic lingers a leaden dawn. By degrees less dark till final grey or all at once as if switched on grey sand as far as eye can see beneath grey cloudless sky same grey. Skull last place of all black void within without till all at once or by degrees this leaden dawn at last checked no sooner dawned. Grey cloudless sky grey sand as far as eye can see long desert to begin. Sand pale as dust ah but dust indeed deep to engulf the haughtiest monuments which too it once was here and there. There in the end same grey invisible to any other eye stark erect amidst his ruins the expelled. Same grey all that little body from head to feet sunk ankle deep were it not for the eyes last bright of all. The arms still cleave to the trunk and to each other the legs made for flight. Grey cloudless sky ocean of dust not a ripple mock confines verge upon verge hell air not a breath. Mingling with the dust slowly sinking some almost fully sunk the ruins of the refuge. First change of all in the end a fragment comes away and falls. With slow fall for so dense a body it lights like cork on water and scarce breaks

3

the surface. Thus then the skull last place of all makes to glimmer again in lieu of going out. Grey cloudless sky verge upon verge grey timeless air of those nor for God nor for his enemies. There again in the end way amidst the verges a light in the grey two white dwarfs. Long at first mere whiteness from afar they toil step by step through the grey dust linked by a litter same white seen from above in the grey air. Slowly it sweeps the dust so bowed the backs and long the arms compared with the legs and deep sunk the feet. Bleached as one same wilderness they are so alike the eye cannot tell them apart. They carry face to face and relay each other often so that turn about they backward lead the way. His who follows who knows to shape the course much as the coxswain with light touch the skiff. Let him veer to the north or other cardinal point and promptly the other by as much to the antipode. Let one stop short and the other about this pivot slew the litter through a semicircle and thereon the roles are reversed. Bone white of the sheet seen from above and the shafts fore and aft and the dwarfs to the crowns of their massy skulls. From time to time impelled as one they let fall the litter then again as one take it up again without having to stoop. It is the dung litter of laughable memory with shafts twice as long as the couch. Swelling the sheet now fore now aft as permutations list a pillow marks the place of the head. At the end of the arms the four hands open as one and the litter so close to the dust already settles without a sound. Monstrous extremities including skulls stunted legs and trunks monstrous arms stunted faces. In the end the feet as one lift clear the left forward backward the right and the amble resumes. Grey dust as far as eye can see beneath grey cloudless sky and there all at once or by degrees this whiteness to decipher. Yet to imagine if he can see it the last expelled amidst his ruins if he can ever see it and seeing believe his eyes. Between him and it bird's-eye view the space grows no less but has only even now appeared last desert to be crossed. Little body last stage of all stark erect still amidst his ruins all silent and marble still. First change of all a fragment comes away from mother ruin and with slow fall scarce stirs the dust. Dust having engulfed so much it can engulf no more and woe the little on the surface still. Or mere digestive torpor as once the boas which past with one last gulp clean sweep at last. Dwarfs distant whiteness sprung from nowhere motionless afar in the grey air where dust alone possible. Wilderness and carriage immemorial as one they advance as one retreat hither thither halt move on again. He facing forward will sometimes halt and hoist as best he can his head as if to scan the void and who knows alter course. Then on so soft the eye does not see them go driftless with heads sunk and lidded eyes. Long lifted to the horizontal faces closer and closer strain as it will the eye achieves no more than two tiny oval blanks. Atop the cyclopean dome rising sheer from jut of brow yearns white to the grey sky the bump of habitativity or love of home. Last change of all in the end the expelled falls headlong down and lies back to sky full little stretch amidst the ruins. Feet centre body radius falls unbending as a statue falls faster and faster the space of a quadrant. Eagle the eye that shall discern him now mingled with the ruins mingling with the dust beneath a sky forsaken of its scavengers. Breath has not left him though soundless still and exhaling scarce ruffles the dust. Eyes in their orbits blue still unlike the doll's the fall has not shut nor yet the dust stopped up. No fear henceforth of his ever having not to believe them before that whiteness afar where sky and dust merge. Whiteness neither on earth nor above of the dwarfs as if at the end of their trials the litter left lying between them the white bodies marble still. Ruins all silent marble still little body prostrate at attention wash blue deep in gaping sockets. As in the days erect the arms still cleave to the trunk and to each other the legs made for flight. Fallen unbending all his little length as though pushed from behind by some helping hand or by the wind but not a breath. Or murmur from some dreg of life after the lifelong stand fall fall never fear no fear of your rising again. Sepulchral skull is this then its last state all set for always litter and dwarfs ruins and little body grey cloudless sky glutted dust verge upon verge hell air not a breath. And dream of a way in a space with neither here nor there where all the footsteps ever fell can never fare nearer to anywhere nor from anywhere further away. No for in the end for to end yet again by degrees or as though switched on dark falls there again that certain dark that alone certain ashes can. Through it who knows yet another end beneath a cloudless sky same dark it earth and sky of a last end if ever there had to be another absolutely had to be.

PART TWO

PART TWO

Tom Mac Intyre

The Man-Keeper

THEY WERE cutting the hay this day. He was pleased – he was generally pleased – and a little drowsy from the heat. He lay down to rest on the fresh grass, leaving the men to it, and dozed off. When he awoke the day was far gone and there was no one in the field but himself.

He rose and made his way home to dinner feeling a little out of sorts: the sleep hadn't refreshed him at all. In the house he decided against having dinner.

—You don't feel well? the daughter asked.

—I don't feel right, he said, I feel like the bed, and that's where I'm going.

—You were working too hard, you tired yourself.

He explained that he'd had a long sleep in the field.

—You've a bit of a chill from lying on the fresh grass, you'll be fine in the morning.

He took the night's sleep but in the morning he felt worse, and complained of a kind of backward and forward movement in his stomach. When evening came and there wasn't the least sign of improvement, they sent for the doctor. The doctor came and questioned and examined. He listened at length to the troubled stomach.

—Now, the patient called out. Can't you hear the backwards and forwards of it?

The doctor could hear nothing.

—He's imagined the whole thing, he told the wife and daughter. He'll be all right in a few days, I believe, but let me know.

He left a bottle, and departed.

9

There was no improvement in a few days; the stirring inside had gone away – that was all that could be said. The doctor was sent for once more, and came several days running. In the end he confessed himself baffled, said he'd come no more, and refused to take a penny for his services.

The house was in a state. A second doctor was sent for, and a third, and a fourth. They came singly, and they came in a bunch. They flourished long names for the illness, prescribed potions and ointments, and charged a lump of money for their attentions, which were to no avail whatever. Quack doctors followed the doctors, one came striding over every hill: they muttered and made signs and left powders and distillations and didn't forget to charge either. The patient continued to fade. Six months had passed: look at him now and all you saw was shadow in a bottle.

Summer came again. The invalid had a habit of sitting by the door a few hours a day in good weather. He was sitting there one day when along came a travelling-woman he knew. They greeted each other, and the travelling-woman couldn't but say what she felt.

—You're a changed man since I saw you last.

—I'm sick, he told her, I'm more than sick, and no cure in the world.

—Doctors?

—They've taken half the farm, and for what?

—Healers?

—Robbers all.

He told her the whole story, how he'd fallen asleep on the fresh grass that day, the upset that followed, all the comings and all the goings.

—Fresh grass?

—Fresh grass.

—Moist maybe?

—No, no.

—A stream close by?

—Yes, a stream close by.

—Can you show me the spot?

The spot. It was the last place he wanted to see. Even as she asked, he remembered that it must be up on a year to the day since he'd risen from sleep and walked away from it. His grave. Must he go with her to point out his grave? He dragged himself to the field. He showed her the exact spot; the hay had just been cut, the fresh grass shone. The travelling-woman studied closely the various weeds and herbs growing there, and before long stood up with a small juicy-looking herb between her fingers.

—Do you see that?

—I do.

—Wherever you find that herb you won't have far to look for what's bothering you.

—Go on.

—You've swallowed a man-keeper.

The travelling-woman met the wife and daughter and gave them her information, and her advice.

—There's only one man can save him and that's the Prince of Coolavin.

—And where's he to be found? the wife asked.

—On the brink of Lough Gara, it's three days from here, no great journey.

A long discussion commenced. The wife and daughter were in favour of making the journey; anything that offered hope must be tried. The invalid was the obstacle: he'd had enough of doctors – and others, he couldn't be cured, he was too weak to travel, let him die in peace. The discussion started over. Finally, the three women convinced him to try it.

The four of them set out the next day, travelling by horse and cart, loaded with provisions. They found lodgings the first night and the second night. They took their fill of rest, especially the invalid, who required constant care. On the third day they arrived at the house of the Prince of Coolavin, a fine house on the brink of the lake. They found the owner at home and the invalid told his story.

—Fresh grass you slept on?

—Fresh grass it was.

—A stream close by?

—A stream close by, yes.

—You've swallowed a man-keeper.

The Prince was having his dinner – the main course that day was corned beef. He sat the invalid down at the table, put a great helping of the corned beef before him, and commanded him to eat. The invalid thanked him but drew back – he'd eaten nothing in months, he couldn't touch it.

—Eat that if it was to choke you.

Forced to it, he got through a third of the plate.

—Fine, said the Prince, rest yourself for a few hours now.

In the late afternoon the Prince led him out to a field near the house. The three women followed. There was a stream running through the field. The Prince put him lying down on the bank of the stream, face directly above the water, mouth open and very close to the water.

—Whatever happens, said the Prince, don't move.

The invalid nodded.

The Prince withdrew, and joined the women a few yards back.

Nothing happened for quite a while. At the end of an hour the invalid felt something stirring inside him, first a backwards and a forwards, then making – at a guess – for the spoon of the breast, on in the direction of the throat, next in his mouth, moving out to the tip of the tongue, next no move at all. About a minute later he felt a stirring in his mouth again, then dart out to the tongue-tip, and this time *plop* with it into the water.

—Don't move, the Prince warned.

The invalid didn't move. In a few minutes he experienced a repeat of the stirrings, first the backwards and forwards, then making headway, up into the mouth, out to the tip of the tongue, sliding back, no move at all, forward again, and *plop* again into the water. It was a procession after that, a dozen in all.

—There's your clutch, said the Prince, now for the mother.

The invalid was close to exhaustion, and growing fretful. When another hour passed without incident, he made to rise, he could take no more. The Prince and the travelling-woman had to go forward and forcibly hold him down, one to each shoulder: there they stayed. The wife and daughter, pale the pair, watched from their same station.

A short time passed, and the invalid felt a stirring inside that surpassed anything so far, a stirring that was almost a tearing, forcing its way up to the throat, through and into the mouth, and resting there. The invalid moved. His hand shot to his mouth but, if he was quick, the man-keeper was quicker: back down the throat with her, gone.

—Didn't I tell you not to move? snapped the Prince, you've maybe frightened her for good.

But he hadn't. She came up again in about twenty minutes, the same tearing and pushing, up into the mouth, timidly there for a minute or two, scouting, back and forth, back and forth, out at last to the tip of the tongue, and *plop* – seven times the plop of any of the others – into the water.

—Well you knew the tub of butter when you found it, the Prince roared after her.

They carried the invalid back to the house. He said nothing for three hours. The first words he said were:

—I'm a new man.

Sean O'Faolain

The Talking Trees

THERE WERE four of them in the same class at the Red
Abbey, all under fifteen. They met every night in Mrs
Coffey's sweetshop at the top of Victoria Road to play the
fruit machine, smoke fags and talk about girls. Not that they
really talked about them – they just winked, leered, nudged
one another, laughed, grunted and groaned about them, or
said things like 'See her legs?' 'Yaroosh!' 'Whamm!' 'Ouch!'
'Ooof!' or 'If only, if only!' But if anybody had said, 'Only
what?' they would not have known precisely what. They
knew nothing precisely about girls, they wanted to know
everything precisely about girls, there was nobody to tell
them all the things they wanted to know about girls and that
they thought they wanted to do with them. Aching and
wanting, not knowing, half guessing, they dreamed of clouds
upon clouds of fat, pink, soft, ardent girls billowing towards
them across the horizon of their future. They might just as
well have been dreaming of pink porpoises moaning at their
feet for love.

In the sweetshop the tall glass jars of coloured sweets
shone in the bright lights. The one-armed fruit machine went
zing. Now and again girls from St Monica's came in to buy
sweets, giggle roguishly and over-pointedly ignore them. Mrs
Coffey was young, buxom, fair-haired, blue-eyed and very
good-looking. They admired her so much that one night
when Georgie Watchman whispered to them that she had
fine bubs Dick Franks told him curtly not to be so coarse, and
Jimmy Sullivan said in his most toploftical voice, 'Georgie
Watchman, you should be jolly well ashamed of yourself, you

are no gentleman,' and Tommy Gong Gong said nothing but nodded his head as insistently as a ventriloquist's dummy.

Tommy's real name was Tommy Flynn, but he was younger than any of them so that neither he nor they were ever quite sure that he ought to belong to the gang at all. To show it they called him all sorts of nicknames, like Inch because he was so small; Fatty because he was so puppy-fat; Pigeon because he had a chest like a woman; Gong Gong because after long bouts of silence he had a way of suddenly spraying them with wild bursts of talk like a fire alarm attached to a garden sprinkler.

That night all Georgie Watchman did was to make a rude blubberlip noise at Dick Franks. But he never again said anything about Mrs Coffey. They looked up to Dick. He was the oldest of them. He had long eyelashes like a girl, perfect manners, the sweetest smile and the softest voice. He had been to two English boarding schools, Ampleforth and Downside, and in Ireland to three, Clongowes, Castleknock and Rockwell, and had been expelled from all five of them. After that his mother had made his father retire from the Indian Civil, come back to the old family house in Cork and, as a last hope, send her darling Dicky to the Red Abbey day-school. He smoked a corncob pipe and dressed in droopy plus fours with chequered stockings and red flares, as if he was always just coming from or going to the golf course. He played cricket and tennis, games that no other boy at the Red Abbey could afford to play. They saw him as the typical school captain they read about in English boys' papers like *The Gem* and *The Magnet*, *The Boy's Own Paper*, *The Captain*, and *Chums*, which was where they got all those swanky words like Wham, Ouch, Yaroosh, Ooof and Jolly Well. He was their Tom Brown, their Bob Cherry, their Tom Merry, those heroes who were always leading Greyfriars School or Blackfriars School to victory on the cricket field amid the cap-tossing huzzas of the juniors and the admiring smiles of visiting parents. It never occurred to them that *The Magnet* or *The Gem* would have seen all four of them as perfect models for some such story as *The Cads of Greyfriars*, or *The Bounders of Blackfriars*, low types given to secret smoking in the spinneys, drinking in the Dead Woman's Inn, or cheating at examinations, or worst crime of all, betting on horses with red-faced bookies' touts down from London, while the rest of the school was practising at the nets – a quartet of rotters fated to be caned ceremoniously in the last chapter before the entire awe-struck school, and then whistled off at dead of night back to their heartbroken fathers and mothers.

It could not have occurred to them because these crimes did not exist at the Red Abbey. Smoking? At the Red Abbey any boy who wanted to was free to smoke himself into a galloping consumption so long as he did it off the premises, in the jakes or up the chimney. Betting? Brother Julius was always passing fellows sixpence or even a bob to put on an uncle's or a cousin's horse at Leopardstown or the Curragh. In the memory of man no boy had ever been caned ceremoniously for anything. Fellows were just leathered all day long for not doing their homework, or playing hooky from school, or giving lip, or fighting in class – and they were leathered hard. Two years ago Jimmy Sullivan had been given six swingers on each hand with the sharp edge of a metre-long ruler for pouring the contents of an inkwell over Georgie Watchman's head in the middle of a history lesson about the Trojan Wars, in spite of his wailing explanation that he had only done it because he thought Georgie Watchman was a scut and all Trojans were blacks. Drink? They did not drink only because they were too poor. While, as for what *The Magnet* and *The Gem* really meant by 'betting' – which, they dimly understood, was some sort of depravity that no decent English boy would like to see mentioned in print – hardly a week passed that some brother did not say that a hard problem in algebra, or a leaky pen, or a window that would not open or shut was 'a blooming bugger'.

There was the day when little Brother Angelo gathered half a dozen boys about him at playtime to help him with a crossword puzzle.

'Do any of ye,' he asked, 'know what Notorious Conduct could be in seven letters?'

'Buggery?' Georgie suggested mock-innocently.

'Please be serious!' Angelo said. 'This is about Conduct.'

When the solution turned out to be *Jezebel*, little Angelo threw up his hands, said it must be some queer kind of foreign woman and declared that the whole thing was a blooming bugger. Or there was that other day when old Brother Expeditus started to tell them about the strict lives and simple food of Dominican priests and Trappist monks. When Georgie said, 'No tarts, Brother?' Expeditus had laughed loud and long.

'No, Georgie!' he chuckled. 'No pastries of any kind.'

They might as well have been in school in Arcadia. And every other school about them seemed to be just as hopeless. In fact they might have gone on dreaming of pink porpoises for years if it was not for a small thing that Gong Gong told them one October night in the sweetshop. He sprayed them with the news that his sister Jenny had been thrown out of class that morning in St Monica's for turning up with a red ribbon in her hair, a mother-of-pearl brooch at her neck and smelling of scent.

'Ould Sister Eustasia,' he fizzled, 'made her go out in the yard and wash herself under the tap, she said they didn't want any girls in their school who had notions.'

The three gazed at one another, and began at once to discuss all the possible sexy meanings of notions. Georgie had a pocket dictionary. 'An ingenious contrivance'? 'An imperfect conception (US)'? 'Small wares'? It did not make sense. Finally they turned to Mrs Coffey. She laughed, nodded towards two giggling girls in the shop who were eating that gummy kind of block toffee that can gag you for half an hour, and said, 'Why don't you ask *them*?' Georgie approached them most politely.

'Pardon me, ladies, but do you by any chance happen to have notions?'

The two girls stared at one another with cow's eyes,

17

blushed scarlet and fled from the shop shrieking with laughter. Clearly a notion was very sexy.

'Georgie!' Dick pleaded. 'You're the only one who knows anything. What in heaven's name is it?'

When Georgie had to confess himself stumped they knew at last that their situation was desperate. Up to now Georgie had always been able to produce some sort of answer, right or wrong, to all their questions. He was the one who, to their disgust, told them what he called conraception meant. He was the one who had explained to them that all babies are delivered from the navel of the mother. He was the one who had warned them that if a fellow kissed a bad woman he would get covered by leprosy from head to foot. The son of a Head Constable, living in the police barracks, he had collected his facts simply by listening as quietly as a mouse to the other four policemen lolling in the dayroom of the barracks with their collars open, reading the sporting pages of *The Freeman's Journal*, slowly creasing their polls and talking about colts, fillies, cows, calves, bulls and bullocks and 'the mysteerious nachure of all faymale wimmen'. He had also gathered a lot of useful stuff by dutiful attendance since the age of eleven at the meetings and marchings of the Protestant Boys' Brigade, and from a devoted study of the Bible. And here he was, stumped by a nun!

Dick lifted his beautiful eyelashes at the three of them, jerked his head and led them out on the pavement.

'I have a plan,' he said quietly. 'I've been thinking of it for some time. Chaps! Why don't we see everything with our own eyes?' And he threw them into excited discussion by mentioning a name. 'Daisy Bolster?'

Always near every school, there is a Daisy Bolster – the fast girl whom everybody has heard about and nobody knows. They had all seen her at a distance. Tall, a bit skinny, long legs, dark eyes, lids heavy as the dimmers of a car lamp, prominent white teeth, and her lower lip always gleaming wet. She could be as old as seventeen. Maybe even eighteen. She wore her hair up. Dick told them that he had met her once at the tennis club with four or five other fellows around her and that she had laughed and winked very boldly all the time. Georgie said that he once heard a fellow in school say, 'She goes with boys.' Gong Gong bubbled that that was true because his sister Jenny told him that a girl named Daisy Bolster had been thrown out of school three years ago for talking to a boy outside the convent gate. At this Georgie flew into a terrible rage.

'You stupid slob!' he roared. 'Don't you know yet that when anybody says a boy and girl are talking to one another it means they're doing you-know-what?'

'I don't know you-know-what,' Gong Gong wailed. 'What what?'

'I heard a fellow say,' Jimmy Sullivan revealed solemnly, 'that she has no father and that her mother is no better than she should be.'

Dick said in approving tones that he had once met another fellow who had heard her telling some very daring stories.

'Do you think she would show us for a quid?'

Before they parted on the pavement that night they were talking not about a girl but about a fable. Once a girl like that gets her name up she always ends up as a myth, and for a generation afterwards, maybe more, it is the myth that persists. 'Do you remember,' some old chap will wheeze, 'that girl Daisy Bolster? She used to live up the Mardyke. We used to say she was fast.' The other old boy will nod knowingly, the two of them will look at one another inquisitively, neither will admit anything, remembering only the long, dark avenue, its dim gas lamps, the stars hooked in its trees.

Within a month Dick had fixed it. Their only trouble after that was to collect the money and to decide whether Gong Gong should be allowed to come with them.

Dick fixed that, too, at a final special meeting in the sweetshop. Taking his pipe from between his lips, he looked speculatively at Gong Gong, who looked up at him with eyes big as plums, trembling between the terror of being told he could not come with them and the greater terror of being told that he could.

'Tell me, Gong Gong,' Dick said politely, 'what exactly does your father do?'

'He's a tailor,' Tommy said, blushing a bit at having to confess it knowing that Jimmy's dad was a bank clerk, that Georgie's was a Head Constable, and that Dick's had been a Commissioner in the Punjab.

'Very fine profession,' Dick said kindly. 'Gentleman's Tailor and Outfitter. I see, Flynn and Company. Or is it Flynn and Sons? Have I seen his emporium?'

'Ah, no!' Tommy said, by now as red as a radish. 'He's not that sort of tailor at all, he doesn't build suits, ye know, that's a different trade altogether, he works with me mother at home in Tuckey Street, he tucks things in and lets things out, he's what they call a mender and turner, me brother Turlough had this suit I have on me now before I got it, you can see he's very good at his job, he's a real dab . . .'

Dick let him run on, nodding sympathetically – meaning to convey to the others that they really could not expect a fellow to know much about girls if his father spent his life mending and turning old clothes in some side alley called Tuckey Street.

'Do you fully realize, Gong Gong, that we are proposing to behold the ultimate in female beauty?'

'You mean,' Gong Gong smiled fearfully, 'that she'll only be wearing her nightie?'

Georgie Watchman turned from him in disgust to the fruit-machine. Dick smiled on.

'The thought had not occurred to me,' he said. 'I wonder, Gong Gong, where do you get all those absolutely filthy ideas. If we subscribe seventeen and sixpence, do you think you can contribute half a crown?'

'I could feck it, I suppose.'

Dick raised his eyelashes.

'Feck?'

Gong Gong looked shamedly at the tiles.

'I mean steal,' he whispered.

'Don't they give you any pocket money?'

'They give me threepence a week.'

'Well, we have only a week to go. If you can, what was your word, feck half a crown, you may come.'

The night chosen was a Saturday – her mother always went to town on Saturdays; the time of meeting, five o'clock exactly; the place, the entrance to the Mardyke Walk.

On any other occasion it would have been a gloomy spot for a rendezvous. For adventure, perfect. A long tree-lined avenue, with, on one side, a few scattered houses and high enclosing walls; on the other side the small canal whose deep dyke had given it its name. Secluded, no traffic allowed inside the gates, complete silence. A place where men came every night to stand with their girls behind the elm trees kissing and whispering for hours. Dick and Georgie were there on the dot of five. Then Jimmy Sullivan came swiftly loping. From where they stood, under a tree beyond the porter's lodge, trembling with anticipation, they could see clearly for only about a hundred yards up the long tunnel of elms lit by the first stars above the boughs, one tawny window streaming across a dank garden, and beyond that a feeble perspective of pendant lamps fading dimly away into the blue November dusk. Within another half-hour the avenue would be pitch black between those meagre pools of light.

Her instructions had been precise. In separate pairs, at exactly half past five, away up there beyond the last lamp, where they would be as invisible as cockroaches, they must gather outside her house.

'You won't be able even to see one another,' she had said gleefully to Dick, who had stared coldly at her, wondering how often she had stood behind a tree with some fellow who would not have been able even to see her face.

Every light in the house would be out except for the fanlight over the door.

'Ooo!' she had giggled. 'It will be terribly oohey. You won't hear a sound but the branches squeaking. You must come along to my door. You must leave the other fellows to watch from behind the trees. You must give two short rings. Once, twice. And then give a long ring, and wait.' She had started to whisper the rest, her hands by her sides clawing her dress in her excitement. 'The fanlight will go out if my mother isn't at home. The door will open slowly. You must step into the dark hall. A hand will take your hand. You won't know whose hand it is. It will be like something out of Sherlock Holmes. You will be simply terrified. You won't know what I'm wearing. For all you'll know I might be wearing nothing at all!'

He must leave the door ajar. The others must follow him one by one. After that . . .

It was eleven minutes past five and Gong Gong had not yet come. Already three women had passed up the Mardyke carrying parcels, hurrying home to their warm fires, forerunners of the home-for-tea crowd. When they had passed out of sight Georgie growled, 'When that slob comes I'm going to put my boot up his backside.' Dick, calmly puffing his corncob, gazing wearily up at the stars, laughed tolerantly and said, 'Now Georgie, don't be impatient. We shall see all! We shall at last know all!'

Georgie sighed and decided to be weary too.

'I hope,' he drawled, 'this poor frail isn't going to let us down!'

For three more minutes they waited in silence, and then Jimmy Sullivan let out a cry of relief. There was the small figure hastening towards them along the Dyke Parade from one lamppost to another.

'Puffing and panting as usual, I suppose,' Dick chuckled. 'And exactly fourteen minutes late.'

'I hope to God,' Jimmy said, 'he has our pound note. I don't know in hell why you made that slob our treasurer.'

'Because he is poor,' Dick said quietly. 'We would have spent it.'

He came panting up to them, planted a black violin case against the tree and began rummaging in his pockets for the money.

'I'm supposed to be at a music lesson, that's me alibi, me father always wanted to be a musician but he got married instead, he plays the cello, me brother Turlough plays the clarinet, me sister Jenny plays the viola, we have quartets, I sold a Haydn quartet for one and six, I had to borrow sixpence from Jenny, and I fecked the last sixpence from me mother's purse, that's what kept me so late . . .'

They were not listening, staring into the soiled and puckered handkerchief he was unravelling to point out one by one, a crumpled half-note, two half-crowns, two shillings and a sixpenny bit.

'That's all yeers, and here's mine. Six threepenny bits for the quartet. That's one and six. Here's Jenny's five pennies and two ha'pence. That makes two bob. And here's the tanner I just fecked from me mother's purse. That makes my two and sixpence.'

Eagerly he poured the mess into Dick's hands. At the sight of the jumble Dick roared at him.

'I told you, you bloody little fool, to bring a pound note!'

'You told me to bring a pound.'

'I said a pound note. I can't give this dog's breakfast to a girl like Daisy Bolster.'

'You said a pound.'

They all began to squabble. Jimmy Sullivan shoved Gong Gong. Georgie punched him. Dick shoved Georgie. Jimmy defended Georgie with 'We should never have let that slob come with us.' Gong Gong shouted, 'Who's a slob?' and swiped at him. Jimmy shoved him again so that he fell over his violin case, and a man passing home to his tea shouted at them, 'Stop beating that little boy at once!'

Tactfully they cowered. Dick helped Gong Gong to his feet. Georgie dusted him lovingly. Jimmy retrieved his cap, put it back crookedly on his head and patted him kindly. Dick explained in his best Ampleforth accent that they had merely been having 'a trifling discussion', and 'our young friend here tripped over his suitcase'. The man surveyed them dubiously, growled something and went on his way. When he was gone Georgie pulled out his pocketbook, handed a brand-new pound note to Dick, and grabbed the dirty jumble of cash. Dick at once said, 'Quick march! Two by two!' and strode off ahead of the others, side by side with Tommy in his crooked cap, lugging his dusty violin case, into the deepening dark.

They passed nobody. They heard nothing. They saw only the few lights in the sparse houses along the left of the Mardyke. On the other side was the silent, railed-in stream. When they came in silence to the wide expanse of the cricket field the sky dropped a blazing veil of stars behind the outfield nets. When they passed the gates of the railed-in public park, locked for the night, darkness returned between the walls to their left and the overgrown laurels glistening behind the tall railings on their right. Here Tommy stopped dead, hooped fearfully towards the laurels.

'What's up with you?' Dick snapped at him.

'I hear a noise, me father told me once how a man murdered a woman in there for her gold watch, he said men do terrible things like that because of bad women, he said that that man was hanged by the neck in Cork Jail, he said that was the last time the black flag flew on top of the jail. Dick! I don't want to go on!'

Dick peered at the phosphorescent dial of his watch, and strode ahead, staring at the next feeble lamp hanging crookedly from its black iron arch. Tommy had to trot to catch up with him.

'We know,' Dick said, 'that she has long legs. Her breasts will be white and small.'

'I won't look!' Tommy moaned.

'Then don't look!'

Panting, otherwise silently, they hurried past the old corrugated-iron building that had once been a roller-skating rink and was now empty and abandoned. After the last lamp the night became impenetrable, then her house rose slowly to their left against the starlight. It was square, tall, solid, brick fronted, three storeyed, and jet black against the stars except for its half-moon fanlight. They walked a few yards past it and halted, panting, behind a tree. The only sound was the squeaking of a branch over their heads. Looking backwards, they saw Georgie and Jimmy approaching under the last lamp. Looking forwards, they saw a brightly lit tram, on its way outward from the city, pass the far end of the tunnel, briefly light its maw and black it out again. Beyond that lay wide fields and the silent river. Dick said, 'Tell them to follow me if the fanlight goes out,' and disappeared.

Alone under the tree, backed still by the park, Tommy looked across to the far heights of Sunday's Well dotted with the lights of a thousand suburban houses. He clasped his fiddle case before him like a shield. He had to force himself not to run away towards where another bright tram would rattle him back to the city. Suddenly he saw the fanlight go out. Strings in the air throbbed and faded. Was somebody playing a cello? His father bowed over his cello, jacket off, shirt sleeves rolled up, entered the Haydn; beside him Jenny waited, chin sidewards over the viola, bosom lifted, bow poised, the tendons of her frail wrist hollowed by the lamplight, Turlough facing them lipped a thinner reed. His mother sat shawled by the fire, tapping the beat with her toe. Georgie and Jimmy joined him.

'Where's Dick?' Georgie whispered urgently.

'Did I hear music?' he gasped.

Georgie vanished, and again the strings came and faded. Jimmy whispered, 'Has she a gramophone?' Then they could hear nothing but the faint rattle of the vanished tram. When Jimmy slid away from him, he raced madly up into the darkness, and then stopped dead half-way to the tunnel's end. He did not have the penny to pay for the tram. He turned and raced as madly back the way he had come, down past her house, down to where the gleam of the laurels hid the murdered woman, and stopped again. He heard a rustling noise. A rat? He looked back, thought of her long legs and her small white breasts, and found himself walking heavily back to her garden gate, his heart pounding. He entered the path, fumbled for the dark door, pressed against it, felt it slew open under his hand, stepped cautiously into the dark hallway, closed the door, saw nothing, heard nothing, stepped onward, and fell clattering on the tiles over his violin case.

A door opened. He saw firelight on shining shinbones and bare knees. Fearfully, his eyes moved upwards. She was wearing nothing but gym knickers. He saw two small birds, white, soft, rosy-tipped. Transfixed by joy he stared and stared at them. Her black hair hung over her narrow shoulders. She laughed down at him with white teeth and wordlessly gestured him to get up and come in. He faltered after her white back and stood inside the door. The only light was from the fire.

Nobody heeded him. Dick stood by the corner of the mantelpiece, one palm flat on it, his other hand holding his trembling corncob. He was peering coldly at her. His eyelashes almost met. Georgie lay sprawled in a chintzy armchair on the other side of the fire wearily flicking the ash from a black cigarette into the fender. Opposite him Jimmy Sullivan sat on the edge of a chair, his elbows on his knees, his eyeballs sticking out as if he had just swallowed something hot, hard and raw. Nobody said a word.

She stood in the centre of the carpet, looking guardedly from one to the other of them out of her hooded eyes, her thumbs inside the elastic of her gym knickers. Slowly she began to press her knickers down over her hips. When Georgie suddenly whispered 'The Seventh veil!' he at once wanted to batter him over the head with his fiddle case, to shout at her to stop, to shout at them that they had seen everything, to shout that they must look no more. Instead, he lowered his head so that he saw nothing but her bare toes. Her last covering slid to the carpet. He heard three long gasps, became aware that Dick's pipe had fallen to the floor, that Georgie had started straight up, one fist lifted as if he was going to strike her, and that Jimmy had covered his face with his two hands.

A coal tinkled from the fire to the fender. With averted eyes he went to it, knelt before it, wet his fingers with his spittle as he had often seen his mother do, deftly laid the coal back on the fire and remained so for a moment watching it light up again. Then he sidled back to his violin case, walked out into the hall, flung open the door on the sky of stars, and straightway started to race the whole length of the Mardyke from pool to pool of light in three gasping spurts.

After the first spurt he stood gasping until his heart had stopped hammering. He heard a girl laughing softly behind a tree. Just before his second halt he saw ahead of him a man and a woman approaching him arm in arm, but when he came up to where they should have been they too had become invisible. Halted, breathing, listening, he heard their murmuring somewhere in the dark. At his third panting rest he heard an invisible girl say, 'Oh, no, oh no!' and a man's urgent voice say, 'But yes, but yes!' He felt that behind every tree there were kising lovers, and without stopping he ran the gauntlet between them until he emerged from the Mardyke among the bright lights of the city. Then, at last, the sweat cooling on his forehead, he was standing outside the shuttered plumber's shop above which they lived. Slowly he climbed the bare stairs to their floor and their door. He paused for a moment to look up through the window at the stars, opened the door and went in.

Four heads around the supper table turned to look up enquiringly at him. At one end of the table his mother sat wearing her blue apron. At the other end his father sat, in his rolled-up shirt sleeves as if he had only just laid down the pressing iron. Turlough gulped his food. Jenny was smiling mockingly at him. She had the red ribbon in her hair and the mother-of-pearl brooch at her neck.

'You're bloody late,' his father said crossly. 'What the hell kept you? I hope you came straight home from your lesson. What way did you come? Did you meet anybody or talk to anybody? You know I don't want any loitering at night, I hope you weren't cadeying with any blackguards? Sit down, sir, and eat your supper. Or did your lordship expect us to wait for you? What did you play tonight? What did Professor Hartmann give you to practise for your next lesson?'

He sat in his place. His mother filled his plate and they all ate in silence.

Always the questions! Always talking at him! They never let him alone for a minute. His hands sank. She was so lovely. So white. So soft. So pink. His mother said gently, 'You're not eating, Tommy. Are you all right?'

He said, 'Yes, yes, I'm fine, Mother.'

Like birds. Like stars. Like music.

His mother said, 'You are very silent tonight, Tommy. You usually have a lot of talk after you've been to Professor Hartmann. What were you thinking of?'

'They were so beautiful!' he blurted.

'What was so bloody beautiful?' his father rasped. 'What are you blathering about?'

'The stars,' he said hastily.

Jenny laughed. His father frowned. Silence returned.

He knew that he would never again go back to the sweetshop. They would only want to talk and talk about her. They would want to bring everything out into the light, boasting and smirking about her, taunting him for having run away. He would be happy for ever if only he could walk every night of his life up the dark Mardyke, hearing nothing but a girl's laugh from behind a tree, a branch squeaking, and the far-off rattle of a lost tram; walk on and on, deeper and deeper into the darkness until he could see nothing but one tall house whose fanlight she would never put out again. The doorbell might ring, but she would not hear it. The door might be answered, but not by her. She would be gone. He had known it ever since he heard her laughing softly by his side as they ran away together, for ever and ever, between those talking trees.

Mary Leland

from *The Killeen*

'THERE WILL be trouble.' Bina put down the *Cork Examiner* and rested it, half-folded, on her knees. At the other side of the fire Father Costello emerged from his abstraction, a haze engendered by the warmth, Bina's silence, and a consciousness of what was going on upstairs.

'No, really, there can't be any doubt about it. Maybe not yet, a few years perhaps, but there must be trouble in Europe, an outbreak of some kind.' Having stated this certainty Bina was prepared to take up the newspaper again, but Father Costello's reply halted her.

'Whose side would we be on, do you think?' It was less of a question than a comment. He was not really interested in the possibility of a war in Europe, being still scarred from the war in Ireland.

'What "we" are we talking about, Father Costello?' Bina raised the end of the question to a challenge. 'Do you mean the Irish government? Or the Irish people? I have no doubts about that. De Valera will either side with England or stay neutral. It will be easier for him to be neutral if England isn't drawn into it, but from what I know' – she bowed her head at him – 'I know it isn't much – of English policies in Europe I feel sure that country will be heavily involved, may even instigate the final confrontation. That will be De Valera's real dilemma; can he really support the British, no matter who the enemy is? I don't think he can, you know, even if he goes on the way he's started.' She rattled the paper and went on. 'But I can answer for the Irish people. Their choice would be Germany. It would have to be.'

The priest envied her certainty even when he didn't share it. All her certainties. She sat here opposite him, legs in ribbed stockings set square under the long tweed skirt, the solidity of her presence a guarantee of utter self-confidence. She discussed Europe with the same efficient assurance she gave to her acid consideration of the Irish parliament, to household management, or to the affairs and gossip of the parish around St Luke's.

'Not that it's my business,' she would say sometimes (he had heard her once outside St Patrick's church on a Sunday morning); 'not that it's my business, it's not my parish. But one must try to help people settle things properly.'

It was the *properly* that mattered. 'Properly' according to Miss Bina Mulcahy was not always what suited the objects of her concern, but then she didn't live in the parish and she didn't have to hear their mutterings. Yet there was no doubt, and she herself would not have doubted it for a second, that the Misses Mulcahy were regarded here in St Luke's with the same classless awe as they were in the South Parish. Inevitably upright, well bred if not well born, propertied, Catholic, educated and powerful. And martyred.

Apart from his son, the Mulcahy sisters were the only living blood relatives of Maurice Mulcahy, hero and martyr, dead in the Curragh military prison camp, on hunger strike. A Republican victim of other Republicans. Sisters of his father, their political lineage was impeccable for eternity.

Father Costello's mother and the mother of Maurice Mulcahy had been sisters; that made him a cousin of the martyr, reduced his acceptability to his bishop and in Cork committed his immediate prospects of preferment to an atmosphere of public sympathy and an intermediate series of chaplaincies. His day would come; even the bishop, in careful nuances, indicated that his day would come. He was simply experiencing a period of adjustment. The fire roasting his trouser legs gave out an added warmth, reminding him of places where he would be welcome, where Earnán would have been welcome.

'She has agreed, she is still in agreement, is she?' He inclined his head sideways and upwards towards the door and the stairs.

'Absolutely.' Miss Bina spoke with resolution. 'That's why we have Dr Douglass with her. Otherwise a midwife would have done. Dr Douglass has a woman waiting to take the child and later will take charge of it herself. When it is older, not needing so much care. She is a busy woman, God bless her.'

Father Costello wondered if Miss Bina did not wonder why he was asking. He had no need to do so; he had been privy to all the plans. So why was he asking, now, when it was all happening? There was no sound in the hall, nothing came from overhead to indicate the turmoil blocked into one small room. The house was calm. He was here only to recognize the child and to baptize it in a quick and necessary ritual. With that out of the way he need have no more dealings with the infant until it was old enough to be educated, and even then he knew that the Misses Mulcahy could be trusted there, they knew what would be required for and from the education of such a child.

Miss Bina's paper rustled again; to forestall another international forecast the priest moved his chair back from the fire by pressing his feet hard on the floor and his lower spine against the studded leather back. The anticipated squeaking shuffle cut across what Miss Bina had been about to say, and Father Costello asked instead: 'Julia is up there, is she?'

Miss Bina did not answer at once. Julia was up there. Miss Bina did not approve, but perhaps, in these very particular circumstances, she should make some allowances in the name of Christian Charity.

'Yes, poor girl, she is so kind. No one is beneath her compassion. A foolish poor girl she is, as we know. But very kind.'

Father Costello was not at all sure that Julia Mulcahy, *née* Watson, was foolish. Most distinctly she was not poor, and although she was discreet about her wealth, this, combined with his uneasy suspicion of more intelligence and certainly more education that her husband's aunts wished to credit, made him carefully civil in his dealings with her. Again in this he admired the aunts, whose assumptions could only be called presumptions by people who felt for Julia's gentility. They treated this composed relic of the dead man with dismissive courtesy. They used the house as if it were their own – but then, Julia allowed that. Thinking about her now, Father Costello suddenly thought that perhaps Julia could behave like that because it didn't matter, her own secret life was contained elsewhere.

So much of her life had been public. There was still intense, if muted, public interest in her wellbeing, and in that of her son, the two-year-old boy the Mulcahys had tried to call Maurice, Julia and her husband had christened Robert Patrick and Julia, determinedly unromantic, always called Pat.

He wondered what could be happening up there. He knew what was happening. For the first time in his life he wondered, nearly, what it was like, the steady waiting time punctured by gasping, tearing pains, the rhythms building with moans and cries, the bursting out with floods of blood and liquids. Yet the house was silent, as if all this sequence of agony and shameful relief and soiled sheets and blood and ordure could be absorbed by the very walls.

The silence grew loud in his ears. His pulse throbbed with heat and the picture grew from the fireplace, a picture more confused and tortured because it was the flesh of imagination. The female legs splayed out, held down by rigorous hands, the black gap between suddenly gushing with blood and birth. Horrible! But he was excited in some way he could not relish, and with a creeping sense of sin he tried to remember the face of the mother, the girl he had last seen leaning against the slate steps in the nuns' garden, her body relaxed and tired as she sat, waiting and still, high up above him when he left the convent cemetery. As he watched her she had stirred, looked down, and she had seen him.

Brown hair waved around her face. She was not conveniently pretty. It was hard to describe the distinctive features which made her appearance memorable. He had pretended all those first months that she had been cheaply attractive but, taking this long look and now embracing what he had seen, he knew that wasn't true. Her face was the face of many Irish girls, healthy, some people might say 'bonny': a white forehead met the brown curls, her deeply lashed eyes were grey under delicate arched brows. The skin of her cheeks had a faint, sunny flush to them, and her mouth was wide, and full, and pale. Then, as he watched her, she shivered and her skirt tightened around the curve of her stomach and he felt distaste rise in his throat. He had turned away to where Julia Mulcahy was waiting inside the porch of the convent, where Margaret was to be met and taken away. To here and now.

'England's difficulty is Ireland's opportunity!' Miss Bina's rejoicing tones reminded him of the great world outside. The world itself was festering; like Miss Bina, like her sister Lou, like Dr Douglass and other men and women scattered in groups large and small through the country, his conviction was that Ireland could be kept pure, unsoiled by what was happening outside. That purity would itself eventually produce a nation strong, inviolable, racially untarnished, Catholic from Bantry to Belfast, the envy of whatever Europe would emerge from the rearrangements now being dreamed, discussed, or witnessed, in Berlin, Paris, London and Rome, even in Madrid.

'I never told her, and that nun swore *she* never told her that I have any connection with the child. Do you think, will Julia tell her?' His question was lightly asked, but anxious.

'Not at all! Julia knows very little about it all, she's not a curious girl, you know. And even if she did know, what difference could it make? Wouldn't all the world see that it is right for a child born in these circumstances to be guarded by his own uncle?'

No nonsense to Miss Bina. She didn't think much of the priest's anxiety on that matter. Earnán was gone, the child was, or would be, here, its mother incapable of caring for 'arrangements'. Naturally her plans must be the best since they included the concern of a priest who was also a relative, a doctor who was also a woman, and herself. Seeing the priest subside more easily in his chair, she went back to the Continent, carefully searching the references to Germany for further signs that the rise of National Socialism offered some helpful guidelines for aspirant and dedicated Irish nationalists.

The high ceiling above them suddenly strummed with hasty steps, then there was silence again.

'How long has it been now?' he asked nervously.

'Only since yesterday afternoon. For a first child that's not so long, I believe. And she's a grand healthy girl. Julia gave her every attention. She should have kept her below in the kitchen like I advised her, but no, she's too kind . . .'

The unspoken rebuke trailed away. Father Costello was counting the hours. Then – 'In sorrow shalt thou bring forth children!' he muttered, reminding himself how justified, in this case, such punishment was.

'The situation here, of course, is bad enough. And it can only get worse, now that he's taken over! Coming like a saviour to his people – as if the entire population of the nation had gone down on their knees to beg him to forget his promises and enter parliament and guide a state so young that it isn't even out of swaddling bonds. De Valera!'

Miss Bina pronounced the name with relish, shortening the second syllable in a ridiculous emphasis.

'We can all see now what's happening with the soldiers he was so friendly with, once upon a time. He's not going to fight for a republic – and it could be done now, you know. It could be done now.'

She hit her hand off the padded wood under her arm.

Her voice rose. The priest shared her disillusionment, but not her anger. His purpose could not be reduced; he brought the sanction of his Church to the drive for unity, for Catholic unity which would be a barrier to alien vices like socialism. He had no need for anger. His staff of life was controlled hate.

'Well, there may not be many the likes of Maurice and Earnán this minute, but they'll come, you mark my words! Maurice has left a legend behind him. The day has to come, Father. My only hope now is that it will come when I can see it, watch it happening.'

She was calm again. Father Costello agreed with her on so many things there was no need for speech. Now he heard the footsteps on the lower stairs, the hand on the door. When it opened, Miss Lou stood there, trailing a thin reek of chloroform.

'All over. A boy, a grand big child. She's asleep, Doctor saw to that. Bring your things, Father, come on.'

The three of them left the room together and went upstairs, to baptize the baby.

Desmond Hogan

from *A Curious Street*

ALAN MULVANNEY did not look unlike a portrait himself November 1943 when his coat was off, in a scarlet V-necked jersey, a shining white shirt always persuasively open at the neck, a green tie striped with yellow and red. Against red velvet hotel couches, against wooden bar pews he sat erect, a dignity and even a derangement about him.

An old man with a toothbrush moustache marched in the middle of the streets of Athlone, giving the Nazi salute. A Jewish family living on the Dublin Road was driven out of town. Two Protestant sisters in the country opened their house as a hospital for cats, they themselves dressed in nurses' uniforms. The romance of Alan Mulvanney and Eileen Carmody settled. Eileen still did not know where it was leading to – an altar, a mound of roses, a bed? – but she trusted its direction. They complemented one another with coats, scarves.

One Sunday evening Eileen picked up a dust-smothered book from the top of a radio and read her first poem.

> When we two parted
> In silence and tears,
> Half brokenhearted
> To sever for years,
> Pale grew thy cheek and cold,
> Colder thy kiss;
> Truly that hour foretold
> Sorrow to this.

The dew of the morning
Sat chill on my brow –
It felt like the warning
Of what I feel now,
Thy vows are all broken,
And light is thy fame;
I hear thy name spoken,
And share in its shame.

They name thee before me,
A knell to my ear;
A shudder comes o'er me –
Why wert thou so dear?
They know not I know thee,
Who knew thee too well: –
Long, long shall I rue thee,
Too deeply to tell.

In secret we met –
In silence I grieve,
That thy heart could forget,
Thy spirit deceive.
If I should meet thee
After long years,
How should I greet thee? –
With silence and tears.

The same evening Alan in his scarlet jersey, white open-necked shirt, green tie, pored over the Bible. 'Intreat me not to leave thee, or to return from following after thee: for whither thou goest, I will go; and where thou lodgest I will lodge: thy people shall be my people, and thy God my God.' Next morning he rose to find Hamburg had been bombed again.

A brother of Eileen's took off to England. Her mother fell on her knees on the stone steps of the lodge house. He was going to be murdered by Adolf Hitler.

Rugby players ran riot on the mental hospital grounds in Eileen's town. Mad people stared out from behind the bars of windows. Fog came to Athlone. It stilled things.

The eighth of December was the Feast of the Immaculate Conception of Mary, therefore a school holiday, and Alan requested Eileen to accompany him to Dublin. She'd been to Galway on a few ragged familial visits, never to Dublin. She cut out a new frock for the occasion, finding the pattern in a pre-war magazine. Foxes crackled in the wood outside. Her mother leaned back and spoke of childhood, one of the first times she spoke freely. Was it a sign she was growing old? Anyway, these days were days of change.

December 8 was a fine day. She took a train as far as Athlone. Alan was waiting on the platform, a figure in a long fawn belted coat, hands in his pockets, the blue air reeling about him. Urchin-like boys offered news of the war, their pale fingers crushing newspaper photographs of fresh blasts of smoke. Alan got on the train. A woman in black beside them, a mother-of-pearl headed pin in her black velvet hat, muttered about the war. A boy in white served them coffee. There were rainbows in the Midland bogs. Men, women, children got on and off the train slowly like refugees. Alan said he came on the wrong day, that his mother had hoped he'd be born today, the Feast of the Immaculate Conception.

'And straight I will repair to the Curragh of Kildare.' White horses cantered by on the Curragh. Alan leaned against the seat opposite, white shirt showing above fawn coat, his face smiling. Suddenly they were in Dublin, his city.

It could be argued that Galway was his city, Galway on a fine morning, Galway where swans lifted themselves as though on magical stilts from quayside steps in early morning, flapping their wings, Galway where white Spanish terraces ran riot, where women in black cloaks and red petticoats observed the sea, philosophically smoking pipes, the Galway of *A Cavalier Against Time*, the Galway his mother had brought him to once or twice, an adolescent boy in a mustard-coloured jersey. But Dublin was the place where all mornings had merged for him into a single morning when he woke and decided to write a novel. This morning Dublin was very blue. The Liffey swept to the outside world. Out there were bombs and people preoccupied with a curious world of sin, if you were to believe Irish priests. Eileen fingered the white green-rimmed cups in Bewley's Oriental Café in Westmoreland Street. She took off her navy coat for the first time to reveal her cornflower-blue dress with its lace collar. Even Alan was dazzled. Women in black from big houses in the country sat over bacon and eggs and old priests sublimated over cherry buns.

The first place they visited was the National Museum where Alan had researched his novel, viewing pistoles, half-pistoles, groats, Venetian glass, two-headed drinking cups behind glass cases as though they had been the matter of a great novel. Looking at her reflection in a glass case, again her navy coat on, Eileen wondered for the umpteenth time why this charade existed, why this novel was locked away. Alan had his own answer that day: a blind accordionist playing 'When Irish Eyes Are Smiling' on O'Connell Bridge, swaying from side to side, a little bent old lady in purple talking about her rotten neighbours to herself as she hobbled along Grafton Street, postcards of Vermeers and Rembrandts in shops by the Liffey; this was the city of his youth, a place closed off. That novel represented this city. Perhaps some day he'd resurrect the novel. Perhaps some day he'd write a new novel and show it to the world, but for now he stared into a glass case containing wine goblets and swords which showed his reflection, curly black hair, his fawn, open-hanging coat. He was still young. There were still roads to travel. There was still time to reveal the space shrouded by trees on Griffith Avenue, a young man in a white shirt at a typewriter, the sun pouring in, the leaves in bloom outside.

Next they looked in on the National Library where Alan wrote some of his novel, reverentially standing as old ladies wrote treatises on the Battle of Aughrim.

They visited Stephen's Green where Alan pointed out an

old astrologer with a white goatee who was speaking to the
ducks. All around were weeping willows and ducks. Eileen
stood as elegantly as possible.

They lunched at the Metropole. All the day Alan was
becoming younger and younger. Eileen wanted to reach to
the youth in Alan's face, stroke it with a black velvet glove.
But each time she made a manifest gesture this quality
receded in Alan.

Eileen, a little drunk, spoke to herself in the mirror in the
ladies. 'Now don't wobble, Eileen, be good.' She fixed her
hat at the same time, finding the right angle with tremendous
difficulty.

The blind accordionist on O'Connell Bridge was playing
'I'll take you home again Kathleen' as they got a bus to the
zoo. Eileen had seen most of the animals before in visiting
circuses, not the rhinoceros. Alan hilariously identified each
of them with an Irish politician or prelate of the time. By the
seal pond, a fat black seal whining behind him, spon-
taneously, red wine on his lips, the whine of the seal
becoming more human, Alan kissed her on the lips. She'd
never forget that kiss. He withdrew. The sun was arctic on
the polar bears.

They had tea in the Shelbourne lounge before leaving.
Eileen was beginning to speak with an upper-class accent in
the course of the day. Here upper society brushed around.
Darkness was falling on Stephen's Green. They walked to the
train. Crowds were pushing out of churches. The Liffey ran
velvet to the sea. Eileen said goodbye to her first glimpse of
the outside world, a red patch over the split where the Liffey
breaks into the sky. On the crowded train home, lights in
country houses, a woman in black beside them recited the
rosary in Irish under her breath 'Se do bheath a Mhuire'. An
ancient language broke through.

The Shannon rose high in December, swans in shadows.
After his display of emotion in Dublin Alan retreated. There
was red in his eyes and red rims about them. He wore his
white, sleeveless, blue-rimmed jersey. His head lay deeply

back in seats. Leningrad was being fought over by the Germans and the Russians. An ancient and elegant city was in mortal peril. Already hundreds of thousands had died. Leningrad became Dublin, became a city of youth, of sacred things. The nature of sacredness itself was being contested in the world.

Alan spoke obsessively of lovers, citing examples from history, Edmund Spenser and Elizabeth Boyle, Geoffrey Keating and Eleanor Laffan, even Cromwell and Elizabeth Bourchier. He spoke of his first poem, a snowman fading away. He spoke of art itself, a perishable thing, a Venetian glass in a glass case in a Dublin Museum, a young man's reflection in the glass case, a would-be artist, a would-be human being. He spoke of the war, of suffering, of the pointlessness of it all. Another of Eileen's brothers slipped away from home, this time to Limerick.

Finally, in this time of war, Alan began to have recourse to history, telling tales of history. Athlone brightened up. But something dug into Alan, the pointlessness of his historical images.

Eileen thought of him one evening, in his red jersey. She thought of a portrait of a young man holding a medallion in a picture Alan had showed her. She thought of Lorcan O'Mahony, holding up a glass of red wine in Galway. She saw Alan as one of these people. She wanted to take him and kiss his lips, red wine on hers. She longed for him now.

How do you make the connection between art and life? Alan wondered. For a moment in Athlone Eileen thought he resembled mad people behind bars in the mental hospital in her town.

Alan wrote a play for his children, a Gaelic nativity play, little children in emerald running about under mistletoe. One little girl made a speech. 'We have come from the courts of Ulster, passing hills of many fires, to seek a child who is born among stone. This child shall change the course of the sea, the imprints of the sand, the direction of the breezes. This child will breathe love on the palms of our hands.' Two days after Christmas there was to be a dance in Athlone. Alan and Eileen decided to go.

A tiny old woman in black, black beret on her head, pushed a pram through the holly in the Blackwoods near Eileen's home on Christmas Eve, collecting firewood. Candles burned in the windows of country houses outside Athlone. More than one tramp was turned away from the doors of these houses.

Eileen went to midnight Mass with her brothers, sisters, parents. Alan went to Mass on Christmas morning with his mother. Eileen had turkey for dinner, Alan goose. Eileen paid a customary visit to the convent crib with her mother, the two of them waiting in the darkness, Eileen in a black coat and black beret, her mother penitantly holding a handbag, pink light on the infant Jesus, a nun's silver star above him, a swish of robes and a rattle of beads in the air as a nun presently approached and ushered them into a room where, as it was Christmas, they were given tea and lady-like slivers of cake. Alan visited the crib in Athlone with his mother. He looked on the child Jesus and wondered at his vulnerability; how could there be birth in a world of war, of annihilation? He thought of a Protestant bishop dining with the O'Neills, his captors in Cavan on a Christmas Day in the 1640s, for one day a warm fire and hot wine. He looked at the infant and was confused by the paradox, bombs, genocide, the mutilation of children. His mother whispered her venial prayers. He wanted to take the chalk child home but it stolidly remained part of the crib, Athlone, Christmas 1943.

Alan and Eileen went to the dance as arranged but Alan's father being with his sister in Roscommon and his mother having taken his brothers to a pantomine in Dublin, Eileen led him home early. In a room full of photographs of priests and nuns, an orange light on, she took off his clothes, one by one, his underpants, bid him kneel, held his head against her waist. Then she took him by the hand, indicated the way, laid him on a bed, removed her own clothes, bent to kiss his mouth, chest, genitals. They were wounded things, his genitals, purple, red. She took them in her mouth and then rose, kissing his mouth again, lingering over it, savouring its smell, toothpaste, grapes, chocolate, kissed his nipples again, took his genitals again, limp in her mouth, became wilder, a goat digging the earth, pressing him, forcing him, confusing him. But Alan just lay there, eyes on the ceiling. After a while she realized. Her stockings lay on a chair. His red jersey lay on another chair in the other room. Alan lay back, his eyes on the ceiling, his mind on dreams of history.

Afterwards it would have more impact for her than war, massacres, concentration camps or, eventually, twin clouds over cities in the Far East. A month later she said goodbye to Alan by the Shannon on a night it was just beginning to snow. She walked her way. She heard again a blind accordionist on a bridge in Dublin. The river was leading now to the outside world.

Francis Stuart

from *Black List, Section H*

WHEN THERE was a jostling among the throng at the far
end of the corridor as two soldiers made their way
along it from the next carriage, he decided that the moment
that for the last three months he'd been expecting had
arrived. But before they had reached his end of the corridor –
what they were looking for, it turned out, wasn't at all what
he'd feared, and they had stopped beside the two German
girls who, however, ignored them in favour of their elderly
fellow countryman – the train restarted with a series of
reassuring jerks.

Around nine o'clock of that November night he got out
at Dornbirn and left the station between two rows of towns-
people who gathered there each evening in the hope of
meeting relatives returning from prisoner-of-war camps, and,
as he started up the Bahnhofstrasse toward the marketplace,
Frau Altdorf caught up with him.

H didn't ask if Halka was still there, and each successive
moment that passed without Frau Altdorf saying that she'd
been sent away was blessed with the growing promise of
reunion. When they came to the bank building she put out
her hand in the dark and took the attaché case from him and,
while he waited outside the door behind whose frosted glass
was no glimmer of light, went upstairs with it.

H stood in the hall taking in the reality, after so many
imaginative returns, of being back, though still not quite
reassured by the landlady's behaviour. Then on the landing
above appeared a plump-seeming girl looking down at him.
Before he'd visually identified her with the longed-for image,

his senses had registered a shock of joy; without appearing to touch the stairs, she flew down the last flight into his arms.

The initial strangeness was accentuated by Halka's having filled out on the quantities of pears and plums that, she explained, she'd eaten while helping her landlady to pick and preserve.

Around midnight they went to bed together without interrupting the talk that had been going on for hours. H counted the strokes he'd feared he'd never hear again as the clock in the market square struck three and, at last, the talking stopped. The silence between them was the almost imperceptible pause that intervenes between ebb and flow, daylight and dusk. The pressures to communicate had been spent; there was a moment when nothing stirred, then the other movement below that of thoughts and their expression set in.

In the intense relief of opening their hearts to each other, unburdening them of the loneliness and fear, the sensation of dumb touch had been forgotten and now rushed back in a shock of delight out of the blue.

In the morning they went through snowy streets to a yard where big, tight-leaved cabbages were being distributed. Halka received a cleanly sliced-through portion as her ration, and as H carried back the icy half-orb with the flat, cut side uppermost with a few snowflakes falling on to the intricate yellow-green pattern, he felt he was holding in his freezing hands a symbol of what he had regained.

A few wintry days of bliss, devoid of almost all normal activity or amenity, between two periods of darkness and dread; not that H foresaw the suddenness of the oncoming of the second of these.

Small happenings that long ago would not have registered now echoed clearly and magically in this pure atmosphere. The one occasion when they left the little room of an evening to attend a recital by a French pianist in a wooden hall a few yards away down a side lane from the bank, they prepared themselves as for an event demanding the most faithful responses. And that is what it turned out, even for H who normally would have dreaded having to sit through a concert or recital. The music of Schumann, Chopin, and Liszt, especially Chopin's 'Barcarole' and the 'Ballade', Opus 47 – he kept the flimsy, single-sheet programme and studied it afterwards – introduced him, as previously only certain works of fiction had done, to new states of perception. Back to the cold room and, hunger forgotten, into bed where her body became a sexual extension of the music and sensations were spiritual-sensual, sacred-obscene, complete as never before.

They had one bad morning when he told her about meeting Susan in Paris, and Halka made him anxious, for he'd an inkling that time was short, by sulking for several hours. And in fact they had hardly recovered from the intensity of the reconciliation when they were startled by a shrill ring of the usually silent bell. A young French lieutenant asked H if his name was Ruark and if Mlle Witebsk lived here too. He then told them to come with him to the street where his *copain* was waiting.

He took them to a car that was stopped, not in front of the bank, but in the market square and spoke to the driver who got out and, as H and Halka returned to the house, followed by the two soldiers, she asked him, 'What's all this about?'

'It's bad,' he said, to prepare her for what was coming.

The quiet room seemed outraged by the presence of the two intelligence officers, as H guessed they were, and questions were put to him in a curiously desultory manner, as if the lieutenant didn't know what to ask and the order had come from Paris or even London, and in French that Halka grasped better than H. He was asked where he came from, had he a gun, how long was he living here; the Frenchman seemed surprised when H said he'd returned from Paris the previous week. He asked Halka if she had been in Marseille during the war, told her to repeat her Christian name and surname, compared them to what was written on the slip he had with him, and then with the same casual air suggested they take a few things with them as they'd be going away for a couple of days.

They were put in the back of the car and driven along the road that for most of the way ran close to the railway line on which they'd so often journeyed to and fro. At Bregenz they were brought to a second-floor office in a building at whose door H had read the sign, 'Securité Territoriale', and Halka was told to take everything out of her handbag; a cutting she'd kept about the trial of William Joyce was studied and commented on in low voices, but H's letters to her care of a Swiss address were ignored. After H had cleared out his pockets and had the contents, including the green booklet of hand-copied psalms, returned to him, a soldier was summoned and, after he was ostentatiously handed a revolver by the lieutenant, they were ordered to accompany him.

They trudged beside their guard – he was carrying a rifle, the revolver had disappeared into his pocket – up a steep street to a part of the town on the hill they had never explored.

'I'm thirsty,' Halka said. What hauntings the word evoked for H!

A high wall full of small, lit windows loomed over them, a barred gate was unlocked and in a stone-flagged, white-washed hallway they were handed over to Austrian prison warders; Halka at once requested not to be separated from H and was told that this wasn't a hotel.

She turned to wave goodbye as she was taken by her humorous gaoler, in a ski suit, up the ancient, winding stairs, and H, after giving up his passport, money, pen and shoe-laces in a tiny office, was also conducted upstairs and down a passage with a red-tiled floor to the last of the metal doors which, unlocked by the stocky little warder, revealed a heavy wooden one – in it, at the level of H's chest, was a small aperture – through which, after a further jingling of keys, H stepped into a cell whose two inmates were waiting in curiosity at this unexpected intrusion.

Sitting on his cot, H answered the tactful questions of the elder of his two fellow prisoners, a tall handsome man in a French uniform from which the insignia had been stripped, who introduced himself as Kestner, whom H later learned from Matukat, his other cellmate, was a colonel of the Algerian regiment who'd done most of the fighting on the way here.

In perfect German Kestner (an Alsatian?) was enquiring the age of H's fiancée as he'd described Halka, and hearing she was in her late twenties, remarked reassuringly, 'Old enough to take what's happened sensibly,' as if that point, rather than curiosity, had prompted the question. He didn't ask H why they had been arrested, not even his nationality, which H mentioned of his own accord.

Kestner returned to a pile of documents on the small table near the wire-guarded bulb over the cell door which, it turned out, the office of the Securité de Territoire gave him to annotate late into the night, and which he was taken there to return during the day – his added notes on the lists of French *collaborateurs*? Every half-hour or so, his bladder reacting predictably again, H had to get up and take the few steps past his chair to the bucket in the corner. When at last H settled himself for the night, Kestner got up and showed him how to arrange his two blankets to the best advantage, remarking that it was an art he'd learned during a North African campaign.

He slept for short intervals and at each awakening reexperiencing the shock of their arrest and incarceration. In the morning at exercise with the other prisoners he had a glimpse of Halka's face behind the bars of one of the second-floor windows and signalled back to her without the warder who stood at the top of the steps from the yard to the back door, or the other stationed under the high outer wall watching the cells, remarking it.

Endless days emptied of all certainty except the fact that they'd fallen into the retributive hands of the victors. H, and Halka because she was involved with him, had been rounded up as one of the plague ridden in the countries being cleaned out. He was not interrogated beyond the brief questioning at their arrest and it did not occur to him to question their right to imprison him, nor even Halka. It wasn't hard for him to see his state of mind as singling him out from the healthy norm at a time when divergence and dissent was doubly suspect. That his inner state was obviously not the factual reason for their imprisonment was irrelevant.

Imperceptibly H got used to the life of the cell, by patience and learning to live on the smallest scraps of reassurance. Listening to Matukat's constant appeals to Kestner, to whom he looked up as someone in authority, a tendency among many Germans that H despised, to examine his dossier at the Securité office, H was encouraged to ask the colonel (ex-colonel?) to try to find out something about his own and Halka's case. He also sent a message to Halka by Matukat, who worked in the kitchen where the women prisoners sometimes peeled potatoes; H described her to his cellmate who dropped the note into her lap as he passed with his buckets. And a few days later a letter came from her in a flimsy bit of paper stuffed into the back binding of her missal, which she was able to send him by the stocky warder known as Pappa Masson, thanks to a benevolence hidden beneath the brisk severity of his exterior.

In the evenings of the days when Kestner had been taken down to the town H waited anxiously for his return. But after the ex-officer had given his usual ambiguous replies to Matukat's importunate questionings, during which he'd have taken off his uniform jacket and stretched on his cot, an ironical smile flickering, it struck H, below his close-cropped moustache, and occasionally farting, he'd take up a book and, while reading, start humming an old German tune. The sentimental words of this song, popular before H's time, about, of all things, a mother swallow and her fledgelings, came to haunt H from having to listen to Kestner singing it below his breath, while seeming to read – to discourage Matukat? – as his hope of hearing something about his and Halka's probable fate dwindled.

Some first prison-impressions: the jingle of keys, the clap of the warder's ski boots on the tiled passage, the cry 'Kübel raus!' at the hour of putting the heavy slop bucket outside the cell, and the refrain of the song:

> *Immerzu, immerzu,*
> *Fliegt die Schwalbenmutter zu,*
> *Ohne Rast und Ruh . . .*

which H translated to himself as:

> *To and fro, to and fro,*
> *Flies the mother swallow*
> *Without rest or peace . . .*

The power of obsessive hunger to give trivialities vital significance: when the shutter in the inner door was slapped down and the tins of gruel or thin soup, containing a few pieces of potato, were passed through to Matukat, H took in exactly how full the one handed on to him was compared with the other two, and a fraction of an inch on the wrong side – Matukat always seemed to manage to put aside the fullest for himself – caused him a pang of disappointment.

The correspondence with Halka, now carried on entirely by missal, which Pappa Masson was not indisposed to take back and forth between their cells, impressed by the pious connotation of the exchange – or pretending to be? – was at first confined to exhortations, on H's part, for her to continue to cling to the somewhat obscure promises of their favourite psalms and not give in to despair. Then, as nothing more drastic happened to them, they began, half shyly at first, to express love and longing for each other and finally, ever regaining a little more outspokenness, there were frank expressions of desire and, finally, of the hope of Halka becoming pregnant at the first opportunity; this bold new idea was an especial reassurance.

When H at last brought himself to ask Kestner if he'd been able to glean anything about their case, he was told, 'They themselves at the Securité are in the dark; the orders for your arrest came from Paris and they're waiting for further instructions.'

H interpreted this as bad news; otherwise why hadn't Kestner volunteered it of his own accord? He was half convinced that the British had asked the French to arrest and, after a short delay, quietly execute him; this, if questioned, could later be explained as a failure in liaison. The idea was strengthened during one of his attempts at what he thought of as facing what was in store by the sensation of the blood gushing from his chest wounds in spurts rather than in a constant flow. Reflecting on this unexpected physical detail, he saw it as an authentic premonition, the effect of the pumping action of the heart which itself hadn't been mortally wounded, and which he thought had been mentioned by the prisoner who'd witnessed the executions at Maryborough.

One morning as he filed with the others back into the building after exercise, he was told to collect his belongings together in readiness to be moved to another cell.

After waiting apprehensively most of the day, for any change that wasn't the essential one was to be dreaded, H was conducted on a winter afternoon to a ground-floor cell that struck him as horribly crowded the moment the door was opened. Unlike the one he'd left, there were no cots in it, but half a dozen straw mattresses lay side by side on a raised and slightly sloping platform at the further end. The warder indicated his as the vacant one on the stone floor.

H had been assimilated into the little community of three in his previous cell, being made to feel somewhat less vulnerable by this tentative solidarity. He'd imagined that Kestner had a certain regard for him, as he didn't treat him with the amused contempt he showed for Matukat; and with

Matukat, largely preoccupied with hero worship for Kestner, H had established a kind of understanding. But here he'd no contacts; he was with a gang of strange men, all young except for a farmer in for selling produce on the black market, who played cards and conversed together in an unfamiliar dialect.

At exercise he looked with nostalgia toward Kestner, when not down at Securité headquarters, and Matukat, and one day managed to join them, by pausing to adjust a piece of purposely torn boot sole, in their part of the slowly perambulating ring. As he did so, a paper pellet fell into the yard not far from them, and Kestner drew H's attention to a shadowy head and shoulders behind the bars of what he said was a punishment cell. On the next circuit H stepped out of line, stooped quickly and picked up the bit of paper.

'Bloody silly taking a risk like that,' Kestner told H; the warder hadn't spotted him.

H was trying to determine whether the woman at the window was or wasn't Halka. He'd only a moment or two at each round of the yard to make up his mind; he daren't draw attention to her by turning his head. Another paper pellet fell into the yard, still miraculously unremarked by Pappa Masson, who'd just been brought the morning's post from the front gate by the female warder.

Unscrewing the first piece of paper before attempting to pick up the second, H found it blank – because her pencil had been taken from her? Had she been able to scribble or scratch a word on the other bit of paper? He was about to try to retrieve that too, but Kestner laid a hand on his arm.

'You're only encouraging the crazy bitch!'

It evidently hadn't crossed Kestner's mind it might be H's 'fiancée' up there, or was he suggesting that as she must be temporarily out of her senses, there was nothing to be gained by H getting himself locked up in another punishment cell?

For nights H was haunted by the apparition at the window. As he lay awake on the floor, everything seemed to indicate that it was Halka; one night he interpreted unaccustomed sounds overhead, where he thought the punishment cells were situated, as the result of her having been found by the warder on his nocturnal rounds, hanging from a window bar. In the mornings he was less sure that it had been her; no one had appeared at the window during exercise again.

At last for the first time since he'd been moved to the new cell, the reason for which he supposed had been the interception of one of their notes, her missal was handed in to him through the aperture in the door. Waiting till his cellmates had returned to their cards, after the expectant pause that always accompanied an unscheduled opening of the Judas hole, he felt inside the back binding with his little finger – a contact that sometimes, but not on this occasion, had for him a subtly sensual connotation – and extracted the piece of toilet paper on which she wrote that she'd heard he would be taken with a transport of prisoners to Paris in a few days.

'I've been promised that we'll be allowed to meet before that happens. But that will be with a warder and we'll have to speak German, so this is to say a few last words of real goodbye.'

With such life-and-death messages and intimations crowding in on him, he gave little thought to a constant need to scratch, registered by what seemed a nerve far away on the fringes of consciousness. But one evening after taking off his trousers before slipping under the blankets he saw that his thigh was covered with burning, itching pimples, still without much concern. He thought that a body already taken over by powerful poisons, as it seemed to him, in the way of psychological by-products wouldn't for long afford a feeding ground for germs.

This theory wasn't borne out, and it was just during the long hours while he waited to be summoned to the prison governor's office to take leave of Halka before joining the batch of French and Belgian prisoners – the latter followers of the Nazi leader Degrelle – whom he'd overheard his cellmates confirm were being sent home for trial, that the rash spread.

When both legs, from hip bones to knees, were covered by tiny, oozing sores he reported his condition, and the following evening at six, which, as at certain other fateful times in the legend, was now the hour when, after an outwardly empty day, the vital events took place, the doors were opened and Pappa Masson accompanied a bespectacled girl into the cell.

Keeping his shirt tucked between his legs, H lowered his trousers and the girl stooped and scrutinized the red pustules. Straightening up, she looked into his face with a fraternal regard that H understood as between two of the contaminated and, after naming the skin disease, told him, in English, that before the war she'd been a medical student in Brussels. Meanwhile the black-market farmer was protesting to the warder at being exposed to an infectious complaint and demanded that H be isolated in a cell where he wouldn't give it to the rest of them.

Now it seemed to H he was shunned by the others in the cell, though it was only the elderly prisoner who folded a sheet of newspaper over the rim of the bucket before he used it. While he spread the black greasy ointment over his thighs and awaited, with increased dread toward evening, the order to put together his belongings, he was aware of having reached the furthest point of loss. All was ending in disaster; he was about to lose Halka, and as for becoming the kind of writer he had hoped to, the prospects might be better than ever but, even if he survived, it seemed it would have to be in a future too remote and unforeseeable to be contemplated except in the fantasies that he sometimes indulged in.

He was again preoccupied by the particular kind of isolation extreme examples of which had obsessed him long ago in Paris when his mind had been attuned for such reflection by the early evening hangovers. He imagined himself relieving the thirst that seemed always suffered by those who, through a misgearing or mistiming that prevented the intermeshing of their consciousness with the ones around them, were exposed either to public or self-condemnation.

In the most frequent fantasy he constructed a machine out of which, like Moses with Aaron's rod, he could cause a sparkling stream to flow. He saw himself trundling his mobile dispenser into precincts reached through a bolted door at the end of tiled corridors, or alongside institutional beds in the endless nights. There were also recipients of the long, cool, citron-flavoured drinks whose faces were not those of complete strangers, though H never defined them too closely.

The second evening after starting the treatment he heard an unusual clamour coming from the window high in the wall and one of the prisoners, by standing on the table and grasping the bars, drew his head level with it and reported that the transport had assembled on the steps; the window overlooked the prison entrance.

Until his muscles couldn't support him any longer, the watcher at the window described the scene under the lights above the front gate as an officer addressed (inspected?) the prisoners and the guards stood below the steps with sub-machine-guns cradled in their arms. Then another of H's cellmates replaced the first and continued the commentary, naming those in the assembled group he recognized.

One was the Belgian girl who'd prescribed the ointment that was already proving efficacious, but the greater shock came with the news that Kestner, known throughout the prison as its most distinguished inmate, was there with the others and, what was more, the only one to be handcuffed.

H was aware of relief that he wasn't after all waiting out there to be taken somewhere where there'd begin an endless legalistic process to decide whether he was to be publicly branded with the sign of the guilty, which couldn't, he thought, have detached him more completely from the community of the just than he now was.

Shortly after the departure of the French and Belgians, on a clear spring morning – he and Halka had now been six months in prison – those in his and the adjoining cells were sent into the vegetable garden at the back of the building to shake out the straw in their mattresses and air their blankets.

The impact of the blinding light – under its high walls the exercise yard was, in comparison, in perpetual twilight – was almost intolerable. After he'd accustomed himself to it he pulled his hand from the slit in the material into which it had been thrust to loosen the straw, and as he straightened his back he saw, floating high above the distant horizon, the pure pale peaks of the Säntis range. In the moment the intimation that the previous summer in the transit camp in Bregenz he'd been on the verge of grasping, but hadn't had the courage for, was being repeated to him.

The cell, on his return, appeared dim and shabby to the point of being uninhabitable, and it was hard to see how he'd ever looked on it, or his own corner of its floor, as a tolerable shelter. But soon he was reconciled to it again. Although he was still far from coming to understand the necessity for what had happened to them, he did begin to see the silence that he had entered as the deep divide between the past and what was still to come. Whatever it was that was at the other end there was no way of telling. It might be a howl of final despair or the profound silence might be broken by certain words that he didn't yet know how to listen for.

Jennifer Johnston

from *The Christmas Tree*

S HE ALWAYS wondered who read her work, the three novels that she had sent hopefully to various publishers. What sort of people were they who took home piles of typescript in the evening and spent a few hours flipping through the pages, letting their eyes stroll through the lines of black words? Hundreds and thousands of useless, wasted words. Someone's dead dreams in the pile on the right, distinct possibilities on the left.

The man had his back to the window as she came in the door, so she was only aware of his height and the paleness and blueness of his suit and the blackness of his hair as she walked the length of the room towards him. He stood there silently, unaccommodating, his hands hanging by his sides, the sunlight shifting through the green leaves on the trees outside the window.

'Sit down.'

She sat on the edge of an elegant chair and looked past him out into the shining garden. After a moment he sat too and turned so that she could at last see his face. He looked fatigued. It must be hell, she thought, at the top. There was so much silence around that she could hear the birds in the garden chirping; if the window had been open she could have heard the grass growing. She pinched the back of her left hand between the nails of her thumb and first finger, just stop, she warned herself, bloody stop. He stretched out a hand and pushed a cigarette box towards her. The silk cuff that covered his wrist was a marginally paler blue than the blue of his suit. If a miracle could translate me back to Notting

Hill again, now, this here moment, now, I might promise never to write another word.

'Umm. No, thanks,' she said, referring to the cigarettes.

He withdrew his hand from the box and let it fall on to the red plastic cover of her typescript that lay in front of him on the desk.

'Why do you write?'

His voice was uninterested.

She opened the catch of her handbag and then closed it again.

He tapped the red cover impatiently as he waited for her answer.

'I ... well ... want to write. That's all I really want to do ... write.'

'But why? Surely you must have some idea why?'

'Isn't it enough just to want to do something ... itch to do it?'

'Have you anything to say?'

'I don't know.'

He looked displeased.

'I mean ... I'll have to find that out as I go along.'

He flipped through the pages in front of him with a finger.

'I like to see the possibles,' he said. 'I like to judge for myself. You can tell. I,' he amended, 'can tell.'

He picked up the typescript and looked at it for a moment before offering it to her across the desk.

'You have a small talent. Quite an original eye. To be quite blunt Miss ... ah ... Keating is it? ... Keating ... there is no point in us publishing a marginal first novel if we don't feel strongly that a second novel will come along, and a third. Growth and development. No point at all. We are not a charitable organization. No.' He allowed himself a slight smile at the thought. 'You have, as I said, a small talent, but I really don't see you developing. In fact, I would be very surprised if you ever wrote anything else.'

She took the papers from him and stood up. Her hands were shaking.

'Thank you,' she said. Her voice sounded thick and ugly. She turned away from the green shining window and walked towards the door. When she reached it, she turned round. He was rubbing fretfully at the hand that had held the red plastic folder, with a pale blue silk handkerchief.

'Goodbye,' she said.

He bowed towards her. No point in wasting more words than were absolutely necessary.

The sun was shining benignly in the windows of the tall houses, little eddies of city dust moved on the pavement. She stood for a moment on the steps outside the door and watched the cars go by. About twenty paces down the street to her right a little basket hung on a lamppost. She walked quickly towards it, the red file in her hand. She shoved it right down amongst the old copies of the *Evening Standard*, the cigarette packets and the paper bags. Maybe, she thought, the man who emptied the bins might take it home and read it, and love it and feel his life was changed for having read it, on the other hand he might not.

'Bloody fucking bastard,' she said inelegantly and walked on.

'Did anything ever come of your writing?'

Her father always asked the same question at the same moment, just after they had ordered their meal and the menus had been removed by the waiter. A glass of pale sherry sat in front of each of them and candles flickered on the small table.

'Not really.'

She had never been able to bring herself to tell him about the interview with the man in the blue suit. She felt she didn't know him well enough to judge whether he would be amused, sympathetic or merely bored. He was mostly bored by their infrequent evenings together when he visited London. Perhaps bored was not quite the right word, uninterested might be more accurate.

'What a shame.' A smile moved his mouth.

I wonder if you love me, she thought as she looked carefully at his handsome, ageing face ... love any of us ... I don't just mean me ... would you have loved a son perhaps?

He raised the glass to his lips. Gold cufflinks, immaculate nails, the skin on the backs of his hands was beginning to wrinkle now, like well-worn gloves.

'Do you mind if I smoke?'

She shook her head. He took a gold case out of his pocket and opened it.

'I take it you haven't acquired the habit?'

'No.'

He took a cigarette from the case and laid it on the table beside the sherry glass and put the case away.

'I once thought seriously of becoming a writer myself.'

She looked at him with amazement as he lit his cigarette.

'Really, Father? When ...?'

'A long time ago. Yes. When I was at Cambridge I wrote a bit. Short stories.' He frowned, regretting, perhaps, his indiscretion. 'A play or two. That was my real interest, writing plays. Only for the university, you understand. I was very keen on theatre in those days.'

'Were they performed, your plays?'

'Oh yes.'

'I wish you'd told me before. Why didn't you?'

'It didn't seem very interesting. My personal failure ... neither interesting nor inspiring in any way. Why did I tell you now, is really the question and I don't know the answer to that. It was a totally unpremeditated remark.'

'Why did you stop?'

He shrugged his shoulders slightly.

'I had to make decisions, my dear. The law seemed more secure. I have never been what you might call a daredevil.'

'And the stories . . . were they published?'

'Oh yes. Quite well received. *The Strand* . . . *Blackwood*'s . . . you know . . . quite well . . .'

'Did Mother know?'

'I had made my decisions before I met your mother. I have never been quite sure whether or not I took the right decision. Over all, I think I did. Yes. I have had a few moments of regret, but only a few. I am not cut out for the artistic life.'

The waiter put two plates of smoked salmon down in front of them. Mr Keating pursed his lips in slight disapproval as he looked at the food.

'So,' he said as he picked up his knife and fork.

Constance watched him.

Carefully he dissected the salmon and put a piece in his mouth.

'I cannot imagine why a restaurant of this calibre gives its customers commercially smoked salmon. Taste it. Taste it.'

'It looks lovely,' said Constance.

'It's poor.' Peevishly he pushed his plate to one side.

'It's delicious, Father.'

'Poor. London has changed.'

'Well, I think it's delicious.'

'So' – he continued as if he had never interrupted himself in the first place – 'it would have given me a certain satisfaction if you had become a writer. Had taken the idea seriously.'

'I did, do, take it seriously, Father. I just don't have the talent, or whatever you'd like to call it.'

'I would have got some pleasure from that all right. There's no denying that. I'm not, of course, suggesting that you and Barbara are not admirable. Admirable. Admirable.'

He obviously regretted his hasty treatment of the smoked salmon. He pulled the plate towards him and began to eat with speed.

'Talent, after all, has to be allied with so many other attributes; drive, persistence, egoism, commitment. I lacked the commitment. I was not prepared to fail. It seems that you, too, feel the same way.' He sprinkled a little red pepper on his salmon.

'A sad thing.'

He broke a piece of brown bread and popped it into his mouth.

'You look at your children as they grow, mature a bit, and will, yes, will, that somehow they will succeed in having some of the attributes that you yourself regret having lacked. At least' – he flushed away the painful taste of the smoked salmon with some sherry – 'some development of the qualities that you find admirable in yourself. Is it a failure of some sort if you only see your own weaknesses in your children? I wonder.'

She felt the question was rhetorical and didn't say a word.

'Your mother would have preferred that I became a judge, but I had no interest, I turned it down. I preferred the bar to the bench. Yes indeed. You and Barbara . . .'

'Bibi and I are all right, Father.'

'You are all right.'

There was a certain contempt in his voice.

'We are the way we want to be. Isn't that all right? As you are. We chose.'

He shook his head.

The waiters surrounded the table. Plates, glasses, knives danced across the white cloth.

'Can I ask you one thing?'

He bent his head slightly, saying neither yes nor no.

'I've always wondered why, when it wasn't really necessary, you went to the war. It might have ruined your career . . . Mother said . . . some people might have taken it amiss. Mother . . .'

'Your mother always believed in people keeping their feet on the ground.'

'It's just something I have always wondered about.'

She paused and looked at his face. He was escaping from

her. She put out a hand as if she might be able to catch some part of him, but laid it down again on the cloth among the glasses and the silver.

'After all, you said yourself, only a moment ago, that you weren't a daredevil.'

His voice was matter-of-fact once more.

'It wasn't that I objected to De Valera's neutrality in any way. On the contrary. It would have been insanity to hurl such a new-born state, and one born out of such pain, into a major war. Insanity. I did, however, feel that I had a duty to perform ... don't get me wrong, I had no political feelings of being West British or anything like that, no Crown fever ... I suppose it was a feeling of duty that I had learnt at school. At Cambridge.'

He sighed.

The waiter poured a few drops of wine into his glass and waited, bottle poised, beside him. He took up the glass and looked at the wine for a moment before touching it briefly with his lips. He nodded to the waiter.

'It was a very personal decision ... to defend, in my own small way, democracy. I know it has its faults. There are many who would totally condemn it, but it was the one thing that gave us, you understand, the freedom to remain neutral, gave me the freedom to choose. So I chose to go, I think it was the right choice. There was a time when we all felt very depressed. You wouldn't remember. You were too young. But there was a time when it seemed possible that Hitler might win. So.'

He picked up his glass and had a drink.

'I wasn't a hero in any way. I can assure you of that. Now that claret is truly excellent.'

He had said too much and the rest of the meal was eaten mostly in silence.

PART THREE

John McGahern

High Ground

I LET THE boat drift on the river beneath the deep arch of the bridge, the keel scraping the gravel as it crossed the shallows out from Walsh's, past the boat-house at the mouth, and out into the lake. It was only the slow growing distance from the ring of reeds round the shore that told that the boat moved at all on the lake. More slowly still, the light was going from the August evening.

I was feeling leaden with tiredness but did not want to sleep. I had gone on the river in order to be alone, the way one goes to a darkroom.

The Brothers' Building Fund Dance had been held the night before. A big marquee had been set up in the grounds behind the monastery. Most of the people I had gone to school with were there, awkward in their new estate, and nearly all the brothers who had taught us: Joseph, Francis, Benedictus, Martin. They stood in a black line beneath the low canvas near the entrance and waited for their old pupils to go up to them. When they were alone, watching us dance, rapid comment passed up and down the line, and often Joseph and Martin doubled up, unable or unwilling to conceal laughter; but by midnight they had gone, and a night of a sort was ours, the fine dust from the floor rising into the perfume and sweat and hair oil as we danced in the thresh of the music.

There was a full moon as I drove Una to her home in Arigna in the borrowed Prefect, the whole wide water of Allen taking in the wonderful mysteriousness of the light. We sat in the car and kissed and talked, and morning was

67

there before we noticed. After the harshness of growing up, a world of love and beauty, of vague gardens and dresses and laughter, one woman in a gleaming distance seemed to be almost within reach. We would enter this world. We would make it true.

I was home just before the house had risen, and lay on the bed and waited till everybody was up, and then changed into old clothes. I was helping my father put a new roof on the house. Because of the tiredness, I had to concentrate completely on the work, even then nearly losing my footing several times between the stripped beams, sometimes annoying my father by handing him the wrong lath or tool; but when evening came the last thing I wanted was sleep. I wanted to be alone, to go over the night, to try to see clearly, which only meant turning again and again in the wheel of dreaming.

'Hi there! Hi! Do you hear me, young Moran!' The voice came with startling clarity over the water, was taken up by the fields across the lake, echoed back. 'Hi there! Hi! Do you hear me, young Moran!'

I looked all around. The voice came from the road. I couldn't make out the figure at first, leaning in a broken gap of the wall above the lake, but when he called again I knew it was Eddie Reegan. Senator Reegan.

'Hi there, young Moran. Since the mountain can't come to Mahomet, Mahomet will have to come to the mountain. Row over here for a minute. I want to have a word with you.'

I rowed very slowly, watching each oar splash slip away from the boat in the mirror of water. I disliked him, having unconsciously, perhaps, picked up my people's dislike. He had come poor to the place, buying Lynch's small farm cheap, and soon afterwards the farmhouse burned down. At once, a bigger house was built with the insurance money, closer to the road, though that in its turn was due to burn down too, to be replaced by the present mansion, the avenue of Lawson cypresses now seven years old. Soon he was buying up other small farms, but no one had ever seen him work with shovel or with spade. He always appeared immaculately dressed. It was as if he understood instinctively that it was only the shortest of short steps from appearance to becoming. 'A man who works never makes any money. He has no time to see how the money is made,' he was fond of boasting. He set up as an auctioneer. He entered politics. He married Kathleen Relihan, the eldest of old Paddy Relihan's daughters, the richest man in the area, Chairman of the County Council. 'Do you see those two girls? I'm going to marry one of those girls,' he was reported to have remarked to a friend. 'Which one?' 'It doesn't matter. They're both Paddy Relihan's daughters'; and when Paddy retired it was Reegan rather than any of his own sons who succeeded Paddy in the Council. Now that he had surpassed Paddy Relihan and become a Senator, and it seemed only a matter of time before he was elected to the Dail, he no longer joked about 'the aul effort of a fire', and was gravely concerned about the reluctance of insurance companies to grant cover for fire to dwelling houses in our part of the country. He had bulldozed the hazel and briar from the hills above the lake, and as I turned to see how close the boat had come to the wall I could see behind him the white and black of his Friesians grazing between the electric fences on the far side of the reseeded hill.

I let the boat turn so that I could place my hand on the stone, but the evening was so calm that it would have rested beneath the high wall without any hand. The Senator had seated himself on the wall as I was rowing in, and his shoes hung six or eight feet above the boat.

'It's not the first time I've had to congratulate you, though I'm too high up here to shake your hand. And what I'm certain of is that it won't be the last time either,' he began.

'Thanks. You're very kind,' I answered.

'Have you any idea where you'll go from here?'

'No. I've applied for the grant. It depends on whether I get the grant or not.'

'What'll you do if you get it?'

'Go on, I suppose. Go a bit farther . . .'

'What'll you do then?'

'I don't know. Sooner or later, I suppose, I'll have to look for a job.'

'That's the point I've been coming to. You are qualified to teach, aren't you?'

'Yes. But I've only taught for a few months. Before I got that chance to go to the University.'

'You didn't like teaching?' he asked sharply.

'No.' I was careful. 'I didn't dislike it. It was a job.'

'I like that straightness. And what I'm looking to know is – if you were offered a very good job would you be likely to take it?'

'What job?'

'I won't beat around the bush either. I'm talking of the Principalship of the school here. It's a very fine position for a young man. You'd be among your own people. You'd be doing good where you belong. I hear you're interested in a very attractive young lady not a hundred miles from here. If you decided to marry and settle down I'm in a position to put other advantages your way.'

Master Leddy was the Principal of the school. He had been the Principal as long as I could remember. He had taught me, many before me. I had called to see him just three days before. The very idea of replacing him was shocking. And anyhow, I knew the politicians had nothing to do with the appointment of teachers. It was the priest who ran the school. What he was saying didn't even begin to make sense, but I had been warned about his cunning and was wary. 'You must be codding. Isn't Master Leddy the Principal?'

'He is now but he won't be for long more – not if I have anything to do with it.'

'How?' I asked very quietly in the face of the outburst.

'That need be no concern of yours. If you can give me your word that you'll take the job, I can promise you that the job is as good as yours.'

'I can't do that. I can't follow anything right. Isn't it Canon Gallagher who appoints the teachers?'

'Listen. There are many people who feel the same way as I do. If I go to the Canon in the name of all those people and say that you're willing to take the job, the job is yours. Even if he didn't want to, he'd have no choice but to appoint you . . .'

'Why should you want to do that for me? Say, even if it is possible.' I was more curious now than alarmed.

'It's more than possible. It's bloody necessary. I'll be plain. I have three sons. They go to that school. They have nothing to fall back on but whatever education they get. And with the education they're getting at that school up there, all they'll ever be fit for is to dig ditches. Now, I've never dug ditches, but even at my age I'd take off my coat and go down into a ditch rather than ever have to watch any of my sons dig. The whole school is a shambles. Someone described it lately as one big bear garden.'

'What makes you think I'd be any better?'

'You're young. You're qualified. You're ambitious. It's a very good job for someone your age. I'd give you all the backing you'd want. You'd have every reason to make a go of it. With you there, I'd feel my children would be still in with a chance. In another year or two even that'll be gone.'

'I don't see why you want my word at this stage,' I said evasively, hoping to slip away from it all. I saw his face return to its natural look of shrewdness in what was left of the late summer light.

'If I go to the Canon now, it'll be just another complaint in a long line of complaints. If I can go to him and say that things can't be allowed to go on as they have been going and we have a young man here, from a good family, a local more than qualified, who's willing to take the job, who has everyone's backing, it's a different proposition entirely. And I can guarantee you here this very evening that you'll be the Principal of that school when it opens in September.'

For the first time it was all coming clear to me.

'What'll happen to the Master? What'll he do?'

'What I'm more concerned about is what'll my children do if he stays,' he burst out again. 'But you don't have to concern yourself about it. It'll be all taken care of.'

I had called on the Master three evenings before, walking beyond the village to the big ramshackle farmhouse. He was just rising, having taken all his meals of the day in bed, and was shaving and dressing upstairs, one time calling down for a towel, and again for a laundered shirt.

'Is that young Moran?' He must have recognized my voice or name. 'Make him a good cup of tea. And he'll be able to be back up the road with myself.'

A very old mongrel greyhound was routed from the leather armchair one side of the fire, and I was given tea and slices of buttered bread. The Master's wife, who was small and frail with pale skin and lovely brown eyes, kept up a cheerful chatter that required no response as she busied herself about the enormous cluttered kitchen which seemed not to possess a square foot of room. There were buckets everywhere, all sorts of chairs, basins, bags of meal and flour, cats, the greyhound, pots and pans. The pattern had faded from the bulging wallpaper, a dark ochre, and some of the several calendars that hung around the walls had faded into the paper. It would have been difficult to find space for an extra cup or saucer on the long wooden table. There were plainly no set meal times. Two of the Master's sons, now grown men, came singly in from the fields while I waited. Plates of food were served at once, bacon and liver, a mug of tea. They took from the plate of bread already on the table, the butter, the sugar, the salt, the bottle of sauce. They spent no more than a few minutes over the meal, blessing themselves at its end, leaving as suddenly as they'd entered, smiling and nodding in a friendly way in my direction, but making little attempt at conversation, though Gerald did ask, before he reached for his hat – a hat I recognized as having belonged to the Master back in my school days, a brown hat with a blue teal's feather and a small hole burned in its side – 'Well, how are things getting along in the big smoke?' The whole effect was of a garden and orchard gone completely wild, but happily.

'You couldn't have come at a better time. We'll be able to be up the road together,' the Master said as he came heavily down the stairs in his stockinged feet. He'd shaved, was dressed in a grey suit, with a collar and tie, the old gold watch-chain crossing a heavy paunch. He had aged since last I'd seen him, the face red and puffy, the white hair thinned, and there was a bruise on the cheekbone where he must have fallen. The old hound went towards him, licking at his hand.

'Good boy! Good boy,' he said as he came towards me, patting the hound. As soon as we shook hands he slipped his feet into shoes which had stood beside the leather chair. He did not bend or sit, and as he talked I saw the small bird-like woman at his feet, tying up the laces.

'It's a very nice thing to see old pupils coming back. Though not many of them bring me laurels like yourself, it's still a very nice thing. Loyalty is a fine quality. A very fine quality.'

'Now,' his wife stood by his side, 'all you need is your hat and stick,' and she went and brought them.

'Thank you. Thank you indeed. I don't know what I'd do but for my dear wife,' he said.

'Do you hear him now! He was never stuck for the charm. Off with you now before you get the back of me hand,' she bantered, and called as we went slowly towards the gate. 'Do you want me to send any of the boys up for you?'

'No. Not unless they have some business of their own to attend to in the village. No,' he said gravely, turning very slowly.

He spoke the whole way on the slow walk to the village. All the time he seemed to lag behind my snail's pace, sometimes standing because he was out of breath, tapping at the road with the cane. Even when the walk slowed to a virtual standstill it seemed to be still far too energetic.

'I always refer to you as my star pupil. When the whole enterprise seems to be going more or less askew, I always point to young Moran: that's one good job I turned out. Let the fools prate.'

I walked, stooping by his side, restraining myself within the slow walk, embarrassed, ashamed, confused. I had once looked to him in pure infatuation, would rush to his defence against every careless whisper. He had shone like a clear star. I was in love with what I hardly dared to hope I might become. It seemed horrible now that I might come to this.

'None of my own family were clever,' he confided. 'It was a great disappointment. And yet they may well be happier for it. Life is an extraordinary thing. A very great mystery. Wonderful . . . shocking . . . thing.'

Each halting speech seemed to lead in some haphazard way into the next.

'Now that you're coming out into the world you'll have to be constantly on your guard. You'll have to be on your guard first of all against intellectual pride. That's the worst sin, the sin of Satan. And always be kind to women. Help them. Women are weak. They'll be attracted to you.' I had to smile ruefully, never having noticed much of a stampede in my direction. 'There was this girl I went home from a dance with once,' he continued. 'And as we were getting closer to her house I noticed her growing steadily more amorous until I had to say, "None of that now, girl. It is not the proper time!" Later, when we were both old and married, she thanked me. She said I was a true gentleman.'

The short walk seemed to take a deep age, but once outside Ryan's door he took quick leave of me. 'I won't invite you inside. Though I set poor enough of an example, I want to bring no one with me. I say to all my pupils: Beware of the high stool. The downward slope from the high stool is longer and steeper than from the top of Everest. God bless and guard you, young Moran. Come and see me again before you head back to the city.' And with that he left me. I stood facing the opaque glass of the door, the small print of the notice above it: *Seven Days Licence to Sell Wine, Beer, Spirits.*

'Do you mean the Master'll be out on the road, then?' I asked Senator Reegan from the boat, amazed still by the turn of the conversation.

'You need have no fear of that. There's a whole union behind him. In our enlightened day alcoholism is looked upon as just another illness. And they wonder how the country can be so badly off,' he laughed sarcastically. 'No. He'll probably be offered a rest cure on full pay. I doubt if he'd take it. If he did, it'd delay official recognition of your appointment by a few months, that'd be all, a matter of paperwork. The very worst that could happen to him is that he'd be forced to take early retirement, which would probably add years to his life. He'd just have that bit less of a pension with which to drink himself into an early grave. You need have no worries on that score. You'd be doing everybody a favour, including him most of all, if you'd take the job. Well, what do you say? I could still go to the Canon tonight. It's late but not too late. He'd be just addressing himself to his hot toddy. It could be as good a time as any to attack him. Well, what do you say?'

'I'll have to think about it.'

'It's a very fine position for a young man like yourself starting out in life.'

'I know it is. I'm very grateful.'

'To hell with gratitude. Gratitude doesn't matter a damn. It's one of those moves that benefits everybody involved. You'll come to learn that there aren't many moves like that in life.'

'I'll have to think about it.' I was anxious to turn away from any direct confrontation.

'I can't wait for very long. Something has to be done and done soon.'

'I know that but I still have to think about it.'

'Listen. Let's not close on anything this evening. Naturally you have to consider everything. Why don't you drop over to my place tomorrow night? You'll have a chance to meet my lads. And herself has been saying for a long time now that she'd like to meet you. Come about nine. Everything will be out of the way by then.'

I rowed very slowly away, just stroking the boat forward in the deadly silence of the half-darkness. I watched Reegan cross the road, climb the hill, pausing now and then among the white blobs of his Friesians. His figure stood for a while at the top of the hill where he seemed to be looking back towards the boat and water before he disappeared.

When I got back to the house everyone was asleep except a younger sister, who had waited up for me. She was reading by the fire, the small black cat on her knee.

'They've all gone to bed,' she explained. 'Since you were on the river, they let me wait up for you. Only there's no tea. I've just found out that there's not a drop of spring water in the house.'

'I'll go to the well, then. Otherwise someone will have to go first thing in the morning. You don't have to wait up for me.' I was too agitated to go straight to bed and glad of the distraction of any activity.

'I'll wait,' she said. 'I'll wait and make the tea when you get back.'

'I'll be less than ten minutes.' The late hour held for her the attractiveness of the stolen.

I walked quickly, swinging the bucket. The whole village seemed dead under a benign moon, but as I passed along the church wall I heard voices. They came from Ryan's Bar. It was shut, the blinds down, but then I noticed cracks of yellow light along the edges of the big blue blind. They were drinking after hours. I paused to see if I could recognize any of the voices, but before I had time Charlie Ryan hissed, 'Will you keep your voices down, will yous? At the rate you're going you'll soon have the Sergeant out of his bed,' and the voices quietened to a whisper. Afraid of being noticed in the silence, I passed on to get the bucket of spring water from the well, but the voices were in full song again by the time I returned. I let the bucket softly down in the dust and stood in the shadow of the church wall to listen. I recognized the Master's slurred voice at once, and then voices of some of the men who worked in the sawmill in the wood.

'That sixth class in 1933 was a great class, Master.' It was Johnny Connor's voice, the saw mechanic. 'I was never much good at the Irish, but I was a terror at the maths, especially the Euclid.'

I shivered as I listened under the church wall. Nineteen thirty-three was the year before I was born.

'You were a topper, Johnny. You were a topper at the maths,' I heard the Master's voice. It was full of authority. He seemed to have no sense at all that he was in danger.

'Tommy Morahan that went to England was the best of us all in that class,' another voice took up, a voice I wasn't able to recognize.

'He wasn't half as good as he imagined he was. He suffered from a swelled head,' Johnny Connor said.

'Ye were toppers, now. Ye were all toppers,' the Master said diplomatically.

'One thing sure is that you made a great job of us, Master. You were a powerful teacher. I remember to this day everything you told us about the Orinoca River.'

'It was no trouble. Ye had the brains. There are people in this part of the country digging ditches who could have been engineers or doctors or judges or philosophers had they been given the opportunity. But the opportunity was lacking. That was all that was lacking.' The Master spoke again with great authority.

'The same again all round, Charlie,' a voice ordered. 'And a large brandy for the Master.'

'Still, we kept sailing, didn't we, Master? That's the main thing. We kept sailing.'

'Ye had the brains. The people in this part of the country had powerful brains.'

'If you had to pick one thing, Master, what would you put those brains down to?'

'Will you hush now! The Sergeant wouldn't even have to be passing outside to hear yous. Soon he'll be hearing yous down in the barracks,' Charlie hissed.

There was a lull again in the voices in which a coin seemed to roll across the floor.

'Well, the people with the brains mostly stayed here. They had to. They had no choice. They didn't go to the cities. So the brains was passed on to the next generation. Then there's the trees. There's the water. And we're very high up here. We're practically at the source of the Shannon. If I had to pick on one thing more than another, I'd put it down to that. I'd attribute it to the high ground.'

Bridget O'Connor

Postcards

And my mother does not sleep at all. And I do not know where my dad is.

W E GET postcards but they are from different places and, sometimes, different lands. It is all lands, there are no people or farms or houses. It is scrubland and coloured hills. There is a man somewhere, or a woman, and that is a job, to paint light and cheer up the country. And some of them are funny. There are blue trees and green skies and some of the clouds have faces. So I think it is the boredom. They must get carried away. And my mother has a boxload. To her they are like love letters. I do not understand this. There is no love there that I can see. I have three of my own. They all say 'Hope you're keeping well.' They arrive on my birthday. Not a day early or a day late. On the right day. I suppose that might be love but I think it is good timing.

And I am the last one now. My sisters have gone and my brother. They have gone Over There, across the water. My mother says they could not wait to Get Out, to Get Away. She says not to mind but I do. The house is very quiet. And in the post come cheques and money orders. My mother will not cash them. And she tears them up into very tiny pieces. She shakes when she does this and hides the pieces in a drawer. 'I would not give them the pleasure,' she says, 'I would not.' I would. I do not see where the pleasure lies but I cannot say that. I cannot say very much to her.

And they went away on boats and planes so I am the

only one left now. And one day I will go, though my mother does not know this yet. There are things you must do first. You need money to leave and exams if you are to get on. That is what Mrs Kinny used to say, 'Exam grades are passports,' she said, 'that or a rich daddy.' But I do not know where my dad is. Mrs Kinny said I have a good brain and I could go far. Mrs Kinny said I must study hard. She liked me a lot. She liked all the unpopular girls because we did not play a lot. And not with each other. I do not have much time to study now. My mother gives me work to do as I am the only one left. She could not do without me, she says, I am her Love and she kisses me and pulls me to her. But she will not let me read or get on. She does not like my head in a book. 'What, with all this work to do.' And there is a lot of work. There is no denying the work to do.

And so, I do not go to school. Sometimes the Inspector comes but nobody can approach us quietly, take us by surprise. The dog barks. It howls and throws back its head. He has a rusty van and the road is not smooth. There are ruts in it and soft mud. And we can hear it cough and sputter and outside the house is gravel. And my mother puts me in the cupboard and folds a coat over my head. There is plenty of time. It is my dad's coat. It smells of my dad and I do not like that. And she pulls a table against the cupboard and sits there. And she is a good liar. She calls him Mister and first he will not sit down or drink her tea. But then he does. She pretends I am Over There with my sisters and my brother. And soon they are talking about the bad road and the storms and the people in the town. He says she must be awful lonely on her own but my mother does not fall for that. My mother does not fall for anything. And when the van is coughing up the road she moves the table back and opens the cupboard door. She slides the coat off my face. BOO she says. That is our joke. And we both laugh.

And my mother does not sleep at all. She does not like to be still. She says she does not know how to be. Every night my sheets are clean. Every day she scrubs them and they are on the line and freeze into walls. And she stands over me at night. I think it is to make sure I have not gone away. She likes to touch my face and put her fingers in my hair. She does this very gently, not to wake me. And it does not wake me now. And I sleep.

And this is what our house is like. It is stone and square and has deep windows. And there is a wooden barn leaning and falling on it. I do not like to go in there. It is my dad's place. It has his things and they are all metals. They are tools and engines and old inventions and they are everywhere in the straw. They are all rusty. It smells of rust and the straw is bad and wet and that smells too. Also, there are rats. When they die they leak a gas and so it smells of that too. I think you can die of that gas so I do not go in there. The light does not go in there either.

And so our house is very windy. This is because the land is flat for miles. And the wind is always wet. It is a soft wet though. You do not know you are wet until you touch your hair. And this is because the land is swamp and this means that my dad should not have built this house because nobody should build a house on a swamp.

And this is what our house sounds like. The wind flaps the sheets so there are sheet noises and a shutter bangs because we do not go into the barn to get the tools to mend it. And the dog barks and splashes in the puddles. And it is my mother who makes all the inside noise. I think this is why she does not stop because otherwise it is very quiet. And it becomes still. The sheets and the shutter and the dog are not noises to us because we do not make them. And we have only two rugs and the floors are cement. When you walk on the floors the dust rises and you cannot see your ankles for clouds. And the sound is hollow. This means that I can hear her feet and she can hear mine. And she is always asking me to get things and to Hurry. I do not see where the Hurry is but she does.

And the things I must bring quickly are old. This is what we do at night. And she calls them her Young Things. And I

know them all by heart. There are dresses and she holds
them up to the lamp and tiny moths fly out and so there are
tiny holes. And I sew up all the holes. And there are
photographs which are yellow and grey and curl up at the
edges. Of my sisters and my brother. I look at their faces but
I do not recognize them. They could not wait to Get Out to
Get Away she says. And there is no picture of me and only
one of my dad. And the one of my dad is after their wedding.
There are other faces in the back but they are blurred. My
mother and my dad are young and they are smiling. And my
mother has white flowers in her hair and pinned on her
blouse. They are so white they are like shining lights so that
is what you notice first. And that is because they are painted.
And my mother saves this picture up till last. And that is
when she cries and goes through the box. To her they are
like love letters but I do not see any love there. And so I go
to bed. And soon the house grows quiet. And it becomes
still.

Bryan MacMahon

A Woman's Hair

ON SUNDAY afternoons when the bar was closed and my father had gone off to a football match my mother would take the opportunity offered by the quiet house to wash her beautiful hair. There were times when she would do so, I realized later, solely to gratify me, her only daughter – and indeed, her only child.

When my mother's hair was washed, rinsed and had almost dried, I would insist on her sitting on a rocking-chair. I would then stand on a chair beside her to catch the cascading hair above the point where it had gently tangled and would resolutely force the comb through it. As accurately as I recall the texture of my mother's hair, I also remember my stolid father's incomprehension of it as a bond between me and her: all he seemed to understand was the filling of spill-over pint glasses for the cartmen and countrymen who made the vacant lot at our gable on the town's edge a stopping-place on their way to the market.

But always between my mother and me, and complementary to the bond of flesh and blood, was the shining spancel of hair. I combed it and plaited it and piled it and experimented with it until my fat father, bustling in and out of the kitchen, scarcely knew whether to laugh or to scowl at such tomfoolery which – to him – was of a piece with my mother's obsession with music and the incomprehensible tock-tock of the metronome on the top of our piano. And when, as ladylike as she had lived, my mother died, I was left with the memory of her hair spread out like a fan on the white linen pillows on either side of her waxen face.

After my mother's death – I was then ten years of age –
I was sent to a boarding school: I pined for home and after
two months was brought back and packed off to the local
convent day school, where I was an irregular attender, being
kept at home on slight pretexts. At this time I was something
of a daydreamer: washing ware at the window of the scullery,
I would look out on to the vacant lot beside our house and
watch the carters unyoke their horses and tie hissing nose-
bags of oats about the animals' necks. I recall seeing a thunder
shower fall on an unprotected box-cart of unslaked lime so
that later the rocks of lime bubbled like molten lava. At
certain times, too, the place grew still more interesting, for it
was a halting-place for the restless of the Irish roads –
umbrella-menders, ballad-singers, knife-grinders, men and
women all subject to the compulsion and tyranny of movement.

One Saturday evening in early January as dusk fell, a
tramp and his wife – more likely his 'woman' – pitched a
crude shelter just below our scullery window. The ice-cold
air and the early evening stars had already given warning
that a night of heavy frost would follow. The shelter was a
crude one – a dirty canvas sheet slung over a ridge-pole held
three feet above the ground by a few curved sally rods with
limestones fallen from our yard wall to keep the soiled skirt
of the camp in place. The shelter could be entered at either
end, simply by groping back the flaps.

The tramp was black-bearded and was sixty if he was a
day while the woman seemed to be in her early twenties. She
had clear-cut features with a weather-worn complexion and
there was in her stare a vacancy that seemed to offer a clue to
such an odd pairing.

But it was her luxuriant dark hair that, despite its tangled
and even filthy nature, attracted my attention. It appeared to
be of a finer texture than my own hair, or indeed than that of
my mother's, but the wind and sun had played havoc with
it. I grimaced at the thought that such hair seemed a waste
on the young woman's head.

As darkness fell, the tramp and his woman entered our bar, squatted on the floor in a corner, and began to drink stolidly, now and again muttering gutturally at each other. My father kept growling half-refusals to their requests for more drink, but the tramp and the woman kept blackmailing him and begging for more. I felt that my father continued to serve them simply because my mother had always pleaded for the 'travellers': 'Don't judge them, Tom – their life is hard. If they get drunk itself,' she would say, 'what harm is it? And they haven't far to go when they leave us – only from the bar to the gable outside.'

So, aloof and alone, the oddly-matched pair drank and muttered and growled and lisped and never spared an upward glance for the other customers.

When closing time was called, and overcalled, the travelling pair, with my father hanging threateningly above them, at last staggered to their feet, bundled themselves out the door and moved towards their shelter, where, swaying giddily, they groped at the flaps and at last fumbled in and down, almost bringing the canvas about their ears with their blundering movements. Watching them from the darkness through the just-open window of the scullery, the night air icy on my face, I wondered at the mystery of the cave in which they slept, with perhaps their bodies oddly tangled in one another. Then I looked up at the frost-polished heavens, shuddered in the night cold, and finally, closing the window without a sound, eased home the brass bolt on it. Thoughtfully I made my way to bed.

In the morning I awoke to find that the frost had painted palm-trees on the window-pane. I prepared the Sunday breakfast, then glanced out at the now glittering canvas of the tent. The frost had made the morning air soundless so that the town seemed unusually still. My father always slept out on Sunday mornings. As I came downstairs after having given him his breakfast in bed I heard a low knocking at the side-door.

I tiptoed out into the hallway. As again the knocking

came, 'Who's out?' I asked sharply. 'Me!' said the deep hoarse voice which I recognized at once as being that of the bearded tramp. 'What do you want?' I asked. 'A knife – or a scissors,' he growled. I paused, a constriction of fear in my heart. 'My father is in bed,' I told him. 'Can you wait till he gets up?' 'I must get it now – we have to be off!' The man's 'We have to be off' assuaged my latent fear that he meant harm, yet I asked: 'What do you want it for?' 'Something that's caught in the frost!' 'Is it the canvas?' 'Give me a knife or a scissors and I'll return it safely,' he muttered in reply.

I stood irresolute. A knife – no! But I could give him the battered black and silver tailor's scissors that was in the drawer of our kitchen table. With a cry of 'Wait!' I ran, rattled open the drawer and going to the door, opened it cautiously and handed out the scissors. A glimpse told me that the man was sober but that his face was haggard and white-cold with traces of drink rust about his lips. Muttering a word of thanks he moved away.

After a time, I ran to the scullery, climbed on a chair and, leaning over the sink, looked out at the shelter. What I saw made me cry out and beat with my knuckles on the frame of the window. I unshot the bolt, swung open the window on its hinges and screamed 'No! No!' at the top of my voice.

The tramp, who was kneeling on the ground at one end of the shelter, looked upwards over his shoulder at me. His black hat was pitched high on his head and a single lock of hair was plastered on to his white sweating forehead. 'No! No!' I screamed again, then leaping off the chair, I raced through the kitchen, tore into the shop, grabbed a claw-hammer from the tool-box under the counter and, opening the hall door, went pelting out.

The man, the scissors still in his hands, was on one knee at the end of the tent. Beneath him, prone on the ground and protruding from under the canvas of the shelter, lay the woman's head and breast. The tumult of her hair was spread out beneath her head. I verified what I had guessed at from my first glimpse through the window, that her hair was frost-locked in a small but comparatively deep pool of water that lay just outside the end of the camp and that the tramp was about to cut the hair so as to release it. The woman's face could have been the one carved in cameo on the brooch my mother wore, but for the fact that the rust of old drink befouled her lips about which an odd not-caring smile now played. The white skin of her lower throat and upper breasts was in startling contrast to her dark complexion and to the soiled ground beneath her head. 'Wait!' I cried again, pushing the man aside; crouching, my fingers verified that the hair was gripped in a frozen pool of animal urine.

I tilted the head sideways and, with the hammer-head, began to hack at the edge of the frozen pool. Under my blows the ice cracked brown-white at its edges. When I had reduced part of the edge of the pool to powder, I tried with the claw of the hammer to lever upwards on the ragged ice block of the frozen pool. Try as I would I failed to gain purchase on the ravelling ice.

The man, still in a kind of animal crouch, was directly behind me and watching me dully. He still held the scissors in his hand. Again I attacked, seemingly as fruitlessly as before, for even the claw of the hammer could do little more than break off futile smithereens. Although I continued to pound and claw, releasing the hair seemed a baffling task.

I paused; then furious and tense, I snatched the scissors from the man's hand. Forcing its two points together to make a single point which I thrust deep under the ice-block, I began to lever the ice upwards. At first I made no impression on it but, at last, hearing the ice squeak, I again inserted the scissors at a different place, this time with its points about an inch apart and then, levering with all my strength, brought the whole irregular frozen block in which the spread of the woman's hair was locked, completely free of the ground.

For a moment or two, utterly spent, I hung above the woman, then I half-dragged, half-helped her to her feet where, smiling grotesquely she continued to regard me sidelong with slightly daft, slightly whimsical, wholly animal eyes. Her neck and shoulders were white and bare and the brown dripping block of ice dangled between her shoulder blades.

Gripping the hammer and scissors I began to push her out into the street and towards our hall-door which still stood ajar. I pushed her into the kitchen where by now the morning range was a grin of fire. Sobbing somewhat, I steered her before me into the scullery. There, standing on a chair, I made her bow her neck as I filled an enamel basin with hot water. Cupping the water in my hands I began to pour it over the matted poll. I kept working furiously until the melting ice began to fall in chunks into the basin. Then I took up a bar of soap and began frenziedly to lather the woman's hair. I found myself working under an odd compulsion.

Not a word passed between us. Again and again I changed the water in the basin until at last as I rinsed the hair, the water poured clearly. I piled a bath-towel about the woman's head, rubbed furiously for some time, and then folding and turning the towel I piled it turbanwise about her head.

She watched dreamily as I took a large oval-shaped zinc bathtub and, setting it on the floor, affixed a length of hose to the nozzle of the hot-water tap and sent steaming water pouring into the vessel. Almost stamping my foot I indicated to the woman that she should stand into the vessel and wash herself. Dully she began to drop her rags to the floor: I tiptoed upstairs and, opening the mahogany wardrobe on the landing, piled a skirt and blouse of my dead mother over one arm and later snatched some underclothes from a drawer beside it. A pair of lizard-skin shoes, old fishnet stockings, these too I took; then, finally, opening a dusty trunk I took out a clutch of hairpins and a fancy comb inset with brilliants.

Returning to the kitchen, I peeped through the keyhole into the scullery; the woman was still standing in the steaming tub, indolently rubbing the cake of soap to her limbs. Young as I was, I realized that she had a beautiful body.

I prepared the breakfast: when I thought that she had

finished washing herself I pushed open the door a little and
left the clothes on the floor inside it. After a time I heard the
basin clank against the trough and the scrape of the woman's
nails as she rinsed the vessel. A little while later she came
slowly out, wearing my mother's clothes.

Holding my breath I watched her walk forward. The
house was without sound. In mid-kitchen she turned and,
looking at the table, indicated that she wished to eat. I placed
food before her. She ate her breakfast slowly and thoughtfully, crumbs falling unheeded to the floor. When she had
finished, I placed the delf on a tray and then pointed to the
rocking-chair by the fire. The woman rose slowly, went and
sat on it. I took the tray to the scullery, piled the ware into a
basin, ran the hot water on it and then returned to the
kitchen. From a press to the left of the fire I took a strong-
toothed comb and standing behind the woman, unwound
the turban and set about combing out the drying hair.

I was patient with the hair, teasing it gently where it had
knotted and working diligently until at last it was a blue-
black thunder-cloud about her head and shoulders. Between
me and the glow of the fire its edges were rimmed with red-
gold. Wholly absorbed, I kept on combing as the hair became
drier and more beautiful – more tractable too, until at last it
glistened and shone and shook and floated and fell in
plenitude about her waist. The woman turned her head quite
sensitively to accommodate me as I worked.

At last I combed the hair back over the woman's ears
and, setting aside the comb, began to plait and pile it,
twisting it this way and that, pinning it at a point that took
my fancy by inserting the comb with the brilliants in it and
then undoing it capriciously as if dissatisfied with the result.
The hair, now wholly dry, was sensual under my fingers, so
that I was reluctant to finish, and time and again with an
exclamation of sham annoyance, I let the piled hair fall. Each
time I broke off, the woman smiled at my feigned disappointment. About us the house grew still more silent.

This went on for some time until I could find no excuse

for continuing. Then the woman's long bare arm curled intuitively about me and drew me gently down on to her lap. At first I was inclined to resist, but her implied certainty that I would obey her was so absolute that I yielded. There was a pause in which my buttocks tested the welcome seat offered by her thighs, then, reassured, I sent my arm over her shoulder and dug my fingers deep into the thicket of hair at the nape of her neck.

Almost imperceptibly at first, but with a mounting sense of rhythm, and muttering, humming and crooning as she moved, the woman began to rock backwards and forwards on the chair with a movement reminiscent of the metronome on the piano-top. I found myself nestling closer to her breasts: of its own volition my head butted intuitively against her and before I knew, or cared, my lips and teeth were on her nipples. I heard myself as at a distance mouthing warm pleasant incoherencies.

So drugged were we both that the vague knocking on the hall door did not disturb us: nor a moment or two later did the sight of my father in the kitchen doorway dressed only in his pants and shirt, with the bearded tramp standing beside him, trouble us in the least. After an uncomprehending glance at us the two men turned away and moved dully into the bar leaving us alone to rock out a solution to one of the many compulsions of our shared womanhood.

Aidan Higgins

from *Balcony of Europe*

POLNISCHE JUDEN: Dangerous to be Jewish in Europe (that ancient bone-heap) in Hitler's day. Doubly dangerous to be Polish-Jewish. For if he hated all Jews, he had a particular hatred for Polish Jews. *Das Armseliges Volk*. A name scraped out from the end pages of the Pentateuch, from the *Familienstammbuch*. And a life that was once, now is no more. No, not even a trace left – the careful blade, the scraper, has made the record clean. The Jew-taint *Judenblut* like bacteria under a microscope. Scraped from the end pages of the *Familienstammbuch*, from the well-thumbed pages of the Pentateuch.

Dangerous to have a Jewish relative, by blood or intermarriage – even a distant relative – in Himmler's day, the Gestapo were digging like weasels into the files. The records were being carefully sifted, Gestapo intelligence tracking back the taint as far back as the Thirty Years War, and only brought to a halt there, the churches pillaged and the records lost.

She might never have come out of Poland, might well have died in Poland: the Lipsky (or Lipski) family only one among many such Polish families perished, the stain wiped out. Jablonski, Handy, Leitgeber, Lilienthal, Kawecki, Morawski, Lipsky (or Lipski) serving only to fertilize Polish earth, by lying dead under it, making it habitable for Germans to live on, walk on. She might have ended her days as a Jewess in Auschwitz. As a child holding on to her mother's skirt, an actress from an old silent movie. A cry of terror, a dismay, a retreat; an appeal, a regret, to say nothing, to beg for life –

it's all too late, they had no pity in dealing with the *Unter-menschen*. Groping, then the shot, the injection, the canister falling, all begins to be lost. They go to join the great Polish dead, the Jewish dead. Charlotte Monowitz, dead; Charlotte Birkenau, dead; Charlotte Dachau, dead; Charlotte Ausch-witz, dead. Lonely sorrowing stations, all lost. A group of victors and vanquished are standing under the shade of spreading limes or oak trees around a Polish manor-house, walking together in some Polish park. A misty scene with the quality of an oleograph, a picture from the past. A lemur-like paw, with shiny digits, pulls aside a half curtain, a little Jewish girl observes them. She has pale Polish eyes. She is there. She is my opposite, yet part of me. She who appears so permanent, is transitory – a souvenir. Lost long ago. I can neither hold her nor let her go.

Somewhere in an apartment in the Jewish sector of Lvov, a child, impervious to all this, too young, moves about. Dangerous to be there; doubly dangerous to be Charlotte Lipsky (or Lipski), one of the Slav *Untermenschen*, Polish or Bulgarian or Pomeranian *Halbaffen* with their polluted blood, Lipski, Lilienthal, Leitgeber, in Hitler's Europe. His agent had sat opposite me, had looked at me out of his troubled bloodshot eyes, had told me that he was his Fuehrer's soldier still, and I believed him.

A blank page, a name scraped out, a life that was once, now is no more. Too late already. Eyes that had looked submissively into Hitler's eyes (full of dead Jewish eyes) had looked into my eyes. In an aloof and surly manner he had indicated that if I were to go too far, say too much, he would tear into me.

But she was fearless (somewhere on the Nida or the Bug a small boat is sailing, Charlotte trails her hand in the water, her father holds the tiller, watching his daughter. I cannot see his face. He does not like Goys, he would have his daughter marry into her own race. The sun is going down. The Bug is the colour of blood. Charlotte Lipski, or Lipsky, trails her hand in the wake of the boat. It's an evening in

Poland in summer, the sun going down. Under the evening clouds a red sail moves; the clouds reach over Poland into Germany, where the preparations are being made).

To flee across the fields and take refuge under the solitary tree where no one has ever died. Kissing in the dry heat, on the track between walls of rock; her glowing face, the urgency and warmth of her embraces. She had come so far; I would take her there. We went away from the river, by caves where livestock were kept. She led the way up the path. Her black slacks unzipped at the back. There, I think, she said, pointing to a kind of wild arbour surrounded by a dry stone wall, a grove of olives and a single carob – like Inishere, but for the trees. We lay down under the carob tree. It's a hardy tree that can grow on top of rock if needs be, in war and famine the people make flour from its seeds (a tree of poor hard countries); otherwise it is used as cattle fodder. Under the carob tree's shade we became one. When I embraced her everything began again. We were on the rough ground. She lay back and smiled. The crickets whirred in the grass. The sun beat on the rock. *Limpia! Limpia!* called the olive picker (who had not stopped singing until then) to someone over the broken wall. When I kissed her there I experienced something comparable to liquification. Her head lay in a small clear area where the earth was a darker colour. Did you ever feel like crying? she asked. When? I asked. After we make love, she said.

Things that a clever girl can find to say.

The tree plain and simple cannot burn away; it cannot resolve itself into its component elements. *Der Apfel fällt nicht weit vom Baum*, the Germans say. Dead trees love the fire. (And on a sudden clear light presented me a face, folded in sorrow.) *Der gute Mann*, Herr Hund, in chamois-tufted (or pheasant feathers) Tyrolean hat, and the stout calves of a resolute killer, slaying deer in the Harz Mountains. The German horn. *Kiefernwald*.

I looked out of the window one morning and saw Daisy Bayless walking on a carpet of morning-glory flowers. The child walked on this incandescent blue. It was not yet eight and the fishing boats were going out. The sound of a donkey-engine meliorated over the water. Daisy called for me to come down. *Morgenschatten in dem Garten. Morgensonne.*

Mary Lavin

Happiness

MOTHER HAD a lot to say. This does not mean she was always talking but that we children felt the wells she drew upon were deep, deep, deep. Her theme was happiness: what it was, what it was not; where we might find it, where not; and how, if found, it must be guarded. Never must we confound it with pleasure. Nor think sorrow its exact opposite.

'Take Father Hugh,' Mother's eyes flashed as she looked at him. 'According to him, sorrow is an ingredient of happiness – a *necessary* ingredient, if you please!' And when he tried to protest she put up her hand. 'There may be a freakish truth in the theory – for some people. But not for me. And not, I hope, for my children.' She looked severely at us three girls. We laughed. None of us had had much experience with sorrow. Bea and I were children and Linda only a year old when our father died suddenly after a short illness that had not at first seemed serious. 'I've known people to make sorrow a *substitute* for happiness,' Mother said.

Father Hugh protested again. 'You're not putting me in that class, I hope?'

Father Hugh, ever since our father died, had been the closest of anyone to us as a family, without being close to any one of us in particular – even to Mother. He lived in a monastery near our farm in County Meath, and he had been one of the celebrants at the Requiem High Mass our father's political importance had demanded. He met us that day for the first time, but he took to dropping in to see us, with the idea of filling the crater of loneliness left at our centre. He did not know that there was a cavity in his own life, much less that we would fill it. He and Mother were both young in those days, and perhaps it gave scandal to some that he was so often in our house, staying till late into the night and, indeed, thinking nothing of stopping all night if there was any special reason, such as one of us being sick. He had even on occasion slept there if the night was too wet for tramping home across the fields.

When we girls were young, we were so used to having Father Hugh around that we never stood on ceremony with him but in his presence dried our hair and pared our nails and never minded what garments were strewn about. As for Mother – she thought nothing of running out of the bathroom in her slip, brushing her teeth or combing her hair, if she wanted to tell him something she might otherwise forget. And she brooked no criticism of her behaviour. 'Celibacy was never meant to take all the warmth and homeliness out of their lives,' she said.

On this point, too, Bea was adamant. Bea, the middle sister, was our oracle. 'I'm so glad he *has* Mother,' she said, 'as well as her having him, because it must be awful the way most women treat them – priests, I mean – as if they were pariahs. Mother treats him like a human being – that's all!'

And when it came to Mother's ears that there had been gossip about her making free with Father Hugh, she opened her eyes wide in astonishment. 'But he's only a priest!' she said.

Bea giggled. 'It's a good job he didn't hear *that*,' she said to me afterwards. 'It would undo the good she's done him. You'd think he was a eunuch.'

'Bea!' I said. 'Do you think he's in love with her?'

'If so, he doesn't know it,' Bea said firmly. 'It's her soul he's after! Maybe he wants to make sure of her in the next world!'

But thoughts of the world to come never troubled Mother. 'If anything ever happens to me, children,' she said, 'suddenly, I mean, or when you are not near me, or I cannot speak to you, I want you to promise you won't feel bad. There's no need! Just remember that I had a happy life – and that if I had to choose my kind of heaven I'd take it on this earth with you again, no matter how much you might annoy me!'

You see, annoyance and fatigue, according to Mother, and even illness and pain, could coexist with happiness. She had a habit of asking people if they were happy at times and in places that – to say the least of it – seemed to us inappropriate. 'But are you happy?' she'd probe as one lay sick and bathed in sweat, or in the throes of a jumping toothache. And once in our presence she made the inquiry of an old friend as he lay upon his deathbed.

'Why not?' she said when we took her to task for it later. 'Isn't it more important than ever to be happy when you're dying? Take my own father! You know what he said in his last moments? On his deathbed, he defied me to name a man who had enjoyed a better life. In spite of dreadful pain, his face *radiated* happiness!' Mother nodded her head comfortably. 'Happiness drives out pain, as fire burns out fire.'

Having no knowledge of our own to pit against hers, we thirstily drank in her rhetoric. Only Bea was sceptical. 'Perhaps you *got* it from him, like spots, or fever,' she said. 'Or something that could at least be slipped from hand to hand.'

'Do you think I'd have taken it if that were the case!' Mother cried. 'Then, when he needed it most?'

'Not there and then!' Bea said stubbornly. 'I meant as a sort of legacy.'

'Don't you think in *that* case,' Mother said, exasperated, 'he would have felt obliged to leave it to your grandmother?'

Certainly we knew that in spite of his lavish heart our grandfather had failed to provide our grandmother with enduring happiness. He had passed that job on to Mother. And Mother had not made too good a fist of it, even when Father was living and she had him – and, later, us children – to help.

As for Father Hugh, he had given our grandmother up early in the game. 'God Almighty couldn't make that woman happy,' he said one day, seeing Mother's face, drawn and pale with fatigue, preparing for the nightly run over to her own mother's flat that would exhaust her utterly.

There were evenings after she came home from the library where she worked when we saw her stand with the car keys in her hand, trying to think which would be worse – to slog over there on foot, or take out the car again. And yet the distance was short. It was Mother's day that had been too long.

'Weren't you over to see her this morning?' Father Hugh demanded.

'No matter!' said Mother. She was no doubt thinking of the forlorn face our grandmother always put on when she was leaving. ('Don't say good night, Vera,' Grandmother would plead. 'It makes me feel too lonely. And you never can tell – you might slip over again before you go to bed!')

'Do you know the time?' Bea would say impatiently, if she happened to be with Mother. Not indeed that the lateness of the hour counted for anything, because in all likelihood Mother *would* go back, if only to pass by under the window and see that the lights were out, or stand and listen and make sure that as far as she could tell all was well.

'I wouldn't mind if she was happy,' Mother said.

'And how do you know she's not?' we'd ask.

'When people are happy, I can feel it. Can't you?'

We were not sure. Most people thought our grandmother was a gay creature, a small birdy being who even at a great age laughed like a girl, and – more remarkably – sang like one, as she went about her day. But beak and claw were of steel. She'd think nothing of sending Mother back to a shop three times if her errands were not exactly right. 'Not sugar like that – that's *too* fine; it's not castor sugar I want. But *not* as coarse as *that*, either. I want an in-between kind.'

Provoked one day, my youngest sister, Linda, turned and gave battle. 'You're mean!' she cried. 'You love ordering people about!'

Grandmother preened, as if Linda had acclaimed an

attribute. 'I was always hard to please,' she said. 'As a girl, I used to be called Miss Imperious.'

And Miss Imperious she remained as long as she lived, even when she was a great age. Her orders were then given a wry twist by the fact that as she advanced in age she took to calling her daughter Mother, as we did.

There was one great phrase with which our grandmother opened every sentence: 'if only'. 'If only,' she'd say, when we came to visit her – 'if only you'd come earlier, before I was worn out expecting you!' Or if we were early, then if only it was later, after she'd had a rest and could enjoy us, be *able* for us. And if we brought her flowers, she'd sigh to think that if only we'd brought them the previous day she'd have had a visitor to appreciate them, or say it was a pity the stems weren't longer. If only we'd picked a few green leaves, or included some buds, because she said disparagingly, the poor flowers we'd brought were already wilting. We might just as well not have brought them! As the years went on, Grandmother had a new bead to add to her rosary: if only her friends were not all dead! By their absence, they reduced to nil all *real* enjoyment in anything. Our own father – her son-in-law – was the one person who had ever gone close to pleasing her. But even here there had been a snag. 'If only he was my real son!' she used to say, with a sigh.

Mother's mother lived on through our childhood and into our early maturity (though she outlived the money our grandfather left her), and in our minds she was a complicated mixture of valiance and defeat. Courageous and generous within the limits of her own life, her simplest demand was yet enormous in the larger frame of Mother's life, and so we never could see her with the same clarity of vision with which we saw our grandfather, or our own father. Them we saw only through Mother's eyes.

'Take your grandfather!' she'd cry, and instantly we'd see him, his eyes burning upon us – yes, upon *us*, although in his day only one of us had been born: me. At another time, Mother would cry, 'Take your own father!' and instantly we'd see *him* – tall, handsome, young, and much more suited to marry one of us than poor bedraggled Mother.

Most fascinating of all were the times Mother would say 'Take me!' By magic then, staring down the years, we'd see blazingly clear a small girl with black hair and buttoned boots, who, though plain and pouting, burned bright, like a star. 'I was happy, you see,' Mother said. And we'd strain hard to try and understand the mystery of the light that still radiated from her. 'I used to lean along a tree that grew out over the river,' she said, 'and look down through the grey leaves at the water flowing past below, and I used to think it was not the stream that flowed but me, spread-eagled over it, who flew through the air! Like a bird! That I'd found the secret!' She made it seem there might *be* such a secret, just waiting to be found. Another time she'd dream that she'd be a great singer.

'We didn't know you sang, Mother!'

She had to laugh. 'Like a crow,' she said.

Sometimes she used to think she'd swim the Channel.

'Did you swim *that* well, Mother?'

'Oh, not really – just the breast stroke,' she said. 'And then only by the aid of two pig bladders blown up by my father and tied around my middle. But I used to throb – yes, throb – with happiness.'

Behind Mother's back, Bea raised her eyebrows.

What was it, we used to ask ourselves – that quality that she, we felt sure, misnamed? Was it courage? Was it strength, health, or high spirits? Something you could not give or take – a conundrum? A game of catch-as-catch-can?

'I know,' cried Bea. 'A sham!'

Whatever it was, we knew that Mother would let no wind of violence from within or without tear it from her. Although, one evening when Father Hugh was with us, our astonished ears heard her proclaim that there might be a time when one had to slacken hold on it – let go – to catch at it again with a surer hand. In the way, we supposed, that the high-wire walker up among the painted stars of his canvas sky must wait to fling himself through the air until the bar he catches at has started to sway perversely from him. Oh no, no! That downward drag at our innards we could not bear, the belly swelling to the shape of a pear. Let happiness go by the board. 'After all, lots of people seem to make out without it,' Bea cried. It was too tricky a business. And might it not be that one had to be born with a flair for it?

'A flair would not be enough,' Mother answered. 'Take Father Hugh. He, if anyone, had a flair for it – a natural capacity! You've only to look at him when he's off guard, with you children, or helping me in the garden. But he rejects happiness! He casts it from him.'

'That is simply not true, Vera,' cried Father Hugh, over-hearing her. 'It's just that I don't place an inordinate value on it like you. I don't think it's enough to carry one all the way. To the end, I mean – and after.'

'Oh, don't talk about the end when we're only in the middle,' cried Mother. And, indeed, at that moment her own face shone with such happiness it was hard to believe that her earth was not her heaven. Certainly it was her constant contention that of happiness she had had a lion's share. This, however, we, in private, doubted. Perhaps there were times when she had had a surplus of it – when she was young, say, with her redoubtable father, whose love blazed circles around her, making winter into summer and ice into fire. Perhaps she did have a brimming measure in her early married years. By straining hard, we could find traces left in our minds from those days of milk and honey. Our father, while he lived, had cast a magic over everything, for us as well as for her. He held his love up over us like an umbrella and kept off the troubles that afterwards came down on us, pouring cats and dogs!

But if she did have more than the common lot of happiness in those early days, what use was that when we could remember so clearly how our father's death had ravaged her? And how could we forget the distress it brought on us when, afraid to let her out of our sight, Bea and I stumbled after her everywhere, through the woods and along the bank of the river, where, in the weeks that followed, she tried vainly to find peace.

The summer after Father died, we were invited to France to stay with friends, and when she went walking on the cliffs at Fécamp our fears for her grew frenzied, so that we hung on to her arm and dragged at her skirt, hoping that like leaded weights we'd pin her down if she went too near the edge. But at night we had to abandon our watch, being forced to follow the conventions of a family still whole – a home still intact – and go to bed at the same time as the other children. It was at that hour, when the coast guard was gone from his rowing boat offshore and the sand was as cold and grey as the sea, that Mother liked to swim. And when she had washed, kissed, and left us, our hearts almost died inside us and we'd creep out of bed again to stand in our bare feet at the mansard and watch as she ran down the shingle, striking out when she reached the water where, far out, wave and sky and mist were one, and the greyness closed over her. If we took our eyes off her for an instant, it was impossible to find her again.

'Oh, make her turn back, God, please!' I prayed out loud one night.

Startled, Bea turned away from the window. 'She'll *have* to turn back sometime, won't she? Unless . . .?'

Locking our damp hands together, we stared out again. 'She wouldn't!' I whispered. 'It would be a sin!'

Secure in the deterring power of sin, we let out our breath. Then Bea's breath caught again. 'What if she went out so far she used up all her strength? She couldn't swim back! It wouldn't be a sin then!'

'It's the intention that counts,' I whispered.

A second later, we could see an arm lift heavily up and wearily cleave down, and at last Mother was in the shallows, wading back to shore.

'Don't let her see us!' cried Bea. As if our chattering teeth would not give us away when she looked in at us before she went to her own room on the other side of the corridor, where, later in the night, sometimes the sound of crying would reach us.

What was it worth – a happiness bought that dearly.

Mother had never questioned it. And once she told us, 'On a wintry day, I brought my own mother a snowdrop. It was the first one of the year – a bleak bud that had come up stunted before its time – and I meant it for a sign. But do you know what your grandmother said? "What good are snowdrops to me now?" Such a thing to say! What good is a snowdrop at all if it doesn't hold its value always, and never lose it! Isn't that the whole point of a snowdrop? And that is the whole point of happiness, too! What good would it be if it could be erased without trace? Take me and those daffodils!' Stooping, she buried her face in a bunch that lay on the table waiting to be put in vases. 'If they didn't hold their beauty absolute and inviolable, do you think I could bear the sight of them after what happened when your father was in hospital?'

It was a fair question. When Father went to hospital, Mother went with him and stayed in a small hotel across the street so she could be with him all day from early to late. 'Because it was so awful for him – being in Dublin!' she said. 'You have no idea how he hated it.'

That he was dying neither of them realized. How could they know, as it rushed through the sky, that their star was a falling star! But one evening when she'd left him asleep Mother came home for a few hours to see how we were faring, and it broke her heart to see the daffodils out all over the place – in the woods, under the trees, and along the sides of the avenue. There had never been so many, and she thought how awful it was that Father was missing them. 'You sent up little bunches to him, you poor dears!' she said. 'Sweet little bunches, too – squeezed tight as posies by your little fists! But stuffed into vases they couldn't really make up to him for not being able to see them growing!'

So on the way back to the hospital she stopped her car and pulled a great bunch – the full of her arms. 'They took up the whole back seat,' she said, 'and I was so excited at the thought of walking into his room and dumping them on his bed – you know – just plomping them down so he could smell them, and feel them, and look and look! I didn't mean them to be put in vases, or anything ridiculous like that – it would have taken a rainwater barrel to hold them. Why, I could hardly see over them as I came up the steps; I kept tripping. But when I came into the hall, that nun – I told you about her – that nun came up to me, sprang out of nowhere it seemed, although I know now that she was waiting for me, knowing that somebody had to bring me to my senses. But the way she did it! Reached out and grabbed the flowers, letting lots of them fall – I remember them getting stood on. "Where are you going with those foolish flowers, you foolish woman?" she said. "Don't you know your husband is dying? Your prayers are all you can give him now!"

'She was right. I *was* foolish. but I wasn't cured. Afterwards, it was nothing but foolishness the way I dragged you children after me all over Europe. As if any one place was going to be different from another, any better, any less desolate. But there was great satisfaction in bringing you places your father and I had planned to bring you – although in fairness to him I must say that he would not perhaps have brought you so young. And he would not have had an ulterior motive. But above all, he would not have attempted those trips in such a dilapidated car.'

Oh, that car! It was a battered and dilapidated red sports car, so depleted of accessories that when, eventually, we got a new car Mother still stuck out her hand on bends, and in wet weather jumped out to wipe the windscreen with her sleeve. And if fussed, she'd let down the window and shout at people, forgetting she now had a horn. How we had ever fitted into it with all our luggage was a miracle.

'You were never lumpish – any of you!' Mother said proudly. 'But you were very healthy and very strong.' She turned to me. 'Think of how you got that car up the hill in Switzerland!'

'The Alps are not hills, Mother!' I pointed out coldly, as I had done at the time, when, as actually happened, the car failed to make it on one of the inclines. Mother let it run back until wedged against the rock face, and I had to get out and push till she got going again in first gear. But when it got started it couldn't be stopped to pick me up until it got to the top, where they had to wait for me, and for a very long time.

'Ah, well,' she said, sighing wistfully at the thought of those trips. 'You got something out of them, I hope. All that travelling must have helped you with your geography and your history.'

We looked at each other and smiled, and then Mother herself laughed. 'Remember the time,' she said, 'when we were in Italy, and it was Easter, and all the shops were chockfull of food? The butchers' shops had poultry and game hanging up outside the doors, fully feathered, and with their poor heads dripping blood, and in the windows they had poor little lambs and suckling pigs and young goats, all skinned and hanging by their hind feet.' Mother shuddered. 'They think so much about food. I found it revolting. I had to hurry past. But Linda, who must have been only four then, dragged at me and stared and stared. You know how children are at that age; they have a morbid fascination for what is cruel and bloody. Her face was flushed and her eyes were wide. I hurried her back to the hotel. But next morning she crept into my room. She crept up to me and pressed against me. "Can't we go back, just once, and look again at that shop?" she whispered. "The shop where they have the little children hanging up for Easter!" It was the young goats, of course, but I'd said "kids", I suppose. How we laughed.' But her face was grave. 'You were *so* good on those trips, all of you,' she said. 'You were really very good children in general. Otherwise I would never have put so much effort into rearing you, because I wasn't a bit maternal. You brought out the best in me! I put an unnatural effort into you, of course, because I was taking my standards from your father, forgetting that his might not have remained so inflexible if he had lived to middle age and was beset by life, like other parents.'

'Well, the job is nearly over now, Vera,' said Father Hugh. 'And you didn't do so badly.'

'That's right, Hugh,' said Mother, and she straightened up, and put her hand on her back the way she sometimes did in the garden when she got up from her knees after weeding. 'I didn't go over to the enemy anyway! We survived!' Then a flash of defiance came into her eyes. 'And we were happy. That's the main thing!'

Father Hugh frowned. 'There you go again!' he said.

Mother turned on him. 'I don't think you realize the onslaughts that were made upon our happiness! The minute Robert died, they came down on me – cohorts of relatives, friends, even strangers, all draped in black, opening their arms like bats to let me pass into their company. "Life is a vale of tears," they said. "You are privileged to find it out so young!" Ugh! After I staggered on to my feet and began to take hold of life once more, they fell back defeated. And the first day I gave a laugh – pouff, they were blown out like candles. They weren't living in a real world at all; they belonged to a ghostly world where life was easy: all one had to do was sit and weep. It takes effort to push back the stone from the mouth of the tomb and walk out.'

Effort. Effort. Ah, but that strange-sounding word could invoke little sympathy from those who had not learned yet what it meant. Life must have been hardest for Mother in those years when we older ones were at college – no longer children, and still dependent on her. Indeed, we made more demands on her than ever then, having moved into new areas of activity and emotion. And our friends! Our friends came and went as freely as we did ourselves, so that the house was often like a café – and one where pets were not prohibited but took their places on our chairs and beds, as regardless as the people. And anyway it was hard to have sympathy for someone who got things into such a state as

Mother. All over the house there was clutter. Her study was like the returned-letter department of a post office, with sacks of paper everywhere, bills paid and unpaid, letters answered and unanswered, tax returns, pamphlets, leaflets. If by mistake we left the door open on a windy day, we came back to find papers flapping through the air like frightened birds. Efficient only in that she managed eventually to conclude every task she began, it never seemed possible to outsiders that by Mother's methods anything whatever could be accomplished. In an attempt to keep order elsewhere, she made her own room the clearing house into which the rest of us put everything: things to be given away, things to be mended, things to be stored, things to be treasured, things to be returned – even things to be thrown out! By the end of the year, the room resembled an obsolescence dump. And no one could help her; the chaos of her life was as personal as an act of creation – one might as well try to finish another person's poem.

As the years passed, Mother rushed around more hectically. And although Bea and I had married and were not at home any more, except at holiday time and for occasional weekends, Linda was noisier than the two of us put together had been, and for every follower we had brought home she brought twenty. The house was never still. Now that we were reduced to being visitors, we watched Mother's tension mount to vertigo, knowing that, like a spinning top, she could not rest till she fell. But now at the smallest pretext Father Hugh would call in the doctor and Mother would be put on the mail boat and dispatched for London. For it was essential that she get far enough away to make phoning home every night prohibitively costly.

Unfortunately, the thought of departure often drove a spur into her and she redoubled her effort to achieve order in her affairs. She would be up until the early hours ransacking her desk. To her, as always, the shortest parting entailed a preparation as for death. And as if it were her end that was at hand, we would all be summoned, although she had no time to speak a word to us, because five minutes before departure she would still be attempting to reply to letters that were the acquisition of weeks and would have taken whole days to dispatch.

'Don't you know the taxi is at the door, Vera?' Father Hugh would say, running his hand through his grey hair and looking very dishevelled himself. She had him at times as distracted as herself. 'You can't do any more. You'll have to leave the rest till you come back.'

'I can't, I can't!' Mother would cry. 'I'll have to cancel my plans.'

One day, Father Hugh opened the lid of her case, which was strapped up in the hall, and with a swipe of his arm he cleared all the papers on the top of the desk pell-mell into the suitcase. 'You can sort them on the boat,' he said, 'or the train to London!'

Thereafter, Mother's luggage always included an empty case to hold the unfinished papers on her desk. And years afterwards a steward on the Irish Mail told us she was a familiar figure, working away at letters and bills nearly all the way from Holyhead to Euston. 'She gave it up about Rugby or Crewe,' he said. 'She'd get talking to someone in the compartment.' He smiled. 'There was one time coming down the train I was just in time to see her close up the window with a guilty look. I didn't say anything, but I think she'd emptied those papers of hers out the window!'

Quite likely. When we were children, even a few hours away from us gave her composure. And in two weeks or less, when she'd come home, the well of her spirit would be freshened. We'd hardly know her – her step so light, her eye so bright, and her love and patience once more freely flowing. But in no time at all the house would fill up once more with the noise and confusion of too many people and too many animals, and again we'd be fighting our corner with cats and dogs, bats, mice, bees and even wasps. 'Don't kill it!' Mother would cry if we raised a hand to an angry wasp. 'Just catch it, dear, and put it outside. Open the window and let it fly away!' But even this treatment could at times be deemed too harsh. 'Wait a minute. Close the window!' she'd cry. 'It's too cold outside. It will die. That's why it came in, I suppose! Oh dear, what will we do?' Life would be going full blast again.

There was only one place Mother found rest. When she was at breaking point and fit to fall, she'd go out into the garden – not to sit or stroll around but to dig, to drag up weeds, to move great clumps of corms or rhizomes, or indeed quite frequently to haul huge rocks from one place to another. She was always laying down a path, building a dry wall, or making compost heaps as high as hills. However jaded she might be going out, when dark forced her in at last her step had the spring of a daisy. So if she did not succeed in defining happiness to our understanding, we could see whatever it was, she possessed it to the full when she was in her garden.

One of us said as much one Sunday when Bea and I had dropped round for the afternoon. Father Hugh was with us again. 'It's an unthinking happiness, though,' he cavilled. We were standing at the drawing-room window, looking out to where in the fading light we could see Mother on her knees weeding, in the long border that stretched from the house right down to the woods. 'I wonder how she'd take it if she were stricken down and had to give up that heavy work!' he said. Was he perhaps a little jealous of how she could stoop and bend? He himself had begun to use a stick. I was often a little jealous of her myself, because although I was married and had children of my own, I had married young and felt the weight of living as heavy as a weight of years. 'She doesn't take enough care of herself,' Father Hugh said sadly. 'Look at her out there with nothing under her knees to protect her from the damp ground.' It was almost too dim for us to see her, but even in the drawing room it was chilly. 'She should not be let stay out there after the sun goes down.'

'Just you try to get her in then!' said Linda, who had come into the room in time to hear him. 'Don't you know by now anyway that what would kill another person only seems to make Mother thrive?'

Father Hugh shook his head again. 'You seem to forget it's not younger she's getting!' He fidgeted and fussed, and several times went to the window to stare out apprehensively. He was really getting quite elderly.

'Come and sit down, Father Hugh,' Bea said, and to take his mind off Mother she turned on the light and blotted out the garden. Instead of seeing through the window, we saw into it as into a mirror, and there between the flower-laden tables and the lamps it was ourselves we saw moving vaguely. Like Father Hugh, we, too, were waiting for her to come in before we called an end to the day.

'Oh, this is ridiculous!' Father Hugh cried at last. 'She'll have to listen to reason.' And going back to the window he threw it open. 'Vera!' he called. 'Vera!' – sternly, so sternly that, more intimate than an endearment, his tone shocked us. 'She didn't hear me,' he said, turning back blinking at us in the lighted room. 'I'm going out to get her.' And in a minute he was gone from the room. As he ran down the garden path, we stared at each other, astonished; his step like his voice, was the step of a lover. 'I'm coming, Vera!' he cried.

Although she was never stubborn except in things that mattered, Mother had not moved. In the wholehearted way she did everything, she was bent down close to the ground. It wasn't the light only that was dimming; her eyesight also was failing, I thought, as instinctively I followed Father Hugh.

But halfway down the path I stopped. I had seen something he had not: Mother's hand that appeared to support itself in a forked branch of an old tree peony she had planted as a bride was not in fact gripping it but impaled upon it. And the hand that appeared to be grubbing in the clay in fact was sunk into the soft mould. 'Mother!' I screamed, and I ran forward, but when I reached her I covered my face with my hands. 'Oh Father Hugh!' I cried. 'Is she dead?'

It was Bea who answered, hysterical. 'She is! She is!' she cried, and she began to pound Father Hugh on the back with her fists, as if his pessimistic words had made this happen.

But Mother was not dead. And at first the doctor even offered hope of her pulling through. But from the moment Father Hugh lifted her up to carry her into the house we ourselves had no hope, seeing how effortlessly he, who was not strong, could carry her. When he put her down on her bed, her head hardly creased the pillow. Mother lived for four more hours.

Like the days of her life, those four hours that Mother lived were packed tight with concern and anxiety. Partly conscious, partly delirious, she seemed to think the counterpane was her desk, and she scrabbled her fingers upon it as if trying to sort out a muddle of bills and correspondence. No longer indifferent now, we listened, anguished, to the distracted cries that had for all our lifetime been so familiar to us. 'Oh, where is it? Where is it? I had it a minute ago! Where on earth did I put it?'

'Vera, Vera, stop worrying,' Father Hugh pleaded, but she waved him away and went on sifting through the sheets as if they were sheets of paper. 'Oh, Vera!' he begged. 'Listen to me. Do you not know—'

Bea pushed between them. 'You're not to tell her!' she commanded. 'Why frighten her?'

'But it ought not to frighten her,' said Father Hugh. 'This is what I was always afraid would happen – that she'd be frightened when it came to the end.'

At that moment, as if to vindicate him, Mother's hands fell idle on the coverlet, palm upward and empty. And turning her head she stared at each of us in turn, beseechingly. 'I cannot face it,' she whispered. 'I can't! I can't! I can't!'

'Oh, my God!' Bea said, and she started to cry.

'Vera. For God's sake listen to me,' Father Hugh cried, and pressing his face to hers, as close as a kiss, he kept whispering to her, trying to cast into the dark tunnel before her the light of his own faith.

But it seemed to us that Mother must already be looking into God's exigent eyes. 'I can't!' she cried. 'I can't!'

Then her mind came back from the stark world of the spirit to the world where her body was still detained, but even that world was now a whirling kaleidoscope of things which only she could see. Suddenly her eyes focused, and, catching at Father Hugh, she pulled herself up a little and pointed to something we could not see. 'What will be done with them?' Her voice was anxious. 'They ought to be put in water anyway,' she said, and, leaning over the edge of the bed, she pointed to the floor. 'Don't step on that one!' she said sharply. Then, more sharply still, she addressed us all. 'Have them sent to the public ward,' she said peremptorily. 'Don't let that nun take them; she'll only put them on the altar. And God doesn't want them! He made them for *us* – not for Himself!'

It was the familiar rhetoric that all her life had characterized her utterances. For a moment we were mystified. Then Bea gasped. 'The daffodils!' she cried. 'The day Father died!' and over her face came the light that had so often blazed over Mother's. Leaning across the bed, she pushed Father Hugh aside. And, putting out her hands, she held Mother's face between her palms as tenderly as if it were the face of a child. 'It's all right, Mother. You don't *have* to face it! It's over!' Then she who had so fiercely forbade Father Hugh to do so blurted out the truth. 'You've finished with this world, Mother,' she said, and, confident that her tidings were joyous, her voice was strong.

Mother made the last effort of her life and grasped at Bea's meaning. She let out a sigh, and closing her eyes, she sank back, and this time her head sank so deep into the pillow that it would have been dented had it been a pillow of stone.

Éilís Ní Dhuibhne

Blood and Water

I HAVE AN aunt who is not the full shilling. 'The Mad Aunt' was how my sister and I referred to her when we were children, but that was just a euphemism, designed to shelter us from the truth which we couldn't stomach: she was mentally retarded. Very mildly so: perhaps she was just a slow learner. She survived very successfully as a lone farm woman, letting land, keeping a cow and a few hens and ducks, listening to the local gossip from the neighbours who were kind enough to drop in regularly in the evenings. Quite a few of them were: her house was a popular place for callers, and perhaps that was part of the secret of her survival. She did not participate in the neighbours' conversation to any extent, however. She was articulate only on a very concrete level, and all abstract topics were beyond her.

Had she been born in the fifties or sixties, my aunt would have been scientifically labelled, given special treatment at a special school, taught special skills and eventually employed in a special workshop to carry out a special job, certainly a much duller job than the one she pursued in reality. Luckily for her she was born in 1925 and had been reared as a normal child. Her family had failed to recognize that she was different from others and had not sought medical attention for her. She had merely been considered 'delicate'. The term 'mentally retarded' would have been meaningless in those days, anyway, in the part of Donegal where she and my mother originated, where Irish was the common, if not the only, language. As she grew up, it must have been silently conceded that she was a little odd. But people seemed to have no difficulty in suppressing this fact, and they judged my aunt by the standards which they applied to humanity at large: sometimes lenient and sometimes not.

She lived in a farmhouse in Ballytra on Inishowen, and once a year we visited her. Our annual holiday was spent under her roof. And had it not been for the lodging she provided, we could not have afforded to get away at all. But we did not consider this aspect of the affair.

On the first Saturday of August we always set out, laden with clothes in cardboard boxes and groceries from the cheap city shops, from the street markets: enough to see us through the fortnight. The journey north lasted nearly twelve hours in our ancient battered cars: a Morris Eight, dark green with fragrant leather seats, and a Ford Anglia are two of the models I remember from a long series of fourth-hand crocks. Sometimes they broke down *en route* and caused us long delays in nauseating garages, where I stood around with my father, while the mechanic tinkered, or went, with my sister and mother, for walks down country lanes, or along the wide melancholy street of small market towns.

Apart from such occasional hitches, however, the trips were delightful odysseys through various flavours of Ireland: the dusty rich flatlands outside Dublin, the drumlins of Monaghan with their hint of secrets and better things to come, the luxuriant slopes, rushing rivers and expensive villas of Tyrone, and finally, the ultimate reward: the furze and heather, the dog-roses, the fuchsia, of Donegal.

Donegal was different in those days. Different from what it is now, different then from the eastern urban parts of Ireland. It was rural in a thorough, elemental way. People were old-fashioned in their dress and manners, even in their physiques: weather-beaten faces were highlighted by black or grey suits, shiny with age; broad hips stretched the cotton of navy-blue, flower-sprigged overalls, a kind of uniform for country women which their city sisters had long eschewed, if they ever had it. Residences were thatched cottages ... 'The Irish peasant house' ... or spare grey farmhouses.

There was only a single bungalow in the parish where my aunt lived, an area which is now littered with them.

All these things accentuated the rusticity of the place, its strangeness, its uniqueness.

My aunt's house was of the slated, two-storey variety, and it stood, surrounded by a seemingly arbitrary selection of outhouses, in a large yard called 'the street'. Usually we turned into this street at about nine o'clock at night, having been on the road all day. My aunt would be waiting for us, leaning over the half-door. Even though she was deaf, she would have heard the car while it was still a few hundred yards away, chugging along the dirt lane: it was always that kind of car. She would stand up as soon as we appeared, and twist her hands shyly, until we emerged from the car. Then she would walk slowly over to us, and shake hands carefully with each of us in turn, starting with my mother. Care, formality: these were characteristics which were most obvious in her. Slowness.

Greetings over, we would troop into the house, under a low portal apparently designed for a smaller race of people. Then we would sit in front of the hot fire, and my mother would talk, in a loud cheery voice, telling my aunt the news from Dublin and asking for local gossip. My aunt would sometimes try to reply, more often not. After five minutes or so of this, she would indicate, a bit resentfully, that she had expected us earlier, that she had been listening for the car for over two days. And my mother, still, at this early stage of the holiday, in a diplomatic mood, would explain patiently, slowly, loudly, that no, we had been due today. We always came on the first Saturday, didn't we? John only got off on the Friday, sure. But somehow my mother would never have written to my aunt to let her know when we were coming. It was not owing to the fact that the latter was illiterate that she didn't write. Any neighbour would have read a letter for her. It was, rather, the result of a strange convention which my parents, especially my mother, always adhered to: they never wrote to anyone, about anything, except one subject. Death.

While this courteous ritual of fireside conversation was being enacted by my parents (although in fact my father never bothered to take part), my sister and I would sit silently on our hardbacked chairs, fidgeting and looking at the familiar objects in the room: the Sacred Heart, the Little Flower, the calendar from Bells of Buncrana depicting a blond laughing child, the red arc for layers' mash. We answered promptly, monosyllabically, the few questions my aunt put to us, all concerning school. Subdued by the immense boredom of the day, we tolerated a further boredom.

After a long time, my mother would get up, stretch, and prepare a meal of rashers and sausages, from Russells of Camden Street. To this my aunt would add a few provisions she had laid in for us: eggs, butter she had churned herself, and soda bread which she baked in a pot oven, in enormous golden balls. I always refused to eat this bread, because I found the taste repellent and because I didn't think my aunt washed her hands properly. My sister, however, ate no other kind of bread while we were on holiday at that house, and I used to tease her about it, trying to force her to see my point of view. She never did.

After tea, although by that time it was usually late, we would run outside and play. We would visit each of the outhouses in turn, hoping to see an owl in the barn and then we'd run across the road to a stream which flowed behind the back garden. There was a stone bridge over the stream and on our first night we invariably played the same game: we threw sticks into the stream at one side of the bridge, and then ran as fast as we could to the other side in order to catch them as they sailed out. This activity, undertaken at night in the shadow of the black hills, had a magical effect: it plummeted me headlong into the atmosphere of the holidays. At that stream, on that first night, I would suddenly discover within myself a feeling of happiness and freedom that I was normally unaware I possessed. It seemed to emerge from some hidden part of me, like the sticks emerging from underneath the bridge, and it counteracted the faint claustrophobia, the nervousness, which I always had initially in my aunt's house.

Refreshed and elated, we would go to bed in unlit upstairs rooms. These bedrooms were panelled in wood which had been white once, but had faded to the colour of butter, and they had windows less than two feet square which had to be propped up with a stick if you wanted them to remain open: the windows were so small, my mother liked to tell us, because they had been made at a time when there was a tax on glass. I wondered about this: the doors were tiny, too.

When I woke up in the morning, I would lie and count the boards on the ceiling, and then the knots on the boards, until eventually a clattering of footsteps on the uncarpeted stairs and a banging about of pots and pans would announce that my mother was up and that breakfast would soon be available. I would run downstairs to the scullery, which served as a bathroom, and wash. The basin stood on a deal table, the water was in a white enamel bucket on the dresser. A piece of soap was stuck to a saucer on the window-sill, in front of the basin: through the window, you could see a bit of an elm tree, and a purple hill, as you washed.

In a way it was pleasant, but on the whole it worried me, washing in that place. It was so public. There was a constant danger that someone would rush in, and find you there, half undressed, scrubbing your armpits. I liked my ablutions to be private and unobserved.

The scullery worried me for another reason. On its wall, just beside the dresser, was a big splodge of a dirty yellow substance, unlike anything I had ever encountered. I took it to be some sort of fungus. God knows why, since the house was unusually clean. This thing so repelled me that I never even dared to ask what it was, and simply did my very best to avoid looking at it while I was in its vicinity, washing or bringing back the bucket of water from the well, or doing anything else. Years later, when I was taking a course in ethnology at the university, I realized that the stuff was nothing other than butter, daubed on the wall after every churning, for luck. But to me it symbolized something quite other than good fortune, something unthinkably horrible.

After dressing, breakfast. Rashers and sausages again, fried over the fire by my mother, who did all the cooking while we were on holiday. For that fortnight my aunt, usually a skilful frier of rashers, baker of bread, abdicated domestic responsibility to her, and adopted the role of child in her own house, like a displaced rural mother-in-law. She spent her time fiddling around in the henhouse, feeding the cat, or more often she simply sat, like a man, and stared out of the window while my mother worked. After about three days of this, my mother would grow resentful, would begin to mutter, gently but persistently, 'It's no holiday!' And my sister and I, even though we understood the reasons for our aunt's behaviour, as, indeed, did our mother, would nod in agreement. Because we had to share in the housework. We set the table, we did the washing up in an enamel basin, and I had personal responsibility for going to the well to draw water. For this, my sister envied me. She imagined it to be a privileged task, much more fun than sweeping or making beds. And of course it was more exotic than these chores, for the first day or so, which was why I insisted on doing it. But soon enough the novelty palled, and it was really hard work, and boring. Water is heavy, and we seemed to require a great deal of it.

Unlike our mother, we spent much time away from the kitchen, my sister and I. Most of every morning we passed on the beach. There was an old boathouse there, its roof almost caved in, in which no boat had been kept for many many years. It had a stale smell, faintly disgusting, as if animals, or worse, had used it as a lavatory at some stage in the past. Even though the odour dismayed us, and even though the beach was always quite deserted, we liked to undress in private, both of us together, and therefore going to great lengths with towels to conceal our bodies from one another, until such a time as we should emerge from the yawning door of the building, and run down the golden quartz slip into the sea.

Lough Swilly. Also known as 'The Lake of Shadows', my sister often informed me, this being the type of fact of which she was very fond. One of the only two fiords in Ireland, she might also add. That meant nothing to me, its being a fiord, and as for shadows, I was quite unaware of them. What I remember most about that water is its crystal clarity. It was greenish, to look at it from a slight distance. Or, if you looked at it from my aunt's house, on a fine day, it was a brilliant turquoise colour, it looked like a great jewel, set in the hills. But when you were in that water, bathing, it was as clear as glass: I would swim along with my face just below the lapping surface, and I would open my eyes and look right down to the sandy floor, at the occasional starfish, the tiny crabs that scuttled there, at the shoals of minnows that scudded from place to place, guided by some mysterious mob instinct. I always stayed in for ages, even on the coldest days, even when rain was falling in soft curtains around the rocks. It had a definite benign quality, that water. And I always emerged from it cleansed in both body and soul. When I remember it now, I can understand why rivers are sometimes believed to be holy. Lough Swilly was, for me, a blessed water.

The afternoons we spent *en famille*, going on trips in the car to view distant wonders, Portsalon or the Downings. And the evenings we would spend 'raking', dropping in on our innumerable friends and drinking tea and playing with them.

This pattern continued for the entire holiday, with two exceptions: on one Sunday we would go on a pilgrimage to Doon Well, and on one weekday we would go to Derry, thirty miles away, to shop.

*

Doon Well was my aunt's treat. It was the one occasion, apart from Mass, on which she accompanied us on a drive, even though we all realized that she would have liked to be with us every day. But the only outing she insisted upon was Doon Well. She would begin to hint about it gently soon after we arrived. 'The Gallaghers were at Doon Well on Sunday,' she might say. 'Not a great crowd at it!' Then on Sunday she would not change her clothes after Mass, but would don a special elegant apron and perform the morning tasks in a particular and ladylike way: tiptoe into the byre, flutter at the hens.

At two we would set out, and she would sit with me and my sister in the back of the car. My sense of mortification, at being seen in public with my aunt, was mixed with another shame, that of ostentatious religious practices. I couldn't bear processions, missions, concelebrated Masses: display. At heart, I was Protestant, and indeed it would have suited me, in more ways than one, to belong to that faith. But I didn't. So I was going to Doon Well, with my aunt and my unctuous parents, and my embarrassed sister.

You could spot the well from quite a distance: it was dressed. In rags. A large assembly of sticks, to which brightly coloured scraps of cloth were tied, advertised its presence and lent it a somewhat flippant, pagan air. But it was not flippant, it was all too serious. As soon as we left the safety of the car, we had to remove our shoes. The pain! Not only of going barefoot on the stony ground, but of having to witness feet, adult feet, our parents' and our aunt's, so shamelessly revealed to the world. Like all adults then, their feet were horrible: big and yellow, horny with corns and ingrown toenails, twisted and tortured by years of ill-fitting boots, no boots at all. To crown it, both my mother and aunt had varicose veins, purple knots bulging hideously through the yellow skin. As humiliated as anyone could be, and as we were meant to be, no doubt, we had to circle the well some specified number of times, probably three, and we had to say the Rosary, out loud, in the open air. And then my mother had a long litany to Colmcille, to which we had to listen and respond, in about a thousand agonies of shame, 'Pray for us!' The only tolerable part of the expedition occurred immediately after this, when we bought souvenirs at a stall, with a gay striped awning more appropriate to Bray or Bundoran than to this grim place. There we stood and scrutinized the wares on display: beads, statuettes, medals, snowstorms. Reverting to our consumerist role, we ... do I mean I? I assume my sister felt the same about it all ... felt almost content, for a few minutes, and we always selected the same souvenirs, namely snowstorms. I have one still: it has a painted blue backdrop, now peeling a little, and figures of elves and mushrooms under the glass, and, painted in black letters on its wooden base, 'I have prayed for you at Doon Well.' I bought that as a present for my best friend, Ann Byrne, but when I returned to Dublin I hadn't the courage to give it to her so it stayed in my bedroom for years, until I moved to Germany to study, and then I brought it with me. As a souvenir, not of Doon Well, I think, but of something.

We went to Derry without my aunt. We shopped and ate sausages and beans for lunch, in Woolworths. I enjoyed the trip to Derry. It was the highlight of the holiday, for me.

At the end of the fortnight, we would shake hands with my aunt in the street, and say goodbye. On these occasions her face would grow long and sad, she would always, at the moment when we climbed into the car, actually cry quietly to herself. My mother would say: 'Sure, we won't feel it now till it's Christmas! And then the summer will be here in no time at all!' And this would make everything much more poignant for my aunt, for me, for everyone. I would squirm on the seat, and, although I often wanted to cry myself, not because I was leaving my aunt but because I didn't want to give up the countryside, and the stream, and the clean clear water, I wouldn't think of my own unhappiness, but instead divert all my energy into despising my aunt for breaking yet another taboo: grown-ups do not cry.

My sister was tolerant. She'd laugh kindly as we turned out of the street on to the lane. 'Poor old Annie!' she'd say. But I couldn't laugh, I couldn't forgive her at all, for crying, for being herself, for not being the full shilling.

There was one simple reason for my hatred, so simple that I understood it myself, even when I was eight or nine years old. I resembled my aunt physically. 'You're the image of your aunt Annie!' people, relations, would beam at me as soon as I met them, in the valley. Now I know, looking at photos of her, looking in the glass, that this was not such a very bad thing. She had a reasonable enough face, as faces go. But I could not see this when I was a child, much less when a teenager. All I knew then was that she looked wrong. For one thing, she had straight unpermed hair, cut short across the nape of the neck, unlike the hair of any woman I knew then (but quite like mine as it is today). For another, she had thick unplucked eyebrows, and no lipstick or powder, even on Sunday, even for Doon Well. Although at that time it was unacceptable to be unmade up, it was outrageous to wear straight hair and laced shoes. Even in a place which was decidedly old-fashioned, she looked uniquely outmoded. She looked, to my city-conditioned eyes, like a freak. So when people would say to me, 'God, aren't you the image of your auntie!' I would cringe and wrinkle up in horror. Unable to change my own face, and unable to see that it resembled hers in the slightest ... and how does a face that is ten resemble one that is fifty? ... I grew to hate my physique. And I transferred that hatred, easily and inevitably, to my aunt.

When I was eleven, and almost finished with family holidays, I visited Ballytra alone, not to stay with my aunt, but to attend an Irish college which had just been established in that district. I did not stay with any of my many relatives, on purpose: I wanted to steer clear of all unnecessary contact with my past, and lived with a family I had never seen before.

Even though I loved the rigorous jolly ambience of the college, it posed problems for me. On the one hand, I was the child of one of the natives of the parish, I was almost a native myself. On the other hand, I was what was known there as a 'scholar', one of the kids from Dublin or Derry who descended on Ballytra like a shower of fireworks in July, who acted as if they owned the place, who more or less shunned the native population.

If I'd wanted to, it would have been very difficult for me to steer a median course between my part as a 'scholar' and my other role, as a cousin of the little native 'culchies' who, if they had been my playmates in former years, were now too shabby, too rustic, too outlandish, to tempt me at all. In the event, I made no effort to play to both factions: I managed by ignoring my relations entirely, and throwing myself into the more appealing life of the 'scholar'. My relations, I might add, seemed not to notice this, or care, if they did, and no doubt they were as bound by their own snobberies and conventions as I was by mine.

When the weather was suitable, that is, when it did not rain heavily, afternoons were spent on the beach, the same beach upon which my sister and I had always played. Those who wanted to swim walked there, from the school, in a long straggling crocodile. I love to swim and never missed an opportunity to go to the shore.

The snag about this was that it meant passing by my aunt's house, which was on the road down to the lough: we had to pass through her street to get there. For the first week, she didn't bother me, probably assuming that I would drop in soon. But, even though my mother had warned me to pay an early visit and had given me a head scarf to give her, I procrastinated. So after a week had gone by she began to lie in wait for me: she began to sit on her stone seat, in front of the door, and to look at me dolefully as I passed. And I would give a little casual nod, such as I did to everyone I met, and pass on.

One afternoon, the teacher who supervised the group was walking beside me and some of my friends, much to my pride and discomfiture. When we came to the street, she called, softly, as I passed, 'Mary, Mary.' I nodded and continued on my way. The teacher gave me a funny look and said: 'Is she talking to you, Mary? Does she want to talk to you?' 'I don't know her,' I said, melting in shame. 'Who is she?' 'Annie, that's Annie Bonner.' He didn't let on to know anything more about it, but I bet he did: everyone who had spent more than a day in Ballytra knew everything there was to know about it, everyone, that is, who wasn't as egocentric as the 'scholars'.

My aunt is still alive, but I haven't seen her in many years. I never go to Inishowen now. I don't like it since it became modern and littered with bungalows. Instead I go to Barcelona with my husband, who is a native Catalonian. He teaches Spanish here, part-time, at the university, and runs a school for Spanish students in Ireland during the summers. I help him in the tedious search for digs for all of them, and really we don't have much time to holiday at all.

My aunt is not altogether well. She had a heart attack just before Christmas and had to have a major operation at the Donegal Regional. I meant to pay her a visit, but never got around to it. Then, just before she was discharged, I learned that she was going home for Christmas. Home? To her own empty house, on the lane down to the lough? I was, to my surprise, horrified. God knows why, I've seen people in direr straits. But something gave. I phoned my mother and wondered angrily why she wouldn't have her, just for a few weeks. But my mother is getting on, she has gout, she can hardly walk herself. So I said, 'All right, she can come here!' But Julio was unenthusiastic. Christmas is the only time of the year he manages to relax: in January, the bookings start, the planning, the endless meetings and telephone calls. Besides, he was expecting a guest from home: his sister, Montserrat, who is tiny and dark and lively as a sparrow. The children adore her. In the end, my sister, unmarried and a lecturer in Latin at Trinity, went to stay for a few weeks in Ballytra until my aunt was better. She has very flexible holidays, my sister, and no real ties.

I was relieved, after all, not to have aunt Annie in my home. What would my prim suburban neighbours have thought? How would Julio, who has rather aristocratic blood, have coped? I am still ashamed, you see, of my aunt. I am still ashamed of myself. Perhaps, I suspect, I do resemble her, and not just facially. Perhaps there is some mental likeness too. Are my wide education, my brilliant husband, my posh accent, just attempts at camouflage? Am I really all that bright? Sometimes, as I sit and read in my glass-fronted bungalow, looking out over the clear sheet of the Irish Sea, and try to learn something, the grammar of some foreign language, the names of Hittite gods, something like that, I find the facts running away from me, like sticks escaping downstream on the current. And more often than that, much more often, I feel in my mind a splodge of something that won't allow any knowledge to sink in. A block of some terrible substance, soft and thick and opaque. Like butter.

Shane Connaughton

Ojus

A s often as he could he escaped from the barracks to roam the drumlin fields or sit with the farmers in hedge or house until the rain had stopped.

There was water everywhere. In the sky, in the lakes, in the light; running off the hills, off the trees, off the roofs and cornered into barrels; in the lime-bottomed well, in the village pump, in the rain gauge at the rear of the station, always in the air and constantly on tap in women's eyes and children's hearts.

'They're born with water in their veins instead of blood,' his father said. Bucketing rain they called 'A damp class of a day'.

In summer he watched George Conlon trying to machine the meadow land and being forced in the end to use a scythe. The swathes lay for weeks trying to dry in the skimpy winds between showers.

A constant net of drizzle hung from hill to hill, the people trapped as fish.

Their lives were moist, their words dry.

'That's a bad downpour.'

'I have me share of it.'

Words gurgled in their mouths like water going down a drain. It was a liquidy language, cranky, flat, sticky as strong tea.

'Why is Butlershill like a springin' cow?'

'Why?'

' 'Cos it's near Cavan.'

'I don't get it.'

'The bull did.'

In his innocence he had left himself wide open for a double punchline. Conlon tried to explain it to him.

'It's a bucolic joke with a sexual bent depending on geographical word-play. The cute hoors love someone like you. They've nothing better to do.'

They lived on dumpy hills rising out of water, along a political Border miles from Dublin or Belfast. Their cut-off lives ran long and narrow as a sheugh but their hearts were open to the boy and from morning until dark he helped them from the ploughtime of the year to harvest home.

'Give that lad a ponger of milk. He's earned it. Are you able for another hunk of bread? Course he is! What'll you have on it?'

'Jam, please.'

'Which one?'

'Rhubarb and ginger, please. It's the best I've ever tasted.'

'Ah-ha, he's the little smiler can charm the missus.'

On the good days when the sun got lost above them he knew it was the greenest country in the world. The golden light magnified the green of grass and ivy, geraniums in window boxes, the glinty eyes of basking pikes. On golden days bone of earth and rock screamed green to the hidden marrow.

'That's an ojus day.'

'You have your share of it.'

His window and the light were out of joint. The sun could only just sneak into his bedroom. It slithered over the sill, down the wall, across the lino, beaming for a few moments into the empty fireplace.

Good days, bad days, being out was freedom from the damp within. In the woods and lakes and hills was happiness. He couldn't bear the thought of being sent away.

The first he heard of it was from George Conlon. They were working in a turnip field, following a horse-drawn slipe, when Conlon stood up to light a fresh cigarette from the butt of the old.

'We'll miss you when you go.'

Puzzled, the boy stared at him. A mesh of drizzle gusted up from behind a hedge, falling sticky on his face like prickly sweat. He hated pulling and snedding turnips. A lumpy cold vegetable, his fingers were the same colour as them – freezing blue. Their tufts of turquoise leaves looked like fantastical wet ears and the sleeves of his cardigan were soaked with touching them. The gungy earth clodded his boots and the water in the shallow drills slurped through his laces.

'I'm not going. Tea won't be ready for ages yet.'

Conlon gasped the smoke into his lungs. Adjusting his brown hat he looked at the boy.

'No. I mean when you go away to school.'

The part of the hat he held when putting it on and off was black from use.

'I am at school sure.'

He could see from Conlon's eyes he regretted having spoken.

'Maybe your mammy hasn't told you yet. She doesn't like the beatings that go on where you are. You're going to a boarding school instead. That's what she told me anyway.'

Lifting the rope reins from the slipe he flapped them over the horse's back. 'Up there.'

The mare rumped along the required few yards, wet earth falling from its huge hooves.

Panic could stab at you anytime, anywhere. Even in a turnip field. In an attempt to keep dry he had a slit potato sack, like a cowl, over his head and back. Throwing if off he bolted across the drills, through a sodden pasture, into the farmyard and out the drive on to the road. He had never known such fear grip his heart. He couldn't imagine his mother wanting to send him away. She needed him. How could there be miles between them, especially at night? It would be like death. And what would be the point of life without his father? He was frightened of him, he hated him but he loved him too.

He loved him in the mornings when he turned round

from shaving, cut-throat in hand, to wink at the boy and laugh when he tried winking back. He loved him when his father held his hand tight, giving him his strength. He loved him when they swam in Kilifanah lake, his father shouting, 'Isn't it grand to be alive?' He loved him when he told him stories of his own father, Black Jack and his uncle Red Mick.

'I saw the pair of them drag a dead horse up on to a cart. With nothing but their bare hands.'

He loved to see him saunter through the village in his dark blue uniform, high and handsome as a star. He loved him when he held his mother's hand and sang as best he could, 'In Pasadena where grass is green now. . . .'

He wasn't going to go away to a boarding school. He would never leave Butlershill and all the people who fed him and let him sit at their open fires until night came down.

Running pell-mell, blind with fear, he came into the village. The tethered goat was crying on the green. He always stopped and spoke to it but now he cut straight past and up the hill to home.

Going by the forge the blacksmith shouted to him.

'How's she cuttin' gossun?'

He was in too much of a hurry and far too angry to reply.

He was so angry he didn't notice the car parked outside the station. Tearing round to the married quarters and without taking his mucky boots off, he hurried straight into the kitchen.

'I'm not going to be sent away and don't try, so I'm not.'

The kitchen was empty. Where on earth was his mother? He was going to roar and shout and kick the furniture when he saw her. He wasn't going to be sent away. She sometimes rested in the afternoon. He ran down the hallway and crashed in through her bedroom door.

He could feel his dirty boots skittering to a halt and his face crumple in amazement.

She was sitting on the bed, her vest and blouse pulled up over her face so he couldn't see her face. Her naked breasts and belly were exposed and a man bent down towards her as if listening to something. The man couldn't hear him and his mother couldn't see him. Her arms crossed over her face held up her garments.

Her belly was white and round, her breasts bigger than he could remember. The man turned and looked at him. It was Dr Langan with a stethoscope hanging from his ears.

'Hello young man.'

His eyes were riveted on his mother's belly. It was round, round as a moon. He was so shocked the world might have stopped turning.

His mother lowering her arms, smiled, embarrassed.

'I thought you were helping George Conlon, darling.'

Something of the utmost importance was happening but his brain was in such a state he couldn't reason it out.

'Well young man, you're not going to be on your own much longer. The baby is coming along very nicely indeed.'

That was it. A baby. His mother was going to have a baby. It was in there in her moony belly, waiting to come out and take his place whilst he was banished to a boarding school. The injustice of it was so startling he couldn't move, ask a question, shout for justice or run from the room and cry for mercy in a ditch.

'Go along, darling, there's some red lemonade in the meat safe. Dr Langan will be going soon.'

Tears squeezed out his eyes and ran down the sides of his nose.

He walked out into the drizzle and stood dumbly staring at his feet. A curlew speared along the hill behind the barracks, its fifing notes drowning behind it in the rain.

Where was his father? He'd appeal to him. His mother wanted him out of the way so she could enjoy the baby unperturbed. If they tried to send him away he'd run into the demesne, climb the trees and live there like a bird.

He went into the barracks, anger swelling his heart. His

father was in the day room with Guard Hegarty. They looked at him in huge amused surprise as he began to rant and rave and stamp the wooden floor.

'I'm not going to no boarding school. I don't want no baby. I'm not leaving here. You want to get rid of me. I'm not going. I'm the big and only bab. I'm not going to be sent to school in Monaghan. I want Mammy. I want Mammy.'

His rage suddenly draining from him he sunk to the floor, tired and breathless.

His father and Hegarty were laughing. He felt a fool. As soon as he felt his father's hand on his head he lashed out with foot and fist trying to hit him. Their guffawing laughter tortured him.

'Begad, Sergeant, he must have got out the wrong side of the bed this morning, hah?'

His father swung him up on to the table and, standing in close to him, imprisoning him, blocked him so he couldn't kick out.

'Now look here, will you calm yourself for Heaven's sake? You're going away for your own good. The school in Monaghan is far better than the one here. Where you won't get thrashed and the teachers won't come in half-shot or hungover. And the baby when it comes will be the best thing ever happened to you. Mark my words. A baby brother? A baby sister? Man alive you won't know yourself.'

His father's face was inches from him, his earnest eyes dancing, his lips now tight and serious, now smiling with conviction.

'Why didn't you or Mammy tell me?'

'We were going to, when we got round to it. Nothing we're going to do is going to be for anything but your own good. You know that, don't you? Hm?'

'I'm not going, I'm not going, I'm not going.'

Dr Langan tapping on the window, his father went out to talk to him.

Hegarty from deep in his trouser pocket handed him some coins.

'There's nothing like a bag of sweets to cure a fellah's heartache.'

He went out the main door, squeezing between his father and Langan who were sheltering from the rain.

They had planned the whole thing behind his back. He'd be sent away and when he came back there'd be someone else in his place, taking his food, stealing his kisses, sleeping by his mother's side. How could his parents betray him so?

He went into the demesne and sat on his hunkers against a tree, his mind grim and desperate.

He hated the baby already. Because he was afraid of it. It would definitely limit his mother's love and his father would be all strutting pride. His father wanted lots of children. His mother had locked her door against him but since he had been forced to sleep on his own, he knew his father was going into her and staying there for a good while before going back to his own bed. He sometimes lay awake listening to his mother's laugh. Laughter in the night burst out of mystery and was always followed by a deep secret silence.

The school he went to in the village he had to admit he didn't like. It had two teachers – a woman and a man. Being young he was in the woman's class but when she wanted children punished she sent them to the Principal's room. There in front of a wall-sized map of Ireland they were beaten without mercy. A cane was used – on hands, legs, back. Ears were twisted, hair pulled out in lumps. He had watched a friend being beaten until he sunk, crushed, to his knees. He had seen pools of urine on the seats, left there by frightened girls.

The boy was terrified. But why should a boarding school be any different? If he was beaten there he wouldn't have his mother to calm and soothe his wounds. They might as well send him away to gaol.

Getting up he walked deeper into the wood. Round by the lake he met Lady Sarah Butler-Coote. She could tell straightaway he was unhappy.

'Oh, treasure, all alone? No chums? Do tell me what's the matter?'

Her old kind face and words turned him on like a tap and his fears came out in such a torrent of self-sorrow, a flock of ducks took fright and shot from the water, wheeling away above the trees.

'Oh my, oh my, oh my. I understand now. Hm. Boarding school? I do not approve of that at all. They sent me to one of those places too. The baby, though, that's golden news. It means you won't be alone in the world. Do you see? I wish I had a brother or sister. I wouldn't be all alone now. Rattling round the house like a pea in a biscuit tin. A baby? Oh yes, I approve of that. And so will you my treasure, believe me you will.'

Her accent was rich and clear as music from a clarinet. He walked away, letting her words swirl round his head, testing them for sense, trying to defeat their purpose. She agreed with him about being sent away and if she was lonely why didn't she buy a husband? She didn't need a brother or sister at all. She loved animals, birds, fish, trees, children. None other came willingly near her. Her looks were legendary and deterred all comers. But surely her vast wealth could blind a desperate man?

When he arrived home, soaking wet, his mother scolded him for his sulking silence.

'You're a big boy now. You have to face up to things. I was a boarder, don't forget. With the nuns in Moyville Abbey. It'll cost money but we want you to have the best. And the day the baby is born, if all goes well, I'll send for you straightaway, kiss you and tell you I love you as much as ever before. Now that's a promise and you know I never break a promise, don't you?'

She was angry when he didn't respond.

'Do you know something? You're just like your father! The image of him in every way.'

Her words chilled him, tumbled his pride. He went to his room and sat on the bed for hours.

Events had hammered him into a corner and hard as he tried to escape over the following weeks, he couldn't. Everybody in the village and the surrounding farms knew about the baby and knew he was being sent away.

'I hear tell the stork's going to be landin' on the barracks chimney.'

'Boarding school? That's ojus altogether.'

Ojus was the most common adjective or adverb. It could be applied positively or negatively to any person, place or thing or stuck in front of any verb. It was a neutral word that could mean anything.

'We're going to miss you somethin' shockin'.'

He was going to miss them, that he knew. He couldn't think how he was going to manage to say goodbye.

His mother let him feel her stomach.

'It'll arrive in three or so months. If all goes well.'

'How do you mean, Mammy? It will go well won't it?'

Without reply she went out and hung a line of clothes stretching the whole length of the garden.

He began to awaken early, and drawing the blinds, lie for hours looking out at the dark clinging to the trees and the pigeons and pheasants striding about the field in the growing dawn.

One morning he saw Tully, the rich publican and shop owner walking quickly past his window. Something must have happened. He was in such a hurry he wasn't even bothering to try and rouse the Guard who slept each night in the barracks dormitory.

The boy hopping out of bed had the halldoor unbolted just as Tully knocked.

'You're a light sleeper, young fellah. Will you tell your daddy there's been a break-in at the lock-up shop out of Scotshouse Cross. Ojus amount of damage and destruction done. You'll not forget will you?'

The lock-up shop was miles from the village and saved the people who lived in its vicinity having to journey for provisions. A shopboy worked in it during the day but at night it was empty.

Tully was the first man up in the morning and the last to go to bed. He thrived on work and worry. As long as he was moving he was making money. It was seven o'clock with a nippy breeze moving through swirls of cold mist. But Tully wore only his brown boots, trousers, braces and an open-necked shirt. He was a lonely bachelor. There was no one to keep him in bed. The boy wondered why he and Lady Sarah didn't get married. Two peas in a biscuit tin were better than one.

Later, he went down to his father and told him about the break-in.

'Well bad cess to them whoever it was. And Tully. Put the kettle on.'

The boy could see he was secretly pleased. This was crime. Not a murder maybe, but a mystery to be cracked. Someone to be trapped by evidence that had to be hunted out. It was what his father loved. His dream of course was murder.

'One good murder is worth a thousand bicycles without tail-lights. It's worth a hundred car crashes. A pub-full of after-hours drinkers doesn't compare. Murder is the only reason police exist.'

He watched his father shave, the cut-throat razor held delicately in his hand as a broken wing. He was humming, pleased with himself. The boy could smell the thick shaving lather from across the other side of the kitchen. It came squeezing out of its tube on to his father's hand like a green caterpillar.

'If it wasn't tinkers did the break-in, then I'm a Dutchman.'

'It might have been a travelling criminal, Daddy.' The boy knew the terms and enjoyed drawing his father out.

'As the Scotsman said, I have me doots. Tully said there was a lot of damage done, didn't he? That's the tinkers for you all right. Housebreaking with destruction – it's bred into them.'

'This can't be housebreaking, can it? A lock-up shop isn't a house, is it?'

'It's classified as such under the Larceny Act, 1916, Section 26.'

'How will you proceed with the investigation when you arrive at the scene of the crime?'

'Light the primus and do me a boiled egg and don't be annoying me. Oh cripes.'

A seed of blood pushed out from a nick on his lip and spread like red ink over his soapy mouth.

'Why is the primus stove made in Sweden, Daddy?'

'Do you want me to cut meself again? I don't know why! It's an impossible question. All I know about Sweden is two things. They're famous for hardy sailors. And they make primus stoves. Nothing else.'

'If there are any footprints at the scene will you take a cast of them?'

'You've reminded me, good boy. Go round to the dormitory and get the bag of plaster of Paris from the top of the wardrobe. I'll be needing it for certain.'

His father was happier than he had ever remembered him. Whistling, relaxed, calm. There were no epileptic roars in the night or moods in the day. He took his daily pill, spooned Milk of Magnesia if his stomach was upset and, after long rides round his sub-district, gulped his glass of barley water.

'Keep the bowels regular and God will look after the rest.'

He rode away from the Station, the bag of plaster of Paris buckled to the carrier by its thin, fraying, leather straps.

His mother calling from her bedroom sent him down to Reilly's for bread, butter and a box of matches. And the newspaper.

Reilly moved slowly behind the counter, letting the day seep gently into his bones. He was tall with handsome smiling looks and a quick temper which he used to poke conversation from all who went into him.

'What are you looking so happy about?'

'I'm being sent away to school.'

'Pity about you. Wasn't I sent to the same school meself?'

'Were you? What was it like?'

'Rough in them days. Not any more from what I've heard.'

'Do they beat you?'

'Only if you shoot the teacher.'

The boy laughed.

'You'll have the time of your life. There'll be fellahs from all over the country, just like yourself. You won't want to know us when you come home on holidays. How is Mammy keeping?'

'Fine thank you.'

He went home knowing his days were numbered. There was no escape. He would have to obey.

Smoke was rising from the Station chimney. Through the day room window he could see Guard Hegarty down on one knee rattling at the fire with a poker.

In the kitchen he put the groceries on the dresser, spread the newspaper on the table and turned on the wireless. Jazz, all the way from New Orleans, blew round him like a hot wind. Standing at the table, listening, reading, he was content.

Thinking he heard his mother call he turned the wireless down. The door opening she staggered in, bent double, clutching her stomach, her face deathly pale.

'Oh no, oh no, oh please God no.'

The boy saw dark water breaking down her legs, then blood.

'Don't be frightened, darling. Get the doctor quick.'

In the day room Hegarty phoned for the doctor and when he raced back to the kitchen his mother was lying in the armchair, her stomach heaving, pain, panic, regret in her eyes.

His blood was running cold, his brain half dead. Low, on the wireless, a clarinet cried.

'A towel, darling.'

He got a towel and a glass of water. Holding her hand he looked at her. She was crying like a child and in her face was enough sorrow for the whole world.

'Please don't die Mammy.'

'Get one of the women.'

He ran to the nearest house and within seconds there was a flock of women running before him.

He hated himself. He had hated the baby and now this was happening. It was all his fault. Evil thoughts became evil deeds. Numb with heartache and guilt he knelt down on the roadside and prayed for his mother and for forgiveness. The occupants of a passing car looked out at him amazed.

Then on Guard Hegarty's three-speed bike he rode out to Scothouse Cross to tell his father.

He rode like a fury, his legs and lungs aching. He didn't care if he crashed. At least he wouldn't have to face his father and see the bad news rooting in his eyes.

He was selfish. Kicking up such a fuss about going away to school! What did it matter? If God would spare his mother he would willingly go the whole way there crawling on his hands and knees.

He shot by the Orange Hall, the quarry, the Protestant church and a scatter of whitewashed houses with a barking dog at every gate. All the fields were pudding-basined hills flagged with ragwort. The pot-holed road was a rotten mouth, the hawthorn hedges on either side long thick lips red with lipstick. Reaching Tully's shop he flung the bike against the wall and went in.

He was aware of the destruction even as his father pierced him with his stare. Sugar crunched under foot. Big-bellied bags of flour were ripped open, their contents spewing. A box of butter was upended and walked on to a mash. The shop counter was littered with broken glass. A radio lay upside down, its back ripped off, the valves and workings kicked to pieces. Plaster of Paris dusted his father's trousers.

'Come quick. There's something wrong with Mammy.'

His father's face turned stone. His body went rigid, his fists tight.

'Sacred heart.'

He went out, mounted his bicycle and methodically rode away.

To the boy it seemed as if his father had been half expecting the news. And knew how to steel himself to the moment. Perhaps it had happened before. Perhaps he was an only child because no other child had managed to make it from his mother's womb.

At the back of the shop, on muddy ground, was a large saucepan upside down as if covering something. On lifting it he saw a plaster of Paris cast. A footprint. The saucepan was to protect the plaster from rain or anyone accidentally treading on it.

The state of the shop was like his own state. Shattered. An alarm clock lying on a shelf began to clatter like a grasshopper, the hammer blurring between two bells. The glass was broken, the minute hand snapped. Abruptly it stopped. The world was a silent, chaotic place.

When he arrived home his mother was in bed, the doctor and his father with her. She was going to be all right. She was going to live. On the floor at the end of the bed was the foetus, wrapped in the *Irish Independent*. A death parcel. His own flesh and blood.

His father told him to dig a hole in the garden. He dug it beside a blackcurrant bush. He didn't want to dig it at the bottom of the garden because that's where they buried the contents of the Elsan lavatory. The ground there was sunken and spongy.

He saw his father coming carrying the parcel. His face was grim and grey as tallow. The corner of his lower lip was gripped in his teeth.

He took the shovel from the boy. Placing the parcel in the hole he began to fill in the clay. Gardening was his favourite pastime. He spent as many hours at it as on police duties. With a shovel in his hand and clay before him he had the grace that comes from power and rhythm.

Patting down the top of the piled clay with the back of the shovel, he turned away and stared at the hill rising from the swampy field on the far side of the garden hedge.

His back seemed to tremble, his shoulders shake. It was the first time the boy had seen him cry.

Going to him he clung round his waist and his father, dropping the shovel, held him tight. They stood as one crying bitter tears, his poor mother watching from her bedroom window.

'You're just like him,' she had said.

He knew his childhood was over. It would lie till Doomsday with his tiny dead brother or sister under the blackcurrant bush.

A week later they walked him to the railway station, where he would get the morning train to Monaghan. He would never have thought it possible but he was glad to be leaving. Since his mother's miscarriage the house was gloomy and dead.

Though it was before eight o'clock doors opened and people rapped on windows.

'Goodbye, we'll be thinking of you.'

'Good luck now.'

'God be with you, you ojus boy.'

To his delight and his father's amazement, as they neared the station, Tully hopped down from a lorry and, shaking the boy's hand, crinkled a pound note into it.

'We'll miss you, gossun, aye man surely.'

'Thank you Mr Tully, thank you very much indeed.'

When they had walked on his father muttered from the corner of his mouth – 'Wonders will never cease.'

'I always told you,' said his mother, 'Tully was a Christian man.'

Waiting for him on the platform was George Conlon. His parents protested when he handed the boy five pounds.

'Get away outa that, Sergeant, he earned every penny of it. And more.'

When they heard the train whistling in the distance his mother began to weep. He put his arms around her neck. She was powdery, perfumed, fresh as apples. He clung to her, dragging her scent down into his lungs, feeling for the last time the heat that warmed his soul.

As in a dream he stepped on to the train and felt outside himself as he waved goodbye.

The engine thundered away with him and just before they went into the deep cutting, he saw Harry, Conlon's twisted brother, waving to him from the turnip field. He would have had to set off very early to make the distance from the house.

There were still stars in the sky and a crescent moon hanging like an incense boat.

The night before when his mother was packing his suitcase, his father came into the room and gave him a plaster of Paris footprint.

'It's my own print. I did it as an experiment. You can show it to your class. I'm sure they'll find it interesting.'

It was an impression of the sole of his boot. The mark of the big seg on the heel was clear, as were the rows of studs. The plaster was the colour of salmon flesh. His father's foot was huge. Police feet. Clowns' feet.

Before he put his case on the rack, he took the footprint out and, leaning from the carriage window, as they crossed the Finn river, threw it in. He would never need reminding of his father's footprints.

Patrick McCabe

from *The Butcher Boy*

I WOKE UP the next morning and went round to the slaughterhouse but it was too early I was waiting for near two hours before Leddy came how long are you here he says a good while Mr Leddy I said. Its near time you'd show your face around here or where in the hell were you! Oh I says I was off rambling. Rambling he says, you'd do well to ramble in your own time Brady I've a mind to kick you rambling down that road. Well says I you won't have to worry for that's the end of it it'll be all over now shortly. He pulled on his apron and says they have a half ton of shite round at that hotel you were supposed to collect it and they have my heart scalded now get round there today and fuckingwell see about it. Right so Mr Leddy I said.

Then we started into the killing and we were working right through till dinnertime. Then he wiped his hands on his apron and says I'm away to my dinner take that cart round now. And make sure and tell them tell them you'll collect on time next week. I will indeed Mr Leddy I says. When he was gone off down the town I took the captive bolt pistol down off the nail where it was hanging and got the butcher's steel and the knife out of the drawer. There was a bucket of old slops and pig meal or something lying by the door so I just stuck them into that and went away with the cart whistling. So Traynor's daughter had been talking to Our Lady again, eh? They were all talk about her going to appear on the Diamond. I heard two old women on about it. We should be very proud says one of them its not every town the Mother Of God comes to visit. Indeed it is not says the

other one I wonder missus will there be angels. I wouldn't
know about that now but sure what odds whether there is or
not so long as she saves us from the end of the world what
do we care? Now you said it missus now you said it.
Everywhere you went: Not long now.

I went by Doctor Roche's house it was all painted up with
big blue cardboard letters spread out on the grass: AVE
MARIA WELCOME TO OUR TOWN. I was wondering could
I mix them up to make THIS IS DOCTOR ROCHE THE
BASTARD'S HOUSE, but I counted them and there wasn't
enough letters and anyway they were the wrong ones.

Tell Leddy to collect this brock on time or its the last he'll get
from us says the kitchen man and stands there looking at me
like I was stealing something off him. I will indeed I said and
started shovelling it into the cart. I shovelled and whistled
away and made sure there wasn't a scrap left so there'd be
no more complaining. Then off I went again on my travels.
Everybody was all holy now, we're all in this together people
of the town, bogmen taking off their caps to women, looking
into prams and everything. This is the holiest town in the
world they should have put that up on a banner.

There was a nice altar on the Diamond. There was three
angels flying over it just in front of the door of the Ulster
Bank.

I never saw the town looking so well. It looked like the
brightest, happiest town in the whole world.

I went round the back swinging my meal bucket. I could see
the neighbour's curtain twitching whistle whistle hello there
Mr Neighbour its me Francie with my special delivery for Mrs
Nugent. Then away she went from the window so I knocked
on Mrs Nugent's door and out she came wearing her blue
housecoat. Hello Mrs Nugent I said is Mr Nugent in I have a
message for him from Mr Leddy. She went all white and

stood there just stuttering I'm sorry she said my husband isn't here he's gone to work oh I said that's all right and with one quick shove I pushed her inside she fell back against something. I twisted the key in the lock behind me. She had a white mask of a face on her and her mouth a small o now you know what its like for dumb people who have holes in their stomachs Mrs Nugent. They try to cry out and they can't they don't know how. She stumbled trying to get to the phone or the door and when I smelt the scones and seen Philip's picture I started to shake and kicked her I don't know how many times. She groaned and said please I didn't care if she groaned or said please or what she said. I caught her round the neck and I said: You did two bad things Mrs Nugent. You made me turn my back on my ma and you took Joe away from me. Why did you do that Mrs Nugent? She didn't answer I didn't want to hear any answer I smacked her against the wall a few times there was a smear of blood at the corner of her mouth and her hand was reaching out trying to touch me when I cocked the captive bolt. I lifted her off the floor with one hand and shot the bolt right into her head *thlok* was the sound it made, like a goldfish dropping into a bowl. If you ask anyone how you kill a pig they will tell you cut its throat across but you don't you do it longways. Then she just lay there with her chin sticking up and I opened her then I stuck my hand in her stomach and wrote PIGS all over the walls of the upstairs room.

I made sure to cover her over good and proper with the brock there was plenty of it they wouldn't be too pleased if they saw me with Mrs Nugent in the bottom of the cart then I lifted the shafts and off I went on my travels again there was more hymns and streams of people up and down Church Hill with prayerbooks. Who did I meet then only your man with the bicycle and the raincoat thrown over the handlebars. He was all friendly this time he was a happy man Our Lady was coming he said. I haven't seen you this long time he says are you still collecting the tax? No I said that's all finished I'm wheeling carts now. You never thought you'd see the day the Mother of God would be coming to this town, eh? he says and looked at me as much as to say it was me arranged the whole thing. No, I did not, I said, its a happy time for the town and no mistake. A happy happy time he says and reached in his pocket to take out his tobacco puff puff what will we talk about now nothing I said the best of luck now I'm away off round to the yard right he says no rest for the wicked that's right I says no rest for anyone only Mrs Nugent in the bottom of this cart. But he didn't hear me saying that.

I left down the cart for a minute and went in to buy some fags the women were there over by the sugar only without Mrs Connolly. I got the fags and I says to the women its a pity Mrs Connolly isn't here I wanted to talk to her about what I said sure I was only codding! I said. What would I go and say the like of that to her for! Me and Mrs Connolly are old friends! Didn't I get a prize off her for doing a dance! A lovely juicy apple! I lit up a fag and puffed it ha ha they said ah sure don't be worrying your head Francie they said we all do things we regret don't we ladies. Yes I said especially Mrs Nugent and laughed through the smoke. Then they said: What? But I said: Oh nothing.

One of them twisted the strap of her handbag round her little finger and said there was no use in people bearing grudges at a special time like this. Now you said it I said, you never spoke a truer word.

Well ladies, I said, I must be off about my business there's no rest for the wicked indeed there is not Francie said the woman with three heads laughing away like in the old days. I had gone through that fag already and the shop was full of smoke I was puffing it all out that fast so what did I do only light another one. Francie Brady – I smoke one hundred cigarettes a day! Yes its true! Francie Brady says! No, it isn't. Only when I'm wheeling Mrs Nooge around. I stuck a little finger in the air and pulled on the fag like something out of the pictures. I say ladies – good day, I said and that started them off into the laughing again. Master Algernon Carruthers and his Nugent cart. OK Nooge let's ride I said, the Francie Brady Deadwood stage is pulling out. The drunk lad went by with another saint in a barrow and ducked down when he seen me.

Stop thief! Come back with that saint! I says and started into the laughing again. Stop that man! He's going to sell that poor saint for drink! Whistling away on I went my old man's a dustman he wears a dustman's hat. I don't know where all the songs came out of. Well its one for the money. I am a little baby pig I'll have you all to know. Yes this is the Baby Pig Show broadcasting on Raydeeoh Lux-em-Bourg!

Hell my good man. Fine weather we're having. What did you order? Two pounds of chump steak?

Or was it a half pound of Mrs Nugent?

Sorry folks, Mrs Nugent's not for sale! She's off on her travels with her old pal Francie Brady.

Where the hell were you says Leddy when I got back to the slaughterhouse yard. Oh, tricking about I says, well trick about in your own time he says I have to go on up to the shop, you take over here. Right, I said, that suits me, and I left down the barrow beside the Pit of Guts and asked Leddy where he'd put the lime. Clear off Grouse! I shouted and he tore off through the gate with a string of intestines. I got the shovel and slit open the bag of lime.

I was whistling away when I looked up and seen Sausage and four or five bogmen police coming across the yard I never seen them before they weren't from the town. One of them kept looking over the whole time sizing me up trying to catch my eye to tell me *by Chrisht you're for it now boy!* but I just went on skinning and whistling. I don't know what I was whistling I think it was the tune from Voyage to the Bottom of The Sea. Leddy was standing in the doorway wiping his hands with a rag then looking over at me with a chalky old face on him. I heard the sergeant saying: *The neighbours seen him going in round the back of the house this morning.*

Next thing what does Leddy do only lose the head. Before the sergeant could stop him he had a hold of me and gives me this push I fell back against the fridge door *I hope to Christ they give you everything that's coming to you! I should never have let you darken the door of the place only I let myself be talked into it on account of your poor mother!* he says standing there shaking with his fists opening and closing. He tried to push me again but I managed to get a hold of his arm I looked right into his eyes and he knew what I was saying to him, Mr Leddy from the Cutting Up Pigs University you better watch who you're pushing Bangkok you were never in Bangkok in your life and you better watch what you're saying about my father plucking my mother or you'll get the same Nugent got would you like that Pig Leddy – Leddy the Pig Man would you fuckingwell like that!

Then I burst out laughing in his face he was so shocked – looking I thought he was going to say O please Francie I'm sorry I didn't mean to say all that it was a slip of the tongue.

What could I say? Such a daft place!

Mr Nugent was shivery and everything I knew he couldn't bear to look at me. Where is she, said Sausage and the bullneck bogmen got a grip of me two on either side. They had me now all right I wasn't fit to move a muscle. Oh I said, this must be the end of the world. I hope the Blessed Virgin comes along to save me!

Where is she? says Sausage again.

Maltan Ready Rubbed Flake, that's the one!, I said to Mr Nugent and I got a thump in the ribs. Then they said right turn this place inside out and that's what they did. They turned it upside down. Those bogmen cops. You could fry a rasher on their necks. How many rashers was that? Four. No – let's make it two rashers and two eggs instead if you don't mind!

I wonder is she in behind this half-a-cow? No, she doesn't appear to be. What about under this septic tank? No, no sign of her. Then they got hysterical. They had to take Mr Nugent away. What have you done with her? I said who and they got worse. They gave me a beating and took me for a drive all round the town. What had they draped across the chicken-house only THE TOWN WELCOMES OUR LADY. I said to them: She must be going to land on the chickenhouse roof and they stuck the car to the road with a screech of brakes by Christ I'll tear that blasphemous tongue out of your head with my bare hands says Sausage. But he didn't, then we were off again where to, the river. Is she out here? Who, I said again. After all that they took me back to the station and gave me the father and mother of a kicking. In the middle of it all what does one of the bullnecks say: Let me have a crack at him and I'll knock seven different kinds of shite out of him!

That finished me off altogether. I started saying it the way he said it. Seven different kinds of shoite! For fuck's sake!

The way they do it they put a bar of soap in a sock and I don't know how many times they gave it to me it leaves no marks. But it still knocks seven different kinds of shite out!

Where is she said Sausage, shaking. Castlebar Sausages – they're the best! I said. Hear them sizzle in the pan – Sergeant Sausage says!

Then they got fed up and said fuck him into the cell we'll get it out of him in the morning. I could hear them playing cards. Foive o' trumps! and all this. That's the besht keeerd you've played thish ayvnin'! I stuck my ear to the wall so as I wouldn't miss any of it. I heard them saying: I wouldn't turn my back on that treacherous fucker not for a second!

*

They kept me in the cell the whole of the next day they were waiting for the detective to come down from Dublin. I could hear them all going by in the street come over here you bastard I shouts to the drunk lad through the bars you owe me two and six the fucker away off then running like the clappers. Hello Mrs Connolly I shouted look where they have me now! Your man with the bicycle, I shouts over: This is what I get for not paying my pig poll tax! It serves me right!

Ha ha he says and nearly drove the bicycle into a wall. Who appears at the window of the cell then only Mickey Traynor and McCooey the miracle worker. I'm praying for you son, says McCooey. He had Maria Goretti propped up against a couple of haybales on the back of the cart he said she was going to bleed at the apparition. Then he says I hear there's been bad trouble in the town this past few days. How are you my son, he says, I'm praying for your immortal soul, never fear. Through the bars I could see Goretti gawking up at the sky with her hands joined. Observe her beautiful eyes, McCooey'd say. Observe the beautiful saint's eyes and then two red red rubies of blood would appear and roll down her white cheeks. Its sad Mr McCooey, I said. What, my son, he said, this vale of tears in which we are all but wanderers searching for home? No, I said, fat old bastards like you wasting all that tomato sauce. O Jesus Mary and Joseph says Mickey and reaches out in case he faints. You're a bad and wicked and evil man and you broke your mother's heart didn't even go to the poor woman's funeral! I said to him what the fuck would you know about it Traynor what do you know you couldn't even fix the television could you well what are you talking about! Do you hear me Traynor? Fuck you! Fuck you and your daughter and The Blessed Virgin! I didn't mean to say that Traynor made me say it the whole street heard me there they were all looking and crossing themselves oh Jesus Mary and Joseph then in came the bullnecks and the detective they gave me another kicking and says we're going for a drive after and you'd better start opening your mouth Brady or by Christ you'll get what's coming to you. I fell into a sort of sleep then after that and I heard Mrs Connolly and them all saying the rosary for me outside in the square. I looked up and there was Buttsy and Devlin looking in between the bars. You better pray they hang you says Buttsy what we're going to do to you we'll string you up like the pig you are. He was all smart but then he starts screeching *what have you done to my sister* till Devlin had to take him away. I said good riddance and read the *Beano* I got one of the children to get me in Mary's shop. General Jumbo he had some army, tiny little robot men he controlled using this wrist panel of buttons made for him by his friend Mr Professor. I used to think: I wouldn't mind having one of them that controlled all the people in the town. I'd march them all out to the river and click!, stop right at the edge. Then just when they were saying: Phew that was a lucky one we nearly went in there, Hi-yah! I'd press the button – in you go youse bastards aiee! and the whole lot of them into the water.

The next time Sausage came in on his own turning the cap round on his lap looking at me with these sad eyes why does there have to be so many sad things in the world Francie I'm an old man I'm not able for this any more. When I seen them eyes, I said to myself, poor old Sausage its not fair. All right Sausage I said I'll show you where she is thanks Francie he said, I knew you would. Its gone on long enough. There's been enough unhappiness and misery. There has indeed Sergeant I said.

The new detective was in the front of the car, Fabian of the Yard I called him after the fellow in the pictures, and I was hemmed in between two of the bullnecks in the back.

Sausage was all proud now that things had worked out and he hadn't made a cod of himself in front of Fabian. I'll be all over shortly now Francie he says you're doing the right thing. I know Sergeant I said. When we turned into the lane he drove slowly to avoid the children what were they at now selling comics on a table it was a comic sale. They stood there looking after us I seen tassels pointing look Brendy its him!

We stopped at the chickenhouse and Fabian says you two men stay out here at the front just in case you can't be too careful. Right they said and me and the sergeant and him and the other two went inside. The fan was humming away and it made me sad. The chicks were still scrabbling away who are all these coming with Francie?

We waded through the piles of woodchips as we went along and I said to them it isn't fair its just down here at the back. Fabian wasn't sure of where he was going it was so dark and when he walked into the light hanging in front of his face it went swinging back and forth painting the big shadows on the walls and the ceilings. I think the chicks must have known what was going to happen for they started burbling and getting excited. I said fuck who put that there and made on to trip and fall down. Watch yourself said Sausage its very dark and when Fabian came over to help me up I had the chain in my hand it had been lying there under the pallets where it always was. I swung it once and Fabian cried out but that was all I needed I tore into the back room and bolted the door. I didn't waste any time I threw the chain there and flung open the window and got out then ran like fuck.

Clare Boylan

Villa Marta

THE SUN rose gently over Villa Marta like a little halfbaked madeleine but by nine o'clock it was a giant lobster, squeezing the pretty pensión in its red claws. Honeysuckle and rose tumbled over the walls of the Villa. The petals fattened and were forced apart. Dismembered blossom dangled in the probing heat. Sally and Rose stumbled down to the patio and ate their hard rolls called bocadillos, and drank bowls of scummy coffee, feeling faintly sick because of the heat and the coffee. The tables on the terrace had been arranged under a filigree of vine and splashes of sun came through, burning them in patches. Behind a cascade of leaves which made a dividing curtain, a group of Swedish boys watched them with pale, intelligent eyes. 'You come out with us,' they hissed solemnly through the vines; 'you come fucky-fuckies.'

They stretched out beside the pool and talked about food and records and sex appeal and sex. Already they had learned a thing or two. Sally had discovered, from a survey in *Time* magazine, that smoking added fifty per cent more sex appeal to a girl. They wondered if you were hopelessly, truly in love, would you know because you would even think a man's thing was nice looking. This was a mystery and also a risk because if such a love did not exist and you spent your life waiting for it, you would be on the shelf, an old maid and hairy.

Built into their contempt for old maids was the knowledge that marriage meant an end to office life and it was so pleasant to lie by the pool, barely disturbed by the prowling vigil of the Swedish boys and the sun rolling over them in bales of heat, that both were intent on a domestic resolution.

It was merely a question of finding the right man or finding the right feelings for some sort of man. When they spoke of their married lives, Sally detailed a red sofa and Japanese paper lanterns. Rose was going to have a television in the bedroom.

Sometimes they fetched a guitar and went and sat among the cacti and sang; 'Sally free and easy, that should be her name – took a sailor's loving for a nursery game.'

In the afternoons, they went for a walk around the streets of Palma. Sally wore a dress of turquoise frills. Rose's frock was white linen. It was the era of the minis but they turned up the hems several times over so that the twitch of their buttocks showed a glimpse of flower-patterned panty. Men followed them up and down the hot, narrow lanes. 'See how they look at you!' Sally shuddered. 'Their eyes go down and up as if they can look right inside you.'

'Why would they want to do that?' Rose said.

In fact she was very aware of their pursuers, of the tense silence in the street behind them as if the air itself was choked with excitement – the stalking whisper of plimsolled feet on cobbles – the hot, shocked breath on the back of the neck. One day one of them captured her as she rounded a corner, caught her by the waist with a hand as brown as a glove and gazed into her face with puzzled eyes and then he kissed her. She slapped his face and ran on giggling to catch up with her friend but all day little fingers of excitement crept up and twisted inside her.

In the evenings they grew despondent for the heat of the day made them lethargic and they did not enjoy the foreign food. 'Drunk-man's-vomit-on-a-Saturday-night,' Sally would sigh, spooning through a thick yellow bean soup.

After dinner there began a long ritual of preparation, of painting eyes and nails, of pinning little flowers and jewelled clips in their hair before going out dancing. They did not bother much with washing because they had dipped in the pool during the day and the showers at the Villa Marta were violent and boiling, but they sprayed recklessly with *L'Air du Temps*.

The dances were not, actually, fun. The boys were young and eager but their desire was not skilfully mounted. They yapped and scrabbled like puppies. They did not know how to make sex without touching so that it hung in heavy droplets on the air. They did not know how to make fire from sticks.

One day on the beach they met a group of Americans, schoolgirls from a convent in Valencia, tall and beautiful although they were only fifteen. They had come to the island for a holiday and the girls pitied them because they still seemed bound by school regulations, crunching the white-hot sand in leather shoes that were the colour of dried blood. The shoes were only taken off when they went into the water and tried to drown one of their companions. The girls joined in splashing the victim who was blonde and tanned and identical in appearance to the others, until they realized that she was terrified and in genuine danger of drowning. 'Stop!' Sally commanded nervously. 'She's afraid!'

'She's a creep,' one of the pretty girls said.

'Why?' Rose pulled the sodden beauty from the floor of the ocean.

'*She* hasn't got oxblood loafers.'

A few days later the Americans came running along the beach, their heavy golden hair bouncing, their feet like aubergines in the shiny purple shoes. 'Hey!' they called out to Rose and Sally who were bathing grittily in the sand. 'There's sailors.'

An American ship had docked in Palma. The girls watched silently as the sailors were strewn along the quay, wonderful in uniforms that were crisp as money. They whistled at the girls and the girls ran after them, their knees shivering on the sweet seductive note. 'Come on, honey,' one boy called to them. 'Where d'you wanna go? You wanna go to a bullfight?' 'Sure!' the American girls agreed, and their leather shoes squeaked and their rumps muscled prettily under little shorts as they ran to catch up.

Sally and Rose had been hoping for something more attractive than a bullfight. Given the opportunity they might have pressed for lunch in one of the glass-fronted restaurants in Palma, where lobsters and pineapples were displayed in the window; but the Americans moved in a tide, scrambling for a bus, juggling with coins and they had to run or get left behind.

Following the example of the giant schoolgirls they pressed themselves down beside the loose forms of two of the young men. 'I'm Will,' the boy beside Sally said, showing wonderful teeth and something small and grey and lumpy like a tiny sheep, which was endlessly ground between them. 'I'm Bob,' Rose's sailor said and laughed to show that names were not to be taken seriously.

The bullring smelled like a cardboard box that had got damp and been left to dry in the sun. It was constructed as a circus with benches arranged in circles on different levels and all of those spaces were crammed with human beings who were waiting for a death. They were pungent with heat and the tension of expectation. This dire harmony wrought a huge hot communal breath which had a little echo in the men who had followed the girls through the lanes of Palma, but here the fear was not exciting and pleasant. Sally and Rose did not believe in death. They sat clammy with dismay, waiting for the animals to be saved.

No matter that it was an honourable sport, that the dead bulls' meat fed the island's orphans; they were unimpressed by the series of little fancy men who pranced around the bewildered animals which lurched and pawed at bubbles of their own blood that bulged brilliantly and then shrank back shabbily into the sand.

How many orphans could so small an island support Rose wondered, as one animal died and then two? She saw the orphans as the left luggage of tourists who had stayed too long in the lanes. She sympathized with this; she too had wanted, in an awful way, to go back alone, without Sally. Her only dismay was for the huge animals crumbling down one by one with hot dribbles and their sides all lacquered red by a pile of little sticks jammed in like knitting needles stuck in a ball of wool.

'He's dead!' Sally accused Will. A third animal folded up its slender legs and rolled in the sticky sawdust.

'Sure is honey,' Will said eagerly and squeezed her fingers. He seemed radiantly happy. 'Say, can I come on back to your hotel?'

Sally gave Rose a careful look. Rose's sailor, Bob, was watching Will for a clue.

Rose thought it wouldn't matter much what happened to Sally since Sally's period was late following some home-based encounter. She calculated some basis on which to make it worthwhile for herself. 'We're late for our dinner,' she said. 'We'd have to have a hamburger.'

'Sure thing,' Bob said amiably.

The girls ate with the speed and concentration of thieving dogs. Their pocket money did not run to delicacies. The sailors treated them to banana splits and the girls thought they should have ordered prawn cocktails and steaks since these men were so rich and so foolish with their money.

On their way back to the hotel after supper they were wreathed in virtue. It was thick around them, like scent over the honeysuckle. Both of them felt like sacrificial virgins although they were not, actually, virgins. In the terms of the understanding, they were going to lie down beside Will and Bob and let them do, within reason, what they wanted. They walked together, no longer feeling a need to be sociable. The sailors were playful in their wake.

When they got to the hotel they let the men into their room and sat with cold invitation on either bed. The sailors took cigarettes from their pockets and asked if there was anything to drink. Rose grudgingly brought a bottle of Bacardi from the wardrobe. 'I gotta girl like you at home,'

Bob said. He rubbed her hand and drew up a linty patch on her burnt skin.

He kissed her then and she could feel his dry lips stretched in a smile even as they sought her mouth. He was the most amiable man she had ever met. She had no notion how to treat or be treated by a man as an equal. Sexual excitement grew out of fear or power. She could only regard him with contempt. 'You like to see my girl?' he said. He brought out his wallet and withdrew some coloured snap-shots of a girl with a rounded face and baby curls.

Will had pictures too. Chapters of American life were spread out on the woven bedspreads and soon the girls were lulled into yawns by the multitude of brothers and sisters, moms and dads, *dawgs* and faithful girlfriends. The sailors spoke of the lives they would have, the houses and children. They had joined the navy to see the world but it seemed that their ship was in a bottle. Soon they would settle down, have families, mow the grass at weekends. The lives ahead of them were as familiar and wholesome as family serials on the television.

Catching Sally's eye, which was hard under the watering of boredom, Rose suddenly suffered an enlightenment. It was herself that she saw in the balding Polaroids – at the barbecue, at the bake sale – squinting into the faded glare of the sky. She was looking at her future.

She gathered in her mind from the assorted periods of films she had seen, a white convertible with a rug and a radio on the back seat, a beach house with a verandah, an orchestra playing round the pool in the moonlight. All Americans had television in the bedroom.

'Bob, put your arms around me,' she said. She swept the photographs into a neat pile and put them prissily face down. Bob's arms fell on her languidly. She drew them back and arranged them with efficiency, one on a breast and one on a hard, brown leg. He gave her a swift look of query but she closed her eyes to avoid it and offered him her open mouth.

'You're as ripe as a little berry. You sure are,' Bob sighed, and for once his smile faded and languor forsook him. He began kissing her in a heavy rhythmic way and his hands pursued the same rhythm on her spine, on her breasts, on her thighs. Rose had a moment of pure panic. She could not think. Her good shrewd plotting mind had deserted her. Clothes, body, common sense seemed to be slipping away and she was fading into his grasp, the touch of his tongue and fingertips, velvety, masterly, liquidy.

She opened her eyes to gaze at him and saw his goodness in the chestnut sweep of his eyebrows and his hair. 'I love you,' was the first thought to return to her head. She reached out to touch his hair.

Bob felt her stillness. He opened his eyes. He found himself staring into blue eyes that were huge with something that he saw as fear. He pushed her away harshly. 'Now don't you go around doing that sort of thing with all the guys,' he said. 'You're a nice girl.'

Rose did not know what to do. Bob shook his head and stood up. He fetched his cigarettes from the dressing table. He tapped the pack on his palm to release one, but he hit it with such violence that all the cigarettes were bent. He lit one anyway and went to the window, opening the shutters and leaning out to sigh long and deeply. Rose, watching the indifferently entwined bodies on the other bed, felt very close to tears.

'Jesus Christmas!' Bob let out a whoop. 'Would you look at that pool!'

In a second, Will had leaped from the disarrayed Sally and joined his friend, his buddy, at the window.

'Holy shit!' Will said with reverence.

'Mind your mouth.' Bob cuffed him good-humouredly. 'Last man in is a holy shit.'

The Villa Marta was constructed on a single storey so the young men were able to let themselves out the window with a soft thump on the cactussy lawn. They breathed muffled swearwords as the cacti grazed their ankles and then ran to the pool, tearing off their beautiful uniforms as they went.

The girls stood at the window watching them playing like small boys in the water. They splashed each other and pulled at one another's shorts. Will jumped from the water, waving his friend's underpants. 'Hey, come back here,' Bob yelled. 'I got a bare ass.'

'Don't worry,' his friend hollered back. 'It's a small thing.'

Bob scrambled from the pool and they tussled on the edge of the prickly lawn. With a cold pang Rose noted that his body was beautiful, every part of it, golden and beautiful. She beat on the shutters savagely with her knuckles. 'You out there! You better go now,' she said.

'Sure thing!' the sailors laughed with soft amusement as they pulled on their clothes.

They came to the window to kiss the girls goodnight and then leaped at the flower-covered wall to scramble on to the street.

'Bob,' Rose howled out softly. Bob dropped back lightly to the ground. He came back to where she was huddled at the window. 'What's up honey?'

'Don't you have a pool at home?' she said. She was troubled by the way he had reacted to the pool at the Villa Marta. All Americans had swimming pools.

'What kind of a question is that?' Bob said. 'We don't have no pool. We live in the hills. We gotta few cows and hens and sheep. We gotta few acres but we ain't got no pool.'

He ran off again but before making his effortless jump at the wall he paused and cried out, 'Wait for me!' and she thought of his chestnut hair and the wild sweetness of his touch and said yes, she would wait, but then she saw the bleak snowfall of blossoms from the wall and she realized that he had been calling out to his buddy. He was gone.

She ran from the room and out into the dark, polish-smelling hall of the Villa. As she stood trying to compose herself, the front door opened and two of the Swedish boys entered. They were immaculately attired in evening dress and carried half-filled bottles of whiskey but both seemed as sober as Mormons.

'Good evening,' one said.

'You like to fuck sailors?' the other enquired respectfully. He had watched the visitors emerging from the wall.

Rose hurled herself at him, slapping his face with both hands in a fury. He delivered his bottle for safe-keeping to his friend and calmly trapped her hands with his. 'You act like the little wolf' – he spoke with detachment – 'but you are really the grandmother in disguise.'

He let her go and she fled through the carved entrance, tearing along the street, down one alley, through the next. She emerged into a long, tree-lined street and there were the sailors. She stood and watched them until the young men had disappeared and only the hipswing of their little buttocks was picked out by the moon like ghostly butterflies in their tight white pants.

'Creeps,' she cried after them.

Glenn Patterson

from *Burning Your Own*

L ES WATCHED him approach, his staring eyes round and guilty. But when he got to the slope up from the playing fields, Les turned his back and went to the bonfire, laying a line of boards and planks from the wide base to the apex where the branches of the outer shell converged. Nearby, Andy was directing Pickles and another boy who were binding with lengths of string the legs of a man-sized doll, made up of old clothes, stuffed with newspaper and dried grass: the Pope for the top of the bonfire.

The young men of the estate, with whom Mucker already played pitch-and-toss sometimes and who this time next year, it was assumed, he would have joined for good and all, were starting to gather now. They drank openly from bottles of cider and cans of beer, hooting at the contingent of girls who passed before them, linked in couples, and trying to catch their skirts with the toes of their shoes. The girls broke formation, arching their backs out of the way, then regrouped further on and passed in front of the boys again, arm in arm.

There were other clumps of people drinking, but they were under-age and sat back from the bonfire in the shade of the first trees, swallowing in quick gulps and setting the bottles on the ground behind them between mouthfuls. Half a dozen teenagers with flutes ran through their repertoire of party tunes, rehearsing for both the night's celebrations and the following day's parades. They stamped their feet in time to their playing and around them jigged a circle of very young children (some no more than toddlers) who wouldn't be allowed to stay up for the fire itself but were making the most of their Eleventh Night anyway.

Mucker was walking between the various groups, swigging from whatever was offered to him. Sonia Kerr hung on to him and took her turn at the bottles and cans when he had finished with them. Drunk, she looked a more awkward mishmash of girl and woman than normal. Her nose, which seemed to be permanently chapped from a head cold, showed up still redder with the alcohol and a thin snailtrail of liquid glistened on her top lip. But, at the same time, there was a coarse, almost muscular, maturity about her and, when she stretched to kiss Mucker's cheek, Mal glimpsed a deep, bluepurple blotch on her neck. He willed the sight away, thinking he had unwittingly discovered a dark secret, and his stomach churned with a curious mixture of repulsion and attraction. He tensed the muscles at the top of his thighs, feeling the weight on his privates of a rat hanging taut on a string.

He was suddenly distressed, lost among so many people. He almost wished Peter had been there, or that Les would make up his mind whether he was sorry or annoyed.

'Yo!'

Andy was beckoning him and he trotted over to the bonfire.

'I want you to shin up there and stick this at the top. Anyone heavier might go through.'

He held the dummy out to Mal. It wasn't a Pope now, but instead, as a piece of cardboard around its neck bore witness, *Gerry Fitt. Agent of Rome.* Mal looked dubiously at the flimsy walkway.

'Go on,' Andy urged him. 'It'll take you no problem.'

'He's scared,' Les said.

'No, I'm not,' Mal told them, though he was.

'Well then.' Andy offered the Gerry Fitt doll. 'Take it.'

Mal started to climb, on all fours, with the dummy slung across his back like a wounded comrade. At the junction of the first and second planks, he felt his wooden footboard shift slightly. The branches below him rustled and sighed. He froze, glancing behind him through his rigid arms. Andy and Les waved him on. He breathed deep, steeling himself, then slowly and carefully continued to the top of the bonfire.

He could be seen now by everyone around the entrance to the woods. Bobby Parker, the bin-lorry driver, was arriving at that moment, lugging his massive Lambeg drum. He set it down and cheered as Mal kneaded the dummy's middle to make it sit straight. The cheer was taken up by the young men drinkers, who raised their bottles and cans. Those who had built the bonfire whoop-whoop-whooped and the tiniest boys and girls jumped up and down, clapping. Mal bowed to them, milking the applause. He felt important and central. Then, all too quickly, the cheering stuttered and died. Mal turned to descend the blind side of the bonfire. But there were no planks, only a stretch of branches, like the blank face of a tall hedge. Les was leaning on one of the boards, while Andy stood looking on, snickering.

'Aw, come on,' Mal pleaded. 'Put them back. How'm I meant to get down?'

'Try jumping,' Les said and laughed his machine-gun laugh.

Mal tried to lower himself, but Andy put a foot on a branch and began to roll it on his instep so that it moved under him. Les joined in, using both feet and his hands until all the branches shifted and swayed. Mal scrabbled to the top again and clung to the effigy. Fear made him dizzy; fear of falling, of crashing down; down through the branches, past the chairs, the mattresses, planks and pallets, the sideboards and thick short logs, the hoopla-ed tyres; and still falling . . .

He heard a muffled thump and a groan and the branches stopped moving. He opened his eyes cautiously. Les was stretched out on the ground, clutching his groin, and Mucker was squaring up to Andy.

'What the fuck are youse at?' he asked.

'It's only a frigging joke,' Andy replied.

'Some joke. Did youse want to pull the whole bonfire down too?'

The flute players interrupted their tune and people drifted round to see what was happening.

'Now wait a minute here,' Andy said. 'Glad you're interested in the welfare of the bonfire again all of a sudden. You weren't so bothered this morning at the chapel. If that priest had called the cops on us they'd have taken our tyres for sure. And then what would we have been left with? You don't know because you never thought about it – and don't forget who it was who organized the building of all this when you were too sulky to be arsed doing anything today.'

'Today?' Mucker shouted. 'What about this past month? How d'you think you were able to do what you did this afternoon? Because I fucking arranged everything weeks ago, that's how.'

Mal watched, fascinated, forgetting his precarious position. It looked like this was it at last: Mucker and Andy were going to have it out. And then Big Bobby stepped between them.

'Okay, okay,' he said, pacifying them. 'Cut it out the both of youse. For Christ's sake, it's the Eleventh Night, let's have no fighting among ourselves. The bonfire's as much due to the one as it is to the other. How's that? Now stop your arguing and have a drink.'

He passed a can of beer to Andy who reluctantly took a pull before holding it out in front of him. Mucker didn't move, so Bobby took the can and offered it more insistently. Mucker ignored him too.

'Put the fucking planks back and let the wee lad down,' he said to Andy.

Andy shrugged.

'I never touched them.'

Les picked himself up sheepishly, one hand still on his groin and, without a word, began to replace the planks on the side of the bonfire. Bobby jerked the beercan towards Mucker a third time. He paused for a long moment, then accepted it and, wiping the mouthpiece with his sleeve, drank from it. The spectators dispersed and Mal descended to the ground, embarrassed now at having been the cause of so much trouble; especially since, once he was down, nobody paid any further attention to him.

He flitted alone through the crowd for the rest of the evening. Darkness rolled off the mountains, seeped through the trees and swallowed the estate. The night air grew chillier and small fires were lit on the slope up from the playing fields. Lights shone in the open doorways of the houses facing the woods as street parties began, and the numbers around the bonfire increased steadily with more and more grown ups coming out to mingle with the young people. There was pressure to light the bonfire early for the benefit of the smaller children, but the boys held out, saying midnight it had always been, and midnight it would be this year.

Mal was becoming drowsy; he had eaten next to nothing all day and felt weak. Only the cold kept him from dropping off, and he was looking for somewhere warm to lie and wait when his father lurched into view with his hand on Bobby Parker's sleeve. It was the first Mal had seen of him since dinner time the night before, and he drew back into the shadows, frightened, for his father was obviously drunk. Mal had known him to be tipsy, but never like this, and never in public. He waved his free hand in the air as he talked loudly.

'These Civil Rights yahoos make me laugh,' he was saying. 'Too lazy to get off their behinds and do things for themselves. Instead they expect to be lifted and laid, have everything done for them. Wait'll I tell you . . . Bobby, is it? Wait'll I tell you, Bobby. I had nothing, and there was nobody took to the streets, demonstrating for me. Ha! If that's what I'd been looking for, I'd still be looking to this day.'

He was going to continue, but Bobby extricated himself, moving out of his reach.

'Oh, you're right there,' he said. 'You're right there, okay. But, here, I must get on: time I was ready with the Lambeg.'

Mr Martin stood alone, pitching forward every now and then and shooting a leg out to steady himself. He was by far and away the neatest person in sight and wore his best navy suit – saved from being unfashionable by a pinkly patterned tie. But his black, slip-on shoes had been scuffed at the toes and, worse, one side of his face was raw and grazed. Mal came out of the shadows to speak.

'Ach, if it isn't me own wee True Blue himself,' his father said thickly. He seemed to want either to hug his son or give him an affectionate pat, but his hands were fumbling and he succeeded only in jiggling him awkwardly.

'What have you done to your face?' Mal asked.

His father pushed him away.

'Oh aye, oh aye,' he said. 'That's your mother's game, is it? I seen her by the pavilion, watching me like a hawk. Spends the afternoon at that brother of hers complaining about me, and now she's sent you snooping. Is that it, hm?'

'I was just worried something had happened to you,' Mal said, hoping he would quieten down.

'Worried?' Mr Martin lowered his face until he was staring directly into Mal's eyes. 'Listen, son, the day I need you to worry for me is the day I'll really start to worry for myself.'

He hauled himself up by his suit trousers and turned away from Mal.

'Did youse hear that?' he appealed to everyone within earshot. 'Worried.'

He tried to buttonhole passers-by and eventually put himself in the path of Sonia and Mucker so that they were obliged to stop and listen to him. Mal sprinted across the playing fields to the pavilion, where he found his mother talking to Mrs Clark. Immediately she saw him, his mother dropped to her knees and hugged him tightly. Looking over her shoulder, Mal noticed Mrs Clark was as uncomfortable as he was.

'Mum,' he said in a low voice.

'Are you not cold?' she interrupted, plucking at his teeshirt.

'I'm all right,' he said. 'Mum, listen.'

'You can't tell them anything,' his mother said.

Mrs Clark smiled awkwardly. 'I know, I know. Our Leslie's the same.'

'Mummy, please,' Mal insisted. 'It's my daddy. He's . . .'

He stopped; he felt exhausted and thought he would fall down at any moment. His mother stared at him, then glanced at Mrs Clark.

'Will you excuse me, Sadie?' she said, strainedly polite, and drew the collar of her coat close to her throat.

Mal led her to the bonfire, where Mr Martin was still holding forth to Sonia and Mucker.

'See, you youngsters, you don't know the meaning of the word. There's only one way to be a success in this world, and that's to *work* for it yourself.'

He swung round abruptly, aware that Mucker was looking at someone behind him. Mrs Martin touched his grazed cheek with the back of her hand. His head recoiled.

'Now don't start,' he threatened her. 'I slipped – fell off a kerb. Anyone could have done it; the state of the footpaths in this place is a disgrace, they're crumbling to bits.'

But it seemed as though Mrs Martin was indeed about to start. Her concern rejected, she was shaping up for a tirade. Somewhat unstably, her husband stood his ground.

'What's that over there?' someone shouted from the edge of the woods.

Beyond the houses at the top of the estate the sky was tinged a light orange.

'And there,' Mucker said.

On the horizon, to the left, the black smoke of burning tyres, denser than darkness, rose in a vertical pall.

Bonfires. It was not quite half eleven, but it did not matter any more. The boys had managed to wait longer than at least some of the neighbouring areas; they had not been the first to give, and now they listened to the calls to for God's sake get on with it and light theirs.

As sticks with petrol-soaked rags wrapped around them were driven in at points around the base of the bonfire, people converged on it from all sides: the Bells, the McMinns, the McMahons and the Crosiers, Tommy Duncan and his family, the Smyllie twins with their wives, the Garritys, the Presses, the Kerrs and the Boyles, the Sinclairs, the Hugheses, the Jamisons and Stinsons, Mrs Clark and old Mrs Parker, the Hemmings, the Taggarts, the Greys, the Whites, all of the Campbells except for the father, the Tookeys, the Clearys, the Kellys and Craigs, McClures, Milligans, Hawthorns and O'Days, the Wheatcrofts, the McDevitts, the Viles, wee Ernie Buchanan with his Bible-tract sandwich boards. More faces in the end than Mal could identify. And when everything was in place, Andy lit a final torch and touched off all the others. The bonfire had begun.

Mal stood between his parents, watching with them, painfully intent. A reverent hush descended as the flames took hold. The dry leaves and twigs of the outer branches crackled and burnt yellow, but they were only the accompaniment to the real fire. The heart of the bonfire began to glow a deep, powerful orange. For what felt like an age, flames hued with fantastical reds, purples, blues and greens from blistering varnish and paintwork burned in circles, rolling round and round as if fuelling themselves, spreading neither upwards nor outwards, while the glow grew ever more bright, ever more intense. Then, on an instant, the flames burst with a whoosh, erupting through the top of the bonfire, engulfing the Gerry Fitt doll.

The silence broke and cheers and whistles pierced the crackling air; the flutes began to trill again, joined now by the monotonous, penetrating rumble of Big Bobby's Lambeg drum: *rat-tat-a-rat-ta-ta-tat, rat-tat-a-rat-ta-ta-tat*. People danced, linking arms and laughing, and Mal felt his parents move closer together behind him. The flames stretched higher and thick smoke belched and billowed up into the night sky above the trees.

Suddenly there was an almighty crash; whiplash flames exploded sideways from the fire and showers of sparks and splinters of burning timber poured down on the scattering, screaming onlookers. The weight of the sides, the devouring intensity of the inner ball of flame, had proved too much for the improvised centrepole and the bonfire had caved in. It blazed on, but it was no longer the bonfire which had been so many weeks in the planning. When the debris settled and the smoke cleared, Mal saw Andy and Les running around the increased circumference of the fire, using long bundles of sticks in a desperate attempt to sweep it back together again. But no sooner did they succeed in shoring up one spot, than another was undermined and subsided; the brushes themselves ignited and were dropped, increasing still further the extent of the fire.

'I knew it,' Mucker grumbled. 'I fucking knew it.'

He was only yards from Mal and his parents.

'Hey, Philip,' Mr Martin shouted, eyes twinkling, reflecting the fire. 'I thought you told me they'd see this one in Lisburn. Have you given them all binoculars?'

Mal could never quite get straight in his mind what exactly happened next. From the flickering, broken images that tumbled before and behind his eyes then, he was able later to piece together only an impression of the rapid movement of silhouettes, jagged flashes of arms and legs and a random scuffling. When it was over, a matter of seconds, no more, his father was on the ground, propelling himself backwards with his elbows, and his mother was stooped over him, crying, trying to protect him.

Mucker seemed to pulsate with rage and his mouth, a firelit gash, worked frantically:

'Don't talk to me about failure, mister, for you're the biggest failure ever drew breath as sure as I'm standing here.'

And then a wall of bodies blotted Mucker from view, and Mal helped his mother lift his father to his feet.

As the family limped across the playing fields, Mal noticed a squat figure emerge from the darkness of the now deserted pavilion. It plodded along at a distance, shadowing them, and then veered away at the bottom of the hill towards the dump.

'Who do you think that is?' Mrs Martin asked, scared in case anyone should try to renew the attack on her husband.

'Nobody I know,' Mal told her, without hesitation.

They started up the hill, followed by the trill of the flute and the dull beat of the Lambeg drum: *rat-tat-a-rat-ta-ta-tat*.

Eugene McCabe

Cancer

TODAY THERE was an old Anglia and five bicycles outside the cottage. Boyle parked near the bridge. As he locked the car Dinny came through a gap in the ditch: 'Busy?'

'From the back of Carn Rock and beyont: it's like a wake inside.'

For a living corpse Boyle thought.

'How is he?'

'Never better.'

'No pain?'

'Not a twitch ... ates rings round me and snores the night long.' Boyle imagined Joady on the low stool by the hearth in the hot, crowded kitchen, his face like turf ash. Everyone knew he was dying. Women from townlands about had offered to cook and wash. Both brothers had refused. 'Odd wee men,' the women said. 'Course they'd have no sheets, and the blankets must be black.' 'And why not,' another said, 'no woman body ever stood in aither room this forty years.' At which another giggled and said 'or lay'. And they all laughed because Dinny and Joady were under-sized. And then they were ashamed of laughing and said 'poor Joady cratur' and 'poor Dinny he'll be left: that's worse'. And people kept bringing things: bacon and chicken, whiskey and stout, seed cake, fresh-laid eggs, whole meal bread; Christmas in February.

In all his years Joady had never slept away from the cottage so that when people called now he talked about the hospital, the operation, the men who died in the ward. In particular he talked about the shattered bodies brought to the

171

hospital morgue from the explosion near Trillick. When he went on about this Protestant neighbours kept silent. Joady noticed and said: 'A bad doin', Albert, surely, there could be no luck after thon.' To Catholic neighbours he said: 'Done it their selves to throw blame on us' and spat in the fire.

It was growing dark at the bridge, crows winging over from Annahullion to roost in the fibrous trees about the disused Spade Mill.

'A week to the day we went up to Enniskillen,' Dinny said.

'That long.'

'A week to the day, you might say to the hour. Do you mind the helicopter?' He pointed up. 'It near sat on that tree.'

Boyle remembered very clearly. It had seemed to come from a quarry of whins dropping as it crossed Gawley's flat. Like today he had driven across this Border bridge and stopped at McMahon's iron-roofed cottage. Without looking up, he could sense the machine chopping its way up from the Spade Mill. He left the car engine running. Dinny came out clutching a bottle of something. The helicopter hung directly over a dead alder in a scrub of egg bushes between the cottage and the river. Dinny turned and flourished the bottle upwards shouting above the noise: 'I hope to Jasus yis are blown to shit.' He grinned and waved the bottle again. Boyle looked up. Behind the curved, bullet-proof shield two pale urban faces stared down, impassive.

'Come on, Dinny, get in.'

He waved again: a bottle of Lucozade.

Boyle put the car in gear and drove North. They could hear the machine overhead. Dinny kept twisting about in the front seat trying to see up.

'The whores,' he screeched, 'they're trackin' us.'

On a long stretch of road the helicopter swooped ahead and dropped to within a yard of the road. It turned slowly and moved towards them, a gigantic insect with revolving swords. Five yards from the car it stopped. The two faces were now very clear: guns, uniform, apparatus, one man had ear-phones. He seemed to be reading in a notebook. He looked at the registration number of Boyle's car and said something. The helicopter tilted sharply and rose clapping its way towards Armagh across the sour divide of fields and crooked ditches. Boyle remained parked in the middle of the road, until he could hear nothing. His heart was pumping strongly: 'What the hell was all that?'

'They could see we had Catholic faces,' Dinny said and winked. There was a twist in his left eye. 'The mouth' McMahon neighbours called him, pike lips set in a bulbous face, a cap glued to his skull. Boyle opened a window. The fumes of porter were just stronger than the hum of turf smoke and a strong personal pong.

'It's on account of Trillick,' Boyle said, 'they'll be very active for a day or two.'

'You'll get the news now.'

Boyle switched on the car radio and a voice was saying: 'Five men in a Land-Rover on a track leading to a television transmitter station on Brougher Mountain near Trillick between Enniskillen and Omagh. Two BBC officials and three workers lost their lives. An Army spokesman said that the booby trap blew a six-foot-deep crater in the mountainside and lifted the Land-Rover twenty yards into a bog. The bodies of the five men were scattered over an area of 400 square yards. The area has been sealed off.'

Boyle switched off the radio and said: 'Dear God.'

They passed a barn-like church set in four acres of graveyard. Dinny tipped his cap to the dead; McCaffreys, Boyles, Grues, Gunns, McMahons, Courtneys, Mulligans; names and bones from a hundred townlands.

'I cut a bit out of the *Anglo-Celt* once,' Dinny said, 'about our crowd, the McMahons.'

'Yes?'

'Kings about Monaghan for near a thousand years, butch-ered, and driv' north to these bitter hills, that's what it said, and the scholar that wrote it up maintained you'll get better bred men in the cabins of Fermanagh than you'll find in many's a big house.'

Boyle thumbed up at the graveyard: 'One thing we're sure of, Dinny, we'll add our bit.'

'Blood tells,' Dinny said, 'it tells in the end.'

A few miles on they passed a waterworks. There was a soldier pacing the floodlit jetty.

'Wouldn't care for his job, he'll go up with it some night.'

'Unless there's changes,' Boyle said.

'Changes! What changes. Look in your neighbour's face; damn little change you'll see there. I wrought four days with Gilbert Wilson before Christmas, baggin' turf beyont Doon, and when the job was done we dropped into Corranny pub, and talked land, and benty turf, and the forestry takin' over and the way people are leavin' for factories, the pension scheme for hill farmers and a dose of things: no side in any of it, not one word of politics or religion, and then all of a shot he leans over to me and says: "Fact is, Dinny, the time I like you best, I could cut your throat." A quare slap in the mouth, but I didn't rise to it; I just said: "I'd as lief not hear the like, Gilbert." "You," says he, "and all your kind, it must be said." "It's a mistake, Gilbert, to say the like, or think it." "Truth," he said, "and you mind it, Dinny."'

He looked at Boyle: 'What do you think of that for a spake?'

They came to the main road and Moorlough: 'Are them geese or swans,' Dinny was pointing. He wound down his window and stared out. On the Loughside field there seemed to be fifty or sixty swans, very white against the black water. Boyle slowed for the trunk road, put on his headlights.

'Hard to say.'

'Swans,' Dinny said.

'Your sure?'

'Certain sure.'

'So far from water?'

'I seen it before on this very lake in the twenties, bad sign.'

'Of what?'

'Trouble.'

The lake was half a mile long and at the far end of it there was a military checkpoint. An officer came over with a boy soldier and said 'Out, please.' Two other soldiers began searching the car.

'Name?'

'Boyle, James.'

'Occupation?'

'Teacher.'

'Address?'

'Tiernahinch, Kilrooskey, Fermanagh.'

'And this gentleman?'

Boyle looked away. Dinny said nothing. The officer said again: 'Name?'

'Denis McMahon, Gawley's Bridge, Fermanagh.'

'Occupation?'

'I'm on the national health.'

The boy beside the officer was writing in a notebook. A cold wind blowing from the lake chopped at the water, churning up angry flecks. The officer had no expression in his face. His voice seemed bored and flat.

'Going where?'

'Enniskillen,' Boyle said.

'Purpose?'

'To visit this man's brother, he's had an operation.'

'He's lying under a surgeont,' Dinny said.

The officer nodded.

'And your brother's name?'

'Joady, Joseph, I'm next-of-kin.'

The boy with the notebook went over to a radio jeep. The officer walked away a few paces. They watched. Boyle thought he should say aloud what they were all thinking, then decided not to; then heard himself say: 'Awful business at Trillick.'

The officer turned, looked at him steadily for a moment and nodded. There was another silence until Dinny said: 'Trillick is claner nor a man kicked to death by savages fornent his childer.'

The officer did not look round. The boy soldier came back from the jeep and said everything was correct, Sir. The officer nodded again, walked away and stood looking at the lake.

Dinny dryspat towards the military back as they drove off. '"And this gentleman!" Smart bugger, see the way he looked at me like I was sprung from a cage.'

'His job, Dinny!'

'To make you feel like an animal! "Occupation" is right!'

Near Lisnaskea Dinny said: 'Cancer, that's what we're all afeerd of, one touch of it and you're a dead man. My ould fella died from a rare breed of it. If he went out in the light, the skin would rot from his face and hands, so he put in the latter end of his life in a dark room, or walkin' about the roads at night. In the end it killed him. He hadn't seen the sun for years.'

He lit a cigarette butt.

'A doctor tould me once it could be in the blood fifty years, and then all of a shot it boils up and you're a gonner.'

For miles after this they said nothing, then Dinny said: 'Lisbellaw for wappin' straw,/Maguiresbridge for brandy./Lisnaskea for drinkin' tay,/But Clones town is dandy/... that's a quare ould one?'

He winked with his good eye.

'You want a jigger, Dinny?'

'I'll not say no.'

Smoke, coughing, the reek of a diesel stove and porter met them with silence and watching. Dinny whispered: 'UDR, wrong shop.'

Twenty or more, a clutch of uniformed farmers, faces hardened by wind, rutted from bog, rock and rain, all staring, invincible, suspicious.

'Wrong shop,' Dinny whispered again.

'I know,' Boyle said, 'we can't leave now.'

Near a partition there was a space beside a big man. As Boyle moved towards it a woman bar-tender said: 'Yes?'

'Two halfs, please.'

'What kind?'

'Irish.'

'What kind of Irish?'

'Any kind.'

Big enough to pull a bullock from a shuck on his own Boyle thought as the big man spat at the doosy floor and turned away. Dinny nudged Boyle and winked up at a notice pinned to a pillar. Boyle read:

Lisnaskea and District Development Association
Extermination of Vermin
1/- for each magpie killed.
2/- for each grey crow killed.
10/- for each grey squirrel killed.
£1 for each fox killed.

Underneath someone had printed with a biro:

For every Fenian Fucker: one old penny.

As the woman measured the whiskies a glass smashed in the snug at the counter end. A voice jumped the frosted glass: 'Wilson was a fly boy, and this Heath man's a bum boy, all them Tories is tricky whores, dale with Micks and Papes and leave us here to rot. Well, by Christ, they'll come no Pope to the townland of Invercloon, I'll not be blown up or burned out, I'll fight to the last ditch.'

All listening in the outer bar, faces, secret and serious, uncomfortable now as other voices joined; 'Your right, George.'

'Sit down, man, you'll toss the table.'

'Let him say out what's in his hand.'

'They'll not blow me across no bog; if it's blood they want

then, by Jasus, they'll get it, all they want, gallons of it, wagons, shiploads.'

'Now you're talking, George.'

The big man looked at the woman. She went to the hatch, pushed it and said something into the snug. The loudness stopped. A red-axe face stared out, no focus in the eyes. Someone snapped the hatch shut. Silence. The big man spat again and Dinny said: 'I'd as lief drink with pigs.'

He held his glass of whiskey across the counter, poured it into the bar sink and walked out. Boyle finished his whiskey and followed.

In the car again the words came jerking from Dinny's mouth: 'Choke and gut their own childer. Feed them to rats.'

He held up a black-rimmed nail to the windscreen.

'Before they'd give us *that*!'

'It's very sad,' Boyle said, 'I see no answer.'

'I know the answer, cut the bastards down, every last one of them and it'll come to that, them or us. They got it with guns, kep' it with guns, and guns'll put them from it.'

'Blood's not the way,' Boyle said.

'There's no other.'

At Enniskillen they went by the low end of the town, passed armoured cars, and the shattered Crown buildings. Outside the hospital there were four rows of cars, two police cars and a military lorry. Joady's ward was on the ground floor. He was in a corner near a window facing an old man with bad colour and a caved-in mouth. In over thirty years Boyle had never seen Joady without his cap. Sitting up now in bed like an old woman, with a white domed head and drained face, he looked like Dinny's ghost shaved and shrunk in regulation pyjamas. He shook hands with Boyle and pointed at Dinny's bottle: 'What's in that?'

'Lucozade,' Dinny said.

'Poison.'

'It's recommended for a sick body.'

'Rots the insides; you can drop it out the windy.'

'I'll keep it,' Dinny said, 'I can use it.'

Boyle could see that Dinny was offended, and remembered his aunt's anger one Christmas long ago. She had knit a pair of wool socks for Joady and asked him about them.

'Bad wool, Miss,' he said, 'out through the heel in a week, I dropped them in the fire.'

She was near tears as she told his mother: 'Ungrateful, lazy, spiteful little men, small wonder Protestants despise them and us, and the smell in that house ... you'd think with nothing else to do but draw the dole and sit by the fire the least they could do is wash themselves: as for religion, no Mass, no altar, nothing ever, they'll burn, they really will, and someone should tell them. God knows you don't want thanks, but to have it flung back in your teeth like that it's ...'

'It's very trying, Annie,' his mother said.

And Boyle wanted to say to his aunt: 'No light, no water, no work, no money, nothing all their days, but the dole, fire poking, neighbour baiting, and the odd skite on porter, retched off that night in a ditch.'

'Communists,' his aunt mocked Joady, 'I know what real Communists would do with those boyos, what Hitler did with the Jews.'

'Annie, that's an awful thing to say.'

There was a silence and then his aunt said: 'God forgive me, it is, but ...' and then she wept.

'Because she never married, and the age she's at,' his mother said afterwards.

Joady was pointing across a square of winter lawn to the hospital entrance: 'Fornent them cars,' he said, 'the morgue.' His eyes swivelled round the ward, 'I heard nurses talk about it in the corridor, brought them here in plastic bags from Trillick, laid them out on slabs in a go of sawdust on account of the blood. That's what they're at now, Army doctors tryin' to put the bits together, so's their people can recognize them, and box them proper.'

The old man opposite groaned and shifted. Joady's voice dropped still lower: 'They say one man's head couldn't be got high or low, they're still tramping the mountain with searchlights.'

'Dear God,' Boyle said.

'A fox could nip off with a man's head handy enough.'

'If it came down from a height it could bury itself in that ould spongy heather and they'd never find it or less they tripped over it.'

'Bloodhound dogs could smell it out.'

'They wouldn't use bloodhound dogs on a job like that, wouldn't be proper.'

'Better nor lavin' it to rot in a bog, course they'd use dogs, they'd have to.'

'Stop!'

Across the ward the old man was trying to elbow himself up. The air was wheezing in and out of his lungs, he seemed to be choking: 'Stop! O God, God, please, I must go ... I must ...'

Boyle stood up and pressed the bell near Joady's bed. Visitors round other beds stopped talking. The wheezing got louder, more irregular, and a voice said: 'Someone do something.'

Another said: 'Get a doctor.'

Boyle said: 'I've rung.'

A male nurse came and pulled a curtain round the bed. When a doctor came the man was dead. He was pushed away on a trolley covered with a white sheet. Gradually people round other beds began to talk. A young girl looking sick was led out by a woman.

'That's the third carted off since I come down here.'

'Who was he?' Boyle asked.

'John Willie Foster, a bread server from beyont Five-mile town, started in to wet the bed like a child over a year back, they couldn't care for him at home, so they put him to "Silver Springs", the ould people's home, but he got worse there so they packed him off here.'

'Age,' Dinny said, 'the heart gave up.'

'The heart broke,' Joady said, 'no one come to see him, bar one neighbour man. He was towld he could get home for a day or two at Christmas, no one come, he wouldn't spake with no one, couldn't quit' cryin'; the man's heart was broke.'

'Them Probsbyterians is a hard bunch, cauld, no nature.'

There was a silence.

'Did he say what about you Joady? . . . the surgeont?'

'No.'

'You asked?'

' "A deep operation," he said, "very deep, an obstruction," so I said "Is there somethin' rotten, Sir, I want to know, I want to be ready?" "Ready for what," says he and smiles, but you can't tell what's at the back of a smile like that. "Just ready," I said.

' "You could live longer nor me," says he.

'He hasn't come next nor near me since I've come down here to the ground . . . did he tell yous anythin?'

'Dam' to the thing,' Dinny said.

And Boyle noticed that Joady's eyes were glassy.

There was a newspaper open on the bed. It showed the Duke of Kent beside an armoured car at a shattered customs post. On the top of the photograph the name of the post read 'Kilclean', Boyle picked up the newspaper, opened it and saw headlines: 'Significance of bank raids'; 'Arms for Bogsiders'; 'Failure to track murderer'; 'Arms role of IRA'.

He read, skipping half, half listening to the brothers.

'In so far as ordinary secret service work is concerned, could be relied on and trusted . . . under the control of certain Ministers. Reliable personnel . . . co-operation between Army intelligence and civilian intelligence . . . no question of collusion.'

'Lies,' Joady said to Dinny, 'you don't know who to believe.' His voice was odd and his hand was trembling on the bedspread. Boyle didn't want to look at his face and thought, probably has it and knows. Dinny was looking at the floor.

'Lies,' Joady said again. And this time his voice sounded better. Boyle put down the paper and said: 'I hear you got blood, Joady.'

'Who towld you that?'

'One of my past pupils, a nurse here.'

'Three pints,' Joady said.

Boyle winked and said: 'Black blood, she told me you got Paisley's blood.'

Joady began shaking, his mouth opened and he seemed to be dry-retching. The laughter when it came was pitched and hoarse. He put a hand on his stitches and stopped, his breathing shallow, his head going like a picaninny on a mission box.

'Paisley's blood, she said that?'

'She did.'

'That's tarror,' he said, but was careful not to laugh again. Boyle stood up and squeezed his arm: 'We'll have to go, Joady, next time can we bring you something you need?'

'Nothin',' Joady said, 'I need nothin'.'

Walking the glass-walled, rubber corridor Boyle said: 'I'll wait in the car, Dinny.'

Dinny stopped and looked at the bottle of Lucozade: 'We could see him together.'

'If you want.'

The surgeon detached a sheet of paper from a file, he faced them across a steel-framed table: 'In your brother's case,' he was saying to Dinny, 'it's late, much, much, too late.' He paused, no one said anything and then the surgeon said: 'I'm afraid so.'

'Dying?'

'It's terminal.'

'He's not in pain,' Boyle said.

'And may have none for quite a while, when the stitches come out he'll be much better at home.'

'He doesn't know,' Dinny said.

'No, I didn't tell him yet.'

'He wants to know.'

The surgeon nodded and made a note on a sheet of paper. Dinny asked: 'How long has he got, Sir?'

The surgeon looked at the sheet of paper as though the death rate were inscribed: 'Sometime this year ... yes, I'm afraid so.'

The Anglia and bicycles were gone now. It had grown dark about the bridge and along the river. Boyle was cold sitting on the wall. Dinny had been talking for half an hour: 'He was never sick a day, and five times I've been opened, lay a full year with a bad lung above at Killadeas; he doesn't know what it is to be sick.'

Raucous crow noise carried up from the trees around the Spade Mill, cawing, cawing, cawing, blindflapping in the dark. They looked down, listening, waiting, it ceased. 'He knows about dying,' Boyle said.

'That's what I'm comin' at, he's dyin' and sleeps twelve hours of the twenty-four, ates, smokes, walks, and for a man used never talk much, he talks the hind leg off a pot now, make your head light to hear him.'

He took out a glass phial: 'I take two of them sleeping caps every night since he come home, and never close an eye. I can't keep nothin' on my stomach, and my skin itches all over; I sweat night and day. I'll tell you what I think: livin's worse nor dyin', and that's a fact.'

'It's upsetting, Dinny.'

It was dark in the kitchen: Joady gave Boyle a stool, accepted a cigarette, and lit it from the paraffin lamp, his face sharp and withered: a frosted crab.

'Where's the other fella gone?'

'I'm not sure,' Boyle said, 'he went down the river somewhere.'

Joady sucked on the cigarette: 'McCaffreys, he's gone to McCaffreys, very neighbourly these times, he'll be there until twelve or after.'

He thrust at a blazing sod with a one-pronged pitch fork:

'Same every night since I come home, away from the house every chance he gets.'

'All the visitors you have, Joady, and he's worried.'

'Dam' the worry, whingin' and whinin', to every slob that passes the road about *me* snorin' the night long, didn't I hear him with my own ears . . .'

He spat, his eyes twisting: 'It's *him* that snores not *me*, him: it's *me* that's dyin', *me*, not him . . . Christ's sake . . . couldn't he take a back sate until I'm buried.'

He got up and looked out the small back window at the night, at nothing: 'What would you call it, when your own brother goes contrary, and the ground hungry for you . . . eh! Rotten, that's what I'd call it, rotten.'

PART FOUR

William Trevor

The Ballroom of Romance

ON SUNDAYS, or on Mondays if he couldn't make it and often he couldn't, Sunday being his busy day, Canon O'Connell arrived at the farm in order to hold a private service with Bridie's father, who couldn't get about any more, having had a leg amputated after gangrene had set in. They'd had a pony and cart then and Bridie's mother had been alive: it hadn't been difficult for the two of them to help her father on to the cart in order to make the journey to Mass. But two years later the pony had gone lame and eventually had to be destroyed; not long after that her mother had died. 'Don't worry about it at all,' Canon O'Connell had said, referring to the difficulty of transporting her father to Mass. 'I'll slip up by the week, Bridie.'

The milk lorry called daily for the single churn of milk, Mr Driscoll delivered groceries and meal in his van, and took away the eggs that Bridie had collected during the week. Since Canon O'Connell had made his offer, in 1953, Bridie's father hadn't left the farm.

As well as Mass on Sundays and her weekly visits to a wayside dance-hall Bridie went shopping once every month, cycling to the town early on a Friday afternoon. She bought things for herself, material for a dress, knitting wool, stockings, a newspaper, and paper-backed Wild West novels for her father. She talked in the shops to some of the girls she'd been at school with, girls who had married shop-assistants or shopkeepers, or had become assistants themselves. Most of them had families of their own by now. 'You're lucky to be peaceful in the hills,' they said to Bridie, 'instead of stuck in a hole like this.' They had a tired look, most of them, from pregnancies and their efforts to organize and control their large families.

As she cycled back to the hills on a Friday Bridie often felt that they truly envied her her life, and she found it surprising that they should do so. If it hadn't been for her father she'd have wanted to work in the town also, in the tinned-meat factory maybe, or in a shop. The town had a cinema called the Electric, and a fish-and-chip shop where people met at night, eating chips out of newspaper on the pavement outside. In the evenings, sitting in the farmhouse with her father, she often thought about the town, imagining the shop-windows lit up to display their goods and the sweet-shops still open so that people could purchase chocolates or fruit to take with them to the Electric cinema. But the town was eleven miles away, which was too far to cycle, there and back, for an evening's entertainment.

'It's a terrible thing for you, girl,' her father used to say, genuinely troubled, 'tied up to a one-legged man.' He would sigh heavily, hobbling back from the fields, where he managed as best he could. 'If your mother hadn't died,' he'd say, not finishing the sentence.

If her mother hadn't died her mother could have looked after him and the scant acres he owned, her mother could somehow have lifted the milk-churn on to the collection platform and attended to the few hens and the cows. 'I'd be dead without the girl to assist me,' she'd heard her father saying to Canon O'Connell, and Canon O'Connell replied that he was certainly lucky to have her.

'Amn't I as happy here as anywhere?' she'd say herself, but her father knew she was pretending and was saddened because the weight of circumstances had so harshly interfered with her life.

Although her father still called her a girl, Bridie was thirty-six. She was tall and strong: the skin of her fingers and her palms were stained, and harsh to touch. The labour they'd experienced had found its way into them, as though juices had come out of vegetation and pigment out of soil: since childhood she'd torn away the rough scotch grass that grew each spring among her father's mangolds and sugar beet; since childhood she'd harvested potatoes in August, her hands daily rooting in the ground she loosened and turned. Wind had toughened the flesh of her face, sun had browned it; her neck and nose were lean, her lips touched with early wrinkles.

But on Saturday nights Bridie forgot the scotch grass and the soil. In different dresses she cycled to the dance-hall, encouraged to make the journey by her father. 'Doesn't it do you good, girl?' he'd say, as though he imagined she begrudged herself the pleasure. 'Why wouldn't you enjoy yourself?' She'd cook him his tea and then he'd settle down with the wireless, or maybe a Wild West novel. In time, while still she danced, he'd stoke the fire up and hobble his way upstairs to bed.

The dance-hall, owned by Mr Justin Dwyer, was miles from anywhere, a lone building by the roadside with treeless boglands all around and a gravel expanse in front of it. On pink pebbled cement its title was painted in an azure blue that matched the depth of the background shade yet stood out well, unfussily proclaiming *The Ballroom of Romance*. Above these letters four coloured bulbs – in red, green, orange and mauve – were lit at appropriate times, an indication that the evening rendezvous was open for business. Only the façade of the building was pink, the other walls being a more ordinary grey. And inside, except for pink swing-doors, everything was blue.

On Saturday nights Mr Justin Dwyer, a small, thin man, unlocked the metal grid that protected his property and drew it back, creating an open mouth from which music would later pour. He helped his wife to carry crates of lemonade and packets of biscuits from their car, and then took up a position in the tiny vestibule between the drawn-back grid and the pink swing-doors. He sat at a card-table, with money and tickets spread out before him. He'd made a fortune, people said: he owned other ballrooms also.

People came on bicycles or in old motor-cars, country people like Bridie from remote hill farms and villages. People who did not often see other people met there, girls and boys, men and women. They paid Mr Dwyer and passed into his dance-hall, where shadows were cast on pale-blue walls and light from a crystal bowl was dim. The band, known as the Romantic Jazz Band, was composed of clarinet, drums and piano. The drummer sometimes sang.

Bridie had been going to the dance-hall since first she left the Presentation Nuns, before her mother's death. She didn't mind the journey, which was seven miles there and seven back: she'd travelled as far every day to the Presentation Nuns on the same bicycle, which had once been the property of her mother, an old Rudge purchased originally in 1936. On Sundays she cycled six miles to Mass, but she never minded either: she'd grown quite used to all that.

'How're you, Bridie?' inquired Mr Justin Dwyer when she arrived in a new scarlet dress one autumn evening. She said she was all right and in reply to Mr Dwyer's second query she said that her father was all right also. 'I'll go up one of these days,' promised Mr Dwyer, which was a promise he'd been making for twenty years.

She paid the entrance fee and passed through the pink swing-doors. The Romantic Jazz Band was playing a familiar melody of the past, 'The Destiny Waltz'. In spite of the band's title, jazz was not ever played in the ballroom: Mr Dwyer did not personally care for that kind of music, nor had he cared for various dance movements that had come and gone over the years. Jiving, rock and roll, twisting and other such variations had all been resisted by Mr Dwyer, who believed that a ballroom should be, as much as possible, a dignified place. The Romantic Jazz Band consisted of Mr Maloney, Mr Swanton, and Dano Ryan on drums. They were three middle-aged men who drove out from the town in Mr Maloney's car, amateur performers who were employed otherwise by the tinned-meat factory, the Electricity Supply Board and the County Council.

'How're you, Bridie?' inquired Dano Ryan as she passed him on her way to the cloakroom. He was idle for a moment with his drums. 'The Destiny Waltz' not calling for much attention from him.

'I'm all right, Dano,' she said. 'Are you fit yourself? Are the eyes better?' The week before he'd told her that he'd developed a watering of the eyes that must have been some kind of cold or other. He'd woken up with it in the morning and it had persisted until the afternoon: it was a new experience, he'd told her, adding that he'd never had a day's illness or discomfort in his life.

'I think I need glasses,' he said now, and as she passed into the cloakroom she imagined him in glasses, repairing the roads, as he was employed to do by the County Council. You hardly ever saw a road-mender with glasses, she reflected, and she wondered if all the dust that was inherent in his work had perhaps affected his eyes.

'How're you, Bridie?' a girl called Eenie Mackie said in the cloakroom, a girl who'd left the Presentation Nuns only a year ago.

'That's a lovely dress, Eenie,' Bridie said. 'Is it nylon, that?'

'Tricel actually. Drip-dry.'

Bridie took off her coat and hung it on a hook. There was a small washbasin in the cloakroom above which hung a discoloured oval mirror. Used tissues and pieces of cotton-wool, cigarette-butts and matches covered the concrete floor. Lengths of green-painted timber partitioned off a lavatory in a corner.

'Jeez, you're looking great, Bridie,' Madge Dowding remarked, waiting for her turn at the mirror. She moved towards it as she spoke, taking off a pair of spectacles before endeavouring to apply make-up to the lashes of her eye. She stared myopically into the oval mirror, humming while the other girls became restive.

'Will you hurry up, for God's sake!' shouted Eenie Mackie. 'We're standing here all night, Madge.'

Madge Dowding was the only one who was older than Bridie. She was thirty-nine, although often she said she was younger. The girls sniggered about that, saying that Madge Dowding should accept her condition – her age and her squint and her poor complexion – and not make herself ridiculous going out after men. What man would be bothered with the like of her anyway? Madge Dowding would do better to give herself over to do Saturday-night work for the Legion of Mary: wasn't Canon O'Connell always looking for aid?

'Is that fellow there?' she asked now, moving away from the mirror. 'The guy with the long arms. Did anyone see him outside?'

'He's dancing with Cat Bolger,' one of the girls replied. 'She has herself glued to him.'

'Lover boy,' remarked Patty Byrne, and everyone laughed because the person referred to was hardly a boy any more, being over fifty it was said, a bachelor who came only occasionally to the dance-hall.

Madge Dowding left the cloakroom rapidly, not bothering to pretend she wasn't anxious about the conjunction of Cat Bolger and the man with the long arms. Two sharp spots of red had come into her cheeks, and when she stumbled in her haste the girls in the cloakroom laughed. A younger girl would have pretended to be casual.

Bridie chatted, waiting for the mirror. Some girls, not wishing to be delayed, used the mirrors of their compacts. Then in twos and threes, occasionally singly, they left the cloakroom and took their places on upright wooden chairs at one end of the dance-hall, waiting to be asked to dance. Mr Maloney, Mr Swanton and Dano Ryan played 'Harvest

Moon' and 'I Wonder Who's Kissing Her Now' and 'I'll Be
Around.'

Bridie danced. Her father would be falling asleep by the
fire; the wireless, tuned in to Radio Eireann, would be
murmuring in the background. Already he'd have listened to
Faith and Order and *Spot the Talent*. His Wild West novel, *Three
Rode Fast* by Jake Matall, would have dropped from his single
knee on to the flagged floor. He would wake with a jerk as
he did every night and, forgetting what night it was, might
be surprised not to see her, for usually she was sitting there
at the table, mending clothes or washing eggs. 'Is it time for
the news?' he'd automatically say.

Dust and cigarette smoke formed a haze beneath the
crystal bowl, feet thudded, girls shrieked and laughed, some
of them dancing together for want of a male partner. The
music was loud, the musicians had taken off their jackets.
Vigorously they played a number of tunes from *State Fair* and
then, more romantically, 'Just One of Those Things'. The
tempo increased for a Paul Jones, after which Bridie found
herself with a youth who told her he was saving up to
emigrate, the nation in his opinion being finished. 'I'm up in
the hills with the uncle,' he said, 'labouring fourteen hours a
day. Is it any life for a young fellow?' She knew his uncle, a
hill farmer whose stony acres were separated from her
father's by one other farm only. 'He has me gutted with
work,' the youth told her. 'Is there sense in it at all, Bridie?'

At ten o'clock there was a stir, occasioned by the arrival
of three middle-aged bachelors who'd cycled over from
Carey's public house. They shouted and whistled, greeting
other people across the dancing area. They smelt of stout and
sweat and whiskey.

Every Saturday at just this time they arrived, and, having
sold them their tickets, Mr Dwyer folded up his card-table
and locked the tin box that held the evening's takings: his
ballroom was complete.

'How're you, Bridie?' one of the bachelors, known as

Bowser Egan, inquired. Another one, Tim Daly, asked Patty Byrne how she was. 'Will we take the floor?' Eyes Horgan suggested to Madge Dowding, already pressing the front of his navy-blue suit against the net of her dress. Bridie danced with Bowser Egan, who said she was looking great.

The bachelors would never marry, the girls of the dance-hall considered: they were wedded already, to stout and whiskey and laziness, to three old mothers somewhere up in the hills. The man with the long arms didn't drink but he was the same in all other ways: he had the same look of a bachelor, a quality in his face.

'Great,' Bowser Egan said, feather-stepping in an inaccur-ate and inebriated manner. 'You're a great little dancer, Bridie.'

'Will you lay off that!' cried Madge Dowding, her voice shrill above the sound of the music. Eyes Horgan had slipped two fingers into the back of her dress and was now pretend-ing they'd got there by accident. He smiled blearily, his huge red face streaming with perspiration, the eyes which gave him his nickname protuberant and bloodshot.

'Watch your step with that one,' Bowser Egan called out, laughing so that spittle sprayed on to Bridie's face. Eenie Mackie, who was also dancing near the incident, laughed also and winked at Bridie. Dano Ryan left his drums and sang. 'Oh, how I miss your gentle kiss,' he crooned, 'and long to hold you tight.'

Nobody knew the name of the man with the long arms. The only words he'd ever been known to speak in the Ballroom of Romance were the words that formed his invita-tion to dance. He was a shy man who stood alone when he wasn't performing on the dance-floor. He rode away on his bicycle afterwards, not saying good-night to anyone.

'Cat has your man leppin' tonight,' Tim Daly remarked to Patty Byrne, for the liveliness that Cat Bolger had intro-duced into foxtrot and waltz was noticeable.

'I think of you only,' sang Dano Ryan. 'Only wishing, wishing you were by my side.'

Dano Ryan would have done, Bridie often thought, because he was a different kind of bachelor: he had a lonely look about him, as if he'd become tired of being on his own. Every week she thought he would have done, and during the week her mind regularly returned to that thought. Dano Ryan would have done because she felt he wouldn't mind coming to live in the farmhouse while her one-legged father was still about the place. Three could live as cheaply as two where Dano Ryan was concerned because giving up the wages he earned as a road-worker would be balanced by the saving made on what he paid for lodgings. Once, at the end of an evening, she'd pretended that there was a puncture in the back wheel of her bicycle and he'd concerned himself with it while Mr Maloney and Mr Swanton waited for him in Mr Maloney's car. He'd blown the tyre up with the car pump and had said he thought it would hold.

It was well known in the dance-hall that she fancied her chances with Dano Ryan. But it was well known also that Dano Ryan had got into a set way of life and had remained in it for quite some years. He lodged with a widow called Mrs Griffin and Mrs Griffin's mentally affected son, in a cottage on the outskirts of the town. He was said to be good to the affected child, buying him sweets and taking him out for rides on the crossbar of his bicycle. He gave an hour or two of his time every week to the Church of Our Lady Queen of Heaven, and he was loyal to Mr Dwyer. He performed in the two other rural dance-halls that Mr Dwyer owned, rejecting advances from the town's more sophisticated dance-hall, even though it was more conveniently situated for him and the fee was more substantial than that paid by Mr Dwyer. But Mr Dwyer had discovered Dano Ryan and Dano had not forgotten it, just as Mr Maloney and Mr Swanton had not forgotten their discovery by Mr Dwyer either.

'Would we take a lemonade?' Bowser Egan suggested. 'And a packet of biscuits, Bridie?'

No alcoholic liquor was ever served in the Ballroom of Romance, the premises not being licensed for this added stimulant. Mr Dwyer in fact had never sought a licence for any of his premises, knowing that romance and alcohol were difficult commodities to mix, especially in a dignified ball-room. Behind where the girls sat on the wooden chairs Mr Dwyer's wife, a small stout woman, served the bottles of lemonade, with straws, and the biscuits, and crisps. She talked busily while doing so, mainly about the turkeys she kept. She'd once told Bridie that she thought of them as children.

'Thanks,' Bridie said, and Bowser Egan led her to the trestle table. Soon it would be the intermission: soon the three members of the band would cross the floor also for refreshment. She thought up questions to ask Dano Ryan.

When first she'd danced in the Ballroom of Romance, when she was just sixteen, Dano Ryan had been there also, four years older than she was, playing the drums for Mr Maloney as he played them now. She'd hardly noticed him then because of his not being one of the dancers: he was part of the ballroom's scenery, like the trestle table and the lemonade bottles, and Mrs Dwyer and Mr Dwyer. The youths who'd danced with her then in their Saturday-night blue suits had later disappeared into the town, or to Dublin or Britain, leaving behind them those who became the middle-aged bachelors of the hills. There'd been a boy called Patrick Grady whom she had loved in those days. Week after week she'd ridden away from the Ballroom of Romance with the image of his face in her mind, a thin face, pale beneath black hair. It had been different, dancing with Patrick Grady, and she'd felt that he found it different dancing with her, although he'd never said so. At night she'd dreamed of him and in the daytime too, while she helped her mother in the kitchen or her father with the cows. Week by week she'd returned to the ballroom, delighting in its pink façade and dancing in the arms of Patrick Grady. Often they'd stood together drinking lemonade, not saying anything, not know-ing what to say. She knew he loved her, and she believed then that he would lead her one day from the dim, romantic ballroom, from its blueness and its pinkness and its crystal bowl of light and its music. She believed he would lead her into sunshine, to the town and the Church of Our Lady Queen of Heaven, to marriage and smiling faces. But someone else had got Patrick Grady, a girl from the town who'd never danced in the wayside ballroom. She'd scooped up Patrick Grady when he didn't have a chance.

Bridie had wept, hearing that. By night she'd lain in her bed in the farmhouse, quietly crying, the tears rolling into her hair and making the pillow damp. When she woke in the early morning the thought was still naggingly with her and it remained with her by day, replacing her daytime dreams of happiness. Someone told her later on that he'd crossed to Britain, to Wolverhampton, with the girl he'd married, and she imagined him there, in a place she wasn't able properly to visualize, labouring in a factory, his children being born and acquiring the accent of the area. The Ballroom of Romance wasn't the same without him, and when no one else stood out for her particularly over the years and when no one offered her marriage, she found herself wondering about Dano Ryan. If you couldn't have love, the next best thing was surely a decent man.

Bowser Egan hardly fell into that category, nor did Tim Daly. And it was plain to everyone that Cat Bolger and Madge Dowding were wasting their time over the man with the long arms. Madge Dowding was already a figure of fun in the ballroom, the way she ran after the bachelors; Cat Bolger would end up the same if she wasn't careful. One way or another it wasn't difficult to be a figure of fun in the ballroom, and you didn't have to be as old as Madge Dowding: a girl who'd just left the Presentation Nuns once asked Eyes Horgan what he had in his trouser pocket and he told her it was a penknife. She'd repeated this afterwards in the cloakroom, how she'd requested Eyes Horgan not to dance so close to her because his penknife was sticking in her. 'Jeez, aren't you the right baby!' Patty Byrne had shouted delightedly; everyone had laughed, knowing that Eyes Horgan only came to the ballroom for stuff like that. He was no use to any girl.

'Two lemonades, Mrs Dwyer,' Bowser Egan said, 'and two packets of Kerry Creams. Is Kerry Creams all right, Bridie?'

She nodded, smiling. Kerry Creams would be fine, she said.

'Well, Bridie, isn't that the great outfit you have!' Mrs Dwyer remarked. 'Doesn't the red suit her, Bowser?'

By the swing-doors stood Mr Dwyer, smoking a cigarette that he held cupped in his left hand. His small eyes noted all developments. He had been aware of Madge Dowding's anxiety when Eyes Horgan had inserted two fingers into the back opening of her dress. He had looked away, not caring for the incident, but had it developed further he would have spoken to Eyes Horgan, as he had on other occasions. Some of the younger lads didn't know any better and would dance very close to their partners, who generally were too embarrassed to do anything about it, being young themselves. But that, in Mr Dwyer's opinion, was a different kettle of fish altogether because they were decent young lads who'd in no time at all be doing a steady line with a girl and would end up as he had himself with Mrs Dwyer, in the same house with her, sleeping in a bed with her, firmly married. It was the middle-aged bachelors who required the watching: they came down from the hills like mountain goats, released from their mammies and from the smell of animals and soil. Mr Dwyer continued to watch Eyes Horgan, wondering how drunk he was.

Dano Ryan's song came to an end, Mr Swanton laid down his clarinet, Mr Maloney rose from the piano. Dano Ryan wiped sweat from his face and the three men slowly moved towards Mrs Dwyer's trestle table.

'Jeez, you have powerful legs,' Eyes Horgan whispered to Madge Dowding, but Madge Dowding's attention was on the man with the long arms, who had left Cat Bolger's side and was proceeding in the direction of the men's lavatory.

He never took refreshments. She moved, herself, towards the men's lavatory, to take up a position outside it, but Eyes Horgan followed her. 'Would you take a lemonade, Madge?' he asked. He had a small bottle of whiskey on him: if they went into a corner they could add a drop of it to the lemonade. She didn't drink spirits, she reminded him, and he went away.

'Excuse me a minute,' Bowser Egan said, putting down his bottle of lemonade. He crossed the floor to the lavatory. He too, Bridie knew, would have a small bottle of whiskey on him. She watched while Dano Ryan, listening to a story Mr Maloney was telling paused in the centre of the ballroom, his head bent to hear what was being said. He was a big man, heavily made, with black hair that was slightly touched with grey, and big hands. He laughed when Mr Maloney came to the end of his story and then bent his head again, in order to listen to a story told by Mr Swanton.

'Are you on your own, Bridie?' Cat Bolger asked, and Bridie said she was waiting for Bowser Egan. 'I think I'll have a lemonade,' Cat Bolger said.

Younger boys and girls stood with their arms still around one another, queuing up for refreshments. Boys who hadn't danced at all, being nervous because they didn't know any steps, stood in groups, smoking and making jokes. Girls who hadn't been danced with yet talked to one another, their eyes wandering. Some of them sucked at straws in lemonade bottles.

Bridie, still watching Dano Ryan, imagined him wearing the glasses he'd referred to, sitting in the farmhouse kitchen, reading one of her father's Wild West novels. She imagined the three of them eating a meal she'd prepared, fried eggs and rashers and fried potato-cakes, and tea and bread and butter and jam, brown bread and soda and shop bread. She imagined Dano Ryan leaving the kitchen in the morning to go out to the fields in order to weed the mangolds, and her father hobbling off behind him, and the two men working together. She saw hay being cut, Dano Ryan with the scythe that she'd learned to use herself, her father using a rake as best he could. She saw herself, because of the extra help, being able to attend to things in the farmhouse, things she'd never had time for because of the cows and the hens and the fields. There were bedroom curtains that needed repairing where the net had ripped, and wallpaper that had become loose and needed to be stuck up with flour paste. The scullery required whitewashing.

The night he'd blown up the tyre of her bicycle she'd thought he was going to kiss her. He'd crouched on the ground in the darkness with his ear to the tyre, listening for escaping air. When he could hear none he'd straighted up and said he thought she'd be all right on the bicycle. His face had been quite close to hers and she'd smiled at him. At that moment, unfortunately, Mr Maloney had blown an impatient blast on the horn of his motor-car.

Often she'd been kissed by Bowser Egan, on the nights when he insisted on riding part of the way home with her. They had to dismount in order to push their bicycles up a hill and the first time he'd accompanied her he'd contrived to fall against her, steadying himself by putting a hand on her shoulder. The next thing she was aware of was the moist quality of his lips and the sound of his bicycle as it clattered noisily on the road. He'd suggested then, regaining his breath, that they should go into a field.

That was nine years ago. In the intervening passage of time she'd been kissed as well, in similar circumstances, by Eyes Horgan and Tim Daly. She'd gone into fields with them and permitted them to put their arms about her while heavily they breathed. At one time or another she had imagined marriage with one or other of them, seeing them in the farmhouse with her father, even though the fantasies were unlikely.

Bridie stood with Cat Bolger, knowing that it would be some time before Bowser Egan came out of the lavatory. Mr Maloney, Mr Swanton and Dano Ryan approached, Mr

Maloney insisting that he would fetch three bottles of lemonade from the trestle table.

'You sang the last one beautifully,' Bridie said to Dano Ryan. 'Isn't it a beautiful song?'

Mr Swanton said it was the finest song ever written, and Cat Bolger said she preferred 'Danny Boy', which in her opinion was the finest song ever written.

'Take a suck of that,' said Mr Maloney, handing Dano Ryan and Mr Swanton bottles of lemonade. 'How's Bridie tonight? Is your father well, Bridie?'

Her father was all right, she said.

'I hear they're starting a cement factory,' said Mr Maloney. 'Did anyone hear talk of that? They're after striking some commodity in the earth that makes good cement. Ten feet down, over at Kilmalough.'

'It'll bring employment,' said Mr Swanton. 'It's employment that's necessary in this area.'

'Canon O'Connell was on about it,' Mr Maloney said. 'There's Yankee money involved.'

'Will the Yanks come over?' inquired Cat Bolger. 'Will they run it themselves, Mr Maloney?'

Mr Maloney, intent on his lemonade, didn't hear the questions and Cat Bolger didn't repeat them.

'There's stuff called Optrex,' Bridie said quietly to Dano Ryan, 'that my father took the time he had a cold in his eyes. Maybe Optrex would settle the watering, Dano.'

'Ah sure, it doesn't worry me that much—'

'It's terrible, anything wrong with the eyes. You wouldn't want to take a chance. You'd get Optrex in a chemist, Dano, and a little bowl with it so that you can bathe the eyes.'

Her father's eyes had become red-rimmed and unsightly to look at. She'd gone into Riordan's Medical Hall in the town and had explained what the trouble was, and Mr Riordan had recommended Optrex. She told this to Dano Ryan, adding that her father had had no trouble with his eyes since. Dano Ryan nodded.

'Did you hear that, Mrs Dwyer?' Mr Maloney called out. 'A cement factory for Kilmalough.'

Mrs Dwyer wagged her head, placing empty bottles in a crate. She'd heard references to the cement factory, she said: it was the best news for a long time.

'Kilmalough won't know itself,' her husband commented, joining her in her task with the empty lemonade bottles.

''Twill bring prosperity certainly,' said Mr Swanton. 'I was saying just there, Justin, that employment's what's necessary.'

'Sure, won't the Yanks—' began Cat Bolger, but Mr Maloney interrupted her.

'The Yanks'll be at the top, Cat, or maybe not here at all – maybe only inserting money into it. It'll be local labour entirely.'

'You'll not marry a Yank, Cat,' said Mr Swanton, loudly laughing. 'You can't catch those fellows.'

'Haven't you plenty of homemade bachelors?' suggested Mr Maloney. He laughed also, throwing away the straw he was sucking through and tipping the bottle into his mouth. Cat Bolger told him to get on with himself. She moved towards the men's lavatory and took up a position outside it, not speaking to Madge Dowding, who was still standing there.

'Keep a watch on Eyes Horgan,' Mrs Dwyer warned her husband, which was advice she gave him at this time every Saturday night, knowing that Eyes Horgan was drinking in the lavatory. When he was drunk Eyes Horgan was the most difficult of the bachelors.

'I have a drop of it left, Dano,' Bridie said quietly. 'I could bring it over on Saturday. The eye stuff.'

'Ah, don't worry yourself, Bridie—'

'No trouble at all. Honestly now—'

'Mrs Griffin has me fixed up for a test with Dr Cready. The old eyes are no worry, only when I'm reading the paper or at the pictures. Mrs Griffin says I'm only straining them due to lack of glasses.'

He looked away while he said that, and she knew at once that Mrs Griffin was arranging to marry him. She felt it instinctively: Mrs Griffin was going to marry him because she was afraid that if he moved away from her cottage, to get married to someone else, she'd find it hard to replace him with another lodger who'd be good to her affected son. He'd become a father to Mrs Griffin's affected son, to whom already he was kind. It was a natural outcome, for Mrs Griffin had all the chances, seeing him every night and morning and not having to make do with weekly encounters in a ballroom.

She thought of Patrick Grady, seeing in her mind his pale, thin face. She might be the mother of four of his children now, or seven or eight maybe. She might be living in Wolverhampton. Going out to the pictures in the evenings, instead of looking after a one-legged man. If the weight of circumstances hadn't intervened she wouldn't be standing in a wayside ballroom, mourning the marriage of a road-mender she didn't love. For a moment she thought she might cry, standing there thinking of Patrick Grady in Wolverhampton. In her life, on the farm and in the house, there was no place for tears. Tears were a luxury, like flowers would be in the fields where the mangolds grew, or fresh whitewash in the scullery. It wouldn't have been fair ever to have wept in the kitchen while her father sat listening to *Spot the Talent*: her father had more right to weep, having lost a leg. He suffered in a greater way, yet he remained kind and concerned for her.

In the Ballroom of Romance she felt behind her eyes the tears that it would have been improper to release in the presence of her father. She wanted to let them go, to feel them streaming on her cheeks, to receive the sympathy of Dano Ryan and of everyone else. She wanted them all to listen to her while she told them about Patrick Grady who was now in Wolverhampton and about the death of her mother and her own life since. She wanted Dano Ryan to put his arm around her so that she could lean her head against it. She wanted him to look at her in his decent way and to stroke with his road-mender's fingers the backs of her hands. She might wake in a bed with him and imagine for a moment that he was Patrick Grady. She might bathe his eyes and pretend.

'Back to business,' said Mr Maloney, leading his band across the floor to their instruments.

'Tell your father I was asking for him,' Dano Ryan said. She smiled and she promised, as though nothing had happened, that she would tell her father that.

She danced with Tim Daly and then again with the youth who'd said he intended to emigrate. She saw Madge Dowding moving swiftly towards the man with the long arms as he came out of the lavatory, moving faster than Cat Bolger. Eyes Horgan approached Cat Bolger. Dancing with her, he spoke earnestly, attempting to persuade her to permit him to ride part of the way home with her. He was unaware of the jealousy that was coming from her as she watched Madge Dowding holding close to her the man with the long arms while they performed a quickstep. Cat Bolger was in her thirties also.

'Get away out of that,' said Bowser Egan, cutting in on the youth who was dancing with Bridie. 'Go home to your mammy, boy.' He took her into his arms, saying again that she was looking great tonight. 'Did you hear about the cement factory?' he said. 'Isn't it great for Kilmalough?'

She agreed. She said what Mr Swanton and Mr Maloney had said: that the cement factory would bring employment to the neighbourhood.

'Will I ride home with you a bit, Bridie?' Bowser Egan suggested, and she pretended not to hear him. 'Aren't you my girl, Bridie, and always have been?' he said, a statement that made no sense at all.

His voice went on whispering at her, saying he would marry her tomorrow only his mother wouldn't permit another woman in the house. She knew what it was like herself, he reminded her, having a parent to look after: you couldn't leave them to rot, you had to honour your father and your mother.

She danced to 'The Bells Are Ringing', moving her legs in time with Bowser Egan's while over his shoulder she watched Dano Ryan softly striking one of his smaller drums. Mrs Griffin had got him even though she was nearly fifty, with no looks at all, a lumpish woman with lumpish legs and arms. Mrs Griffin had got him just as the girl had got Patrick Grady.

The music ceased, Bowser Egan held her hard against him, trying to touch her face with his. Around them, people whistled and clapped: the evening had come to an end. She walked away from Bowser Egan, knowing that not ever again would she dance in the Ballroom of Romance. She'd been a figure of fun, trying to promote a relationship with a middle-aged County Council labourer, as ridiculous as Madge Dowding dancing on beyond her time.

'I'm waiting outside for you, Cat,' Eyes Horgan called out, lighting a cigarette as he made for the swing-doors.

Already the man with the long arms – made long, so they said, from carrying rocks off his land – had left the ballroom. Others were moving briskly. Mr Dwyer was tidying the chairs.

In the cloakroom the girls put on their coats and said they'd see one another at Mass the next day. Madge Dowding hurried. 'Are you OK, Bridie?' Patty Byrne asked and Bridie said she was. She smiled at little Patty Byrne, wondering if a day would come for the younger girl also, if one day she'd decide that she was a figure of fun in a wayside ballroom.

'Good-night so,' Bridie said, leaving the cloakroom, and the girls who were still chatting there wished her good-night. Outside the cloakroom she paused for a moment. Mr Dwyer was still tidying the chairs, picking up empty lemonade bottles from the floor, setting the chairs in a neat row. His wife was sweeping the floor. 'Good-night, Bridie,' Mr Dwyer said. 'Good-night, Bridie,' his wife said.

Extra lights had been switched on so that the Dwyers could see what they were doing. In the glare the blue walls of the ballroom seemed tatty, marked with hair-oil where men had leaned against them, inscribed with names and initials and hearts with arrows through them. The crystal bowl gave out a light that was ineffective in the glare; the bowl was broken here and there, which wasn't noticeable when the other lights weren't on.

'Good-night so,' Bridie said to the Dwyers. She passed through the swing-doors and descended the three concrete steps on the gravel expanse in front of the ballroom. People were gathered on the gravel, talking in groups, standing with their bicycles. She saw Madge Dowding going off with Tim Daly. A youth rode away with a girl on the crossbar of his bicycle. The engines of motor-cars started.

'Good-night, Bridie,' Dano Ryan said.

'Good-night, Dano,' she said.

She walked across the gravel towards her bicycle, hearing Mr Maloney, somewhere behind her, repeating that no matter how you looked at it the cement factory would be a great thing for Kilmalough. She heard the bang of a car door and knew it was Mr Swanton banging the door of Mr Maloney's car because he always gave it the same loud bang. Two other doors banged as she reached her bicycle and then the engine started up and the headlights went on. She touched the two tyres of the bicycle to make certain she hadn't a puncture. The wheels of Mr Maloney's car traversed the gravel and were silent when they reached the road.

'Good-night, Bridie,' someone called, and she replied, pushing her bicycle towards the road.

'Will I ride a little way with you?' Bowser Egan asked.

They rode together and when they arrived at the hill for which it was necessary to dismount she looked back and saw in the distance the four coloured bulbs that decorated the façade of the Ballroom of Romance. As she watched, the lights went out, and she imagined Mr Dwyer pulling the metal grid across the front of his property and locking the two padlocks that secured it. His wife would be waiting with the evening's takings, sitting in the front of their car.

'D'you know what it is, Bridie,' said Bowser Egan, 'you were never looking better than tonight.' He took from a pocket of his suit the small bottle of whiskey he had. He uncorked it and drank some and then handed it to her. She took it and drank. 'Sure, why wouldn't you?' he said, surprised to see her drinking because she never had in his company before. It was an unpleasant taste, she considered, a taste she'd experienced only twice before, when she'd taken whiskey as a remedy for toothache. 'What harm would it do you?' Bowser Egan said as she raised the bottle again to her lips. He reached out a hand for it, though, suddenly concerned lest she should consume a greater share than he wished her to.

She watched him drinking more expertly than she had. He would always be drinking, she thought. He'd be lazy and useless, sitting in the kitchen with the *Irish Press*. He'd waste money buying a secondhand motor-car in order to drive into the town to go to the public houses on fair-days.

'She's shook these days,' he said, referring to his mother. 'She'll hardly last two years, I'm thinking.' He threw the empty whiskey bottle into the ditch and lit a cigarette. They pushed their bicycles. He said:

'When she goes, Bridie, I'll sell the bloody place up. I'll sell the pigs and the whole damn one and twopence worth.' He paused in order to raise the cigarette to his lips. He drew in smoke and exhaled it. 'With the cash that I'll get I could improve some place else, Bridie.'

They reached a gate on the left-hand side of the road and automatically they pushed their bicycles towards it and leaned them against it. He climbed over the gate into the field and she climbed after him. 'Will we sit down here, Bridie?' he said, offering the suggestion as one that had just occurred to him, as though they'd entered the field for some other purpose.

'We could improve a place like your own one,' he said,

putting his right arm around her shoulders. 'Have you a kiss in you, Bridie?' He kissed her, exerting pressure with his teeth. When his mother died he would sell his farm and spend the money in the town. After that he would think of getting married because he'd have nowhere to go, because he'd want a fire to sit at and a woman to cook food for him. He kissed her again, his lips hot, the sweat on his cheeks sticking to her. 'God, you're great at kissing,' he said.

She rose, saying it was time to go, and they climbed over the gate again. 'There's nothing like a Saturday,' he said. 'Good-night to you so, Bridie.'

He mounted his bicycle and rode down the hill, and she pushed hers to the top and then mounted it also. She rode through the night as on Saturday nights for years she had ridden and never would ride again because she'd reached a certain age. She would wait now and in time Bowser Egan would seek her out because his mother would have died. Her father would probably have died also by then. She would marry Bowser Egan because it would be lonesome being by herself in the farmhouse.

Molly Keane

from *Good Behaviour*

R OSE SMELT the air, considering what she smelt; a miasma of unspoken criticism and disparagement fogged the distance between us. I knew she ached to censure my cooking, but through the years I have subdued her. Those wide shoulders and swinging hips were once parts of a winged quality she had – a quality reduced and corrected now, I am glad to say.

'I wonder are you wise, Miss Aroon, to give her the rabbit?'

'And why not?' I can use the tone of voice which keeps people in their places and usually silences any interference from Rose. Not this time.

'Rabbit sickens her. Even Master Hubert's first with his first gun. She couldn't get it down.'

'That's a very long time ago. And I've often known her to enjoy rabbit since then.'

'She never liked rabbit.'

'Especially when she thought it was chicken.'

'You couldn't deceive her, Miss Aroon.' She picked up the tray. I snatched it back. I knew precisely what she would say when she put it down on Mummie's bed. I had set the tray myself. I don't trust Rose. I don't trust anybody. Because I like things to be right. The tray did look charming: bright, with a crisp clean cloth and a shine on everything. I lifted the silver lid off the hot plate to smell those quenelles in a cream sauce. There was just a hint of bay leaf and black pepper, not a breath of the rabbit foundation. Anyhow, what could be more delicious and delicate than a baby rabbit? Especially after it has been forced through a fine sieve and whizzed for ten minutes in a Moulinex blender.

'I'll take up the tray,' I said. 'When the kettle boils, please fill the pink hot-water bottle. It makes a little change from the electric blanket. Did you hear me? Rose?' She has this maddening pretence of deafness. It is simply one of her ways of ignoring me. I know that. I have known it for most of my life.

'I see in today's paper where a woman in Kilmacthomas burned to death in an electric blanket. It turned into a flaming cage, imagine.'

I paid no attention to the woman in the blanket and I repeated: 'When the kettle boils and not before.' That would give me time to settle Mummie comfortably with her luncheon before Rose brought the hot-water bottle and the tale of the woman in Kilmacthomas (who I bet did something particularly silly and the blanket was quite blameless) into her bedroom.

Gulls' Cry, where Mummie and I live now, is built on the edge of a cliff. Its windows lean out over the deep anchorage of the boat cove like bosoms on an old ship's figurehead. Sometimes I think (though I would never say it) how nice that bosoms are all right to have now; in the twenties when I grew up I used to tie them down with a sort of binder. Bosoms didn't do then. They didn't do at all. Now, it's too late for mine.

I like to sing when nobody can hear me and put me off the note. I sang that day as I went upstairs. Our kitchen and dining-room are on the lowest level of this small Gothic folly of a house. The stairs, with their skimpy iron banister, bring you up to the hall and the drawing-room, where I put all our mementoes of Papa when we moved here from Temple Alice. The walls are papered in pictures and photographs of him riding winners. Silver cups stand in rows on the chimney-piece, not to mention the model of a seven-pound sea trout and several rather misty snapshots of bags of grouse laid out on the steps of Temple Alice.

Mummie never took any proper interest in this gallery, and when her heart got so dicky, and I converted the room into a charming bed-sit for her, she seemed to turn her eyes away from everything she might have remembered with love and pleasure. One knows sick people and old people can be difficult and unrewarding, however much one does for them: not exactly ungrateful, just absolutely maddening. But I enjoy the room whenever I go in. It's all my own doing and Mummie, lying back in her nest of pretty pillows, is my doing too – I insist on her being scrupulously clean and washed and scented.

'Luncheon,' I said cheerfully, the tray I carried making a lively rattle. 'Shall I sit you up a bit?' She was lying down among her pillows as if she were sinking through the bed. She never makes an effort for herself. That comes of having me.

'I don't feel very hungry,' she said. A silly remark. I know she always pretends she can't eat and when I go out makes Rose do her fried eggs and buttered toast and all the things the doctor says she mustn't touch.

'Smell that,' I said, and lifted the cover off my perfect quenelles.

'I wonder if you'd pull down the blind' – not a word about the quenelles – 'the sun's rather in my eyes.'

'You really want the blind down?'

She nodded.

'All the way?'

'Please.'

I went across then and settled her for her tray, pulling her up and putting a pillow in the exact spot behind her back, and another tiny one behind her head. She simply refused to look as if she felt comfortable. I'm used to that. I arranged the basket tray (straight from Harrods) across her, and put her luncheon tray on it.

'Now then,' I said – one must be firm – 'a delicious chicken mousse.'

'Rabbit, I bet,' she said.

I was still patient: 'Just try a forkful.'

'Myxomatosis,' she said. 'Remember that? – I can't.'

I held on to my patience. 'It was far too young to have myxomatosis. Come on now, Mummie' – I tried to keep the firm note out of my voice – 'just one.'

She lifted the small silver fork (our crest, a fox rampant, almost handled and washed away by use) as though she were heaving up a load of stinking fish: 'The smell – I'm—' She gave a trembling, tearing cry, vomited dreadfully, and fell back into the nest of pretty pillows.

I felt more than annoyed for a moment. Then I looked at her and I was frightened. I leaned across the bed and rang her bell. Then I shouted and called down to Rose in the kitchen. She came up fast, although her feet and her shoes never seem to work together now; even then I noticed it. But of course I notice everything.

'She was sick,' I said.

'She couldn't take the rabbit?'

Rabbit again. 'It was a mousse,' I screamed at the old fool, 'a cream mousse. It was perfect. I made it so I ought to know. It was RIGHT. She was enjoying it.'

Rose was stooping over Mummie. 'Miss Aroon, she's gone.' She crossed herself and started to pray in that loose, easy way Roman Catholics do: 'Holy Mary, pray for us now and in the hour of our death . . . Merciful Jesus . . .'

She seemed too close to Mummie with that peasant gabbling prayer. We should have had the Dean.

'Take the tray away,' I said. I picked Mummie's hand up out of the sick and put it down in a clean place. It was as limp as a dead duck's neck. I wanted to cry out. 'Oh, no—' I wanted to say. I controlled myself. I took three clean tissues out of the cardboard box I had covered in shell-pink brocade and wiped my fingers. When they were clean the truth came to me, an awful new-born monstrosity. I suppose I swayed on my feet. I felt as if I could go on falling for ever. Rose helped me to a chair and I could hear its joints screech as I sat down, although I am not at all heavy, considering my

height. I longed to ask somebody to do me a favour, to direct
me; to fill out this abyss with some importance – something
needful to be done.

'What must I do now?' I was asking myself. Rose had
turned her back on me and on the bed. She was opening the
window as high as the sash would go – that's one of their
superstitions, something to do with letting the spirit go
freely. They do it. They don't speak of it. She did the same
thing when Papa died.

'You must get the doctor at once, Miss Aroon, and Kathie
Cleary to lay her out. There's no time to lose.'

She said it in a gluttonous way. They revel in death . . .
Keep the Last Rites going . . . She can't wait to get her hands
on Mummie, to get me out of the way while she helps Mrs
Cleary in necessary and nasty rituals. What could I do against
them? I had to give over. I couldn't forbid. Or could I?

'I shall get the doctor,' I said, 'and Nurse Quinn. *Not* Mrs
Cleary.'

She faced me across the bed, her great blue eyes blazing.
'Miss Aroon, madam hated Nurse Quinn. The one time she
gave her a needle she took a weakness. She wouldn't let her
in the place again. She wouldn't let her touch her. Kathie
Cleary's a dab hand with a corpse – there's nothing missing
in Kathie Cleary's methods and madam loved her, she loved
a chat with Kathie Cleary.'

I really felt beside myself. Why this scene? Why can't
people do what I say? That's all I ask. 'That will do, Rose,'
I said. I felt quite strong again. 'I'll telephone to the doctor
and ask him to let Nurse know. Just take that tray down and
keep the mousse hot for my luncheon.'

Rose lunged towards me, over the bed, across Mummie's
still feet. I think if she could have caught me in both her
hands she would have done so.

'Your lunch,' she said. 'You can eat your bloody lunch
and she lying there stiffening every minute. Rabbit – rabbit
chokes her, rabbit sickens her, and rabbit killed her – call it
rabbit if you like. Rabbit's a harmless word for it – if it was a

smothering you couldn't have done it better. And – another thing – who tricked her out of Temple Alice? Tell me that—'

'Rose, how dare you.' I tried to interrupt her but she stormed on.

'. . . and brought my lady into this mean little ruin with hungry gulls screeching over it and two old ghosts (God rest their souls) knocking on the floors by night—'

I stayed calm above all the wild nonsense. 'Who else hears the knocking?' I asked her quietly. 'Only you.'

'And I heard the roaring and crying when you parted Mr Hamish from Miss Enid and put the two of them in hospital wards, male and female, to die on their own alone.'

'At the time it was totally necessary.'

'Necessary? That way you could get this house in your own two hands and boss and bully us through the years. Madam's better off the way she is this red raw minute. She's tired from you – tired to death. Death is right. We're all killed from you and it's a pity it's not yourself lying there and your toes cocked for the grave and not a word more about you, God damn you!'

Yes, she stood there across the bed saying these obscene, unbelievable things. Of course she loved Mummie, all the servants did. Of course she was overwrought. I know all that – and she is ignorant to a degree, I allow for that too. Although there was a shocking force in what she said to me, it was beyond all sense or reason. It was so entirely and dreadfully false that it could not touch me. I felt as tall as a tree standing above all that passionate flood of words. I was determined to be kind to Rose. And understanding. And generous. I am her employer, I thought. I shall raise her wages quite substantially. She will never be able to resist me then, because she is greedy. I can afford to be kind to Rose. She will learn to lean on me. There is nobody in the world who needs me now and I must be kind to somebody.

'You're upset,' I said gently. 'Naturally you're upset. You loved Mrs St Charles and I know you didn't mean one word you've just said to me.'

'I did too, Miss Aroon.' She was like a drowning person, coming up for a last choking breath. 'God help you, it's the flaming truth.'

'Don't worry,' I answered. 'I've forgotten ... I didn't hear ... I understand. Now we've both got to be practical. We must both be brave. I'll ring up the doctor and you'll take that tray to the kitchen, and put the mousse over a pot of boiling water – it may be hours till lunchtime.'

She took up the tray, tears pouring down her face. Of course I had expected her to obey me, but I won't deny that before she turned away from the bed, the tray, as it should have been, between her hands, I had been aware of a moment of danger. Now, apart from my shock and sorrow about Mummie, a feeling of satisfaction went through me – a kind of ripple that I needed. I needed it and I had it.

I went into the hall and picked up the telephone. While I waited for the exchange (always criminally slow) to answer, I had time to consider how the punctual observance of the usual importances is the only way to behave at such times as these. And I do know how to behave – believe me, because I know. I have always known. All my life so far I have done everything for the best reasons and the most unselfish motives. I have lived for the people dearest to me, and I am at a loss to know why their lives have been at times so perplexingly unhappy. I have given them so much. I have given them everything, all I know how to give – Papa, Hubert, Richard, Mummie. At fifty-seven my brain is fairly bright, brighter than ever I sometimes think, and I have a cast-iron memory. If I look back beyond any shadow into the uncertainties and glories of our youth, perhaps I shall understand more about what became of us.

Neil Jordan

Last Rites

ONE WHITE-HOT Friday in June at some minutes after five o'clock a young builder's labourer crossed an iron railway overpass, just off the Harrow Road. The day was faded now and the sky was a curtain of haze, but the city still lay hard-edged and agonizingly bright in the day's undiminished heat. The labourer as he crossed the overpass took note of its regulation shade of green. He saw an old, old negro immigrant standing motionless in the shade of a red-bricked wall. Opposite the wall, in line with the overpass, he saw the Victorian façade of Kensal Rise Baths. Perhaps because of the heat, or because of a combination of the heat and his temperament, these impressions came to him with an unusual clarity; as if he had seen them in a film or in a dream and not in real, waking life. Within the hour he would take his own life. And dying, a cut-throat razor in his hand, his blood mingling with the shower water into the colour of weak wine he would take with him to whatever vacuum lay beyond, three memories: the memory of a green-painted bridge; of an old, bowed, shadowed negro; of the sheer tiled wall of a cubicle in what had originally been the wash-houses of Kensal Rise Tontine and Workingmen's Association, in what was now Kensal Rise Baths.

The extraordinary sense of nervous anticipation the labourer experienced had long been familiar with him. And, inexplicable. He never questioned it fully. He knew he anticipated something, approaching the baths. He knew that it wasn't quite pleasure. It was something more and less than pleasurable, a feeling of ravishing, private vindication, of exposure, of secret, solipsistic victory. Over what he never asked. But he knew. He knew as he approached the baths to wash off the dust of a week's labour, that this hour would be the week's high-point. Although during the week he never thought of it, never dwelt on its pleasures – as he did, for instance on his prolonged Saturday morning's rest – when the hour came it was as if the secret thread behind his week's existence was emerging into daylight, was exposing itself to the scrutiny of daylight, his daylight. The way the fauna of the sea-bed are exposed, when the tide goes out.

And so when he crossed the marble step at the door, when he faced the lady behind the glass counter, handing her sevenpence, accepting a ticket from her, waving his hand to refuse towel and soap, gesticulating towards the towel in his duffle bag, each action was performed with the solemnity of an elaborate ritual, each action was a ring in the circular maze that led to the hidden purpose – the purpose he never elaborated, only felt; in his arm as he waved his hand; in his foot as he crossed the threshold. And when he walked down the corridor, with its white walls, its strange hybrid air, half unemployment exchange, half hospital ward, he was silent. As he took his place on the long oak bench, last in a line of negro, Scottish and Irish navvies, his expression preserved the same immobility as theirs, his duffle bag was kept between his feet and his rough slender hands between his knees and his eyes upon the grey cream wall in front of him. He listened to the rich, public voices of the negroes, knowing the warm colours of even their work-clothes without having to look. He listened to the odd mixture of reticence and resentment in the Irish voices. He felt the tiles beneath his feet, saw the flaking wall before him, the hard oak bench beneath him, the grey-haired cockney caretaker emerging every now and then from the shower-hall to call 'Shower!', 'Bath!' and at each call the next man in the queue rising, towel and soap under one arm. So plain, so commonplace, and underneath the secret pulsing – but his face was immobile.

As each man left the queue he shifted one space forward and each time the short, crisp call issued from the cockney he turned his head to stare. And when his turn eventually came to be first in the queue and the cockney called 'Shower!' he padded quietly through the open door. He had a slow walk that seemed a little stiff, perhaps because of the unnatural straightness of his back. He had a thin face, unremarkable but for a kind of distance in the expression; removed, glazed blue eyes; the kind of inwardness there, of immersion, that is sometimes termed stupidity.

The grey-haired cockney took his ticket from him. He nodded towards an open cubicle. The man walked slowly through the rows of white doors, under the tiled roof to the cubicle signified. It was the seventh door down.

'*Espera me*, Quievo!'

'*Ora, deprisa, ha*?'

He heard splashing water, hissing shower-jets, the smack of palms off wet thighs. Behind each door he knew was a naked man, held timeless and separate under an umbrella of darting water. The fact of the walls, of the similar but totally separate beings behind those walls never ceased to amaze him; quietly to excite him. And the shouts of those who communicated echoed strangely through the long, perfectly regular hall. And he knew that everything would be heightened thus now, raised into the aura of the green light.

He walked through the cubicle door and slid the hatch into place behind him. He took in his surroundings with a slow familiar glance. He knew it all, but he wanted to be a stranger to it, to see it again for the first time, always the first time: the wall, evenly gridded with white tiles, rising to a height of seven feet; the small gap between it and the ceiling; the steam coming through the gap from the cubicle next door; the jutting wall, with the full-length mirror affixed to it; behind it, enclosed by the plastic curtain, the shower. He went straight to the mirror and stood motionless before it. And the first throes of his removal began to come upon him. He looked at himself the way one would examine a flat-handled trowel, gauging its usefulness; or, idly, the way one would examine the cracks on a city pavement. He watched the way his nostrils, caked with cement dust, dilated with his breathing. He watched the rise of his chest, the buttons of his soiled white work-shirt straining with each rise, each breath. He clenched his teeth and his fingers. Then he undressed, slowly and deliberately, always remaining in full view of the full-length mirror.

After he was unclothed his frail body with its thin ribs, hard biceps and angular shoulders seemed to speak to him, through its frail passive image in the mirror. He listened and watched.

Later it would speak, lying on the floor with open wrists, still retaining its goose-pimples, to the old cockney shower attendant and the gathered bathers, every memory behind the transfixed eyes quietly intimated, almost revealed, by the body itself. If they had looked hard enough, had eyes keen enough, they would have known that the skin wouldn't have been so white but for a Dublin childhood, bread and margarine, cramped, carbonated air. The feet with the miniature half-moon scar on the right instep would have told, eloquently, of a summer spent on Laytown Strand, of barefoot walks on a hot beach, of sharded glass and poppies of blood on the summer sand. And the bulge of muscle round the right shoulder would have testified to two years' hod-carrying, just as the light, nervous lines across the forehead proclaimed the lessons of an acquisitive metropolis, the glazed eyes themselves demonstrating the failure, the lessons not learnt. All the ill-assorted group of bathers did was pull their towels more rigidly about them, noting the body's glaring pubes, imagining the hair (blond, maybe) and the skin of the girls that first brought them to life; the first kiss and the indolent smudges of lipstick and all the subsequent kisses, never quite recovering the texture of the first. They saw the body and didn't hear the finer details – just heard that it had been born, had grown and suffered much pain and a little joy; that its dissatisfaction had been deep; and they thought of the green bridge and the red-bricked walls and understood —

He savoured his isolation for several full minutes. He

allowed the cold to seep fully through him, after the heat of clothes, sunlight. He saw pale, rising goose-pimples on the mirrored flesh before him. When he was young he had been in the habit of leaving his house and walking down to a busy sea-front road and clambering down from the road to the mud-flats below. The tide would never quite reach the wall and there would be stretches of mud and stone and the long sweep of the cement wall with the five-foot-high groove running through it where he could sit, and he would look at the stone, the flat mud and the dried cakes of sea-lettuce and see the tide creep over them and wonder at their impassivity, their imperviousness to feeling; their deadness. It seemed to him the ultimate blessing and he would sit so long that when he came to rise his legs and sometimes his whole body would be numb. He stood now till his immobility, his cold, became near-agonizing. Then he walked slowly to the shower, pulled aside the plastic curtain and walked inside. The tiles had that dead wetness that he had once noticed in the beach-pebbles. He placed each foot squarely on them and saw a thin cake of soap lying in a puddle of grey water. Both were evidence of the bather before him and he wondered vaguely what he was like; whether he had a quick, rushed shower or a slow, careful one; whether he in turn had wondered about the bather before him. And he stopped wondering, as idly as he had begun. And he turned on the water.

It came hot. He almost cried with the shock of it; a cry of pale, surprised delight. It was a pet love with him, the sudden heat and the wall of water, drumming on his crown, sealing him magically from the world outside; from the universe outside; the pleasurable biting needles of heat; the ripples of water down his hairless arms; the stalactites gathering at each fingertip; wet hair, the sounds of caught breath and thumping water. He loved the pain, the total self-absorption of it and never wondered why he loved it; as with the rest of the weekly ritual – the trudge through the muted officialdom of the bath corridors into the solitude of the shower cubicle, the total ultimate solitude of the boxed,

sealed figure, three feet between it and its fellow; the contra-
dictory joy of the first impact of heat, of the pleasurable pain.

An overseer in an asbestos works who had entered his cubicle
black and who had emerged with a white, blotchy, greyish skin-hue
divined the reason for the cut wrists. He looked at the tiny
coagulation of wrinkles round each eye and knew that here was a
surfeit of boredom; not a moody, arbitrary, adolescent boredom, but
that boredom which is a condition of life itself. He saw the way the
mouth was tight and wistful and somehow uncommunicative, even
in death, and the odour of his first contact with that boredom came
back to him. He smelt again the incongruous fish-and-chip smells,
the smells of the discarded sweet wrappings, the metallic odour of
the fun-palace, the sulphurous whiff of the dodgem wheels; the
empty, musing, poignant smell of the seaside holiday town, for it
was here that he had first met his boredom; here that he had wandered
the green carpet of the golf-links, with the stretch of grey sky
overhead, asking, what to do with the long days and hours, turning
then towards the burrows and the long grasses and the strand,
deciding there's nothing to do, no point in doing, the sea glimmering
to the right of him like the dull metal plate the dodgem wheels ran
on. Here he had lain in a sand-bunker for hours, his head making a
slight indentation in the sand, gazing at the mordant procession of
clouds above. Here he had first asked, what's the point, there's only
point if it's fun, it's pleasure, if there's more pleasure than pain;
then thinking of the pleasure, weighing up the pleasure in his
adolescent scales, the pleasure of the greased fish-and-chip bag
warming the fingers, of the sweet taken from the wrapper, the
discarded wrapper and the fading sweetness, of the white flash of a
pubescent girl's legs, the thoughts of touch and caress, the pain of
the impossibility of both and his head digging deeper in the sand he
had seen the scales tip in favour of pain. Ever so slightly maybe, but
if it wins then what's the point. And he had known the sheep-white
clouds scudding through the blueness and ever after thought of them
as significant of the preponderance of pain; and he looked now at the
white scar on the young man's instep and thought of the white
clouds and thought of the bobbing girls' skirts and of the fact of
pain—

The first impact had passed; his body temperature had risen and the hot biting needles were now a running, massaging hand. And a silence had descended on him too, after the self-immersed orgy of the driving water. He knew this shower was all things to him, a world to him. Only here could he see this world, hold it in balance, so he listened to what was now the quietness of rain in the cubicle, the hushed, quiet sound of dripping rain and the green rising mist through which things are seen in their true, unnatural clarity. He saw the wet, flapping shower-curtain. There was a bleak rose-pattern on it, the roses faded by years of condensation into green: green roses. He saw the black spaces between the tiles, the plug-hole with its fading, whorling rivulet of water. He saw the exterior dirt washed off himself, the caked cement-dust, the flecks of mud. He saw creases of black round his elbow joints, a high-water mark round his neck, the more permanent, engrained dirt. And he listened to the falling water, looked at the green roses and wondered what it would be like to see those things, hear them, doing nothing but see and hear them; nothing but the pure sound, the sheer colour reaching him; to be as passive as the mud pebble was to that tide. He took the cake of soap then from the grilled tray affixed to the wall and began to rub himself hard. Soon he would be totally, bleakly clean.

There was a dash of paint on his cheek. The negro painter he worked beside had slapped him playfully with his brush. It was disappearing now, under pressure from the soap. And with it went the world, that world, the world he inhabited, the world that left grit under the nails, dust under the eyelids. He scrubbed at the dirt of that world, at the coat of that world, the self that lived in that world, in the silence of the falling water. Soon he would be totally, bleakly clean.

The old cockney took another ticket from another bather he thought he recognized. Must have seen him last week. He crumpled the ticket in his hand, went inside his glass-fronted office and impaled it onto a six-inch nail jammed through a block of wood. He flipped a cigarette from its packet and lit it, wheezing heavily. Long hours spent in the office here, the windows running with condensation, had exaggerated a bronchial condition. He let his eyes scan the seventeen cubicles. He wondered again how many of them, coming every week for seventeen weeks, have visited each of the seventeen showers. None, most likely. Have to go where they're told, don't they. No way they can get into a different box other than the one that's empty, even if they should want to. But what are the chances, a man washing himself ten years here, that he'd do the full round? And the chances that he'd be stuck to the one? He wrinkled his eyes and coughed and rubbed the mist from the window to see more clearly.

White, now. Not the sheer white of the tiles, but a human, flaccid, pink skin-white. He stood upwards, let his arms dangle by his sides, his wrists limp. His short black hair was plastered to his crown like a tight skull-cap. He gazed at the walls of his own cubicle and wondered at the fact that there were sixteen other cubicles around him, identical to this one, which he couldn't see. A man in each, washed by the same water, all in various stages of cleanliness. And he wondered, did the form in the next cubicle think of him, his neighbour, as he did. Did he reciprocate his wondering. He thought it somehow appropriate that there should be men naked, washing themselves in adjacent cubicles, each a foreign country to the other. Appropriate to what, he couldn't have said. He looked round his cubicle and wondered: what's it worth, what does it mean, this cubicle – wondered was any one of the other sixteen gazing at his cubicle and thinking, realizing as he was: nothing. He realized that he would never know.

Nothing. Or almost nothing. He looked down at his body; thin belly, thin arms, a limp member. He knew he had arrived at the point where he would masturbate. He always came to this point in different ways, with different thoughts, by different stages. But when he had reached it, he always realized that the ways had been similar, the ways had been the same way, only the phrasing different. And he began then, taking himself with both hands, caressing himself with a familiar, bleak motion, knowing that afterwards the bleakness would only be intensified after the brief distraction of feeling – in this like everything – observing the while the motion of his belly muscles, glistening under their sheen of running water. And as he felt the mechanical surge of desire run through him he heard the splashing of an anonymous body in the cubicle adjacent. The thought came to him that somebody could be watching him. But no, he thought then, almost disappointed, who could, working at himself harder. He was standing when he felt an exultant muscular thrill run through him, arching his back, straining his calves upwards, each toe pressed passionately against the tiled floor.

The young Trinidadian in the next cubicle squeezed out a sachet of lemon soft shampoo and rubbed it to a lather between two brown palms. Flecks of sawdust – he was an apprentice carpenter – mingled with the snow-white foam. He pressed two handfuls of it under each bicep, ladled it across his chest and belly and rubbed it till the foam seethed and melted to the colour of a dull whey, and the water swept him clean again, splashed his body back to its miraculous brown and he slapped each nipple laughingly in turn and thought of a clean body under a crisp shirt, of a night of love under a low red-lit roof, of the thumping symmetry of a reggae band.

There was one intense moment of silence. He was standing, spent, sagging. He heard:

'Hey, you rass, not finished yet?'

'How'd I be finished?'

'Well move that corpse, rassman. Move!'

He watched the seed that had spattered the tiles be swept by the shower-water, diluting its grey, ultimately vanishing into the fury of current round the plug-hole. And he remembered the curving cement wall of his childhood and the spent tide and the rocks and the dried green stretches of sea-lettuce and because the exhaustion was delicious now and bleak, because he knew there would never be anything but that exhaustion after all the fury of effort, all the expense of passion and shame, he walked through the green-rose curtain and took the cut-throat razor from his pack and went back to the shower to cut his wrists. And dying, he thought of nothing more significant than the way, the way he had come here, of the green bridge and the bowed figure under the brick wall and the façade of the Victorian bath-house, thinking: there is nothing more significant.

Of the dozen or so people who gathered to stare – as people will – none of them thought: Why did he do it? All of them, pressed into a still, tight circle, staring at the shiplike body, knew intrinsically. And a middle-aged, fat and possibly simple negro phrased the thought:

'Every day the Lord send me I think I do that. And every day the Lord send me I drink a bottle of wine and forget 'bout doin that.'

They took with them three memories: the memory of a thin, almost hairless body with reddened wrists; the memory of a thin, finely wrought razor whose bright silver was mottled in places with rust; and the memory of a spurting shower-nozzle, an irregular drip of water. And when they emerged to the world of bright afternoon streets they saw the green-painted iron bridge and the red-brick wall and knew it to be in the nature of these, too, that the body should act thus—

Bernard MacLaverty

Between Two Shores

IT WAS dark and he sat with his knees tucked up to his chin, knowing there was a long night ahead of him. He had arrived early for the boat and sat alone in a row of seats wishing he had bought a paper or a magazine of some sort. He heard a noise like a pulse from somewhere deep in the boat. Later he changed his position and put his feet on the floor.

For something to do he opened his case and looked again at the presents he had for the children. A painting by numbers set for the eldest boy of the *Laughing Cavalier*, for the three girls, dolls, horizontal with their eyes closed, a blonde, a redhead and a brunette to prevent fighting over who owned which. He had also bought a trick pack of cards. He bought these for himself but he didn't like to admit it. He saw himself amazing his incredulous, laughing father after dinner by turning the whole pack into the seven of clubs or whatever else he liked by just tapping them as the man in the shop had done.

The trick cards would be a nice way to start a conversation if anybody sat down beside him, so he put them on top of his clothes in the case. He locked it and slipped it off the seat, leaving it vacant. Other people were beginning to come into the lounge lugging heavy cases. When they saw him sitting in the middle of the row they moved on to find another. He found their Irish accents grating and flat.

He lit a cigarette and as he put the matches back in his pocket his fingers closed around his wife's present. He took it out, a small jeweller's box, black with a domed top. As he clicked back the lid he saw again the gold against the red satin and thought it beautiful. A locket was something permanent, something she could keep for ever. Suddenly his stomach reeled at the thought. He tried to put it out of his mind, snapping the box shut and putting it in his breast pocket. He got up and was about to go to the bar when he saw how the place was filling up. It was Thursday and the Easter rush had started. He would sit his ground until the boat moved out. If he kept his seat and got a few pints inside him he might sleep. It would be a long night.

A middle-aged couple moved into the row – they sounded like they were from Belfast. Later an old couple with a mongol girl sat almost opposite him. The girl was like all mongols. It was difficult to tell her age – anywhere between twenty and thirty. He thought of moving away to another seat to be away from the moist, open mouth and the beak nose but it might have hurt the grey-haired parents. It would be too obvious, so he nodded a smile and just sat on.

The note of the throbbing engine changed and the lights on the docks began to move slowly past. He had a free seat in front of him and he tried to put his feet up but it was just out of reach. The parents took their mongol daughter 'to see the big ship going out' and he then felt free to move. He found the act of walking strange on the moving ship.

He went to the bar and bought a pint of stout and took it out on to the deck. Every time he travelled he was amazed at the way they edged the huge boat out of the narrow channel – a foot to spare on each side. Then the long wait at the lock gates. Inside, the water flat, roughed only by the wind – out there the waves leaping and chopping, black and slate grey in the light of the moon. Eventually they were away, the boat swinging out to sea and the wind rising, cuffing him on the side of the head. It was cold now and he turned to go in. On a small bench on the open deck he saw a bloke laying out his sleeping bag and sliding down inside it.

He had several more pints in the bar sitting on his own, moving his glass round the four metal indentations. There were men and boys with short hair, obviously British soldiers. He thought how sick they must be having to go back to Ireland at Easter. There was a nice looking girl sitting alone reading with a rucksack at her feet. She looked like a student. He wondered how he could start to talk to her. His trick cards were in the case and he had nothing with him. She seemed very interested in her book because she didn't even lift her eyes from it as she sipped her beer. She was nice looking, dark hair tied back, large dark eyes following the lines back and forth on the page. He looked at her body, then felt himself recoil as if someone had clanged a handbell in his ear and shouted 'unclean'. Talk was what he wanted. Talk stopped him thinking. When he was alone he felt frightened and unsure. He blamed his trouble on this.

In the beginning London had been a terrible place. During the day he had worked himself to the point of exhaustion. Back at the digs he would wash and shave and after a meal he would drag himself to the pub with the other Irish boys rather than sit at home. He drank at half the pace the others did and would have full pints on the table in front of him when closing time came. Invariably somebody else would drain them, rather than let them go to waste. Everyone but himself was drunk and they would roar home, some of them being sick on the way against a gable wall or up an entry. Some nights, rather than endure this, he sat in his bedroom even though the landlady had said he could come down and watch TV. But it would have meant having to sit with her English husband and their horrible son. Nights like these many times he thought his watch had stopped and he wished he had gone out.

Then one night he'd been taken by ambulance from the digs after vomiting all day with a pain in his gut. When he wakened they had removed his appendix. The man in the next bed was small, dark-haired, friendly. The rest of the ward had nicknamed him 'Mephisto' because of the hours he spent trying to do the crossword in *The Times*. He had never yet completed it. His attention had first been drawn to Nurse

Mitchell's legs by this little man who enthused about the shortness of her skirt, the black stockings with the seams, clenching and unclenching his fist. The little man's mind wandered higher and he rolled his small eyes in delight.

In the following days in hospital he fell in love with this Nurse Helen Mitchell. When he asked her about the funny way she talked she said she was from New Zealand. He thought she gave him special treatment. She nursed him back to health, letting him put his arm around when he got out of bed for the first time. He smelt her perfume and felt her firmness. He was astonished at how small she was, having only looked up at her until this. She fitted the crook of his arm like a crutch. Before he left he bought her a present from the hospital shop, of the biggest box of chocolates that they had in stock. Each time she came to his bed it was on the tip of his tongue to ask her out but he didn't have the courage. He had skirted round the question as she made the bed, asking her what she did when she was off duty. She had mentioned the name of a place where she and her friends went for a drink and sometimes a meal.

He had gone home to Donegal for a fortnight at Christmas to recover but on his first night back in London he went to this place and sat drinking alone. On the third night she came in with two other girls. The sight of her out of uniform made him ache to touch her. They sat in the corner not seeing him sitting at the bar. After a couple of whiskeys he went over to them. She looked up, startled almost. He started by saying, 'Maybe you don't remember me . . .'

'Yes, yes I do,' she said laying her hand on his arm. Her two friends smiled at him then went on talking to each other. He said that he just happened to be in that district, and remembered the name of the place and thought that he would have liked to see her again. She said yes, that he was the man who bought the *huge* box of chocolates. Her two friends laughed behind their hands. He bought them all a drink. And then insisted again. She said, 'Look I'm sorry I've forgotten your name,' and he told her and she introduced

him to the others. When time was called he isolated her from
the others and asked her if she would like to go out for a
meal some night and she said she'd love to.

On the Tuesday after carefully shaving and dressing he
took her out and afterwards they went back to the flat she
shared with the others. He was randy helping her on with
her coat at the restaurant, smelling again her perfume, but he
intended to play his cards with care and not rush things. But
there was no need, because she refused no move he made
and her hand was sliding down past his scar before he knew
where he was. He was not in control of either himself or her.
She changed as he touched her. She bit his tongue and hurt
his body with her nails. Dealing with the pain she caused
him saved him from coming too soon and disgracing himself.

Afterwards he told her that he was married and she said
that she knew but that it made no difference. They both
needed something. He asked her if she had done it with
many men.

'Many, many men,' she had replied, her New Zealand
vowels thin and hard like knives. Tracks of elastic banded
her body where her underwear had been. He felt sour and
empty and wanted to go back to his digs. She dressed and he
liked her better, then she made tea and they were talking
again.

Through the next months he saw her many times and
they always ended up on the rug before the electric fire and
each time his seed left him he thought the loss permanent
and irreplaceable.

This girl across the bar reminded him of her, the way she
was absorbed in her reading. His nurse, he always called her
that, had tried to force him to read books but he had never
read a whole book in his life. He had started several for her
but he couldn't finish them. He told lies to please her until
one day she asked him what he thought of the ending of one
she had given him. He felt embarrassed and childish about
being found out.

There were some young girls, hardly more than children,

drinking at the table across the bar from the soldiers. They were eyeing them and giggling into their vodkas. They had thick Belfast accents. The soldiers wanted nothing to do with them. Soldiers before them had chased it and ended up dead or maimed for life.

An old man had got himself a padded alcove and was in the process of kicking off his shoes and putting his feet up on his case. There was a hole in the toe of his sock and he crossed his other foot over it to hide it. He remembered an old man telling him on his first trip always to take his shoes off when he slept. Your feet swell when you sleep, he had explained.

The first time leaving had been the worst. He felt somehow it was for good, even though he knew he would be home in two or three months. He had been up since dark getting ready. His wife was frying him bacon and eggs, tiptoeing back and forth putting the things on the table, trying not to wake the children too early. He came up behind her and put his arms round her waist, then moved his hands up to her breasts. She leaned her head back against his shoulder and he saw that she was crying, biting her lip to stop. He knew she would do this, cry in private but she would hold back in front of the others when the mini bus came.

'Don't,' she said. 'I hear Daddy up.'

That first time the children had to be wakened to see their father off. They appeared outside the house tousle-headed and confused. A mini bus full of people had pulled into their yard and their Granny and Granda were crying. Handshaking and endless hugging watched by his wife, chalk pale, her forearms folded against the early morning cold. He kissed her once. The people in the mini bus didn't like to watch. His case went on the pryamid of other cases and the mini bus bumped over the yard away from the figures grouped around the doorway.

The stout had gone through him and he got up to go to the lavatory. The slight swaying of the boat made it difficult to walk but it was not so bad that he had to use the handles above the urinals. Someone had been sick on the floor, Guinness sick. He looked at his slack flesh held between his fingers at the place where the sore had been. It had all but disappeared. Then a week ago his nurse had noticed it. He had thought nothing of it because it was not painful. She asked him who else he had been sleeping with – insulting him. He had sworn he had been with no one. She explained to him how they were like minute corkscrews going through the whole body. Then she admitted that it must have been her who had picked it up from someone else.

'If not me, then who?' he had asked.

'Never you mind,' she replied. 'My life is my own.'

It was the first time he had seen her concerned. She came after him as he ran down the stairs and implored him to go to a clinic, if not with her, then on his own. But the thought of it terrified him. He had listened to stories on the site of rods being inserted, burning needles and worst of all a thing which opened inside like an umbrella and was forcibly dragged out again. On Wednesday the landlady had said someone had called at the digs looking for him and said he would call back. But he made sure he was out that night and this morning he was up and away early buying presents before getting on the train.

He zipped up his fly and stood looking at himself in the mirror. He looked tired – the long train journey, the sandwiches, smoking too many cigarettes to pass the time. A coppery growth was beginning on his chin. He remembered her biting his tongue, the tearing of her nails, the way she changed. He had not seen her since.

Only once or twice had his wife been like that – changing that way. He knew she would be like that tomorrow night. It was always the same the first night home. But afterwards he knew that it was her, his wife. Even though it was taut with lovemaking her face had something of her care for his children, of the girl and woman, of the kitchen, of dances, of their walks together. He knew who she was as they devoured each other on the creaking bed. In the Bible they knew each other.

Again his mind shied away from the thought. He went out on to the deck to get the smell of sick from about him. Beyond the rail it was black night. He looked down and could see the white bow wave crashing away off into the dark. Spray tipped his face and the wind roared in his ears. He took a deep breath but it did no good. Someone threw a bottle from the deck above. It flashed past him and landed in the water. He saw the white of the splash but heard nothing above the throbbing of the ship. The damp came through to his elbows where he leaned on the rail and he shivered.

He had thought of not going home, of writing to his wife to say that he was sick. But it seemed impossible for him not to do what he had always done. Besides she might have come to see him if he had been too sick to travel. Now he wanted to be at home among the sounds that he knew. Crows, hens clearing their throats and picking in the yard, the distant bleating of sheep on the hill, the rattle of a bucket handle, the slam of the back door. Above all he wanted to see the children. The baby, his favourite, sitting on her mother's knee, her tulle nightdress ripped at the back, happy and chatting at not having to compete with the others. Midnight and she the centre of attention. Her voice, hoarse and precious after wakening, talking as they turned the pages of the catalogue of toys they had sent for, using bigger words than she did during the day.

A man with a woollen cap came out on to the deck and leaned on the rail not far away. A sentence began to form in his mind, something to start a conversation. You couldn't talk about the dark. The cold, he could say how cold it was. He waited for the right moment but when he looked round the man was away, high stepping through the doorway.

He followed him in and went to the bar to get a drink before it closed. The girl was still there reading. The other girls were falling about and squawking with laughter at the slightest thing. They were telling in loud voices about former nights and about how much they could drink. Exaggerations. Ten vodkas, fifteen gin and tonic. He sat down opposite the girl reading and when she looked up from her book he smiled at her. She acknowledged the smile and looked quickly down at her book again. He could think of nothing important enough to say to interrupt her reading. Eventually when the bar closed she got up and left without looking at him. He watched the indentation in the cushioned moquette return slowly to normal.

He went back to his seat in the lounge. The place was smoke-filled and hot and smelt faintly of feet. The mongol was now asleep. With his eyes closed he became conscious of the heaving motion of the boat as it climbed the swell. She had said they were like tiny corkscrews. He thought of them boring into his wife's womb. He opened his eyes. A young woman's voice was calling incessantly. He looked to see. A toddler was running up and down the aisles playing.

'Ann-Marie, Ann-Marie, Ann-Marie! Come you back here!'

Her voice rose annoyingly, sliding up to the end of the name. He couldn't see where the mother was sitting. Just a voice annoying him. He reached out his feet again to the vacant seat opposite and found he was still too short. To reach he would have to lie on his back. He crossed his legs and cradled his chin in the heart of his hand.

Although they were from opposite ends of the earth he was amazed that her own childhood in New Zealand should have sounded so like his own. The small farm, the greenness, the bleat of sheep, the rain. She had talked to him, seemed interested in him, how he felt, what he did, why he could not do something better. He was intelligent – sometimes. He had liked the praise but was hurt by its following jibe. She had a lot of friends who came to her flat – arty crafty ones, and when he stayed to listen to them he felt left outside. Sometimes in England his Irishness made him feel like a leper. They talked about books, about people he had never heard of and whose names he couldn't pronounce, about God and the Government.

One night at a party with ultra-violet lights someone with rings on his fingers had called him 'a noble savage'. He didn't know how to take it. His first impulse was to punch him, but up till that he had been so friendly and talkative – besides it was too Irish a thing to do. His nurse had come to his rescue and later in bed she had told him he must *think*. She had playfully struck his forehead with her knuckles at each syllable.

'Your values all belong to somebody else,' she had said.

He felt uncomfortable. He was sure he hadn't slept. He changed his position but then went back to cupping his chin. He must sleep.

'Ann-Marie, Ann-Marie.' She was loose again. By now they had turned the lights down in the lounge. The place was full of slumped bodies. The rows were back to back and some hitch-hikers had crawled on to the flat floor beneath the apex. He took his raincoat for a pillow and crawled into the free space behind his own row. Horizontal he might sleep. It was like a tent and he felt nicely cut off. In the next row some girls sat, not yet asleep. One was just at the level of his head and when she leaned forward to whisper her sweater rode up and bared a pale crescent of her lower back. Pale downy hairs moving into a seam at her backbone. He closed his eyes but the box containing the locket bit into his side. He turned and tried to sleep on his other side.

One night when neither of them could sleep his wife had said to him, 'Do you miss me when you're away?'

He said yes.

'What do you do?'

'Miss you.'

'I don't mean that. Do you do anything about it? Your missing me.'

'No.'

'If you ever do, don't tell me about it. I don't want to know.'

'I never have.'

He looked once or twice to see the girl's back but she was huddled up now sleeping. As he lay the floor increased in hardness. He lay for what seemed all night, his eyes gritty and tense, conscious of his discomfort each time he changed his position. The heat became intolerable. He sweated and felt it thick like blood on his brow. He wiped it dry with a handkerchief and looked at it to see. He was sure it must be morning. When he looked at his watch it said three o'clock. He listened to it to hear if it had stopped. The loud tick seemed to chuckle at him. His nurse had told him this was the time people died. Three o'clock in the morning. The dead hour. Life at its lowest ebb. He believed her. Walking the dimly lit wards she found the dead.

Suddenly he felt claustrophobic. The back of the seats closed over his head like a tomb. He eased himself out. His back ached and his bladder was bursting. As he walked he felt the boat rise and fall perceptibly. In the toilet he had to use the handrail. The smell of sick was still there.

How could his values belong to someone else? He knew what was right and what was wrong. He went out on to the deck again. The wind had changed or else the ship was moving at a different angle. The man who had rolled himself in his sleeping bag earlier in the night had disappeared. The wind and the spray lashed the seat where he had been sleeping. Tiny lights on the coast of Ireland winked on and off. He moved round to the leeward side for a smoke. The girl who had earlier been reading came out on deck. She mustn't have been able to sleep either. All he wanted was someone to sit and talk to for an hour. Her hair was untied now and she let it blow in the wind, shaking her head from side to side to get it away from her face. He sheltered his glowing cigarette in the heart of his hand. Talk would shorten the night. For the first time in his life he felt his age, felt older than he was. He was conscious of the droop in his shoulders, his unshaven chin, his smoker's cough. Who would talk to him – even for an hour? She held her white raincoat tightly round herself, her hands in her pockets. The tail flapped furiously against her legs. She walked towards the prow, her head tilted back. As he followed her, in a sheltered alcove he saw the man in the sleeping bag, snoring, the drawstring of his hood knotted round his chin. The girl turned and came back. They drew level.

'That's a cold one,' he said.

'Indeed it is,' she said, not stopping. She was English. He had to continue to walk towards the prow and when he looked over his shoulder she was gone. He sat on an empty seat and began to shiver. He did not know how long he sat but it was better than the stifling heat of the lounge. Occasionally he walked up and down to keep the life in his feet. Much later going back in he passed an image of himself in a mirror, shivering and blue lipped, his hair wet and stringy.

In the lounge the heat was like a curtain. The sight reminded him of a graveyard. People were meant to be straight, not tilted and angled like this. He sat down determined to sleep. He heard the tremble of the boat, snoring, hushed voices. Ann-Marie must have gone to sleep – finally. That guy in the sleeping bag had it all worked out – right from the start. He had a night's sleep over him already. He tilted his watch in the dim light. The agony of the night must soon end. Dawn would come. His mouth felt dry and his stomach tight and empty. He had last eaten on the train. It was now six o'clock.

Once he had arranged to meet his nurse in the Gardens. It was early morning and she was coming off duty. She came to him starched and white, holding out her hands as she would to a child. Someone tapped him on the shoulder but he didn't want to look round. She sat beside him and began to stroke the inside of his thigh. He looked around to see if anyone was watching. There were two old ladies close by but they seemed not to notice. The park bell began to clang and the keepers blew their whistles. They must be closing early. He put his hand inside her starched apron to touch her breasts. He felt warm moistness, revolting to the touch. His hand was in her entrails. The bell clanged incessantly and became a voice over the Tannoy.

'Good morning, ladies and gentlemen. The time is seven o'clock. We dock at Belfast in approximately half an hour's time. Tea and sandwiches will be on sale until that time. We hope you have enjoyed your . . .'

He sat up and rubbed his face. The woman opposite, the mongol's mother, said good morning. Had he screamed out? He got up and bought himself a plastic cup of tea, tepid and weak, and some sandwiches, dog-eared from sitting over-night.

It was still dark outside but now the ship was full of the bustle of people refreshed by sleep, coming from the bath-rooms with toilet bags and towels, whistling, slamming doors. He saw one man take a tin of polish from his case and begin to shine his shoes. He sat watching him, stale crusts in his hand. He went out to throw them to the gulls and watch the dawn come up.

He hadn't long to go now. His hour had come. It was funny the way time worked. If time stopped he would never reach home and yet he loathed the ticking, second by second slowness of the night. The sun would soon be up, the sky was bleaching at the horizon. What could he do? Jesus what could he do? If he could turn into spray and scatter himself on the sea he would never be found. Suddenly it occurred to him that he *could* throw himself over the side. That would end it. He watched the water sluicing past the dark hull forty feet below. 'The spirit is willing but the flesh is weak.' If only someone would take the whole thing away how happy he would be. For a moment his spirits jumped at the possibility of the whole thing disappearing – then it was back in his stomach heavier than ever. He put his face in his hands. Somehow it had all got to be hammered out. He wondered if books would solve it. Read books and maybe the problems won't seem the same. His nurse had no problems.

The dark was becoming grey light. They must have

entered the Lough because he could see land now on both sides, like arms or legs. He lit a cigarette. The first of the day – more like the sixty-first of yesterday. He coughed deeply, held it a moment then spat towards Ireland but the wind turned it back in the direction of England. He smiled. His face felt unusual.

He felt an old man broken and tired and unshaven at the end of his days. If only he could close his eyes and sleep and forget. His life was over. Objects on the shore began to become distinct through the mist. Gasometers, chimney-stacks, railway trucks. They looked washed out, a putty grey against the pale lumps of the hills. Cars were moving and then he made out people hurrying to work. He closed his eyes and put his head down on his arms. Indistinctly at first, but with growing clarity, he heard the sound of an ambulance.

Mary Beckett

Heaven

To Hilary in her sixties, heaven was an empty house.
She loved to come in from shopping and shut the door
behind her knowing that there was nobody in any of the
seven neat rooms and that nobody would arrive home until
her husband did, shortly after six. A daughter-in-law might
wish to call on her for some service but she had insisted from
the beginning that they telephone first to arrange a suitable
time. She noticed sometimes her opposite neighbour being
visited by people who turned the key in the door and walked
in. That, to Hilary, would have been intolerable. Occasionally
someone said to her that she must be lonely with her four
sons grown and gone. She smiled and murmured something
about keeping busy and anyway when her sons were healthy
and happy that was all that mattered.

She had appeared always as a devoted mother. When
she was young her pram had been polished, the pillow
immaculate, the blankets fluffy, the baby perfect. The nappies
on the line were white and square like a television advertisement. The standard in the district was high except for a few
unfortunate backsliders but Hilary was out on her own. Her
little boys playing with the other children got dirty in the
normal way but it was obviously newly acquired dirt on clean
clothes, not general grubbiness. She was fortunate perhaps
in that they all had her blonde pink and white appearance.
None of them had inherited their father's dark hair and
shadowed skin although they were tall like him and thin.
Hilary often said then that she should slim but instead she
dressed in drifty floaty clothes, and before hats went out of

fashion she wore black gauzy hats with red cherries, or pink hats with veils or green hats with roses. She dressed up every afternoon to wheel out the pram and do the shopping. Some of the neighbours admired her style, and others criticized that but admitted she had great spirit.

The effort of all this perfectionism drained her each day so that when the children were eventually in bed she sat down by the fire and her husband sat in the opposite chair. She glanced at magazines and ate sweets and sighed or yawned every now and again. He read the papers in their entirety and switched the television from snowy channel to foggy channel and back so that it blared all evening until it closed down for the night. At least then the noise came from one place only. Later, when the boys were in their teens, Hilary had to tolerate transistors in bedrooms and tape-recorders as well as the television and record-player. So long as she stayed in her kitchen she had some slight refuge but it was there that the younger boys brought their troubles with sums, or spellings to hear or Irish passages to learn, while the older ones brought their complaints about unfair teachers or biased referees.

These worried her. It upset her to see their soft curved mouths drawn down in ugly resentment. She tried to persuade them not to feel aggrieved so readily, that it would become a habit and give them indigestion. She had to laugh them out of it because they would have been very embarrassed if she had confessed that she feared the harm it would do their souls. She never said such things to anyone. The only time she spoke out was at a parents' meeting once in the boys' school. There had been an alarming increase in rugby injuries to boys' spines, not in the school but in the country generally, news of brilliant boys paralysed for life. Some of the parents asked the priests who ran the school how their boys were safeguarded. The priests marshalled reassurances and the parents failed to put forward sensible objections. Hilary said she thought rugby an uncivilized game anyway, and the rivalry between schools concerning rugby and between the priests involved was completely unchristian. There was a murmur of dissent and then several men shouted no, no.

'If anything happens to any of my boys on the rugby field,' Hilary persisted, 'I will go and howl outside the priests' house day and night.'

The other parents laughed but Hilary did not laugh and the priests did not really laugh either and none of her boys made much progress at rugby from that time on.

They did well at everything else, though, much better in their exams than their teachers ever expected going by their class marks and by their judgements to Hilary during parent–teacher meetings. They went to university and there followed years of counting every penny to keep them there, of going without new clothes, of wearing cheap shoes long after they were broken and spread. Her husband had to keep his old car when it was a daily torment of refusing to start in the mornings or even at traffic lights, and people pushing it and looking as if they might get heart attacks. But they did well so that their father often wondered aloud how far he too might have gone in this world if he had had the chances they were getting. Hilary never had such thoughts about herself. She fed them nourishing food morning and night, worried about their not having enough sleep, listened to their panic about exams, and to relieve the terrible feelings of impotence she had about them began going to Mass every morning to pray for their success. Then they were all finished, all with jobs except the youngest who was awarded a grant to do a PhD in an American university and insisted on marrying before he went, to his father's disgust. He fumed and fussed and denounced it as lunatic but Hilary was relieved because she had read novels about American universities and she could hardly believe such depravity existed. A wife would keep him safe.

Even before the others married she found herself alone in the house for long hours during the day. At first she would stand in the hall with her hands clasped, looking into empty rooms and wondering how she would celebrate. She generally finished up making herself tea and cake or eating a bar of chocolate with a feeling that there was something she was missing. Gradually she realized that this was not an occasional luxury, this solitude, but a routine. So she fixed a time every morning to sit and relish the quiet. As the days passed she grew more intense about it so that frequently the blood surged in her ears and she was whirled into a great cone of silence and stayed there suspended. She had no thoughts, no contemplations. She was not aware of the happiness it induced until she resumed her household activities and found herself smiling. She began hurrying home in the mornings to shut herself in. Only years of discipline insisted that she cleaned, washed and cooked as she always did. Sometimes the silence caught her up out of doors so that she drifted past people without seeing them or speaking to them.

She began thinking of heaven. She imagined deep silence. Innumerable people stood in rapture, no one touching another, backed and divided by pillars and arches as in Renaissance paintings, drawn, she supposed, to God whom she could not imagine, but still and complete in themselves. She was confident she was going there, seeing herself as a middle-aged to elderly ewe in the middle of the flock giving no trouble at all to the shepherd. She had never had any great temptations; she was unlikely, she thought, to have any now. At funeral Masses she happily saw herself as the dead person and arranged in her mind how things should be done about food, flowers and cars. No one would miss her, she had done all that had been asked of her, she could fade out any time.

She did do baby-sitting for the grandchildren whenever she was asked, until her eldest son took his wife off for a holiday to celebrate her getting a job and left their three-year-old boy with Hilary for a fortnight. By the end of the first week she was consumed by the same desire for perfection in everything to do with this grandson as with her sons more than twenty years before. His hair must shine, his teeth must gleam, his clothes must grace his little straight sturdy body. When she watched him concentrating on a toy she contemplated the possibility of his being lonely at any time in the future or unhappy or unsuccessful and could hardly bear the pain. When her son came to collect him he congratulated her on the child's fine appearance.

'It'll be all right to leave him round on Monday morning when Pauline and I are going to work, won't it?' he asked casually, and Hilary said, 'No, not at all,' sharply, and then made excuses that she was too old, that he'd be better in his own home with someone in to look after him. 'We don't know anybody suitable,' her son protested. 'It's risky to let in someone we don't know. She might not care for him properly.'

'He is your child,' she said tartly. 'He is your responsibility, yours and Pauline's. You cannot shift it on to me. You'll just have to pay somebody well and hope for the best.'

He seized on that. 'But we have every intention of paying you. Of course we had. You mustn't think . . .'

'How much would you have thought of? Five pounds a week? No, no, no, money wouldn't make any difference.'

They had actually thought that if there were any question of money they should offer twenty pounds a month – it would be better paid by the month – but that indeed it was unlikely she would take any money. What would she want money for? She never bought anything except just the necessary food. She would be so glad of the child's company during her long empty day. He would give her a fresh interest in life and they'd pick him up most evenings after work.

They did not forgive her. The child was left in a playschool in the mornings and collected by a neighbour who minded him with her own children until his parents came home. It was not satisfactory, really. Hilary, after a week or two of sleepless nights, managed to put him out of her mind most of the time. A year later, tidying a drawer, she came across a silly affectionate birthday card given to her by one of her sons when he was young and felt a pang. It was nice after all when she was of use to them so that they loved her.

One morning her husband opened a letter that made him laugh first and then angered him.

'What is it?' she said with only a polite interest. He hesitated for a minute and then handed it over. It said:

> Dear Sir,
> You should know your wife is an alcoholic. She is being talked about all over the district. She hurries home in the morning without talking to her neighbours and shuts herself in the house. Some of these days she will disgrace you.
>
> Signed
> A Wellwisher

She was alarmed, even though the letter-writer had mistaken the object of her addiction.

'I shouldn't have shown it to you,' he said, looking at her in surprise. 'It's upset you. Sure we all know you drink nothing but coffee and tea, although you drink plenty of them. It's only some crank.' He was watching her, though, and when he came home from work he continued to watch her. He suggested they go for a walk. She refused, murmuring something about tired feet. The next night he thought they should go for a drive. She hadn't been in the car for years except for Sunday Mass or Friday-night shopping.

'What would we do that for?' she asked, embarrassed. 'It's threatening rain.' The attention unnerved her, making it more difficult for her to escape into silence, but she could cope so long as he was there only in the evening.

Then he retired. She had known for years the date of his retirement but refused to face it, as did he.

He would give full attention to the garden, he said, and he tramped in and out of her kitchen, needing water when she was at the sink, wanting her hand to hold a line for beds he was digging. He grunted and groaned and held his hand to the small of his long back. He didn't enjoy it. He had no company. His dark face grew more and more saturnine. Hilary dreaded coming home to him. He had stopped watching her but he continued the recent invitations to walks, drives, meals out. They were no longer a lifeline for her but for himself. She refused, regardless. She had always an excuse; she was tired, she had no clothes. She had never revived her interest in clothes, suppressed while the money was needed for her growing family. She wore black trousers with an elastic waistband and any kind of tunic on top. He urged her to buy something else but she put it off.

One rainy day, when he was sitting in the kitchen rubbing continuously at the threadbare places on the knees of his trousers, he asked, 'Hilary, why did you marry me?'

'Such a thing to ask, out of the blue,' she said, taken aback. 'Have you nothing better to think about than ancient history?'

'It's not ancient history. Whatever there was then surely keeps on now. You don't love me now; you can't stand me around the place. Did you love me ever, that's what I want to know? That's what I have to know.'

'For goodness' sake, it's just that I'm not used to somebody under my feet in the daytime. You're miserable yourself – you should think of something to get you out among other men.'

'You're not answering me.' He kept on so that she snapped at him, 'And I'm not going to answer you. How can I remember what it was like when I was young?'

He said no more but sat there, hunched.

She was uncomfortable, remembering clearly what it was like to see her twenties speeding by, and in spite of her blonde hair and pink cheeks and Ballybunion and Salthill and Tramore and numerous escorts nobody had offered to marry her. She had seized on the prospect of marriage with him as the only way to a real life – her old life had no sense or meaning. They had been well suited, neither until now interested in the other. She had had her children, her house and then her silence. He had had his job and his children to a certain extent. Now he had nothing and, she thought indignantly, he was busy seeing that she'd have nothing either.

While he was about the house she never sat down until nighttime. She polished and cleaned things that were already shining. She hovered over the cooker as it cooked their simple meals. He was either in the kitchen reading his paper or in and out of the garden. His breathing banished silence from the house. The smallest sounds impinged on her – the gentle bong of a Venetian blind upstairs at an open window, the click of a thermostat in the bathroom as it turned itself on or off, the ticking of clocks all over the house, unsynchronized.

Before the winter set in she told the priest at her monthly Confession, 'I have feelings of hatred for my husband, murderous feelings. I am afraid I will do him an injury – I have carving knives and heavy casseroles in the kitchen.' The priest told her to pray about it, to see a doctor, to get a hobby for herself or her husband. 'But,' he warned her, 'don't let hatred enter into your soul or you'll be fighting it until your dying day.' She was afraid then of losing her peace in heaven as well as the peace in her home. All the beautiful broad shining avenues of silence would be shut off from her and she would be condemned to some shrieking cacophonous pit.

She urged the buying of a garden shed and a greenhouse to occupy him. He was not enthusiastic about them but he consented after long deliberations on the back mat over where they were to go and then what was to go in them. She tried putting a chair in the shed and bringing out his morning coffee and afternoon tea, but she could not put him out of her mind. Every time she glanced out of the window she could see his shape, stooped. She could even see the sun sparkling on the drip at the end of his nose.

She resigned herself and rang up her daughters-in-law. 'I will mind your children after playschool,' she told them.

'I need my mornings for messages and housework but I'll have them on a regular basis from lunchtime until you come home from work. I don't want any money for it. Their grandfather can collect them. He'll help me with them. I'll not find them too much for me while he is there.'

They were stiff. They were dubious. 'You would need to be sure you're not just using our children to cover your own loneliness,' Pauline said.

'I have never been lonely, Pauline, never in my life,' she answered mildly, so they allowed themselves to be persuaded and every afternoon five children aged between two and six invaded her life.

She had one of her sons go up to the roof-space and bring down all the toys and books stored there since his own childhood, and because there were no girls' playthings she produced her old green and rose-petalled hats so they could dress up. She put a load of builders' sand in the back garden and saw it tramped everywhere. She was vigilant that they didn't rub it into one another's eyes or use the spades as weapons. She hugged them when they cried and loved their hot damp foreheads pressing into her neck. After their tea she sorted them out from the debris, packed them into the car and her husband delivered them to their three separate homes. Apart from collecting and delivering the children he took no interest in them. When the elder son of his eldest son put his hand on his knee and said, 'Come on out and kick football, Grandfather,' he almost blushed but made an excuse and went up to the bathroom, no refuge with five children in the house. One evening he told her that he was tired of the arrangement, too old to suffer all those children. He would still act as chauffeur but he had met another grandfather at the playschool and they had decided to go to a bowling-green not far away on good afternoons and to a quiet pub if it rained. He would not be at home at that time for the foreseeable future. There were plenty of things to do for a retired man still active and alert. Hilary agreed, told him he was perfectly right, and sat down exhausted every evening when she had cleaned up the mess left by the children, far too tired to do anything but leaf through a magazine or glance now and then at her husband's choice of television programmes, six clear channels now, one always blaring.

Now and again, though, she did catch a distant glimpse of calm corridors and vaulted roofs all soundless and it gave her a feeling of great sweetness in anticipation.

Val Mulkerns

Memory and Desire

T HE TELEVISION people seemed to like him and that was
a new feeling he found exciting. Outside his own work
circle he was not liked, on the whole, although he had a
couple of lifelong friends he no longer cared for very much.
The sort of people he would have wished to be accepted by
found him arrogant, unfriendly, and not plain enough to be
encouraged as an oddity. His wealth made him attractive
only to the types he most despised. He was physically gross
and clumsy with none of the social graces except laughter.
Sometimes his jokes were good and communicable. More
often they were obscure and left him laughing alone as
though he were the last remaining inhabitant of an island.

Sometimes, indeed, he wondered if he spoke the same
language as most other people, so frequently were they
baffled if not positively repelled. He liked people generally,
especially physically beautiful people who seemed to him
magical as old gods. Sometimes he just looked at such people,
not listening or pretending to listen to what they said, and
then he saw the familiar expression of dislike and exclusion
passing across their faces and he knew he had blundered
again. Now for several weeks he had been among a closely
knit group who actually seemed to find his company agreeable. He knew nothing about television and seldom watched
it. But because his father's small glassmaking business had
blossomed under his hand and become an important element
in the export market, the television people thought a programme could be made out of his success story, a then-and-
now sort of approach which seemed to him banal in the

extreme. He had given his eventual consent because time so often hung on his hands now that expansion had progressed as far as was practical and delegation had left him with little to do except see his more lucrative contacts in Europe and the United States a couple of times a year.

The only work he would actually have enjoyed during these days was supervising the first efforts of young glass-blowers. Two of the present half-dozen were grandsons of his father's original men. At a time when traditional crafts were dying out everywhere or falling into strange (and probably passing) hands, this pleased him. He tried to show signs of his approval while keeping the necessary distance right from the boys' first day at work, but this was probably one of the few places left in Ireland where country boys were shy and backward still, and their embarrassment had been so obvious that nowadays he confined himself to reports on them from the foreman. It had been different in his father's time. The single cutter and the couple of blowers had become personal friends of his father and mother, living in the loft above the workshop (kept warm in winter by the kiln) and eating with the family in the manner of medieval apprentice craftsmen. During holidays from boarding school, they had become his friends too, gradually and naturally passing on their skills to him, and so listening without resentment to the new ideas on design he had in due course brought back with him from art school and from working spells in Sweden. Gradually over the years of expansion after his father's death he had grown away from the men. Now since the new factory had been built in Cork he knew very few of them any more.

The odd thing about the television people was that right from the beginning they had been unawed and called him Bernard, accepting that he had things to learn about their business and that he would stay with them in the same guest-house, drink and live with them during the shooting of the film, almost as though they were his family and he an ordinary member of theirs. It had irritated and amused and baffled and pleased him in rapid progression and now he even found it hard to remember what his life had been like before them or how his days had been filled in. Their youth too had shocked him in the beginning; they seemed like children at play with dangerous and expensive toys. The director in particular (who was also the producer and therefore responsible for the whole idea) had in addition to a good-humoured boy's face an almost fatherly air of concern for his odd and not always biddable family. What was more remarkable, he could discipline them. The assistant cameraman who had got drunk and couldn't be wakened on the third day of the shooting had not done it again. When Eithne, the production assistant, had come down to breakfast one morning with a streaming cold and a raised temperature, Martin had stuffed a handful of her notes into the pocket of his jeans and sent her back up to bed, weeping and protesting that she was perfectly all right and not even her mother would dare to treat her like that.

Martin was very good with uncooperative fishermen, and with the farmer on whose land the original workshop still hung over the sea. A nearby hilly field had recently been sown with oats, and the farmer began with the strongest objection to a jeep laden with gear coming anywhere near it. He had agreed to it during preliminary negotiations, but shooting had in fact been delayed (delayed until more money became available) and that field, the farmer said, was in a delicate condition now. If they'd only come at the right time – Martin it was who finally talked him around with a guarantee against loss which would probably land him in trouble back in Dublin. But Martin (the Marvellous Boy was Bernard's private label for him) would worry about that one when he came to it and he advised Bernard to do the same about his fear of appearing ridiculous in some sequences. Not even half the stuff they were shooting would eventually be used, Martin said, and anyhow he'd give Bernard a preview at the earliest possible moment. Bernard stopped worrying again. Most of the time he had the intoxicating illusion of drifting with a strong tide in the company of excellent seamen and a captain who seemed to know his business.

The actual process of remembering was actually painful, of course. His only brother Tom had been swept away by a spring tide while fishing down on the rocks one day after school, and at first Bernard hadn't believed any reference to it would be possible when the script finally came to be written. Martin had come back to it casually again and again however, and finally one day of sharp March winds and flying patches of blue sky he had stood with Bernard on the headland near the roofless house.

'Let me show you what I have in mind,' Martin said gently, the south Kerry accent soft as butter. 'It will be very impressionistic, what I've in mind, a mere flash. A spin of sky and running tides, a moment. If you'd prefer, it won't need anything specific in the script. Just a reference to this friendly big brother mad about fishing, who knew about sea birds and seals and liked to be out by himself for hours on end. Maybe then, a single sentence about the nature of spring tides. The viewers generally won't know that spring tides have nothing to do with spring. You may say we're telling them about a successful glass industry, not about the sea, but the sea takes up a large part of your own early background and this piece is about you too. I'd write you a single sentence myself for your approval if you wouldn't mind – just to show you what I think would work – OK?'

'"These are pearls that were his eyes" – you could end like that, couldn't you?' Bernard heard himself sneering and almost at once regretted it. The director actually blushed and changed the subject. In a few seconds it was as if the moment had never happened, but it seemed to Bernard that a kind of bond had been perversely established.

Two days later a spring tide was running and he watched a few sequences being shot that might well be used for the passage he knew now he was going to write. He walked away from the crew when he found he could no longer watch the sort of sling from which the chief cameraman had been suspended above the cliffs to get some of the necessary angles. The whole thing could have been done better and more safely by helicopter but Martin had explained about the problems he had encountered after overrunning the budget for the last production. It wasn't of course that he wanted to make Bernard's backward look a cheaper affair; you often got a better end result (in his own experience) by using more ingenuity and less money: he thought he knew exactly how to do it. The somewhat unconvincing argument amused and didn't displease Bernard, who thought it more than likely that something less conventional might finally emerge. The last he saw of the crew was that crazy young man, clad as always when working in a cotton plaid shirt, suspending himself without benefit of the cameraman's sling to try to see exactly what the lens saw.

A fit of nervousness that had in it something of the paternal and something else not paternal at all made him walk the seven miles around to the next headland. He hadn't thought like a father for five years. For half of that isolated time he hadn't brought home casual male encounters either because nothing stable had ever emerged from them and more often than not he was put off by the jungle whiff of the predator and managed to change direction just in time. Now he tried to resist looking back at the pair of boys busy with their games which they apparently regarded as serious. The head cameraman was even younger than Martin. He had a fair freckled face and red hair so long that it would surely have been safer to tie it back in a girl's ponytail before swinging him out in that perilous contraption. Bernard turned his face again into the stiff wind and looked back at the receding insect wriggling above the foaming tide, man and technology welded together in the blasting sunlight. The weird shape drew back his eyes again and again until a rock they called the Billygoat's Missus cut it off and he was alone for (it seemed) the first time in several weeks.

For the first time as in a camera's framed eye he saw his own room at home. Tidy as a well-kept grave, it was full of spring light from the garden. There were daffodils on his desk. Spangles of light from the rocky pool outside danced on the Yeats canvas that took up most of one wall and struck sparks from the two early balloons which he treasured. Five poplars in a haze of young green marked the end of his garden. Beyond it, the sharp-breasted Great Sugarloaf and eventually the sea. The room had been tidy for five years now. No maddening litter of dropped magazines, no hairpins, no shoes kicked off and left where they fell: left for the woman next morning to carry to the appropriate place in the appropriate room because she was born to pick up the litter of other people's lives, paid for it as the only work she knew. One night in a fit of disgust he had kicked into the corner a black leather clog, left dead centre on the dark carpet awaiting the exact moment to catch his shin. Uncontrolled fits of violence he despised. Recovering quickly he had placed the shoes side by side outside the door as though this were an old-fashioned hotel with a dutiful boots in residence. She had come in laughing later on, both clogs held up incredulously in her hand, laughing and laughing, tossing them finally up in the air to fall where they might before she left the room. As perhaps she had done last night and would do again tomorrow. Wherever she was.

A rising wind drove before it into the harbour a flock of black clouds that had appeared from nowhere, and when drops of rain the size of old pennies began to lash down he sought refuge in the hotel which had been small and unpretentious in its comfort when he was a child. His father's clients had often stayed here. He had sometimes been sent on messages to them with his brother. Now the place had several stars from an international guide book and was famous both for its seafood and the prices that foreign gourmets were willing to pay for it.

He sat in the little bar full of old coastal maps and looked out at the sea; alone for the first time in two weeks he was no less content than in the casual company of the television people. Their young faces and their voices were still inside his head. As though on cue, Martin suddenly came through into the bar, also alone. The wind had made any more shooting too dangerous for today he said, and the girls had gone off to wash their hair. He had his fishing gear in the boot, but he doubted if he'd do much good today.

'Have lunch with me, then, and eat some fish instead,' Bernard invited, and was amused to see a flash of pure pleasure light up the director's face. Beer and a sandwich usually kept them going until they all sat down together at the end of the day.

'This place has got so much above itself even since the last time I was down here that I expect to be asked my business as soon as I set foot inside the door,' Martin grinned.

'They wouldn't do that in late March,' Bernard assured him. 'Neither the swallows nor the tourists have arrived yet, so I fancy even people in your state of sartorial decay would be encouraged.'

Martin took an imaginary clothes brush out of the jeans pocket (too tight to hold anything larger than a toothbrush) and began to remove stray hairs from that well-worn garment which had seaweedy stains in several places and looked slightly damp. The boy walked with a sort of spring, like a healthy cat, and there was no trace yet of the flab which his pint-drinking would eventually bring. He ate the bouilla-baisse and the fresh baked salmon which followed with the relish of a child brought out from boarding school for the day and determined to take full advantage of it. He praised the Alsace wine which was apparently new to him and Bernard decided that one of the great remaining pleasures of money was never to have to worry about the cost of anything one suddenly wanted to do. Bernard listened abstractedly to a little house politics over the coffee and then at the end of the first cognac he spoke one unwary line about buying all those bandy little boss men for a next birthday present for Martin should he wish it. The sea-reflecting blue eyes opposite him narrowed coldly for a moment before they closed in a bellow of laughter and the moment passed, like the rain outside.

The sea was too uneasy, however, in the whipping wind to yield anything, but Bernard remembered one good story about his dead brother on a long-ago trip to Kinsale. Martin made a note in biro on the back of the wrist which held his fishing rod and Bernard knew it would be transferred to the mounting heaps of papers back at the hotel. More and more in the course of the programme he was being his own production assistant.

Mr O'Connor had carried in a mountain of turf for the fire and Eithne rather liked to listen to the rattle of the rain outside by way of contrast. Her hair was dry by now but spread all over the hearthrug and she swung it back in a tickling blanket over the recumbent John D. who was still struggling with the *Irish Times* crossword.

'Give that over and sit up,' she said, fetching her eternal dice-throwing version of Scrabble which she had bought somewhere in Holland.

'I was just going to work out another angle for that last shot to put to Martin when he gets back.'

'Martin is probably half-way to France by now on an ebbing tide. We'll find his pathetic little bits and pieces in the morning.'

'Stop that!' John D. was superstitious as well as red-haired. He was nervous about things like that. 'All right, I'll give you three games and that's it.'

'Nice John D. Did you notice Bernard's face today when you were strung up over the cliff, by the way?'

'I had other things to worry about. Is "cadenza" allowed?'

'It's not English but I suppose it's in the OED like everything else – it's virtually been taken over, after all.'

'OK it's allowed.' John D. formed the word.

'But no *brio* or *allegro molto*,' Eithne warned.

'No *brio* or *allegro molto* – I haven't the makings of them anyhow. What sort of look did Bernard have on his unlovely mug?'

'A bit nervous for you, I think. I think that's why he walked away.'

'Arrogant bastard a lot of the time.' John D. swept up the dice after totting his score. 'Are capitalists human? You should put that theme to Martin some time.'

'More a Neville sort of line, surely? But I think you're wrong. He's shy and he's only just stopped being uneasy with us.'

'Just in time to say goodbye then,' said John D. with satisfaction. 'There's hardly a week in it, if the weather lifts a bit.'

'If,' Eithne said, scooping a single good score. It was her game, her thing, but the others always won. 'I think he's lonely, which only goes to show you money isn't everything.'

'You can be miserable in much more comfort though. He looks to me like a bod who's had it off wherever he pleased with one sex or t'other, despite his ugly mug. He has the brazen confidence you only get from too much money.'

'I think you're wrong and the death of his brother is still bothering him after all these years. It's something I just have a hunch about. And then of course his wife walked out on him a few years ago. Prime bitch they say she was too. He came home one night and found not as much as a hairclip left behind, and his baby gone too.'

'"Hunch" is not a permissible word all the same. Thirties slang,' said John D. with finality. 'Why wouldn't she walk out on him when he's probably given to buggery?'

'It's much more permissible than "cadenza". How about to hunch one's shoulders?'

'Go and ask Mr O'Connor if he has a dictionary then.'

'You go. My hair isn't dry yet.'

'Your hair is practically on fire, lady,' John D. said, settling himself comfortably on the hearthrug again. A car crunched in the sandy drive outside and Eithne gave a long sigh.

'Thank God. I couldn't have borne the smell of good country roast beef much longer.'

'There'll be frogs' eyes to follow.'

'At worst there'll be stewed apples, at best apple pie. Doesn't your nose tell you anything except whether a pint's good or bad?'

In out of the rain and the early dusk, Bernard was touched all over again by the sight of two apparent children playing a game beside the fire. He came over very willingly to join them when Eithne called and Martin went upstairs to look over his notes before dinner. He would call Evelyn on his way down, he said.

Later they all went in the pouring rain to the pub and listened while a couple of local Carusos rendered songs like 'Two Sweethearts' – one with hair of shining gold, the other with hair of grey – or the endless emigrant laments favoured by local taste. Whiskey chasing several pints made John D. a bit quarrelsome and he shouted for a song from Bernard just to embarrass him. To everybody's surprise, Bernard was not embarrassed. He stood up, supported only by two small Jamesons (the second of which he was still nursing) and gave the company a soft-voiced but not untuneful version of 'Carrigfergus' which was vociferously applauded by the locals and earned him delighted approval from the team. Eithne thought they ought maybe incorporate 'Carrigfergus' into the soundtrack, and John D. wanted to know why they couldn't all move up to Carrigfergus and let Bernard do his party piece with his back against the castle walls. This suggestion was received with the contempt it deserved, but Bernard wasn't discomfited.

That happened only when they got back to the guest-house and he heard Martin telling Mrs O'Connor that they would almost certainly be finished shooting by the end of the week and would hardly stay over the weekend. The sinking of the heart was like what came long ago with the necessity of facing back to school after the long summer holidays. He felt ashamed of his emotion and unsure how to conceal it, so he went up early to his room. Normally they would hang about for hours yet, reading the newspapers they hadn't had time for during the day, swapping stories, doing crossword puzzles, discussing the next day's work. Usually he didn't contribute much to the conversation; like a silent member of a big family he was simply there, part of what was going on, perfectly content to sit up as long as they did.

Now there was something symbolic about hearing the murmur of their voices from downstairs. The script had still to be written and there would be consultations in Dublin about it, hopefully with Martin, but (give or take a few days from now) the thing was over. Next week they would all be busy taking somebody else through his mental lumber-room. The little family would re-form itself around another fire, and it would have nothing to do with him. And soon it would be April, breeding lilacs out of the dead land, mixing memory and desire. Time perhaps to go away; he had promised himself a few weeks in April. On the other hand, why not stay on here?

He let down the small dormer window and looked out over the water. This house echoed, in almost exact detail, that other, roofless, house; the murmur of voices, even, was like his sisters' voices before they settled down for the night, all together in the big back bedroom. His own small room above the harbour used to be shared with his brother. The rain had stopped now and there was almost no sound from the sea and he wasn't surprised when Martin came to his door to say the weather forecast had been very good for the south-west and they might get in a full day's shooting tomorrow.

'Come in and have a nightcap,' he invited, and Martin said he wouldn't stay long but happily didn't refuse the brandy when it was taken from the wardrobe.

'What will you do next?' Bernard asked, just for a moment unsure of how to begin.

'A bit of a break before I join Current Affairs for a short stint,' the boy smiled. 'Yours is the last programme in the present series. No more now until next season.'

'You mean you're going to take a holiday?' He strove to

make his voice sound casual, although he was suddenly aware of the beating of his heart.

'Unless something untoward crops up, yes.'

'Why not join me in Greece, then, since that's where I'm heading next week or the week after? The place I have on Ios needs to be opened up after the winter and there's plenty of room I assure you. Also two local women waiting to cook and clean for us.' Bernard saw the refusal before it came; it was only a question of how it would be framed, how lightly he would be let down.

'It's a tempting offer, and there's nothing I'd enjoy more, all things being equal. Never been further than Corfu as a matter of fact. But my wife has organized a resident babysitter for the two boys and we're off on a busman's holiday to Canada as soon as I'm free. Laura is Canadian you know. I met her when I was training in London with the BBC. When we get back, maybe you'd come over for supper with us some evening? Laura's an unpredictable cook, but you'll agree that doesn't matter too much when you meet her. Is it a deal?'

He drained the glass and got up off Bernard's bed with the same catspring which was noticeable also in the way he walked.

'It's a deal. Many thanks. And maybe you'll both join me some time in Greece?'

Martin made the appropriate noises and didn't go at once, but started talking about a painter called Richard Dadd who (somebody had told him) had probably given Yeats his Crazy Jane themes. He hadn't seen the paintings himself at the Tate but Bernard had, so this kept them going until the door closed behind him, and on his youth, and on the hollow promise of knowing him as one knew every line of one's own hand. There was a lot of the night left and, fortunately, a lot of the brandy too.

The weather behaved as the weathermen said it would and the rest of the shooting went without a hitch. During this couple of weeks the year had turned imperceptibly towards summer, primroses in the land-facing banks, sea-pinks along the cliffs and an air about the television people that Bernard had seen before and couldn't quite place. Only when he went with them for the final day's shooting did he pin it down; a fairground the day after the circus. The television gear was more easily moved, of course; no long hours were needed for the pull-out. But the feeling was the same. They didn't believe him when he said he was staying on and they seemed shocked, which amused him, when he determinedly heaped presents on them the morning they were going: his Leica for Eithne who (incredibly) had never owned a camera of her own, a sheepskin jacket for John D. because his own was in flitters from the rocks, a silver brandy flask (circa 1840), a cigarette lighter and a gold biro scattered apparently at random among the rest. The vulgarity of the largesse amused Bernard himself because such behaviour was not usual and he didn't entirely understand his impulse. But he understood perfectly why he gave Martin his signed first edition of *The Winding Stair*, a volume which for a year or more had lived in the right-hand door-pocket of his car for no better reason than that he liked to have it there. He had bought it somewhere along the quays of Cork.

> 'Fair and foul are near of kin
> And fair needs foul,' I cried,
> 'My friends are gone and that's a truth
> Nor grave nor bed denied
> Learned in bodily loneliness,
> And in the heart's pride.'

A former owner had marked that with a small star in the margin, and Martin smiled slightly as he read it aloud in gratitude when the book fell open.

'I often have a disturbing feeling when I finish a job like this that I know –' he searched patiently for the words he wanted and his hesitation seemed to Bernard like comfort consciously given for some loss he could understand. 'That I know almost enough to begin all over again. Properly.' He didn't smile at all when they shook hands so that the handgrip seemed warmer. 'Until soon, in Dublin,' were his last words, a rather childish farewell which would have left a pleasant glow behind if Bernard had not known by now that they would not meet again. The vanful of technology went on ahead of the boy's unreliable little red sports car, and watching from the drive of the guesthouse, Bernard had the feeling of the fairground again after the circus caravans have rolled away. It was peaceful, though, with the blue sea breathing quietly all around him and a few mares' tails of cloud slowly unravelling in the sky.

He was leaning over the wall considering how he would fill his remaining time when the guesthouse owner strolled by, indicating the blue boat which bobbed at the end of its mooring rope below them. 'You could take the aul' boat out fishing any day you had a fancy for it, Mr Golden. You're more than welcome to her any time though I wouldn't recommend today, mind you.'

'I'm much obliged to you, Stephen. I have all the gear I need in the boot of the car so I might do just that. But why not today?'

'She'll rise again from the south-west long before evening,' his host said positively. 'And she'll blow herself out if I'm not mistaken. 'Twould be a dangerous thing to go fishing out there today.'

'The weather men last night didn't mention any gales blowing up.'

'The weather men don't live around this Hook either,' O'Connor said drily. 'I've caught those same gentlemen out once or twice, and will again with the help of God.'

'You might be right at that, I suppose. But if I do go out, I'll only fish for a short while, I promise you.'

A pleasant man, Stephen O'Connor, a retired Civic Guard with an efficient wife to make a business out of the beautiful location of their house and her own hard work. Bernard remembered him vaguely from childhood, pedalling wet and fine around the coast roads, stopping here and there for a chat, missing nothing. It was he who had brought the news that Tom's body had been washed ashore somewhere near Kinsale. It was he who had in fact identified it. On remembering this Bernard toyed with the idea of having an actual conversation with this kindly man whose memories touched his own at one black juncture. The moment passed, however, and Stephen made a little more chat, lingering with natural courtesy just long enough for a guest to make up his mind whether or not further company would be welcome, and then he ambled contentedly in the direction of the greenhouse for a day's pottering. Old man, old man, if you never looked down again at a drowned face of my father's house it would be time enough for you. Forgive me, Stephen O'Connor.

The first warm sun of the year touched Bernard's eyes and he smiled, sitting up on the sea wall. No more Aprils, no more lilacs breeding out of the dead land, no more carnal awakenings. He felt peaceful then a little surprised that the image behind his closed eyelids was not of his brother or of the young Martin or even of the caravans pulling out. It was the small wilful face of his daughter in the act of breaking away when one tried to hold her. He didn't know where she was, or even how she looked now, whether she still mirrored her mother in every gesture. He had a perfect right to know for the mere trouble of enforcing it. He hadn't done that, at first put off by the refusal of maintenance, by the eternal sound of the phone ringing in an empty flat and by two or three unanswered letters. He hadn't made a very energetic effort to keep in touch. As one year became two or three and now five, it had always seemed too late, but it would be untrue to pretend he greatly cared. It was just that, not being able to understand why the child's face should be so vivid in his mind, he was bothered as by some minor irritation, a door that slammed somewhere out of sight, a dripping tap. It wasn't until he was actually aboard the boat starting up the engine in a freshening breeze that he realized why he couldn't rid himself of his daughter's face today, of all days.

Mary Dorcey

The Husband

THEY MADE love then once more because she was leaving him. Sunlight came through the tall, Georgian window. It shone on the blue walls, the yellow paintwork, warming her pale blonde hair, the white curve of her closed eyelids. He gripped her hands, their fingers interlocked, his feet braced against the wooden footboard. He would have liked to break her from the mould of her body; from its set, delicate lines. His mouth at her shoulder, his eyes were hidden and he was glad to have his back turned on the room; from the bare dressing-table stripped of her belongings and the suitcase open beside the wardrobe.

Outside, other people were going to Mass. He heard a bell toll in the distance. A man's voice drifted up: 'I'll see you at O'Brien's later,' then the slam of a car door and the clatter of a woman's spiked heels hurrying on the pavement. All the usual sounds of Sunday morning rising distinct and separate for the first time in the silence between them. She lay beneath him, passive, magnanimous, as though she were granting him a favour, out of pity or gratitude because she had seen that he was not after all going to make it difficult for her at the end. He moved inside her body, conscious only of the sudden escape of his breath, no longer caring what she felt, what motive possessed her. He was tired of thinking, tired of the labour of anticipating her thoughts and concealing his own.

He knew that she was looking past him, over his shoulder towards the window, to the sunlight and noise of the street. He touched a strand of her hair where it lay along the pillow.

She did not turn. A tremor passed through his limbs. He felt the sweat grow cold on his back. He rolled off her and lay still, staring at the ceiling where small flakes of whitewash peeled from the moulded corners. The sun had discovered a spider's web above the door, like a square of grey lace its diamond pattern swayed in a draught from the stairs. He wondered how it had survived the winter and why it was he had not noticed it before. Exhaustion seeped through his flesh bringing a sensation of calm. Now that it was over at last he was glad, now that there was nothing more to be done. He had tried everything and failed. He had lived ten years in the space of one – altered himself by the hour to suit her and she had told him it made no difference – that it was useless whatever he did because it had nothing to do with him personally, with individual failing. He could not accept that, could not resign himself to being a mere cog in someone else's political theory. He had done all that he knew to persuade, to understand her, he had been by turns argumentative, patient, sceptical, conciliatory. The night when, finally, she had told him it was over, he had wept in her arms, pleaded with her, vulnerable as any woman, and she had remained indifferent, patronizing even; seeing only the male he could not cease to be. They said they wanted emotion, honesty, self-exposure but when they got it, they despised you for it. Once and once only he had allowed the rage in him to break free; let loose the cold fury that had been festering in his gut since the start of it. She had come home late on Lisa's birthday and when she told him where she had been blatantly, flaunting it, he had struck her across the face; harder than he had intended so that a fleck of blood showed on her lip. She had wiped it off with the back of her hand, staring at him, a look of shock and covert satisfaction in her eyes. He knew then in his shame and regret that he had given her the excuse she had been waiting for.

He looked at her now, at the hard pale arch of her cheekbone. He waited for her to say something but she kept silent and he could not let himself speak the only words that were in his mind. She would see them as weakness. Instead, he heard himself say her name, 'Martina', not wanting to, but finding it form on his lips from force of habit; a sound, a collection of syllables that had once held absolute meaning and now meant nothing or too much, composed as it was of so many conflicting memories.

She reached a hand past his face to the breakfast cup that stood on the bedside table. A dark, puckered skin had formed on the coffee's surface but she drank it anyway. 'What?' she said without looking at him. He felt that she was preparing her next move, searching for a phrase or gesture that would carry her painlessly out of his bed and from their house. But when she did speak again there was no attempt at prevarication or tact. 'I need to shower,' she said bluntly, 'can you let me out?' She swung her legs over the side of the bed, pushing back the patterned sheet, and stood up. He watched her walk across the room away from him. A small mark like a circle of chalk dust gleamed on the muscle of her thigh – his seed dried on her skin. The scent and taste of him would be all through her. She would wash meticulously every inch of her body to remove it. He heard her close the bathroom door behind her and a moment later the hiss and splatter of water breaking on the shower curtain. Only a few weeks ago she would have run a bath for them both and he would have carried Lisa in to sit between their knees. Yesterday afternoon he had brought Lisa over to her mother's house. Martina had said she thought it was best if Lisa stayed there for a couple of weeks until they could come to some arrangement. Some arrangement! For Lisa! He knew then how crazed she was. Of course, it was an act – a pretence of consideration and fairmindedness, wanting it to appear that she might even debate the merits of leaving their daughter with him. But he knew what she planned, all too well.

He had a vision of himself calling over to Leinster Road on a Saturday afternoon, standing on the front step ringing the bell. Martina would come to the door and hold it open staring at him blankly as if he were a stranger, while Lisa ran to greet him. Would Helen be there too with that smug, tight, little smile on her mouth? Would they bring him in to the kitchen and make tea and small talk while Lisa got ready, or would they have found some excuse to have her out for the day? He knew every possible permutation, he had seen them all a dozen times on television and seventies' movies but he never thought he might be expected to live out these banalities himself. His snort of laughter startled him. He could not remember when he had last laughed aloud. But who would not at the idea that the mother of his child could imagine that this cosy Hollywood scenario might become reality? When she had first mentioned it, dropping it casually as a vague suggestion, he had forced himself to hold back the derision that rose to his tongue. He would say nothing. Why should he? Let her learn the hard way. They would all say it for him soon enough – his parents, her mother. The instant they discovered the truth, who and what she had left him for, they would snatch Lisa from her as ruthlessly as they would from quicksand. They would not be shackled by any qualms of conscience. They would have none of his need to show fine feeling. It was extraordinary that she did not seem to realize this herself, unthinkable that she might not allow it to influence her.

She came back into the room, her legs bare beneath a shaggy red sweater. The sweater he had bought her for Christmas. Her nipples protruded like two small stones from under the loose wool. She opened the wardrobe and took out a pair of blue jeans and a grey corduroy skirt. He saw that she was on the point of asking him which he preferred. She stood in the unconsciously childish pose she assumed whenever she had a decision to make, however trivial, her feet apart, her head tilted to one side. He lay on his back watching her, his hands interlaced between the pillow and his head. He could feel the blood pulsing behind his ears but he kept his face impassive. She was studying her image in the mirror, eyes wide with anxious vanity. At last she dropped the jeans into the open case and began to pull on the skirt. Why – was that what Helen would have chosen? What kind of look did she go for? Elegant, sexy, casual? But then, they were not into looks – oh no, it was all on a higher, spiritual plane. Or was it? What did she admire in her anyway? Was it the same qualities as he did or something quite different, something hidden from him? Was she turned on by some reflection of herself or by some opposite trait, something lacking in her own character? He could not begin to guess. He knew so little about this woman Martina was abandoning him for. He had left it too late to pay her any real attention. He had been struck by her the first night, he had to admit, meeting her in O'Brien's after that conference. He liked her body; the long legs and broad shoulders and something attractive in the sultry line of her mouth. A woman he might have wanted himself in other circumstances. If he had not been told immediately that she was a lesbian. Not that he would have guessed it – at least not at first glance. She was too good-looking for that. But it did not take long to see the coldness in her, the chip on her shoulder; the arrogant, belligerent way she stood at the bar and asked him what he wanted to drink. But then she had every reason for disdain, had she not? She must have known already that his wife was in love with her. It had taken him a year to reach the same conclusion.

She sat on the bed to put on her stockings, one leg crossed over the other. He heard her breathing – quick little breaths through the mouth. She was nervous then. He stared at the round bone of her ankle as she drew the red mesh over it. He followed her hands as they moved up the length of her calf. Her body was so intimately known to him he felt he might have cast the flesh on her bones with his own fingers. He saw the stretch marks above her hip. She had lost weight this winter. She looked well but he preferred her as she used to be – voluptuous, the plump roundness of her belly and arms. He thought of all the days and nights of pleasure that they had had together. She certainly could not complain that he had not appreciated her. He would always be grateful for what he had discovered with her. He would forget none of it. But would she? Oh no. She pretended to have forgotten already. She talked now as though she had been playing an elaborate game all these years going through ritual actions to please him. When he refused to let her away with that kind of nonsense, the deliberate erasure of their past and forced her to acknowledge the depth of passion there had been between them, she said yes, she did not deny that they had had good times in bed but it had very little to do with him. He had laughed in her face. And who was it to do with then? Who else could take credit for it? She did not dare to answer but even as he asked the question he knew the sort of thing she would come out with. One of Helen's profundities – that straight women use men as instruments, that they make love to themselves through a man's eyes, stimulate themselves with his desire and flattery but that it is their own sensuality they get off on. He knew every version of their theories by now.

'Would you like some more coffee?' she asked him when she had finished dressing. She was never so hurried that she could go without coffee. He shook his head and she walked out of the room pulling a leather belt through the loops of her skirt. He listened to her light footstep on the stairs. After a moment he heard her lift the mugs from their hooks on the wall. He heard her fill the percolator with water, place it on the gas stove and after a while its rising heart beat as the coffee bubbled through the metal filter. He hung on to each sound, rooting himself in the routine of it, wanting to hide in the pictures they evoked. So long as he could hear her moving about in the kitchen below him, busy with all her familiar actions, it seemed that nothing much could be wrong.

Not that he believed that she would really go through with it. Not all the way. Once it dawned on her finally that indulging this whim would mean giving up Lisa she would have to come to her senses. Yes, she would be back soon enough with her tail between her legs. He had only to wait.

But he would not let her see that he knew this. It would only put her back up – bring out all her woman's pride and obstinacy. He must tread carefully. Follow silently along this crazy pavement she had laid, step by step, until she reached the precipice. And when she was forced back, he would be there, waiting.

If only he had been more cautious from the beginning. If only he had taken it seriously, recognized the danger in time, it would never have reached this stage. But how could he have? How could any normal man have seen it as any more than a joke? He had felt no jealousy at all at the start. She had known it and been incensed. She had accused him of typical male complacency. She had expected scenes, that was evident, wanted them, had tried to goad him into them. But for weeks he had refused to react with anything more threatening than good-humoured sarcasm. He remembered the night she first confessed that Helen and she had become lovers; the anxious, guilty face, expecting God knows what extremes of wrath, and yet underneath it there had been a look of quiet triumphalism. He had had to keep himself from laughing. He was taken by surprise, undoubtedly, though he should not have been with the way they had been going on – never out of each other's company, the all-night talks and the heroine worship. But frankly he would not have thought Martina was up to it. Oh, she might flirt with the idea of turning on a woman but to commit herself was another thing. She was too fundamentally healthy, and too fond of the admiration of men. Besides, knowing how passionate she was, he could not believe she would settle for the caresses of a woman.

Gradually his amusement had given way to curiosity, a pleasurable stirring of erotic interest. Two women in bed together after all – there was something undeniably exciting in the idea. He had tried to get her to share it with him, to make it something they could both enjoy but out of embarrassment, or some misplaced sense of loyalty, she had refused. He said to tease her, to draw her out a little, that he would not have picked Helen for the whip and jackboots type. What did he mean by that, she had demanded menacingly. And when he explained that as, obviously, she herself could not be cast as the butch, Helen was the only remaining candidate, she had flown at him, castigating his prejudice and condescension. Clearly it was not a topic amenable to humour. She told him that all that role playing was a creation of men's fantasies. Dominance and submission were models women had consigned to the rubbish heap. It was all equality and mutual respect in this brave new world. So where did the excitement, the romance come in, he wanted to ask. If they had dispensed with all the traditional props, what was left? But he knew better than to say anything. They were so stiff with analysis and theory, the lot of them, it was impossible to get a straightforward answer. Sometimes he had even wondered if they were really lesbians at all. Apart from the fact that they looked perfectly normal there seemed something overdone about it. It seemed like a public posture, an attitude struck to provoke men – out of spite or envy. Certainly they flaunted the whole business unnecessarily, getting into fights in the street or in pubs, because they insisted on their right to self-expression and that the rest of the world should adapt to them. He had even seen one of them at a conference sporting a badge on her lapel that read: 'How dare you presume I'm heterosexual.' Why on earth should anyone presume otherwise unless she was proud of resembling a male impersonator?

And so every time he had attempted to discuss it rationally they had ended by quarrelling. She condemned him of every macho fault in the book and sulked for hours but afterwards they made it all up in bed. As long as she responded in the old manner, so he knew he had not much to worry about. He had even fancied that it might improve their sex life – add a touch of the unknown. He had watched closely to see if any new needs or tastes might creep into her lovemaking.

It was not until the night she had come home in tears that he was forced to rethink his position.

She had arrived in, half drunk, at midnight after one of their interminable meetings and raced straight up to bed without so much as greeting him or going in to kiss Lisa goodnight. He had followed her up and when he tried to get in beside her to comfort her she had become hysterical, screamed at him to leave her alone, to keep his hands away from her. It was hours before he managed to calm her down and get the whole story out of her. It seemed that Helen had told her that evening in the pub that she wanted to end the relationship. He was astonished. He had always taken it for granted that Martina would be the first to tire. He was even insulted on her behalf. He soothed and placated her stroking her hair and murmuring soft words the way he would with Lisa. He told her not to be a fool, that she was far too beautiful to be cast aside by Helen, that she must be the best thing that had ever happened to her. She was sobbing uncontrollably but she stopped long enough to abuse him when he said that. At last she had fallen asleep in his arms but for the first time he had stayed awake after her. He had to admit that her hysteria had got to him. He could see then it had become some kind of obsession. Up to that he had imagined it was basically a schoolgirl crush, the sort of thing most girls worked out in their teens. But women were so sentimental. He remembered a student of his saying years ago that men had friendships and women had affairs. He knew exactly what he meant. You had only to watch them, perfectly average housewives sitting in cafés or restaurants together, gazing into each other's eyes in a way that would have embarrassed the most besotted man, the confiding tones they used, the smiles of flattery and sympathy flitting between them, the intimate gestures, touching the other's hand, the little pats and caresses, exasperating waiters while they fought over the right to treat one another.

He had imagined that lesbian lovemaking would have some of this piquant quality. He saw it as gently caressive – tender and solicitous. He began to have fantasies about Martina and Helen together. He allowed himself the delicious images of their tentative, childish sensuality. When he and Martina were fucking he had often fantasized that Helen was there too, both women exciting each other and then turning to him at the ultimate moment, competing for him. He had thought it was just a matter of time before something like it came about. It had not once occurred to him, in all that while, that they would continue to exclude him; to cut him out mentally and physically, to insist on their self-sufficiency and absorption. Not even that night lying sleepless beside her while she snored, as she always did after too many pints. It did not register with him finally until the afternoon he came home unexpectedly from work and heard them together.

There was no illusion after that, no innocence or humour. He knew it for what it was. Weeks passed before he could rid his mind of the horror of it; it haunted his sleep and fuelled his days with a seething, putrid anger. He saw that he had been seduced, mocked, cheated, systematically, cold-bloodedly by assumptions she had worked carefully to foster; defrauded and betrayed. He had stood at the bottom of the stairs – his stairs – in his own house and listened to them. He could hear it from the hall. He listened transfixed, a heaving in his stomach, until the din from the room above rose to a wail. He had covered his ears. Tender and solicitous had he said? More like cats in heat! As he went out of the house slamming the door after him he thought he heard them laughing. Bitches – bloody, fucking bitches! He had made it as far as the pub and ordered whiskey. He sat drinking it – glass after glass, grasping the bowl so hard he might have snapped it in two. He was astounded by the force of rage unleashed in him. He would have liked to put his hands around her bare throat and squeeze it until he had wrung that noise out of it.

Somehow he had managed to get a grip of himself. He had had enough sense to drink himself stupid – too stupid to do anything about it that night. He had slept on the floor in the sitting room and when he woke at noon she had already left for the day. He was glad. He was not going to humiliate himself by fighting for her over a woman. He was still convinced that it was a temporary delirium; an infection that, left to run its course, would sweat itself out. He had only to wait, to play it cool, to think and to watch until the fever broke.

She came back into the room carrying two mugs of coffee. She set one down beside him, giving a little nervous smile. She had forgotten he had said he did not want any. 'Are you getting up?' she asked, as she took her dressing gown from the back of the door. 'There's some bread in the oven – will you remember to take it out?'

Jesus! How typical of her – to bake bread the morning she was leaving. The dough had been left as usual, of course, to rise overnight and she could not bring herself to waste it. Typical of her sublime insensitivity! He had always been baffled by this trait in her – this attention, no matter what crisis, to the everyday details of life and this compulsion to make little gestures of practical concern. Was it another trick of hers to forestall criticism? Or did she really have some power to rise above her own and other people's emotion? But most likely it was just straightforward, old-fashioned guilt.

'Fuck the bread,' he said and instantly regretted it. She would be in all the more hurry now to leave. She went to the wardrobe and began to lift down her clothes, laying them in the suitcase. He watched her hands as they expertly folded blouses, jerseys, jeans, studying every movement so that he would be able to recapture it precisely when she was gone. It was impossible to believe that he would not be able to watch her like this the next day and the day after. That was what hurt the most. The thought that he would lose the sight of her – just that. That he would no longer look on while she dressed or undressed, prepared a meal, read a book or played with Lisa. Every movement of her body familiar to him, so graceful, so completely feminine. He felt that if he could be allowed to watch her through glass, without speaking, like a child gazing through a shop window, he could have been content. He would not dare express it, needless to say. She would have sneered at him. Objectification, she would call it.

'A woman's body is all that ever matters to any one of you, isn't it?' And he would not argue because the thing he really prized would be even less flattering to her – her vulnerability, her need to confide, to ask his advice in every small moment of self-doubt, to share all her secret fears. God how they had talked! Hours of it. At least she could never claim that he had not listened. And in the end he had learned to need it almost as much as she did. To chat in the inconsequential way she had; curled together in bed, sitting over a glass of wine till the small hours – drawing out all the trivia of personal existence: the dark, hidden things that bonded you for ever to the one person who would hear them from you. Was that a ploy too? A conscious one? Or merely female instinct to tie him to her by a gradual process of self-exposure so that he could not disentangle himself, even now, when he had to, because there was no longer any private place left in him, nowhere to hide from her glance, nowhere that she could not seek out and name the hurt in him. It was this knowledge that had let her see the pain in him, when she woke this morning, behind his closed eyes, that had caused her to make love with him. Another of those little generous acts: handing over her body as you would a towel to someone bleeding. And he had accepted it, idiot that he was – little fawning lap-dog that she had made of him.

She was sitting at the dressing-table brushing her hair with slow, attentive strokes, drawing the brush each time from the crown of her head to the tips of her hair where it lay along her shoulder. Was she deliberately making no show of haste, pretending to be doing everything as normal? It seemed to him there must be something he could say; something an outsider would think of immediately. He searched his mind but nothing came to him but the one question that had persisted in him for days: 'Why are you doing this? I don't understand why you're doing this?' She opened a bottle of cologne and dabbed it lightly on her wrists and neck. She always took particular care preparing herself to meet Helen. Helen, who herself wore some heavy French scent that clung to everything she touched, that was carried home in Martina's hair and clothing after every one of their sessions. But that was perfectly acceptable and politically correct. Adorning themselves for each other – make-up, perfume, eyebrow plucking, exchanging clothes – all these feminine tricks took on new meaning because neither of them was a man. Helen did not need to flatter, she did not need to patronize or idolize, she did not need to conquer or submit and her desire would never be exploitative because she was a woman dealing with a woman!

Neither of them had institutionalized power behind them. This was the logic he had been taught all that winter. They told one another these fairy stories sitting round at their meetings. Everything that had ever gone wrong for any one of them, once discussed in their consciousness-raising groups, could be chalked up as a consequence of male domination. And while they sat about indoctrinating each other with this schoolgirl pap, sounding off on radio and on television, composing joint letters to the press, he had stayed at home three nights a week to mind Lisa, clean the house, cook meals, and read his way through the bundles of books she brought home – sentimental novels and half-baked political theses that she had insisted he must look at if he was to claim any understanding at all. And at the finish of it, when he had exhausted himself to satisfy her caprices, she said that he had lost his spontaneity, that their relationship had become stilted, sterile and self-conscious. With Helen, needless to say, all was otherwise – effortless and instinctive. God, he could not wait for their little idyll to meet the adult world; the world of electricity bills, dirty dishes and childminding, and see how far their new roles got them. But he had one pleasure in store before then, a consolation prize he had been saving himself. As soon as she was safely out of the house, he would make a bonfire of them – burn every one – every goddamn book with the word woman on its cover!

She fastened the brown leather suitcase, leaving open the lock on the right hand that had broken the summer two years ago when they had come back from Morocco laden down with blankets and caftans. She carried it across the room, trying to lift it clear of the floor, but it was too heavy for her and dragged along the boards. She went out the door and he heard it knocking on each step as she walked down the stairs. He listened. She was doing something in the kitchen but he could not tell what. There followed a protracted silence. It hit him suddenly that she might try to get out of the house, leave him and go without saying anything at all. He jumped out of bed, grabbed his trousers from the chair and pulled them on, his fingers so clumsy with haste he caught his hair in the zip. Fuck her! When he rooted under the bed for his shoes she heard and called up: 'Don't bother getting dressed, I'll take the bus.' She did not think he was going to get the car out and drive her over there, surely? He took a shirt from the floor and pulled it on over his head as he took the stairs to the kitchen two at a time. She was standing by the stove holding a cup of coffee. This endless coffee drinking of hers; cups all over the house, little white rings marked on every stick of furniture. At least he would not have that to put up with any longer.

'There's some in the pot if you want it,' she said. He could see the percolator was almost full, the smell of it would be all over the house now, and the smell of the bloody bread in the oven, for hours after she was gone.

'Didn't you make any tea?'

'No,' she said and gave one of her sidelong, maddening looks of apology as though it was some major oversight, 'but there's water in the kettle.'

'Thanks,' he said, 'I won't bother.'

He was leaning his buttocks against the table, his feet planted wide apart, his hands in his pockets. He looked relaxed and in control at least. He was good at that – years of being on stage before a class of students. He wondered if

Helen would come to meet her at the bus stop or was she going to have to lug the suitcase alone all the way up Leinster Road? He wondered how they would greet each other. With triumph or nervousness? Might there be a sense of anti-climax about it now that she had finally committed herself after so much stalling? Would she tell Helen that she had made love with him before leaving? Would she be ashamed of it and say nothing? But probably Helen would take it for granted as an insignificant gesture to male pride, the necessary price of freedom. And suddenly he wished that he had not been so restrained with her; so much the considerate, respectful friend she had trained him to be. He wished that he had taken his last opportunity and used her body as any other man would have – driven the pleasure out of it until she had screamed as he had heard her that day, in his bed, with her woman lover. He should have forced her to remember him as something more than the tiresome child she thought she had to pacify.

She went to the sink and began to rinse the breakfast things under the tap.

'Leave them,' he said, 'I'll do them,' the words coming out of him too quickly. He was losing his cool. She put the cup down and dried her hands on the tea towel. He struggled to think of something to say. He would have to find something. His mind seethed with ridiculous nervous comments. He tried to pick out a phrase that would sound normal and yet succeed in gaining her attention; in arresting this current of meaningless actions that was sweeping between them. And surely there must be something she wanted to say to him? She was not going to walk out and leave him as if she was off to the pictures? She took her raincoat from the banister and put it on but did not fasten it. The belt trailed to one side. She lifted up the suitcase and carried it into the hallway. He followed her. When she opened the door he saw that it was raining. A gust of wind caught her hair, blowing it into her eyes. He wanted to say 'Fasten your coat – you're going to get cold,' but he did not and he heard himself ask instead, 'Where can I ring you?' He had not intended that, he knew the answer. He had the phone number by heart.

She held open the door with one hand and set down the case. She stared down at his shoes and then past him the length of the hallway. Two days ago he had started to sand and stain the floorboards. She looked as if she was estimating how much work remained to be done.

'Don't ring this weekend. We're going away for a while.'

He felt a flash of white heat pass in front of his brain and a popping sound like a light bulb exploding. He felt dizzy and his eyes for a moment seemed to cloud over. Then he realized what had happened. A flood of blind terror had swept through him, unmanning him, because she had said something totally unexpected – something he had not planned for. He repeated the words carefully hoping she would deny them, make sense of them.

'You're going away for a while?'

'Yes.'

'Where to, for God's sake?' he almost shrieked.

'Down the country for a bit – to friends.'

He stared at her blankly, his lips trembling and then the words came out that he had been holding back all morning:

'For how long? When will you be back?'

He could have asked it at any time, he had been on the verge of it a dozen times and had managed to repress it because he had to keep to his resolve not to let her see that he knew what all this was about – a drama, a show of defiance and autonomy. He could not let her guess that he knew full well she would be back. Somewhere in her heart she must recognize that no one would ever care for her as much as he did. No one could appreciate her more or make more allowances for her. She could not throw away ten years of his life for this – to score a political point – for a theory – for a woman! But he had not said it, all morning. It was too ridiculous – it dignified the thing even to mention it. And now she had tricked him into it, cheated him.

'When will you be back?' he had asked.

'I'll be away for a week, I suppose. You can ring the flat on Monday.'

The rain was blowing into her face, her lips were white. She leaned forward. He felt her hand on his sleeve. He felt the pressure of her ring through the cloth of his shirt. She kissed him on the forehead. Her lips were soft, her breath warm on his skin. He hated her then. He hated her body – her woman's flesh that was still caressive and yielding when the heart inside it was shut like a trap against him.

'Goodbye,' she said. She lifted the case and closed the door after her.

He went back into the kitchen. But not to the window. He did not want to see her walking down the road. He did not want to see her legs in their scarlet stockings, and the rain-coat blown back from her skirt. He did not want to see her dragging the stupid case, to see it banging against her knees as she carried it along the street. So he stood in the kitchen that smelled of coffee and bread baking. He stood over the warmth of the stove, his head lowered, his hands clenched in his pockets, his eyes shut.

She would be back anyhow – in a week's time. She had admitted that now. 'In a week,' she had said, 'ring me on Monday.' He would not think about it until then. He would not let himself react to any more of these theatrics. It was absurd the whole business. She had gone to the country, she was visiting friends. He would not worry about her. He would not think about her at all, until she came back.

Edna O'Brien

What a Sky

THE CLOUDS – dark, massed and purposeful – raced across the sky. At one moment a gap appeared, a vault of blue so deep it looked like a cavity into which one could vanish, but soon the clouds swept across it like trailing curtains, removing it from sight. There were showers on and off – heavy showers – and in some fields the water had lodged in shallow pools where the cows stood impassively, gaping. The crows were incorrigible. Being inside the car, she could not actually hear their cawing, but she knew it very well and remembered how long ago she used to listen and try to decipher whether it denoted death or something more blithe.

As she mounted the granite steps of the nursing home, her face, of its own accord, folded into a false, obedient smile. A few old people sat in the hall, one woman praying on her big black horn rosary beads and a man staring listlessly through the long rain-splashed window, muttering, as if by his mutters he could will a visitor, or maybe the priest, to give him the last rites. One of the women tells her that her father has been looking forward to her visit and that he has come to the front door several times. This makes her quake, and she digs her fingernails into her palms for fortitude. As she crosses the threshold of his little bedroom, the first question he fires at her is 'What kept you?', and very politely she explains that the car ordered to fetch her from her hotel was a little late in arriving.

'I was expecting you two hours ago,' he says. His mood is foul and his hair is standing on end, tufts of grey hair sprouting like Lucifer's.

'How are you?' she says.

He tells her that he is terrible and complains of a pain in the back from the shoulder down, a pain like the stab of a knife. She asks if it is rheumatism. He says how would he know, but whatever it is, it is shocking, and to emphasize his discomfort he opens his mouth and lets out a groan. The first few minutes are taken up with showing him the presents that she has brought, but he is too disgruntled to appreciate them. She coaxes him to try on the pullover, but he won't. Suddenly he gets out of bed and goes to the lavatory. The lavatory adjoins the bedroom; it is merely a cupboard with fittings and fixtures. She sits in the overheated bedroom listening, while trying not to listen. She stares out of the opened window; the view is of a swamp, while above, in a pale untrammelled bit of whey-coloured sky, the crows are flying at different altitudes and cawing mercilessly. They are so jet they look silken, and listening to them, while trying not to listen to her father, she thinks that if he closes the lavatory door perhaps all will not be so awful; but he will not close the lavatory door and he will not apologize. He comes out with his pajamas streeling around his legs, his walk impaired as he goes towards the bed, across which his lunch tray has been slung. His legs like candles, white and spindly, fore-shadow her own old age, and she wonders with a shudder if she will end up in a place like this.

'Wash your hands, Dad,' she says as he strips the bedcovers back. There is a second's balk as he looks at her, and the look has the dehumanized rage of a trapped animal, but for some reason he concedes and crosses to the little basin and gives his hands, or rather his right hand, a cursory splash. He dries it by laying the hand on the towel that hangs at the side of the basin. It is a towel that she recognizes from home – dark blue with orange splashes. Even this simple recollection pierces: she can smell the towel, she can remember it drying on top of the range, she can feel it without touching it. The towel, like every other item in that embattled house, has got inside her brain and remained there like furniture inside a room. The white cyclamen that she has brought is staring at her, the flowers like butterflies and the tiny buds like pencil tips, and it is this she obliges herself to see in order to generate a little cheerfulness.

'I spent Christmas Day all by myself.'

'No, Dad, you didn't,' she says, and reminds him that a relative came and took him out to lunch.

'I tell you, I spent Christmas Day all by myself,' he says, and now it is her turn to bristle.

'You were with Agatha. Remember?' she says.

'What do you know about it?' he says, staring at her, and she looks away, blaming herself for having lost control. He follows her with those eyes, then raises his hands up like a supplicant. One hand is raw and red. 'Eczema,' he says almost proudly. The other hand is knobbly, the fingers bunched together in a stump. He says he got that affliction from foddering cattle winter after winter. Then he tells her to go to the wardrobe. There are three dark suits, some tweed jackets, and a hideous light-blue gabardine that a young nun made him buy before he went on holiday to a convent in New Mexico. He praises this young nun, Sister Declan, praises her good humour, her buoyant spirit, her generosity and her innate sense of sacrifice. As a young girl, it seems, this young nun preferred to sit in the kitchen with her father, devising possible hurley games, or discussing hurley games that had been, instead of gallivanting with boys. He mentions how the nun's father died suddenly, choked to death while having his tea, but he shows no sign of pity or shock, and she thinks that in some crevice of his scalding mind he believes the nun has adopted him, which perhaps she has. The young nun has recently been sent away to the same convent in New Mexico, and the daughter thinks that perhaps it was punishment, perhaps she was getting too fond of this lonely, irascible man. No knowing.

'A great girl, the best friend I ever had,' he says. Wedged among the suits in the cupboard is the dark frieze coat that belongs to the bygone days, to his youth. Were she to put her hand in a pocket, she might find an old penny or a stone that he had picked up on his walks, the long walks he took to stamp out his ire. He says to look in the beige suitcase, which she does. It is already packed with belongings, summer things, and gallantly he announces that he intends to visit the young nun again, to make the journey across the sea, telling how he will probably arrive in the middle of the night, as he did before, and Sister Declan and a few of the others will be waiting inside the convent gate to give him a regal welcome.

'I may not even come back,' he says boastfully. On the top shelf of the wardrobe are various pairs of socks, and handkerchiefs – new handkerchiefs and torn ones – empty whiskey bottles, and two large framed photographs. He tells her to hand down one of those photographs, and for the millionth time she looks at the likeness of his mother and father. His mother seems formidable, with a topknot of curls, and white laced bodice that even in the faded photograph looks like armour. His father, who is seated, looks meeker and more compliant.

'Seven years of age when I lost my mother and father, within a month of each other,' he says, and his voice is now like gravel. He grits his teeth.

What would they have made of him, his daughter wonders. Would their love have tamed him? Would he be different? Would she herself be different?

'Was it very hard?' she asks, but without real tenderness.

'Hard? What are you talking about?' he says. 'To be brought out into a yard and put in a pony and trap and dumped on relations?'

She knew that were she to really feel for him she would enquire about the trap, the cushion he sat on, if there was a rug for his knees, what kind of coat he wore, and the colour of his hair then; but she does not ask these things. 'Did they beat you?' she asks, as a form of conciliation.

'You were beaten if you deserved it,' he says, and goes on to talk about their rancour and how he survived it, how he developed his independence, how he found excitement and sport in horses and was a legend even as a young lad for being able to break any horse. He remembers his boarding school and how he hated it, then his gadding days, then when still young – too young, he adds – meeting his future wife, and his daughter knows that soon he will cry, and talk of his dead wife and the marble tombstone that he erected in her memory, and that he will tell how much it cost and how much the hospital bill was, and how he never left her, or any one of the family, short of money for furniture or food. His voice is passing through me, the daughter thinks, as is his stare and his need and the upright sprouts of steel-coloured hair and the over-pink plates of false teeth in a glass beer tumbler. She feels glued to the spot, feels as if she has lost her will and the use of her limbs, and thinks, This is how it has always been. Looking away to avoid his gaze, her eyes light on his slippers. They are made of felt, green and red felt; there are holes in them and she wishes that she had bought him a new pair. He says to hand him the brown envelope that is above the washbasin. The envelope contains photographs of himself taken in New Mexico. In them, he has the air of a suitor, and the pose and look that he has assumed take at least thirty years off his age.

At that moment, one of the senior nuns comes in, welcomes her, offers her a cup of tea, and remarks on how well she looks. He says that no one looks as well as he does and proffers the photos. He recounts his visit to the States again – how the stewardesses were amazed at his age and his vitality, and how everyone danced attendance on him. The nun and the daughter exchange a look. They have a strategy. They have corresponded about it, the nun's last letter enclosing a greeting card from him, in which he begged his daughter to come. From its tone she deduced that he had changed, that he had become mollified; but he has not, he is the same, she thinks.

'Now talk to your father,' the nun says, then stands there, hands folded into her wide black sleeves, while the daughter says to her father, 'Why don't you eat in the dining room, Dad?'

'I don't want to eat in the dining room,' he says, like a corrected child. The nun reminds him that he is alone too much, that he cries too much, that if he mingled it would do him some good.

'They're ignorant, they're ignorant people,' he says of the other inmates.

'They can't all be ignorant,' both the nun and the daughter say at the same moment.

'I tell you, they're all ignorant!' he says, his eyes glaring.

'But you wouldn't be so lonely, Dad,' his daughter says, feeling a wave of pity for him.

'Who says I'm lonely?' he says roughly, sabotaging that pity, and he lists the number of friends he has, the motorcars he has access to, the bookmakers he knows, the horse trainers that he is on first names with, and the countless houses where he is welcome at any hour of day or night throughout the year.

To cheer him up, the nun rushes out and shouts to a little girl in the pantry across the way to bring the pot of tea now and the plate of biscuits. Watching the tea being poured, he insists the cup be so full that when the milk is added it slops over onto the saucer, but he does not notice, does not care.

'Thank you, thank you, Sister,' he says. He used not to say thank you and she wonders if perhaps Sister Declan had told him that courtesy was one way to win back the love of recalcitrant ones. He mashes the biscuits on his gums and then suddenly brightens as he remembers the night in the house of some neighbours when their dog attacked him. He had gone there to convalesce from shingles. He launches into a description of the dog, a German shepherd, and his own poor self coming down in the night to make a cup of tea, and this dog flying at him and his arm going up in self-defence, and the dog mauling him, and the miracle that he was not eaten to death. He charts the three days of agony before he was brought to the hospital, the arm being set, being in a sling for two months, and the little electric saw that the county surgeon used to remove the plaster.

'My God, what I had to suffer!' he says. The nun has already left, whispering some excuse.

'Poor Dad,' his daughter would say. She is determined to be nice, admitting how wretched his life is, always has been.

'You have no idea,' he says, as he contrasts his present abode, a dungeon, with his own lovely limestone house that is going to ruin. He recalls his fifty-odd years in that house – the comforts, the blazing fire, the mutton dinners followed by rice pudding that his wife served. She reminds him that the house belongs to his son now and then she flinches, remembering that between them, also, there is a breach.

'He's no bloody good,' he says, and prefers instead to linger on his incarceration here.

'No mutton here; it's all beef,' he says.

'Don't they have any sheep?' she says, stupidly.

'It's no life for a father,' he says, and she realizes that he is about to ask for the guarantee that she cannot give.

She takes the tea tray and lays it on the hallway floor, then praises the kindness of nuns and of nurses and asks the name of the matron, so that she can give her a gift of money. He does not answer. In that terrible pause, as if on cue, one crow alights on a dip of barbed wire outside the window and lets out a series of hoarse exclamations. She is about to say, about to spring the pleasant surprise. She has come to take him out for the day. That is her plan. The delay in her arrival at the nursing home was due to her calling at a luxurious hotel to ask if they did lunches late. When she got there from London, late the previous night, she had stayed in a more commercial hotel in the town, where she was kept awake most of the night by the noise of cattle. It was near an abattoir, and in the very early hours of the morning she could hear the cattle arriving, their bawling, their pitiful bawling, and then their various slippings and slobberings, and the shouts of the men who got them out of the trailers or the lorries and into the pens, and then other shouts, indeterminable shouts of men. She had lain in the very warm hotel room and allowed her mind to wander back to the time when her father bought and sold cattle, driving them on foot to the town, sometimes with the help of a simpleton, often failing to sell the beasts and having to drive them home again, with the subsequent wrangling and sparring over debts. She thinks that indeed he was not cut out for a life with cattle and foddering but that he was made for grander things, and it is with a rush of pleasure that she contemplates the surprise for him. She had already vetted the hotel, admitting, it is true, a minor disappointment that the service did not seem as august as the gardens or the imposing hallway with its massive portraits and beautiful staircase. When she visited to enquire about lunch, a rather vacant young boy said that no, they did not do lunches, but that possibly they could manage sandwiches, cheese or ham. Yet the atmosphere would exhilarate him, and sitting there in the nursing home with him now, she luxuriates in her own bit of private cheer. Has she not met someone, a man whose very voice, whose crisp manner fill her with verve and happiness? She barely knows him, but when he telephoned and imagined her surrounded by motley admirers, she did not disabuse him of his fantasy. She recalls, not without mischief, how that very morning in the market town she bought embroidered pillowcases and linen sheets, in anticipation of the day or night when he would cross her bedroom doorway. The thought of this future tryst softens her towards the old man, her father, and for a moment the two men revolve in her thoughts like two halves of a slow-moving apparition. As for the new one, she knows why she bought pillowslips and costly sheets: because she wants her surroundings not only to be beautiful for him but to carry the vestiges of her past, such sacred things as flowers and linen, and all of a sudden, with unnerving clarity, she fears that she wants this new man to partake of her whole past – to know it in all its pain and permutations.

The moment has come to announce the treat, to encourage her father to get up and dress, to lead him down the hallway, holding his arm protectively so that the others will see that he is cherished, then to humour him in the car, to ply him with cigarettes, and to find in the hotel the snuggest little sitting room – in short, to give him a sense of well-being, to while away a few hours. It will be a talking point with him for weeks to come, instead of the eczema or the broken arm. Something is impeding her. She wants to do it, indeed she will do it, but she keeps delaying. She tries to examine what it is that is making her stall. Is it the physical act of helping him to dress, because he will, of course, insist on being helped? No, a nun will do that. Is it the thought of his being happy that bothers her? No, it is not that; she wants with all her heart to see him happy. Is it the fear of the service in the hotel being a disappointment, sandwiches being a letdown when he would have preferred soup and a meat course? No, it is not that, since, after all, the service is not her responsibility. What she dreads is the intimacy, being with him at all. She foresees that something awful will occur. He will break down and beg her to show him the love that he knows she is withholding; then, seeing that she cannot, will not, yield, he will grow furious, they will both grow furious, there will be the most terrible showdown, a slanging match of words, curses, buried grievances, maybe even blows. Yes, she will do it in a few minutes; she will clap her hands, jump up off the chair, and in a sing-song voice say, 'We're late, we're late, for a very important date.' She is rehearsing it, even envisaging the awkward smile that will come over his face, the melting, and his saying, 'Are you sure you can afford it, darling?' while at the same moment ordering her to open the wardrobe and choose his suit.

Each time she moves in her chair to do it, something

awful gets between her and the nice gesture. It is like a phobia, like someone too terrified to enter the water but standing at its edge. Yet she knows that if she were to succumb, it would not only be an afternoon's respite for him, it would be for her some enormous leap. Her heart has been hardening now for some time, and when moved to pity by something she can no longer show her feelings – all her feelings are for the privacy of her bedroom. Her heart is becoming a stone, but this gesture, this reach will soften her again and make her, if not the doting child, at least the eager young girl who brought home school reports or trophies that she had won, craving to be praised by him, this young girl who only recited the verses of 'Fontenoy' in place of singing a song. He had repeatedly told her that she could not sing, that she was tone-deaf.

Outside, the clouds have begun to mass for another downpour, and she realizes that there are tears in her eyes. She bends down, pretending to tie her shoe, because she does not want him to see these tears. She saw that it was perverse not to let him partake of this crumb of emotion, but also saw that nothing would be helped by it. He did not know her; he couldn't – his own life tore at him like a mad dog. Why isn't she stirring herself? Soon she will. He is talking non-stop, animated now by the saga of his passport and how he had to get it in such a hurry for his trip to America. He tells her to fetch it from the drawer, and she does. It is very new, with only one official entry, and that in itself conveys to her more than his words ever could: the paucity and barrenness of his life. He tells how the day he got that passport was the jolliest day he ever spent, how he had to go to Dublin to get it, how the nuns tut-tutted, said nobody could get a passport in that length of time because of all the red tape, but how he guaranteed that he would. He described the wet day, one of the wettest days ever, how Biddy the hackney driver didn't even want to set out, said they would be marooned, and how he told her to stop flapping, and get her coat on. He relives the drive, the very early morning, the floods, the fallen boughs, and Biddy and himself on the rocky road to Dublin, smoking fags and singing, Biddy all the while teasing him, saying that it is not a passport that he is going for but a mistress, a rendezvous.

'So you got the passport immediately,' the daughter says, to ingratiate herself.

'Straightaway. I had the influence – I told the nuns here to ring the Dáil, to ring my TD, and by God, they did.'

She asks the name of the TD, but he has no interest in telling that, goes on to say how in the passport office a cheeky young girl asked why he was going to the States and how he told her he was going there to dig for gold. He is now warming to his tale, and she hears again about the air journey, the nice stewardesses, the two meals that came on a little plastic tray, and about how when he stepped out he saw his name on a big placard, and later, inside the convent gate, nuns waiting to receive him.

Suddenly she knows that she cannot take him out; perhaps she will do it on the morrow, but she cannot do it now; and so she makes to rise in her chair.

He senses it, his eyes now hard like granite. 'You're not leaving?' he says.

'I have to; the driver could only wait the hour,' she says feebly.

He gets out of bed, says he will at least see her to the front door, but she persuades him not to. He stares at her as if he is reading her mind, as if he knows the generous impulse that she has defected on. In that moment she dislikes herself even more than she had ever disliked him. Tomorrow she will indeed visit, before leaving, and they will patch it up, but she knows that she has missed something, something incalculable, a moment of grace. The downpour has stopped and the sky, drained of cloud, is like an immense grey sieve, sieving a greater greyness. As she rises to leave, she feels that her heart is in shreds, all over the room. She has left it in his keeping, but he is wildly, helplessly looking for his own.

PART FIVE

Roddy Doyle

from *The Snapper*

IT WAS half-six and Sharon was home from work. She was
standing on the Burgess's front step. She was afraid she
was making a mistake but she rang the bell again before she
could change her mind.

Pat Burgess slid back the aluminium door.

—Yeah?

—Is Mister Burgess there?

—Yeah.

—Can I see him for a minute?

—He's still havin' his tea.

—Only for a minute, tell him.

Sharon looked in while she was waiting. It was a small
hall, exactly the same as theirs. There were more pictures in
this one though, and no phone. Sharon could hear children
and adult voices from the kitchen. She could see the side of
Missis Burgess's back because she was sitting at the end of
the table nearest the door. Then she saw Missis Burgess's
face. And then she heard her voice.

—Is it George you want, Sharon?

God! thought Sharon.

—Yes, please, Missis Burgess. Just for a minute.

She wanted to run. Jesus, she was terrified but she
thought Mister Burgess probably was as well. The kitchen
door closed for a second and when it opened again Mister
Burgess was there. There was a napkin hanging from his
trousers. He looked worried all right. And angry and afraid.
And a bit lost.

Looking at him, Sharon felt better. She knew what she

was going to say: he didn't. She wasn't disgusted looking at him now. She just couldn't believe she'd ever let him near her.

Mister Burgess came towards her.

—Yes, Sharon? he said. To Missis Burgess.

—I want to talk to you, Sharon said quickly when he got to the door.

He wouldn't look at her straight.

—Wha' abou'?

—YOU know.

—I'll see yeh later.

—I'll tell Missis Burgess.

Mister Burgess looked back into the hall. A lift of his head told her to come in.

—Come into the lounge, Sharon, he shouted.—Sharon's here abou' Darren.

—Hiyeh, Sharon.

It was Yvonne, from somewhere in the kitchen.

—Hiyeh, Yvonne, Sharon called back.

—See yeh later.

—Yeah, okay.

She walked into the front room. Mister Burgess shut the door. He was shaking and red.

—Wha' do yeh think you're up to, yeh little bitch? he hissed.

—What' d'yeh think YOU'RE up to, yeh little bastard?

He didn't hiss now.

—Wha'?

—Wha' were yeh sayin' about me to your friends? said Sharon.

—I didn't say ann'thin' to annyone.

It was an aggressive answer but there was a tail on it.

—You said I was a ride. Didn't yeh?

George Burgess hated that. He hated hearing women using the language he used. He just didn't think it was right. It sounded dirty. As well as that, he knew he'd been snared. But he wasn't dead yet.

—Didn't yeh? said Sharon.

—Are yeh mad? I did not.

—I can tell from your face.

It wasn't the first time he'd been told that. His mother had said it; Doris said it; everyone said it.

—I was only jokin'.

—I'm a great little ride.

The word ride made him snap his eyes shut.

—I didn't mean anny harm. I only—

—Wha' else did yeh say about me?

—Nothin'.

—Maybe!

—I swear. I didn't. On the Bible. I didn't say annythin'. Else.

She was nearly feeling sorry for him.

—Yeh stupid bastard yeh.

He looked as if he was being smacked.

She went on.

—You got your hole, didn't yeh?

He shut his eyes again. He got redder.

—Wha' more do yeh want?

—I swear on the Bible, Sharon, I didn't mean anny harm, I swear. True as God now.

—Wha' did yeh say?

—Ah, it was nothin'.

—I'll go in an' tell her.

He believed her.

—Ah, it was silly really. Just the lads talkin', yeh know.

Sharon knew that one step towards the door would get her a better explanation, so she took one.

—We—they—we were havin' a laugh, abou' women, yeh know. The usual. An' the young lads, the lads on the team, they were goin' on abou' the young ones from around here.——An' that's when I said you were a—I said it.

He looked at the carpet.

—Yeh dope. Wha' did yeh say tha' for?

—Ah, I don't know.

He looked up.

—I was showin' off.

——Wha' else?

—Nothin', I swear. They laughed at me. Some o' them didn't even hear me. They'd never believe that I got me —— have—Off you.

He was looking at the carpet again.

—They thought tha' I was jokin'.

He jumped when the door was opened by Missis Burgess.

—There y'are, love, he roared at her.

—Hello, Sharon, said Missis Burgess.

—Hiyeh, Missis Burgess, said Sharon.

—I was just tellin' Mister Burgess abou' Darren.

—That's righ', Mister Burgess nearly screamed.

—Is somethin' wrong with Darren?

—He has a bit of a cold just.

—A cold, said Mister Burgess.

—Maybe flu.

—We'll just have to hope he's better for Saturday, said Mister Burgess.—God knows, we'll need him.

—I didn't know there was flu goin' around, said Missis Burgess.—I hope there isn't, ——now. Will you tell your mammy I was askin' for her?

—I will, yeah, Missis Burgess.

—When are yeh due, Sharon? Missis Burgess asked.

—November. The end.

—Really? You look sooner. ——D'you want a boy or a little girl?

—I don't mind. A girl maybe.

—One of each, wha', said Mister Burgess.

Missis Burgess looked at Mister Burgess.

—I'm off to my bingo now, George.

—Good, said Mister Burgess.—That's great. Have you enough money with yeh, Doris?

—My God, he's offerin' me money! He's showin' off in front of you, Sharon.

Sharon smiled.

—Bye bye so, Sharon, said Missis Burgess.

—See yeh, Missis Burgess.

—Don't forget the grass, George.

—No, no. Don't worry.

—Remember to tell your mammy now, Missis Burgess told Sharon.

Then she was gone.

Sharon knew what he was going to say next.

—Phew, he said.—Tha' was close, wha'.

—It'll be closer the next time if yeh don't stop sayin' things abou' me.

—There won't be a next time, Sharon, I swear to God. I only said it the once. I'm sorry. ——I'm sorry.

—So yeh should be. ——I don't mind bein' pregnant but I do mind people knowin' who made me pregnant.

——So ——you're pregnant, Sharon?

—Fuck off, Mister Burgess, would yeh.

They stood there. Sharon was looking at him but he wasn't looking at her, not really. She wanted to smile. She'd never felt power like this before.

—Sorry, Sharon.

Sharon said nothing.

She was going to go now, but he spoke. His mouth was open for a while before words left it.

——An', Sharon—

He rubbed his nose, on his arm.

—Yeah?

—I never thanked yeh for—yeh know. Tha' nigh'.

He was looking at the carpet again, and fidgeting.

—I was drunk, said Sharon.

She wanted to cry now. She'd forgotten That Night for a minute. She was hating him again.

—I know. So was I. I'd never've ——God, I was buckled. ——Em—

He tried to grin, but he gave up and looked serious.

—You're a good girl, Sharon. We both made a mistake.

—You're tellin' me, said Sharon.

—Hang on a sec, Sharon, he said.—I'll be back in a minute.

He went to the door.

—Wait there, Sharon.

Sharon waited. She was curious. She wasn't going to cry now. She heard Mister Burgess going up the stairs, and coming down.

He slid into the room.

—That's for yourself, Sharon, he said.

He had a ten pound note in his hand.

Sharon couldn't decide how to react. She looked at the money.

She wanted to laugh but she thought that that wouldn't be right. But she couldn't manage anger, looking at this eejit holding out his tenner to her.

—Do you think I'm a prostitute, Mister Burgess?

—God, no; Jaysis, no!

—What're yeh givin' me tha' for then?

—It's not the way yeh think, Sharon. Shite! ——Em, it's a sort of a present—

The tenner, he knew now, was a big mistake.

—Yeh know. A present. No hard feelin's, yeh know.

—You've some fuckin' neck, Mister Burgess, d'yeh know tha'?

—I'm sorry, Sharon. I didn't mean it the way you're thinkin', I swear. On the Bible.

He was beginning to look hurt.

—We made a mistake, Sharon. We were both stupid. Now go an' buy yourself a few sweets—eh, drinks.

Sharon couldn't help grinning. She shook her head.

—You're an awful fuckin' eejit, Mister Burgess, she said. —Put your tenner back in your pocket.

—Ah no, Sharon.

He looked at her.

—Okay, sorry ——You're a good girl. And honest.

—Fuck off!

—Sorry! ——Sorry. I'll never open me mouth about you again.

—You'd better not.

—I won't, I swear.

Then he remembered something.

—Oh yeah, he said.

He dug into his trousers pocket.

—I kept these for yeh. Your, em, panties, isn't tha' what yis call them?

He was really scarlet.

—Me knickers!

Sharon was stunned, and then amused. She couldn't help it. He looked so stupid and unhappy.

She put the knickers in her jacket pocket. Mister Burgess, she noticed, wiped his hand on his cardigan. She nearly laughed.

—What' were yeh doin' with them? she asked.

—I was keepin' them for yeh. So they wouldn't get lost.

He was purple now. His hands were in and out of his cardigan pockets. He couldn't look at her.

—Don't start again, said Sharon.—Just tell us the truth.

—Ah Jaysis, it was stupid really. Again. ——A joke—I was goin' to show them to the lads.

—Oh my—!

—But I didn't I didn't, Sharon! I didn't.

He coughed.

—I wouldn't.

Sharon went to the door.

—I've changed me mind, she said.—Give us the tenner. I deserve it.

—Certainly, Sharon. Good girl. There y'are.

Sharon took the money. She stopped at the door.

—Remember: if you ever say annythin' about me again I'll tell Missis Burgess wha' yeh did.

—Yeh needn't worry, Sharon. Me lips are sealed.

—Well—Just remember. ——Bye bye.

—Cheerio, Sharon. Thanks, ——very much—

She was a great young one, George decided as Sharon shut the door after her. And a good looker too. But, my God——! He sat down and shook like bejaysis for a while. She'd do it; tell Doris. No problem to her. He'd have to be careful. Think but: he'd ridden her. And he'd made her pregnant. HE had.

—Jaysis.

He was a pathetic little prick, Sharon thought as she went back across the road to her house. He was pathetic. He wouldn't yap anymore anyway. He'd be too scared to.

David Park

Oranges from Spain

Iᴛ's ɴᴏᴛ ᴀ fruit shop any more. Afterwards, his wife sold it and someone opened up a fast food business. You wouldn't recognize it now – it's all flashing neon, girls in identical uniforms and the type of food that has no taste. Even Gerry Breen wouldn't recognize it. Either consciously or unconsciously, I don't seem to pass that way very often, but when I do I always stop and look at it. The neon brightness burns the senses and sears the memories like a wound being cauterized; but then it all comes back and out flows a flood of memory that nothing can stem.

I was sixteen years old and very young when I went to work for Mr Breen in his fruit shop. It was that summer when it seemed to rain every day and a good day stood out like something special. I got the job through patronage. My father and Gerry Breen went back a long way – that always struck me as strange, because they were so unalike as men. Apparently, they were both born in the same street and grew up together, and even when my father's career as a solicitor took him upmarket, they still got together occasionally. My father collected an order of fruit every Friday night on his way home from work, and as children we always talked about 'Gerry Breen's apples'. It's funny the things you remember, and I can recall very clearly my mother and father having an argument about it one day. She wanted to start getting fruit from the supermarket for some reason, but my father wouldn't hear of it. He got quite agitated about it and almost ended up shouting, which was very unlike him. Maybe he acted out of loyalty, or maybe he owed him some kind of favour, but whatever the reason, the arrangement continued.

If his name is mentioned now they never do it in front of me. It's almost as if he never existed. At first it angered me – it was almost as if they thought I would disintegrate at its sound – but gradually I came to be grateful for it. I didn't even go to the funeral, and from that moment it was obvious my family sought to draw a curtain over the whole event. My mother had taken me away for a week's holiday. We stayed with one of her sisters who lives in Donegal, and I've never had a more miserable time. Inevitably, it rained every day and there was nothing to do but mope around and remember, trapped in a house full of women, where the only sounds were the clink of china cups and the click of knitting needles. It was then the dreams started. The intervening years have lessened their frequency but not their horror. When I woke up screaming for about the tenth time, they took me to a special doctor who reassured them with all the usual platitudes – I'd grow out of it, time was a great healer, and so on. In one sense I did grow out of it – I stopped telling anyone about the nightmares and kept them strictly private. They don't come very often now, but when they do only my wife knows. Sometimes she cradles me in her arms like a child until I fall asleep again.

I hadn't even really wanted a job in the first place. It was all my father's idea. He remembered the long weeks of boredom I had complained about the summer before and probably the nuisance I had been as I lazed about the house. I walked right into his trap. He knew I'd been working up to ask if I could have a motorbike for my next birthday. The signs weren't good, and my mother's instinctive caution would have been as difficult a barrier to surmount as the expense, so it came as a surprise when my father casually enquired if I'd be interested in starting to save for one. I took the bait, and before I knew what was happening, I'd been fixed up with a summer job, working in Gerry Breen's fruit shop.

I didn't like the man much at first. He was rough and ready and he would've walked ten miles on his knees to save a penny. I don't think he liked me much either. The first day he saw me he looked me up and down with unconcealed disappointment, with the expression of someone who'd just bought a horse that wasn't strong enough to do the work he had envisaged for it. He stopped short of feeling my arm muscles, but passed some comment about me needing to fill out a bit. Although he wasn't tall himself, he was squat and had a kind of stocky strength about him that carried him through every physical situation. You knew that when he put his shoulder to the wheel, the chances were the wheel would spin. He wore this green coat as if it was some sort of uniform, and I never saw him in the shop without it. It was shiny at the elbows and collar, but it always looked clean. He had sandy-coloured hair that was slicked back and oiled down in a style that suggested he had once had an affinity with the Teddy boys. The first time I met him I noticed his hands, which were flat and square, and his chisel-shaped fingers. He had this little red pen-knife, and at regular intervals he used it to clean them. The other habit he had was a continual hitching-up of his trousers, even though there was no apparent prospect of them falling down. He was a man who seemed to be in perpetual motion. Even when he was standing talking to someone, there was always some part of him that was moving, whether it was transferring his pencil from one ear to the other, or hoisting up the trousers. It was as if there was a kind of mechanism inside him. Sometimes I saw him shuffle his feet through three hundred and sixty degrees like some kind of clockwork toy. For him sitting still would have been like wearing a strait-jacket, and I don't think any chair, no matter how comfortable, ever held him for more than a few minutes.

On my first morning, after his initial disappointment had worn off and he had obviously resolved to make the best of a bad job, he handed me a green coat, similar to his own but even older. It had a musty smell about it that suggested it had been hanging in a dark cupboard for some considerable time, and although I took it home that first weekend for my mother to wash, I don't think the smell ever left it. The sleeves were too long, so all summer I wore it with the cuffs turned up. My first job was chopping sticks. As well as fruit and vegetables, he sold various other things, including bundles of firewood. Out in the back yard was a mountain of wood, mostly old fruit boxes, and for the rest of that morning I chopped them into sticks and put them in polythene bags. At regular intervals he came out to supervise the work and caution me with monotonous regularity to be careful with the hatchet. It was obvious I wasn't doing it to his satisfaction; his dissatisfaction was communicated by a narrowing of his eyes and a snakelike hiss. As far as I was concerned, there weren't too many ways you could chop sticks, but I was wrong. Unable to restrain his frustration any longer, he took the hatchet and proceeded to instruct me in the correct technique. This involved gently inserting it into the end of the piece of wood and then tapping the other end lightly on the ground so that it split gently along the grain. When he was assured I had mastered the method, he watched critically over my first efforts.

'Too thick, son, too thick. Did your da never teach you how to chop sticks?'

It was only when I had produced a series of the thinnest slivers that he seemed content. I suppose it meant he got more bundles of firewood, but you wouldn't have got much of a fire out of them. It made me feel guilty somehow, like I was an accessory to his stinginess. 'Did your da never teach you how to?' was a phrase I heard repeatedly that summer, and it inevitably prefaced a period of instruction in the correct technique and subsequent supervision.

The rest of my time that first morning was divided between sweeping up and humping bags of spuds from the yard into the store-room. No matter how often I brushed that shop floor, it always seemed to need to be done again. I must have filled a whole dump with cauliflower leaves, and I never stopped hating that smell. Perhaps, if I'm honest, I felt the job was a little beneath me. By the time the day was over, my back was aching and I was still trying to extract splinters from my hands. The prospect of a summer spent working like that filled me with despondency, and the attraction of a motorbike lost some of its appeal. I thought of telling my father I didn't want to go back, but was stopped by the knowledge that I would have to listen to eternal speeches about how soft young people were, and how they wanted everything on a plate. That I didn't need, and so I resolved to grit my teeth and stick it out.

The shop was situated at the bottom of the Antrim Road, and while it wasn't that big, every bit of space was used, either for display or storage. It started outside on the pavement where each morning, after carrying out wooden trestles and resting planks on them, we set out trays of fruit, carefully arranged and hand-picked, designed to attract and entice the passer-by. Above all this stretched a green canvas canopy which was supported by ancient iron stanchions, black with age. When it rained it would drip on to the front displays of fruit and so all that summer I had to carry them in and out of the shop. Inside was a long counter with old-fashioned scales and a till that rang as loudly as church bells. Under the counter were paper bags of every size, miles of string, metal hooks, bamboo canes, withered yellow rubber gloves, weights, elastic bands and a paraphernalia of utensils of unfathomable purpose. On the wall behind the counter was an assortment of glass fronted shelving, sagging under the weight of fruit and vegetables. Above head height, the walls were covered in advertising posters that had obviously arrived free with consignments of fruit and looked like they had been there since the shop opened. On the customer side was more shelving and below it a clutter of wooden and cardboard boxes that seemed designed to ladder tights or catch the wheels of shopping trolleys. If there was any kind of logical system in the layout, I never managed to work it out. I got the impression it had evolved into a sprawling disorder and that so long as everything was close at hand, the owner saw no reason to change it.

In the back of the shop was a store-room where among merchandise and debris stood a wooden table, two chairs, a gas cooker and a sink. The only other room was a small washroom. Beyond this was a small cobbled yard, enclosed by a brick wall topped with broken glass. Over everything hung the sweet, ripe smell of a fruit shop, but in Mr Breen's shop it was mixed with a mildewed mustiness, a strange hybrid that stayed in my senses long after I had left the scene.

I worked my butt off that first day and it was obvious he intended getting value for money out of me. Maybe my father had told him it was what I needed – I don't know. It was nearly time to close and the shop was empty. He was working out some calculations on the back of a brown paper bag and I was moving fruit into the store-room, when he glanced up at me with a kind of puzzled look, as if he was trying to work out what I was thinking.

'Sure, son, it's money for old rope. Isn't that right?'

I gave a non-committal nod of my head and kept on working. Then he told me I could go, and I could tell he was wondering whether he would see me the next day. Returning to his calculations again, he licked the stub of the pencil he was using and hitched up his trousers. I said goodbye and just as I was going out the door he called me back.

'Do you want to know something, son?'

I looked at him, unsure of what response he expected. Then, signalling me closer, he whispered loudly, 'My best friends are bananas.' I forced a smile at his joke, then walked out into the street and took a deep breath of fresh air.

The fruit shop did steady business. Most of the trade came from the housewives who lived in the neighbourhood, but there was also a regular source of custom from people who arrived outside the shop in cars, and by their appearance didn't live locally – the type who bought garlic. He knew them all by name and sometimes even had their order already

made up, always making a fuss over them and getting me to
carry it out to their car. They were obviously long-standing
customers, and I suppose they must have stayed loyal to him
because they were assured of good quality fruit. He had a
way with him – I had to admit that. He called every woman
'madam' for a start, even those who obviously weren't, but
when he said it, it didn't sound like flattery, or like he was
patronizing them. It just sounded polite in an old-fashioned
way. He had a great line in chat as well. If he didn't know
them it was usually some remark about the weather, but if he
did, he would ask about their families or make jokes, always
cutting his cloth according to his audience. When a gaggle of
local women were in, it was all 'Now, come on, ladies, get
your grapes. Sweetest you can taste. Just the thing for putting
passion into your marriage,' or 'Best bananas – good enough
to eat sideways.' They all loved it, and I'm sure it was good
for business. Whatever their bills came to, he always gave
them back the few odd pence, and I'm sure they thought he
was very generous. As far as I was concerned, I thought
he was one of the meanest men I'd ever met. For a start, he
never threw anything away – that was one of the things that
was wrong with the shop. Whether it was a bit of string or a
piece of wood, he stored it carefully, and if he saw me about
to throw something away, he'd stop me with a 'Never know
when it might come in useful, son.' Most of the produce he
collected himself from the market early in the morning, but
whenever deliveries were made, he inspected each consign-
ment rigorously, with an energy that frequently exasperated
the deliverer. If he found a damaged piece of fruit, he would
hold it up for mutual observation and, wrestling up his
trousers with the other hand, would say something like,
'Now come on George, are you trying to put me out of
business?' and he'd haggle anew over already arranged
prices. Watching him sniffing out flawed produce would
have made you think he'd an in-built radar system. And he
was always looking for something for nothing. Sometimes it
was embarrassing. If the Antrim Road had still had horses

going up and down it, he'd have been out collecting the droppings and selling them for manure.

One day Father Hennessy came into the shop. Mr Breen's faced dropped noticeably and about half a dozen parts of his body seemed to fidget all at once.

'Hello, Father. What can I do for you?'

'Hello, Gerry. How's business?'

'Slow, Father, very slow.'

The priest smiled and, lifting an apple, rubbed it on his sleeve, the red bright against the black.

'I'm popping over to the Mater to visit some parishioners. I thought a nice parcel of fruit would cheer them up. Help them to get better.'

He started to eat the apple and his eyes were smiling.

'Of course, Father. A very good idea.'

With well-disguised misery, he parcelled up a variety of fruit and handed it over the counter.

'God bless you, Gerry. Treasure in heaven, treasure in heaven.'

With the package tucked under his arm, and still eating the apple, the priest sauntered out to his car. If he had looked back, he would have seen Mr Breen slumped on the counter, his head resting on both hands.

'The church'll be the ruin of me. He does that about three times a month. Thinks my name's Mr Del Monte, not Gerry Breen. Treasure in heaven's no use to me when I go to pay the bills at the end of the month.'

The frustration poured out of him and I listened in silence, knowing he wasn't really talking to me.

'Does he go up to Michael Devlin in the bank and ask him for some money because he's going to visit the poor? Since when did it become part of my purpose in life to subsidize the National Health system? I pay my taxes like anyone else.'

I think he'd have gone on indefinitely in a similar vein, but for the arrival of a customer, and then it was all smiles and jokes about the rain.

'Do you know, Mrs Caskey, what I and my assistant are building out in the yard?'

Mrs Caskey didn't know but her aroused curiosity was impatient for an answer.

'We're building an ark! And whenever it's finished we're going to load up two of every type of fruit and float away up the road.'

'Get away with you, Gerry. You're a desperate man.'

And then he sold her tomatoes and a lettuce which he described as 'the best lettuce in the shop'. I'd almost have believed him myself, but for the fact that I'd already heard the same phrase on about three previous occasions that day.

Gerry Breen was very proud of his shop, but he took a special pride in his displays outside, and he did this expert printing with whitening on the front window. Not only did he fancy himself a bit of an artist, but also as a kind of poet laureate among fruiterers. He had all these bits of cardboard – I think they were backing cards out of shirts – and on them he printed, not only the names and prices of the fruit, but also descriptive phrases meant to stimulate the taste buds of the reader. Grapes might be described as 'deliciously sweet' or strawberries as 'the sweet taste of summer' while Comber spuds were always 'balls of flour'. The front window always looked well. Bedded on a gentle slope of simulated grass rested the various sections of produce, complete with printed labels. Each morning when he had arranged it he would go out on the pavement and stand with his hands on his hips, studying it like an art critic viewing a painting. Inside he had other signs saying things like 'Reach for a peach', 'Iceberg lettuce – just a tip of the selection' or 'Fancy an apple – why not eat a pear?'

After the first week or so we started to get on a little better. I think he realized that I was trustworthy and prepared to pull my weight. He probably thought of me as being a bit snobbish, but tolerated it so long as he got good value for his money. I in turn became less critical of what I considered his defects. Gradually, he began to employ more of my time on less menial jobs. After three weeks I had progressed to serving customers and weighing their fruit, and then a week later I was allowed to enter the holy of holies and put my hand in the till. I still had to chop sticks and brush up of course, but whenever the shop was busy I served behind the counter. I almost began to feel part of the business. The continual wet weather stopped me from missing out on the usual activities of summer and I was increasingly optimistic that my father would reward my industry with a motorbike. Mr Breen didn't much like the rain – he was always complaining how bad it was for business. According to him, it discouraged passing trade, and people didn't buy as much as they did in warm weather. He was probably right. Sometimes, when a lull in trade created boredom, I tried to wind him up a little.

'Mr Breen, do you not think it's wrong to sell South African fruit?'

'Aw, don't be daft, son.'

'But do you not think that by selling their fruit you're supporting apartheid?'

He swopped his pencil from ear to ear and did what looked a bit like a tap dance.

'I'm only supporting myself and the wife. Sure wouldn't the blacks be the first to suffer if I stopped selling it? They'd all end up starving and how would that help them?'

I was about to provoke him further when a customer appeared and I let him have the last word.

'God knows, son, they have my sympathy – don't I work like a black myself?'

The customer turned out to be Mr Breen's wife. She was all dressed up in a blue and white suit and was on her way to some social function. She had one of those golden charm bracelets that clunked so many heavy charms I wondered how her wrist bore the strain, and while she hardly looked sideways at him, she made an embarrassing fuss over me, asking about my parents and school, and gushing on in a slightly artificial way. When she finished whatever business she had, she said goodbye to me and warned Gerald not to work me too hard. I smiled at the name Gerald, and I could see him squirming behind the counter. A heavy shower came on and we both stood in the doorway watching it bounce off the road. He was unusually silent and I glanced at him a few times to see if he was all right. When he spoke, his voice was strangely colourless.

'Never get married, son – it's the end of your happiness.'

I didn't know whether he was joking or not, so I just went on staring at the rain.

'My wife's ashamed of me,' he said in the same lifeless voice.

I uttered some vague and unconvincing disagreement and then turned away in embarrassment. I started to brush the floor, glancing up from time to time as he stood motionless in the doorway. In a minute or so the rain eased and it seemed to break the spell, but for the rest of that afternoon, he was subdued and functioned in a mechanical way. He even closed the shop half an hour early – something he'd never done before.

Nothing like that ever happened again, my first experience of work slipped into an uneventful routine. One day, though, comes clearly to mind. One afternoon when business was slack he asked me to deliver fruit round to a Mrs McCausland. The address was a couple of streets away and I felt a little self-conscious as I set off in my green coat. It wasn't a big order – just a few apples and oranges and things. I followed the directions I had been given and arrived at a terraced house. Unlike most of its neighbours, the front door was closed, and the net curtain in the window offered no glimpse of the interior. At first, it seemed as if no one was in, and I was just about to turn and leave, when there was the slow undrawing of a bolt and the rattle of a chain. The door opened wide enough to allow an old woman's face to peer out at me, suspicion speckling her eyes. I identified myself and showed the fruit to reassure her. Then there was another pause before the door gradually opened to reveal an old woman leaning heavily on a walking stick. Inviting me in, she hobbled off slowly and painfully down the hall and into her tiny living room. She made me sit down and, despite my polite protests, proceeded to make me a cup of tea. The room resembled a kind of grotto, adorned with religious objects and pictures. Her rosary beads hung from the fireplace clock and a black cat slept on the rug-covered sofa. She talked to me from the kitchen as she worked.

'Isn't the weather terrible?'

'Desperate – you'd never think it was the summer,' I replied, smiling as I listened to myself. I had started to sound like Gerry Breen's apprentice.

'Summers never used to be like this. I can remember summers when the streets were baked hot as an oven and everyone used to sit on their doorsteps for you could hardly get a breath. If you sat on your doorstep these past few days you'd get pneumonia.'

She brought me a cup of tea in a china cup, and a slice of fruit cake, but nothing for herself. She sat down and scrutinized me intently.

'So you're working for Gerry for the summer. I'm sure that's good fun for you. You work hard and maybe he'll keep you on permanent.'

I didn't correct her misunderstanding, but I laughed silently inside.

'He says if it keeps on raining he's going to start building an ark.'

She smiled and rearranged the cushion supporting her back.

'Gerry's the salt of the earth. Do you see that fruit you brought? He's been doing that for the best part of fifteen years and nobody knows but him and me.'

She paused to pour more tea into my cup and I listened with curiosity as she continued, her words making me feel as if I was looking at a familiar object from a new and unexpected perspective.

'I gave him a wee bit of help a long time ago and he's

never forgotten it, not through all these years. I don't get out much now, but sometimes I take a walk round to the shop, just to see how he's getting on. He's a great man for the crack, isn't he?'

I smiled in agreement and she shuffled forward in her seat, leaning confidentially towards me.

'Have you met Lady Muck yet? Thon woman's more airs and graces than royalty. She was born and bred a stone's throw from here and to listen to her now you'd think she came from the Malone Road. I knew her family and they didn't have two pennies to rub together between the lot of them. Now she traipses round the town like she was a duchess. You'll never catch her serving behind the counter.'

It was obvious that the woman wanted to talk – she was probably starved of company – and no matter how often I attempted a polite exit, she insisted on my staying a little longer, assuring me that Gerry wouldn't mind. I wasn't so sure, but there was no easy escape, as she produced a photograph album and talked me through a maze of memories and mementoes.

Parts of it were interesting and when she told me about the Belfast blitz I learned things I hadn't known before. Before I finally got up to go, she returned to the subject of the weather, her voice serious and solemn.

'This weather's a sign. I've been reading about it in a tract that was sent to me. It's by this holy scholar, very high up in the church, and he says we're living in the last days. All these wars and famines – they're all signs. All this rain – it's a sign too. I believe it.'

When she opened the front door it was still raining and I almost started to believe it too. I ran back quickly, partly to get out of the rain and partly because I anticipated a rebuke about the length of my absence.

There were no customers in the shop when I entered and he merely lifted his head from what he was reading, asked if everything was all right with Mrs McCausland, and returned to his study. It surprised me a little that he said nothing about the time. He was filling in his pools coupon and concentrating on winning a fortune, so perhaps he was distracted by the complexities of the Australian leagues. He had been doing them all summer and his approach never varied. He did two columns every week, the first by studying the form and this forced him to ponder such probabilities as whether Inala City would draw with Slacks Creek, or Altona with Bulleen. For the second column, he selected random numbers, his eyes screwed up and an expression on his face as if he was waiting for some kind of celestial message. On this particular afternoon, reception must have been bad, because he asked me to shout them out. Out of genuine curiosity, I asked him what he would do if he did win a fortune. He looked at me to see if I was winding him up, but must have sensed that I wasn't, because, on a wet and miserable Belfast afternoon, he told me his dream.

'It's all worked out in here,' he said, tapping the side of his head with a chisel-shaped finger. 'I've it all planned out. Thinking about it keeps you going – makes you feel better on days like this.'

He paused to check if I was laughing at him, then took a hand out of his coat pocket and gestured slowly round the shop.

'Look around you, son. What do you see?'

A still, grey light seemed to have filtered into the shop. The lights were off and it was quiet in an almost eerie way. Nothing rustled or stirred, and the only sound was the soft fall of the rain. In the gloom the bright colours smouldered like embers; rhubarb like long tongues of flame; red sparks of apples; peaches, perfect in their velvety softness, yellows and oranges flickering gently.

'Fruit,' I answered. 'Different kinds of fruit.'

'Now, do you know what I see?'

I shook my head.

'I see places. A hundred different places. Look again.' And as he spoke he began to point with his finger. 'Oranges from Spain, apples from New Zealand, cabbages from

Holland, peaches from Italy, grapes from the Cape, bananas from Ecuador – fruit from all over the world. Crops grown and harvested by hands I never see, packed and transported by other hands in a chain that brings them here to me. It's a miracle if you think about it. When we're sleeping in our beds, hands all over the world are packing and picking so that Gerry Breen can sell it here in this shop.'

We both stood and looked, absorbing the magnitude of the miracle.

'You asked me what I'd do if I won the jackpot – well, I've got it all thought out. I'd go to every country whose fruit I sell, go and see it grow, right there in the fields and the groves, in the orchards and the vineyards. All over the world!'

He looked at me out of the corner of his eye to see if I thought he was crazy, then turned away and began to tidy the counter. I didn't say anything, but in that moment, if he'd asked me, I would have gone with him. All these years later, I still regret that I didn't tell him that. Told him while there was still time.

Four days later, Gerry Breen was dead. A man walked into the shop and shot him twice. He became another bystander, another nobody, sucked into the vortex by a random and malignant fate that marked him out. They needed a Catholic to balance the score – he became a casualty of convenience, a victim of retribution, propitiation of a different god. No one even claimed it. Just one more sectarian murder – unclaimed, unsolved, soon unremembered but by a few. A name lost in the anonymity of a long list. I would forget too, but I can't.

I remember it all. There were no customers when a motorbike stopped outside with two men on it. The engine was still running as the passenger came towards the shop. I was behind the counter looking out. He had one hand inside his black motorcycle tunic and wore a blue crash helmet – the type that encloses the whole head. A green scarf covered the bottom half of his face, so only his eyes were visible. Only his eyes – that's all I ever saw of him. Mr Breen was standing holding a tray of oranges he had just brought from the back.

Suddenly, the man pulled a gun out of his tunic and I thought we were going to be robbed, but he never spoke, and as he raised the gun and pointed at Mr Breen, his hand was shaking so much he had to support it with the other one. It was then I knew he hadn't come for money. The first shot hit Gerry Breen in the chest, spinning him round, and as he slumped to the floor the oranges scattered and rolled in all directions. He lay there, face down, and his body was still moving. Then, as I screamed an appeal for mercy, the man walked forward and, kneeling over the body, shot him in the back of the head. His body kicked and shuddered, and then was suddenly and unnaturally still. I screamed again in fear and anger and then, pointing the gun at me, the man walked slowly backwards to the door of the shop, ran to the waiting bike and was gone. Shaking uncontrollably and stomach heaving with vomit, I tried to turn Mr Breen over on to his back, but he was too heavy for me. Blood splashed his green coat, and flowed from the dark gaping wound, streaming across the floor, mixing with the oranges that were strewn all around us. Oranges from Spain.

They say help arrived almost immediately. I don't know. All I can remember is thinking of the old woman's words and hoping it really was the end of the world, and being glad and asking God to drown the world, wanting it to rain for a thousand years, rain and rain and never stop until all the blood was washed away and every street was washed clean. There were voices then and helping hands trying to lift me away, but no one could move me as I knelt beside him, clutching frantically at his green coat, begging God not to let him die, praying he'd let Gerry Breen live to build his ark and bring aboard the fruit of the world. All the fruit of the world safely stored. Oranges from Spain, apples from the Cape – the sweet taste of summer preserved for ever, eternal and incorruptible.

Eoin McNamee

If Angels had Wings

WE'VE ALL done it, imagined our own funerals. Inevitably the church is overflowing. There is unrestrained weeping. A mysterious woman dressed in black stands at the back of the crowd, then steps forward to lay a wreath. The face is veiled, but the hands are beautifully manicured, the nails long and red, cuticles stripped with orange stick and the skin so fine it is almost transparent so that the tips of her fingers are drops of milky water. There is some scandalized whispering, and men eye their wives wishing it to be over, earth rustling like sheets on the lid of the coffin.

At least that's how I imagine it. Other people probably have their own way. That's why, when they were burying Deeds I stood eyeing the crowd expectantly. If anyone had earned a beautiful stranger it was him. All I saw were familiar faces. Like Boyle, the teacher, who had got Deeds by the throat once, and thrust his chalky, bald head into his face hissing 'Your misdeeds will be the death of me.' That's how he got the name Deeds.

They were lowering the coffin into the ground. A few years ago they excavated an ancient graveyard in the middle of the town to build a new roundabout. There were graves exposed everywhere, the lids of the coffins as thin as old parchment. Deeds selected four or five skulls and lined them up on a wall. They were grinning at him and he was grinning back as he blasted them to dust and fragments with an air rifle.

'The living revenge themselves upon the dead,' he said, and laughed.

It all had a beginning in the Harbour Cafe one Saturday afternoon. The stainless steel urn steamed, fogging the windows. Greasespots separating and merging on the surface of the tea in front of me. Wadding a cigarette between finger and thumb and smoking it into a tight ducks arse.

Ten of us met there every Saturday, all wearing white tartan scarves which were Deeds' idea. We had been planning for some weeks to ambush a youth called Annett. Annett's father was the richest man in the town, but it wasn't as if Annett himself had done anything in particular.

We finished our tea and walked the hundred yards to the top of the Harbour road. Deeds stood in a doorway and the rest of us crouched behind a wall. We waited for a long time. I remember JB turning to me and remarking how cold it was.

After another length of time we heard Deeds whistle. It was the signal, and the rest of them turned to look at me. I looked down and saw a beetle climbing over a dead leaf. I flipped the leaf and counted to ten. Before I had finished the beetle had come out from underneath. I flipped the leaf again and climbed over the wall with the rest of them behind me.

It worked perfectly. Annett was trapped halfway between Deeds, who had stepped out from the doorway, and the rest of us. He was tall and stupid looking with small eyes in a big, spade shaped head. I lit a cigarette and sat on the wall. Annett looked at Deeds, then looked back at the rest of us and stopped walking. He took his hands out of his pockets but left them swinging by his sides.

Deeds walked right up to him and hesitated, wanted Annett to strike first, but he didn't move so Deeds turned sideways to him, swivelled on one foot and kicked him hard in the crotch with the other. Annett took two steps backwards cradling his balls but not saying anything. Then Deeds swung his fist.

It was a quiet winter's day going on towards evening. Everything was slate-grey and very still. There was the sound that an apple makes when you pull the two halves apart. Annett went down with blood on his mouth.

It was counterfeit and we all knew it. I started to see faces, photographs, men behind barbed wire, a woman with a child on her hip and flies on her eyes, a man watching a plume of smoke rising above hills that weren't far enough away. Mortals. I wanted to know what we were doing there.

Deeds just stood looking at the body at his feet as if it were a crack that had opened in the pavement. Then he turned and walked past us as if we were invisible.

Afterwards he said that he had felt as if he had suddenly lost touch with everything. Not that anything had changed, but that he himself had become unreal, like a ghost. I looked at his big round face and his expression as if butter wouldn't melt in his mouth and I laughed.

Whatever about ghosts, when we got back to the Harbour Cafe I felt as if I were a giant ten feet tall. No one had anything to say about the fight and most of us drifted home. Deeds went off to inspect his loft.

Deeds spent a lot of time in the loft, in the clatter of pigeons' wings and the soft sounds they made to themselves. Deeds and Jammy had built it on the roof of an old warehouse by the river. Jammy was the son of an alcoholic. He had shoulder length brown hair, a speech defect and a chinful of pimples on the verge of bursting. He followed Deeds around and treated the pigeons as if they were his children.

The river itself was dirty and shallow, full of old prams, slime-covered rocks and fish heads. Deeds and Jammy had found the wood they needed along its banks and had painted the loft with scraps of paint, tar and creosote. Inside they kept bags of meal, pliers for ringing the pigeons' legs, carrying baskets and ointment for toe-rot and other diseases. And pigeons: blues, greys, fantails.

Deeds would take a pigeon in his cupped hands like water to blow its breastfeathers apart or stroke them against the grain with his forefinger. 'Look at that,' he would say, 'if an angel was going to fly like a pigeon it would have to have a chest ten feet wide to get off the ground.'

The loft was also where he brought Anne-Marie Clarke,

the waitress from the Harbour Cafe. She had olive skin and huge breasts, the blue and white nylon of her apron shifting and hissing as she moved among the tables. She had big eyes and a small mouth and rarely spoke.

Almost a week after the fight with Annett Deeds and Jammy climbed up to the loft. To safeguard the approach Deeds had devised a system of ladders which would come away from the wall, holes in the roof disguised by loose tiles, gutters weakened so that if you put a foot wrong it would tilt you into the river seventy or eighty feet below. Snakes and Ladders he called it.

It hadn't worked this time. You've seen footage of great disasters on television with the victims laid out on the floor of an aircraft hangar or church hall, covered with blankets. It was like that. The pigeons were lined up in neat rows, each one with its neck broken and a tiny bubble of dried blood on its beak.

It must have been Annett's workmen, or the owner of the warehouse acting under Annett's instructions.

It was worse for Jammy. Deeds used to take the birds to a field outside the town and release them, watching them fly in a tight homing circle. Jammy hated it, thinking that they wouldn't come back.

Deeds carried the corpses to the edge of the roof and dropped them into the river.

Jammy wasn't missed until the next day. Deeds found him floating face up in the river. Everyone assumed that Jammy had stumbled blindly into one of the traps and had been thrown into the river below. The police wanted to talk to Deeds.

Later that evening I was walking along the Banks when I met Deeds. The Banks are brick coloured cliffs overlooking a shingle beach near the Harbour. There are grass clippings, old bottles and builders rubble piled up at their foot. Deeds was smoking a cigarette and staring out to sea. The waves raked through the shingle.

We were silent for a while, then Deeds started to talk. He

told me how he'd found Jammy wedged between rocks with head pointing downstream, the current rolling it from side to side as if he was being interrogated by an invisible hand. The blood had drained from his face so his complexion was clear and his hair streamed out behind him. Deeds swore he looked beautiful. Then he told me that Jammy hadn't slipped. The other thing hadn't occurred to me.

That was the last conversation I had with him. Later that night he had gone to the Annett house which was a tall red-brick building at the edge of town with a tree-lined drive and neat lawns. He had a petrol bomb with him.

There is a way of holding a petrol bomb when you throw it so that the petrol doesn't spill down your arm. You don't overfill it and you hold it the correct way. Deeds taught me that.

But the next thing Deeds went up in flames directly in front of the sitting room window. Old man Annett puts down his paper, his wife sets aside her bridge cards, and they come to the window and stand in silence to look out to where Deeds is burning a hole in their lawn. The next day they had a gardener sowing grass seed on the burnt patch.

I stayed behind in the graveyard after the funeral. After a while two men strolled up with shovels, rolled up the artificial grass and started to fill in the grave. I heard the earth strike the coffin, and felt as if they were throwing everything in. Fish heads, old prams, grass clippings, builders rubble, old bottles. Anything to make him stay down there. I left them to it and went home.

A few weeks later I went down to the Banks with Anne-Marie. There were no formalities with her. You walked in silence until you found a spot and then you lay down. Once she got into her stride you knew that you might as well be anyone. It was almost as if you could get up and walk away and she would still be lying there, her eyes closed and her soft little mouth probing the air like the snout of some half blind night creature.

We were on a patch of grass half way down the cliff path.

On our right the sodium arc-lights over the Harbour reflected on the underside of low cloud, making the night seem twice as dark. They reminded me of flames and I felt uneasy.

Suddenly I remember some picture that Deeds had torn from some porn magazine and stuck on the wall of the loft. It was of a tomb in Paris. The man had been a founder of a fertility cult, Deeds told me, and the place was still a shrine. He was cast in bronze, lying on his back in a frock coat and top hat. The girl in the photograph wore a black veil. She had hitched up her black dress and straddled the lying figure, crushing her pink genitals against the bronze crotch.

I opened my eyes and saw that Anne-Marie had hers open. She was staring over my shoulder at the spot where I had last talked with Deeds. I felt a chill run through me, then I took her head in both my hands and forced her eyes to mine and her mouth to mine and kissed her and kissed her again. As far as I was concerned there were no beautiful strangers, and the only ghosts in this town were the ones that were walking the streets.

Benedict Kiely

from *Proxopera*

BUT KYRIE ELEISON what is this on the road on a Sunday
morning, smoke rising from the smouldering stump of
what's left of the Orange Hall where once that love-bewil-
dered young Protestant provoked a riot by footing the light
fantastic with a papist girl. In this present Ulster world there's
little place for the light fantastic: close to Newry town the
UVF or was it the UDA murdered a showband.

My road drops down, doing a double bend, into a saucer
of a valley. High, green, terraced banks, no turn left or right,
no turning back, no way out except straight through: *There
we were like two Robinson Crusoes far away from Fireagh Orange
Hall. Though we starved on that rock for a fortnight, not a ship ever
came within call.* Fireagh, here I come. And the Orange Hall
has just gone. Up in smoke. Thirty or so people are in and
around what's left of it. As close to the smouldering ruins as
they dare to go. The flames have blackened the bushes on
the high bank above. Sweet sight for a Sunday in a good
autumn. No soldiers around. This is a fire. Not a fight. Thank
God for that. But for what? One policeman raises his blue-
black arm. What can I do but stop? No use to say to him halt
me at your peril. And the peril of everybody in this little
valley. And of my son and his wife and Gary and Catherine
and Minnie, Minnie Brown we're home again from Dungloe
town.

—Good morning, Mr Binchey. Bit of a surprise to see
you at the wheel.

A decent fellow. I drank with his father. Also in the force.
And a brother of his, a plain-clothes man, murdered in the

town, twelve months ago. Sitting reading the paper at a bar-counter when two gunmen walked in. Into a pub in which he had had his first drink. And in which on my way from teaching I used to drink with his father, at the same counter at the same place. Tried to pull his gun. They shot him once. Crawled into the gents. They followed him and finished the job and shouted: We have you in the right place on the shithouse floor.

That pub would never be the same again.

—Good morning, constable. I wouldn't be at the wheel only necessity knows no law.

How true, how bloody true.

—We got back from Donegal last night. Margaret wasn't feeling too well. Robert's on the suspended list. As you know. So old grandad has to head off to the chemist. But I'm taking it easy.

—It's the best thing to do these days, Mr Binchey. If you can. What do you think of that on a Sunday morning?

The engine purrs. He's afraid to cut it off. God only knows what restarting might do. The constable is a squat solid civil fellow with a squint, and his face smudged from the fire the way the soldiers, now and in this place, smudge their faces on night patrol, in my own town, dear God, battledress and camouflage in my own town. Could I tell him that time is ticking away? Could I tell him that someone in the crowd is watching?

—What happened, constable?

—IRA. I'd say, a reprisal for the Catholic church at Altamuskin. The UVF tossed a bomb into that.

—Oh, what a wonderful war.

—So now the UVF will bomb another Catholic church. Or a Catholic pub. Then the IRA will shoot a policeman or bomb a Protestant pub. And then the UVF . . .

—Was the brigade here?

—Couldn't make it. Fire's everywhere this bloody morning. All a few miles outside town. Cornstacks. Barns. Anything.

Aha, the grand strategy, get the brigade away from the town, make straight the path for Binchey the Burner. Time's ticking away.

—They could be up to something else, Mr Binchey. All this could be a diversion.

It sure as God could, except that diversion is not the word that Mr Binchey, his ass squelching in a pool of sweat, his stomach frozen with fear, his mind running crazily on irrelevancies, would have chosen. What at the moment is relevant? Time's ticking away. Time's relevant. How long have I left? How long has anybody left? Half an hour after I place the bomb even at the remoter place, the Judge's house, say fifty minutes to an hour, constable, constable let me pass or I'll wet my pants or my heart will stop.

—These are queer times, Mr Binchey, pubs and churches, women and children, my own brother, the Tower of London, and in London too the Ideal Homes Exhibition, a bomb by the escalator, sixty-five mutilated and eleven of them Irish, bad, mad times.

With utterly resigned terror Mr Binchey recalls that the constable's father was an amiable long-winded man. In the smouldering wreckage another constable has discovered something and the crowd has gathered around him. So if I go up I'll only bring this boy with me. The watcher, whoever he is, will be watching from a safe distance. That's the name of the game. Proxopera. Proxopera. He spells it to himself as a sort of charm to move the man to let him pass. But, hands on the door of the car, stooping down, square head half in the window, smudged face still smelling of good aftershave lotion, the young man in blue-black uniform one of the last surviving symbols of an empire gone forever into the shadows, is preparing to talk to Mr Binchey, as venerable, as respectable, as comforting as the face of the town clock: this is an historic moment and I was a teacher of history and Latin and English literature, and time is ticking away.

—But one of the worst things of all, Mr Binchey, was that business in the Catholic graveyard at Lisnagarda on the outskirts of Scarva in County Down. Even in the bloody graveyard nothing's sacred.

She sleeps, waiting for me, in new Drumragh, I come, I come, my heart's delight.

—I didn't hear about that.

—It happened, I'd say, when you were in Donegal. The caretaker of the graveyard, sixty-one years of age, a woman, walking in the graveyard in the morning, sees a wreath lying on the path. Purple plastic chrysanthemums and white roses. Thinks it was blown from a new grave. Picks it up. Boom. Boobytrapped. Sure as Jesus. Could you beat that, Mr Binchey?

An awkward question, in the silvery can, constable my constable, time is ticking away, I'm boobytrapped like the white roses and purple plastic chysanthemums, we may boom and go aloft together.

—Only a part of it went off or the poor woman was done for. As it was, hands, legs and body severely injured. An old lady. Sixty-one. In a consecrated graveyard. Blood running out of her, she staggered three hundred yards to the nearest cottage, rapped on the window and collapsed. Only one shoe and stocking on, blood everywhere. Something, she said, hit me on the foot when I lifted the wreath. God in heaven, wouldn't you think an old woman would be safe in a graveyard?

Every spring we lay on her grave a bunch of daffodils, a branch of green and golden whin.

—Nothing's sacred, Mr Binchey. But I'd better not hold you up.

You'd better not, indeed.

—And the odd thing, Mr Binchey, is that a lot of these fellows, IRA or UVF or UDA or ABCDEXYZ, if left alone wouldn't hurt a cat or a child. But get a few of them together and give them what they think is a leader or an ideal and they'd destroy Asia and themselves and their nearest and dearest.

A military truck comes from the direction of the town.

—Good luck, Mr Binchey. And I hope young Mrs Binchey will be well soon.

—Thank you, constable. And so do I.

Two soldiers walk towards them. They wave casually at Mr Binchey as he goes on his way towards the town he was reared in.

Those two soldiers looked like lizards, protective colouring to be worn in the emerald isle, Ireland of the welcomes and the bomb in the pub and the bullet in the back. He remembers a time when the soldiers in the town dressed smartly, pipe-clayed belts and shining brass badges, polished nailed boots, puttees rolled with precision, peaked caps at an exact angle, walking cane under the oxter the way you'd truss a chicken. They were part of the town then, too, even if they were also part of the far-flung empire: the Royal Irish, the Royal Inniskillings, the pipes playing Adieu to Bellashanny and the Inniskilling Dragoon as they marched from the barracks to the railway station and thence to Aldershot and India or Egypt or the West Indies or Hong Kong or the Burma Road itself. A soldier out for the evening could talk to friends on the street although regulations did not encourage them to loiter at street corners. They drank with the people in the pubs and no madman gloried in shooting them dead in the shithouse. They relaxed with the girls in and around a public park. Or, better still, in whatever private place a poor man could find. Nobody thought of them as an invading hostile army. No girl had her head shaved or was tarred and feathered.

But then we always had with us Bertie's father and the like of him.

Curious thing, but the only book I ever saw in the hands of Bertie's father was a copy of *Mein Kampf*. Not in his hands exactly, but under the oxter where the soldiers kept the canes. He had a stiff left leg and always wore a brown belted overcoat, and had no brains, and through 1939 and 1940 he was never without that book. Never did I see him open it to peek at the treasures within. Was he like the vagrant who was washed and treated at a delousing centre and was delighted to discover, buried under alluvial mud in his navel, a collar-stud he had lost six years before? Yet he carried, even if he didn't read, *Mein Kampf*, because since the Jerries were marching against and going to invade England, Hitler had to be a republican. Declare a republic, Mr Binchey. Oh la–dee–da, says my father, and goes on stirring the porridge. And about the same time there was a crazy missionary father going around, a roaring beanpole of a man, preaching missions in rural and even urban churches, the purest Goebbels who had noebbels at all, and all about the Jews and the Freemasons, and the real names of the rulers of Russia, all ending in ski, until his religious superiors had to put a stop to his gallop and lock him up or something. Oh never fear for Ireland, boys, for she has soldiers still.

No pipeclayed belts, no shining brass badges, no girls in the park, no drinks with the people in the pubs. But soldier boys like lizards on a sunny Irish Sunday against a background of scorched hedgerows and a burned-out Orange Hall, black wicked guns carried at an angle, pointing upwards, Martian antennae. They hold on to their guns as if they might rocket into space. They whistle through their teeth so as to seem carefree. Young fellows from the other island who scarcely know where they are or what they're doing here or what in hell it's all about. Their boots are dull-black, rubber-soled. They can move as quietly as cats round corners or along alleys. In the old days you could hear the clatter of the nailed boots half a mile away: evil secrecies of the world we have lived into. Forty shades of green, ironically, the green above the red, over trousers and combat jacket. And over the bullet-proof vest, a life-jacket for very dry land, and tied down back and front. But only a black beret protects the head and where have all the tin hats and helmets gone?

*

Christ hear us, Christ graciously hear us, I'm gripping the wheel so hard that my left arm has gone completely numb, it's not there, it's amputated, I've only one arm remaining and the road is empty and the sun bright and high and I swelch in sweat but I'll make the bridge where the railway used to be before I rest long enough to shake and rub and exercise that arm back into existence. In Jefferson County jail in Alabama there's a prisoner who's in for using an artificial arm to kill a man – like the joker who killed Miss Kilmannsegg with and for her precious golden leg. He has two artificial arms and he complains that the people who run the prison won't let him wear them so that he can't eat, shave, brush his teeth, change his clothes or clean himself after crapping: but the prison people say that if he had his arms he'd hurt somebody, and there you are, like Ulster, an insoluble problem, and my left arm now hurts like hell so it must still be there but, *exaudi nos domine*, there's the bridge around a pastoral corner, lambs on the green hills gazing at me and many a strawberry grows by the salt sea and many a ship sails the ocean, and up a slight slope, and once up there I can survey the morning smoke of my own town.

There below me as I lean on the parapet and puff and sweat and sip the last of the brandy, the blood of Hennessy the God, is the Grand Canyon of my boyhood, now a choked-up formidable dyke where weeds and wild trailing brambles have smothered the magic well at the world's end. No train will ever again go through there bringing noisy happy summer crowds to the breakers at Bundoran. The world is in wreckage and these madmen would force me to extend that wreckage to my town below, half-asleep in the valley, my town, asleep like a loved woman on a morning pillow, my town, my town, my town. Declare a republic, Mr Binchey, destroy the town, Mr Binchey. Who's watching me now? Where are they? And down in the Grand Canyon I ate sweet raw turnips and drank, from the rock, water as cool as Moselle. That spring will never be the same again, yet for what civilization, my town, is now worth, we still have inherited something, we have many good memories. Now I see. Let them watch and damn them to the lowest pit.

Here where I lean, the parapet was once shattered by a runaway truck and during the repairs a boy wrote in the soft concrete the name he imagined himself by: Black Wolf. And I'm the man who was the boy who wrote Black Wolf, and the concrete hardened, as is its nature, and there the name still is, and would Black Wolf ever submit to what the madmen are now trying to force on me, and go on for the rest of his life remembering that to save his own family he had planted death in his own town which is also his family? And even if every blade of grass were an eye watching me, to hell with them, let the grass wither in the deepest Stygian pits of gloom, and blast and blind the bastards and Bertie Bigboots and Mad Minahan and that creepy half-literate Corkman. Now I see. Mud in the eyes is a help and, more than my son and his son, or the bees in the pink oxalis, I see there my town and all its people, Orange and Green, and the post office with all its clerks and postmen and red mail vans, and the town hall and its glass dome and everybody in it – from that fine man, my friend, town clerk, or mayor, for forty-odd years, down to the decent tobacco-chewing man who swabs out the public jakes in the basement, my people, my people. Under that glass dome I played as a young man in amateur theatricals, the Coming of the Magi, the Plough and the Stars, the Shadow, God help us, of a Gunman, and the return of Professor Tim and the Monkey's Paw and the shop at Sly Corner and Look at the Heffernans, and all the talk and all the harmless posturing and laughter, my people. Hissing into a sock or something Corkman couldn't know what a town is. Even by consenting for a moment to drive this load of death I've given these rotten bastards some sort of a devil's right over the lives of my people. What, after my death, will they say about me in the local papers, what would they remember: that I carried a bomb on a sunny Sunday to the town hall and the post office or to the door of Judge Flynn who's one of the best men in the north and who goes every day in danger: they've already murdered a good Judge at his door in the morning and in the presence of his seven-year-old daughter, and now I see and there she is, the virgin, the sleeping beauty inaccessible in a sleeping wood, and thorns and thorns around her and the cries of night? Did she stir in her sleep? Did her guts rumble? My left arm stings but it is alive again.

He places his left hand, palm flat, on the creamery can. He strokes her as if she were a cat. He recalls harmless tricks of boyhood, putting carbide in tins, boring holes in the tins, clamping down the lids, dripping water through the holes, listening for the hiss, putting matches to the holes, and delighting in the bangs and the soaring tins: or tossing squibs over the garden fences of crabbed old men. Down in the valley his town is at peace and blue peace is on the hills beyond. This may be farewell forever, the end of my ill-fated cruise on the treacherous waves of Lough Muck. He says to the can that, daughter of Satan, you'll never get to where you were sent. The beleaguered white house is far away in another world, her grave is very near. He closes the boot carelessly, turns the car sharply on the road, and drives back towards the nameless lake of the mad old women.

Maeve Kelly

Orange Horses

ELSIE MARTIN'S husband beat her unconscious because she called him twice for his dinner while he was talking to his brother. To be fair, she did not simply call him. She blew the horn of the Hiace van to summon him.

He had never beaten her unconscious before. He was surprised and a little frightened when she lay down and did not get up. He was a small man but she was even smaller, weighing barely seven stone, and she was further handicapped by being five months pregnant. Afterwards his mother said that if Elsie had fed herself better instead of wasting good money on them fags she'd have been able to take the few wallops and get over them the way any normal woman would.

'He didn't mean nothin',' the elder Mrs Martin said. 'He got a bit ahead of himself. But she shouldn't have blown the horn at him that way. A man won't take that kind of treatment from any woman and I wouldn't expect him to. He has his pride.'

She leaned on the caravan door while she spoke, staring out at the twisted remains of a bicycle, a rusty milk churn, a variety of plastic containers, three goats, two piebald ponies all tethered to an iron stake, and a scattering of clothes hanging on the fence which separated her domain from the town dump. Behind her, Elsie lay stretched. Her jaw had been wired in the hospital and was still aching. The bruises on her legs were fading and the cut in her head had been stitched and was healing nicely now, thank God.

'You'll be grand again, with the help of God,' her mother-in-law said, watching the ponies reach for a fresh bit of grass on the long acre. 'Grand,' she repeated with satisfaction as if by saying the word she made it happen, God's help being instantly available to her. 'You're grand. I'll be off now and I'll cook him a bit myself. I'll get one of the young ones to bring you over a sangwich. You could manage a sangwich.'

Elsie closed her eyes, trying to squeeze out the pain. Her stomach had not shrunk back to normal. The baby was only gone a week. She folded her hands over the place where he had been. She was sure he had been a boy, the way he kicked. She grieved quietly for him, for his little wasted life that never got the chance to be more than a few small kicks and turns inside her body. But she was sorry for herself too, because she had had a feeling about him, that he would be good to her. He might have been the one to protect her when the others were married with their own wives. She could tell by the older boys that they would hit their wives to control them. She wouldn't interfere but she would not stay around to watch her history being repeated. She had planned a life for herself with this baby. The plan would have to be changed.

Brigid, her eldest daughter, stepped lightly into the caravan and stood beside her. 'Nana says would you like a drink of tay with your sangwich.'

'Shut the door,' Elsie said crossly. 'You're letting the wind in. And sweep out the place. Didn't I tell you to do it this morning? Do you ever do anything you're told?'

'I did it. Them childer have it destroyed on me?'

'Who's minding them? Are they all at your Nana's? Where's Mary Ellen? Where's your father?'

'I dunno.' The child took the sweeping brush and began to sweep the floor. Her sullen expression annoyed her mother almost more than the careless way she swept the bits of food through the caravan door and out on to the green. A dog poked hopefully through the crumbs, then looked up expectantly at Brigid. She said, 'Geraway outa that,' without enough conviction for him to move. He placed a paw on the step. She pushed it off and stared maliciously at him. 'I'll tell my daddy on you, you little hoor,' she whispered and then, a living image of her grandmother, leaned on the brush handle surveying the scene.

'Look, Mama,' she called. 'The sky is orange. Why is it orange?'

Elsie lay back, floating between waves of pain, bathing herself in its persistence. She tried anticipating its peaks, the way she had been learning to anticipate the peaks in labour pains for the baby who was born dead. For the first time in her sixteen years of childbearing she had attended an ante-natal class. It had all come to nothing. She should have known better. Her husband hadn't wanted her to go. He had been persuaded by the social worker to let her try it. But he had grumbled a lot after her visits and told her she was getting too smart. Baby or no baby, he said, you're due a beating. Keeping in with the country people isn't going to do you any good. And they don't care for you anyway. You're only a tinker to them.

She turned her head to see what Brigid was up to. The child had dropped the brush and was standing very still staring at something. 'What are you staring at?' the mother called.

'The pony is orange too,' Brigid said softly. 'The pony is orange.' She had cross eyes of a strange pale grey and the glow of the sunset lit them and changed their colour to a near yellow. One of the ponies suddenly tossed his head and flicked a quick look in her direction before turning his attention back to his patient grazing. Brigid wondered what it would be like to ride him. She was never allowed to try. If she did, her brothers knocked her off. She was beginning to think that she didn't want to ride. She would soon forget that she had ever had such a desire. Her brothers rode like feudal lords, galloping through wastelands and even through the crowded streets, proud and defiant. Brigid fixed her sombre gaze on the pony's back. It must be like the wind, she thought. It would be like racing the wind. That's why her brothers were so proud and cocky. They could race the wind, and she couldn't. Her father did it once. Her mother never did it. Her mother got beaten and had babies and complained. Her mother was useless.

Elsie called out. 'What are you sulking about now? Would you take that look off your face? If you can't do anything for me would you go away and leave me in peace.'

When she was gone, Elsie wanted her back. Brigid, she cried hopelessly, Brigid. It was a pity she wasn't lovable so that Elsie could cuddle her and tell her she was sorry for being cross. But what was the point? Brigid was eleven years of age and she should be doing things for her mother. What did she do all day? Gave them their breakfast in the morning and pushed the small ones in the buggy but beyond that – nothing. She spent most of the day moping around, listening to the gossip in the other caravans.

The caravans were arranged in a circle around the small caravan owned by Hannah, Elsie's mother-in-law. When her children married and had their own caravans they took their place in the circle whenever they came for a gathering. Their father was dead. There were nine surviving sons and seven daughters. When the father was sixty he stopped beating Hannah and got religion very bad. He paid frequent visits to the holy nun in the convent who could cure everything but death. He died peacefully, like a baby asleep, and had a huge funeral. From England and Scotland and all over Ireland the relations came to bury him. The casualty department in the hospital was kept going for two days with the results of the mourning. Hannah was very proud, though she wept for weeks, being supported by all her daughters and all but two of her daughters-in-law, Elsie and Margaret Anne.

Elsie remembered Margaret Anne, the way she used to drink the bottles of tawny wine so that she wouldn't feel the beatings. One night she drank a full bottle of vodka and choked on her own vomit. She was twenty-three. There were no fights after her funeral. There was no public lamentation. Her children cried and her husband cried and took the pledge for six months. Two years later he married her youngest sister and they went away t'England. There were plenty of sites in London for them. They would simply break down a gate, pull the caravan in and stay put until they were evicted. England, Elsie's youngest sister said, was a grand place. They had been put up in the best hotels for months because they were homeless.

Elsie often thought of staying in the best hotels too. Her husband called it one of her notions. His sisters said, 'That one has too many notions.' She had notions about not wanting to do the houses with them, about not wanting to stay home, night after night, while her husband went drinking with his brothers. The worst notion of all was when she arranged to get her dole money split so that she got her own share and the share for half the children. The welfare officer gave her dire warnings that if she changed her mind again, as she had done before, she would be left with nothing. Her husband coaxed, threatened and beat her but she would not surrender.

She had notions about Fonsie when she met him at the horse fair in Spancel Hill. Her parents had pulled their caravan into a by-road a few miles from the village. It was a scorching day when she saw Fonsie tussling with a colt, backing him up, jerking his head to show his teeth, running his hands down his fetlocks, slapping his flanks. The animal reared and bucked and frightened bystanders.

'Aisy, aisy,' a farmer said, 'you'll never sell him that way.'

'I'm not asking you to buy him,' Fonsie said smartly.

'You're not, for I wouldn't,' said the man. 'I never saw any good come from a tinker.'

'You wouldn't have the price of him,' Fonsie said and turned his head and winked at Elsie. His red hair was like a mad halo and his eyes were a blazing blue. She was like a rabbit hypnotized by a weasel. She followed him everywhere. She badgered her parents until they consented to the wedding. She was fifteen. She ignored all their warnings about his bad blood. He was the middle of the brothers and above and below him they were all the same. Always drinking. Always in trouble. Always dodging the law, frequently in jail or facing the judge and getting some smart solicitor to get them off on a technicality.

Fonsie never went to jail. He was too smart. But he didn't want her to be too smart. Smart women annoy me, he said. So be smart and stay stupid. One night when she was three months pregnant, he hit her because she was too smart by half, an ugly bitch who gave him the eye at Spancel Hill and was probably after being with someone else and the child could be anyone's.

There were different notions in her head then when she picked herself up from the floor and cried for her own people who were travelling up north. Through one of her sisters-in-law she got word to her own sisters. One of them travelled to see her and give her advice.

'Don't be saying anything to him when he is drunk.'

'I didn't say anything,' Elsie said.

'Well maybe you should have. Did you look at him? A man can hate a hard look. He'll take it as an insult.'

'I looked at the floor,' Elsie said. 'I was afraid to look at him.'

'Well, there you are then. That's how it happened,' her sister said triumphantly. 'You didn't spake to him and you didn't look at him. Sure that explains it.'

'He says the child isn't his.'

'An old whim he has. His brothers putting him up to it. They're too much together. They should be at home with their wives instead of always in each other's company. They're terrible stuck on each other.'

Elsie knew that was the trouble. A man was all right on his own with a woman but put him in with the herd of men, especially the herd of his own family, and he lost his senses.

Her sisters had always given her plenty of advice. Don't get too fat or you won't be able to run away when he wants to bate you. Learn the houses that are good to the travellers.

Don't try them too often. Don't look for too much the first time. Always bring a baby with you. If you haven't one, borrow one. Keep half of the money for yourself. Her mother gave her one piece of advice. Keep silent and never show a man the contempt you feel for him. It is like spitting in the face of God.

It was good advice, especially the bit about the money. Her sisters had not told her how to keep the money, where to hide it, what to do with it. For them that was the simplest part. They could thrust their hands down into the recess between their breasts and pull up a wad of notes worth a couple of hundred pounds. When a caravan was needed their men would call on them as others would call on a banker. Their interest rates were negotiable and were never paid in kind but in behaviour or favours granted. Her sisters knew how to control their husbands but they were simple men and not as cute as hers. He always seemed to know when she had money accumulated and usually managed to beat it out of her. His spies were everywhere, his sisters and mother always prying and asking questions of the children. She stopped bringing the small children on her rounds. In spite of warnings it was easy for them to let out important information, like where she had been for the few hours of her absence. Elsie knew that she was one of the best of the travellers for getting money from the settled people. They liked her because she was polite and handsome and clean. She didn't whine and she didn't exaggerate. Pride and a certain loyalty to her own people wouldn't allow her to tell the truth about her husband's drinking and beatings. For some of her regulars it wasn't necessary. Her black eyes and bruises were enough.

The latest accumulation was lying under a stone in the mud bank, twenty paces from her caravan. £353.00 in twenty-pound notes and ten-pound notes and five-pound notes and one-pound notes. She had counted it lovingly, feeling the notes, smoothing them out, folding them into twenty-pound bundles held in place by elastic bands, the whole lot wrapped in a plastic supermarket bag. If her husband moved the caravan her treasure was still measurable. It was thirty-five paces from the third cement pole, holding the last section of fencing around the dump. If someone moved the poles it was a hundred paces from the bend in the new road. If the country people decided to change the road, as she knew from experience was a likely occurrence, it was two hundred paces from the last brick house on the estate. If that went then it was straight under the last rays of the setting sun on 23 September. If there was no sun on 23 September she would dig the bank from dump to road in the middle of the night until she found it. If there was no bank – If someone came with a bulldozer – She sat up suddenly. She wanted to rush out to claw at the clay, scrabbling like a dog crazy for his buried bone, in the mud and bare-rooted trees.

She lay down again, her secret like a flame to be kept alive but not so alive that it would leap up and consume her. At long last she had learned discipline. At long last she had learned her mother's secret of silence. When she used the Hiace horn she almost broke the secret. The sound of the horn had its own words and her husband understood them. Only that morning he had looked at her and said, 'You're due a beating and when I have time I'll give it to you.' She should have been there waiting for him, dinner ready, whenever he turned up. She should always wait around the caravan, never farther away from his mother's or his sisters' vans. He didn't like her going to his brothers' vans where she might gossip or plot treason with their wives, or worse, be unfaithful with one of the brothers.

Once only had Elsie and the sisters-in-law plotted. The great idea came to them that they would run away together and leave all the children to Hannah. There were forty-three children under the age of twelve. They sat contemplating the idea in wonder on a sunny morning when the men had gone to collect their dole money and the sisters were gossiping with Hannah. The idea had been thrown out by Mary Teresa and when the magic of it had been chewed over and gloried in it was Mary Teresa who began to destroy it. She said my Danny would never be able to look after himself. After that it was a landslide of surrender. Kathleen said her two boys were wild already and if she left them to their father, no knowing what would become of them. They'd end up in trouble with the law. Bridie said her fellow wouldn't take a bite from anyone only herself. Eileen said mine are all at school. He'd never bother sending them and they'd lose all the schooling they had. And she'd never mind them – meaning Hannah. She's all talk. When it comes down to it she won't look after another woman's children even if they are her grandchildren. All talk, that's all she is. Elsie thought uncomfortably of Brigid and how she hadn't got around to giving her all the loving she should have done and how her father had eyed her a few times but she couldn't put that thought into words. She said I'd be worried about Brigid. Then suddenly all the women remembered their daughters in surprise and confusion and began to name them off, one by one, picturing each child, pretty or plain, cross-eyed or red-haired, loving or defiant, as if naming them became their remembrance.

Elsie lay thinking about all of this as the sunset deepened into a scarlet glow, filling the caravan with its radiance, bouncing off her brass ornaments and mirrors, turning her faded blanket into a brilliant rug, a kaleidoscope of purest wonder. She dozed for a while, soothed by the sun's strange lullaby. She was disturbed by shouts and the thunder of hooves around the caravan. She twitched the curtain to peer out. The magic had gone out of the sky but over the town the pale shape of a crescent moon could just be seen. The pickers were beginning to set fire to the dump and its acrid-smelling smoke drifted in a long low swathe towards the housing estate. The cries of the children at a last game before bedtime reached her and above them came the shouts of her two eldest sons who waved their arms and ran after one of the piebald ponies. As Elsie peered through the window she could see the animal tearing away into the distance, towards the high church steeple, with its rider hanging on for dear life.

More trouble, Elsie thought. Someone had stolen the pony.

Then the door was pushed in and Johnny and Danny burst upon her, pulling at her blankets, crying, 'Get up, get up, Brigid has taken the pony.'

Fonsie was after them, face red with rage, shouting, 'That's your rearing for you, the little bitch has gone off riding like a tinker on the piebald.'

Well then, thought Elsie, stroking her wired-up jaw, here's a right how do ye do. The little bitch is up on a pony and away like the wind.

'Wait till I lay hands on the little rap,' Fonsie said bitterly. 'Bringing disgrace unto the whole family. She's your daughter all right. But is she mine? Answer me that will you?'

'She is yours,' Elsie said. 'She didn't get that wild blood from me. Did you ever see one of my sisters up on a pony? Have any of my family got red hair? Every one of us has brown eyes. 'Twasn't from the wind she got the blue eyes and the hair.'

'She could be Danny's. From day one he was hanging around you. From the minute I brought you back.'

'He was twelve then,' Elsie said, wearily playing the chorus to an old tune.

'What has that got to do with it? You were fifteen. Brigid's near twelve now. She's not like a girl at all. There could be something wrong with her. When your jaw is better let you see to it and when she gets back here I'll give her a lesson she won't forget. Don't give me any of your old guff.'

'Supposing she doesn't come back?' Elsie had started to say, but he didn't want to hear it and he jumped off the step and joined his brothers who had gathered to grin at his discomfiture. Elsie watched them, a few thrusts of fists, a few raised voices, another soothing voice and they climbed into Danny's van and drove away.

One of the pickers stopped by her window, his sack full

of bits of copper and aluminium, the wheel of a bicycle hanging like a huge medallion down his back.

'You've got a bold one there,' he said. 'And to look at her you'd think butter wouldn't melt in her mouth, cross eyes and all. Have they gone to fetch her?'

'Gone to Old Mac's,' Hannah joined in, leaning her large behind against the caravan, looking the picker up and down. 'Did you get much today? That's a miserable old wheel you got. I'll take it off your hands for 50p.'

'Go back to your knitting, old woman,' he said scornfully. 'I have a buyer for this. A proper bicycle dealer.'

'Well that shifted him,' Hannah said, as he heaved his load up on his bicycle and wobbled away down the road, disappearing like a ghost in the fog of burning plastic bags and litter. 'Poking his nose in where he isn't wanted. I hope you told him nothing.'

Elsie turned her face to the wall and groaned.

'Hurts you, does it?' Hannah asked. 'You shouldn't have let that black doctor put the wire in. I wouldn't let a black doctor next or near me. Nor one of them women doctors either. But you were always the one with notions. I'll go away now and look after your poor childer for you. They're crying with the hunger, I expect, if they're not watching the telly.'

The blessed peace when she had gone flowed over Elsie, better than any painkiller. The second pony munched near her window, stretched the full length of his tether. Brigid could have fallen off by now. She could be lying on the road with a broken arm or leg. In the distance the siren of an ambulance screamed hysterically. That's probably her, Elsie thought. They have picked her broken little body up and brought her to hospital. She's unconscious or maybe dead. I'll never see her again.

The dark closed in on the caravan. Elsie listened for the voices of her children as they made their different ways to their aunts' caravans. If Brigid were here she would come and say goodnight to her. She would cuddle up against her and she would not push her away impatiently. Brigid, Brigid, she groaned aloud.

'I'm here, Mama.' Brigid was beside her, hopping up and down on the bed. 'Did you see me? I never fell off once. Did Dada see me?'

Exasperation filled every inch of Elsie's body. It took charge of the pain. She wanted to sit up and shake Brigid till her teeth rattled. She opened her mouth to say your father'll kill you and good enough for you when Brigid said, 'I wouldn't have done it if he hadn't turned orange. The sun turned him orange and I wanted to ride him while he was that colour.'

'He wasn't that colour at all,' Elsie said. 'You only thought he was that colour.'

'He was. I saw him,' Brigid insisted, her crossed eyes glinting with temper. 'Can I cuddle into you, Mama? Can I sleep here with you?' What was the use of anything, thought Elsie. The child was safe and sound and wanting to sleep beside her and she didn't want anyone in the bed with her. She wanted to toss and turn and groan in privacy.

'I might keep you awake.'

'You won't, Mama. And I'll get you anything you want. Will I make you a sup of tay? Did the fellas see me? What did they say?'

Elsie began to laugh. 'Oh my God,' she groaned, 'don't make me laugh. My jaw aches. They were raging. They'll kill you when they get their hands on you.'

'I don't care,' Brigid said. 'It was worth it. I'll kick them and I'll ride the pony again and again. I've him tethered now. I fell off loads of times but I got up again. It's easy. I'll practise. If they see I'm good, they'll let me do it. I'm not like you, Mama. I'm like my Dada and no one will bate me into the ground. You shouldn't let Dada hit you.'

Oh Mary, Mother of God, intercede for me at the throne of mercy, prayed Elsie silently. Give me patience. Help me to say the right thing. She said nothing. She thought of the money wrapped tightly under the stone waiting to liberate her.

Brigid was almost asleep. She flung an arm across Elsie's stomach and said, 'I'll make money for you when I'm big and you'll be able to buy anything you like.'

'Won't you want to buy things for yourself? Maybe your own pony?'

'When I'm big I won't care about the pony,' Brigid said. 'When I'm big.' She was already asleep. Elsie looked down at her pale freckled skin and carrotty eyelashes and she smiled. An orange sun and an orange horse and orange hair. She looked with love at Brigid and she understood her world. For a moment she had a glimpse of some meaning beyond the caravan and the dump and the pile of money buried under the bank. Was it heaven that she was thinking about? Some place up there, way beyond the sky where you could go to bed and rest easy, a place like the Dallas of the telly without the fighting and arguing. All the arguing would wear you out. You either got worn out or as fat as a pig like some of her sisters-in-law who stuffed themselves even when they weren't hungry. It was the opposite with her. Her stomach couldn't take food when the arguing and shouting was going on. After a beating she couldn't eat for weeks.

An orange horse was like a flame, she thought. It would burn the air up as it raced by your window. It would warm your heart but never singe your soul. It could fly up to the clouds and down again. It could give you more notions than anyone would ever know. You could touch it and not feel it. You could feel it and not touch it. It could have a meaning that you might never understand but knowing it was there would change your life. It would help you find a way to spend the money you saved. It would save your life if you let it. It would make your jaw ache less. It was better than the holy nun, God forgive her for thinking such a thing. If Margaret Anne had seen it she might never have choked on her own vomit. An orange horse that never was could be the greatest secret of all. She stroked Brigid's hair and fell asleep.

People in the town said afterwards that the flames of the fire turned the sky the maddest orange they had ever seen.

Three of the caravans went up together but the only casualties were a mother and daughter. Their caravan went up first. The heat was so intense it was a wonder the whole lot of them didn't go up. A gas cylinder exploded. The police were questioning a man who had thrown a can of petrol into the first caravan and set it alight. He was drunk. He didn't know what he was doing. There were screams from the caravan, terrible screams that those who heard them would never forget. But the firemen found nothing. It was the heat, they said. It was an incinerator. A Hiace van was burned and left a carcass of twisted metal. A pony died and left a charred body but in the caravan there was nothing. Nothing.

Dermot Bolger

from *The Journey Home*

ALTHOUGH THE minister's name never appeared on any business documents it became obvious to me that he was a silent partner in all of his brother Pascal's ventures. Sitting in that kitchen waiting for them to emerge on the evenings I was paid to drive Pascal, I began to piece together a thumb-nail sketch of their lives from what I had heard there and from what my mother had told me.

Patrick had been two years a national schoolteacher in the suburb when his elder brother returned from England in the early sixties with capital and ambition. Soon he had Patrick selling encyclopaedias to the parents of his pupils, checking up on their home backgrounds to give Pascal leads for his new business of selling door to door. In those days the two brothers were inseparable. Although Pascal was a year older, my mother said they looked like twins. At dances girls had problems telling them apart. But soon they were rarely to be seen at dances. They moved into lodgings with an old bachelor on the North Road where the light in the living-room was still burning no matter how late you passed the house.

By 1966 Pascal had opened the garage and found others to go from door to door for him. The fiftieth anniversary of the Easter Rising that year was the making of them. From his native Mayo they dragged up their grandfather, Eoin, who had been thirty-eight during the rising and was eighty-eight then. They brought him around the estates to meet the people. One night when we were drinking heavily, Pascal described him to me. Eoin had come to Dublin in 1916 looking for work and joined with Connolly's men only on the morning of the rising. He had stuck to his new leader's side and even helped to carry Connolly down when he was shot on the roof of the GPO. Before arriving in Dublin he had known nothing, but he came out of the internment camp in Wales a confirmed socialist. Wounded six times in the War of Independence, he had not died. Pascal used to repeat this bitterly. If only his grandfather had been killed I think he felt they could have both won seats.

After the dust had settled in 1923 he was still a socialist and still spoke out as one. They gave him medals reluctantly and eventually a pension, but he was not there in the carve up of jobs and power. At the time of the Graltan affair in Leitrim, he too had been denounced from the pulpits as a Bolshevik. Graltan on the run had often hidden in his house, and when he was deported to America the newspapers cried out for Eoin Plunkett to be dispatched as well. He survived, the aura of holiness around his Easter medal protecting him, until one night the locals set fire to his house. The brothers' mother had died giving birth to Patrick and their father had brought them to live with Eoin. After the fire, their father cursed Eoin, took the only suitcase and went to England. The sons never heard from him again. Eoin took them to his sister's house in Kerry near where my own father was born, left them there and was arrested and sent home when trying to board a boat to join the International Brigade in Spain. In 1939, when his grandsons were in their late teens, the police came for him again. He came out of the Curragh Internment Camp, a grey-haired man of sixty-seven, when peace was declared.

The brothers always resented the poverty they grew up in when they knew how easy it would have been for Eoin to secure a well-paid niche. He could barely walk when they got him reluctantly back up to the city but they quickly learnt how much he despised their new activities. Eventually, in desperation, each evening before they took him on their rounds of the estates they would remove his false teeth so that the people mistook his tirades against the snugness of the new state for the standard pieties they expected.

They shipped him home when the bunting came down, and in the next election Patrick Plunkett slipped into the last seat on the twelfth count. Eoin died as the first bombs exploded on Derry's streets. They forgot to remove the tricolour from his coffin when they lowered it down, and shovelled the clay on top of it. The local priest claimed a bedside conversion. I always wondered if he had prised the teeth out first.

In April the party had an emergency Ard-Fheis, giving rise to speculation of a snap election. At the last minute Patrick Plunkett was dropped from the list of speakers. That night, after the leader's speech he arrived at Pascal's house. I could see he had been drinking heavily. The brothers withdrew into the drawing-room, muttering angrily to themselves. After an hour Patrick emerged from the drawing-room and told his driver to go. Through the open door I could hear Pascal on the phone placing a bet with someone. I had been idling in the kitchen for hours, waiting to be told to go home. When I heard the receiver being replaced I reached for my coat and was zipping it up when Pascal came in.

'You're working late tonight Hanrahan,' he said, his manner abrupt as always in his brother's presence. 'Drive us back into the city.'

I could smell whiskey like a fever in the back of the car as I drove. It was after one o'clock when we got there, the streets almost deserted with the burger huts closed and the night-clubs still churning out music. We drove by Liberty Hall, crossed the river and cruised along Burgh Quay. Near the public toilets they beckoned for me to stop. Three youths leaned on the quayside wall, watching for men, obviously for sale. The eldest might have been sixteen. I could sense the brothers staring at them before they motioned me to move on.

Maybe twenty-five years ago it had been impossible to tell them apart, but the grooming of political power had lent

Patrick a veneer of cosmopolitanism at odds with his brother's instinctive raw aggression. That night though, as they sat impassively behind me, it was like the polish had slipped away and they were one again. I drove slowly, with a sickness in my stomach, along the quays and down alleyways where dirty children huddled in groups with bags of glue and plastic cider bottles. Some spat at the slow car, others watched with mute indifference. Neither man spoke beyond instructing me to slow down or drive on. At times we moved at a funeral pace and those badly lit alleyways could have been some ghostly apparition of a dead city which we were driving through. Murky lanes with broken street lights, the ragged edges of tumbledown buildings, a carpet of glass and condoms, of chip papers and plastic cartons and, picked out in the headlights, the hunched figures of children and tramps wrapped in blankets or lying under cardboard, their hands raised to block the glare of headlights.

Twice we paused where a figure lay, down a laneway between the ancient cathedral and the ugly squatting bunkers of the civic offices, before I was ordered to stop. Patrick Plunkett was bundled up in an old overcoat and hat. In the semi-dark of the car he could have been anyone or no one. This is what death looks like when it calls, I thought, watching him in the mirror, a black figure with no face. Pascal got out and approached the youth on the ground who tried to shuffle away when he bent to talk to him. He was perhaps eighteen. I saw him shake his head repeatedly before Plunkett produced two twenties and a ten pound note from his wallet which he held up and then placed carefully back among the wad of notes. Both were still for a moment before the youth picked himself up and folded the blanket under his arm. Plunkett caught his shoulder and, after arguing briefly, the youth turned and carefully hid the filthy covering behind some rubble in the lane.

He sat between the two brothers in the back. I could tell from his face in the mirror how scared he was. He wanted to ask them questions but was intimidated by the brothers' silence. Occasionally Pascal murmured to him, reassuring the youth as you would a frightened animal, or called out directions to me. Otherwise we made the journey in silence.

I thought I knew North County Dublin until that night. I know we passed near Rolestown and much later I glimpsed a signpost for The Naul, but generally the lanes we travelled were too small to be signposted. Two cars could not have passed on them and I had to negotiate by following the ridge of grass which grew down the centre. Just when they seemed to peter out they would switch direction. At one crossroads another set of headlights emerged and began to tail us, and this was repeated again and again until we too caught up with a procession of tail lights streaking out into the darkness ahead of us.

The cars slowed almost to a halt and we turned off the tarmacadam and were bumping our way across gravel and then grass. In the field ahead of us a semi-circle of light was formed by the headlights of parked cars. We took our place and those behind followed until a rough circle of blazing light was completed. Men stood about in the grass. Patrick Plunkett addressed me for the first time since leaving the city.

'Get out!'

He climbed into the driver's seat and donned the chauffeur's hat from the glove compartment which I had never been asked to wear. He slammed the door and fixed his eyes through the windscreen on the trampled floodlit grass. Pascal had got out and was standing beside the open boot with the youth who was now stripped to the waist and shivering. Pascal was rubbing liquid from a bottle on to the youth's chest. He handed it to me with a sponge and plastic container of water, then placed his hand on the youth's shoulder to steer him out into the circle. From the far side of the ring of light I saw a second youth being led out, as scared looking as the first. I knew the man at his side, a wholesale fish merchant named Collins from Swords who occasionally did business with Plunkett. He called out jeeringly:

'Is that the best you can do, Plunkett? You must have fierce weak men up in the city.'

'Are you sure a grand won't bust your business Collins?' Plunkett called back. 'I know it's a lot of money for a small man like yourself to lose.'

The two youths eyed each other, desperate to make a deal between themselves. But even if they had tried to run they would have been pushed back into the ring by the circle of well-fed men who were closing in around them. A referee, stripped to his waistcoat, was rolling up his sleeves.

'Where did you get him?' he asked Plunkett.

'Back of Christchurch.'

'And yours?' He turned to Collins.

'Knackers. Camped out near The Ward.'

'Fifty pounds to the winning boxer. I want twenty-five each off you now.'

He turned to the youths.

'Nothing to the loser. Do you understand? No using your feet, you break when I tell you and the first to surrender is out. Now you've got five minutes.'

We returned to the boot of the car. Plunkett put a jacket over the youth's shoulders and fed him instructions on how to weave and hit. Two men approached us and he walked off to cover their bets. The youth kept glancing at me as though I were his jailer. I wanted to tell him to run but I was too terrified, afraid that if he did escape I would be thrust into the ring in his place. The winning purse was less than the smallest bet being placed around me. The laughter and shouting, as if by an unconscious signal, died down into a hush of anticipation. Plunkett returned and pushed the youth forward.

'Fifty pounds son. Fifty smackers into your hand. Don't let me down now.'

I walked behind, noticing that Patrick had left the car and was standing unobserved a small way off from the crowd. A man staggered over to offer me a slug of Southern Comfort and thump me on the back.

'Good man yourself,' he shouted in my ear. 'I've a hundred riding on your man, but watch it, them knackers fight fierce filthy.'

There was a roar as both youths entered the ring. They circled cagily while the referee encouraged them forward. For over a minute they shadowed each other, fists clenched and raised, tongues nervously exposed. The crowd grew angry at the lack of action. They cursed and called the fighters cowards. Then the Gypsy ducked low to get in close and swung his fist up. He caught the youth above the eye as he moved back and flailed at the Gypsy who danced away. It had begun.

There were no gloves, no rounds, both fighters punching and clinging to each other as the men around them screamed, until after five or six minutes the Gypsy was caught by a succession of blows and fell over on to the ground. I expected the referee to begin a count but Collins just pulled him up and wiped the sponge quickly over his face. Plunkett grabbed the water from me and raised it to his fighter's lips.

'Don't swallow, just spit,' he said. 'It's going to be a long night.'

Then they were thrust back into action, a graceless, headlong collision of blows and head butts. Both bled badly from the face. More frequently now they fell and the fight was stopped for a few seconds. After half an hour, the Gypsy got in under his opponent's defence and rained blows against his rib cage. He stepped back and the youth fell, doubled up on the ground. He kept trying to stay down as Plunkett pulled him up.

'Me ribs mister, they're broken, broken.'

'Get back in there. I've money riding on you. Finish the cunt off or you'll leave this field in a box.'

The youth stumbled forward with one hand clutching his side. Money was flowing on to the Gypsy. He approached, grinning now through the blood, sensing that his ordeal was nearly over, but as he swung his fist the youth caught him with his boot right in the balls and, as he fell to his knees, again in the face. There was a near riot of indignation among the crowd around me, their sense of fair play abused. Both youths knelt on the ground while the referee shouted at Plunkett.

'Once more Plunkett and I'm giving it to Collins. Do you hear me?'

The youth rose reluctantly and looked back to where I stood. I lowered my eyes and walked towards the gate of the field. I could bear to watch no more. To the south the lights of the city were an orange glow in the sky. The wind blew against my face. A tree was growing by itself in the ditch. I pressed my face against its cold bark, remembering suddenly the old woman's story of the oak trees in her wood that she would embrace to find strength in times of crisis. I closed my eyes and I could see her, not as that ancient figure I had abandoned, but a young mother in the early light running between trees. I saw her so clearly, as if her image had always been locked away inside me, part of the other me I never allowed myself to think of. I wanted him back, the person I kept nearly becoming – in her caravan, with Shay in the flat. From the shouts behind me I knew that the Gypsy was finishing it. Every eye would be watching the final grisly moments before clustering round the bookmakers. I wrapped my whole body against the base of the tree. I had nobody left to pray to so I prayed to it and to her and to me: to the living wood itself, to the old woman of the fields, to the memory of someone I had almost once been.

When the noise died down, I turned and walked back. The youth was lying against the side of the car. He was crying. I found his clothes, helped him to dress. I wanted to ask him his name but it seemed too late to do so. I helped him up and opened the back door where the brothers sat.

'Put him in the front,' Pascal shouted.

I eased him gently into the passenger's seat and started the engine.

'Leave us home,' Pascal said, 'then dump that tramp back where you found him. Bring the car into work at lunch-time.

One word about this and your family will be living on sawdust.'

I let them out at his house. Both slammed their doors, disgruntled and, now they were alone, bowed their heads together to discuss the fight. I drove into the city. The Mater Hospital was on casualty. It was almost dawn but still the benches were jammed with drunks, with lonely people hoping to fool their way into a bed, with girls in party dresses who cried waiting for word of their friends behind the curtains. He hadn't wanted to go in and, if I hadn't sat there, would have stumbled his way back to his blanket hidden in the laneway.

Even the nurses were shocked at his appearance. They called him in ahead of those waiting. When he rose I pushed whatever money was in my pockets into his hand. I knew that Plunkett had given him nothing. He looked at me but we did not shake hands. I watched the nurses help him on to the bunk and, staring back at me with mistrust, pull the curtain shut.

It was daylight outside. I thought of my brothers and sisters. At twelve o'clock I would be waiting at the garage to drive him, but now I left his car there and walked the two miles home in some futile gesture of penance, even though I knew that nothing would be changed.

Colm Tóibín

from *The Heather Blazing*

H E WOKE during the night and went downstairs to his study. He had been dreaming, but now the dream had escaped him. He went into the kitchen and took some cold water from a plastic bottle in the fridge. He sat at the kitchen table for a while and then went back into the study. It was a warm night.

He sat at his desk and looked down at the judgment he had written in longhand on foolscap pages. It was ready to be delivered. He wondered for a moment if he should have it typed, but he was worried about it being leaked. No one knew about it; even as he sat down to write it himself he did not know what he would say, what he would decide. There was so little to go on, no real precedent, no one obviously guilty. Neither of the protagonists in the case had broken the law. And that was all he knew: the law, its letter, its traditions, its ambiguities, its codes. Here, however, he was being asked to decide on something more fundamental and now he realized that he had failed and he felt afraid.

He took a biro from a drawer and began to make squiggles on a pad of paper. What was there beyond the law? 'Law'; he wrote the word. There was natural justice. He wrote the two words down and put a question mark after them. And beyond that again there was the notion of right and wrong, the two principles which governed everything and came from God. 'Right' and 'wrong'; he wrote the two words down and then put brackets around them and the word 'God' in capitals beside them.

Somehow here in the middle of the night with the moths

and midges drawn to the window, the idea of God seemed more clearly absurd to him than ever before; the idea of a being whose mind put order on the universe, who watched over things, and whose presence gave the world a morality which was not based on self-interest, seemed beyond belief. He wondered how people put their faith in such a thing, and yet he understood that the courts and the law ultimately depended for their power on such an idea. He crossed out the word 'God'. He felt powerless and strange as he went back to read random passages of his judgment. He decided to go to bed and sleep some more: maybe he would be more relaxed about his judgment in the morning.

Carmel did not stir in the bed when he came into the bedroom, but he knew that she had woken. When he got into bed he put his arms around her. She kissed him gently on the neck and then turned away from him, letting him snuggle against her. She fell back asleep, and he lay there for a while holding her until he grew drowsy and fell asleep as well.

He was wakened by the alarm clock and reached across her to turn it off. They both lay there without moving or speaking, as though still asleep.

'Are you in court today?' she finally asked, almost whispering.

'Yes,' he said.

'Do you have a full day?'

'There's a lot of work to get through.'

Another last day of term; another year gone by. He hoped that all the urgent applications for injunctions would go elsewhere. He knew that the press would be in his court today. This case was newsworthy. He hated the journalists' faces looking up at him, eager for something instant which they could grasp and simplify. He snoozed for a while and when he woke he found that Carmel had left the bed. He moved over to her side and lay in her heat until he knew that it was time to get up.

It was a fine morning. Thin wisps of white cloud hung in

the sky like smoke, and the sun was already strong. He realized as he tested the water in the shower that he would like to get into his car now and drive with Carmel to Cush and never set foot in the court again.

She was still in her dressing-gown when he came downstairs. She poured tea for him.

'I think everything is ready now,' she said. 'Are you looking forward to getting away?'

'Yes, I am. I was just thinking that I'd be delighted never to set foot in the court again.'

'You'll feel differently at the end of the summer.'

He went into his study again and sat at the desk. He thought that he should read the judgment over again before going into the court, but he could not face it. He felt unsure about it, but as he left the house and drove into the city the uncertainty became deep unease. It was not yet nine o'clock when he arrived at the Four Courts, and he was not due to deliver his judgment until eleven, or maybe later, depending on what injunctions were being sought.

The line of reasoning in his judgment was clear, he thought. It had not been written in a hurry; evening after evening he had sat in his study and drafted it, working out the possibilities, checking the evidence and going over the facts. Even so, he was still not sure.

He stood at the window of his chambers and looked out at the river which was low now because of the tide and because of the good summer. He watched a boy moving between lorries and cars on a horse, riding bareback with confidence. When the lights changed to green, the boy and his horse joined the flow of traffic towards Capel Street.

He had taken the judgment from his briefcase and placed it on the table. He went over and looked at it again. The case had happened in one of the border towns. A lot of people must live on the edge there, he thought, with strange upheavals, odd comings and goings. But this had nothing to do with the case, as far as he knew. The case was simple: a sixteen-year-old girl attending a convent school had become pregnant and been expelled. She was due to have the baby over the summer and wished to return to the school for the final year, but the school had made it clear that she would not be re-admitted. The girl and her mother sought a court order instructing the school to take her back.

The girl was clever, according to the school reports which had been produced in evidence. Her becoming pregnant had been a great trauma and she had confided in nobody until it became obvious. Both the girl and her mother had given evidence. The mother seemed surprisingly young, but had been very confident in the witness box as she told of her visits to the school to talk to the principal and her long discussions with her daughter about her pregnancy and her future. She seemed sincere and deeply upset about her daughter's expulsion.

It would have been easier for everyone, she said, if her daughter had had an abortion. But because they decided to have the child and bring it up in the town, her daughter was being made to suffer. She would have to go to the Vocational School or travel every day to another town. She was being victimized, stigmatized, her mother said. She told the court that the principal had been more interested in keeping the pregnancy a secret than in her daughter's welfare or the welfare of the unborn child.

The daughter was a smaller, softer version of her mother, but just as articulate and just as sure that an injustice had been done to her. She liked the school, she said, she had a good relationship with all of her teachers, she expected to go to university after her final year. She told the court about her worry when she thought she might be pregnant, how she hoped she would have a miscarriage and wondered if she could get away and have an abortion without anyone discovering. When her mother found out, she said, she told her that all the family would support her. Her father had been upset for a few days but he said nothing bad to her.

The principal was new, she said, she had replaced a nun who had run the school for years. She was young and everybody liked her. So she was not afraid when she was called into the office. But she was very surprised, the girl told the court, when she was informed that she could not come back that term. It was a few days later that the principal told her mother that she would not be allowed back to the school the following year. She was shocked by this and hurt, the girl said. She didn't want to go out and began to feel ashamed and depressed.

She told counsel for the school that she knew what she had done was wrong. And she agreed that it was a bad example for younger girls, especially in a Catholic school. She told everyone she was sorry, she said. No one wanted to expel the boy, she said, although some people knew who he was. She felt being expelled from the school stigmatized her.

He had spent three days listening to the case. The principal could only have been in her late twenties. She, too, was calm, assured and articulate. She was employed to run a Catholic school, she said. It was an educational establishment, but with a very specific ethos. She was prepared to forgive anybody a transgression, she said, and it was for God, not her, to judge, but she had to protect the school's ethos. There were, she told the court, great pressures on the girls in a changing world, but some things were still not acceptable to her as principal, to her board of management or to the majority of the parents. She had the right to decide if a girl should be expelled and she had decided to exercise that right.

Parents who had children in the school spoke for both sides. Some said that the girl should be forgiven and treated as a normal student in her final year. Others said that a teenage pregnancy should not be looked upon as normal or acceptable, and allowing the girl to return to school would have an abiding effect on her fellow students.

Eamon was aware as the case went on that the costs were rising and if the girl and her family lost it would be a great financial blow to them. He was disturbed by the case, which was widely reported on radio, television and in the newspapers. He remembered how calm the young girl had been, how vulnerable. He realized that this was one of the few cases he had heard where both sides were clearly telling the truth and were not afraid of the truth. All the witnesses were sincere, no one wished to hide anything.

He listened carefully to the counsel's submissions about various articles of the Constitution, but there was no argument about facts or truth, guilt or innocence. In the end he was not the legal arbiter, because there were so few legal issues at stake. Most of the issues raised in the case were moral: the right of an ethos to prevail over the right of an individual. Basically, he was being asked to decide how life should be conducted in a small town. He smiled to himself at the thought and shook his head.

As he worked on the judgment, he realized more than ever that he had no strong moral views, that he had ceased to believe in anything. But he was careful in writing the judgment not to make this clear. The judgment was the only one which he could have given: it was cogent, well argued and, above all, plausible.

He went to the window again and stood there looking out. How hard it was to be sure! It was not simply the case, and the questions it raised about society and morality, it was the world in which these things happened which left him uneasy, a world in which opposite values lived so close to each other. Which could claim a right to be protected?

He went over to his bookshelves and took down the sacred text: *Bunreacht na hEireann*, the Irish Constitution. This contained the governing principles to which the law was subject. The preamble was clear about the Christian nature of the state, it specifically referred to the Holy Trinity. He thought about it again, how the school had a duty to defend Christian principles, and indeed a right to do so, under its own articles of association and also under the general guidance of the Constitution.

Surely these rights and duties were greater than any rights a single individual, whose presence in the school might undermine the school's ethos and principles, could lay claim to?

His tipstaff came with tea. He began to think again. He wrote down three words in a note-pad: charity, mercy, forgiveness. These words had no legal status, they belonged firmly to the language of religion, but they had a greater bearing on the case than any set of legal terms. Opposite them he wrote three other words: transgression, sin, scandal. He sighed.

One other matter began to preoccupy him. The family, according to the Constitution, was the basic unit in society. He read the words in the Constitution: 'a moral institution possessing inalienable rights, antecedent and superior to all positive law'. What was a family? The Constitution did not define a family, and at the time it was written in 1937 the term was perfectly understood: a man, his wife and their children. But the Constitution was written in the present tense, it was not his job to decide what certain terms – he wrote 'certain terms' in his note-pad, underlined it and wrote 'uncertain terms' below that – such as 'the family' had meant in the past. It was his job to define and redefine these terms now. Could not a girl and her child be a family? And if they were, did the girl have rights arising from her becoming a mother, thus creating a family, greater than the rights of any institution?

He thought about it for a while and the consternation it would cause among his colleagues, a broadening of the concept of the family. The girl would have to win then, and the school lose. The idea seemed suddenly plausible, but it would need a great deal of thought and research. It had not been raised as a possibility by counsel for the girl and her mother. Lawyers, he thought, knew that he was not the sort of judge who would entertain such far-fetched notions in his court.

If he were another person he could write the judgment, but as eleven o'clock grew near he knew that the verdict he had written out on his foolscap pages was the one he would deliver, and it would be viewed by his colleagues as eminently sensible and well reasoned. But he was still unhappy about the case because he had been asked to interpret more than the law, and he was not equipped to be a moral arbiter. He was not certain about right and wrong, and he realized that this was something he would have to keep hidden from the court.

The downstairs corridors of the Four Courts were like some vast marketplace. He had to push his way through the passage leading to the side door of his court.

'The courtroom is packed, my lord,' his tipstaff said.

'Are we ready then?' he asked.

He tried to act as businesslike as possible when he came into the courtroom and everybody stood up. He sat down, arranged his papers in front of him, put on his reading-glasses, and consulted with the clerk, learning that there were several barristers seeking injunctions. He tried to deal with them promptly, realizing that, if he hurried, he could be finished by one o'clock, which meant that he could be in Cush by four, or half past four, and if the weather was warm enough he could have a swim. He told the clerk that he was ready to begin the judgment. He surveyed the court for a moment: the press benches were full as he had expected, and the public benches were also full. He knew that this judgment would be news. It would be carried on the radio and there would probably be editorials in the newspapers. He would certainly be attacked in *The Irish Times*. As he settled down to read the judgment, sure now of his conclusions, he thought about how ill-informed and ignorant the comment would be, and how little of the processes of law the writers would understand.

He did not intend his judgment to be dramatic, but he wished to set out the facts first, clearly and exactly. The argument at times, he knew, was close and dense and it would be difficult for most people in the court to follow, but a great deal of it was clear. After half an hour, when he had set out the facts and paused for a drink of water, he was

aware that no one in the court knew which side he was about
to come down on. He could feel the tension; and the few
times he looked up he could see them watching him carefully.
He caught the mother's eye only once: she had the resigned
look, he felt, of someone who knew that she was going to
lose. People would have warned her that he was not a judge
who would rule in her favour. He avoided eye contact with
the girl.

As he read on and came near the passage which would
make the result clear he found that he was enjoying the
tension and noticed that he had begun to speak more distinctly, but he stopped himself and went back to the rigorous
monotone which he had adopted at the beginning.

A murmur started in the court as soon as it became clear
that he had decided in favour of the school; from the bench it
sounded like the murmur in a film, and he felt that he should
bang the desk with a gavel and shout 'Order in the court',
but he continued as though there had not been a sound.

When he had finished, counsel for the school was on his
feet immediately, his face flushed with victory. He was
looking for costs. There was no choice, he could delay it until
the new term, but it would be pointless and he wanted to
have done with the case. The costs would be high, he listened
to the submission from the other side. When he looked over
he saw that the mother and father were holding each other,
and both were looking up at him as though afraid.

'Costs follow the event and I see no reason why it should
be different on this occasion,' he said. The mother began to
cry. Although he had awarded costs against her, he thought
she would probably not have to pay all of them. He wondered
as he gathered up his papers if she would appeal, but he
thought not; he had based a great deal of his judgment on
matters of fact rather than law, and the Supreme Court could
not dispute many of his findings. She would not have much
chance of winning an appeal, he felt.

Back in his chambers he went to the telephone immediately.

'I'm ready now,' he said as soon as Carmel answered.

'We're going to pick up Niamh in Rathmines. She's decided to come down with us today. She's taking the carrycot and all the things so we'll need to collect her,' Carmel said.

'I thought she wasn't coming,' he said.

'She's finding it very hard,' Carmel said, as though he had complained about her coming.

'I'll be there in half an hour,' he said. He sat down at his desk and put his head in his hands. He could feel the sweat pouring down his back and his heart beating fast. He tried to control his breathing, to breathe calmly through his nose. He tried to relax. He remembered Niamh best when she was fourteen or fifteen, when she was still growing; even then she was tall for her age and interested in sports; hockey, tennis, swimming. They had pushed her too hard, Carmel said, forced her to study when she did not want to. She had studied social science when she failed to get the points for entry to study medicine. She had become a statistician, working on opinion polls and surveys of social change. She had become independent and distant from them until she was pregnant, when she and Carmel became closer, but he did not believe that she had felt any affection for him since she was in her early teens.

He sat at his desk as his heart kept pounding. He wondered if he was going to have a heart attack, and he waited for a dart of pain, or a sudden tightness, but none came and slowly the heartbeat eased.

Niamh was standing at the door of a small house down a side street in Rathmines. She waved when he beeped the horn and shouted that she would not be long.

'I thought she was living in a flat,' he said.

'Yes,' Carmel said, 'but there are three flats in the house and she knows the other people, they're all friends. They're very good to her, they babysit and help out.'

Niamh came out of the front door with the baby. He

noticed that she had lost weight and let her hair grow longer. She smiled at them.

'I hope there's loads of space in the boot because I have to take the computer as well as the baby, and that's not forgetting the go-car and the cot.' She handed the baby to Carmel. Eamon went into the hall, brought out the cot and put it in the boot.

'The computer will have to go on the back seat,' he said. 'Are you sure you need it?'

She went past him without answering. He carried a suitcase and put it into the boot. He stood there then looking at the baby who looked back at him sullenly and curiously, fixing on him as something new and strange. Suddenly, the baby began to cry, and continued to roar as they arranged the go-car on the roof-rack and set off through Ranelagh and Donnybrook. 'He's very big,' he said after a while when the child had quietened down. 'He's much bigger than I expected him to be.' He looked behind at the child who began to cry again.

'It's better maybe if you don't look at him when he's like that,' Niamh said.

He knew as they drove past Bray that if they turned on the radio they would get the three o'clock news which would probably report on the judgment. Carmel would want to know about it, she would want to discuss his reasons for ruling in favour of the school, she would go away and think about it and want to discuss it further. With Niamh in the house it would be worse. He realized that he would prefer if they never found out about it. It would be difficult to explain.

'Who else is living in the house with you?' he asked Niamh. There had been silence in the car for some time. Both women told him to keep his voice down.

'The baby's asleep,' Niamh said.

At Arklow he took a detour to avoid the traffic in the town. It was close to four o'clock, and it was only now that he became relaxed enough to enjoy the good weather, the clear light over the fields and the heat which he knew would persist for at least two more hours, despite the clouds banked on the horizon. When they passed Gorey, the baby woke and began to make gurgling sounds.

'You should teach him "The Croppy Boy",' he said and laughed to himself as they passed a sign for Oulart. Niamh said that she would have to change his nappy, so they stopped the car and got out. He walked up and down taking in the heat as the two women busied themselves around the child, who had begun to cry again.

When they reached Blackwater Carmel said that she wanted to stop to get some groceries and to order *The Irish Times* for the duration of their stay. The baby was asleep again and he and Niamh sat in the seat without speaking. He closed his eyes and opened them again: in all the years there had been hardly any changes in the view from here up the hill. Each building was a separate entity, put up at a different time. Each roof was different, ran at a different angle, was made of different material: slate, tile, galvanized. He felt that he could be any age watching this scene, and experienced a sudden illusion that nothing in him had changed since he first saw these buildings.

They drove towards the sea at Ballyconnigar and then turned at the hand-ball alley to Cush. There were potholes on the narrow road and he had to drive carefully to avoid them.

'What's for dinner?' he asked.

'I'm not making any more dinners,' Carmel said and laughed.

'I hope you can cook, Niamh,' he said.

'It's time men pulled their weight,' Niamh said drily.

There was always that moment when he saw the sea clearly, when it took up the whole horizon, its blue and green colours frail in the afternoon light. The road was downhill from then on. He drove along the sandy road, saluting a few people as he passed.

'I want to unload really quickly,' he said, as he stopped the car beside the house, 'because I want to go for a swim before the sun goes in.'

'I'd love to go for a swim too,' Niamh said.

'I'll take the baby if you both empty the car,' Carmel said.

Niamh had gone to change, and he stood waiting for her. There was a sweet, moist smell from the high grass in front of the house. He was tired and felt the burden of the day in his back muscles and his eyes. Suddenly he looked up and his eye caught the rusty red paint on the galvanized iron of the gate. He liked the colour, and it seemed familiar as he stood there and took in the scene: the rutted lane, the tufts of grass clinging to the sandy soil of the ditch, and the sound of a tractor in the distance. He stood there for a moment fixing on nothing in particular, letting each thing in the landscape seep towards him as he tried to rid himself of everything that had happened that day.

Down on the strand they could see as far as Curracloe. Niamh wore only a light dress over her swimming-suit, so she was already in the water while he was still undressing. When he took off his shoes he felt an instant release as though a weight had been lifted from him. Most of the strand was in shadow. He left his clothes on a boulder of dried marl and walked towards the sunlight on the foreshore, stepping gingerly over the small, sharp stones which studded the sand.

The water was cold; Niamh waved to him from way out. He watched her long, thin arms reach up from the water as she swam parallel to the shore. He was tempted, as usual, to turn back, but he waded in farther, jumping to avoid a wave, and then he dived in and swam hard out, gliding over each swell as it came. He turned and put his head back, letting it rest on the cold, blue water, and opening his eyes to stare up at the sky. He breathed in deeply and floated on the waves, relaxed now and quiet. He curled back towards the water after a while, and swam farther out, each movement half instinct, half choice.

He cast his eye down the coast and noticed as he turned that a family was moving slowly up the strand towards the gap, carrying rugs and babies, struggling as they reached the cliff. He watched Niamh wading out and drying herself. She waved to him. No one else would come until the morning, except maybe a tractor using the strand as a short cut. He was tired now; the swimming would be easier the next day and the day after that. He changed to a dog paddle which consumed less energy than the breast stroke. A cloud passed over the sun and left him in shadow so that he could feel a cold edge to the wind on his face. He turned again and floated, keeping his eyes closed for as long as he could, not knowing whether the water was taking him in or out. For a few seconds he forgot himself, sustained by the rise and fall of the waves and the knowledge that it would carry him as long as he relaxed and remained at peace.

As soon as he arrived back at the house he knew that Carmel and Niamh had been listening to the six-thirty news.

'Well, you were busy this morning,' Niamh said.

'Was it on the news?' he asked, as if it was a routine matter.

'Do you think I should be expelled as well?' she asked.

'Your father's on his holidays, Niamh,' Carmel said.

'That's not what you said before he came in. My father thinks that unmarried mothers shouldn't be allowed to go to school,' she laughed bitterly.

'What exactly is biting you?' he asked.

'That poor girl. How could it be right to expel her and never let her back?'

'Read the judgment and find out,' he said.

'Did you bring it with you?' she asked.

'Of course I didn't.'

'I think it's a disgrace, that's what I think,' Niamh said. 'It's an outrage.'

'But you would think that, wouldn't you?'

'I know about it. I know what it's like to be a woman

in this country, and I know what it's like to have a child here.'

'And I suppose you're a legal expert as well.'

They had supper in silence, which was broken only by the whimpering of the baby. He faced the window and noticed the first throbbing rays of the lighthouse glinting in the distance. He wanted to ask Carmel what she had said about him and his judgment before he came in, but he realized that he could gain nothing by doing so.

'Do you want more tea?' Carmel asked him.

'Yes, please,' he said. He tried to make his voice sound neutral, as though he was not annoyed with them. He was too tired now to want any further argument. He sat at the table as they cleared away the dishes.

'We're going to take Michael for a walk,' Carmel said to him. 'Are you staying here?'

'Yes,' he said.

'Are you all right?' she put her hand on his shoulder.

'I'm tired,' he said. 'I'm glad to be here.'

He stood up and walked into their bedroom, and rummaged through the suitcases until he found a book. He lay down on the bed, but as soon as he opened the book he knew that he was too tired to read. He knew that he would sleep. He took off his jacket and his shoes and rested on his side, facing away from the window.

She woke him when she turned on the bedside lamp. He felt heavy and tired as he turned towards her.

'It's all quiet now,' she said. 'You were fast asleep.'

'Is it late?'

'It's after ten. You were on the news again. Not you, but there was a report about you.'

'Nothing that they haven't said before.'

'The Irish Council for Civil Liberties – Niamh says that Donal is a member – have issued a statement.'

'Our son and our daughter,' he said and laughed.

'They're fine people, both of them,' Carmel said.

'I suppose I'm the one who's wrong?'

'No, you're all right, too,' she stood over him and smiled. 'After a few days here you'll be fine, but I don't understand your judgment. It seems wrong to me.'

She lay down beside him, not bothering to take off her shoes.

'I'm tired too,' she said, as she turned towards him and put her arms around him. 'I don't know why I'm so tired.'

Joseph O'Connor

Mothers Were All the Same

I MET CATRIONA again on the train in from Luton. I had noticed her on the plane, just before we came in to land, leafing through the lousy in-flight magazine – 'a great big top o'the morning from Delaney's Irish Cabaret' – while the old lady beside her worried about air disasters. The hostess told her to calm down and held her bony little hand. The old lady's hand, that is. Not Catriona's. Catriona's hands weren't bony at all. They were cute.

She said it was statistically impossible. She said you had more chance of being kicked to death by a mule than dying in an air crash. The old lady said to tell that to Yuri Gagarin, but the hostess just giggled and said, 'Who's he when he's at home? Something to do with glasnost, is it?' Catriona looked over at me. She grinned, and she rolled her beautiful eyes.

The plane screeched in, bucked as the wheels skimmed the ground, and shuddered to a halt outside the arrivals terminal. Catriona was ahead of me as we shuffled in off the tarmac, collars raised in the cold. Two police cars emptied. The plainclothes men stared and scribbled like crazy on their clipboards as we filed past them.

I told the customs guy I'd just arrived from Dublin, and I didn't know how long I'd be staying. That was true all right. He glared under his peaked cap, making me feel guilty. He had a face like the 'Spitting Image' puppet of Norman Tebbit, but without the charm. I mean, I hadn't done anything, but the way he looked at me made me feel like some kind of terrorist, just the same. Then he asked me to write down my full name, and he slouched off into a back room. That's it, I thought, I'm finished now. I gazed around the baggage lounge, full of wailing babies and neon signs. LUTON: GATEWAY TO THE SOUTH EAST. RYANAIR TO THE REPUBLIC OF IRELAND. LOADZA LUVVERLY LOLLY IN THE SIZZLING SOARAWAY SUN. Then I saw her staring at me. Just for a second, but she was definitely looking at me. I smiled back, but she turned away to look for her bags. I made up my mind to ask her later, if I got the chance.

'Right,' said the customs man, and he told me to report my address to the local police as soon as I had one. I was going to ask why. But you don't bother, do you? You're so relieved that your name hasn't somehow crept into their bloody computer that you just smile politely and say thanks very much. He said he hoped I had a nice trip, and he was sorry for holding me up. But it was for everyone's good, if I knew what he meant. I knew what he meant.

I only had my rucksack, so I caught up with her on the other side of customs. I saw her immediately, looking in the window of the Sock Shop.

A troop of boy scouts was lined up at the burger counter, screaming curses and waving banknotes. Three football fans were drunk and singing in the corner, beer all over their England shirts. Soldiers walked up and down with machine guns in their hands. Actually, there were uniforms everywhere, now that I think of it. That's one thing I noticed straightaway, everybody seemed to be wearing a uniform. Customs, police, pilots, cleaners, waitresses, delivery boys, hostesses, all rushing around the hall. Above it all was the sound of the loudspeaker, announcing late flights and missing passengers.

I said, 'Excuse me,' and she turned around, looking a little surprised.

'Yeah?' she said.

I asked if I had seen her somewhere before. I was hoping she wouldn't think this was some big corny pick-up line, but I really did think I had seen her somewhere before and I couldn't remember where. I said I couldn't help noticing her

on the plane and she looked familiar. She said she really
didn't think so, and she looked away. I said I was sure. She
turned again and scrutinized me. Then she asked if I was a
friend of Johnny Reilly, by any chance. I said, yeah, I was.
Used to be anyway. Recognition dawned on her face. That
party he had – last Christmas? I was there with a blonde-
haired girl. Susan. Yes. She remembered me now. I was
pretty flattered, actually, until she pointed out the reason she
remembered me. I was the one who had puked over the
aspidistra in the hall.

I grinned. She pursed her lips and looked at her watch. I
said it was a small world. She said, yeah, it was a small
world, but she wouldn't like to have to paint it. There didn't
seem to be much else to say. She'd just come over for the
weekend. What about me? I was here looking for a job. Who
wasn't? I told her I didn't know how long I'd stick it. She just
kept staring at that watch so eventually I just said bye, and
she wished me luck and dragged her case outside to the bus
stop for Luton station.

I waited for the next bus. Well, if she wanted to be like
that, fine, I didn't really feel like being friendly anyway. Too
many things on my mind. I didn't feel like some big conversation. OK, OK, so I had Aunt Martha's place, but that was
only good for a few weeks at most, the old bat. I'd have to
get a job soon. Then my own place. I never knew the folks
would be so upset about me going, either. When I told them
first they were delighted. But the morning I left it was a
different story. Tears and scribbled addresses and folded-up
tenners in the suit pocket. The whole emigrant bit. You'd
have sworn I was going to the moon, the way they went on.
The whole thing was like some bloody Christy Moore song
come to life in our front room. On the way out to the airport
I actually thought my father was going to tell me the facts of
life. It was that bad.

At least the suit wasn't too hick. Still fitted me, anyway.
Just about. Though I'd really have to go on a diet. All the
drinking I'd done in the weeks I was saying my goodbyes

was catching up fast. I must have put on eight pounds. But everyone insists on buying you pints, so what can you do? Everyone except Johnny Reilly, of course, the tight shit. My father got me the suit the week I started college. It was hanging over the back of my door when I reeled in that night. He said I'd need a good suit. I wore it twice in three years. Once for Granny's funeral and once for my graduation. He said to bring it with me to London anyway. He said I'd need it for all the interviews.

On the bus I thought about Una Murray. I'd never known she was into me until it was too late. But after our farewell drink she lunged at me on Capel Street Bridge, with the wind from the Liffey blowing through her hair like in a movie or something. Shit. If only I'd known before. Well, it wouldn't have made any difference. Still, would have been nice to know. Susan would have been jealous as hell.

When I got to Luton station, the London train was just pulling in, and the scramble of passengers was milling around the doorways. I fought my way on, dragging the rucksack behind, and I made a rush for the one spare seat. There were posters everywhere, saying that unattended luggage would be removed by the cops and blown up.

There she was, sitting opposite me as I squeezed in. Catriona. She was reading a book. *The Ultimate Good Luck* by Richard Ford. She looked up and smiled again. She said we must stop meeting like this. I tried to think of something smart but nothing came. I just grinned back like an idiot and I think I blushed as I offered her a duty-free cigarette. She shook her head and took off her glasses and pointed to another sign. NO SMOKING. An old man with a moustache glared at me.

'Haven't you heard of King's Cross?' he said.

We got talking again. She asked me where I was staying in London. Strange, but I said I didn't know. I don't know why I said that. Because I did know. But as Johnny Reilly says, I can't give anyone a straight answer, and I must admit that much is true. I suppose I was afraid she'd have nowhere to stay and want to come to Aunt Martha's with me. Look, I know it's stupid, but I'm funny like that. I like my space. Crazy, I know, but what can you do? I think it's because everyone at home asks so many bloody questions. Where were you? Until when? Who were you with? And the great bloody existential conundrum of course: just who do you think you are? All that stuff is enough to make anyone defensive. I'm not saying it's right. I'm just saying that's the way it is.

I needn't have worried. She was fixed up already, staying in some hotel near the station. It was a small place, she said, but it was hunky-dory. I couldn't remember the last time I'd heard that expression. Hunky-dory. As the train pulled in I asked if she needed any help with her bags. I knew she didn't, but I thought I'd ask anyway. She said she could manage on her own. So I shook hands with her on the platform and said goodbye again. Her hand was cold. She smiled, because I was being so formal, I suppose, with the handshake and everything. She said she might see me around. I shrugged and said I hoped so. She told me she hoped I'd find somewhere to stay, and I said good luck, see you, and walked off.

'Eddie,' she shouted, as I walked through the ticket barrier. I turned and saw her trotting towards me, dragging her case, panting. She said she was sorry, that I must have thought she was really rude. I wondered what she meant. She said if I really had nowhere to stay why didn't I come with her? She said that was the obvious thing. She was sure they'd have another room. It was a really cheap place too, and if I needed somewhere to sleep for a few nights, until I found something else, it was probably OK. I hesitated. I knew I couldn't afford to stay in any hotel, no matter how cheap, not even for one night. Three nights would nearly clean me out. But then I thought, to hell with it. Why not? Nothing ventured, all of that. I just felt like doing something different. I don't know why. Something spontaneous after all the weeks of planning every last moment. That's what I wanted. And I suppose I have to admit I thought she was pretty cute, too. I asked whether she was sure she wouldn't mind. She said, of course not. She'd love the company. I could come with her now, and maybe she could show me some of the sights over the weekend. All right. I said I would.

She was amazed that I'd never been to London before. She'd come over every summer for three years. She had a job over there whenever she wanted it, in some trendy lefty bookshop on Charing Cross Road. She might come over for good next year, she said. But she knew what it was like to be in London on your own. It was such an overwhelming place. So huge and anonymous and impersonal. So different from Dublin. Yeah, I told her, that's why I came over.

Then she wanted to know what Johnny Reilly was doing these days. I said I didn't know. I was going to tell her about our big falling out, but I didn't bother. I just said I hadn't seen him for a while, and I hadn't a clue what he was up to, but it was probably either illegal or a waste of time.

'That sounds like Johnny all right,' she said.

So we went over together to the El Dorado Hotel and we signed in. The Greek guy behind the counter told us he rented rooms by the hour. You didn't have to have them for the whole night. There were no questions asked here, not blooming likely. I blushed like a sap and she made some joke. The Greek laughed out loud and apologized. Then he said he did have separate rooms to spare and he'd show us the way. Creaking up the stairs I whispered that I wasn't so crazy about this kip. But she told me not to be so silly, that old Zorba was only joking about the hourly rate. I said I thought he was pretty serious, and she sighed and said she knew, but for seven-fifty a night you couldn't expect The Ritz. I coughed knowledgeably and said I supposed she was right.

While she changed and unpacked, I slipped downstairs and outside and phoned Aunt Martha. The phone box was plastered with stickers advertising masseuses and prostitutes and kinky nuns and 'corporal punishment specialists'. I thought it must be great to be a specialist at something. Aunt Martha's businesslike voice buzzed down the line. I was to come over immediately. She had the dinner on and my cousins were just dying to meet me again. I imagined Uncle Frank and her and Alvin and Sharon sitting around the table. I could just see them all – waiting for me. I reconsidered, just for a second.

But I just couldn't face it. I told Aunt Martha I was sorry but I was still in Dublin airport and I couldn't make it until Monday. It was the fog, I said. Everything was screwed up because of the fog. I felt bad about lying, but what can you do? She sounded so disappointed though. Soon as I'd said it, I regretted it, but it was too late then. She said they'd just have to wait. I said I was really sorry. She said she should think so too. All the trouble she'd gone too, not to mention the expense. I noticed her weird accent. She nearly didn't sound Irish at all.

The funny thing was, though, as soon as I put the phone down I knew in my heart that this whole thing was a big mistake. I really did. I just had this feeling, you know? Like God was going to get me for lying to Aunt Martha. Not that I believe in God. But still. You never know.

Back at the El Dorado things were looking up. My room was fine. It was small, but you could see Tower Bridge in the distance, and there was a television in the corner. I flicked the switch but nothing happened. You had to put a pound coin in the slot to make it work. Well, it looked good. And although I didn't want to watch anything, it made me feel good knowing that I could, if I wanted to, if I had a pound to spare.

I sat down and bounced on the bed. Gently. Yeah, this was great. God, I thought, if my mother could only see me now. Holed up with a strange woman in a King's Cross knocking shop. I felt like a Harold Robbins hero.

I said this to Catriona on the Tube up to Leicester Square that night. She said she wasn't familiar with the Harold Robbins *oeuvre* – she was a little sarcastic really – but she knew what I meant about the El Dorado. It hadn't been quite as sleazy last time she was there. Still, never mind. It was all part of our little adventure, she said. We walked around the square for a while, looking at the lights and the posters in the cinema windows.

I bought her an ice cream in a little place in Soho. She said this was a really trendy area now, and the shops were way too expensive. I said she didn't have to tell me, the ice creams had cost six-fifty. She smiled and said she'd give me the money. I told her not to be so silly, but she insisted, so I took it. I gave the waiter a two-quid tip. Well, I didn't want her to think I was mean. She said, 'You only did that because you don't want me to think you're mean.' I tried to be as offended as possible but she just slipped her arm through mine and laughed again, and there was something about her made me want to be happy. So I admitted it and she sighed with mock desperation that men were so transparent.

Catriona was beautiful when she sighed. Wearing jeans and Doc Martens and a Public Enemy T-shirt, she was far more elegant than any of the women we watched swanning out of the opera house in pearls and fur. Her eyes were kind of soft and sparkling, the kind you read about in books. Her face was lightly freckled. She had a way of talking fast and avoiding my eyes that was just irresistible. And she was funny, too. In the wine bar she made sarcastic comments about the posers and yuppies in the corners.

I told her about home and Susan and everything. It's funny how much you can trust and say to a total stranger. And I told her I wasn't really sure what kind of job I was looking for, just something a bit more interesting than sitting in Dublin on the old rock and roll. She said she still had a year to go in art school, then she'd probably come over here and do some course or another. She had lots of friends over here already. In fact, she knew more people over here than she did in Dublin. Lots of people. Bucketloads of them. She'd never be stuck in London, she said.

The thing that got me was this. When we were talking

about gigs and holidays and stuff I noticed she said 'we' all the time. We did this. We saw that. Some lucky bastard was obviously going out with her back home, and I suppose she kept dropping this 'we' shit to let me know that. Half-way through the second bottle of wine I plucked up the courage to ask her. She said he was a brilliant guy, Damien, they were really happy together and all that. A really wonderful pass-the-sickbag relationship.

'So, what's happening?' I asked her, pretending not to be jealous as hell. 'I mean, are we talking wedding bells or what?'

'Maybe,' she admitted, 'when he qualifies.'

'And kids and everything?'

'Yeah,' she said. 'I'm sure we'll have children. I mean, why wouldn't we?'

'I don't know,' I said, 'why would you? I mean, why?'

'What is this,' she said, 'twenty fucking questions?'

I suppose I shouldn't have been so pushy and everything. It's not good to pry. I know that, but you know, it was just the booze really. Booze makes some people happy or sad or horny. It makes me curious. Always has. Outside in the rain I felt uneasy and confused. She seemed very quiet now, like there was something on her mind. The mood of things had changed. The feel of the night was suddenly weird and different now. Maybe this hadn't been such a great idea. I told her I was sorry for asking so many personal questions. She just stood there outside the Hippodrome chewing her fingernails and saying nothing.

'Do you want me to go away?' I asked.

She smiled then. She slipped her hand into mine. She said she was sorry too. She didn't know what had come over her. She had things on her mind. She couldn't say. Maybe she'd tell me some other time. She was really sorry, though. Here she was spoiling my first night in London. I told her that was rubbish, and if it wasn't for her I'd be having an awful time. I said come on, here I was in London with a gorgeous woman and not a care in the world. She smiled and looked up at me then. She asked me if I meant the gorgeous bit.

'Yeah,' I said. I did. She said she'd been called beautiful before, but never gorgeous. 'They're not the same thing,' I said, 'not the same thing at all.'

'Charmer,' she said, in a sad voice, 'you're just like Damien.' I said I was sure I wasn't. She said I was, but for one night it didn't matter.

That night Catriona and I made love in the El Dorado Hotel. I had no condoms but she said it was safe. We held each other tight as the bedsprings gave us away. I didn't care. I didn't think about anything except her. I couldn't. Afterwards we lay in each other's arms. I asked her is she sure it was safe. She said yes. Her voice sounded weird. Like she was about to shout. Then I touched her face and she softened. She held my hand very hard.

When I woke up I didn't know where I was. My head hurt and my mouth was numb. She was sitting at the dressing table, putting her earrings in. She said she was going out for the day and wouldn't be back until teatime. She had to see this friend of hers. I asked if it was a guy. She laughed and said no. But she wouldn't let me come. It was just girl talk, she said.

'I'll probably tell her all about you,' she smiled, 'all about how I seduced you.' She kissed me before she slipped out of the room. She said she'd see me back here at eight.

'Yeah,' I said, 'mind yourself.' She said she would.

Down in the breakfast room the Greek grinned lasciviously as he ladled a large sausage on to my plate.

'Eat it all up,' he said. 'You will need all your strength, yes?'

I spent the day dossing around. On Oxford Street the shop windows were full of cheap suits and grim-looking dummies. A guy in sunglasses was selling gold chains from a cardboard box outside the HMV Megastore. 'Any shop in the West End, ladies and gents they'd costya two hundred nicker straight up but here it's not two hundred, it's not one hundred and fifty, it's not seventy-five or fifty or even thirty. A pony, ladies and gents. First twenty-five pound down gets it.' Nobody moved. 'Come on now, loves,' he said, 'before Mister Plod comes back, who'll give me twenty-five for one of these lovely items?' I walked away and bought a postcard of Princess Diana for my mother. I wrote it over coffee in a little place on Russell Street. I told her I'd arrived safely, and that I was fine, and already making friends. I smiled when I wrote that. I couldn't find a post office open anywhere so I put the card in my pocket and forgot all about it. I never sent it. I still have it in my pocket somewhere, all crumpled up and torn. I've always kept it.

When Catriona came back that night she had an upset stomach. She was bleary-eyed and pale. She told me she'd eaten some awful burger or something, and it hadn't agreed with her at all. I told her to watch it. I told her catching salmonella is the national fucking sport over here. But when she tried to laugh it really creased her up. She had to lie down. She had to get some sleep. Soon as she said that she leaned over and vomited on the floor. I was worried. She walked into the room and flopped on to the bed, shivering and clutching her stomach. She really was in a bad way. When I put my arms around her she started all of a sudden – I mean for absolutely no reason – to cry. I asked her to tell me what was wrong. Had she had some row with her friend? She said, no, she hadn't even seen her. Why not? She snapped at me then. I mean, she nearly bit my fucking head off. She really got weird on me, started saying she had no friends and she was on her own. I said I was her friend and she laughed and said, yeah, things were that bad. Then she said she was sorry. I held her hand as she eased painfully under the sheets, with all her clothes still on. I asked if it was something to do with her period.

'Oh my God,' she sighed, 'spare me the new man bit.' She laughed out loud then, really laughed the bloody roof down. No, she said, if there was one thing it had nothing to do with, it was that. Then she told me she just had to get some sleep. I was to come back and see her later on.

In my room I walked up and down, chain-smoking and flicking ash all over the carpet. I didn't care. Then I lay on my bed and stared out at the lights on the street. What the hell was wrong? Would she be all right? Jesus, say if she bloody died or something. I got up and poured myself a glass of duty free. The tumbler was dirty and it tasted like tooth-paste. But I drank it anyway. Then I had another one. Then I had a double. She'd probably be OK. Just some bug or something, that was all. In fact I wasn't feeling so terrific myself. I fed a pound into the television. I watched a documentary about a tribe in the Amazon that eat monkeys.

The bed was wet when I woke up. The stench of the whisky was everywhere. The clock on the wall said ten-past eleven. Shit. I must have dozed off holding the bottle. It was nearly all spilt. My jeans stuck to my legs. I splashed water over my face. I stared in the mirror. I looked awful. My face was pale and my tongue felt all furry. Maybe it was that ice cream we'd had the night before. I don't know. Six-quid-fifty for strawberry-flavoured botulism. Or too much cheap red wine. Yeah. That was probably what was wrong with her. Just a hangover.

When I stumbled in she was sitting up in the bed and wearing my pyjama top. I sat down beside her and asked how she was. She had been crying again. She wrapped her arms around me. The smell of drink filled my head. I told her not to worry. I said everything would be all right. She said my name a few times while I tried to kiss her. She was so beautiful. I couldn't help it.

'Please,' she said, taking my hands off her. She couldn't. It wasn't that she didn't want to. She just couldn't. 'Don't you understand anything?' she said, with tears in her eyes. 'I mean, do I have to paint you a picture?'

I said if she wanted to be like that she could stay on her own. It wasn't my bloody fault she was sick. I told her I bet old Damien wouldn't have stood for this bloody primadonna crap. Who the hell did she think she was, anyway? She told me to get out. I said I was sorry. She started screaming, 'Get out, you shit. Get out of my room.' She picked up a glass and pitched it at me; it smashed on the wall.

When I came back later and knocked on her door there was no answer. I stood in the corridor, apologizing through the keyhole. No sound came from the room. The Greek came by and saw me on my knees.

'The ladies, my friend,' he shrugged, 'what can you do with them?' I said nothing.

Next morning Catriona was gone. She'd checked out at seven-thirty, taken all her stuff, ordered a cab for Luton airport. The Greek said he was terribly sorry. I said I hadn't known her that well anyway.

'Still,' he said, 'a very sad situation.' I asked him what he meant. He said no offence, but it was just very sad, a young girl like her.

Breathless, I stood in Catriona's room, staring at the made-up bed and the open windows. My pyjama top lay on the chair by the window. There was a brown bloodstain on it. The Greek's wife came in with an armful of clean white towels.

The young lady had been very ill in the night, she said. They were going to call me but Catriona had insisted that they shouldn't. She begged them not to. She couldn't let anyone find out. If her parents discovered, they would kill her. She explained everything and said it was nothing to worry about. The nurses had told her all this would happen. What she needed now was rest. No worry, and plenty of sleep. It was all over now. But a little discomfort was only to be expected.

The Greek's wife told me she was terribly sorry. She'd thought I would have been aware of things. If only she'd known, she would have broken it more gently. I felt like my whole body was turning to water. She asked me if I wanted a drink. I said no, I still had some duty free left.

I arrived at Aunt Martha's place at lunchtime on Sunday. The door opened and I fell in. She was furious with me. What did I mean, turning up in this drunken state? Did I think this was some kind of boarding house? And where had I been, anyway? She'd phoned Dublin on Friday night to see whether the fog had lifted. My mother had been worried sick about me. I'd better have a good explanation. They were just about to call the police. My father was searching the house for a photo to give them for *The News*. The only one he could find was the one they took the day of my graduation. They didn't know what kind of trouble I was in. Out in the hall I rang home. I said I'd bumped into Johnny Reilly, a guy I once knew in college, who was living over here now. I'd decided to stay a few nights with him. My mother said she wanted me back home on the next plane. She said it was patently obvious that I couldn't be trusted to look after myself.

Alvin and Sharon said it was good to see me. Sharon had purple hair now, and Alvin had a ring through his nose. I managed to croak that I was sorry for all the trouble I'd caused. They shrugged and said not to worry. They said London was all about enjoying yourself. They said I shouldn't let my mother guilt-trip me. In the kitchen someone made me a cup of strong coffee. Alvin said not to pay any attention to Aunt Martha either. He said mothers were all the same. Then Sharon put her arms around me and told me to stop crying. She was sure it would all blow over soon. We'd be laughing about it, she said, in a few weeks.

I went to bed and stared at the ceiling. I wrapped the blanket tight around me. Really tight. Over my head. So tight that it felt like a second skin. And the whole world was shut out now, on the other side of the darkness.

Sara Berkeley

The Sky's Gone Out

BEFORE HE opened his paper, he glanced down the row of faces opposite. He was not looking for anything. His mind was on an incident at the office that is lost to him now if he tries to recall. It amused him how the English scrutinized each other in the Underground, planted in their rows like beans. He liked to catch two people watching one another without their eyes ever meeting. Yet when he was caught looking someone full in the face, he quickly averted his eyes. If it was a woman, even a plain woman, he was aware he often blushed. Frequently when the carriage was empty he played the game with himself in the window opposite. On good days he risked a wink or a wry smile. In general, he was troubled by his weight and thinning hair, and looked quickly away.

He liked to see a pretty face on the tube. He liked to know without looking that a slender leg was three feet from his own; the hollow of an ankle could arouse in him a peculiar melancholy that was pleasant. Sooner or later he always became engrossed in his paper. Sometimes he thought of his wife for a little: not in clear pictures, but in words and abstractions. She was a gentle woman.

He had a theory: on days when a lovely woman sat across from him, there would invariably be three or four more in the carriage. On these days he did not notice the twelve stations go by. Even the men seemed exemplary specimens. He would smile to himself, thinking what a flaw in the design he was. The lower buttons on his shirt gaped, his trouser legs rode up. He didn't mind. If, on the other hand, an ugly woman sat opposite, her companions were likely to be drab. Everyone's hair looked greasy. Dandruff prevailed.

The train was full but not crowded, and he got a seat at once: his favourite, at the end. With pleasure he folded his paper and patted it down in his lap. In his first, cursory glance he saw her, but the tiny sound he made involuntarily in his throat was swallowed easily by the train's hum. Suddenly, he had no desire to scan the rest of the faces opposite, nor to make out the reflections of his neighbours in the windows. He looked quickly at his paper. He had read the first paragraph twice. He felt a strong desire to look at her again. She might be getting off at the next station; like hundreds before her, she would disappear in the crowd. Beauty was made to be gratefully admired. He raised his eyes. She was staring an inch to the left of him. She looked transfixed, the word came to him, clear as a bell. Hurriedly he looked away, annoyed with himself, but at the same time acutely troubled. He felt a sensation at the back of his neck and knew it must be the beginning of a blush. Her look! He stared at a point on the door, struggling to think why her look troubled him so greatly. Certainly she was striking. She had the bone structure of a very lovely woman, her hair was silky and escaped from her black felt hat in the kind of tangled curls he particularly liked. Who did she resemble? No one. He realized he had never seen another woman like her. But it was not her face that kept him in this suddenly heightened state – it was her expression. She had stared a little to one side of him with a look of wildness, there was no other way to describe it.

Stiffly, he returned to his paper and read the same paragraph. His eyes fixed on the last word, unseeingly, as he realized that the train was slowing at a station. Once again, she might get off. She might leave. In ten seconds he could be staring at an empty seat, unable to believe she was no longer there. He had to look at the face one more time. His sense of foolishness was uncomfortable, but as the train stopped and she did not move, he let relief embolden him and glanced across. Her eyes were closed.

He did not hear the babble of alighting and movement in the train around him. For a moment he held his breath. He felt a brief, unidentifiable ache in his abdomen. She sat very still, almost stiffly, with her hands loose on her lap. Her clothes were dark – he took them in confusedly, tensely aware that at any second she might open her eyes and look at him. An infinitesimal scene tripped through his head: she saw him, she was angry, she shouted something, reached across and slapped his face. He felt a hot blush spreading from the roots of his hair, he could feel the tingling on his cheek that followed the sharp impact of her hand.

On her lap, the fingers of one hand clenched suddenly into a fist, then relaxed. She wore no rings. Her eyes were still closed: he allowed himself three agonizingly long seconds taking in the lashes, the cheekbones, the perfect skin, then looked dazedly back down at the paper in his lap. He brought one hand out from under it and studied his nails with care. Details like the white of his cuticles brought him slowly back to rational thought. My god she's lovely. He thought the words once, loudly, then felt a delicious, tantalizing power. If he read his paper for a little longer, before they reached the next station, he could turn the page and take the natural opportunity to glance idly round the carriage. It bothered him that someone might have seen him staring at her, seen the incriminating blush. He wanted to look around defensively, aggressively even, to subdue any knowing looks he might receive. But I am ridiculous, he thought, and again the words came loud and clear. Ridiculous. An old ass. He thought with a smile of his son's latest phrase: a spa. You're a spa daddy. He had rebuked him for using it just the other day.

The train slowed and all thoughts were wiped from his mind. He turned the page of his paper with difficulty. Despite years of practice the paper refused to fold. It rucked in the middle, the inside pages slipped sideways; it was a mess, and the train had stopped. Still, she did not move and he felt absurdly like laughing. One more, then, one more indulgence. At last he got the paper straight. She was staring down now, directly at his feet. He felt his toes stiffen. Briefly he tried to picture his shoes: which ones was he wearing? What colour socks? Her hands were moving in her lap now, a vague fumbling movement – but her eyes ... did she never blink? Abruptly she lifted her head, but in the moment before he turned his away, he saw that she was looking distractedly to one side, listening to an announcement from the platform. The train would take one of two branches at the next station. Some-times they changed their minds, you had to listen. The doors closed and he hadn't heard. Let it be! If she alighted at the next station, well, he could too! It didn't matter which line he took. They joined up later and he rode on for several stops.

On the second page of the paper his eye was caught by pictures of the war; tanks, explosions, soldiers, the waste sickened him. His eyes felt irritated and smarted as though stung by the desert sand. The whole world gone mad, and for what? Life went on. Take the woman: it was plain to him she was caught up in some close drama of her own – what might it be? By the cut of her clothes she was a well-bred woman. He winced as two lines of thought crossed in his head: here he was, calmly wondering what sort of calamity might have befallen her that she could look so stricken; at the same time, his thoughts were a hotbed of fantasies. He pictured her crossing a bridge in the wind, her dark coat billowing, her hair blowing across her face. For a moment, as his mind focused sharply on this scene, it seemed unbearable that this woman should be someone he had casually sat opposite not ten minutes ago on a train. How had he worked himself to such a fever pitch in that time? How had the few glimpses of her face worked so powerfully, and stirred such agitation, such peculiar excitement as he was now feeling?

In a moment he had decided: if she left the train at the

next station he would follow. He would casually cross to the other branch, as though it was something he naturally had to do. If she crossed too, perhaps they could continue their journey together in harmless, one-sided companionship, in a sort of secret union; it was, after all, harmless and so . . . harmless . . . her calves were crossed and elegant in dark stockings, the skirt long, the knees shapely through the light fabric; the train was slowing, he frowned and clutched his paper. Should she move, he must be ready to follow quickly; so easy for a figure to be swallowed in the crowd, the teeming carnival of the underground . . .

She was not getting off. She was looking above him, her mouth a little open, and he imagined in the brief glimpse he allowed himself that her breath was coming in short gasps. Perhaps she was ill! Again he felt his scalp prickle as he stared intently at the newsprint. He hated illness in public places. But she did not look ill. He was sure she wasn't ill. It was something else. A matter of love, surely, a matter of the heart. In spite of himself, he felt like smiling; a middle-aged gent on his way home from the office, making up stories about a pretty face. Strangers on a train. The doors closed. He really had intended to get off the train if she had! What would he do, follow her? She would have left the station, and then where would he be? Stranded, on the platform, the picture of foolishness. It was not like him to risk looking foolish. In this way, he tried to swallow it down, the rise of his feelings, the lightness that took hold. The next stop was Waterloo: he thought of that picture of the bridge in purple smoke and dusk. She would get off at Waterloo. She would cross the bridge in the evening with the sky and the water turning just those lurid colours: a dark, threatening cumulus of blues and purples.

Far underground, where seven tunnels met in a wide passage, seven streams of people merged and massed at the foot of the escalator. She took the right hand side. She was a swift and accurate mover in a crowd. He trod on toes and elbowed people out the way, distantly amazed at his own rudeness. He almost lost her on the steps behind a group of boys. He almost lost her again passing through the ticket barrier. Caught behind an old man, his impatience turned to panic. There was only one reason he was emerging from Waterloo station at five on a Tuesday and it was itself so elusive he had difficulty keeping it in his grasp. She was slipping away from him. Gritting his teeth, he pushed through the crowd, muttering excuses, his eyes fixed on the black hat thirty yards away. 'All right, all right,' the ticket collector said, and an old lady nearby clucked reprovingly.

The black hat was still visible beyond the people walking the long corridor at the back of the concourse. Red railings. White tiles. It was a long time since he had been in Waterloo station. A beautiful building, with its latticework and gables. He remembered it well and knew if he glanced to his right, past the telephones, he would glimpse the lofty iron trellis-work of the roof. She was now turning towards the York Road exit.

His shoes sounded smartly on the tiles and for the length of the corridor he allowed himself to feel as full of purpose as he sounded. In fact, he was in a strange state. His rational side was sitting back, far back in the shadow of this thing, whatever it was, that was driving him forward in her pursuit. Having left the train he knew there was no turning round. The balance tipped, his excitement tampered with the valves of his heart, he was passing through fire. He could just see the tails of her coat billow as she turned the corner. He racked his brains to recall the geography of the place: another flight of stairs and then a confusion of turnings and exits – the red iron gates folded back from the main exit ahead. He would surely lose her there. The humiliation of turning back now! He broke into a heavy run.

It had begun to rain, an unsteady drizzle, and commuters were pouring into the station. By the taxi rank, he stood a moment, out of breath already, searching for her. She had

broken free from the crowd and was heading for Waterloo
Bridge. Years before, he had worked for a while with the
homeless on the Embankment. He and a group of others had
brought them food, sat around the fires when they were
welcome, listened to the stories. Memories of that time
flooded him as he descended to the riddle of subways and
emerged on the great bowl, wet now and bleak as ever. She
was entering the far tunnel, the one that led up to the bridge
itself. To follow her, he would have to pass them, the
shambling figures round their fires, huddled in their blankets. Suddenly, he felt his face begin to burn with shame.
Once he had come here with time and food to offer the
hopeless. Now he hurried blindly across the concrete, his
thoughts in uproar. Follow her! Follow her you fool! Soon
she will be gone. Soon you will walk by the river, by the
Queen Mary and Cleopatra's Needle, to Embankment station
to catch the next train; for that is what you are going to do,
you sad old man. No more of this. You are a plain man. No
more of this madness then. It does not belong in the vessel
of your life. It was not meant.

Ahead, he saw them, overcoated men, hanging around
by the bottom of the ramp. They watched her pass by, hands
in their pockets, and he imagined their eyes, dull and
hooded. They let her go by, no one made a move. His face
was still burning, though he knew they could not see, and
his hands hung stiffly by his side. No time, he muttered to
himself as he approached. One of the men moved his hand,
scarcely bothering to make a supplicatory gesture. He shook
his head quickly. No time now to fumble in pockets for a coin
and shrug off the response in a welter of discomfort and
shame. She was on the bridge. Let me go now, he pleaded
silently to the hunched figures, let me go.

The crowd moved from North to South. She walked by the
rails and people stepped aside to make way for her. It was
difficult to see distinctly, but he thought that people turned

as she passed and he understood this. Like him, they could not help taking a second look. He imagined the whole flow of city workers coming to a halt, piling into one another, trying to turn back and follow her. It seemed as though only he was going in the right direction. I am walking to Embankment station, he told himself, but he knew it was not so. He was following this woman. Something in a stranger's face had made it impossible to remain on the train he travelled on every evening to his home in Woodside Park. He had done something unaccountable; now he felt as though the gesture had launched him into an uninterruptable state. With the wind hitting him hard downriver and the rain blowing on his face, he knew now he could make no mistake. He was carried forward, against the crowd, his eyes continually seeking and finding the woman ahead. He was filled with a sense of irony, but it had no object.

It was simple on the bridge. He even gained on her, making up for the gap that had widened in the station. She was now ten yards ahead, no more. He could see her ankles, the dark heels of her shoes on the wet pavement. Her hat sat crookedly and the wind blew her hair exactly as he had imagined. He laughed aloud, and the sound was carried away on the wind. Now he had a chance to look around him – the vast panorama of the Thames, Westminster to Blackfriars, the proud riverbanks. It was years since he had walked here. He felt tiny. They were all specks, hurrying across this great structure, pendulously draped across the expanse of rolling water. Even the river was tiny, a blue streak on a map, dividing the grey stain that was London. Only she was something, this woman. By her very rejection of everything around her, she became something herself. He was nothing, he knew that, and he did not mind. She was something and he had understood. Now he was allowed to follow her; for a brief span of both their lives he would bind them together. It was irrelevant that only one of them knew. One was enough. And besides, he thought, I'm glad it is me. After all, what if she were following *me* across Waterloo Bridge towards the rich promise of the city beyond? I would never have seen those eyes. I would be less than I am.

It remained with him, this inexplicable feeling of well-being, all the way across the bridge. Rain was damping his hair down. There were dark streaks on his coat, his briefcase was bubbled with tiny drops. He was able to keep up without effort. As they neared the city side, his thoughts began to roam around the hub of streets leading to Covent Garden and the West End. Still, he did not allow himself to speculate where she was going. His thoughts were dreamlike, everything unpleasant was submerged.

It came as a shock when she made a rapid turn and began to descend to Victoria Embankment. A quick decision was needed: on the bridge, where there were hundreds of people, it was easy to follow her without being noticed. On the Embankment there were few people; he would be conspicuous keeping ten, even twenty yards behind a lone woman. He stopped by the parapet where it curved out to the steps down. She had already disappeared but she would emerge below; he could see then where she went. Once again, he told himself that he was going to walk to Embankment station. His eyes on the dirty blue and white of the *Queen Mary*, he waited until she would have emerged below. Yes, she was there, heading upriver towards Cleopatra's Needle. The stairs were wet and the passage smelt dank. He could hear the cars passing outside, but for a few seconds he was alone on the staircase, clattering down, his hand out in case he slipped – and she was out of sight. Now, he thought, imagine she is gone. When you emerge, she is nowhere to be seen, the bond is severed and you carry on ... as though ... nothing ... In the moment he reached the street, his eyes sought her avidly. She was still there, crossing at the lights, walking straight in the rain. He followed, grateful, absurdly relieved; happy again.

The gap was wider than ever. He could scarcely make

out the details her hair made against hat and collar. Her hands were pale marks against her coat. The lights had changed again and he could have done a dance of impatience as he waited for a break in the traffic to dash across. But there she was, familiar now, he held her warmly with his eyes. He wished to speak to her, silently in his head, but he could find no words. I am here, he wanted to say. Whatever it is, do not despair. But they sounded like the words of a foolish middle-aged man in a mac, and he was no such man. He was nothing.

She was approaching Cleopatra's Needle now, they were rounding the river together, and for the first time her steps faltered. So used to the pace now, he faltered momentarily too. What to do? It was raining: he couldn't sit on a bench, he couldn't stop, it was out of the question. Such an interruption now would lift the lid on a scene of great emptiness. She was walking quite slowly now, with none of the purpose that had carried them across the bridge. Her hands hung limply by her sides. Rain drove in gusts against their faces. He was blinded and he felt at risk. Great peril, somewhere, just behind him, breathing on his neck. Instinctively, he raised a hand to the back of his neck as though to swat a fly and at the same moment she stopped. She had reached the sphinx, the first of the two that flanked Cleopatra's Needle. She put a hand out as though to touch the stone, but it touched nothing. As he watched in disbelief, walking as slowly as he dared now, she turned and descended the few steps to the parapet overlooking the river. Standing there, she put her hands flat on the broad wall. The wind chose that moment for a vicious squall that lifted her hat and carried it in a trice up, somersaulting once, and then swiftly out over the river and down until it was lost from view. She did not seem to notice. He could see one side of her face, close enough now to make out that her eyes were open and staring across the river, wild as they had seemed on the train, staring at his own feet.

There was no alternative. He must pass her by, leave her

behind. It never entered his head to do otherwise. But his eyes were fixed on her. If he had to tear himself away, he would see her until the last possible moment. She looked tragic now, standing like that, with her hands spread out, flat on the stone, and her hair blowing unchecked across her face. As he reached the sphinx, once again as close to her as he had ever been since leaving the train, able to make out the curve of cheek and neck, she tipped back her head and shouted. The words were blown to him, fouled by the same wind that carried them. He made out sounds, sounds only, they made no sense. For a blind moment, it occurred to him to stop, approach her, touch her shoulder. As soon as it was conceived, the idea of intruding on her distress revolted him. Turning his collar up, he began to walk quickly, past Cleopatra's Needle, past the second sphinx, up the bank of the Thames River towards Embankment station.

Before the bridge he crossed and entered the station in a crowd of others. Through the ticket barrier and down, mechanically following the black arrows. All at once, he was on another train platform, waiting in the close air for another train. On the surface, his thoughts were childishly simple. He observed several things: on the opposite platform, a man shook out his umbrella with a grimace. A child skipped close to the platform edge. He felt the need to urinate. Deep in his brain, the sounds he had heard were being swapped and juggled, echoing in patterns that veered close to sense, then back to unintelligible sounds. But before the train reached the station, while it was still rumbling through the dark, something clicked and he could clearly understand what she had said. The headlights were visible now and a grubby wind blew. They were suddenly obvious, the words, and he felt momentarily exalted. Turning a little, catching the last moment of quiet before the air filled, he began to say them over and over, softly, to no one in particular.

Robert McLiam Wilson

from *Ripley Bogle*

B IG RIVERBEND HERE. Passing now under the crumble of
Putney Bridge. Putney to Barnes. Yes. I dribble away
from the city. I check out the Fulham Palace on the other
bank. It wobbles and jives in this heat-shimmer. That way
Parsons Green and Brompton lie. Not for me, they don't.

Well, it's another belter today. Hot. The active, super-
luminous sun poaches me in my own sweat and grease. I
have to pant and wheeze to catch the stale, warmed-up urban
air. In the circumstances, I feel it's hardly worth the effort.

Perry is getting worse. This morning was bad, really bad.
I'm not in the mood for the startled confusion of the aged
underdog. After last night's wickedness, I'm finding it hard
to play upon my sympathies. Perry's getting worse, though.
He really is.

It's so hot at the moment that the heat haze is about eight
feet high and four feet distant. Or maybe it's because my
eyelids are all cocked-up. Alternately crusty or slimy and
constantly painful. Perhaps it is close-up goo and not heat
haze that I am, in fact, seeing right now. It's surprisingly
hard to tell. I should clean my eyes up a bit, I know, but I
just can't find the courage.

Notwithstanding, it is still very, very hot. What is going
on here? I don't know what it is with the weather these days.
I suspect that it has some obscure meteorological grudge
against me. It sounds potty, I agree, but I'm almost certain.
I've worked it out. I know all about the weather. I'm au fait
with the physics and chemistry of the upper air, its temperature, density, motions, composition, chemical processes,

reactions to solar and cosmic radiation, etc. I've done my homework.

The perfect trampweather is that mild autumnal dullness that we get in September and early October. No cold, no heat, no rain and little wind. The happy medium must be struck and struck hard. Tranquillity and quietude are what we chiefly love. Summer's too hot and dry and dirty. We simmer in filth and corporeal corruption. We thirst and we croak and we catch really unusual diseases. Winter is, predictably, much too cold. We freeze and thaw and freeze again. Hypothermia, frostbite, bronchitis, pneumonia and gangrene all say hello. Bladders pack in all over the shop and pauperdeaths litter the seamier sides of town. Spring is too wet. Getting pissed on becomes depressing after a while. That's the season of trenchfoot, exposure, rigor, polio, cystic-fucking-fibrosis and the bubonic plague! (I nearly crapped myself this morning when I discovered this monstrous bubo on my neck. Fuck me, I thought, this is it! The big B. The plague no less! Of course, it was only an outsize pimple, a semi-boil. A tramp hill. It was big though, really enthusiastic, a yellow-topped baked bean, an astrobleme!)

As I was saying about the weather: the seasons are all buggered up at the minute. If I'm not fighting with frostbite, I'm struggling with sunstroke. There is no intermediate stage – it's straight from polar pain to tropical toil. Every hour the weather winds up some new inclement gimmick to do me harm. Perhaps it's on account of this new Ice Age that all the boffins are wetting their trunks about. Yes, that might be it. However, I still can't help feeling that it is simple supernatural malice. Someone up there is no fan of mine.

Christ almighty! Last night was a stinker! Lardwit, I got plastered and blew the sad remnants of my treasured dosh. I'm a cretin, I declare to God I am. Six final, necessary quid pissed away on soapy booze! And what did I get? A pound of pain in my brainbone and a slap on the gob from some crazy Irish bastard who claimed to know me. A fiver and more for that! Where am I keeping my brains these days?

Subsequently, what I'm experiencing on this fine June morning can scarcely be described as a hangover. Dear me, no. Alcoholic excess is but one of the Attendant Lords in the Revenger's Tragedy that my grumpy body is enacting. Chronic Emphysema plays the virulent, inexorable lead, well-supported by the superslim Scurvy as the anorexic usurper who lusts after the luxurious Gynaecomastia, Queen of the Hormonal Confusions. Melanoma steals the show as the fresh-faced Chorus while Subacutebacterialendocarditis toothily disappoints as the Romantic Interest.

I feel a major headache heralding its cruel intent. My neck aches bitterly and my spinal ropes groan and creak. This is Migraine Time. This is going to lay me out. My brain will bend and stretch in agony. (You would not believe the extent of my cranial elasticity when it comes to pain!) The sky is boiling already and the air is heavy, deplorable, weighing down on the burgeoning pain in my skull. The atmosphere is tense and attentive. Stormwaiting. While my own personal tempest rages unabated.

Wheeeee! I feel a clumsy ball of nausea unfurl in my throat and I have a strong and sickening urge to defecate. My abdomen is swollen and taut. Hiding gurgling, bubbling slime and obscenity. I've got to move a motion. Cessbag to latrine. Brother to brother. I need a crap. That's it. All too familiar. Shitting. Migraine. Strain and pain. Nausea. Eggs-in-thorax. Gloom.

Penniless, fecal, nauseous, I trail off the riverbank on to the Richmond Road now. Why am I moving away from the city, you might justifiably ask. What possible joy can I find in the leafy glades of Roehampton or Mortlake? None, I freely admit. I am escaping the city because today is Saturday and London Town on Saturdays gets on my tits amazingly. The whole weekending business. The shoppers, the Salvation Army, the housewives meeting each other for their monthly visit to the choirboy brothels, the nose-eye-ear picking adolescents, the Saturdayfreed schoolgirls strutting their precocious prepubescent stuff, the daytripping hickprovincials gawping at the metropolitan mayhem, the happy, shirt-sleeved policemen, the park-playing families, the youthful couples (bastards!), the sportsmen, the grotbags, the promenaders, the people, the people!

Worst of all – the tramps, the beggars and the cripples. The rejects, the drop-outs, the addicts and the tragedies. Saturday is their best begging day. The period of optimum fruitful scrounging. It's an abhorrent sight which I try to avoid. Saturday is everyone's good mood day. People grow charitable. They give in plenty from their plenty. Nice enough but still gets me down.

This is why I tend to hang out on the fringes of the Saturday capital. It probably seems pompous but like I say, I hate to see my homeless colleagues letting the side down.

(Actually, the real reason that I avoid the greater populace on Saturdays is because I'm terrified of seeing someone I know. Someone from my past. Someone who doesn't know I'm a tramp. The mere thought makes me gibber in terror. Cheap, huh?)

I slouch wittily along, young and carefree. I can feel the noisome juices in my belly percolating moistly through my squirting bowels. Shit!

London simmers, gently sweating as the huge orb of the fiery sun hangs white and merciless in the low sky. Concrete buildings and pavements shimmer dishonestly in the brightness. Shops hang gaudy canopies over their windows. All of a sudden, the city has a festive, summer air. The sun beats and beats in a spurious, mediterranean masquerade. The pale, mask-like London faces have begun to tinge and reflect the glow of the sun. In hot, sticky little cafés, prudish old women glare venomously at the prevalence of youth and flesh. They console themselves with thoughts of winter, their season. And still the sun falls and spreads its smellsetting rays throughout.

*

The Serpentine boils and bakes in heavy heat. The water is splashed and striped with light and there are lots of swelling semi-dressed girls lolling on the grass and precariously in boats. Multitudes of ice-cream vendors loudly ply their sugary wares and children's vests are dribblestained with snot, tears and melted lollies. Their plaintive, inarticulate clamour is harsh in this heat and their mothers are running out of sweat and patience. Old folks lounge on ranks of deckchairs and young bloods play desultory games of soccer on sloping grass. They hope to attract the sunbathing beauties. I'm feeling mainly less than up to this.

The day has slowed its march. It lopes now. It danders on, it jazzwalks. Various cassette devices blare differing, tuneless songs. It should be discordant but merges neatly into a heated hymn to this young day; this hot, heavy, slow day. I look at the youths around me. I share their age. I share their suitability to this day. Or I should but don't. I stare with sad longing at the deckchaired oldsters. That's where I should be. I'm not feeling up to this promenade of youth.

Despite all this dusty discomfort this is one of the better places to be today. This health-giving sunshine seems less onerous here than it did in the streets. In the microwave jumble of glass, concrete and dust. In the citystew. Nonetheless, I need a rest. I've had a bad afternoon. I want to watch its death in comfort. A little sit-down is what I require.

I passed out again, you see. I lit out. It was much worse this time. I had a deal of bad dreams. Nasty, depressing dreams. All about things I didn't want to know or learn. What is it with these dreams of mine? Why do they wish me this harm? I didn't invite the bastards. They're free to leave when the fancy strikes them. They never do. What do they want with me? I've got it bad enough already. Where is my auctorial control?

This passing out business is beginning to worry me somewhat. This time loss of mine has been on the up and up in recent weeks. For instance, last Friday I didn't actually pass out as such (I think) but I had a complete memory lapse between noon and evening. I suddenly found myself in Victoria coach station (not somewhere I'd willingly go, poor as I am). I was bewildered and frightened. I had no idea where I'd been or what I'd been doing. This temporal manque both surprised and depressed me. I knew what it meant – more or less. At the very least, I knew that it wasn't good news. I probably hadn't done very much that would be fun to remember – it was just the principle. I'm not sanguine enough about my life to write off the odd bad day here and there. I need all of my days, good or bad.

You can imagine that this kind of thing makes you think a little. I wondered to what I owed this new diversion. Hunger? Exhaustion? Poverty? Boredom? God knows.

Needless to say, my bad dreams were all about Laura. They were very bad dreams indeed. Not a lot of romance to be had. They all came to their squalid, graceless end without resort to pleasure of any kind. Nasty loveless Laura. Hardly fair. When you dream about women, you generally expect some kind of sex, good or bad.

Upon waking from this most recent of my sad little trances, I felt so dreadful that I mosied on back to town. I was no longer in the mood for the metropolitan outskirts. Not in that mood at all. So now here I am, traipsing around the heated Serpentine, dodging the families, the doggies and the joggers. It's hardly ideal but probably the best of my day's swaps. Barn Elms was getting me down.

Now I seek a bench, I seek my sit-down. I want a rest. I can manage one of those, I think. I trundle through the trees, eyes swivelling and feet super-blistered. This is deckchair land all right. They charge money for the use of these spindly, rickety seats. So, I can't take one of those. Obviously. I haven't the courage needed to defy the merest deckchair attendant, be he ever so infirm. I slouch grassily past the seated ranks of OAPs, fat businessmen and bored, defiant non-paying punks. I revise my options and try to find a tree against which I may sit. That's it. I find it easily. Midway on the slope backing from the boating lake, it stands in tall splendour, free of satellite chairs. It spreads high above me, leafy, immense and free of charge. I plant my arse amongst its roots and ease my knobbly back on to its yielding bark. I breathe and smile, relieved. My poor feet inflate and my knees click and clack in unexpected luxury. This is the happiness I've wanted.

Contentedly, I watch the boating lake palpitate in the dying heat and the dawdling, baked crowds slip away. The broom of lassitude sweeps me up and cools me off a little. My sweat bubbles and dries. The afternoon fades, tired and grateful. It will be dark soon. Saturday night and fun will be had. Even by me. In a way – of its sort. We know that nights are usually bad news for me and Saturday is especial but I have a feeling that this one will be cool and welcome. Friendly and forgiving. Come. I need a little night.

It has to be said I am feeling appreciably worse – older, sadder and less buoyant than I have felt for a very long time. The asperity of my decline is breathtaking, its projected speed delightful. I was a fool to think that this indigence would fail to take its toll. I'm starting to suffer now. I'm growing replete with jaded beggary. It occurs to me of a sudden that I can scarcely be a quarter of the fellow I claim to be. It's sad. All, I trust, will end in tears.

No, I must not dissemble when it comes to the tale of my deterioration but I must be wary of the hyperbole of intermittent self-pity. It's not that I'm spreading myself too thinly. It's just that there's little left to spread.

This lowslung sun has fallen further and now fringes the lower reaches of the gleaming horizon. Folk shade their eyes from the slanting glare and stand in weird silhouette tableau. The bustle has eased with the heat and the afternoon palls hard. Late Saturday afternoons are always like this. Strange, limbo-like, disaffected. Glamourless and restive, time for the football results and dressing for the night's excesses. It's never much of a nice time. Composed of dust, beer smells and boredom, it used to get me down when I was a kid. It's like that now. The proletarian smell of ironing board, the dust and the flat glad glare.

Hugo Hamilton

from *Surrogate City*

Street Light

THINGS WERE beginning to get a bit hot over in Wolf and Hadja's place. I could see it coming. I could see it was not a good place for a pregnant woman to stay. It was only a matter of time before Hadja caught on to Wolf and the apartment would become uninhabitable, thrown into open warfare. Wolf had begun to mess around with a student called Lydia; meeting her in the afternoons in cafés, or at night. And because I work so closely with Wolf, I know what's going on all the time. I was there when he first met this woman, Lydia. Wolf tells me everything. The trouble is that Hadja has also begun to realize that, which is why she comes to me whenever she wants to know something about Wolf, and I have to be very careful what I say.

At the end of the month, Wolf has a big concert on at the Aula Max in the Free University of Berlin. The posters have been up for some time now. Wolfgang Ebers: *Liedermacher*. Hadja has been doing most of the work so far. The phone never stops ringing in their apartment, and she is working herself into a frenzy, organizing newspaper coverage, more posters etc. Everything she achieves has to be acknowledged and spoken about, otherwise she is likely to fly into a rage. There is a genuine excitement in the apartment, because this is an important time for Wolf. The Aula Max is a big one. But the tension has also increased hundredfold. Which is why I think Wolf has picked a really bad time to have a fling with Lydia. It's none of my business, but I can see what's coming.

One thing was certain; Hadja and Wolf's place was no place for Helen. I could see Hadja's suspicion. There would be war. I told Helen she could stay in the spare room at Sonnenallee until she found a place of her own. I said it to her a few times, casually. I wasn't pushing her. I just thought things would be quieter in my apartment because I'm hardly ever there. She thanked me and said she would think it over, and I could only presume that she was still thinking of going back home to Ireland; that she wasn't going to stay in Berlin since she hadn't found who she was looking for. Anyhow, the offer stood and I said no more. But I took the precaution of telling Wolf never to bring Lydia around to my apartment, even in the afternoon. Besides, I didn't want Hadja discovering them in my apartment; the apartment which Hadja had given me. I was too much a collaborator already.

You have to know who your real boss is. I work with Wolf. I'm a lighting operator. I also do the sound for him at times, but my real occupation is lighting. If I wanted to give myself a real title I would be calling myself lighting consultant. Since Hadja has become manager, it is she who pays my wages and she who determines everything I do, so I can't really ignore the reality that she is my employer. I do some odd jobs for her as well, whenever she asks. For instance, once a week she goes over to collect the rent in one of her father's houses and she needs an escort. I'd say she would be a lot tougher than me if anything were to happen, but she likes the idea of male security. And I'm not really in a position to refuse work, particularly when Wolf can't justify a full-time lighting operator yet. So I'm a bit of everything at the moment. Lighting op. Sound op. Roadie. Bodyguard. Rent collector.

I did have a full-time job in lighting with one of the opera houses here in Berlin. But that only lasted for three months. I was in charge of one spotlight, and every night, at a given time, I was expected to direct the spot on one man, the broad-chested Don Giovanni, as he prepared to go to Hell. That was a good job. Working for Wolf is even better.

Before that I worked with a stage and location lighting company with nothing on its mind but lighting fashion shows and fashion photography. We were expected to think of models only in terms of how their legs could be lit up for maximum effect while providing for sufficient shadows to maintain the myth. I was assigned to a photographer who dealt only with women. A little more Bermuda on her left, he would say to me. Or else he'd say: Give her the Michelangelo from the top. His lighting directions were atmospheric. He would assess the wardrobe, assess the girls and then call out lighting instructions which I was meant to understand by instinct. London rain with Ugandan oranges. Or else, if he wanted a model lit from underneath, he would ask for her to be river-reflected. Float her on the Nile, he would say.

With another photographer I once had the pleasure of lighting up the set for the portrait of a prominent industrialist whose left ear had been damaged during the war. He asked us not to show his bad side. So I blew that left ear off altogether with darkness.

Wolf is turning me into a liar. Every lie that he tells Hadja is backed up by my silence. How can he elude suspicion? The truth of his affair with Lydia must be written on his face. Or written on my face.

Lydia has high cheekbones. She is best lit from above. Her blonde hair and hazel eyes might benefit from a blue glare on the left. With proper lighting, I could make her look more pensive, more mature and perhaps more hurt looking. I could give her eyes more substance; make her look older and less like a student. With a strong backlight, I could give her a Polish grandmother, or some Russian origins at least.

Wolf says she looks very different without her clothes.

*

Nakedness is a sign of intimacy. It can also be a sign of hostility, which amounts to the same thing. Whenever football supporters expose their backsides to pedestrians from passing buses, it must be a gesture of affection and defiance at the same time. Whenever Hadja walks around the apartment naked, it becomes a show of friendship and fearlessness at the same time. A sign of territorial advantage.

On the morning that Helen decided to move out of Wolf and Hadja's place, this is just what happened. The phone rang in the hallway and Hadja went to answer it without any clothes on. It's summer, of course, but that's no reason. Hadja spoke for a while on the phone as though she were fully clothed, and the person on the other end of the line couldn't possibly have known that Hadja was naked, leaning against the wall, occasionally running the flat of her hand across her stomach and occasionally running the sole of her foot along her shin.

Helen was in the kitchen. The door was open, giving her a full view of Hadja's broad bottom as she argued on the phone.

Helen had already been to the shop to buy fresh rolls. She had made coffee and was having breakfast. She had her clothes on, which makes it very obvious when somebody else doesn't. The smell of fresh coffee must have challenged Hadja's nostrils, because instead of going back to her bedroom, she went straight into the kitchen and sat down.

Ah – Kaffee, she said, reaching up into the cupboard for a cup.

Hadja has very large breasts. Sheer size is enough sometimes to attract attention. And they cannot fail to entrap Helen, who has small breasts herself, into a grotesque fascination. Large breasts are hard to believe, even with your own eyes. The same way that hostility is hard to believe, even if it is compelling and you can't stop looking for it once you see it.

Hadja took one of the fresh rolls and cracked it open with two thumbs. Placed a piece of *Wurst* in the middle and began to eat. She groaned with satisfaction at the first bite.

I'm starving, she said. Bouncing makes you hungry, she added with her mouth full. Then she laughed.

Helen found it hard to believe what she heard. She stopped eating, because eating is such an impulsive thing and it's so easy to put a pregnant woman off eating. Helen could only look at Hadja's huge breasts, which were staring back at her.

Scheisse, Hadja said. They promised the extra posters this morning. Now I won't have them until this evening.

Hadja speaks as though everyone is interested in what she has to say. The same way that she thinks her body would be attractive to everyone. Helen sipped her coffee. She had something on her mind.

Hadja, she said. There's something I have to tell you.

Yes. What is it?

I've found a new place to stay, Helen said. Then, almost as though she wanted to retract an unintended insult, she thanked Hadja for everything she had done. But there was also that sense of joy associated with leaving things behind.

Oh, well, that's great, Hadja said. I'm delighted for you. Where are you moving to?

Helen hesitated.

Well, she said. I've been offered a room in Alan Craig's apartment. He's got lots of space and I think it will be quieter over there.

Hadja immediately began to laugh out loud. Her breasts were flung around, even sideways with laughter. She leaned back so that Helen began to think it was Hadja's breasts that were doing all the laughing.

Into Alan Craig's apartment ... Hadja chanted. This I cannot believe.

Did you hear that, Wolf? Hadja went on speaking and laughing into the hallway. She's moving in with Alan Craig.

But Wolf was already pushing out the first alphabet of notes through his saxophone in the sitting room.

That day, everything seemed to Helen like the end of a film. In the afternoon, she stood alone for a moment in the hallway of Wolf and Hadja's place, thinking quite consciously that this was the end of something. Something was over. Then she walked out and shut the door behind her. She had to shut the door three times. It wasn't that easy. And later on, she stood for a moment in the darker, far narrower hallway of my apartment in Sonnenallee. She didn't have many belongings. She brought some groceries; cheese, eggs, a jar of strawberry jam and some fresh mayonnaise, which, she said, should go straight into the fridge.

Some people would call me a light-jockey. Same as a DJ except with lights. But I prefer lighting operator as a title. My job is to illuminate chosen objects. To present everything with a swollen look.

A spotlight is like an extended eye or an antenna which gives a preliminary, unspoken name to everything it touches.

Berlin bei Nacht. I've seen most of Berlin by night. Sometimes, working in the music business with Wolf, I don't see much daylight at all. I've often come home first thing in the morning; on the first *U-Bahn*, with people beginning to go to work. Things are so silent in the morning. It's too bright. And people make you feel like you're going in the wrong direction. Even if I changed places with them I'd feel I was going in the wrong direction.

On the way home in the morning, I often see people out with their dogs for an early walk. One morning, walking through Schöneberg, I passed a man with two poodles. But there was something about him that made me think he wasn't the owner; something awkward, something in the way he looked into the distance down towards Innsbrücker Platz. He was a

Turk. I knew by the cheekbones, brown eyes and moustache. It must have been part of his job to walk his owner's dogs. There was something strained and unnatural about his appearance. He was too tall to own poodles.

Nobody ever looks comfortable doing somebody else's job.

Early in the morning, the first signs of daylight often make things look idiotic and irrelevant. The lights, which looked so good all over the city at night, begin to pale and weaken in the morning. Light is a fraud. In the morning, everything you see is reduced to half its size. Everything swells under lights.

I walked down Tauentzienstrasse with Helen one night. We were larger than life, swollen in the oncoming lights of traffic. We walked slowly, just talking about things; noticing Berlin the way visitors do. The sky must have covered over with clouds, because there was a reddish hue above us, reflecting the glow of the city. The lights of the street must have flooded our faces as we walked. Neon faces. As we got on the *U-Bahn* at Wittenbergplatz, the strong brightness in the carriage seemed to force a universal equality and silence on all passengers.

Everything ages rapidly under light.

When we got back to the apartment in Sonnenallee, we sat down at the round table in the sitting room with a cup of tea. I left the window open and the lights off. Only the light from the kitchen seeped around the door. It was enough for us to see each other and to keep talking about anything that came into our heads. Helen talked about her father and mother.

Her brother. Her uncles. I talked about work. Music. Friends I had. One by one, outside in the courtyard, we could see the lights of neighbouring apartments being switched off.

Helen still couldn't believe that the light goes off inside the fridge when you shut the door. She never will. Her brother explained it to her when she was young, but she never believed it. Which goes to show that you can believe something and not believe it at the same time. The same way that you can voluntarily allow yourself to do something you've been telling yourself not to do all along. I told her there was no way out but for her to get inside the fridge and shut the door.

Helen is light-sensitive. She turns her back instinctively on strong headlights as though light caused pain. She flinches when lights are switched on. She knows that light can be used as a weapon because she remembers her brother going out at night when they were down in the country at their uncle's house near a river where the local boys used to go and blind fish with torches and then gaff them. Her brother used to tell her a lot about fishing. He told her why fish usually have freckled backs and white bellies, so they can't be seen from above or below.

Helen has a fair complexion. Curly hair. Large round eyes. A smile that hints towards the left. Wears little jewellery; a ring, a watch and a chain at most. Her clothes are practical bordering on festive. Her hands are small and thin. Other distinguishing features: vertical forehead, white skin and a lot of freckles, mainly around her shoulders and arms. She is light-shy. Undresses away from the light and turns her back. She likes to leave a light or even a radio on long after she falls asleep.

*

Hadja phoned me early one morning and asked me if I knew about it. I was only half awake at the time but I knew immediately what she was on about. It had to happen. I just act dumb.

What?

This woman?

What woman?

Wolf's woman, who else? Come on, Alan. Don't act stupid.

Wolf's woman?

Come on, Alan, I want to know everything. Am I the last to find out about it? I suppose the whole world knows except me. And you knew all along and wouldn't tell me either.

Hadja, what are you talking about? I still wasn't sure if she was bluffing or not.

You know what I'm talking about, she said. I'm talking about Lydia Stanjeck. That is her name, isn't it?

Look, Hadja, I said. This is none of my business really. I don't interfere with anybody's private life.

Alan, don't move. I'm coming over, she said. I want to talk to you about this. I'll be there in ten minutes.

Hadja was breathless when she arrived at my apartment. Breathless because there is no lift in the block. She came in and sat down at the round table without a word. Some of the breakfast things were still on the table. There was a plate with a ransacked eggshell and some scattered salt. I took them all away and asked Hadja if she wanted coffee or tea. Helen wasn't up yet.

When I came back from the kitchen with coffee in my hand, I saw Hadja sitting straight, rigidly looking down at a photograph she had just taken from her bag. She looked up at me with accusation in her face. But she waited until I had poured the coffee until she stuck the photo out towards me.

Is this her? she asked, looking intensely into my eyes.

I wouldn't know, Hadja, honestly, I said. I don't know why you're asking me these things.

Come on, Alan, don't be a fool, she said. You know everything Wolf does. You're with him all the time. Tell me, is that her?

Look, Hadja, why don't you ask Wolf himself? It's nothing to do with me.

No answer is also an answer. Hadja must have been able to read my mind because she withdrew the photograph and replaced it in her bag.

I don't want him to know that I know, she said. The bastard. I'll get him for this. Whatever you do, Alan, don't tell him that I know who she is or anything. Tell him nothing, you hear?

Everything that Hadja does is designed to give her answers. She looked around the apartment. She saw boxes by the window in which I keep my equipment; spare bulbs, cables, switches, spots, lighting mixer. Beside an armchair, she would have seen Helen's shoes. Hadja looked out over the courtyard. She must have seen herself as the former occupant of the apartment. It must have reminded her of certain things. Early days. But her mind was blocked with one single thought.

Say nothing to Wolf, she said. Is that clear? Not a word. I'll get him for this.

Everything can be turned into an advantage. Hadja has the skill to reverse any disadvantage, no matter what the circumstances.

I wish I could say the same for myself. Instead, sometimes I am convinced that it is the person who acts who becomes the victim. It's the person who operates the lights who gets blinded. There I was throwing the spotlights on Don Giovanni every night for months, but after a while I found it was me who was going down to Hell every time.

Same way that I now feel trapped because I know what's going to happen to Wolf. The game is up. Hadja is on to him.

I noticed a new row of posters right outside the entrance to the university as I walked in. Wolfgang Ebers! Wolfgang Ebers! He looks different in duplicate. And the posters are really superfluous because the concert was a complete sellout anyway.

I spent the morning setting up the lighting rigs. We had hired extra sets of colour spots so it took a lot longer than usual. But it's going to look a lot more impressive too. I just worked quietly beside the sound operator Willy, from Westphalen. Hadja was in early as well.

In the afternoon, Wolf arrived for a sound and light check. He insists on choreographing the sound and light show for the performance in advance, which suits me because everything is perfectly planned out. No room for hitches. It's an important concert. Hadja was everywhere. She's even more fussy than I am. She's a perfectionist. She stood by and watched the whole rehearsal. All afternoon, I couldn't get near Wolf on his own. I wanted to get some kind of message to him. Eventually, I was able to slip into the toilets after him to give him a small warning.

She's on to you, Wolf, I told him. And I wonder sometimes why I was so loyal to him. He didn't seem surprised at all. He remained calm, almost impervious. I suppose he had more on his mind at the time. Perhaps he could think of nothing else but his music.

Wolf, do you hear me? Hadja knows about you and Lydia, I said.

There is a strange loyalty or comradeship between men when they piss in parallel at urinals. There are these duplicitous sideways and downward glances: fraternal acknowledgement. Otherwise there is little else to look at except the tiles in front of you.

I see, Wolf said, staring at a tile only inches away from his eyes. So Hadja knows. Yes . . . well just play along with her. Don't worry. Just play along.

When I got back to the rig later on, the Aula was beginning to fill up. Hadja was there already. She was rushing around the auditorium, and when she came up to me, she handed me the photograph of Lydia. Why was she giving me the photograph? I refused it. She insisted. And then I realized that it was a duplicate, one of which she had also given to Willy, the sound operator, and to each of the security men as well.

If you see her, let me know immediately, she said.

I put the photograph away and ignored it. It's none of my business. The next I saw of Wolf was when he arrived on stage with his guitar. Wolf is fond of the light. He wouldn't be a professional singer if he didn't have such a high tolerance for exposure. It's good to work with somebody who is not light-shy.

The Aula was jammed. There were people standing along the aisles to the side. I occasionally caught sight of Hadja near the doors or down at the front of the stage. She had free movement throughout the auditorium. Wolf's fifth song was the one about the Atlantic. I had the list in front of me. Not that I really have time to listen to the songs any more when I'm working. They merely become reference points for specific lighting performance. The Atlantic song gets a cold, blue background while Wolf is picked out in a strong white spot. I can make him stand right on the edge of the Cliffs of Moher. And if I switched off the white spot, he would disappear; the audience would think he had fallen in. Wolf's face is serious as he sings, as though he is singing out into a strong wind that carries a trace of salt.

I noticed Hadja coming up beside me, but I concentrated on the end of the song where the light is meant to fade like an accelerated sunset.

I have her, she whispered. I have the bitch.

A moment later, the song was over and the Aula broke into unified applause. Wolf disappeared in semi-darkness.

I have the bitch, Hadja kept whispering to me. More like shouting. I pretended not to hear her, but I kept hearing the word bitch, so I eventually had to listen.

There, at the door, she shouted as the applause began to die down. There she is at the door.

I want you to put the spot on her, Hadja demanded.

I didn't move.

Put the spot on her, she demanded again.

I can't do that, I said. I pretended to look busy. The applause had ceased.

Put the spot on her, she repeated. I will do it FUCKING myself, if you don't.

It was no time to laugh at a linguistic mistake. I knew she was serious. I did what she asked and turned the spot.

Lydia was picked out beautifully in a thin white beam. The rest of the lights were left on very low. The house lights were out. The applause died out completely and left a vacuum. The sound was switched off, too, which left Wolf without a mike, and nothing to say.

I was almost proud of Lydia, blinded by the force of the spotlight and by the eyes of the audience who followed the light and looked around at her. Lydia didn't move. She stood still. If she had moved sideways by a metre, she would have fallen out of light.

Michael O'Loughlin

A Rock-'n'-Roll Death

WHATEVER WAY you look at it, it was the chance of a lifetime, and he blew it. There he was, our man on the spot, the man with the inside story. I held the press till the last moment, having already plastered his name all over the cover, but there was nothing. I tried frantically to contact him but he had vanished, gone AWOL in Amsterdam, leaving the biggest story we ever had to handle hanging. I thought at first that something terrible must have happened to him, to tell you the truth, but I figured that if it had I would have heard. But no, it was just too big for him and he blew it.

It was his first really big assignment after he had done more or less everything else, from making the tea to reviewing showbands. He had a great style, like Flann O'Brien on speed, and a great nose for bands. In fact it was he who wrote the first review of Sheila's, a late night pub gig somewhere in Dame Street, and he raved about her long before anyone else thought she would get that big. It all happened very quickly. A big record deal, the album hitting the charts like a rocket, the American tour lined up. Within a year of Dave's review, she had become the biggest thing out of Ireland since U2 – and she was a lot better-looking. So I sent Dave off with her on her big European tour. You know the kind of thing I was after – the inside story of the band on the road, sex, drugs and diarrhoea. Because Sheila, though her music was very new, was a bit of an old-style rocker, slightly out-of-synch in these puritanical times, some people might say. She wasn't a junkie or anything like that, but she certainly did keep a few Bolivian farmers off the dole, and she did have a penchant for tall, blond, muscular teenagers – in which the continent, as we know, abounds. A great story, I thought, the girl from the steppes of Donegal in Paris, Amsterdam, Berlin . . . but of course, it ended in Amsterdam.

I couldn't believe it when I got the news that night. I was half-asleep, it being the middle of the night, and as the phone babbled in my ear I swear I saw a neon sign light up in front of me, saying: ROCK-'N'-ROLL DEATH! It's not that I'm callous or anything, but it's my job, and I immediately saw all the implications. Rock-'n'-roll death is always sexy, but this one was our own. She was a great girl, Sheila, but I just saw it in front of me: Dean, Hendrix, Joplin, Sid Vicious, and now, our very own Sheila Shanahan. I was a bit surprised when they said drugs, but of course, as it came out later, that was not the whole story. Some kind of tumour in the brain, combined with the exhaustion and the big dose of coke, and she just blew her fuses. And unbelievably, our man was on the spot. This was the sort of thing you wait all your life for. First I'd run the story in a special edition, and then sit back and let the phone ring from New York, London, wherever.

But it didn't happen. I managed somehow, between busting a gut trying to contact Dave, to piece together something from the files and Martin did a great last-minute job. You never would have guessed. I, in the meantime, was phoning every hotel and pub in Amsterdam in an attempt to find my scribe. But no Dave. It was weird, he'd just sent in a great piece on the Paris concert, which Martin had performed plastic surgery on. But after that – nothing. Like I said, I thought at first that something must have happened to him, but not hearing anything, I figured that this was probably not the case. I was puzzled. I told Colm Doyle in the pub the night we put the magazine to bed, and asked him what he thought. He gave me his evil grin and said: 'Sure Ciaran, it's as plain as the nose on your face. Your erstwhile employee has gone to ground in good old Amsterdam, and is holed up in some back-street hotel with his trusty Olivetti. At present he is roughly halfway through his magnum opus: 30,000 words of delirious prose on Sheila Shanahan – Death In Amsterdam, which will out-Hunt Thompson and outrun Wolfe. Ambitious young fellow, our Dave. One of these days you'll be getting a nasty surprise on the cover of *Rolling Stone*!'

Christ! Of course I didn't believe this for a minute, it being par for the course, you know what Dublin is like. But anyway, I decided to go to Amsterdam and have a look myself. I could do a bit of background on an article.

I got a flight next morning, and when I arrived in Schiphol, I took a taxi straight to the hotel where Sheila had snuffed it, so to speak. When I was checking in, I asked straight away about the room it had happened in, but I got the Dutch equivalent of a dirty look. The guy claimed not to know anything about it! And in a way it was peculiar, but the hotel seemed to be just going on like normal, the usual businessmen, whores and Japanese tourists, and all the rest. I don't know what I had expected, but somehow it was a bit strange. I got a young lad, clever me, to carry my bag, and bribed him shamelessly.

'That Irish singer? It was one of the rooms on the second floor, I think.'

I had known that much before leaving Baggot Street.

'Yeah, that's right. Do you think I could take a look?'

'I'm sorry, but all the rooms are occupied. Maybe tomorrow you could try.'

Occupied? Three days later? Ah well, you know us Irish, very sentimental about death we are. From my room I rang up a guy I knew, editor of a Dutch music mag. I'd helped him out when he was over in Dublin doing a story on Geldof, so he owed me one. I arranged to meet him in a pub in half an hour. Sitting there over a drink, we talked about Sheila and agreed on how tragic it was. He'd been at the concert that night and said it was brilliant. He had talked to her too at the press conference in the afternoon before the concert and had taken a great fancy to her – in fact, he said, they had all been enchanted by her.

'She was something special that girl, you know. And her music was so great also. It was that kind of Irish wild mystic thing, sort of like Van Morrison, no? When she sang that song with the words in Irish, like nobody could understand it, but it was so expressive, everybody felt sad but in a happy way, you know what I mean?'

Then I realized that he might have met Dave at the press do. When I asked him, he said no, but some of the other rock journalists had, they had mentioned it to him for some reason or other.

'Who?' I asked, taking out my notebook, feeling like a private eye. 'Can you remember their names?'

I imagined myself tracking them down through the bars and nightclubs of Amsterdam.

'No problem. They will all come in here some time today. You want another beer?'

So I sat there all afternoon as people drifted in and out. It turned out that a couple of music press people did remember him, and one had even had a drink with him later at the concert. But none of them had seen him since. And then a guy came in who had:

'Funny thing, I saw him last night. I think it was him, the Irish guy. I didn't talk with him because I was with some people, but I recognized him. He didn't look too good, you know, drinking a lot and just sitting there alone.'

I got him to mark down on my street map where the bar was, and then I headed for it. It was just outside the last circle of canals, a bar that stayed open late. It took me quite a while to find it, what with all the canals looking the same. When I finally got there, of course there was no Dave. So I tried the next bar, and the next one, consuming a lot of fizzy yellow beer in the process. By now it was eleven o'clock and I was tired out, so I got a taxi back to the hotel. As I walked through the lobby, I glanced through the doorway into the bar and saw Dave's famous yellow linen jacket on a barstool, with Dave in it.

I stormed in, and you can imagine what I said. A full five

seconds after I had started half-shouting at him, he slowly turned his head towards me. He looked bad – unshaven, hair in bits. He was drinking the local firewater, but he didn't seem drunk. His eyes were just strange, all lit up, and it was clear there was something seriously wrong with him. I decided to cool it. I climbed up on a stool and ordered a Perrier with a twist of lemon. When I asked him what he was having, he didn't react, so I ordered him more of the same. Something told me not to say anything. And then he started talking, in his normal voice.

'I was sitting here in this bar having a drink after the concert. It was something else, the concert. Amazing. You know, she was wearing this red leather suit, and she was like a flame. I don't mean that she looked like a flame – she was a flame. Do you understand?'

He turned and looked at me, and I mumbled some kind of affirmation.

'It's like she, she herself, was a flame, and her body was what was burning in it. But not like a match, I mean, not consumed, it's like the flame burning was her body, and then around it was her voice, the aura around a flame. It wasn't just me, you know, we all felt it, everybody who was at the concert. The crowd went crazy, made her do encore after encore until she stopped, they wouldn't let her go. They lit matches and lighters, like an answer or something to her flame, to relight her.'

He picked up his glass and emptied it in one swallow, then went on:

'Anyway, we all came back here afterwards, we got rid of the journalists and the rest. We were still buzzing. After every concert I did a quick interview with her, kind of like a running commentary while we were still all high from the concert, instead of the usual dark glasses sitting in the plane kind of thing. I wanted to get a different kind of feel into it. She said she was a bit tired, but we agreed to do it anyway. First she wanted to lie down for a minute, and then I would go up to her room and we would do it there. I had another drink. One of the roadies came down in a few minutes and said she was ready. So I picked up the tape recorder and went upstairs. I walked along the corridor till I came to her door. I knocked and went in. As I walked in she smiled at me. She was lying on her side on the bed. She was naked, and she was white, completely white, except for her finger-nails and toenails, and her lips. You've never seen anything so beautiful, she was like a statue of warm, white flesh.' Suddenly he stopped and looked at me again.

'Have you ever been in love?' he asked.

'Sure.' I said. He gave me a strange smile.

'It's funny how words don't really mean anything. You know, as she lay there smiling at me, everything suddenly fell into place. It was like I had just woken up out of a dream. Before, I was nothing, absolutely nothing, running around like a headless chicken, not even knowing it, not even knowing that all the time I was missing something. But now, everything was all right. I saw how it all worked out. I knew who I was, and who she was. I was a different person, she was smiling at me, and I was smiling at her.'

Suddenly it dawned on me and I blurted out:

'You mean – but she was dead—'

Again he gave me that smile.

'Death is just a word, it has nothing to do with this. I was standing there a long time, I don't know how long, and sure, I saw that word floating about somewhere at the back of my mind, but you know, it only made me smile.'

Smiling, he stopped speaking.

I didn't say anything.

He asked abruptly:

'You did English Lit at UCD, didn't you?'

The question surprised me. Like Dave a few years later, I had spent three years mainly listening to records before scraping through my exams. I nodded.

'Did you have O'Neill for Elizabethan Drama?'

A bit disorientated, I nodded again.

'He was a great reader. I remember him reading out a bit

of a play one day. I never read the thing, but one line stuck in my memory.'

In a low voice, he said:

'*Cover her face; mine eyes dazzle; she died young.*'

The whole bar, the whole city, seemed to fall silent.

He leaned towards me and put his hand on my arm. With that smile on his face again, he said:

'Ciaran, I'm dazzled.'

Deirdre Madden

from *Remembering Light and Stone*

I OFTEN USED to wonder if Adolfo, the waiter in the café that I used to go to in S. Giorgio, ever guessed that there was a reason for my early morning visits, and what that reason was. Probably not. He never showed any signs of doing so. I only went there when I felt I had to. I would often call in of an evening, or after work, to sit on the spindly gilt chairs and read the papers there. But I never dropped in so early in the morning without my reason for doing so. Sometimes I would wake early at that period in my life, feeling very depressed, and then not be able to get back to sleep, so I would go to the bar to have a coffee and cake, and try to get myself ready to face the day. It usually helped to some degree.

It was barely seven when I went into the bar on that particular morning. I said hello to Adolfo and ordered a *cappuccino* and a *cornetto* with jam. I watched him as he made the coffee with a few deft movements, some bangs and hisses from the chrome coffee machine, and then the cup was set on the steel counter before me with a flourish. He flicked open the lid of the metal sugar container on the counter, and I helped myself, with the aid of one of the abnormally long spoons in it. Patting some chocolate powder on to the top of the milky foam he said, 'The cakes are arriving now,' and nodded towards the door.

A man was coming into the bar as he spoke, carrying on his shoulder a long shallow cardboard box, which he put down on the counter. Adolfo immediately started to lift the cakes from it, with rapid fluent movements of a pair of tongs, and to arrange them in the glass-fronted case directly under the counter.

'*Ecco!*' He had arrived at the *cornetti* and handed me one across the counter, wrapped in a small paper napkin. I took it, and continued to watch him while I ate, and drank my coffee.

Sometimes I would feel it was foolish to take not just such interest, but such solace, from this spectacle. There is something ridiculous about it, like buying yourself something small when you feel down, a bar of Swiss chocolate or some expensive soap, and absurdly feeling a bit better because of it. I pulled the *cornetto* apart. It was still warm and flaky because it was so fresh. It oozed apricot jam. I watched Adolfo as the man kept carrying in boxes of cakes, and carrying out empty ones when Adolfo had finished with them. The glass case quickly filled up with flat tarts full of yellow custard and scattered with crushed almonds; pies covered with heavily glazed fruit; rolls of apple strudel full of spice, sultanas and pine-nuts. The last box carried in contained savoury things, which were set in a space reserved for them on the left: crisp bread rolls with cheese and salami protruding from them; long savoury pastries full of smoked ham and egg. I admired the speed and neatness with which Adolfo emptied the boxes and filled the case, gently layering some of the flat cakes like tiles on a roof. I felt safe and contented to be there, in the warmth, with all the colours and the smells of the cakes. I felt as Hansel and Gretel must have done before they realized that the witch in the gingerbread house was going to eat them. Below the cakes there was a closed glass case, where there was a display of bottles of champagne, surrounded by paper streamers. Behind Adolfo there were glass shelves, laden with boxes of chocolates and expensive biscuits, together with glass jars filled with chocolate money, silver dragees, sugared almonds, and sweets wrapped in coloured foil.

The preceding afternoon, it had clouded over, and started to rain. It was seldom showery in S. Giorgio, and when the rain did begin, it could settle down without stopping for two days. This time it rained heavily, steadily, and I stood by the window looking out at it, until the apartment seemed to be totally enclosed by the weather, wrapped in greyness and darkness, and it triggered off in me a sense of desolation. Everything in my life – everything I valued and had struggled for, suddenly struck me as reprehensible. My independence, my job, my apartment, the books and music which meant so much to me, the whole external aspect I presented, all struck me as absurd. I thought of all the effort and energy I had expended and still needed to exercise every day to keep this whole show together, and it seemed pointless and foolish. I felt that I didn't have the energy to keep it all going. My life was fuelled by pure will. Nothing was left to chance, everything was willed, worked for, and yet it wasn't making me happy, it was just a new trap I had made for myself.

I felt my life beginning to unwind around me in a way that was no less terrible for it having happened many times before. I started to think of Ireland, of my family, my home; started to remember all the things I was trying to forget. I couldn't control my own mind, the old self-loathing, the familiar, bitter dissatisfaction with everything. The grey rain hammered down, driving in against the windows. I was too conscious of my self, of my own body, and I wanted desperately to flee myself, even if only for a short time. The rain was nailing me in, I felt as if I were in a cage. The rain sheeted across the square. It was too cold and dark to go out, and in any case, I was already too far gone, and where was there to go? I tried twice to call Ted but he wasn't there. On both occasions I could hear the phone ring and ring in the empty apartment. What good would it have done even if I had spoken to him? What difference would it have made, even if he had been there with me in S. Giorgio that night? When these fits of desolation came upon me, I felt completely isolated, irrevocably lonely, and to be with someone, particularly someone I liked, only made me more aware of how cut off I was from them, how isolated.

It wasn't other people who bothered me, it all came from inside myself, and the feeling was so strong that it was as if there were another person inside me, a dark self who tormented me. My self was split in two, and one half threatened the other, the weaker half.

And then, there in the apartment while the rain hammered down, the strangest thing happened. I felt that this other self was no longer in me, but felt secure enough of her tight hold over me to risk slipping outside, to show me she was real and powerful. Now she was there in the room with me, standing behind me. I felt as you do when you go into an empty building, and you know that it's not really empty, that there is someone else there. You can sense their presence, even though you can't see or hear them. I thought that if I was to turn around, I would see her standing there right behind me, that other person. I could imagine that physically she would look completely unlike me, with an expression on her face somewhere between merriment and malice. 'But what's wrong with you? Frightened of your own shadow, just like you always were. Still a coward? Still frightened of your own self? What is there to be afraid of? Don't you know me? Don't you recognize me?'

The door bell rang. I didn't want to answer but it rang again. It was the bell immediately outside the apartment, at the top of the stairs, so I knew that it must be Franca or some of the family. I got up. The creature behind me melted away.

It was Lucia. She had borrowed a dictionary from me earlier that evening to do her English homework, and she had come to return it. As I spoke to her, I hoped that I was hiding efficiently what I was feeling. It was like someone who is held hostage in their own home, and is sent to the door to pay the milkman, but is warned not to tell him what is happening, or give any indication that something is wrong.

I looked at Lucia as if she were a being from another

dimension. She seemed to me more unlikely than the person I had thought was standing behind me. I looked with wonder at her happy face, from which you could plainly see that she did not know torment, that she would never understand what it was to feel haunted. Her thick dark curls were pinned back with a plastic clip, with a white artificial flower attached to it. She was wearing jeans and a sweatshirt that said on it in English 'Winter Warmth', against a background of russet and orange leaves. There was a thin coloured Brazilian good-luck charm around her wrist, that some boy had given her, and which she always wore.

'*Tutto bene, Aisling?*'

I said that I was fine. She smiled and left.

I slept badly that night, and had terrible dreams. I often have nightmares, but even by my standards these were exceptional. Towards morning, I dreamt that I was combing my hair. My scalp was very itchy, and I didn't know why. Then I saw that impaled on the teeth of the comb were two big fat maggots, and I realized that the pain was coming from their gnawing my scalp. So I took a brush and brushed and brushed to get them out, and I did it so violently that my scalp was torn to pieces, my hair seeping with blood. And then I woke up.

I was in my room. It was still raining, it had rained all through the night. I looked at all the things around me – the clothes I had taken off the night before draped over a chair; a basket on the dressing table full of hairslides and bows; a long regular row of shoes; lipsticks and jars of face-cream and perfume bottles and hairbrushes. It struck me that I wouldn't be there for ever, and I wondered how I would ever find the energy to move. I thought it would be easier to just walk out of it some day and leave everything there, start all over again from scratch somewhere else. Then I remembered leaving Paris, and I knew that it couldn't be done, you couldn't slip out of your life like a snake shedding a skin. You could try, but at the end of the day, you'd still be the same person. It was myself that I wanted to get away from, and you can't do that just by abandoning a few pairs of shoes and some old cosmetics.

I made myself get up, and washed and dressed. It was still dark when I left the house, and walked through the narrow streets to the bar. In spite of the dream, in spite of having slept badly, I felt a bit better than I had done the night before. I was at a point when I felt it could be useful to go where there were other people, other things, where it was bright and warm and comforting, and where I could sit quietly for a while.

What was I going to do about this? I had already tried so hard. I had tried to be sensible, rational, told myself that I was depressed, that it was an illness like any other, and should be treated like any other.

The doctor I'd gone to see had a black leather bag with a long metal bar across the top and a complicated lock, the sort of bag that doctors were traditionally supposed to use to carry new babies to their parents. The doctor himself was staring at the bag while I spoke to him. He heard me out, and then gave a magnificent shrug.

'È la nostalgia,' he said, picking up his pen. 'Homesickness.'

The best thing to do, he said, would be for me to go back home to where I came from, back home to my mamma. I told him she was dead. He frowned, but went on writing and said that I should probably go back anyway. I could see he thought I was being unreasonable. If I went away from my own home, what could I expect, only unhappiness and loneliness? Until such time as I did return, he said, I could take these, and he handed me a prescription for some tranquillizers. I got them from the chemist, but I hardly ever used them. I didn't like the effect they had on me, and of course they didn't solve the problem. They couldn't make me feel less unhappy, just dulled, as if I had been hit on the head with something. Sometimes I was grateful for that.

So what was I to do? I still hoped that life itself would cure it. I thought that to go back to Ireland wouldn't help at all, because it was something that had been caused by my early life, it was a northern problem. I had tried to help myself as unhappy north Europeans had tried to help themselves for years: by going south. I wanted to believe that it had helped. It wasn't that the doctors of the south couldn't cure me – and of course they couldn't – but I couldn't be cured either by being close to what had hurt me in the first place.

I thought of the fresco of the man vomiting the devil. I thought of Don Antonio and his pendulum. If I had been living in some countries, I'd have been taken out to the edge of a wood, and left there, so that the dark things could come in the night and take away my evil. But I knew what caused my troubles. I had always known. The thing was, to try to change it. I had, I thought, spent all my adult life trying to work to that end, but on a night like last night it seemed to have all been in vain. I just didn't know what I should do instead.

I looked at my watch. I had to go home and get my things ready for work, or I'd be late. I said '*Ciao*' to Adolfo, and he said, 'See you tomorrow.' I thought, I hope not, as I walked out into the rain.

Sebastian Barry

from *The Engine of Owl-Light*

A WOODEN wordless man kept the door of the bar, with its elegant sign, leaning *Topless* into the mauve evening. His skull was shaved, except for a rabbity run of hair in the middle, and his eyes had a raw bladed look too. But he wasn't connected with the warmth of the place – not quite the heat of the ordinary night outside, but something by the way and solitary added to it.

The moving nakedness of a dancer was the first thing to avoid staring at, at least to start with. Entering with Ali gave me the sensation of being a regular friend to the bar, not a gawking patron. But Ali paused open-handedly and watched the dancer for a few moments.

We perched up at the counter and as always Ali was saluted as a fixture, and I got the little side honey of that. A popular dance record was being given a new surrounding and meaning, and a careful exact lighting steadily made sure to reveal all angles of the performer, without shadows.

The drinks were on the house, as the bar woman presumed I had no money, since I was with Ali. This made no difference to her.

A tallish server stopped beside us, and complimented Ali on his dreadlocks. Ali replied smoothly and pleasantly to her, drawing her into his geometric benign friendship. I tried to concentrate on admiring her face, but the lack of clothes made my old eyes topple to her body. And the way she was decked out had me thinking not of making love to her, but of fucking her. The verb fitted the clothes, or what there was of clothes.

And yet her palliness was distant, Moll, and quietly fenced, and looking was the order of the night. We were there to gaze, and even if in other conditions we had been allowed to touch and possess, here everyone was reduced to an insular voyeurism. Actually it gave me quite a sensation of freedom. I knew I didn't have to attract any of the women in here, or plot to make them not see my strangeness. Because they tried, as much as possible, to treat all the customers in the same prejudiced manner. For the sake of sanity, the basic reason of the establishment was considered within the boundaries, but further lowering of things was invisibly prevented. Any notion of a hand reaching out to finger was quickly made shameful and rather awful, as if touching might cause a severe disappearance or suchlike in the toucher, or as if touching might suddenly call the procedures of crotching and bottoming on the sanded floor into question.

Ali and I preserved our professional position at the bar, which was a little outside the main area of heat. The pattern of dancing was straightforward. A girl appeared from the dressing-room when her predecessor had done, and began to thump her body to whatever rhythm the music could imagine. She danced in her cramped square and the young men occupied the seats at the table-height railings, drinking beer and almost filming the dancer with pleasant blotting-paper smiles. Most of them had a little sheaf of dollar bills beside their drinks, and when they wanted to draw the dancer, they waved one of these greenly. The woman moved through the clear shadowless glare, that bared her even to the pimples on her bottom. She paused with her crotch thrust out, so the happy man could slip the folded bill under the drawn line of her G-string. Then the dancer turned her back on him, and dropped straight over, so her arse was stuck neatly in his flooded face. Off then to dance, till the next carrot was raised. I was fairly certain that these tips were the wages of the dancers.

It was a bit curious for me to watch these transactions, all done with smiles on the part of the women, and bigger smiles on the part of the young men. And they were very young men, not bad looking, and probably sailors in port for a few days. There were none of the grubbier types that you see in such places in the big cities. In fact there was a sinister sense of innocence about it, a quaint obscene ceremony that wasn't obscene because it didn't belong to humanity – and yet there it was. Its accepted boundaries made it real, but only inside the alien bar.

Mostly it was hugely exciting and attractive and I was completely shuffled into it after a while, and waited impatiently at the bar for my 'favourite' dancer to come round and round in her turn. For there were only three women in all, and the one I liked was the server who had spoken to Ali. Her figure was ordinary and her breasts took a brief stretched dip just before the nipples, but she seemed overloaded with energy, and her particular lure was a mad scatty smile that she reserved for her tippers. It really was the most hair-raising and cock-raising flourish.

That was the business of the place – a sort of ordered protracted arousal of the men, which became after an hour or two a clear alternative to actual fucking, and gained a satisfaction and addiction of its own. It didn't lose its potency because there was never any form of climax. Given the stamina and the right measure of beer and food, I might have sat there at the welcoming bar for weeks. The lack of furtiveness was reviving, and because I hadn't spent much time in such joints before, I was surprised by the everyday way the show progressed, and the ordinary and even special camaraderie of the people enclosed for the night among the green performances. It was a love affair of a kind, and when I was eventually locked at the pit with my single dollars, and had tried the action of tipping the dancer, my head was quite lost to its whole logic. It wasn't money in my hands but a sort of language, a formula to beckon over the symbol of simple desire. And under the crippled music, and after a fair number of bills had been bestowed into the strings, the premium among rewards was a plain pat on the head and a muss of the hair from my beloved. No gesture could have a more supreme value. Because as touching was barred, the act of touching on her part became a profound expression of her acceptance and her admiration. I began to feel both privileged and rather handsome inside that cocoon, and confused myself and my life with the abrading lonely troubles of the briefly-contented young sailors.

Johnnie kept his shell-blue cap on at all times, because you could see, Moll, that there was no hair to slip down from under it, and the best guess was that he was bald. We were out on the deep emotional waters of the bay, and Ali held his short rod idly, but with a definite expertise. Yet another of his skills had become apparent. We fished in the thick-looking water, while Johnnie attended slowly to the wheel, and the light insect of the engine. A rich blue colour jumped off the water into the air, which was almost sore on the daytime eye. The blue gushed up like a huge geyser, but it was motionless too. Ali's hedgy beard grabbed his chin, but apart from that his body was dipped and switched-off in the chair.

'Hey, Ali,' said Johnnie. 'I wanted ta ask ye. You're what they call a rasta-man, right?'

'That's right. Rasta-man,' said Ali. 'Dat's what I am.'

'Right, but, now, what do you guys do when it comes to gettin marriage, or such?'

'It's like anywan, Johnnie: the woman is for the man, and that's the end of the story.'

'Right, right. I was just wondering.'

And then for a long while we didn't offer a word to the held blue energy of the bay.

'The children are important too,' said Ali.

Johnnie looked at him quickly, and said *uh-huh*, and let his eyes yawn out to sea again. The sun in the boat and the sun outside the boat felt like two different sorts of metal.

Johnnie whistled in a little stream. The tune was *Alabama Bound*, and he had quite a few grace notes to throw against its famous monotony. He liked its monotony though. Then he sang a few lines of it all under his breath:

'I'm Alabama bound, I'm Alabama bound, I'm Alabama, silk pyjama, Alabama bound.'

He sang with a wooden private lack of tone, like a madman's whisper. His round brown face turned to us, and he laughed at something. The boat purred on over the careless businesslike surface. Johnnie made a noise in his teeth, and blew some tuneless air out of his mouth in a sort of sighless sigh. He was still talking to himself really, but suddenly he said:

'Well, Ali, what would it be now if a man in your place were a queer, you know, a gay guy?'

Ali lay calm like a big safe tiger for another bit. He didn't seem to be thinking it over, but rather waiting for Johnnie's words to reach him. The air was very solid, and the words had to be strong blue birds to cross the soupy boat.

'In rasta,' he said, 'in rasta it doesn't happen. No. It wouldn't be. The men go with the women.'

'Oh yeh, well, and if there is a guy, you know, if there just is one.'

'There isn't one,' said Ali, without any emphasis. 'It doesn't happen.'

'Hell, Ali boy, there's always queers, I'm tellin ye.'

Johnnie had got a little excited about this and only his hand on the wheel had remained as before. He spoke as if someone might be listening, and although he wasn't whispering, he adopted the attitude of a whisperer.

'It's nature's law, Ali,' he said.

'No,' said Ali again. 'It cannot be, man, because rasta does not allow.'

'Okay, okay, and when it just so happens that a rastaman falls in love, Jesus Christ, with another regular man, what then?'

'It doesn't happen, because if it did, we would have to kill him.'

Ali's words slipped over the side of the boat, and sank like a bait into the sea.

'You'd kill him? Aw, come on,' said Johnnie.

'Oh yes, mon, we'd just remove him. But you see, mon, it never happens.'

'It happens, of course it happens,' said Johnnie. 'Holy shit, you sit there like a statue with a tape-recorder stuffed up its ass, and you tell me one of the most, the most natural things in the world, in the whole world, never happens.'

Ali moved his shoulders in a cottony shrug. He was still wearing the exact same clothes he had on when I first met him. He washed them out every few days, and between their age and the bleaching sun they were looking pretty thin and light. His black skin rose out of the shirt almost aggressively, as if there wasn't any true connection between him and the poor clothes he had to wear. But this great self-possession of his was clearly a first-rate weapon in an argument, because while Johnnie got more and more sure of what he said, Ali remained as sure as he had been at the start, which isn't the same thing. I thought myself that Johnnie was probably right, but Ali, by dint of simple stillness, was making being right a very dubious value.

'So, did you ever have to kill a queer guy? I mean, you say it never happens. But did you ever do that?'

'No. Not me,' said Ali. 'But I've seen it. An it was all right to do that, because if we didn't, then maybe all of rasta would come to an end. You have to be clear, mon, you have to be clear.'

'God Jesus, I don't believe you,' said Johnnie, 'You're too fuckin much, Ali, you know that? Shit, you go around killin people because they're different, and you. Ah, shit.'

Johnnie glared out over the clean colour, and let his heart slow down for a while. He really hated Ali talking like that. Ali's rod did a quick strong flip, and Johnnie was over in a second, and talking to him like he was a lover. Ali didn't need the advice, and seemed to know already about the brake on the reel, and whatever else Johnnie had to say. But he listened with obvious attention. They had got themselves into a bit of a bad corner with the argument, and neither of them had wanted the argument, and now it could be forgotten in the arrival of the strike. They were close now, like lovers. But they weren't remotely that at all. Because since Ali had all borders and allotments exactly drawn, his brand of friendship could be as intimate as his silent belief wished. He and Johnnie could have slept naked in the same bunk, one on top of the other, and it would never enter Ali's mind that there was something sexual involved in it. It didn't happen so therefore it couldn't be, and if it did happen, you killed it. I wondered if Johnnie so was gay, as his talk half-suggested. But I knew from Ali that he had a young whore that he lived with noisily in the harbour.

Johnnie liked Ali, but he didn't like him to be so strange about such a straightforward natural thing. He liked him to be strange about most other things though. It was better to see them working the fish together.

After a full pulled minute the rod returned to its stiff passionless state, and Ali slumped back without surprise, in the canvas seat.

'Ah shit,' said Johnnie, 'we could have used that fish.'

'It doesn't matter. It didn't happen,' said Ali.

It was a simple siesta-ing groggy Key West afternoon, and Ali and I had come down by the yellow-flowered road to sit on the planked pier that pointed a bit pointlessly towards Cuba, and to hang our legs from it. No boats, either pleasure- or fishing-, moored there, because it was open sea, and the reasonably happy blue water accepted the brighter thinner colour of a vanishing sky. The inks up there seeped away more and more, as the hour or two drifted, and the paper bleached in its own sunlight. The sea transferred its flat bulk from right to left, so you thought the whole key was adrift and heading out into the Atlantic. Away to the right was a private shore of luxury houses, and to the left the public beach, where cheap fried sandwiches could be got – and an ageing gay sulked in the loo – and a big highwaylike pier that waded out into deep water, and rightangled there, and stopped.

Dope-pedlars liked to meet there, Ali said, because at night only the soft wool of the lamps was visible, and any car with or without headlamps could be prepared for if it set tyre on to the ramp. As we talked, a far-away stick of black strolled on motionless threadthin limbs into a corner of the marooned end. Like a piece of dirt in someone's eye, the figure seemed to float rather than propel itself, and it slipped into obscurity among the boulders of the pier's bulwarks. Ali followed this charcoal smudge with a superior professional concentration.

'He don't even have a car, mon. Look at him.'

'What's he waiting for, do you think?'

'He's waiting for no one. He thinks he's waiting for his customer, but it's too early.'

But along the wide palmed searoad, a large American-built car was trailing a closing tunnel of shimmer and exhaust. Ali was silent. Under my palms the grainy wood was warm and somehow soft – in the night it would be stone-hard. Two girls in parrot-bright bikinis treaded past us without heeding us. At the lip of our pier they stepped carefully down the seaweedy rungs, and flung themselves one after the other into the quiet stewing glitter. Their heads sleeked up from their dives, and they snaked in overarm straight out into nowhere. They turned about three hundred yards from shore and swam diagonally to the wriggling coast.

The big car meanwhile had got as far as the elbow in the large pier. It had paused there, and two men, or two straws we took to be men, detached themselves from the tiny blackness of the automobile. I supposed the first arrival had been luckier than Ali's doubting prophecy, because his figure reappeared clearly on the stricken whitened tar, and slid again in that odd legless way towards the similarly-floating newcomers. We heard the tiniest noise, like the top of an egg being tapped by the moon, but just once – and it sounded as unimportant as a seagull's bark.

'Shit mon,' said Ali.

The single man, who had not been let down, fell down instead, and his two customers flicked back to their car, and we imagined we could catch the swell of the engine as they reversed and calmly retraced their tracks.

'We didn't see that,' said Ali. 'You hear me?'

'What happened?' I said, very puzzled.

'It's useful for dat too,' said Ali. 'A little bit of business put straight again and no one the wiser.'

'But they just shot him. They just blew him away.'

'Mon, they have ten of these a month here. And it's not as bad as Fort Lauderdale. Forget you saw it. Forget it.'

'But they're crazy!'

'It's drugs, mon. The drugs people are really bad – really gone loose in the head. You can stay away from them and live a reasonably long life, but not in their company.'

Nothing happened on the searoad or the seapier. The black mark remained toppled over, and the car purposefully gained the further houses and gardens, and glimmered out of sight, the roof talking to the sun. No one came and no alarm appeared to be raised. We hung our legs and the sea moved from right to left, as if we were a great rocky raft, and the girls started to swim back towards us. Just nothing happened. There was no reaction on the part of the general scenery to this rapid smooth death, that had occurred as an item at the extreme range of our sleepy eyes. Its unimportance was bewildering. I felt nothing. It hadn't really taken place. The figure was there but if you let your gaze blur a little, the merest bit, it fuzzed and became part of the surface – it might have been a different-colour tar laid as a patch, or a trick of the light. Nowhere in my mind could I see it as a man of this or that height, with a well-placed bullet somewhere vital in his corpse. There would be blood steaming from the wound, gathering in a widening invisible shape, and dyeing into his light summer clothes. He might be panting a final morsel of air. The sky might be unbearable, and exaggerated to a furnace in his shocked unable pupils. But more certainly none of these things could be unfolding, at such a distance – nothing could be real so far away and stagelike. It hadn't altered the progress of our inaction, nor impressed the seabirds, or been noticed by the only other moving intelligences in the vicinity, who were even now pulling their varnished unattractive forms from the blind sea.

'What does he do now? Just lie there?' I said.

'What you want to do? Run over? And what? He's dead. Someone will find him who saw nothing, and they'll call for a cop, and the cop will haul him away, and won't find out who did it, or if they do it won't matter because the killers will be dead too, or I don't know. You can't do anything. These are mad people and dangerous and not important.'

I felt a short splatter of drops on the back of my shirt as the swimmers mutely passed. Their feet darkened the pale wood. Other bits of liquid pattered through into the sea. Maybe we didn't exist for them, like the dead man didn't for us. If someone crawled up now and blasted the two of us, we'd probably be left on these boards bleeding unimportantly into the water. It was a brand-new thought for me. It reminded me of what Captain Collins said once about Asian people – that at home in Thailand and so on they had no respect for human life at all, and killed each other freely and without bitterness. It was because there were so many of them, he said, fifty million in a small area. But in Africa, Asian colonists changed, because they were abruptly so few. But this didn't explain an unceremonious murder in an ordinary Florida afternoon. Cuba was the next piece of good land, and the whole shoaling deep of civilized America thundered up to the Great Lakes at our backs. There wasn't any way out of this. Ali understood it and I didn't. He knew there was nothing to understand. It had stopped long ago being humanly understandable.

Brian Moore

The Sight

Cassandra's gift is of course a curse. The Trojan priestess who could foretell the future (but whom no one would believe) is haunted by the evils that will come and the knowledge that nothing can prevent them. She shares her curse with the condemned in Hell – they also know what they can expect from the days ahead, and they also lack all hope. In Brian Moore's story, Cassandra appears in an unexpected light.

Brian Moore has written a number of highly successful novels – including The Lonely Passion of Judith Hearne, Catholics, The Great Victorian Collection *– and is claimed as a national writer by Ireland (where he was born), Canada (where he worked) and the United States (where he now lives).*

BENEDICT CHIPMAN never took a drink before five and never drank after midnight. He ate only a light lunch, avoided bread and potatoes, and drank decaffeinated coffee. These self-regulations were, he sometimes thought, the only set rules he observed. Otherwise, he did as he liked.

Yet on the morning he returned to his eight-room apartment on Fifth Avenue after four days in hospital, his first act was to tell his housekeeper to bring some Scotch and ice into the library. When she brought it, he was standing by the window, looking out at Central Park. He did not turn around.

'Will that be all, sir?'

'Yes, thanks, Mrs Leahy.'

Chipman was fifty-two and a partner in a New York law firm. A few weeks ago, during his annual medical check-up, his doctor had noticed a large mole on his back and had recommended its removal. The operation was minor but, for Chipman who had never been in hospital before, the invasion of his bodily privacy by doctors, nurses, and attendants had been humiliating and vaguely upsetting. Then, to complicate matters, while the biopsy showed the mole to be probably benign, the pathologist advised that 'to be completely sure', the surgeon should repeat the procedure but, this time, make a wider incision. The second biopsy had been scheduled for the end of the month. 'There's nothing to worry about,' the surgeon said. 'Just relax and come back ten days from now.'

But Chipman did not feel like relaxing. He felt nervous and irritable. As he poured the Scotch, he looked at the tray containing his mail. The first letter on the pile was postmarked Bishopsgate, N. H. He had been born in Bishopsgate and for some reason he could not explain the sight of the postmark disturbed him. The letter was from his brother, Blake, who wrote that he and his wife were coming to New York to visit their son Buddy, a journalism major at Columbia. Buddy, it seemed, had learned that his uncle had been in hospital and Blake wrote that all three of them would like to call tomorrow afternoon. The letter irritated Chipman. He had no wish to see Blake and his family. He thought of his brother as a man who had never in his life owned a hundred dollars he didn't know about and whose relations with himself were sycophantic rather than fraternal, largely because of loans which Blake had not repaid.

At the library door, Mrs Leahy announced herself with a small prefatory cough. 'Mrs Kirwen is here, sir.'

'Show her in. And ask if she'd like something to drink.'

As he put his brother's letter down and rose to greet Geraldine, he heard her chatting with Mrs Leahy in the front hall.

'Is *he* having one? Oh, well then, a sherry, I think. By the way, how's your nephew, Mrs Leahy?'

'He still has the pleurisy, ma'am. But he'll be all right.'

'Good, that's good news.'

'Thank you, Mrs Kirwen.'

I never knew Mrs Leahy had a nephew, Chipman said to himself. But, come to think of it, he didn't know much about Mrs Leahy, although she had been with him for almost ten years. Lately, he had decided that his interest in other people was limited to the extent of their contributions to his purse, his pleasure, or his self-esteem. He had a weakness for such aphoristic judgements. But in this instance he also remembered another aphorist's warning: lack of interest in others is a first sign of age.

'Ben, darling, how are you? Shouldn't you have your feet up or something? You mustn't overdo it on your first day home.'

'Stop fussing.'

'I'm not fussing. Dr Wilking told me you should take it easy.'

'When was Wilking talking to *you*?'

'I met him in the corridor yesterday. Remember, he thinks I'm your wife.'

The surgeon, who did not know Chipman, had come in on them unexpectedly the night after the biopsy and found Geraldine, the buttons of her dress undone, lying on the hospital bed with Chipman. The surgeon had tactfully assumed she was Chipman's wife and had addressed her as such in the subsequent conversation. No one had contradicted him. 'That was a mistake,' Chipman said now, remembering. 'I should have said something.'

'Oh, what's it matter?'

'Well, my own doctor, Dr Loeb, knows I'm not married.'

'Oh, Ben. Who cares nowadays?'

At that point Mrs Leahy brought Geraldine's sherry. Geraldine, sipping it, put her long legs up on a yellow silk footstool. In this posture her skirt fell back, revealing her elegant thighs. Although impromptu erotic views normally pleased Chipman, this morning he was not pleased: he was irritated. 'Why can't you sit properly?'

'That's not a very nice thing to say when I've given up an important job to be with you today.'

'What job?'

'Remember I tried out for the Phil Lewis show last week? Well, my agent called and said they want me for a second audition this afternoon. He says that usually means you've got the job. But, I'm not going.'

'Why not?'

'Because if I got the job it would mean I'd be on the coast for the next seven weeks. I'm not going to be three thousand miles away while you're in and out of hospital.'

'I'm not in and out of hospital. I'm just going back for a couple of days, that's all. Now, be a good girl. Phone and say you'll be glad to audition this afternoon.'

'No,' she said, suddenly looking as though she might begin to cry.

'But why not?'

'Because I've realized something, Ben. I'm in love with you. I don't want to be separated from you.'

In love with him? He remembered La Rochefoucauld's maxim that nothing is more natural or more mistaken than to suppose that we are loved. He knew Geraldine did not love him. She was an unsuccessful young actress, divorced from a television producer and in receipt of a reasonable alimony. His own role in her life was that of a suitable escort, an older man capable of providing presents and a good time, a friend who was good for a small loan and might not expect to see his money again. This sudden protestation of love was, he decided, no more than the familiar feminine need to justify having gone to bed with him. Geraldine would not give up her alimony: he did not want her to. The present arrangement suited him perfectly.

Nevertheless when she said that she loved him, for one moment he felt strangely elated. Then put his glass back on the silver tray and in its surface saw his face, which seemed distorted, white, old. This foolishness must stop. 'Now, don't talk nonsense. Go and phone those people.'

'Are you trying to get rid of me?'

'Of course not. But if you go out to Hollywood this week it might work out very well. I was thinking of going to Puerto Rico. I thought I'd take a vacation. Lie in the sun until I have to go back into hospital.'

'Do you know people in Puerto Rico, is that it?'

'No. No. Look, Geraldine, you're *not* in love with me. My God, I'm twenty years older than you.'

'Age has nothing to do with being in love with someone.'

'Maybe not at your age. But at my age it has everything to do with it. Now go and make that phone call. Then I'll take you out and buy you lunch.'

She stood and picked up the otter coat he had helped pay for, trailing it behind her on the carpet as she moved across the room. At the door, she turned. 'So that's what you want? To go to Puerto Rico alone?'

'Yes.'

'OK.'

She went into the hall. He listened to hear the tinkle as she picked up the phone, but instead heard the front door slam. He started across the room, thinking to go after her and bring her back, but stopped. He realized that he was close to the almost forgotten sensation of tears. Dammit, he'd just invented Puerto Rico to help her make up her mind about the audition. But now, as he felt himself tremble with anger – or was it weakness? – he decided a short vacation in the sun might be the ideal way to wait out the next ten days. Maybe with Geraldine. He decided to suggest it at the office when he went in tomorrow.

There might be a little ill-feeling, though. He had already had a long vacation this summer. But what could they do? In the seventeen years he had been a member of the firm he had frequently demonstrated that his interests were not the law or the success of the partnership, but women, music, and his collection of paintings. However, on the day he joined the partnership he brought with him, as a wedding present from his father-in-law, an insurance company which dwarfed all other clients the firm did business with. And although his marriage had subsequently broken up (his wife died eight years later in an alcoholic clinic, driven there, some said, by Chipman's behaviour with other women) his father-in-law had not held it against him. He still represented the insurance company and this power, coupled with his disregard for the firm's other clients, had driven his partners to revenge themselves on him in the only way they knew. They no longer invited him to their homes or, indeed, to any social function. Their boycott amused him: they bored him. They knew that he was amused and bored. Their dislike of him, he guessed, had long ago turned to hatred.

Yet on the following morning when he went to the office he was surprised to see George Geddes, the senior partner, come in at his doorway, eager, out of breath, and smiling like a job applicant. 'Ben, how are you, how're you feeling?'

'Hello, George.'

'So, how did it go?'

Directly behind Geddes, Chipman's secretary was at her desk in the outer office. He did not want her to hear what he had to say and so beckoned Geddes in and shut the door. 'Matter of fact, George, I wanted to have a word with you about that. Everything went very well, but they want me to go back, just as a precaution, and have a wider excision made. They've scheduled it for the thirty-first. I don't know. I'm feeling a little knocked out. I thought, if you don't mind, I might go and lie in the sun for a week. Not really come back to the office until next month.'

As he spoke he noticed that Geddes was already nodding agreement as though helping someone with a speech impediment. 'Of course, Ben, of course. No sense sitting around here. Good idea.'

'Well, thanks. Of course there are a few things I can clear up before I go.'

'No, no,' Geddes said. 'Let the juniors do some work for a change. Get on your feet again, that's the main thing.'

After Geddes had left, Chipman phoned a travel agency.

He booked a double room with patio and pool in a first-class Puerto Rico resort hotel, starting the following Monday. He called in his juniors and reviewed their current handling of his clients' affairs. At noon he told his secretary that he was leaving and would not be back until the first week in December. Then he took a taxi to his apartment and for the second morning in a row broke his rule and made himself a drink.

But now his reason was celebratory. What a relief it had been to find Geddes agreeable for once. And there was a note saying Geraldine had telephoned. Obviously, her temper tantrum had not lasted. After pouring a Scotch he picked up the phone and dialled her number.

'Geraldine? Ben. First of all, I'm sorry about yesterday.'

'No, darling, it was my fault. Why shouldn't you go on a trip if you want to? When are you going, by the way?'

'No, tell me first, how was your audition?'

'I didn't go. It's a long story, I won't bore you with it.'

'Does that mean you might be free to join me in Puerto Rico?'

'Ben, do you mean it?'

'Of course. I booked a double room with patio and pool in the Caribe Imperial. Or would you rather I got you a room of your own?'

'No, no.'

'Good. And what about the week-end? Are you free?'

'Do you mean now? Yes. Completely.'

'Well, so am I. Or, almost. I have to be here tomorrow afternoon when my brother and his family are coming. But that shouldn't take more than an hour.'

'Are we thinking of the same thing?'

'I hope so.'

'All right, darling. Come on down. I'll be waiting.'

'I'll be right there.'

*

His brother's hand, tentative at first, went out to finger the Steinway's polished surface, then boldly stroked the wood. His brother's head turned, afternoon sunlight merciless on the thin grey hair, the pink skull-cap of skin beneath. His brother smiled, ingratiate and falsely intimate. 'Beautiful piano, eh, Ben?' his brother said. 'You must play something for us before we go. I mean, if you feel up to it.'

'Oh yes, Ben, you must,' said his brother's wife who, he knew, did not care at all for music.

If he felt up to it. What would they say if they knew he had come up from the village two hours ago after a night of screwing that would exhaust anyone? Perhaps it would not exhaust Blake's wife, though. One summer, when their son Buddy was still a brat in rompers, Chipman had gone to visit them at their summer cottage on Cape Cod. He was sunbathing in the dunes when Blake's wife came up from the beach, drying her hair on a towel, her shoulder-straps undone, her swimsuit wet from the sea. She did not see him until she stumbled on him and when he reached up and pulled her down she did not say a word. Later they walked hand in hand over the dunes towards the cottage. Blake was sitting on a deck-chair on the lawn, reading a book, and the child was on the porch playing with an old inner tube. Man and child looked up and his brother's wife at once let go of his hand and ran to kiss her child. She avoided Chipman for the rest of that evening and the following morning he thought it wise to pretend a business engagement in Boston. He had not been to stay with them since.

'Let Buddy play something,' he said, knowing that Buddy's atrocious playing would please them much more than his own. And so Buddy obediently flopped down on the piano bench, looked disdainfully at the music scores in front of him, then poised his large hands over the keys. 'What'll it be, Uncle Ben?'

'You choose,' Chipman said. Years ago, prodded by Blake's wistful hints about the child's musical inclinations, he had paid for a series of piano lessons for Buddy. The money had been wasted for Buddy's musical talents were a myth, the first of a long series of efforts on his parents' part to make Chipman feel a special affection for the boy. All had failed. Buddy's only effect on his uncle was to relieve him of any regrets about not having had a son of his own.

But now he pretended to listen as Buddy stumbled through some Cole Porter tunes, noticing as he mimed attention that Buddy's parents seemed nervous as though they had quarrelled before coming and were now trying to cover it up by a surfeit of polite remarks to each other. Chipman was uninterested. He simply wanted them to go and so, when Blake glanced at last in his direction, he pretended drowsiness. It worked. As his son thumped to a pause in the music, Blake stood up. 'Thanks, Bud, but we'd better not overtire your uncle. Besides, your mother and I want to catch that Wyeth show at the Met before our train leaves.'

Then he turned to Chipman. 'Ben, could I have a word with you?'

As on signal both Buddy and his mother left the room. It was, Chipman knew, the usual prelude to Blake's asking for money, but today a loan seemed well worth it to get rid of them. He went to his desk, aware that Blake, if left to his own devices, would take at least five minutes to come to the point. He opened a drawer and took out his cheque-book.

'What's that for?' Blake asked sharply.

'Nothing.'

'Put that away, will you,' Blake said. 'I'm ashamed that I owe you so much. As a matter of fact, Ben, it wasn't that at all. It was just that we wondered if you'd like to come up to Bishopsgate to convalesce until you go back into the hospital.'

'Thanks, but I'm going to Puerto Rico.'

'Oh. Puerto Rico?'

'Yes, I thought I'd like to lie in the sun for a few days.'

'Oh, that's a pity, we were looking forward to the thought

of having you. You and I haven't spent much time together these last years.'

'I know. Well, maybe some other time.'

'Any time,' Blake said. 'I'd like us to go for walks around the old place and have talks and all that. I'd like that a lot.'

And then, abruptly, Blake took hold of his hand and squeezed it. 'I'd really like it, Ben.'

'Well, we'll do it,' Chipman said, uneasily, beginning to move towards the hallway where the others waited. As they came out he saw Blake's wife glance at her husband and saw Blake give a small, almost imperceptible shake of his head. Buddy came forward, hand out, smiling. 'Goodbye, sir.'

'Goodbye,' Chipman said. 'Goodbye, Blake.'

His sister-in-law came towards him. He held out his hand. She ignored it and reached up to kiss him on the cheek. He was astonished. 'Goodbye,' his sister-in-law said. 'Take care of yourself.'

The elevator came. They went down.

Confused, Chipman closed the door of his apartment. It was as though he had found an interesting passage in a dull book and had seen it snatched away before he had time to finish it. Why had Blake's wife kissed him, she who had so carefully avoided kissing him ever since that summer on the beach? And why had Blake come up with this unprecedented invitation to visit them at Bishopsgate? Why were they being so kind all of a sudden? Come to think of it, everyone had been abnormally kind these past two days – Geraldine, Geddes, Blake. It was irritating, dammit, to be treated as though, all of a sudden, he were made of glass. How did La Rochefoucauld put it? *Pride does not wish to owe, nor vanity to pay.* He didn't want favours from anyone. So, why did they try?

He had reached the library door before the thought and the answer came to him. He was going to die. That was why they were all being so gentle. They knew something he didn't know. A wider excision, that was what the surgeon said. 'To be completely sure,' the pathologist said. They hadn't told him the truth, that was it. 'Just relax,' the surgeon said.

He must not panic. He must call Dr Loeb, his internist, and put the question to him quite casually, implying that he already knew all about it. He must go to the phone now and clear things up.

He went into his bedroom and closed the door so that Mrs Leahy would not overhear him. He phoned Dr Loeb but the answering service said Dr Loeb was out of town for the weekend and a Dr Slattery was taking his calls. So that was no use. The surgeon's name was Wilking. He looked up the number. The answering service said Dr Wilking wasn't in, but would he leave a message. He left his name and number and lay down on the bed, worrying. After five minutes he telephoned again and said it was an emergency. He must reach Dr Wilking at once. This time, the answering service gave him a number to call. Dr Wilking answered.

'Dr Wilking, this is Benedict Chipman speaking. Now, I know this may sound silly to you, but was there anything about that operation of mine that I should know about?'

'Why do you ask, Mr Chipman?'

'I just want to know the truth. It's important, doctor.'

'Well, look, Mr Chipman, it's pretty much as I told you. I don't think you have anything to worry about.'

'Is that the truth? I want the truth.'

'Yes, what can I say? Look, Mr Chipman. The best thing you can do now is relax. Your wife mentioned you might go off for a short vacation. I think that's a good idea.'

'How the hell can I take it easy? For God's sake, doctor, that's like telling a man to take it easy in the condemned cell while you decide whether or not he's to be reprieved.'

'Oh, come on now, Mr Chipman, I wouldn't say that.'

'Of course, you wouldn't,' Chipman shouted. 'And that girl isn't my wife, do you hear? So anything you have to say, just say it to me!'

He put the receiver down without waiting to hear the surgeon's reply. He looked at his bed. This was the bed he might die in. He turned from it and went into his library. Small picture-lights lit his collection of Krieghoff landscapes. When he died these pictures would be sent to the Bishopsgate Art Gallery to be exhibited in a special room with a brass plaque over the door, identifying him as their donor. They would arrive after his body, which would be buried under a plain headstone in the episcopal cemetery, next to his parents' grave. How many people ever read donors' plaques or the names on headstones? A year from now he would be forgotten.

But wasn't that jumping the gun, giving in to a bad case of jitters unsupported by any evidence? How could they know he was going to die when they hadn't even done the second biopsy yet? What were they keeping from him? Whatever it was had frightened Geraldine into suddenly declaring her love. But she doesn't love me, Chipman decided, she pities me. Pity is what everyone feels for me now: Geraldine, Geddes, Blake, Blake's wife. Yet how could they all know this thing about me? Geraldine has never met Geddes. Or Buddy. Who told Buddy, for instance?

Chipman went to his desk, searched it, and then went to the telephone table in the hall. He knew he had a number for Buddy someplace, and when he found it and dialled it, it was a fraternity house. No one answered for a long time and then some boy told him Buddy wasn't in, and that he didn't know when he would be back. As Chipman replaced the receiver, Mrs Leahy passed him in the hall, going down the corridor to her own room. Only one person might have spoken to Buddy, to Geddes, to Geraldine. One person who would answer the phone when people called here to ask how he was. He went down the corridor to the far end of the apartment and stopped outside Mrs Leahy's door. He almost never came into this part of the apartment, near the pantry and wine cellar, and past the kitchen. He stood for a moment and then, without knocking, he opened the door.

He had not seen the inside of Mrs Leahy's room for years. Sometimes he heard the television sound, turned low, and sometimes she would leave the door open, at night, when she went to answer the phone. Now, his eyes went from the television set to the horrid rose and green curtains, the cheap coloured lithograph of some saint, to the crucifix, entwined with fading palm, which hung over what seemed to be a sewing-table. It was the sort of room he used to glimpse through upper-storey windows, years ago, when he still rode the subways, a room which screamed a sudden mockery of all other rooms in his elegant apartment. And its occupant, her back to him, unaware of his presence, was the perfect figure in this interior. In her pudgy fingers, the surprise of a cigarette: on her lap, inevitably, the garish headlines of the *Daily News*.

'Mrs Leahy?'

She turned. Her grey head was that of a stranger's, utterly changed by the absence of her uniform cap. 'Oh, did you ring, sir? Is the bell not working?'

'No, I didn't ring.'

'Can I get you something, sir? Are you all right?'

By this time she had stubbed her cigarette and had pinned on the familiar housemaid's cap. 'A little whisky?' she said. 'Or, are you hungry, sir? Would you like a sandwich?'

'Whisky,' he said. 'And I want to talk to you.'

'Yes, Mr Chipman.' Swiftly she moved past him going down the corridor to the monastic neatness of her kitchen. She did not, of course, expect him to follow her into the kitchen and looked up, surprised, when he did.

'A little water with it, sir? I'll bring it into the library, will I?'

'No. Sit down, Mrs Leahy. Please.'

As she placed the bottle of Scotch, ice, and a glass and pitcher of water on a tray, he drew out one of the chrome and leather kitchen chairs, indicating that she should sit in at the table. As she did, he saw a red rash of embarrassment rise from her neck to her cheeks. They had never been informal together. He sat opposite her and poured himself a

Scotch. 'Now,' he said. 'Let me ask you something. Are you the person who's been telling people I have cancer?'

'Me, sir?'

'Yes, you.'

She did not answer him at once. She put her veiny old hands on the table, joined them as in an attitude of prayer, then looked at him with the calculating, ready-to-bolt caution of a rodent. He had never before noticed this animal quality of hers. Why, she's a hedgehog, he decided. She's Mrs Tiggy-winkle.

'Yes, sir. It was me.'

He must keep calm. He must not let her know that he was ignorant of all the facts of his illness. 'I see. And who told *you* that I might have cancer?'

'Mrs Kirwen, sir.'

'And what did she say, exactly?'

'Ah, she didn't say you had cancer, she said they were going to operate on you again just to be sure. There was always the chance, she said. And I said to her I thought I should let Mr Buddy know. On account of your brother, sir. And then Mr Geddes rang up about you. And I told him. To let him know, like.'

'Oh, you did, did you? Well, I like the way you let them know. They think I'm going to die. I could see it on my brother's face this afternoon. He thinks I'm going to die.'

'I'm very sorry, now, Mr Chipman.'

'Mrs Kirwen *didn't* say to you I had cancer, did she? She didn't say the doctors had told her something they hadn't told me. Or, did she?'

'Ah, no, sir. Mrs Kirwen never said you were going to die. 'Tis not Mrs Kirwen's fault at all. 'Tis my fault, and I'm very sorry now.'

'Tell me Mrs Leahy. Do you dislike me?'

'Oh, no, sir.'

'Then why did you tell these people that I'm going to die?'

'Ah, well, sir, that's a long story. And I'm very sorry to

455

be bringing you news like that. But them doctors don't know everything, now do they?'

'What do you mean?' He was shouting, but he could not stop himself. 'Just exactly what the hell do you mean, Mrs Leahy?'

Mrs Leahy, avoiding his eye, stared down at her joined hands. 'Well, sir, you see, I have something now, something not many people have. And there's times I wish I didn't, let me tell you.'

'Didn't what? Didn't have what?'

'I have the sight, sir. The second sight.'

'Second sight?' Chipman repeated the words with the joy of a man repeating the punch line of a joke. 'Well. And there I was . . .' Beginning to shake with amusement, he lifted his glass and drank a great swallow of whisky. 'You mean you dreamed it, or something like that?'

'Yes, sir. Last Monday, the night before your operation.'

'Now let me get this straight,' Chipman said. 'Mrs Kirwen told you nothing except what you've told me. The truth is nobody *knows* I have cancer. There's absolutely no proof of it at all.'

'That's right, sir.'

'My God, do you realize the mischief you've caused?'

'I'm very sorry, now. I see I shouldn't have said anything. I beg your pardon, sir.'

'It was a disgraceful thing to do!'

'Yes, sir. I'm sorry, sir. Maybe I should give you my notice?'

'No, no.' Chipman poured himself a second drink. Suddenly, he felt like laughing again. 'Well, now,' he said. Unconsciously, and for the first time in their acquaintance, he found himself slipping into an imitation of her Irish brogue. 'And how long have you had this "sight"?'

'Ah, a long time, now. I noticed it first when I was only fourteen.'

'You dream about things and then they happen, is that it?'

'In a way, sir.'

'What do you mean? Tell me.'

'I'd rather not, now, sir. I'm sorry about speaking to those people. I only meant it for your sake, sir.'

'Now, wait. I'm just interested in this premonition of yours. Now, what happened in my case? You had a dream?'

'Yes, just the dream, sir. Nothing else.'

'What do you mean, nothing else?'

'Well you see, first there's the dream. And then, later on, you see, there's a second sign.'

'And what's this second sign?'

'It's a look I do see on the person's face.'

'A look?'

'Yes. When the trouble is very close.'

Chipman, in the act of downing his second Scotch, looked at her over the rim of his glass. Ignorant, stupid old creature with her hedgehog eyes and butterfat brogue. Some primitive folk nonsense, typically Irish, he supposed; it was their religion that encouraged these fairy-tales. 'When it's close,' he said. 'What does that mean?'

'When it's close to the time, sir.'

'So, I take it you haven't seen this look on my face. Not yet.'

'That's right, sir.'

'When do you think you'll see it?'

'I don't know that, sir. Better not be asking me things like that. It's no pleasure to me to be seeing the things I do see. That's the God's own truth, sir.'

'But how do you know you'll see it? Do you always see it after you have this dream?'

'I'd say so, sir.'

'Give me an example.'

'Well, I saw it on my own sister, sir, the night before she died. I had a dream and saw her in the dream, and when I woke up she was sleeping in the bed with me and I lit the lamp and looked at her face. I saw it in her face. And the very next night she was killed by a bus on her way home. I was fourteen at the time.'

'Tell me about another time.'

'Ah, now, what's the use, sir?'

'No, you started this, Mrs Leahy. I want to hear more.'

'And I don't want to tell you, sir.'

'But you told Mrs Kirwen and Mr Geddes and my nephew. You weren't afraid to tell them this fairy-tale.'

'Ah, I didn't tell them that at all, sir. Sure they wouldn't believe it. I just said I had information, I couldn't say more. But that the doctors were very worried about you.'

'*Did* you?' Again, he felt furious at her. 'How dare you, Mrs Leahy!'

'I'm sorry, sir. I wanted to be a help to you, sir. I mean I wanted Mrs Kirwen, and your family and all, to be good to you now in your time of trouble.'

I must *not* lose my temper with a servant, Chipman told himself. 'All right,' he said. 'You told me about your sister. Give me another example.'

'My husband, sir, God rest his soul. I dreamed about him June second, 1946, and he was took on the second of November, the same year. And on the first of November I saw the look on his face. I begged him not to go to work the next day, but he didn't heed me. He fell off a scaffolding. He never lived to see a priest.'

'Wait,' Chipman said. 'Both these deaths were from accidents, not illnesses.'

'Yes, sir.'

'Well, have you had any premonitions about deaths from illness?'

'Well, Jimmy, one of the doormen in this building. I saw him in a dream four months before he died of heart disease. And on the day he was taken I went to see him in the hospital. And I saw the look on him.'

'Indeed.' Slowly, Chipman finished his Scotch.

'Of course, 'tis not always departures. Deaths. Sometimes I do see arrivals. Do you remember, sir, the night you came home from Washington, last New Year's it was? I had your dinner waiting for you. I dreamed the night before that you would come at nine, wanting your dinner. And you did.'

As a matter of fact, Chipman thought, I remember it well. I remember thinking she'd prepared that roast lamb for herself and some crony. Extra-sensory perception, premonition: of course all that was only one jump away from teacup reading, table turning, spiritualistic quacks. But she dreamed of my death.

'So, Mrs Leahy. You dreamed of me, again, the other night. But this time it wasn't about my arrival?'

She nodded.

'Tell me the dream.'

'Ah, don't be asking, sir.'

'But I am asking. If you go around telling false stories to people about my death, you have the obligation to tell me the truth about what prompted you to do it. Now, what did you see in this dream?'

'I saw the shroud, sir. You came in the room and you were wearing the shroud.'

'A shroud. That means death.'

'Yes, sir.'

'When?'

'Ah, now, I don't know that, sir.'

'But you will know, as soon as you see this look on my face, is that it?'

'Yes, sir. I'd know the time, then.'

'I see,' Chipman said. 'And now I suppose you'd like me to cross your palm with silver, so that you'll tell me when I must make my funeral arrangements. Well, Mrs Leahy, I'm going to disappoint you. A few minutes ago, when I thought of the mischief you've done and the worry you've caused my family and friends, I was quite prepared to let you go. But, believe me, I wouldn't let you go now for all the gold in Fort Knox. A year from now, Mrs Leahy, you and I will sit here together. We'll have a drink together, this time, this date, one year from now.'

'God willing and we will, sir.'

He stood up, suddenly feeling his drink, his chair making a screeching noise on the linoleum floor. 'And now,' he said, 'I'd better phone Mrs Kirwen and those other people and explain what's really happened.'

'Yes, sir. I'm very sorry.'

He went back into the library. There was no point in being angry with her, it was a joke really. He should be celebrating. The doctors weren't alarmed, and even if they found some malignancy, there are all sorts of treatments, cobalt bombs, chemotherapy and so on. To think that stupid old hedgehog had set all this in motion – Geddes, Buddy, even Geraldine. Poor Geraldine.

He went to his shelves, took down a volume of the *Encyclopaedia Britannica* and read the entry under *cancer*. He then read the entry under *clairvoyance*. When he had finished, he replaced the books and rang the bell.

'Yes, sir.'

She stood at the door, her uniform cap on straight, the perfect housekeeper, a treasure, his women friends said. 'I'd like some ice and water,' he said.

She nodded and smiled. Mrs Tiggy-winkle. When she came back with the tray, he tried to affect a bantering tone. 'Now, just in theory, mind you, just for curiosity's sake. When do you think you'll see that look on my face?'

'I don't know, sir. I hope it will be a long, long time off. Was there anything else, sir?'

'No.'

'Goodnight, sir.'

She bobbed her head in her usual half-curtsey of withdrawal. When she had gone he made himself a fresh drink, then went to the window and stood looking down at Fifth Avenue. People in evening dress were getting out of rental Cadillac limousines in front of his building, laughing and joking, going to some function.

An hour later, he was still standing there. The room

behind him was quite dark. He heard no sound in the apartment. He walked into the lighted hallway and went towards the kitchen. She was not there. He went past the kitchen, going towards her room. He stood in front of her door, trembling with excitement. He knocked.

'Yes, sir.'

She was sitting in her armchair, stitching the hem of an apron. The television set had been turned off.

'You were waiting for me, weren't you?'

'No, sir. Would you be wanting dinner, sir?'

'You should know I don't want dinner. I thought knowing things like that was one of your specialities.'

She bent to her sewing.

'Mrs Leahy, I want to ask you something. What if I fired you tonight? You'd never see the look, would you?'

'I suppose not, sir.'

'Then you'd never know if you'd been right. I mean supposing you never saw my death in the paper. You wouldn't know, would you?'

She bit the edge of her thread.

'Well, answer me.'

'Yes, sir, I'd know.'

'Look at me!' Even to himself, his voice sounded strange. 'You haven't looked at me since I came into the room.'

She folded the apron, placed it on the sewing-table and turned around. He went towards her, his face drained. As her eyes met his, he thought again of an animal. An animal does not think: it knows or it does not know. He sat on the edge of a worn sofa, facing her.

'Well?' His voice was hoarse.

'Well what, sir?'

'You know what. Am I still all right?'

'Yes, sir.'

'Mrs Leahy,' he said. 'You wouldn't lie to me, would you? I mean, you'd tell me if you saw it?'

'I suppose so, sir. I might be afraid to worry you, though.'

His hands gripped hers. 'No, no, I want to know. You must tell me. Promise me you'll tell me when the time comes?'

Tears, the unfamiliar tears of dependence, blurred his vision: made the room tremble. Gently, she nodded her head.

Aidan Mathews

Incident on the El Camino Real

JOSEPH SAW the woman from about two hundred yards. She had her thumb out and she was moving it quite lazily as if she had been there a long time. But it was still early morning, and people going to work had other things on their minds. The best time for hitching was in the evening when the homebound traffic was inching along slowly, and the people driving out of the city were starting to feel lonely and frightened again as they made their way back to their wives and children. Then it was nice to have company: college kids only had to look semi-normal to get a ride, and if a good-looking one just wiggled her butt a bit, she could cause a pile-up. At the start of the day, it was different: you were either bone-weary from the night before, or you were bent on making that day, that particular day, the one that would mark the change, the one that would bring about the difference, the one that would for ever divide the days of your life into those that came before and those that followed after. The last thing you wanted was to volley pleasantries with a perfect stranger as you shot on course and on target down the arrow-straight stretches of the Camino Real.

As it happened, Joseph had climbed between the sheets at a reasonable hour the night before; and he had long since given up on the early morning buzz. One day was much like another, and he liked it that way. He had been through the guess-what-tomorrow-might-bring phase, but that was sophomore territory. He was into a futility syndrome now. Life was a pain in the ass. You minimized the pain and you maximized the ass; that way, Tuesday passed into Wednesday, Wednesday into Thursday, with little comment and less crisis. Weekends, you partied. Also, Joseph had people in his life: he loved the woman he was living with, and he kind of liked her child too. He had never known what it was to have a kid brother. Now he could talk to Benjamin, and tell him stories about the Bible and space-wars, and promise to take him to Disneyland some day, and teach him the difference between coniferous and deciduous, and about whales, and Marconi, and why capital punishment is wrong.

'But why is it wrong?' Benjamin would say.

'Because,' Joseph would tell him. 'Anyhow, how would you like to have your head chopped off?'

'But they don't do that now. What they do is they fry you in the chair, or they inject you.'

'That's worse,' Joseph said. 'That's a perversion of medical progress.'

And they would go on and on.

Joseph checked the time. He had an hour before that Freshman Composition class. All he had to do was be there on time. No students were coming to see him, their papers were graded, he had the handouts done already. There might even be time to let a coffee get cold while he read the *Chronicle* in the University coffee-house. He liked that slow-start approach to the day. So he swung over to the kerb, and pulled up. The woman ran the few feet to the car. Joseph only had seconds to realize that his first impressions had been overly negative: she was more than average, she was nice. Twenty-five, twenty-seven, good teeth, blondish, biggish boobs, cord trousers, boots. As she ducked her face down to the window, she held her hair back with her hand. He could see the slim tan-mark of a wrist-watch.

'Where to?' Joseph said.

'That depends,' said the woman, getting in.

Even before he had reached across her to close the door, the scent of whatever she was wearing filled the car.

To begin with, they talked shop.

'Do you go to school?' she said to Joseph.

'I used to go to school,' he said. 'Now I teach. I teach at a Jesuit place.'

'You're not a priest, are you?'

'No,' Joseph said. 'My father was a wealthy Jew from New York. He was a very lugubrious man.'

'Are you a wealthy Jew?' she asked.

'My finances are so-so,' he said. 'I am not neurotic about them.'

She was quiet for a few minutes. Joseph thought she might be nervous. She was holding her cotton handbag tightly, and staring out the window as if she had never seen such interesting store-fronts. Yet she was tapping her foot to the music on the radio. If she was agitated, she would hardly keep time to a pop song, let alone a pop song that was so mediocre. Joseph switched to another band, to a news update. Her foot kept tapping.

'Are you all right?' he said to her.

'Uh huh.'

She didn't have a gun in the bag, did she? Was she crazy? If it was a heist, she would surely team up with some other guy. She couldn't pull it off all by herself. Maybe she was just a bit odd, a bit uptight. Maybe she thought he was bizarre because he had used the word 'lugubrious'. Or perhaps she had personal problems. She hadn't just come from anywhere. She had come out of a situation, a background, a context.

'Lugubrious means kind of woeful, very down,' Joseph said.

She had made up her mind about something. She turned to look at him.

'Ever feel very horny in the morning?' she said to him. 'I mean, first thing in the morning, do you ever feel like pussy?'

'Don't talk like that,' Joseph said.

She was taken aback, baffled even.

'You mind me talking about sex?'

'The topic is fine with me,' said Joseph. 'I guess I'm a romantic about it. I don't much like dirty language. "Horny", and "pussy", and that stuff.'

The woman might not have anticipated this contingency, but she adapted to it, and coped with it. That was because she was flexible.

'When you wake up,' she said to him, 'and you're on your own, do you ever want to be with a woman, to share what you have to give with a woman, to have a relationship with her?'

'Why do you ask?'

'Because I could make you very happy for a few minutes, if you wished it. I could bring something special into your drive to work. I mean, it wouldn't delay your getting there on time. You wouldn't have to pull in, or go somewhere. You could just keep driving.'

Joseph looked at her critically. She seemed to be for real. She spoke nicely, her skin was clear, she dressed neatly, almost stylishly, and she smelled like a perfume counter. But what did that tell you? You could be beautiful, and still psychotic. Look at Catherine the Great, who copulated with stallions. Or you could be handsome, a fine-looking man, and be deranged. Look at the Joint Chiefs of Staff. There was one who might have been Rembrandt with less hair, and who liked nothing better than to throw out a strike-first line at Commencement Days. Colour schemes and well-shaped fingernails proved nothing. Inside a person's head was a mystery, a closed book.

'Are you a Fairy Godmother?' Joseph asked her. 'Or a professional?'

'I'm just an ordinary girl,' she said. 'This is a whole new thing for me.'

'Are you attracted to me? Is it my aftershave, or my mouthwash, or maybe the fact that I drive a European car?'

'Questions, questions,' she said. 'I can give you a handjob for twenty-five bucks. But please stop asking me questions.'

'I hate that word too. I hate that word "handjob".'

'I can satisfy your manhood. I can release the passion in your loins.'

'I prefer that,' he said. 'I like appropriate diction. It confers dignity on things.'

'Twenty dollars is not much. You would pay more for a parking violation. But thirty is thirty. So I thought twenty-five.'

'Twenty-five is all right,' Joseph said. He was beginning to feel comfortable with the situation. It was not everyday, of course, but it was not extraordinary either. What made it seem unusual was the hour of the day. It was still early. The guy in the next lane was shaving, one hand on the wheel, his neck arched high while he ran the battery razor up and down the sides of his Adam's apple. That was what made for the sense of unreality. If it was dark, you would not give it a second thought. After all, he had been relieved of his tensions in automobiles on maybe a half-dozen occasions. The cars had all been stationary at the time, it was true. Still, Joseph was a safe driver. In fact, he had the lowest premium of any thirty-year-old he knew. Anyhow, even with the risk, it would be a hell of a story.

'How are we off for time?' said the woman.

'We're fine for time,' he said. And he waited to see what she would do next. It crossed his mind that she might be a police officer, but it seemed unlikely. After all, the courts had ruled against that kind of harassment, and this was not New York. This was the Camino Real, the distance between A and B, the forty minutes of easy music and a sluggish stick shift between home, where the garden sprinklers made a sound like coffee-vending machines, and work, where the coffee-vending machines made a noise like garden sprinklers. This was not hallowed ground: it was safe ground. So Joseph waited. He could afford to.

At first, she rummaged in her handbag, taking out compacts and atomisers. Finally she found the packet she was looking for.

'I can't wear condoms,' Joseph said. 'They dishearten me. Anyhow, I live a perfectly above-suspicion, clean-living kind of life. Sometimes I think that I may marry the woman I am sharing everything with right now, and that would prove my altruism, because I have had quite a few not-nice-at-all experiences with ladies.'

The woman went through her bag again, and came up with a double-fold cotton diaper. Perhaps she had a baby, or perhaps she diapered clients. After all, the most colourful oddballs flourished along the Camino Real, not to mention the City. Joseph just wished that the woman would put away those awful prophylactics.

'Careful now,' he said to her as she tugged at his zip. 'Mind my hairs.'

'It's a very strong zip,' she said. 'Can you lift up off the seat a bit, so I can get your trousers down?'

Joseph tried this, but it was difficult. His foot sank a little hard against the pedal, and the car surged forward. The chap who was shaving looked annoyed; then his own car picked up speed, drew level, pulled ahead.

'This is ridiculous,' Joseph said. 'I can't drive with my trousers round my knees. I'll do it.'

He got his zip down, but he couldn't pull his briefs aside to free his penis. Why did he wear such tight underwear? Apart all together from that talk about cancer of the testis, it let you down so badly at moments like these. No wonder he was beginning to feel vulnerable.

'I know how,' said the woman, and she did too. Joseph winced a little as she worked him loose. While still an adolescent, he had had a traumatic encounter with a zip fastener. These things went deep.

'There now,' said the woman. 'Where have you been hiding?'

Joseph switched lanes. There was a Santrams bus coming

in fast behind him; he could do without a burst of bluecollar applause. All those people on buses ever did was look into cars in a bored, accusing manner. It would put anybody off.

'What do you call him?' the woman said.

'What do you mean "Call him"?'

'It, then. Most men have a name for it. Their own name.'

Certain things are sacred. Joseph was not about to make free with something as intimate as a name. Even the woman he lived with called him by his special word rarely.

'I'm not most men,' Joseph said. He said it nearly as well as Joseph Cotten had said it the night before, on that film he could not remember the title of. In fact, he thought he gave it an extra something, a frisson.

But the woman spread the diaper out on his lap, and touched him here and there, deftly.

'You can tell me,' she said.

'Excalibur,' he said.

'He looks his name,' she said. 'If I had to think of a name, that is the one I would think of.'

'It is from the Arthurian cycle,' said Joseph. 'From the King Arthur legends. It has nothing to do with guns.'

Already, in his heart of hearts, he was sorry he had told her. But it was too late now. Besides, there was a good chance she would forget. It was a long word. So Joseph closed his eyes as often as he could, when the road ahead was clear, and he thought about the second girl in the Dairy Produce advertisement that he had seen five times, spanking the dark girl with the little mole on her throat, who hardly ever said anything in class and always asked for an extension on her assignments.

The woman beside him kept on talking.

'Have you something you want to give me, Excalibur?' she said. 'I have the strangest feeling you want to give me something.'

Joseph checked his rear-view mirror. The bus was way behind him. Then he shut his eyes again. This time, he reversed the spanking scenario. Now he had the girl with the mole smacking the woman in the milk commercial. Actually, that was much nicer.

'What's happening?' he heard her say. 'What's happening?'

Joseph was feeling generous as he backed into his space in the faculty parking area.

'Would you like a cup of coffee?' he said to the woman. She had been quiet for a time, glancing out the side-window, her thumbs flicking open and snapping shut the catch of her handbag. It was strange how she moved from reserve to the other. She was a complete mystery to him. If he had met her at a function, he would probably have been attracted to her. At none of the parties he attended would she have seemed in any way out of place, a rank outsider. She would have fitted in more easily than some of his own colleagues, especially the guys from the Art Department, or the women in Linguistics.

'That would be nice,' she said.

Joseph wondered about the money. He suspected she would want it now. Over coffee and bagels it would be inappropriate to count out dollar bills. It might even draw attention to them. Better to pay her, and have done with it. Still, he waited. He hoped she might ask him for the twenty-five bucks. That would signal the close of business, the end of the contract. He would prefer her to say it, because that would identify her more clearly. As it was, she was beginning to seem remote, complex even. She had a faraway, very alert expression, which bothered him. It would be nicer if she was nonchalant, and bantered with him.

'What's your name?' she said to him.

'Jon,' he said. 'My parents say Jonathan, my friends say Jonnie.'

'Jonathan is nice,' she said.

'I can live without it,' Joseph said. 'I like Jon better.'

He liked the woman well enough, but you had to be

careful. Names were dynamite. Joseph was still a little unhappy that he had given away Excalibur. It was true that women could worm anything out of you. The Samson story said it all. Malory was full of it too.

'My name is Elinor,' said the woman.

Joseph thought that was most unlikely.

'I knew two Elinors, back east,' he said. 'Elinor is a neat name.'

They said nothing for a few minutes. Joseph could hear the hood ticking as it cooled, and the woman breathing through her nose. She had a slight sinus problem.

'Were they like me?' she said finally.

'More or less,' Joseph said.

Joseph's mistake was to offer her food as well. Still, it was typical of him: he was basically good-natured. She chose a portion of taramasalata in a ramekin dish, and some ripe Dolcelatte from the cheeseboard. These things were not inexpensive. He was tempted to take it out of her twenty-five. The taramasalata on its own was four dollars, almost twice the cost of the vegetable rissole he had pointed out to her.

'If you want to eat the taramasalata out of the ramekin, you have to pay ten dollars indemnity,' the assistant at the check-out said to Elinor. Joseph made her go back, and scoop the salad into a styrofoam bowl.

'There is a notice to that effect,' said the assistant.

'I know,' Joseph said. 'It's been a strange morning.'

The woman who called herself Elinor reappeared at his side. Joseph checked his watch against the clock over the check-out. He had fifteen minutes.

'Ramekin is a nice word,' the woman said. 'That's two new words inside an hour.'

It vexed him that she was still holding on to that private pet-name. As an endearment, it would be finito if she uttered it again.

'Yes?' he said.

'Ramekin,' she said. 'And before that, lugubrious.'

That was the topic he settled on, to steer him over the fifteen minutes. Words, and what happens to them. Actually, it was Joseph's territory. Besides, it was a warm-up exercise, a work-out before class. He was going to talk about meaning, and then hand back their assignments. He might as well start now.

'You were saying you like "lugubrious",' he said.

She talked through the taramasalata.

'Me, I love words too,' Joseph said. 'I look around, and I see the saddest things happening to them. Once you created the cosmos, now you create a hairstyle. To speculate was to think, to wonder, to live the life of the mind, to mind the life of the mind.'

Joseph thought that was rather good.

'Uh huh,' she said, through the taramasalata.

'Now it's to buy real estate, or to fool around with venture capital. The same thing happened to "rationalize". I mean, just look at it. To reason, to order the world in a scientific manner. Now they use it to lay off people.'

'It's terrible,' she said.

'I hate to see language being prostituted,' Joseph said.

As he said this, a young girl approached the table. She would have to be the dark one with the little mole on her throat; and she was.

'Joseph,' she said. 'I wanted to catch you before class. I need an extension.'

'We'll talk later,' he said.

When she moved on, the woman who called herself Elinor looked at him. She had really demolished that taramasalata.

'Joseph?' she said.

'I am Joseph here,' he said. 'In my other job, I am Jon. I moonlight. My tax is very convoluted. Joseph is my second name.'

'That's strange,' she said. 'My second name is Elinor. We seem to like second names, the two of us. We share a lot.'

'You want us to be on first-name terms?' said Joseph.

'No,' she said. 'I've known you as Jon for so long, I couldn't begin to think of you as Joe. Joey perhaps, or Little Joe. Maybe even Jo-Jo.'

Joseph was at a loss what to say. Even if she was not a hooker, she could hardly have a sense of irony. People with a sense of irony did not go around the place, relieving other people of their tensions. More likely she was being nice, and grateful for the taramasalata. When you thought about it, she could only be dull average at best.

'I must go now,' he said. He opened his wallet, and counted out thirty dollars in six five-dollar bills. Back home, he could say it had been stolen.

'You're a nice person,' he said. 'The extra five is to say that.'

'You go,' she said. 'I have to finish my cheese.'

'Couldn't you take it with you?'

'I want to wash up after my cheese,' she said. 'I can't hitch a ride back to where you picked me up, smelling of cheese and salad.'

That floored him. The idea had never entered his head. Obviously, he was not dumbfounded. Nowadays, people tend not to be. Surprise is very uncommon. Still, he was taken aback. If necessary, the class could wait a few minutes.

'Are you going to go through this whole routine again?' he said.

'What did you think? Did you think I was going to ride a bus?'

'But how can you do that? How can you do it again? A second time?'

'Third,' she said.

'I find this revolting. I am not highly strung, but I find this too much.'

'You know any other way to raise four hundred dollars by six o'clock tonight?'

'You need four hundred dollars by six?'

'I need three hundred twenty dollars,' she said.

Joseph had not forgotten his simple arithmetic.

'You got fifty dollars from some guy?'

'I got fifty dollars from a guy with a button-down shirt and a pearl necktie pin.'

Simple arithmetic did not, however, extend into fractions.

'How often can you do this in a day?' Joseph asked her.

'As often as I meet people like you,' she said. 'Are there many people like you?'

'After I buy you breakfast, you ridicule me,' he said. 'After I buy you taramasalata at four dollars.'

He could not endure her now. He stood up and strode off. The whole affair had been a mistake: picking her up, telling about Excalibur, the line about Jon, the salad and cheese, the extra five bucks. He had been born yesterday. He would never learn sense. If you were kind, if you opened up to other people, they would only manipulate and exploit you. Then they would add insult to injury by abusing you to your face. He should have thrown her out of the car as soon as she had said 'That depends'. To think that she had just climbed out of another car. That was the most sordid part.

At the swing-door of the coffee house, he looked back briefly. She was sitting over her Dolcelatte, holding her head with both hands as if it had broken off and she was waiting, trying not to move, until the glue hardened.

All the way home in the car, Joseph thought about her. What kind of a person could spend her day driving up and down the Camino Real, performing sexual acts with complete strangers? She must have been very crazy. She may even have been psychotic. If he read in the morning paper about some poor guy who had been stabbed a billion times, he would know where to point the finger. It was only a matter of time before she showed herself in her true colours. The way she disguised herself was effective, but she could not keep it up forever. Neat clothes and clear skin might deceive for a time; sooner or later, her fidgeting would give her away. He could properly be thankful that she had not been violent in the car. Even allowing for his superior strength as a male, she might have caused a pile-up in the few seconds of confused tussling while he sought to restrain her. These were not pleasant thoughts, but they had to be faced.

Joseph stopped at the only florist's which was still open.

'Something really nice,' he said to the man in the store. 'Up to thirty dollars.'

'For thirty dollars,' the man said, 'we can do something very special.'

There was another possibility. It too had to be confronted. She might attempt to blackmail him. She knew his first name, she knew where he worked, she had probably made a note of the car registration. If she wanted to, she could find out where he lived.

'These are not honeysuckle,' the man said, 'but you would have to be in the business to tell the difference.'

She could not have spread infection. She had only touched him with her hands, not with her mouth. But what if the other guy had been dirty, and had left some germs on her fingers or under her nails? How long could germs live in the light? These days, you heard the most horrific stories about diseases. To listen to them would put you off your food. When he got home, he would wash in very hot water. If necessary, he would almost scald himself. Somewhere in the house was a new bottle of hydrogen peroxide.

'Put in more of the blue ones,' he said to the florist.

One explanation covered everything. She was a drug addict. How else could you explain her having to make up four hundred dollars by six o'clock? True, she didn't look like a junkie, but things were so deceptive in this world. She might be as full of puncture marks as a pin-cushion. He hadn't seen very much of her, and she was hardly going to shoot herself in the face or hands. Four hundred bucks would probably supply the fix she needed.

'More of the pink too,' Joseph decided.

'You don't want your colours to clash,' said the florist. 'You want them to co-operate.'

Finally, it was done. It was a lovely arrangement.

'Whoever the significant other in your life may be,' the man said, 'he or she is going to love this.'

'She deserves them,' Joseph said, accenting the pronoun.

'A woman in a thousand,' the florist said.

'A woman in a thousand,' Joseph agreed.

When Joseph got home again, it was already dark. He parked in the car-port and sat a while at the wheel, feeling the wet from the flower arrangement soak into his trouser-leg. He wished he had stayed in bed that morning. He wished he had woken with a strep throat or a sore tooth, and turned away from the window back into the warm duvet. And he wished he had washed his mouth or maybe eaten a Granny Smith and then made love to the woman he was living with, after Benjamin had gone out the pantry door to start his paper round. Because he was feeling strange now, like the way he did when he read the Psalms or the small side-columns in the Sunday papers about river blindness in African infants. He was feeling lost and found; he was feeling sad and singular; he was feeling shit.

He walked across the drive under starlight. Snails were mating on the tarmacadam under the porch-front canopy. Joseph picked his route delicately among their soapy huddles, but he couldn't avoid standing on one, and then of course he had to mash it into the pavement with the heel of his boot to make quite certain it was really dead and not left suffering. He had a conscience about these things, and about the eco-system too. He was not all bad.

Inside the house, Benjamin was watching the television. He was in the lotus position, and didn't look round. Only when Joseph plonked his briefcase on the loose floorboard and made the picture snow, did the boy turn toward him.

'They bar-be-cued that black guy in Miami this morning,' Benjamin announced. 'You know, the one that made the woman eat the parish letter.'

Joseph was not listening. When had he last brought her flowers, and would she suspect him for doing so? He had heard about that happening to a guy in Modern Languages. He had arrived home with fresh flowers, and his wife had only said: 'So, who's the competition?' She had been right too, but that was not the point. The point was that the woman he lived with had not been given flowers since the time she had terrible PMT, and threw the television out the bedroom window. Mind you, it was only a portable. And that was at least six months ago.

Anyhow, he gave them to her. She was in the kitchen, steeping a mohair cardigan. Her hands were red from the hairs, but that always happened. It was no use getting uptight about it. At least she liked the arrangement.

'Are these from Excalibur?' she asked him softly.

'Sort of,' Joseph told her. Why did she have to go and bring up Excalibur? There was no need.

The woman he was living with put her arms around him.

'I'll sit on your face tonight,' she said. 'As a special treat.'

Joseph tried to smile the way he was supposed to. It was difficult.

'I'll be back in a second,' he said. 'A call of nature.'

He went into the bedroom and lay on the bed. Then he got up and opened the mirrored doors of the double wardrobe. He opened them as wide as they would go, and held them back with shoes and a hatbox. He needed to lie down, but he could not bear to look at his own face while he did so.

PART SIX

Anne Enright

Men and Angels

THE WATCHMAKER and his wife live in a small town in Germany and his eyesight is failing.

He is the inventor of the device which is called after him, namely 'Huygens' Endless Chain', a system that allows the clock to keep ticking while it is being wound. It is not perfect, it does not work if the clock is striking. Even so Huygens is proud of his invention because in clocks all over Europe there is one small part that bears his name.

Two pulleys are looped by a continuous chain, on which are hung a large and a small weight. The clock is wound by pulling on the small weight, which causes the large weight to rise. Over the hours, the slow pull of its descent makes the clock tick.

The small weight is sometimes replaced by a ring, after the fact that when Huygens was building the original model, his impatience caused him to borrow his wife's wedding ring to hang on the chain. The ring provided a perfect balance, and Huygens left it where it was. He placed the whole mechanism under a glass bell and put it on the mantelpiece, where his wife could see the ring slowly rise with the passing of the hours, and fall again when the clock was wound.

Despite the poetry of the ring's motion, and despite the patent which kept them all in food and clothes, Huygens' wife could not rid herself of the shame she felt for her bare hands. She sent the maid on errands that were more suited to the woman of the house, and became autocratic in the face of the girl's growing pride. Her dress became more sombre and matronly, and she carried a bunch of keys at her belt.

Every night Huygens lifted the glass bell, tugged his wife's ring down as far as it would go, and left the clock ticking over the hearth.

Like Eve, Huygens' wife had been warned. The ring must not be pulled when the clock was striking the hour. At best, this would destroy the clock's chimes, at worst, she would break the endless chain and the weights would fall.

Her mistake came five years on, one night when Huygens was away. At least she said that he was away, even though he was at that moment taking off his boots in the hall. He was welcomed at the door by the clock striking midnight, a sound that always filled him with both love and pride. It struck five times and stopped.

There are many reasons why Huygens' wife pulled the ring at that moment. He put the action down to womanly foolishness. She was pregnant at the time and her mind was not entirely her own. It was because of her state and the tears that she shed that he left the ruined clock as it was and the remaining months of her lying-in were marked by the silence of the hours.

The boy was born and Huygens' wife lay with childbed fever. In her delirium (it was still a time when women became delirious) she said only one thing, over and over again: 'I will die. He will die. I will die. He will die. I will die FIRST,' like a child picking the petals off a daisy. There were always five petals, and Huygens, whose head was full of tickings, likened her chant to the striking of a clock.

(But before you get carried away, I repeat, there were many reasons why Huygens' wife slipped her finger into the ring and pulled the chain.)

When his first wife died, Sir David Brewster was to be found at the desk in his study, looking out at the snow. In front of him was a piece of paper, very white, which was addressed to her father. On it was written 'Her brief life was one of light and grace. She shone a kindly radiance on all those who knew her, or sought her help. Our angel is dead. We are left in darkness once more.'

In Sir David's hand was a dull crystal which he held between his eye and the flaring light of the snow. As evening fell, the fire behind him and his own shape were reflected on the window, a fact which Sir David could not see, until he let the lens fall and put his head into his hands.

There was more than glass between the fire, Sir David and the snow outside.

There was a crystalline, easily cleavable and non-lustrous mineral called Iceland spar between the fire, Sir David and the snow, which made light simple. It was Sir David's life's work to bend and polarize light and he was very good at it. Hence the lack of reflection in his windows and the flat, non-effulgent white of the ground outside.

Of his wife, we know very little. She was called MacPherson and was the daughter of a famous (in his day) literary fraud. MacPherson senior was the 'translator' of the verse of Ossian, son of Fingal, a third-century Scottish bard – who existed only because the age had found it necessary to invent him. Ossian moped up and down the highlands, kilt ahoy, sporran and dirk swinging poetically, while MacPherson read passages of the Bible to his mother in front of the fire. MacPherson was later to gain a seat in the House of Commons.

All the same, his family must have found sentiment a strain, in the face of the lies he propagated in the world. I have no reason to doubt that his daughters sat at his knee or playfully tweaked his moustaches, read Shakespeare at breakfast with the dirty bits taken out, and did excellent needlepoint, which they sold on the sly. The problem is not MacPherson and his lies, nor Brewster and his optics. The problem is that they touched a life without a name, on the very fringes of human endeavour. The problem is sentimental. Ms MacPherson was married to the man who invented the kaleidoscope.

Kal eid oscope: Something beautiful I see. This is the simplest and the most magical toy; made from a tube and two mirrors, some glass and coloured beads.

The *British Cyclopaedia* describes the invention in 1833. 'If any object, however ugly or irregular in itself, be placed (in it) ... every image of the object will coalesce into a form mathematically symmetrical and highly pleasing to the eye. If the object be put in motion, the combination of images will likewise be put in motion, and new forms, perfectly different, but equally symmetrical, will successively present themselves, sometimes vanishing in the centre, sometimes emerging from it, and sometimes playing around in double and opposite oscillations.'

The two mirrors in a kaleidoscope do not reflect each other to infinity. They are set at an angle, so that their reflections open out like a flower, meet at the bottom and overlap.

When she plays with it, her hand does not understand what her eye can see. It can not hold the secret size that the mirrors unfold.

She came down to London for the season and met a young man who told her the secrets of glass. The ballroom was glittering with the light of a chandelier that hung like a bunch of tears, dripping radiance over the dancers. She was, of course, beautiful, in this shattered light and her simple white dress.

He told her that glass was sand, melted in a white hot crucible: white sand, silver sand, pearl ash, powdered quartz. He mentioned glasswort, the plant from which potash is made; the red oxide of lead, the black oxide of manganese. He told her how arsenic is added to plate glass to restore its transparency, how a white poison made it clear.

Scientific conversation was of course fashionable at the time, and boredom polite, but David Brewster caught a spark in the young girl's eye that changed all these dull facts into the red-hot liquid of his heart.

He told her how glass must be cooled or it will explode at the slightest touch.

After their first meeting he sent her in a box set with velvet, Lacrymae Vitreae, or Prince Rupert's Drops: glass tears that have been dripped into water. In his note, he explained that the marvellous quality of these tears is that they withstand all kinds of force applied to the thick end, but burst into the finest dust if a fragment is broken from the thin end. He urged her to keep them safe.

Mr MacPherson's daughter and Dr (soon to be Sir) David Brewster were in love.

There is a difference between reflection and refraction, between bouncing light and bending it, between letting it loose and various, or twisting it and making it simple. As I mentioned before, Sir David's life's work was to make light simple, something he did for the glory of man and God. Despite the way her eyes sparkled when she smiled, and the molten state of his heart, Sir David's work was strenuous, simple and hard. He spent long hours computing angles, taking the rainbow apart.

Imagine the man of science and his young bride on their wedding night, as she sits in front of the mirror and combs her hair, with the light of candles playing in the shadows of her face. Perhaps there are two mirrors on the dressing table, and she is reflected twice. Perhaps it was not necessary for there to be two, in order for Sir David to sense, in or around that moment, the idea of the kaleidoscope; because in their marriage bed, new forms, perfectly different, but equally symmetrical, successively presented themselves, sometimes vanishing in the centre, sometimes emerging from it, and sometimes playing around in double and opposite oscillations.

(One of the most beautiful things about the kaleidoscope is, of course, that it is bigger on the inside. A simple trick which is done with mirrors.)

Perhaps because of the lives they led, these people had a peculiar fear of being buried alive. This resulted in a fashionable device which was rented out to the bereaved. A glass ball sat on the corpse's chest, and was connected, by a series of counterweights, pulleys and levers, to the air above. If the body started to breathe, the movement would set off the mechanism, and cause a white flag to be raised above the grave. White, being the colour of surrender, made it look as if death had laid siege, and failed.

Death laid early siege to the bed of Sir David Brewster and his wife. She was to die suitably; pale and wasted against the pillows, her translucent hand holding a handkerchief, spotted with blood. It was a time when people took a long time to die, especially the young.

It is difficult to say what broke her, a chance remark about the rainbow perhaps, when they were out for their daily walk, and he explained the importance of the angle of forty-two degrees. Or drinking a cup of warm milk with her father's book on her lap, and finding the skin in her mouth. Or looking in the mirror one day and licking it.

It was while she was dying that Sir David stumbled upon the kaleidoscope. He thought of her in the ballroom, when he first set eyes on her. He thought of her in front of the mirror. He built her a toy to make her smile in her last days.

When she plays with it, the iris of her eye twists and widens with delight.

Because of her horror of being buried alive, Sir David may have had his wife secretly cremated. From her bone-ash he caused to be blown a glass bowl with an opalescent white skin. In it he put the Lacrymae Vitreae, the glass tears that were his first gift. Because the simple fact was, that Sir David Brewster's wife was not happy. She had no reason to be.

Sir David was sitting in his study, with the fire dying in the grate, his lens of Iceland spar abandoned by his side. He was surprised to find that he had been crying, and he lifted his head slowly from his hands, to wipe away the tears. It was at that moment that he was visited by his wife's ghost, who was also weeping.

She stood between him, the window and the snow outside. She held her hands out to him and the image shifted as she tried to speak. He saw, in his panic, that she could not be seen in the glass, though he saw himself there. Nor was she visible in the mirror, much as the stories told. He noted vague shimmerings of colour at the edge of the shape that were truly 'spectral' in their nature, being arranged in bands. He also perceived, after she had gone, a vague smell of ginger in the room.

Sir David took this visitation as a promise and a sign. In the quiet of reflection, he regretted that he had not been able to view this spectral light through his polarizing lens. This oversight did not, however, stop him claiming the test, in a paper which he wrote on the subject. Sir David was not a dishonest man, nor was he cold. He considered it one of the most important lies of his life. It was an age full of ghosts as well as science, and the now forgotten paper was eagerly passed from hand to hand.

*

Ruth's mother was deaf. He mouth hung slightly ajar. When Ruth was small her mother would press her lips against her cheek and make a small, rude sound. She used all of her body when she spoke and her voice came from the wrong place. She taught Ruth sign language and how to read lips. As a child, Ruth dreamt about sound in shapes.

Sometimes her mother would listen to her through the table, with her face flat against the wood. She bought her a piano and listened to her play it through her hand. She could hear with any part of her body.

Of course she was a wonder child, clever and shy. Her own ears were tested and the doctor said 'That child could hear the grass grow Mrs Rooney.' Her mother didn't care. For all she knew, the grass was loud as trumpets.

Her mother told Ruth not to worry. She said that in her dreams she could hear everything. But Ruth's own dreams were silent. Perhaps that was the real difference between them.

When Ruth grew up she started to make shapes that were all about sound. She wove the notes of the scale in coloured strings. She turned duration into thickness and tone into shape. She overlapped the violins and the oboe and turned the roll of the drum into a wave.

It seemed to Ruth that the more beautiful a piece of music was, the more beautiful the shape it made. She was a successful sculptor, who brought all of her work home to her mother and said 'Dream about this, Ma. Beethoven's Ninth.'

Of course it worked both ways. She could work shapes back into the world of sound. She rotated objects on a computer grid and turned them into a score. This is the complicated sound of my mother sitting. This is the sound of her with her arm in the air. It played the Albert Hall. Her mother heard it all through the wood of her chair.

As far as people were concerned, friends and lovers and all the rest, she listened to them speak in different colours. She made them wonder whether their voices and their mouths were saying the same thing as their words, or something else. The whole message was suddenly complicated, involuntary and wise.

On the other hand, men never stayed with her for long. She caused the sound of their bodies to be played over the radio, which was, in its way, flattering. What they could not take was the fact that she never listened to a word they said. Words like: 'Did you break the clock?' 'Why did you put the mirror in the hot press?' 'Where is my shoe?'

'The rest is silence.'

When Ruth's mother was dying she said 'I will be able to hear in Heaven.' Unfortunately, Ruth knew that there was no Heaven. She closed her mother's eyes and her mouth and was overwhelmed by the fear that one day her world would be mute. She was not worried about going deaf. If she were deaf then she would be able to hear in her dreams. She was terrified that her shapes would lose their meaning, her grids their sense, her colours their public noise. When the body beside her was no longer singing, she thought, she might as well marry it, or die.

She really was a selfish bastard (as they say of men and angels).

Gerardine Meaney

Counterpoints

THE OLD man's voice rose and fell, rose again slow, melodious dripping of long ago and far from this into the cool, sour, clean place where he now sat, rocking, slow forth and back and back again. The old man's voice was hoarse, sometimes seeming stuck in an ever tightening chamber where sounds, when one is young, reverberate and flow. What the old man spoke, no one could know.

'Nonsense, yes.' It seemed to satisfy the plump physician. 'Totally withdrawn. It must have been precipitated by whatever stroke or accident brought him in here thirty years ago or so. Perhaps he was mad already.'

'Any family?'

'No one ever claimed him, poor old devil. He's no trouble at all, muttering away to himself. But there's nowhere to send him, you know, so he must stay with us.'

Giggling noises and a peal of little rasped-out chuckles followed the slight and somewhat disturbed young student and her instructor out of the ward.

Next day the old man seemed livelier. The laugh like little chiming bells greeted his observers. He babbled then, politely, with the air of a man returning to their puzzled or amused comments, urbane and civil comments of his own. When they stopped he stopped too. All looked at each other and the old man uttered a single sound as they turned and were gone.

All night the student tossed and wondered why that sound reverberated in her brain. It rang there, a call and a cipher. It sounded as the call to prayer might sound, high and alien and clear to one who has never slept before in the vicinity of a mosque.

Early, before the duty rounds, when the nurses were busy elsewhere, she went and stood before the old man. She said it. There now. He answered her. There could be no doubt, for he nodded and smiled with what seemed to her the gratitude of a fellow countryman met, lost and alone, among strangers. He spoke further, earnestly, and now it was her turn to smile and nod, grateful but helpless.

Later, on the rounds again, she asked her senior colleague if there was any possibility that the old man spoke a real but little-known language, perhaps one that had died out altogether. A frown of interest, then he dismissed it as not feasible, not now.

'A century ago, even half a century. Have you ever looked up old case histories for misdiagnosis on those grounds?'

Half a century ago. Not so long as that. She addressed the old man with a word for farewell she had learned as a child. He replied, adding a few courteous phrases beyond her repertoire.

'Don't mock the poor fellow.' The older doctor was stern, shocked.

'It's the old speech of my people, I'm not sure what people really.' Embarrassed, she was gazing beyond the old man. 'My grandparents remembered some stories. And some words. My grandmother taught me bits of the language, whatever she could remember. It is her language he is speaking.'

Not fifty, not even twenty years. 'And do you want an apple now? And how do you say "I want" in Granny's tongue?' Grandmother had coaxed and bribed and bullied what her daughter called 'that nonsense' into the child's head. The old woman regretted volubly that she had not known what she had to give her own children when she had remembered more.

'Are you sure?'

She had gone far away and the old man and the doctor were looking straight at her. Could she be sure after so many years from fables and childhood and even family? The woman who taught her this lost language was remembered only as a large lap that had smelt warm and nurturing, that had turned sour in that last year or so, dying.

'I can't be positive. I was only a toddler when my grandmother died. I haven't heard this dialect, or whatever it is, since then. Even she seemed to have only words and a few phrases.' She felt curiously bereft.

'Why didn't you tell me this the first day we came in here?' Had this stammering little know-all been making a fool of him? Making a fool of the poor old man too, pretending not to understand. Cruel.

'I didn't know. I told you I'm still not sure, but I thought I heard him bid us farewell. Yesterday. So this morning I greeted him – I can remember that much – and he understood and answered me.'

'You said the word first, gave him a cue, as you did just now?'

'Yes, yes, I suppose so.'

'Perhaps we had better talk this over.'

The voice rose and fell and fell again, dropped to a murmur, crooning and rasping, scrub – vicious and thorned – singing in the thrush's warble. The old patient's eyes were sympathetic and tolerant as a hand on her shoulder.

'Better jumping to conclusions than with no imagination in this game, after all.' No need for the senior man to be too hard on her. 'All young once and so on. Cramming for exams, are we?'

The old man breathed in and out; breathily he chirped her farewell.

When she said she wanted to research a paper on language loss, as he had suggested, the doctor took it, as she had intended, as a compliment. He had talked her out of that lost language nonsense, shown her the scientific basis. Couldn't remember suggesting a paper though.

'Trauma and loss of linguistic capacity,' he suggested now. 'Very good, very good. Plenty of material here, you know, plenty of case studies.'

She studied only one. He was surprised to see her back. Recording his old voice proved easy. He spoke ceaselessly, smiling at her, occasionally and incomprehensibly admonishing.

In the beginning he had babbled good-humouredly on. One day his voice rose, booming sonorous and solemn, washing the sterile ward with waves of sound. The old man had an innate grasp of acoustics, she had learned. He stopped himself now, forcibly, and looked at her. She had during the previous evening's 'research' recognized or seemed to recognize some handful of words. Using what she remembered and what he reminded her, she communicated haltingly with him, having recourse time and again to sign language. The old man appreciated her efforts, rewarding them with the song of his punctuated warbling.

Now she was missing some signal: he wanted something from her. She sat waiting and he sat opposite her, waiting also. *What* was still beyond her vocabulary. You want? She wasn't sure if she had said *you want* or *I want* or simply *want*. But relieved, delighted, he echoed her word and again began the long flow of his speech, ending not in sleep, as on other evenings, but interrupted when the night nurse asked her to leave.

On the following evening he was looking out for her, anxious. She was still setting up her recording equipment when he began, excitedly, impatient. She understood little. His tone, however, she recognized as different: gesturing, agitated at first, then slowing to a dirge-like strain, more dismal than she had heard it before. The pace speeded up a little, lilting along in a half-humorous, half-sad tone, his flow interrupted here and there by little intimate chuckling asides to her that ended in a sigh. Love. He was speaking of love, as the old speak of love to the young. Not rambling, not any longer. Or had he ever? She would have to listen again to the earlier tapes. Now, hour after hour, she heard the cadences, the rhythms and ornaments, the varying paces and tones of anger, adventure, danger, love and death. My old friend is a storyteller. He told and kept on telling until long after she should have left. A slow crescendo to the final coda and then the old man began to snore, grumbling through his nose. She called a nurse and left him sleeping in his chair.

Now when she arrived he awaited her word. Repeating it, he began his story. Using up her meagre store, she offered him words of his own, for he needed a start, a challenge. Perhaps this was some old storytelling game and he the champion. Whatever the word, the same themes, or rather the same tones and moods, shadows and light on the voice, recurred. He learned over the weeks to mould his art to the times of the hospital regimen. The flickering electronic numbers on the opposite wall were no match for his inventiveness. Mutating ever the sequence and particular quality of each of his timeless preoccupations, he cheated the timepiece that she had feared would come to measure the sensuous whisper of the grey and deathly skin still hugging its bones in the chair.

No repetition of her leading words was possible. She had once or twice attempted to offer a word used weeks before for a second tale and his reaction had been that of a man who has caught a dear friend cheating him at cards. He recoiled, he was silent; disappointed, he sulked. Presents or her faltering attempts at apology only insulted him further. Starved for her tale, her gift, she had learned to reproduce, slowly, sounds from her tapes, searching for the combination in which he would find sense and from which he could begin. Soon she could control this, choosing the potential words from moods in previous stories that matched her own moods. When he realized this he reached and put his hands on her head, as priests once conferred blessing.

She offered him one night a word, a sound from a mood that, unlike others, surfaced only occasionally and in what she recognized as the most demanding tales for the teller and for herself. It was a guess, chance; she had begun to attempt to isolate syllables from those words she was sure were words. These two 'syllables' seemed to recur, though never in immediate juxtaposition, in the mood that matched her own as she sought a tale from the old man and thought her training here was nearly over. She uttered two sounds that seemed in any case to overlap. He gasped or sighed, not in pain, and his eyes were unbearably steady on and in hers. She wouldn't move. Recollecting all of herself to the present, she concentrated on the sound she had made, trying to connect it with what his eyes, telling more than he had told in all these months, told now. He held her thus in his gaze and gazing into the word for only a moment, as long as she could bear it. Then he was content. He was content. He nodded, raised his hand and closed his eyes. The tale was over for tonight.

Next day the nurses told her he had died in the early morning. No pain, just exhausted and old. 'We all thought you were marvellous, giving him all that attention, all he wanted really.'

The old man's voice rose and fell, fell again, melodies dripping of long ago and far from this, dropping to a whisper filling her room in the night. His flowing lilt was interrupted as it commenced, a whirr as she rewound her recording to repeat itself.

She sat at a wide table, papers flying. She thought she had an alphabet now and the patterns of sound had wider patterns, not sentences perhaps. Sometimes it all broke down to lovers and dangers and death and the tales, it seemed, were telling themselves.

Sometimes she could distinguish no patterns, no figures, no words, not even individual sounds. Then there were two high, clear notes that seemed to overlap and a crooning, murmuring, rasping counterpoint.

Leland Bardwell

The Hairdresser

L ONG AGO they had painted the houses. Pale pastel shades – mauves, pinks, greys. The estate had expanded up Trevor's Hill, across the old sheep-field, curling back down like an anvil until it seemed the mountain had grown a second crust. Attempts to divert the streams had failed and water ran freely into the residents' gardens and rotted the foundations of the houses.

Paint cracked, window frames warped: there seemed no wisdom in the continuous building of new dwellings but after the last of the city clearances, the Local Authority brought out their trucks, their cranes, their earth-movers and packed them in the road that ran directly through the estate till it could run no more and ended, T-shaped beneath the higher slopes.

Electric wires, pylons blew down in the storms and were seldom repaired so the estate lay mostly in darkness during the winter. There were strange happenings behind those closed doors at night. Many of the middle-aged women, whose husbands had taken off or been gaoled, took in men – those who roamed the country homeless – with whom they shared their bed and welfare payments. Occasionally a daughter would return with a new brood. Those men came and went; domestic unease, lack of money, young children crowding and squabbling would drive them out after a few months.

The women did their best and it was not unusual to see a middle-aged woman perched on her roof, trying to pin over a piece of plastic or rope up a bit of guttering. Like many another family, Mona and her mother had one of the houses on the higher slopes. Victims of the worst winter weather, they spent hours, plastering, drying, mending window frames and replacing slates. With one difference, however; Mona was the only one in the estate who attended secondary school. A rather plain girl with dry ribbed hair and a boxy figure, she was something of a scholar. Her mother was a gaunt angular woman with fierce energy.

Unlike the other women she attracted a certain type of man, more chaotic, more unprincipled than the average. She responded passionately to these men and was thrown into despair when they left.

To Mona, her mother gave the recurring excuse that 'they were safer with a man about'. Mere excuse, of course, because the marauding gangs had 'cased' every house and in theirs there was little left to steal. To eke out their dole they had sold their furniture, their television, their kitchen appliances one by one. They now made do with the barest necessities. An old kitchen table, over which hung a thin plastic cloth, a few upright chairs, mattresses and one cupboard sufficed for their basic needs. Only Mona's room was spotless. Her fastidious nature forswore squalor, and to this room, as soon as she had cooked the dinner, she would retire, her lesson books spread before her, a stub of a candle lighting up the immediate circle on the floor and with her stiff hair tied back in a knot she would concentrate on her studies to the exclusion of all else.

For some weeks now a new man had established himself in their household. Although he combined all the complexities and evil ways of his forerunners he was as yet an unknown quantity to Mona. Her mother forever alert, listened to his speeches – he made speeches all day long claiming an intellectual monopoly on every subject. This irked Mona who had a fine mathematical brain and disagreed with many of his illogical conclusions. However, for the sake of her mother she held her peace.

Today she had decided to scrub the lino. As she scraped

and picked between the cracks she could feel his gaze upon her as if it were a physical thing. She rose in confusion; there were rings on her knees from the muddy floor.

'Why don't you kneel on something?' he barked, looking down at her legs as if she were a yearling in the ring.

'Ah shut up,' she said; for once she lost her temper. 'If you'd shift your arse I'd get on more quickly.' He gazed at her angrily, his eyes still as glass; they were his most unsettling feature.

All this time her mother was sitting on the edge of her chair watching him, with the air of one who waits for her child to take its first few steps; she said nothing nervously lighting one cigarette from the tip of another.

Mona went to the sink to wring out her cloth: she looked round at him, sizing him up once again. There was madness there, she felt, in this posture, his teeth grinding, the occasional bouts of pacing; he was leaning over, elbows on knees, his stained overcoat folded back like the open page of an almanac. His hands were gyrating as though he were shuffling a pack of cards. He had strangely delicate hands, his fingers tapered into neat girlish nails yet he had huge tense shoulders. His face was stippled and pocked from long hours spent in the open. Yes, this man was not like the others – ruthless, fighting for survival – there were qualities within him, seams of impatience and rage that were beyond his control. Mona knew it was dangerous to answer him back; she wished she had held her tongue. Yet far from antagonizing her mother, his rages seemed to make her more submissive, more caressing, more loving than ever. Or perhaps she, too, sensed danger; Mona wasn't sure.

When they were alone she would try to warn her mother but the latter would touch her own brow with the hand of a lover and with her other hand take Mona's and say, 'Don't worry, darling. It will all be over one day.'

Winter crawled. Snow came, dried off and fell again. It was no longer possible to patch the roof so they caught the water in buckets placed under the worst of the leaks. On a sleety February afternoon, Mona returning from her long journey back from school – it was dole day and they had bought cider – she found them both slightly drunk. They sat by the fire – one more chair had been burnt – and there was a glow of frivolity between them. But on her entry he addressed her rudely, finishing up by shaking his fists and saying 'You're a nasty piece of work.' Mona snapped back, 'You're a fucking creep, yourself.'

There was silence. The skin on her mother's cheeks darkened with fear but she rose – an animal hoisted from its lair – and slowly picked up the flagon. He automatically held out his glass but she ignored it and poured the cider into his eyes.

The kitchen exploded. Chairs, table, went flying, and they were both on the floor, his fingers, those mobile fingers, closing, closing on her mother's throat and Mona's screaming, kicking him from behind till he fell back howling in his effort to wipe his eyes with his sleeve. In a second her mother was up, apologizing, begging for 'another chance'. But he was up too and heading for the door, his large frame bent like a sickle, his arms held stiffly from his body, he banged out of the house. The stricken women stood face to face as though waiting for a message that would never come. But her mother was already straining to go after him.

'Let him, mammy, let him go, for God's sake,' Mona grasped the wool of her mother's jersey.

'No, no, I must save him. Save him from the police,' and she slipped out of her jumper like a snake shedding its skin and she, too, ran out of the house.

The cold mountain air crept into the hall; gusts ran under the mat and up her legs as she shouldered shut the door. She stood for a while, knowing now that her life was beyond the ken of the two people out there. Who was she now? Mona the lucky one, she used to call herself, the only member of the family to forestall the fate that had swallowed up the rest of them. One brother killed in a hit-and-run, another in Mountjoy Gaol for armed robbery, a sister dead – from medical malpractice, another gone to England for an abortion who never returned. Mona the lucky one who had long ago made a pact with herself: to work and work, to use her ability to study, to use her interests that lay beyond this hinterland, so that one day, one far off day, she could take her mother and herself away from this no-man's territory where rats and dogs got a better living than they did. Along with this pact she'd promised herself that she would never allow her neat parts to be touched by the opposite sex, never succumb to the martyrdom of sexual love. In all the other houses, mile upon mile, children had given birth to children and were already grandmothers in their thirties. But she, Mona, treaded a different path. Or did she? Should she not just pack her bags, go, too, into the recondite night, join the packs of boys and girls, small criminals, who got by by 'doing cheques' or robbing the rich suburbs on the other side of the city.

She climbed the stair, the re-lit candle dripping hot wax over her hand. In her room, her books, her friends, all stacked neatly, were suddenly strangers, strangers like the two people who had fled into the unyielding darkness. She went on her knees, taking each book and fondling it. The ones she cared for most, those on quantitive or applied mathematics, she held longingly, opening them, smoothing out the pages. But it was no use; they denied the half of her that was her pride. She threw them from her, went to the window, hoping to see her mother returning alone. But the street was dark, the houses down the hill, derelict as an unused railway station. She left the window open and sank down on the bed.

A little while later she heard them; they came into the hall. They spoke in low tones; the fight had been patched up and Mona knew that once again she'd get up, shop, make the dinner and act as if nothing had happened.

In the shop she would spend the few coins that she had, money that she earned from her better off student friends, the ones she helped with their homework; most of her mother's dole went on cigarettes and drink and lasted for about a day. So it was up to her to keep them from the edge of starvation.

She skirted the heaps of rubble, piles of sand that had been there for years. She used her memory to avoid the worst of the puddles and potholes. Even so her shoes filled up with icy water. The journey to the shop usually took about twenty minutes – it was over a mile away – and as it was nearly six Mona began to run.

The fierce cold of that day was the one thing that struck in Mona's memory above all else. How dirty papers had flared up in front of her feet as she'd run the last few paces home; how the unending gale had pierced her chest and how she had clasped her inadequate coat collar round her chin. It had always been difficult to fit the yale into the keyhole and it seemed to take longer than usual as her white fingers grappled and twisted. But with the help of the wind the door blew in and a glass fell at the end of the passage – a glass of dead flowers – and water dripped quickly on to the floor. At first she had not seen her mother; the man had gone from the kitchen and Mona assumed they had gone upstairs to continue their moments of reparation.

So Mona had begun to unwrap the food before she saw the blood. In fact it was when she was about to throw the plastic wrapping into the rubbish bin that her eyes lit on the dark expanding pool. And before the horror had fully struck her her first thought had been that the body contains eight pints of blood – a gallon – and that this is what will now run over the floor, sink into the cracks of the lino, make everything black and slimy. Yes, he had slit her throat with the kitchen knife and left the body curled up half hidden by the piece of plastic cloth that hung down over the back of the table.

But the years had now passed. That murder had just become another legend in the estate, one of the many legends of killings and rapings. The football pitch, which had once been a place of recreation, had now become a graveyard for the people who died daily of diseases brought on by malnutrition and were bundled into the ground. There were thousands of dogs who crowded the 'funerals' and who, when night came dug up the corpses and ate them. Soon the people had ceased to care and left the bodies unburied for the scavengers. Everyone pretended they had not eaten human flesh.

And what of Mona?

After her mother's murder the madman had disappeared and was never found – no doubt he had holed up with some other lonely woman. Mona had left school and gone to work in a better off suburb as a hairdresser's assistant. She had continued to live in the same house which was now neat and tidy, the roof well patched and the gutters straightened. She had no friends and seldom went out after dark. But as the country fell further and further into the well of poverty, the rich, behind their gun-towers and barbed wire, grasping to themselves their utopian 'freedom', jobs in the better suburbs folded one by one, so for want of something to do, Mona took over the old hardware shop and turned it into an establishment of her own. Nobody could pay so she accepted anything they could offer from watercress, which still proliferated on the hills – to bits of food stolen from the itinerants, whose powers of survival were stronger than theirs.

People would do anything to get their hair fixed by Mona. It was the only entertainment left to them. Men, women and children flocked in happy to queue for hours, their absent expressions momentarily lit by narcissistic anticipation. Yes, there was nothing for them to do. The revolution that once people had hoped for had petered out in the nineties. The only way in which they might have expressed themselves would have been to fight the gangs of vigilantes who held the city in a grip of violence. But that would have meant a long trek into town and people were too underfed to face it. So Mona cut and dyed and permed from nine to six; the mathematician in her enjoyed the definition of a pleasant hairdo. She had grown gaunt, like her mother, and her strong brown eyes would survey her 'customers', assessing the sweep of their locks with the same fixed gaze as that which her mother had used to pin down her men-friends.

The smell from the football pitch would waft in while people admired their reflections in the mirror; at times the purple fissure and cracks enhanced or disguised their grey features, their hollow eye-sockets, their sagging skin.

But Mona didn't care about any of this but she cared, oh so deeply about her own expertise. If a person moved his head suddenly she'd get into a stifling rage. One day, she knew, she would kill one of her customers with the scissors, she would murder them as cold-bloodedly and as bloodily as her mother had been murdered. She'd clip them inch by inch, first the ears, then she'd shove the scissors up their nostrils and so on and so forth.

John Banville

from *Mefisto*

O LAMIA, MY DEAR, my darling, Lamia, my love. How diligent you were, how well you cared for me. I can see you still, your smooth skin of tenderest mauve, your insides white as white, your name in wonderfully clear, minute print, and that coy little letter R, enclosed in a ring, like a beauty spot on your glossy cheek. You melted under my tongue, you coiled yourself around my nerves. What would I have done without my Lamia, how would I have borne my season in hell? There were others that ministered to me, but none that gave such succour. Here is Oread, white nymph of forgetfulness, and Lemures, the deadeners, like little black beans, and skittish, yellow-hued Empusa, hobgoblin to the queen of ghosts. They are angels of a lesser order, but precious for all that.

I slept, it was a kind of sleep. Deep down, in the dark, an ember of awareness glowed and faded, glowed again. A word would enter, or a flash of light, and ramify for hours. I was calm, mostly, feeling nothing. Outside the dome of numbness in which I lay I sensed something waiting, like an animal waiting in the darkness. That was pain. Pain was the beast my angels kept at bay.

They came to me, my guardians, in endless file down their transparent ladder, into my arm, when at last I opened my eyes I saw the sun shining in the plastic bag above me, a ball of white fire streaming outwards in all directions. The room was white, a thick cream colour, really, but it seemed white to my eyes, so accustomed by now to black. Splinters of metallic light coruscated on walls and ceiling, like reflections from a glittering sea.

Water. The thought of water.

At first I was a mind only, spinning in the darkness like a dynamo. Then gradually the rest of me returned, rolling up its sleeves and spitting on its hands with the grim enthusiasm of a torturer. I watched the liquid in the plastic tube, a fat tear trembling on its steadily thinning stalk. Then the stalk snapped, the drop fell. Pain pounced.

How to describe it? Not to. I was Marsyas, lashed to my tree, the god busy about me with his knife, whistling through his teeth as he worked. I was alone, no one could help me. The difference, the strangeness. This was a place where I had never been before, which I had not known existed. It was inside me. I came back each time a little more enlightened. Now for the first time I saw the world around me radiant with pain, the glass in the window suffering the sun's harsh blade, the bed like a stricken ox kneeling on its stumps, that bag of lymph above me, dripping, dripping. The very air seemed to ache. And then the wasps dying, the moths fumbling at the window, the dog that howled for a whole night. I had never known, never dreamed. Never.

The loneliness. The being-beyond. Indescribable. Where I went, no one could follow. Yet someone managed to hold my hand. I clung to her, dangling above the abyss, burning.

Never known, never dreamed.

Never.

Scorched hands, scorched back, shins charred to the bone. Bald, of course. And my face. My face. A wad of livid dough, blotched and bubbled, with clown's nose, no chin, two watery little eyes peering out in disbelief. Yes, they let me see myself. That was later. They gave me a hand mirror, I wonder where it came from? It was round, with a pink plastic handle and a back in the fan shape of a sea shell. I don't think, no, I don't think it belonged to her, though it was she who put it into my swollen paw. When I had finished marvelling at my face I angled the glass downwards, and was dazzled by the glare of metal.

– Tinfoil, Dr Cranitch said. To prevent heat loss. A new technique.

But that was later again.

I liked the nights. The silence was different than by day, when it was not really silence, but suspension, as if things around me were holding their breath, appalled, speechless with wonder. At night a great nothingness blossomed like a flower. The room was faintly illumined. When I turned my head, when I was able to turn my head, I could see the open doorway, and then another room, or a corridor, in darkness, at the far end of which there was a desk, and someone sitting at it, dressed in white, who never moved, but kept her vigil all the long night long. A green-shaded lamp stood on the desk, throwing its rays downwards, only her shoulders and the sleeves of her white coat could be seen, and something around her neck that shone. A path of light lay along the polished floor, like a shimmer of moonlight on black water.

By day my door was kept shut. I strained to catch the vague hubbub from beyond it, voices and footsteps, the hum of machinery. There was a stairs nearby, and overhead people walked up and down. How busy they seemed! Once someone cried out, a long, desolate wail that rose up and up, like a red rocket, then wavered, and sank back slowly to a gurgle. That was the apogee of those days, the day of the scream. I was not alone.

I howled too, making someone else's day, no doubt, bringing him a little solace, a sense of companionship. It was clear then I would survive: if I could scream, I would live. She came running at once, on her rubber soles, and emptied an ampoule of double-strength Lamia into my dripfeed. It was night when I woke again. She was at her desk, as always, headless in the lamplight. I imagined it was always she. All hands were her hand, all voices her voice. It was a long time before I began to distinguish the others, to distinguish them from her, I mean. I took scant notice of them in themselves. It was she who had kept me alive. She held on to me, and would not let go her grasp, until at last I scrambled up, out of the pit.

Weeks, weeks. I could feel the summer passing by outside, the slow days falling, one by one. At evening the visitors came. I heard them traipsing along the corridors, their heavy, swinging tread. I thought of a religious procession. Sometimes I even caught a whiff of the flowers they brought. They did not stay long, and passed by again, with a lighter step. A few stuck it out until the bell went. Then the tea was brought around, the skivvies singing. A mutter from the chapel as the rosary was recited. I listened, hardly breathing. I thought of the others, for I knew there must be others, straining like me after these last sounds, these last few drops, dripping into the sand.

Now I could not sleep, I who had slept for so long. I built up walls of number, brick on brick, to keep the pain out. They all fell down. Equations broke in half, zeros gaped like holes. Always I was left amid rubble, facing into the dark.

Father Plomer visited me. I opened my eyes and there he was, sitting beside my bed, with his legs crossed under the shiny black skirts of his cassock and his large, pale, hairless hands clasped on his knee. He smiled at me, nodding encouragingly, as if he were a hypnotist, and I his subject, coming out of a trance. I could not see his eyes behind the flashing lenses of his spectacles. He leaned forward, with a confidential air, and spoke softly.

– And how are you, young man?

– I want to die, I said.

– What's that?

I tried again, getting my blubber lips around it.

– Die, I said, I want to die.

– Oh now. They tell me you're doing fine.

In sleep the sirens had sung to me, I could still hear their sweet song.

– Don't die, the priest said, and smiled blandly, gently wagging his head at me. Not a good idea.

The nurses were cheerful, cheerful and brisk, or else preoccupied. Not she. She moved with slow deliberation, saying little. Her hands were broad. She was young, quite young, or not old, at least. It was hard to tell. They laughed at her behind her back, called her a cow. She spoke to them quietly, in a stiff, formal tone, never looking at them directly. Yes, matron, they would say primly, their lips tightening. And she would turn away. Her face was covered with freckles, big coffee-coloured splashes, the back of her hands too. She wore a cross on a fine gold chain around her neck. It dangled above me the day she cut me out of my metal wrappings. It took a long time. She plied the scissors and then the swab, turn and turn about. Her face was impassive, fixed in concentration. I could hear no sound anywhere around us, as if the whole hospital had been emptied for the occasion. Full summer sunlight streamed in the window. A nickel dish glinted. The tinfoil crackled, a cocoon breaking open. I wept, I moaned, I pictured a ribbon of raw, red stuff winding endlessly out of my mouth. Dr Cranitch appeared above me, his hands in the pockets of his white coat.

– Well, he said. You've pulled through.

PART SEVEN

Dermot Healy

The Death of Matti Bonner

CATHERINE WAS thirteen the day that Matti hanged himself from a tree midway between the Catholic chapel and the Presbyterian church. She was first down the steps of the church to face his contorted visage.

At the beginning she did not realize what had happened.

He was like a climber reaching out for the next branch, or someone hiding up a tree, but then she saw that his two boots were resting on nothing. She had left the church because religious gatherings often made her sick. Now, filling her lungs with air, she saw Matti Bonner's face. She came forward a bit. The right hand, that was missing a middle finger, seemed to stir imperceptibly. Behind her an organ played and a choir was singing a hymn.

'Daddy!' she screamed.

In convulsions she ran back to the church.

'Daddy! Daddy!' she screamed, and men, embarrassed, stood up to let Jonathan Adams through to his daughter.

Jonathan Adams ordered everyone to remain where they were. Then, knowing Matti Bonner to have been a parishioner of St Mary's, he stepped quietly into the sour-cream smell of the Catholic chapel to tell those standing at the back what had happened. As the communicants were coming down the aisle a labourer cut the dead man down, Jonathan Adams received him and an on-duty RUC man laid him out on the ground.

By then the congregations of both churches had been

released, though each Sunday, morning service began in one when Mass in the other was nearly over. The two were timed so that the congregations would not meet, either going or returning. But this morning the service had ended abruptly when Catherine ran in; the Mass had faltered after communion. The parishioners gathered round the dead man, they studied the tree, the cut of the knot, and fended off certain political thoughts. The Presbyterians looked on remotely as the priest whispered into Matti's ear.

The Catholics appeared awed.

But for all there this death was uninspiring. It did not lead to awesome thoughts about the hereafter. It disputed grief. It seemed the work of a man intent on turning his face away from God.

It was the third suicide in two years. A young reservist had been washed up at Dernish Island on the Erne, a girl had cut her wrists in a shed. Both of these were Protestant deaths. The first brought on by manic depression, the second by domestic trouble. But this was the first time in recent history that a Catholic had taken his own life in that territory.

Matti Bonner's death gave the Loyalist village an insight into how vulnerable the enemy was.

The Presbyterian elders who were standing under the birch tree felt both alienated and aggrieved. His death had somehow exposed them. Even though this suicide should have been a reproach to the Catholics, they felt it was directed at them. It involved them all. There was a curse in what he'd done. It was a sign. He wanted to remain for ever in their minds.

And as for the Catholics, who moved round his death with an easy familiarity, they, at a further remove, felt let down. By his suicide he had gone over to the other side. He had smashed the idol of life itself. By his death he had turned informer. They were embarrassed by the obvious grief of Jonathan Adams, while they themselves were not so moved. Matti Bonner had even robbed them of their right to mourn.

That he should have hanged himself facing the Catholic chapel meant he was pointing the finger at them.

He was saying: In the chapel there is no peace.

And there were some who privately understood Matti Bonner's despair.

He had picked that spot and that time and those two churches, and said: *I've had enough – one day you go out alone and marry death.* Matti Bonner was not saying he died because of politics, or economics, or because of a broken heart. He was saying that God had failed him in his despair. And so he risked the concept of everlasting mercy. *I am not staying around,* said Matti Bonner from the tree, *I've had enough.*

So, because of neighbourliness, or secret approval of his sense of courage and drama, or out of plain curiosity to see whether the Catholics would bury him in consecrated ground since it was rumoured that his church might not, Matti Bonner had a big funeral. People of most beliefs appeared, at least to walk the short distance behind the hearse. It was a time when all sects could attend each others' funerals. Ecumenism was in the air, and the war had only just begun. Some of the more severe Presbyterians did disappear at some point on the street. They were still, for the moment, survivors. Others, the apologists, stood in the doorway of the chapel till the funeral Mass was over. Over the heads of the congregation they watched with fascination all that their forebears had forsworn take place on the altar. Lighted candles. Chalices. Beads in prayer. Instead of a supper that was a memorial, here was a feast that was a sacrifice. The ecumenical men looked on bemused at all the trappings, while others, like Jonathan Adams, watched with distaste the red gorge of the priest billow out like a frog's as he drank the wine. His fingers fumble with the wafer. How he dusted his hands and knelt with a rustle and turned and blessed the congregation.

The just shall live by faith alone, Jonathan Adams said to himself.

The congregation could feel the priest's embarrassment as he sprinkled holy water over the suicide and invited the soul to enter heaven. *An eternity of the tabor.* Four labouring men shouldered Matti high, and as the mourners walked behind, they looked at each other to see who was weakening. His death modified the Protestant strut, the Catholic lurch. The mourners did not grieve. Decency made it proper that they attend, not to grieve but to observe each other about their rituals. The warp of superstition attending this lone man into the grave. But then they were shocked to find that they were following the coffin of a man who by his death had belittled their existence. His suicide was preying on their minds.

And when they buried him, it was into a deep compartment of the mind that they put Matti Bonner, a place where the existence of God has never been fully resolved, nor their own lives really authenticated. His death triggered off in their pysches questions about the meaning of the word *everlasting*, the meaning of *despair*, and the meaning of the concept of *redemption*. There could be no uplift of the spirit in burying a man who had died by his own hand opposite two churches on Thanksgiving Day. Even the earth that was thrown on his coffin was somehow transparent, made of nothing. And the prayers for the dead seemed the final blasphemy.

Matti Bonner hanged himself from a birch that to the north commanded a view of a field where the Reverend Ian Paisley had come at midnight with torches and flares and flute bands to summon up votes for his entry into Stormont. Under it, Catholics usually stood smoking after Mass and watched the other sects file past. To the west was a small soccer pitch.

From a distance the tree looked like a man taking off his feathered hat with a flourish.

Some names had been cut into the bark with a penknife. The most famous of them now was Matti Bonner's own, undated, dark and deep.

The Irish for the townland was *Cul Fada*. The English was Cullada. In the fields behind the birch Matti Bonner used to turn hay for his Protestant neighbours when they went off to celebrate the twelfth of July. He would have known the birch from all sides. Now, when the Catholics passed the tree they made the sign of the cross, and when the Adams girls talked in their rooms they talked of Matti Bonner the bachelor, who used to walk the back garden of his house with his flies undone. They'd saunter up the road to stare at the tree where the bit of a rope without its noose still hung; they'd pick their way down to the untidy house and peer into the rooms with dizzy stomachs, see the porringers and cups, the milk pail by the door. They'd see the old black Ford tipped into a ditch, the red, upturned cart, the TV aerial cocked back at an angle after a severe gust in a storm, the Christmas cards still on the mantel and, despite the hostile Catholic spirit, they'd feel a twinge of sentiment. Then they came across the skull of a dead cow under the apple trees and thought it was his; they stood petrified in his galvanized shed in a fall of hail and knew God existed, and yet whispered hard, uncaring things.

They were trying to outwit their fear.

They could see his house from theirs, for theirs was next along, just a field away that he used to march with Reilly at his heels, and the house since his death seemed to have grown enormous. For now that he had died, his consciousness seemed to inhabit the place more fully. At night they could hear Matti whistling to his dog. From their upstairs bedroom they looked over towards his house and swore they saw a Sacred Heart lamp burning. Congealed blood began to drip from the heart of Christ in his kitchen. His house grew more barbaric and profane than when he'd been alive.

Because now, added to their disdain, came pity that turned to revulsion at the Catholic appetite for suffering.

And because of what she had seen – this Catholic nightmare – and for fear the face of the dead man would haunt her, Catherine was allowed to sleep next to Sara, and from Sara's window the girls now watched his house till the edge of the buildings gave off a blue haze. His sudden whistling could be heard through the trees. The poor man's scandalous image of Christ burned through the night like a

Christmas fairy. The hair stood on their heads. He was in Hell.

'Is he there for ever?' Catherine, terrified, ran in and asked her father.

Jonathan Adams considered the word that gave rise to that concept of everlasting, αιωϑιοσ, meaning eternal, age-long. Was the absolute eternity of evil affirmed? Was there a difference between everlasting and eternal? He sought a psalm that might alleviate Matti Bonner's suffering and calm his daughters' fears.

'For his anger endureth but a moment: in his favour is life: weeping may endure for a night, but joy cometh in the morning,' their father read from the book of Psalms.

And then he considered the words for hell. *Sheol*: the world beyond the grave. *Tartarus*: an intermediate state prior to judgment. *Hades*: the unseen world. And *Gehenna*, the word the Lord had used: the common sewer of a Jewish city where the corpses of the worst criminals were flung and fires lit to purify the contaminated air.

That was where Matti Bonner was, the girls decided as they stood by their window looking out into the darkness. And it was everlasting. Matti Bonner was in the Valley of Hinnom; his unburied corpse had been cast forth amid the worms and fires of the polluted valley. The stench of the dead reached them, and their cries, and then the yelps of a barking dog.

In time Matti Bonner's animals crossed the fields to the Adams' house.

His hens came. His white nanny-goat, langled as she was, came over the walls on her knees. Finally, came his dog. But the dog only came for food. Always he returned to his old house to search around. Lights would go on, and lights would go off. Catholic relations trooped through the rooms like grave robbers. At midnight the dog would whine till all hours. He startled the geese who began honking and screeching. Cocks were crowing the night through. Reilly tore away with his claws at Matti Bonner's kitchen door. 'Let me in!' he yelled, 'Let me in!' Then the seagulls chasing seed in the fields began barking like dogs. Reilly turned cross. The night was full of barking, followed by long mournful whining, till it felt as if only an animal could really mourn a human's passing.

If the girls went near the house during the day Reilly would turn on them, though he knew them both. He was cross, possessed, his spine drawn back like a bow. Yet when he came across to the Adams' he would straight away roll on his back for them, baring his loins and smiling. By night the dog became the curse of the countryside. The girls would call him from their window. 'Reilly,' they'd call. He'd stop a minute then carry on whining. The geese would screech. All manner of birds would wake. The night air filled with disturbance.

The girls would lie in Sara's bed listening to the dog and wondering at the nerve of a man who could hang himself opposite the two churches. They wondered how he felt as he walked to make his protest. The Protestant boys in the village said that when a man hangs himself his cock stands. They said that Matti Bonner, the Taig, had his trousers open at the flies the day he died facing the Catholic chapel.

That was what Sara wanted to know. Was it true? Had Catherine seen his mickey standing? Catherine said she thought she had seen something white like his belly. She could not be sure. But in time she came to believe she had. Yes, it was a stiff white cock. Not a married, fatherly cock, nestling quiet and brown on her father, but something foreign, something even independent of Matti Bonner. His cock took on a life of its own. In the dark she'd see it, the male penis that only stood when a man was hanged. First she'd see his face scowling and then his frail white member hanging, not standing, but childlike. Then, as the rope stiffened, so did his penis.

'Could you see any hair? He had red hair,' said Sara seriously.

'Yes,' she'd seen hair where his trousers had been torn by barbed wire. She saw the scratch marks on his skin. Their scandalous whispers grew enthralled by fear. *Outside were dogs*. Catherine's lies and Sara's imagination kept them hallucinating tiredly while they grew acquainted with Matti Bonner, the first real person they'd known to die. They grew to like their fear of this man as night fell. He had been such a man that if you looked away you would not remember him. He was a small house with poor walls, a name, a Catholic yard, a white bleating goat, a way of walking, a way of talking with bothered outbursts, a bachelor with a missing digit on the right hand. Someone they could look down upon. Now he was an immense frightening figure in a state of eerie erection whose pathetic dog, night after night, whinged on the step of his house.

One night, the girls not only saw lights in Matti Bonner's house, but furniture being hurled through the windows. The dog was frantic. Then, there was the sudden discharge of a shotgun, a terrifying shriek from Reilly, another shot and then silence. The countryside at last went quiet. The torment of his soul had suddenly ended.

The next day Jonathan Adams said: 'That's it. Tonight, Catherine, go back to your own room.'

'Daddy, I'm afeared.'

'And what's there to be afeared of?'

'Matti Bonner.'

'Go long.'

'I am.'

'That's enough out of ye, once is enough Catherine for me to tell ye. Matti is in heaven.'

'He's in hell.'

'Stop it, Catherine. Tonight you'll hike yourself back to your room.'

'But Daddy, he'll folly me.'

'Foll-ow!' the Sergeant said correcting her.

'Follow,' said Catherine, 'he'll *follow* me.'

'There's no one going to folly ye, daughter.' He took her by the hand and the two stepped briskly along. 'Once you start that kinda talk, you're asking for it. People should learn when wee to be alone.'

So Catherine went back to her room and strangely enough Matti Bonner did not visit her that night. It was the ghost of the dog haunted her and Sara, till eventually the dog backed off, as a dog will in terror from the unknown. Reilly was forgotten. Matti's house housed animals, his furniture sat in his nephew's garage. The gap leading to the subconscious was filled in, and finally the land was sold to a Free Presbyterian from Tyrone who scoured the walls and the floors clean of all signs of Catholic possession and painted on the gable, RIGHTEOUSNESS IS OF THE LORD.

Across the fields Matti Bonner now lay in consecrated ground.

But Catherine knew he was out there somewhere trying to get back in.

The first time she lay tight against Jack Ferris she remembered the Catholic bachelor silently hanging from the tree and again imagined his member standing softly up out of his navy-blue trousers. It was not true, it had never happened in reality. But it did happen in her dreams. The erect penis meant death by hanging. Often in years to come she would jump awake covered in sweat to recall that a second before she had been making love to a disembodied penis. It was the penis of someone who wasn't there. Only this male member jammed into her. She'd reach out to hold the person only to find him missing. The shock would bring her awake.

Then she'd realize with a terrible sense of unease that there had been no man there a few seconds before, only this disembodied penis making love to her. And her unease would be greater when she'd remember that the penis belonged to Matti Bonner. He, she'd realize in terror, had been the strange elusive man she had been reaching out to embrace and comfort. But in her dreams there was never anyone there but a nameless spirit in a state of arousal. In panic she'd flail out either side of her to touch him, and wake terrified to find no one, only this distant sexual joy receding fast from her scalded thighs. A phantom penis had been sent to pleasure her in her sleep from the world of the dead.

John MacKenna

Absent Children

THERE ARE times, when you come face to face with raw emotion, when you don't know what to say, so you say little or nothing. And there are other times when you're drawn into saying something that surprises you, leaves you in awe at your own daring.

It was like that with me. I was sitting in the yard of the house with the boy's mother. I knew her, knew her well. We'd met through all kinds of committees and things but we weren't on any kind of intimate level, we'd never had an intimate conversation in all our years. But I was sitting there with her, in the yard, two or three days after he'd been buried.

I was away when the accident happened, on a course, so when I got back and heard about it I called up to sympathize. I wasn't looking forward to it, I can tell you. But you have to get these things done. Anyway, we sat there, drinking tea, under a sunshade. The heat was just amazing. I had never experienced anything like it. I kept thinking about how difficult it must have been for the gravediggers with the ground so hard.

She was talking and talking about the little fellow and about how every time she stepped out in the street she imagined there were flecks of his blood in the ruts of the tar.

And she stopped talking for a moment and then she said: 'You've no idea what it's like, have you?'

I was about to say, no, I haven't, but something stopped me.

'I think I have,' I said.

She looked at me. She hadn't expected me to say that.

I started telling her a story that I hadn't thought about for years, a story about four boys setting out one winter evening, it must have been in the end of January. Four ten-year-olds tramping out the road from Castledermot, the three miles to Mullaghcreelan Hill to sledge down the slopes in the frozen snow.

It must have been after four when we left the village. Each of us had something to slide on. A sack, two sacks, a wooden board, a car bonnet.

We were singing Christmas carols, well out of season – is anything more unseasonal than a carol in January? I asked this woman, sitting in the eighty-degree heat.

We weren't the only ones walking. There were dozens of people coming and going and no cars on the frozen, snow-locked roads between the village and the hill.

It was a blue-white evening with an almost complete moon hanging up over Ballyvass bog. Every tree in Mullagh-creelan wood was clear in its own space. I had never seen the trees so individually set before.

We traipsed up the path through the trees, following the shouts that guided us to where the procession of sledges shot down the incline and into the flattened furze bushes at the base of the hill.

The summit was a milling collection of hats, scarves, laughing figures whose faces were dark in the shadow of the moon.

We joined the queue and took our turns at screaming out into the chilled air and shooting helplessly into the frozen furze. It was worth the wait and worth the three-mile walk.

The stream of voices crying in helpless laughter went on and on and as one group disappeared home for tea another replaced it.

I don't remember exactly what I was doing when it happened, the accident. I may have been twenty yards away, on the other side of the hill, and then everything seemed to go silent and I turned and saw the adult figures disappearing awkwardly now, all their grace at sliding gone, over the edge of the hill. The children stood on the brow, staring down. I ran across to join them. A huddle of coats stood at the bottom of the slippery run, out beyond the furze, where the snow gave way to the darkness of the evergreens. Somewhere between them a figure lay on the whiteness.

'She went out over the furze,' someone whispered, as if what the figure had done was deserving of awe.

We stood there for seven, ten, minutes and then one of the men at the foot of the hill took off his heavy overcoat and draped it across the dark figure on the ground and we knew, without being told, that the girl was dead.

I remember her name. Miriam Thompson.

Another of the men came up the hill and took the car bonnet we had and brought it down and lifted the girl's body onto it. He and two other men began to carry it down through the trees.

The four of us followed, I think only because the bonnet was ours and we were determined not to lose it.

The men carried it down and hoisted it over the stepping stones onto the road.

'No cars coming in this weather,' one of them said and they set off walking for Castledermot.

We followed behind, gradually closing in on them.

At one point, coming through Hallahoise, one of them slipped and the coat slid from the girl's face. It was perfectly white in the moon and there was one slight bruise on her temple.

'That couldn't have killed her,' I said.

'She broke her neck,' one of the men said.

I didn't understand what that meant but I nodded anyway.

The longer we walked the colder it got, and the colder it got inside me. I began to shiver and I wished the men would walk faster. Coming in to Castledermot we met a group coming out. They already knew about the accident, though how I never knew. One of them was her father. Miriam

Thompson's father. He took one corner of the bonnet, never lifted back the coat or anything, just took the corner, as if it had been left for him all those miles.

I was too numb to cry. I just let the procession drift away from me, ahead of me, and I turned at MacDonald's corner and walked home alone.

'You still have no idea what it's like,' the woman said.

I have, I have, I kept thinking. But I said nothing.

Mary Morrissy

Divided Attention

HE RANG FIRST three months ago – at three in the morning. The phone blundered into my fogged brain and I lay in bed not sure if the burring was in my ears or the vestige of a dream phone. But then, phones in dreams ring, don't they? They're usually the old, black, bakelite models – as if the fixtures of our dreams are awaiting modernization. It continued for several minutes, not a demon of sleep but a whimpering child waiting to be picked up. Alarmed, I padded to the kitchen. It could only be death at this hour, death or bad news, or ... you. I shook the thought away. I was no longer a woman waiting for the phone to ring. I lifted the receiver.

'Hello?'

Silence.

'Hello?' I heard my own puzzled tone echo back at me.

Still nothing.

'Hello?' Mild aggravation now – I know that tone from the receiving end. 'Who is this?'

The silence persisted. Why is it so disconcerting on the phone? Why does it yawn so? Minutes gape.

'Hello!'

There was a shifting sound. I got the impression of a large bulk wedged into a small space. Then an exerted breathing. It was laboured, distressed even. Was someone hurt, wounded in some way? I conjured up pictures of a street fight, or a mugging, a man stumbling into a phone box clutching a bloody side and dialling the first number that came into his head. Was it someone I knew? Victor, I thought.

A friend of mine, an asthmatic with a comic book name, prone to late night, melancholy drinking. You wouldn't know him. When he is distressed he makes this gnawing sound, a device he uses to reassure himself that he will draw the next lungful.

'Victor, is that you, Victor?'

The breathing intensified, louder now, more protesting.

'Are you all right, Victor? Are you hurt? What's wrong?'

There was a harrumphing noise like a horse snorting and the breathing shifted up a gear, quicker, more jagged. I heard in it a rising panic, an urgency that had not been there before. And then, only then, I realized. This was an obscene call. I slammed the receiver down. I was shaking. The phone sat there, implacable. Flat as a pancake, the little square buttons in their serried rows, the receiver safely in its snug depressions, the letter-box window stoutly declaring my number, the coy curl of its flex. How often had I sat staring at it, willing it to ring, cursing it for its refusal. But then it had been a co-conspirator, imbued with a delicious imminence as if it too was longing to hear from you. It was traitorous sometimes, but never *this*, never spiteful. Now it had invited a pervert into my home. How could I ever trust it again?

You would have said, change your number, that's what you would have said. I know exactly the tone you would use – emphatic, overlaid with a professional concern. You managed that combination well. A sort of alms-giving affection. Go ex-directory, you would have said, like me. What a relief, you once said, no more crank calls. Precisely! You didn't know I had your number, did you? I got it by stealth. Oh, I looked in the directory hoping to find your name there carelessly among imposters. There are five who share your name in the book, all of whom could have been you but none of them were. I pitied those who were not you, I pitied anyone who thought one of these frauds was you. But that was early on. It was only later that I pitied myself.

*

It started innocently, I swear. I had not intended ever to use your number. Having it alone was enough. I carried it around it my wallet, taking it out from time to time and contemplating it, wondering what it would be like for this particular conjunction of figures to be familiar – oh, let's not beat around the bush – to be *mine*. I wanted them to spell out home. It soothed me to have it; it was connection, that was all, just connection. And it served as my lucky charm, like a rabbit's foot, which had the power to conjure you up and granted me an ownership which you knew nothing about. As long as I had your number, I would be safe.

Celia told me to report the call.

'You must protect yourself,' she said. Her stout face flushed angrily, her perm bounced. 'The bastard!'

Much like what she said of you.

You once remarked that she had the sort of looks that would have won a bonny baby competition. Ruddy cheeks, plump arms, a stolid, ready smile, those curls. Can't you see her in bonnet and pantaloons, you said. Watch the birdie, Celia! I used to smile when I saw her and remembered that, a sly, complicitous smile, a smile for *you*. It was part of our language, the secret, mocking language of lovers. Now I look at Celia squarely in the face and think – she is here; you are not.

I didn't report it. I don't know why. Laziness, perhaps, embarrassment. But no, it was more than that. I was resisting this man, and his method of entry into my life. I didn't want him to force me into changing my number. I didn't want him to have the power to make me fear my own telephone. I didn't want the notion of him to make any difference to me – echoes, echoes. And anyway, I couldn't bring myself to describe the call. If I put it into words, it would sound flat and neutral. What was it but a series of silences punctuated by heaving and gasping? Who would understand the great gap between what it was and how it made me feel? Perhaps it *had* been Victor. He would ring soon and say shamefacedly, 'look, about the other night . . .'

But my biggest fear was that the policeman logging the call down in the large ledger of misdemeanours would look up at me and know that I too have been a caller in my time.

I rang your number first as an experiment, simply to see if I could. And I was curious too, about your other life. The Wife, the Two Daughters, the Baby. *She* answered.

'809682, hello?'

I heard the sun in her voice; it spoke to me of gaiety and ease. I saw a blonde woman, hair scraped back in a workaday pony-tail (that you might later loosen), a floral dress, bare legs and sandals. She was slightly out of breath as if she had run in from the garden. In the background a child was wailing. She said 'excuse me' and put her hand over the mouthpiece.

'Emily,' I heard her say, 'give Rachel the teddy. You must learn to share.'

'Hello?' she said again slightly crossly.

I put the phone down swiftly.

Of course, it didn't stop there. Curiosity knows no boundaries. The first call had rewarded me with your daughters' names – you had always referred to them as The Children, an anonymous troop of foot-soldiers. But then, I suppose, my name was never uttered in your household.

I picked times when I knew you wouldn't be there. You see, it was not you I wanted, but your world. Sometimes, Emily – or was it Rachel? – answered. They would deliver your number in a piping voice before the receiver was taken away. I got to know the sounds of your house. Your doorbell has chimes. Your hallway has no carpet – I have heard the tinny crash of toys falling on a hard surface. The television is in a room close to the phone. I have heard its muffled explosions, the clatter and boom of cartoons before your wife says: 'Emily, *please* shut the door.'

*

He rang again. Same time. He's a creature of habit. This time I was awake. I had come in from a party – yes, I'm getting out now, mixing, meeting people. I was making coffee. There was a vague drumming in my temples that would later become a hangover. I was still in my finery, or some of it. I had kicked off my shoes and was removing my earrings when the phone trilled. I lifted it and knew immediately it was him. The quality of *his* silence is different; it is the silence of ambush. This time I said nothing, remembering with shame my response the first time, my babbling concern for Victor which had exposed me as a stupid woman who didn't recognize an obscene call even in the middle of it. I thought too that if I said nothing, *he* would be forced to speak.

As time went by, I got more adventurous, or desperate. I rang once at three a.m. – the witching hour! Nothing malicious, I promise; I simply wanted to hear your voice. You answered almost immediately. There must be another phone by the bed. You must have been awake. Perhaps you had just made love to her and you were having a cigarette, resting the ashtray on your chest and blowing smoke-rings into the air, your arm lazily around her shoulder. *This*, I know.

'Hello?' you said.

'Larry,' I heard her whisper, 'who is it?'

Larry, she calls you Larry.

And then, there was another sound. The gurgling of a baby, the drowsy, drugged stirrings of a child suckling. The night feed.

'Don't know,' I heard you say thoughtfully.

Was that suspicion in your voice?

I imagined you withdrawing your arm from around her.

'Just a wrong number,' I heard you say before the line went dead.

*

528

They say that you should laugh at flashers. Cuts them down to size, literally. But with a caller, my caller, it was more difficult. He operated on my imagination. I wondered what he did in the phone box. (I always thought of him in a phone box though he could have been ringing from the comfort of his own home.) I imagined him fumbling with his fly as I answered, then rubbing himself, abandoning himself to his own grim joy while I listened. He wanted me – anyone – to listen. And what did he get out of it? Horror, fear, abuse maybe. Perhaps that's what drove him on. That was another thing; he never reached a climax. Maybe he couldn't and that was his problem. Or maybe my silence, my intent listening inhibited him.

I remember once hearing my mother make love. She had been out and came home late. I heard the scrape of the key in the lock and the sound of coarse whispering in the hall. The stairs creaked. The loose floorboard on the landing, which I knew how to avoid, groaned. My mother giggled. I imagined her leading someone by the hand, a blind man not familiar with the obstacles of our house – the low chest on the landing, the laundry basket that held the bathroom door ajar. He stumbled against something.

'Ssh,' she urged, 'the children!'

I lay, stiff with wakefulness, as they went into her room. A thin wall separated us. In the darkness I manufactured pictures. A skirmish in a cobbled square, her bed a high-sprung carriage rocked by a baying crowd. A cry! My mother's, sharp and high. Has someone hurled a stone? The crowd sets to with more vigour, heaving, pushing. She cries again but it is muffled as if she is being thrown against the coach's soft upholstery. I hear the tramp of boots on oily cobbles – left, right, left, right – the icy whip of bayonets, the vicious sheen of blades. A groan. He staggers; she cries out 'no!' I hammer with my fists against the wall. Stop, stop!

*

I rang the night of the party. New Year. Tradition, you said, we always have a crowd in. You looked at me ruefully.

'I'd much prefer to be with you, you know that.' You shrugged.

I called close to midnight. A guest answered. I felt safe to speak your name.

'Hold on,' she said gaily, 'I'll get Laurence. Laurence . . . it's for you.'

The receiver was put down. For several minutes I was a gatecrasher at your party. Oh, how festive it sounded! There was a noisy crescendo of conversation, the ring of laughter, a male voice above the din calling plaintively, 'the opener, has anyone seen the bottle opener?'

I saw plates of steaming food being handed across a crowded room, glasses foaming at the rim, streamers trailing from your hair.

'Hello!' you cried triumphantly – several drinks on. 'Excuse the noise. Party!'

I could have spoken then but I didn't. What would I have said? Happy New Year from a well-wisher? No, then you would have known the power I had over you, the power to betray *you*.

'Oops,' I heard a woman cry, 'careful!'

I didn't, of course, betray you. But knowing that I could changed things. I had to stop ringing for fear I would blurt it out – our secret. The snatched moments, the meetings in pubs, the subterfuge. Instead, I have to admit it, I went to your house. Just once. Once was enough.

It was at night. I took the train. I crossed the metal bridge at your station imagining your gaze on its familiar struts. The stationmaster snoozed in his booth, his chin resting on his soiled uniform. He didn't check my ticket. This made me feel invisible, convinced me that I wasn't really doing this – making a pilgrimage to the shrine of your home. You see, even at the height of what I felt for you I realized how foolish

I'd become. As I trod down the leafy passage leading from the station I heard the singing of the rails as another train approached, the train my sensible self would have boarded for the city. But it pulled away without her; there was no going back now. I picked my way through the quiet, darkening streets. It was late spring, fragrant after rain. Petals floated in the kerbside puddles. A fresh breeze soughed in the trees. I passed the lighted windows of other homes. Their warm, rosy rooms were on display. Sometimes I glimpsed a family tableau. A father in an armchair, one child on his lap, another perched on the armrest. A granny with a walking frame and sagging face – a stroke victim, I guessed – being hauled to her feet by a young woman plump with goodness. Two blonde girls sitting cross-legged on a window-seat plaiting one another's hair.

You live on a high, sloping avenue overlooking the bay. The lights of the city jostled on the skyline, beacons flooding the water with silent messages, mouthing like goldfish. I approached your house like a thief, with darting looks up and down the street. I cringed at the creak of the gate, slipping quickly around it to hide behind the large oak, the only tree in the garden. I leaned gratefully against its bark. There was a muddied bare patch at its base as if it had sheltered others before me and I knew I would find hearts and arrows carved on its trunk. Your house stands on its own. Pleasing, symmetrical, five windows around an arched doorway. It was ablaze with light. I must have stood there for hours growing chilled and stiff as the night closed in, the sky turning to indigo. The swift stealth of the moon threw the garden into relief.

I was rewarded – finally. The front door opened. An orange beam of light flooded down the path. I peered from my fronds of shadow. And then your voice.

'. . . and then it's straight to bed!'

You were holding the hand of a dark-haired child of about five. Rachel, or at least I decided it was Rachel.

'Amn't I a good girl, Daddy, amn't I?'

'Yes, of course you are.'

'Am I your favourite?'

A dog bounded down the garden. I froze. You never told me you had a dog. He frisked on the lawn and Rachel whooped delightedly.

'Look, Daddy, look at Brandy!' (Brandy – what a name for a dog. Why didn't you go the whole hog and call it Smirnoff?) Brandy trailed towards the gate.

'Brandy, Brandy,' you called.

I stiffened, fearing the dog would smell the stranger in your midst and would expose me, panting victoriously at my feet. I imagined you finding me there, cowering in the undergrowth. How could I explain? There was no explanation except that I wanted to see you. I held my breath, terrified. You were close now. I could smell you, but it seemed that I had stood there for so long that my odour of fear and longing had been taken up by the very veins of the leaves and belonged now to the garden itself. Rachel saved me.

'Daddy,' she wailed. 'Daddy, where are you? I can't see you.'

'It's all right, darling, I'm here.'

'Daddy?'

'It's okay.' You halted, a hair's breadth away. 'I'm still here.'

You turned away and walked into a sudden shaft of moonlight. Seeing you thus, I ached to be discovered, to share in the tenderness you saved for this little girl. The dog scampered up the path ahead of you. Rachel rushed out of the gloom and clung to your waist. You lifted her up and carried her inside drawing the train of light in after you. The door closed.

I was alone, shut out where I belonged, in the pit of the garden.

*

I've told all this to my caller. I've named him Larry in your honour. I've had to battle against his groaning and heaving but I've persisted. He keeps ringing so it must do something for him. It's therapy for me, you could say. Therapy, indeed! I can see you wrinkle your nose disdainfully. I needed to tell someone. I needed to tell *you* – but he's a good second best. I address the noisy static that is his frustration. I am happier that he is preoccupied – as you were in your way – and that he is not listening exclusively to me. I could not bear undivided attention.

Last week I threw your number away. The paper on which it was written was yellowed and grubby and ragged along the folds. The ink had almost faded away. I found it had lost its power. Does this mean I'm cured? Of you, perhaps.

Colum McCann

Through the Field

SEE, THE THING about it is, that klein grass was about going out to head. It was hot out there – like Kevin says it was hotter than a three-peckered goat – and I was keen on getting the whole dadgum job done as soon as possible, before we got ourselves a rain and lost all the nutrient to seed. I never seen a field look so good, a big sweep of grass almost four foot tall, running itself along down to the creekbed where Natalie found that rattler one time. When the sun fell on it right and the wind blew from up along the creek it looked like something out of a movie.

I wished I owned it, but we were renting it from Cunningham. It was going to take about three days, what with all the cutting, crimping and swathing. We'd have ourselves about forty, fifty round bales and we were going to make ourselves a nice little profit, I could tell. Kevin figured on maybe buying some wallpaper for his Natalie's bedroom – she's gone outgrown that pink kind – or maybe just him and Delicia having a little easier living, put their feet up some. I was wanting to get a valve job done on my pick-up.

We were only able to work the field at the weekend, Kevin and me, seeing as how we were working at the State School during the week. That Friday night Kevin was hollering to get the tractor filled with gas so we could get a start. He's a hard worker, Kevin is, with big thick arms. He's always itching to get going. You watch him, even at lunchtime, and his foot's tapping. I was ready too. I had my new boots that Ellie bought me at Reid's. We wanted to cut as much as we could, right up until it got dark. We were filling

the tractor right enough, but then we started getting into all
that stuff about Stephen Youngblood, the kid that murdered
that guy over near Nacadoches. Kevin, he got the chills when
I told him what that boy told me. He started shivering, Kevin
did, and he went on home to gather up mine and his family.
That night we hardly got nothing done.

I been doing the grounds maintenance at the State School for
best part of three years now, and in all that time I ain't never
seen a man want to know something so bad. Ferlinghetti, he
come down from the University of Texas, like they sometimes
do, for his work study. He got assigned the Juvenile Capital
Offenders. He wasn't young like the rest of the students. He
was about my age. He was kinda fat and one day I heard one
of the boys say that he was nothing but ten pounds of shit
wrapped in a five-pound bag. Which made me laugh. But he
wasn't *that* fat and his hair was going back, and he had these
blue eyes, blue as the blue you get on a winter's morning.
But, boy, could he get those kids to talk.

Truth be told, most staff at the State School don't much
like the social-work students. They come in, on their work
placement, thinking they can save the world. Ain't nobody
can save the world except maybe Jesus, but even Jesus must
have had a off-day when he made most of the kids at the
State School. And maybe when He made the place itself,
'cause it don't much look like a prison. It's like a complex
with a fence around it and cottages where the kids live. But
it's big and open, with grass and trees and flowers, which I
guess is good 'cause it gives me and Kevin a job. There ain't
no uniforms on the kids neither. The thing that shocks people
the most is that it don't shock them. It just looks ordinary.
The kids out there, walking along in double-file groups along
the sidewalk, with the security guards going around in vans
and station-wagons. And no guns, not a one.

Most those kids – even the ones in there for murder –
look like the sort of kids you see hanging out down by Sonic

or skateboarding outside the 7-Eleven. I guess Stephen Youngblood was just another one that got caught up in a mess and couldn't get out. But Ferlinghetti, he knew he was onto something big for him and the head-shrinking business.

Stephen was a small blond wiry kid with acne all over. You could drown this kid just by spitting on him. He had eyeglasses, but he kept them hid in his back pocket, embarrassed I guess. He walked all the time with his head down, like he's hiding some sort of sick animal in his pocket. You wouldn't believe that he done what he done. Most days him and Ferlinghetti would be out there, on the bench under the oak tree. Ferlinghetti'd be grilling him, staring right at him, his hands on his belly, nodding his head up and down. He looked like a buzzard on a branch looking for some dead meat for himself.

These kids supposed to get at least twenty-five minutes of counselling every week, but Ferlinghetti, damnit, he must have talked Stephen's ear off for at least a couple of hours each time.

I was out there the first time they talked, working on a flower bed near the park bench, and Stephen was giving him the normal stuff the kids give new counsellors. 'I took the life of William B. Harris on December 9th two years ago. I got a thirty-year determinate sentence.' They learn to say it that way in the Capital Offenders Group. After a while they just say it, not a hint of emotion, 'cause they said it hundreds of times.

Stephen was just flicking that blond hair away from his eyes, staring straight ahead when Ferlinghetti just, boom, changed the subject. Now, most of them counsellors they get all serious and sad-like, then say: 'Would you like to talk about it, Stephen?' And Stephen'd say, 'yeah, s'pose so', just 'cause he knows he'd be up the creek without a goddamn paddle if he says no. Then the counsellor would say: 'Well, Stephen, how do you *feel* about it?' And Stephen he'd say:

'Bad.' And on and on, until the counsellor goes off to write up his CF 114.

But not Ferlinghetti. Ferlinghetti just looks at him and nods. Then he starts talking about baseball, football, and heavy metal. I damn near shit myself laughing, kneeling down there with the trowel in my hand. I just stayed down there in that flower bed and listened and what they talked about was some drummer from England who done got his arm chopped off in a car accident. Then Ferlinghetti just said bye, walking off, his big ass waddling like a duck. And Stephen, he looked like he'd been slapped with a stick.

After that they started meeting all the time. And always on the concrete bench under the oak tree. Most of the other counsellors, they like to get one of the SSA's office or something, for some privacy, but not Ferlinghetti. Out in the open, that was him. And, man, did he get that kid to talk up a storm.

Me and Stephen, we worked together sometimes too. The kids, they get to do some of the flowers and the weedeating, depending on their level. Stephen was doing pretty good – he was a senior – and he got to work with me. There's about three hundred kids, maybe twenty capital offenders, and you hear it all. There's some kids in there did nothing more than piss on their Momma's toothbrush. But there's one who hung babies up by Christmas wrapper ribbons when a drug deal went wrong one time. Strangled them clean dead. Others who just blow their friends away for a vial of crack. One girl knifed her old man four hundred times.

Kevin, he's different than me. He's been working there twelve years, and he doesn't like to hear the stories no more. He says after a while you don't want to hear anything. You walk around with your hands over your ears and you mow the lawn with the noisiest goddamn lawnmowers you can find, so that your head gets to ringing and you can't even hear the bell sounding for lunch-time. Even when his Delicia comes along to pick him up at the front gates every day he just gets in the front of that station-wagon, she asks him what's going on, and he just says same ol' same ol' darling.

Me and Kevin planted the field in spring. Chuck Anderson lent us the tractor and the other equipment, and we ploughed it in late March, then sowed the klein grass the next day. That night, when we finished the sowing, we took ourselves a bottle and sat down at the edge of the creek and had ourselves a good time.

We took care of that field, Kevin and me, even though we didn't own it. Lord knows why we wanted to do it. One night we was just sitting around, shooting the shit, and both of us got to talking about ranching. See, last year there was a drought and some of the ranchers were low on hay for the cattle. We just wanted to start off with something small. Next year we're going to plant ourselves a proper crop. But Kevin has a friend works in the feed store down on Polk Street who said he could get us some free grass seed and we said okay. The field was five miles down the road, towards Manor, and it was laying idle. We called old man Cunningham and he laughed at first. Said he didn't have time for fooling around. But we got it, in the end, pretty darn cheap too.

At night we'd come home from the State School and take ourselves a few beers and sit down and watch the dadgum thing grow. Klein grass has a broad leaf and a narrow stem. It gets up to near four foot.

It was mighty nice out there. We'd sit on the back of my pick-up and watch those stars. Sometimes, when the sky was clear, Kevin would point out the satellites just moving on through the stars. Every now and then you'd hear a coyote howl. I wanted to shoot those critters – used be you could get some money for killing them – but Kevin said they never done anyone any harm. I suppose he's right. There's enough killing without having to start on the coyotes. When Kevin started in the State School, twelve years ago, there was hardly any kids who had done murder. Now they all over the place. He says there's so much killing going on that sometimes you just got to wonder what's happening.

Kevin brings little Natalie and Myron out to the field a lot. They play on the dirt road and sometimes climb trees. But it scared the living daylights out of Kevin one day when Natalie found that rattlesnake down in the creekbed. She was six then and damn nearly got bit. I leave my Robert at home. He's just four years old and don't need to be messing around with snakes.

That Friday night we were supposed to start cutting the field. The following day we was going to cut some more, then crimp it and lay it out in nice neat swaths. Then we was going to turn it so it dried evenly and, the next day, bale it. As it turned out we ended up being mighty late with the whole deal, seeing how Kevin took the story about Stephen. At first he wasn't listening much. I was just babbling on. But then, when I told him about what Stephen said, he stared at me, bug-eyed, like I'd told him the end of the world was coming.

Ferlinghetti got everything out of Stephen except why he gave himself up. I never seen anyone work a kid so hard for a tiny bit of information. I started to listen most days that I could, when they were there on the park bench. What I can't believe is how this kid just opened up to Ferlinghetti, telling him nearly every dang bit, but not the bit he wanted.

Once I seen Ferlinghetti hand him some Red Man, which is against the rules. It was raining pretty heavy but Ferlinghetti had himself an umbrella and they were huddled up pretty close on that bench. I was walking over to one of the cottages and I see him take the pack of Red Man out of his overcoat and give it to Stephen. But I do that too, sometimes. I have a can of Skoal and some kid's working with me, just dying for

a dip, you give him a pinch. It's only human. I suppose
Ferlinghetti knew he could get Stephen to talk if he gives him
some tobacco.

Stephen was fourteen at the time of the murder, living in
a trailer out near the Piney Woods. He'd been in one of them
chicken-eating Baptist homes for a few years, after some
petty thievery. But his Momma had taken him back. He'd
watch a lot of teevee and play with computer games. His
Momma was whoring around while his father was off out
west, working the oilfields. She was getting these pretty
regular visits from this Bill Harris guy who's married and
lives outside Nacadoches.

Nothing but this cheap plyboard in the rooms and Stephen, he can hear all of it, the grunting and moaning and
slapping and screaming. He gets mad and takes a baseball bat
to Harris who's laying in bed. He gets a couple of licks in,
but Harris ups and kicks Stephen in the mouth, sends him to
hospital, where he has to get eight stitches.

Stephen gets himself out of hospital and decides to take
a visit over to Harris' wife to tell her what her husband's at.
He gets on his ten-speed Huffy and rides over there. Except
he gets tired halfway and decides to steal himself a truck, one
of these TOYOTA pick-ups that just has YO on the back
tailgate. He speeds on over there. This woman, Mrs Harris,
or whatever her name is, takes Stephen into her trailer house.
She sits him down at the kitchen table.

Stephen tells Ferlinghetti that the weird thing is that this
Mrs Harris – she's a redhead – don't even flinch when she
finds out her husband's screwing around. She rises up from
the table, puts her arms around Stephen, then starts rubbing
her fingers up and down his chest, saying thank you thank
you for telling me. Opening the buttons and all. Working her
way down to his zipper. He's fourteen. Walks around all day
long with a boner anyway, let alone when some old lady is
doing him.

He's telling Ferlinghetti all this. That's what's killing me.

He's telling Ferlinghetti about how he's getting done and all, how she's leaving lipstick on Russell the Love Muscle, how she looks like Woody Woodpecker down there with the red hair. Ferlinghetti lets him say things like that. Both of them look very serious, out there on the park bench.

Anyway, Harris comes home early to his trailer house that afternoon. Stephen is there, lying in bed with his wife, like a regular soap opera. Harris picks the kid up out of the bed and slaps him around. Stephen gets beat up pretty bad again and leaves in the YO truck. When he comes back two hours later he's got a hunting rifle, a Marlin, that he's stolen from another pick-up. It was in the gun-rack. Parks the truck. Goes around the back. Stands up on the ball of the trailer which looks into the back bedroom. Harris is there boning his wife. Stephen, who's done himself some hunting before and says that he's an ace with the rifle on Nintendo, hits him straight in the forehead. Harris flops to the floor. Stephen opens the door of the trailer and tells Mrs Harris that she should get packed, that they're leaving. She's going plumb crazy. He wants her to go to Florida. He's seen Florida on the teevee.

Harris is still alive on the floor. Stephen wants Mrs Harris to say 'I love you, Stephen', in front of her old man. He's flipped out, Stephen has. She's bent over her husband, sobbing. Then Stephen shouts at her: 'Kiss me!' He's fourteen years old. She gets up and kisses him. Then he goes over to Harris, puts the gun down the man's throat, pulls the trigger and kills him. Then he shoots Harris twice more, in the heart. All the time Mrs Harris is just standing there, screaming.

You hear these stories all the time working at the State School. I suppose what makes them worse than those murders on the teevee is that they're true, but still you get pretty used to them after a while. Kevin normally don't even listen when I get to rambling about who done this and that and when. But what got to Kevin that night when we were due to fire up the tractor and cut our field, was the thing that Ferlinghetti broke his ass trying to find out, but never did.

Ferlinghetti, I guess he sees it as one of these mother complex things, because he's asking Stephen if he loves his Mom and if he thought Mrs Harris was his Mom, that sort of thing. But, more than that, he's wondering all the time what happened afterwards and why Stephen gave himself up to the cops. They're sitting on the park bench a couple of days a week and he keeps coming at it all sorts of different ways. Eventually he just says it straight out.

'So, dude,' – that's what's cracking me up, this guy Ferlinghetti says 'dude' and 'dissing' and 'cool' and 'wild' and all – 'why did you give yourself up to the cops?'

And Stephen, he don't say nothing. He just keeps on saying 'because' over and over.

Stephen already told him about how he ran into the forest after he shot and killed Old Man Harris. How the cops came and flooded the place. How he hid himself behind a tree and was just waiting for a chance to go back and ask the redhead if she wants to go to Florida. That's all he wants, to go down to them beaches with all the skinny women. How he wasn't scared of the cops, not a bit. He was sure they was going to get away. He was going to even leave a note for his Mom. *Gone to Florida, see ya soon.* The cops and the ambulances and the fire people are there, all over the place.

Once he gets so goddamn daring that he sneaks up to the back of the trailer and peeks in the window where the cops are taking photographs. Ferlinghetti don't believe that, I can tell, but Stephen doesn't care. He just says what's the point in lying? I killed the man, everybody knows that.

After looking in the window he goes back into the forest. The sun is going down. A couple of hours later he just walks up to the police, who are all having coffee on the front steps of the trailer house, chatting. Stephen gives himself up.

Ferlinghetti, he asks again, says it's very important to

him, starts giving this crap about how Stephen needs someone to respect him, that sort of thing, but still Stephen says
'because'. I'm just sitting there, in the flower bed, listening
to all this. Once or twice Stephen turns around and looks at
me. I just look down, pretending I'm not interested.

Later in the afternoon we're out there digging and raking
in a flower bed, me and Stephen. There's some other workers
there too, but they're feeling lazy, taking themselves a load
off their feet. I'm just digging away and Stephen, he's sort of
puttering with the rake. He's got those long skinny arms. For
some reason he's wearing his eyeglasses, which he don't
normally do. He's got some of that brown powder stuff on
his face that the kids use to cover up the zits. He looks awful
sad. It takes him a long old time to pull that rake along the
ground even just a little bit.

Kevin's way over on the other side of the fence, near the
staff houses, weedeating. So I'm asking Stephen what he
thinks of the Cowboys and the Oilers and all, except I get to
thinking that the kid must think I sound like Ferlinghetti,
asking all these questions, so I stop. I don't want to sound
like no shrink. I'm just turning some soil, whistling away,
thinking about how that night me and Kevin are due to start
work on the field. I think maybe I'll go home and get myself
a big old plate of steak, maybe some of that Gatorade that
keeps you going. I'm looking at the sky and thinking it may
stay clear, when Stephen turns to me. He looks straight at
me.

'I was scared of the dark,' he says.

First thing I'm thinking he's saying something about a
darkie, which is weird since I think they only use that word
in old movies. But then I catch on. He's still looking at me,
but I have no dadgum idea why he's telling me this. I ain't
never asked him but maybe he saw me listening to him and
Ferlinghetti, so he figures I want to know. But he's just
staring away into space. His mouth is quivering. His eyes are
all red around the edges. This don't look like a kid who put a
gun in a man's mouth and spilled his brains out on the floor,

who stole them trucks, slept with women, all those things. He just looks like an ordinary kid. He's just standing there, with the rake in his hands, staring out over the fence.

'I was out there in the forest and it got dark,' he says. 'I'd never been in the dark like that before.'

I just took to digging a little deeper in the soil and said nothing. I thought about Ferlinghetti and what he might get out of that. This kid was scared of nothing else – not scared of killing a man, that's for sure, or stealing, or boning away whenever he got the chance. I knew it was weird. Guess he didn't have his teevee or nothing out there. Guess that's what maybe he was scared of. I just nodded my head and said I know what you mean, man, I know what you mean.

I'm telling Kevin all this and his face just drains. We're standing there putting the gas in the tractor. He's holding the big red five-gallon can and I got the funnel. For some reason Kevin, his hands start to shake like he's got the chills and some of that gas is spilling itself down the side of the tractor. 'Scared of the dark,' says Kevin, not like a question, just repeating it over and over. He puts the last drop of gas in that tank and then he tells me that he'll be back in a moment. I see him hightail off towards my pick-up truck and slam the door. He leaves a trail of dust on the dirt road that runs through the centre of our field. I get up on the tractor to fire her up, but Kevin has the dadgum keys.

So I just sit myself down on the ground and poke a little stick in a mound of fire ants and watch them little bastards scuttle. Millions of them. I heard someone say once that they can build a mound that goes fifteen feet down in the ground. They can also kill a baby if enough of them get on the baby's body. They start to crawl up my boots, so I climb up on the tractor and look out over the field.

It sure is getting late. I can see some red sky in the west. There's even a star up there already. The last of the buzzards are taking themselves down off the thermals. I wonder where it is they sleep at night. One thing for sure, those crickets don't sleep. They started chirping so it sounded like a song. I don't know how long I sat there for, but it was almost fully night when I looked up and there was Kevin coming down the road in the pick-up truck. He had his whole family with him, the whole dadgum lot, his wife Delicia, his sons Lawrence and Myron, his girl Natalie. Then I see, sitting in the back of the truck, my Ellie and my little boy, Robert. Everyone quiet. Normally they all shouting up a storm and laughing when they get together.

Kevin gets out of the truck with this strange look on his face. He's wearing his working shirt and the sleeves are rolled way up on his shoulders. His face full of wrinkles. His eyes all serious. He gets everyone to line up at the edge of the field behind him, in a row. Ellie's in her gown and slippers. Her hair is in curlers. Delicia, she has to carry Myron in her hands because he's so small. Lawrence has himself a small football tucked under his arm. I do a little shadow boxing with my Robert, but he's quiet as a mouse. That klein grass is so big that it's over all the kids' heads. Nobody's saying anything. It's all quiet as can be. Except for the crickets.

Kevin gets me to stand at the end of the line and then he just starts walking through the field. Everyone just steps on along behind him, but pretty soon he gets to jogging and everyone jogs along behind him, brushing away the grass with their hands, until it gets faster and faster and we're hightailing through that field, the grass parting along in our way. I hear all the kids laughing, then Delicia giving a chuckle, then Ellie hollering something crazy. I'm holding on to Robert's hand. He's kicking at the stalks as we go. Kevin is whooping for some reason. My own body gets kind of loose and I find myself damn near dancing through the field. I haven't danced like that since the club in Giddings burnt down.

Well, it must have looked plumb stupid, us running through the field like that, with our kids, when we had so much work to do. But I was stumbling along, hearing everyone laughing, holding on to my little boy, then I looked up beyond the top of the grass and I noticed how dark the sky was, how big and heavy it was, how much it had come down on top of us. We were laughing, and I knew right there and then what Kevin was doing. He was no fool.

PART EIGHT

Antonia Logue

from *Shadow Box*

THE FIRST TIME I knew what my life would be like I was standing on sewerage watching a white man pack a wicker suitcase with a worn-out blue linen suit. Forty thousand people were shouting coon-boy and nigger-shit and a man called Jack London was sitting five feet away from me telling me to get my black ass back to Georgia. I'm from Texas. A few years later Belle bought me a whole shopful of his books and that black ass has never been warmed with such satisfaction. It was supposed to be Hughie Mc Intosh's night, he was the man who'd finally agreed to shut the black boy up once and for all and let the people pay to see Jack Johnson put in his grave. Hughie's idea of making money was to pay his own guy the full pocket, pay the contender, me, not a dollar, and make himself referee so his man didn't lose the title. Sydney didn't have anywhere that suited Hughie, so in ten days he had Rushcutter's Bay stadium built. It frightened some people, but forty thousand good Australians were game enough to climb in and shout abuse at $5 a head. Hughie had it built in the open air on thirty-foot stilts over the municipal swamp so while the city's sewage sludge fermented underneath us, Tommy Burns and I were saying our hellos to our welcoming crowds.

Burns wasn't a bad fighter, and that is what people like to forget now. Burns had a low right uppercut that if it got the solar plexus it could take the fight out of a man long enough to dose him with a punch that floored him. He understood how to distract an opponent with only half of what was coming. He was onto the instalment plan. But he was small and loved to drink, and not all the eight-mile runs and sparring bouts could tighten up that softness in his belly that would lure him into a bar to souse himself. So I was careful to be seen drinking in twice as many bars as he was, but only Jim Fitzpatrick knew what was in my glass. Back then I was like a gored bull about getting that title, and in 1908 it was Tommy Burns who gave it to me. That and a lot more besides.

Just to give it an extra sharpness it poured torrents on Christmas Eve, so when we all got to the stadium the next morning the stench was ripe as a plague corpse. It added atmosphere, Mc Intosh said. He'd taken to lugging round a piece of lead pipe wrapped in a shirt; to kill the black bastard when he jumps me in an alley, he said. If winning the World Championship wasn't enough, that it wiped out Mc Intosh within two years made it a glory even greater.

Something happened at that fight that spun me right around, and left me ready for anything. I could take abuse, shouts, insults, easy hatred, all of that fired me up, the more I got the fiercer, more focused I got, tens of thousands of mouths opening and closing round you yelling coon ... but that day when I came out of the tunnel shack they got me, for a split second they got me. They went silent. They all sat back, forty thousand bastards, and eyeballed me, stared out at the sky, looked at the ring, as if seized by a maniacal fury that had soldered their vocal chords, tonsils, lips. Just a few shouts, less than thirty or forty spread all across the stadium making the silence even more acute. Designed to put fear in me, and if not fear they scored momentary shock, an ability for life to depend on nothing, not even the surest thing. But of course Belle got me on that one.

The silence lasted maybe a minute, far longer than felt human while I kept strolling towards the ring as if they were cheering me their hero, as if deafened by the bawl of them, caught inside but not for even a second in my gait, in what was visible to them. So I had them, arms up high above my head as if acknowledging their rapture and about four hundred feet from the ring they exhaled in a long hard bellow of nigger bastard, faces contorted with the violence of getting the words out loud as they could, the objects coming at me, newspapers rolled tight, beer bottles ... but I was in the ring blowing kisses and grinning like it was my birthday, until they got so fired up they didn't even notice Burns at the mouth of the tunnel shack waiting for a space in the noise to make his entrance. Then Mc Intosh shoved him in the back to get him going and they all erupted all over again, Tommy jogging down to the ring like a paperboy, all grins and dimples and triumph, bashful as a virgin, all this for me? And all of us looking at him like he is an imbecile just escaped, for Tommy in his daftness is head to toe in a three-piece suit in pale blue linen, hands all bandaged and looking as if he's ready for an honest day's work.

I jog on the spot, spar the air, flex my hands in readiness for the compression of the gloves while Tommy climbs in the ring and starts a rigorous striptease that shows just how many real ones he's missed. With the concentration of a coal miner testing a shaft in the dark he takes off first the jacket, then the waistcoat, then the ruffled shirt ... and folds each piece immaculately and places it in a wicker suitcase resting on Mc Intosh's knee, raising his arms to the crowd's roar with each garment, while our impartial referee looks up at him with a thrill on his face like it's a lap-dance. I feel like I'm at a cabaret, and as the crowd tire of Tommy and remember why they're here, I jog around the ring punching air with a glaze on my eyes as if I don't see them, and I understand this is how it will be. Absolute hatred everywhere, cured in an instant of the naivety that the way I fight, the power of it, will level things, will make titles seem my due, earned glory. That day in Australia I get the first full force of how things are to be, knowing as I punch the stench that I'm walking away with the Championship of the World in a matter of minutes, and the short little boy scout packing his case and all his clan have no idea of the impact I am about to have on their world. I am about to punch my way into history and not one of them will ever stop me.

In the end it was majestic. Tommy had drawn out the prelims even further by checking my hands for hard tape eight or nine times, then covering his elbows in the stuff so we'd a wrangle over that for near-on ten minutes. Mc Intosh knew the crowd was restless so he just pulled the tape off Tommy himself. Then we were tied into our gloves and the bell rang out for history.

I was pretty sharp, even for me. I reckoned it would be short and I wanted to lull him, so I measured the distance with a few flick punches, then drew back and let him come to me. I let him have the centre of the ring and danced around him telling him to come and get it. My legs were able for it, and I knew they wouldn't have to last up any distance, so he thought he was on the up, that he had me doing the sidesteps while he reigned confident on the centre spot. Then I cuffed him.

But I was after a knock-out, I wanted absolute humiliation so I eased up on him, rebounded a few back open-handed, facing the palms of my gloves in close to his face so he thought he was getting me on the defensive, deflecting his blows. Then he lunged, but I stepped aside, and when he came back at me, I feinted a long left hook, could even see his eyes follow it, and I dipped down with my right, took a step in closer and came up from the shoulder with a right uppercut that rammed his jaw up into his nose. He was still following the left, leaning into the right to evade it, leaning into the right so it caught him like a speeding car. And that was it. Mc Intosh might have been able to turn a blind eye to fouls or over-ruled my corner, but there's not much protection you can give to your assets when they're lying in a stupor looking at the Sydney sky like it's about to fill with angels. You can't disallow a knock-out like that, you just kick the sorry bastard who fell for it.

Burns was tough. Not to beat, that was easy, but tough to

humiliate because he kept coming back for more. I'd busted
his eyes and cut up his mouth but he still kept throwing these
big swaying punches at my belly, like I hadn't watched him,
hadn't learned everything there was to know about the World
Champion in those three years I'd chased him round the
world for these moments. I'd earned him, earned the right to
frighten them, so he could aim at my solar plexus all he liked.
That was the key. It wasn't in the fists. It was in the head. I
saw a lot of guys who had it in the fists, not as good as me
but close enough if they'd stayed at it, but nothing in the
head. So Burns there was swiping at me like a dog-catcher
and couldn't work it out when I was never there to take the
blow. I gashed all over his face with everything from light
warning grazes to megalithic power punches that started a
foot back from the shoulder, ones where you felt your muscles
tighten and quiver like an overtuned cello string when the
punch landed, but up Tommy bobbed, no matter what. It was
the Chinese torture routine, and all the small gashes together
spewed so much blood it trickled thickly down Tommy's neck
and onto his chest, splattered Mc Intosh and all the ringside
hacks when he took a blow. There were parts of the canvas
that became part of the strategy for us, places where the blood
made it hard to keep afoot for sliding. Now and again he'd
hit a good punch and I'd taunt him with it, challenge him to
better it, to make it hurt, to draw blood, tease him for his
natty suit all folded up, offer to teach him how to fight when
we got home, grinning at him like I'd just won the Derby,
congratulating him when he managed to stand straight,
complimenting him on his lovely wife. I laughed like I was
at the vaudeville when he'd try and shout back at me, telling
me I was a dirty dawg, a nigger bastard, a coon cur, telling me
to fight like a white man. If I had ever in my life fought like
a white man I'd never have got out of the Galveston dock-
yards. And the more of that nigger shit he threw at me and
the crowd roared at me, the less of a knock-out I wanted,
the passion boiling in me for a big long drawn-out bastard of
a fight. Burns' jaw was hanging off him like dribble by the

eighth round, the blood flowing out of one eye so much I was sure they'd row in and pull him out, but they kept slapping champagne on his face between rounds like it was a miracle healer, so for a few seconds at the start of each round the molecules of sweat and dried blood would be coated in a tight champagne glaze. He looked ready for the oven. His legs were from a comedy show, wobbling every time I touched him as if his own weight was too much to bear and it was now, him having to dance around the outside while I stood centred turning this way and that, confusing him, and still the blood came out of that eye and still they refused to acknowledge the humiliation, so in the fourteenth I just threw a power right cross at his left cheekbone, and when he hit the canvas the cops crowded in and scraped him off, Tommy screaming like a kid sent to bed that he was still good, he'd still beat that nigger, he could still win it. And around him there was the hush of embarrassment, a shock more real than anything electric, a stunned, frightened, silenced crowd of forty thousand brains slowly understanding that Tommy beat meant the black man had won. Their nigger coon was Heavyweight Champion of the World. And there was nothing they could have done to have stopped it.

Jeffries was twenty pounds out of shape when they first got on his back to come out and flatten me. It was London who started it, writing all this mindless gallery-playing stuff about battering the golden smile off my face, rescuing the white race, finding the Great White Hope. I let them at it. I was Champion now, I'd them scared but it didn't matter too much then, it was being Champion that woke me up at night just out of sheer hammered excitement, this curl in my belly that gave me the runs sometimes it'd get so away with itself when I thought about it all. Which was all the time.

The parties and the parades weren't too hectic when I got back from Australia. You'd have thought they'd all have gone mad but word was out that I kept in with white women and didn't pay much heed to the ones who thought I'd do a better job keeping in with my own. Did I care. They'd all this palaver lined up in Galveston, I was to come up the river on a great boat and there'd be bands and classy hoopla on the docks and a big calvacade but then, even before we'd left Australia, we got a telegram asking who was this Hattie Mc Stay woman and was it true she was a white woman. Well, that was that. Mind their own damn business. Truth was, I was bored with Hattie, she'd taken the edge off the newness of Australia for me, but she talked a lot, idiot talk most of the time. But I kept her by my side every time we went out after I got back to Chicago, every time I saw a photographer I'd kiss her or take her hand and lay it on my thigh. And then I met Belle.

The Everleigh Club was the smartest place of its kind in America. When I opened my own place, I modelled that side of things on what I'd heard the Everleigh sisters had done in their club. Pure class. Of course, the problems in my life more or less started that March night I got turned away from it, when this gorgeous piece of tight laughing ass called Belle Schreiber came out into the light with a customer and I moved in on him right there on the doorstep. She was a good judge of circumstances, Belle, though I sure as hell wasn't where she was concerned. Nothing would be the same for me after Belle.

I used to race cars with Cravan in Spain during the war, he was good, and he asked me one day if I hated her. If I blamed her. I said damn right I did, two-bit whore, and he laughed at me and said that was all bullshit. She was the only woman I'd ever loved, he said. He had this cynicism about love that he had decided would stop him from ever finding it. He believed in it like some philosophy about death that you would live your life by and then be thrown down a hole in a wooden box the day you actually knew if you were right about it all. It was a head thing with him. Love was something he had worked out the same as his fuel-to-speed ratio and his acceleration potential on a wet road. It could be rationalized and understood, aspired to and controlled, dealt with as a fact. I didn't think anyone would ever crack him. But then I was wrong.

And he was wrong about Belle. I never loved her. I don't

think I have it in me, I used to assume I had, but then your wedding in Mexico made me appreciate that whatever it's been that got me in and out of people's lives all these years, it has never been that. Not even now, and I love Irene, do I use the word like it was invented to be used. It buys affection, it fills in gaps, it offers you a bond with someone you have time for, someone you might lust after or want to get into bed for every kind of reason you can think of, even spite, it puts someone at the other end of the phone when you want to talk late at night on the road, it seduces loyalty, it gives you a feeling, a sense of spontaneity and purpose. It does all those things. But my kind of love doesn't bring calm, it doesn't make the lines in your head stop leaping around and settle into shapes, it doesn't fill that sense in yourself that whatever you have done you are missing an instinct, a way of waking up and filling your heart with somebody else, somebody not you, somebody whose angle you never need to work out because it isn't there. Someone you want to fill yourself so full of that you forget about yourself more often than you remember. Someone to change for. And I've never found that. Back then Cravan could think that my hatred of Belle was unrepentant love, but back then, Mina, he knew just about as much about it as I did. He didn't know you.

After Australia I needed money. You'd have thought they'd have been throwing it at me, boxing promoters all over the place wanting to get in with the Champion of the World and set up his fights, name his price, take their cut . . . but not with me they weren't. Not yet. I'd ditched Jim Fitzpatrick back in Australia, he had more of a problem with the white women than anyone, kept leaping at me about it, he kept dancing this word propriety around. Sex embarrassed him, he'd think up the dirtiest moves in the game for you, but outside of training he was pure prude. And the fact was, I liked sex a lot, I liked the excitement and the anticipation, and yeah, I liked the authority, the ways of getting a woman to do whatever you wanted. More than anything, it was fun, always different, always mutinous. All those reasons explain the prostitutes, and the fact was, I got on well with those women, and I never saw marriage as anything to tighten up for. I didn't have any wives at that point anyway, Fitzpatrick's logic was just down to me being mad for sex, and him being impotent. Then this whole white women business began and he started in on me, said I was only doing it to stir trouble, that to me it all had the same result anyway no matter what colour the woman, so why couldn't I just keep it all quiet, keep it to my own. Jim didn't last long after that. I never fired him, it wasn't like that, he just got sick of me, and I got sick of the sight of him, so we agreed to make our separate ways back to America. And that was that. A World Champion without a manager and not a vulture in miles looking to swoop.

The real problem was that there was no one good enough for me. Anyone up to staying a few rounds, I'd already fought, because they were black men, Sam Langford, Joe Jeanette, Ed Martin, Peter Jackson, Sam Mc Vey . . . and I didn't see much point in fighting them again. I was the one who made it to the title, and I was the one who broke the white hold on it. They could have made their chance just like I did. They just didn't want it like I did, weren't up to it, not in the fists or in the dream of it. You can do anything if you want it badly enough, and I wasn't backtracking to the old days for anyone. Anyhow, nobody paid to see a pair of black men fight, even if one of them was World Champion. The money was in luring the white prey in, playing on all that hatred till it made me rich. It had to be a white challenge, and they didn't have one. They all had their heads tucked under their arms in a huddle in New York, while I kept the pressure up by telling every reporter I knew that I was out to pulverize Ketchel, Kaufman and Jeffries. But not a word came back.

I needed some easy money, so I decided to set something up myself. I had a look around at some of the fading ladies who'd go up against me just to keep their name in lights, the ones who were past being noticed by the big guns in New York. Philadelphia Jack O'Brien got picked to do the job. He

was only about 165 pounds but he'd been the Light Heavyweight Champion once, and he'd been fairly hot in his day, a
bit of a looker who liked to dress up and act the debonair. A
man I could like. Of course he was like all the rest of them,
saying to reporters that he was only taking the fight on to belt
the nigger back into the pit he belonged in. It was a slow cup
of coffee the morning I read that. I had a bit of fun with him
though, being World Champion and all that, I made him come
to Pittsburgh right into the back room of the dirtiest shabbiest
bar in the coloured district to sign for the fight. It belonged to
a guy I knew, and I was fond of it, but just like we planned,
O'Brien was disgusted and held his nose on the way in like
some silly wife crossing a puddle. The fight wasn't much
better for him. I went on the beer the night before – how could
you train to fight Jack O'Brien – and so we had a bit of a
dance inside the ropes, I roughed him up a bit, put in six
rounds like the contract said, and went out on the town with
the $5,000 purse that night. Didn't make for much of a
spectacle, but it did make it onto film, and the idea was to get
the New York boys all complacent about me so they'd set up
a fight with one of the big guns so I'd be looking at a mega-
buck title fight by the year's end. Meanwhile I got $5,000 for
my efforts. I got myself a fairly great diamond ring and the
nicest little speed roadster I could find. That just about cleaned
me of that purse, so we were on for another one, as many as
they wanted to see until temptation got too much for them. I
did in Tony Ross next, an Italian who decided he'd hit the big
time a lot sooner if he ditched the Italian and went for a solid
Irish name. Didn't do poor old Antonio much good. I broke
his nose with the first punch I laid on him, busted his lip with
near on the second. I went easy to make it last the six rounds
in the contract, just like before, but there wasn't much to it.
More money.

Eventually the bait got bit. First up was young Kaufman.
He was up for nothing, so that got disposed of easily enough,
a lot of blood and daftness. But a month later the big goods
arrived in the shape of the Assassin Stanley Ketchel. He was a

mean bastard. When he was a kid he'd found his father in a barn with his throat slit, and a couple of months later his mother went the same way. He didn't hang around much. He traipsed around the country working on the logging rivers and watching his back, winding up Middleweight Champion for the things he learnt on the way. He had a taste for blood, boxed like a stunned crazed fox in a chicken coop, tearing flesh and pounding open wounds till they pumped blood onto his gloves, going for ribs like he was hatcheting at an eighty-foot tree.

I did a deal. I knew I'd finish him in two rounds, which was giving him his dues and a bit of space for leeway, and no promoter wants a film with a couple of rounds on it. The money at the gate was beer-money compared to the film potential on a fight like this. Here was the nigger they all loved to think had climbed down off a tree in some jungle out the Galveston way, and here was a savage bastard of a fighter whom everyone knew hated me like I'd killed his father myself. Fight films were the hottest thing in the business, they got screened in theatres all round the country with more deference than newsreels. And Sunny Jim Coffroth who was putting the fight together hadn't fallen for those stunts on O'Brien and Ross. He knew how good I was, and he sure as hell wasn't going to have me flatten Ketchel in two rounds. No. So we sat down and talked. I got a big fat percentage of the film revenue on top of $40,000 if I kept it going for twenty rounds. If not, I took $25,000. Either way, poor little Stanley got $18,000 and a beating, and wasn't going to know a thing about any of it.

It happened in a place called Colma, just outside San Francisco. Belle came with me to the training camp, and juiced me up for the fight. She'd have been about twenty-four around the time of the Ketchel fight, and more beautiful than any other woman I'd ever seen. She knew what to make of that compliment. She had this platinum hair all curled up at her shoulder and she'd wear these suits that caught her waist like a pinch of the ass and made her legs seem like they went on for miles, ankles that could make me go hard just seeing them twirl gently at the top of her heel, all wrapped in silk like the rest of those legs. The day of that fight she wore a little hat with a veil and a tweed suit, I remember the roughness of it against my face when she came in as I was sitting getting my hands bandaged ready to go out. They hadn't let her in to the dressing rooms at first, thought this elegant blonde was all confused, thought she'd got lost trying to find her seat or her husband. She got through by flicking her heels into their calves, told them she was my wife and I suppose she was the nearest I had to it at the time. Maybe if I'd married her she'd have kept her mouth shut, but you'd never get a girl like Belle to change. Others, sure, like Lucille, but not Belle.

Ketchel was such a bad bastard his trick was to come out and act like the crowds weren't there, ignore them, fight, leave. But this one wasn't about Ketchel, it was about demolishing me, so the crowds were manic, they cheered for him and yelled for him and applauded him and roared for him and when he came out to all that noise he burst out crying, these big wet softman tears pouring down his face like he'd just given birth to a healthy baby boy, this big tough bastard of a fighter blubbing at the emotion of so much damn support and will for him to win. That was the only surprise of the night. I was wearing my lucky belt, the US flag, and they hissed at me all the way down to the ring, spat, all the usuals, I smiled back like I was being introduced to the lifers in an asylum all trussed up in their straitjackets, forty-eight thousand of them. And me with my arms free, swinging them back and forth over my shoulders to loosen up. I just kept smiling at them. Stanley had got his nose wiped and his eyes dried for him, even after the gloves went on his corner kept popping out to wipe up his nose because he was fumbling about with a bit of cotton with the big thug gloves on him trying to do it himself like a geriatric. Then he pulled himself together and marched slowly round the ring close to the ropes locked into a world of his own, head down, staring out the bugs on the canvas, getting his concentration back, pretending the noise wasn't there and psyching up every bit of ruthless bastardness he had in him. I knew what he was at. Everyone does it, the key was to do it on your own, to come out and face them with your head hard and resolute, not to need the last moments before the bell to draw in your strength. It's too late by then.

It started slow because I had to draw him out twenty rounds. I'd give him a pounding every now and again to make it look like there was somebody else in the ring with me, but most of the time in those early rounds I'd dip out of easy flooring punches, try to close up the spaces Ketchel made so it didn't look like I was too obviously avoiding good chances, covering up his mistakes where I could have cleaned him out with an uppercut to the side of his head. I feinted a lot, sent him round the ring after punches that never came, had him flailing round like a windmill after me, but I'd just stand back and laugh when that caper got going. I got his nose running again but red now, and his mouth too, but the ribs and the gut and the brains were all still fairly intact by the time we hit the twelfth.

I came out of the corner when the bell went and dandered over to him with a left jab under the chin, a tickle almost. This got him mad but he let in another before Rudy Maxwell his trainer yelled at him NOW, STANLEY, and next thing he landed a meteor on the skullbone behind my left ear and I stumbled back with the force of it, using my right hand to break the fall, which could have been the stupidest thing I ever did but no damage was done and the second my ass grazed the canvas I was up again, the referee suspended mid-breath with his finger in the air ready to guillotine the seconds, but Stanley thought he had me, that I was still recovering from the punch so he raced at me ready to pound me back onto the canvas. Stupid Stanley. He ran from one side of the ring straight into my volley of punchbag blows rhythmic as a set-dance, and then one fast hard right uppercut that he opened his mouth for so when I pulled back my hand the leather was all torn with these two yellow-white pearls embedded in the stuffing, while Ketchel fell back like he'd been harpooned, hitting the canvas a deadweight. I was sure I'd killed him, the whiteness of him, the lifelessness, the way everyone was rushing around him, round the referee who was counting him out, while I stood to the side and watched over, wishing the bastard would just wake up. They dragged him over to his corner and started with the smelling salts and the rum until poor old Stanley fluttered open his eyes like a Southern coquette, and realizing what had happened just closed them again and got ready in his head to walk the walk of shame out through the crowd. He turned out to be alright after that. Sunny Coffroth had cut him into the film deal too, a tenth of what he promised me, but still, enough so Stanley thought he'd one over me, and I never told him different. We went gambling that night the pair of us and I let him win $1100 dollars off me at craps. A year later he got caught screwing the wrong girl and her husband came and ripped out his heart with a single bullet. And that was Stanley. Poor stupid Stanley, fodder for the big fight and the saddest man I ever met.

Seamus Deane

from *Reading in the Dark*

STAIRS

February 1945

O N THE STAIRS, there was a clear, plain silence.

It was a short staircase, fourteen steps in all, covered in lino from which the original pattern had been polished away to the point where it had the look of a faint memory. Eleven steps took you to the turn of the stairs where the cathedral and the sky always hung in the window frame. Three more steps took you on to the landing, about six feet long.

'Don't move,' my mother said from the landing. 'Don't cross that window.'

I was on the tenth step, she was on the landing. I could have touched her.

'There's something there between us. A shadow. Don't move.'

I had no intention. I was enthralled. But I could see no shadow.

'There's somebody there. Somebody unhappy. Go back down the stairs, son.'

I retreated one step. 'How'll you get down?'

'I'll stay a while and it will go away.'

'How do you know?'

'I'll feel it gone.'

'What if it doesn't go?'

'It always does. I'll not be long.'

I stood there, looking up at her. I loved her then. She was small and anxious, but without real fear.

'I'm sure I could walk up there to you, in two skips.'

'No, no. God knows. It's bad enough me feeling it; I don't want you to as well.'

'I don't mind feeling it. It's a bit like the smell of damp clothes, isn't it?'

She laughed. 'No, nothing like that. Don't talk yourself into believing it. Just go downstairs.'

I went down, excited, and sat at the range with its red heart fire and black lead dust. We were haunted! We had a ghost, even in the middle of the afternoon. I heard her moving upstairs. The house was all cobweb tremors. No matter where I walked, it yielded before me and settled behind me. She came down after a bit, looking white.

'Did you see anything?'

'No, nothing, nothing at all. It's just your old mother with her nerves. All imagination. There's nothing there.'

I was up at the window before she could say anything more, but there was nothing there. I stared into the moiling darkness. I heard the clock in the bedroom clicking and the wind breathing through the chimney, and saw the neutral glimmer on the banister vanish into my hand as I slid my fingers down. Four steps before the kitchen door, I felt someone behind me and turned to see a darkness leaving the window.

My mother was crying quietly at the fireside. I went in and sat on the floor beside her and stared into the redness locked behind the bars of the range.

READING IN THE DARK

October 1948

The first novel I read had a green hardboard cover and was two hundred and sixteen pages long. On the flyleaf my mother had written her maiden name. I stared at it. The ink had faded, but the letters were very clear. They seemed strange to me, as though they represented someone she was before she was the mother I knew, who might not even have been the same person who wrote the shopping lists and counted up the grocer's book every week and rolled her eyes and said what I took to be prayers and aspirations under her breath. Underneath her name, she had written *Eucharistic Congress, Dublin, 1932*. I didn't know what a Eucharistic Congress was, and when I asked the answers seemed very vague. They all seemed to be about St Patrick and a Count John McCormack, who sang a hymn called 'Panis Angelicus' over and over again, for most of 1932 as far as I could understand.

The novel was called *The Shan Van Vocht*, a phonetic rendering of an Irish phrase meaning The Poor Old Woman, a traditional name for Ireland. It was about the great rebellion of 1798, the source of almost half the songs we sang around the August bonfires on the Feast of the Assumption. In the opening pages, people were talking in whispers about the dangers of the rebellion as they sat around a great open-hearth fire on a wild night of winter rain and squall. I read and re-read the opening many times. Outside was the bad weather; inside was the fire, implied danger, a love relationship. There was something exquisite in this blend, as I lay in bed reading while my brothers slept and shifted under the light that shone on their eyelids and made their dreams different. The heroine was called Ann, and the hero was Robert. She was too good for him. When they whispered, she did all the interesting talking. He just kept on about dying and remembering her always, even when she was there in front of him with her dark hair and her deep golden-brown eyes and her olive skin. So I talked to her instead and told her how beautiful she was and how I wouldn't go out on the rebellion at all but just sit there and whisper in her ear and let her know that now was forever and not some time in the future when the shooting and the hacking would be over, when what was left of life would be spent listening to the night wind wailing on graveyards and empty hillsides.

'For Christ's sake, put off that light. You're not even reading, you blank gom.'

And Liam would turn over, driving his knees up into my back and muttering curses under his breath. I'd switch off the light, get back in bed, and lie there, the book still open, re-imagining all I had read, the various ways the plot might unravel, the novel opening into endless possibilities in the dark.

The English teacher read out a model essay which had been, to our surprise, written by a country boy. It was an account of his mother setting the table for the evening meal and then waiting with him until his father came in from the fields. She put out a blue-and-white jug full of milk and a covered dish of potatoes in their jackets and a red-rimmed butter dish with a slab of butter, the shape of a swan dipping its head imprinted on its surface. That was the meal. Everything was so simple, especially the way they waited. She sat with her hands in her lap and talked to him about someone up the road who had had an airmail letter from America. She told him that his father would be tired, but, tired as he was, he wouldn't be without a smile before he washed himself and he wouldn't be so without his manners to forget to say grace before they ate and that he, the boy, should watch the way the father would smile when the books were produced for homework, for learning was a wonder to him, especially the Latin. Then there would be no talking, just the ticking of the clock and the kettle humming and the china dogs on the mantelpiece looking, as ever, across at one another.

'Now that,' said the master, 'that's writing. That's just telling the truth.'

I felt embarrassed because my own essay had been full of long or strange words I had found in the dictionary – 'cerulean', 'azure', 'phantasm' and 'implacable' – all of them describing skies and seas I had seen only with the Ann of the novel. I'd never thought such stuff was worth writing about.

It was ordinary life – no rebellions or love affairs or dangerous flights across the hills at night. And yet I kept remembering that mother and son waiting in the Dutch interior of that essay, with the jug of milk and the butter on the table, while behind and above them were those wispy, shawly figures from the rebellion, sibilant above the great fire and below the aching, high wind.

PISTOL

January 1949

In that dark winter, there were two police cars, black and black, that appeared to have landed like spaceships out of the early morning light of the street. I saw their gleaming metal reflected in the lacquered window glass of the house next door as they took off with us. But first there was the search. A bright figure, in a white rain-cape, came through the bedroom door and stood with his back to the wall, switching the light on and off. He was shouting, but I was numb with shock and could see only his mouth opening and closing. I dressed within that thin membrane of silence. They were, I knew, looking for the gun I had found the afternoon before in the bottom drawer inside the wardrobe of the room next door, where my sisters slept.

It was a long, chill pistol, blue-black and heavy, which I had smuggled out the back to show to some boys from Fahan Street, up near the old city walls. They had come over to play football and afterwards we had an argument about politics. I had been warned never even to mention the gun which, I was told, had been a gift to my father from a young German sailor, whose submarine had been brought in to the port at the end of the war. He had been held with about thirty others in Nissen huts down by the docks, and my father used to bring him extra sandwiches or milk every lunch-time when he was helping to wire up the huts for light and heat. Before he went away the young sailor gave my father the gun as a memento. But since we had cousins in gaol for being in the IRA, we were a marked family and had to be careful. Young as I was, I was being stupid.

While we were gathered round the gun, hefting it, aiming it, measuring its length against our forearms, I had felt eyes watching. Fogey McKeever, known to be a police informer, was at the end of the lane, looking on. He was a young, open-faced man of twenty or so with a bright smile and wide-spaced, rounded eyes. He looked the soul of candour. He had seen me bring the gun back into the house.

I waited ten minutes and then brought it out again, wrapped in an old newspaper, and buried it in one of the stone trenches up the field. I was so sure that was enough that I had forgotten about it even before I went to sleep. But now, here were the police, and the house was being splintered open. The linoleum was being ripped off, the floorboards crowbarred up, the wardrobe was lying face down in the middle of the floor and the slashed wallpaper was hanging down in ribbons.

We were huddled downstairs and held in the centre of the room while the kitchen was searched. One policeman opened a tin of Australian peaches and poured the yellow scimitar slices and the sugar-logged syrup all over the floor. Another went out to the yard and split open a bag of cement in his ransack of the shed. He came walking through in a white cloud, his boots sticking to the slimy lino and the cement falling from him in white flakes. I was still in the silence. Objects seemed to be floating, free of gravity, all over the room. Everybody had sweat or tears on their faces. Then my father, Liam and I were in the police cars and the morning light had already reached the rooftops as a polished gleam in the slates that fled as we turned the corner of the street towards the police barracks, no more than a few hundred yards away.

Where was the gun? I had had it, I had been seen with it, where was it? Policemen with huge faces bent down to ask me, quietly at first, then more and more loudly. They made my father sit at a table and then lean over it, with his arms outspread. Then they beat him on the neck and shoulders with rubber truncheons, short and gorged-red in colour. He told them, but they didn't believe him. So they beat us too, Liam and me, across the table from him. I remember the sweat and rage on his face as he looked. When they pushed my chin down on the table for a moment, I was looking up at him. Did he wink at me? Or were there tears in his eyes? Then my head bounced so hard on the table with the blows that I bit hard on my tongue.

For long after, I would come awake in the small hours of the morning, sweating, asking myself over and over, 'Where is the gun? Where is it? Where is the gun?' I would rub the sleep and fear that lay like a cobweb across my face. If a light flickered from the street beyond, the image of the police car would reappear and my hair would feel starched and my hands sweaty. The police smell took the oxygen out of the air and left me sitting there, with my chest heaving.

Philip Casey

from *The Water Star*

KARL

July–September 1950

THE WHISTLE BLEW. Karl laid as many bricks as he had cement for and washed his trowel. He did not want company. He was going into himself and needed to be alone. Hugh was animated, he could see that, but he did not respond. He needed desolation, empty of the living, peopled only by ghosts. On the way home, he forced himself to speak.

'Go ahead. Please excuse me.'

He turned and left Hugh, walking quickly down a side road. He knew and did not know where he was going. At a junction, he turned left, ignoring the occasional bombed house. At last he found what he was looking for. To be it! God in heaven! Did he know what that meant?

Behind a bombed house was a ruinscape. He stumbled blindly across the loose rubble and thousands of bricks, intact, fallen into beautiful configurations, but tangled with weeds, until he came to a clearing, embedded with weeds and wild flowers, and lay down. He closed his eyes, stilled his mind, and raising his arms to the sky, waited for them. The city was blacked out, but somewhere an accordion was playing. He could hear the waters of a canal lapping against its walls. Then the dogs started howling and the sirens wailed, and he heard the drone build louder and louder.

I am waiting, he thought. I am waiting patiently. The searchlights locked on to the sky, catching the terrified seagulls, which veered away. He was lying on a small bridge over a canal, tall buildings rising behind and in front of him. The curves of the canal's railing were visible as his eyes became accustomed to the darkness. There was a streetlamp in a recess from which, if they never came, he could hang himself. The searchlights streamed into the night and the guns started, but still the bombs would not fall. The searchlights turned to a point above him and he was filled with hope, so that his body rose to meet the bombers; but still they would not come. The railings, he could now see, had fine lattice work in continuous cruciform and, dimly, he could perceive fire in the buildings further down the canal, their tall windows a beautiful series of rectangular frames for the conflagration. Even in horror there was beauty.

So the bombs must have fallen, but it was all too dim and he could no longer even hear the guns, and had felt no shock from any explosion. It was happening, but without him. He opened his eyes to pacific daylight, and felt sick. It was gone. He stood with difficulty, and looked around him, puzzled. It was gone. It had never truly come. And where was he to go now? Home? He had a home in this enormous city, he knew, but he could only vaguely sense Elizabeth, as if he had not seen her for many years. Nevertheless, he went home, climbed the unfamiliar stairs to his room, and fell rapidly into a deep sleep.

The weeks passed, and he shared Elizabeth's bed several times, though they did not always make love. He had recovered, even if at the back of his mind there still floated ghosts engulfed in flames, pressing him into inertia. She noticed, even when he had succeeded in making love to her. She stroked his face, gazing on him as if he were a newborn.

'My poor Karl,' she whispered. 'Where are you? Where have you been? Tell me.'

When he did not respond, as always her anxiety turned to anger, a more appropriate response.

'Why do you lock me out like this?'

If he could answer that, he would be a free man.

One Sunday evening while he was alone in the house, he went to the shed and took the effigies from the sack. He hadn't forgotten them, but had gone too far down to care. Now, like a convalescent, he was finding the strength to at least try to care. He took out his knife, and began to carve the effigy of his sister, and as her face, in its light and shadow, emerged, unconsciously, like fresh water on a parched shore, love touched him. He carved all afternoon, until he saw her before him. She was not finished, but she gave him peace, and he would finish her another time, when he most needed peace again.

When Elizabeth returned, she made dinner as usual, but only for two.

'Where's Hugh?'

'At the cinema. Something called *The Actress*, but Jean Simmons is in it and he likes the look of her, as he says.' She laughed to herself.

So they were alone. There would be no Hugh in his room, perhaps listening. He touched her hand and she stopped laughing, and their eyes met.

'Finish your meal,' she whispered. They ate, and she did not look at him again, but her tranquillity moved him. It was good to feel this love, and not just gratitude, or a wanting to love. She cleaned the dishes and washed them, while he never moved. When she had finished, she stood behind him, put her arms around his neck, and kissed his head. They went to her room and made love slowly, their fingers deliberating on the other's skin, their kisses unhurried, the blood in their lips exquisite. In this way they were together for hours, until they heard Hugh come in and go to his room. The outside world had returned, and with it his foolishness.

'I owe you so much,' he said.

'Stop that, Karl.'

'No, I have to say it. Without you I would be mad or probably dead.'

'Stop.'

She was uncomfortable now, and he knew she hated it, but he couldn't help himself.

'You took me in. You saw that I was a man before I was German. You fed me, brought me back to life, listened to me. And although I hardly dare to say it, you loved me. I want you to know that in my own crippled way, I love you in return.'

She smiled. 'That's the first time . . .'

'Yes. It is long overdue, but I want you to know that whatever happens, I always will.'

'What might happen, Karl?'

'You might love someone else, for example.'

For the first time since he had known her, she turned crimson, and did not reply. His finger played a circle around her nipple as she stared at him in silence. 'You have loved a young Irishman before now,' he added after a time. She pushed him away.

'You weren't supposed to know that. And I didn't love him.'

'And I didn't mind, Elizabeth. You didn't exclude me, so I didn't mind.'

'Why do you have to ruin everything?' She threw back the blankets, dressed and left the room.

Yes, he knew that. As he lay there for some time, he knew he had ruined everything. It was his destiny.

On Saturday evening they were sitting in the yard together. They were all reading. Hugh, he noticed, read earnestly and took a long time to turn a page. Elizabeth was reading her usual diet of magazines. This one had a Hollywood actor on the cover. He put aside his papers and lit his pipe. There was nothing he would rather do than finish Gertrud's effigy. He supposed that Elizabeth must know, that she had been discreet. Perhaps one day, when she was angry, she would spit it into his face. And what about those statues. Who do you think you are – Frankenstein? Ah yes, Elizabeth, you were cruel if you were hurt. She had not spoken more than a few words to him all week. Worse, she was polite, and even, in her actions, kind. She was playing the landlady, as if they had never been friends, much less lovers.

'Oh,' she said out loud, but really to herself. 'It says here that Gene Kelly is happily married to film actress Betsy Blair. That rings a bell.'

Hugh looked up from his book and gazed at her. It was obvious that he was in love with her, although Karl doubted if he knew it.

A goods train rumbled along the embankment and Karl returned to his papers, at one point getting a pen to work out the crossword.

'Hugh, would you like to come with me to the market tomorrow?' She said it so quietly, that Karl wondered if he had imagined it. He glanced at Hugh, who looked like a startled calf.

'That'd be great,' Hugh said.

'Eleven o'clock?'

'Right.'

'Right,' she half-mimicked him, grinning.

Satisfied, she went indoors. Karl heard the bath running.

Careless now as to whether he was seen or not, he folded his paper and went to the shed, took Gertrud from her sack and began carving in front of Hugh. He was curious to know if Elizabeth worked. He closed his book and went indoors. Karl pressed the knife too hard against Gertrud's cheek, and sliced away a deep groove. This stopped him. He ran his finger up and down the jagged groove and shook his head. 'My poor Gertrud,' he whispered. 'What have I done to you?'

It was time he stopped this. It was past time. If he could not bear to feel, he must not drag Elizabeth with him. It must stop. Say it, Karl, say it. They will be lovers and you, you Karl, will be happy for her. He fought to maintain an exterior calm, though his spirit twisted like a blanket wrung between washerwomen. It was the time. It was the time to know that Elizabeth needed vitality, a head on her pillow that was not a dead-weight. He tried to smile. He didn't feel an appropriate emotion, but yes, he could smile. He would smile for Elizabeth. He practised it again. His jaw ached, and he wondered if his smile being false would be grotesque.

He went inside and paused at the foot of the stairs as Elizabeth descended, closing her robe. He smiled, but she cast down her eyes and went into her room. He lay on his bed, smiling. Then he went into the bathroom, being careful to lock the door, and forced himself to look in the mirror, realizing that he had forgotten how he looked. His hair had receded, and the revealed pate was tanned but scaled by the elements. He smiled, and yes, his smile was grotesque. He had fine teeth, but his cheekbones rose to almost obliterate his eyes and the furrows on his forehead rose to his scalp in a pyramid of steps. He practised: jolly – no; broad – worse still. It seemed that a meagre smile suited him best. After a few tries he was satisfied with this, and he went to sleep wearing his new smile.

He woke in mid-afternoon. He had dreamt that he had been thrown to the ground by a demon and that he had bitten into its waxy jaw to fight him off. He emptied his bladder and went downstairs, still heavy with sleep. Elizabeth was sitting at the table. Without thinking, he smiled, and she smiled back.

'You are not at Millie's.'

'No. Not today.'

He stripped and washed at the sink as he had done in the old days, his braces hanging down his legs, and sang as he washed. 'O Mensch! O Mensch! Gib acht! Gib acht!'

She had his Sunday newspapers and he read them over tea, a few hours later than usual. She was fidgety, sitting and standing. He lowered his paper.

'Elizabeth, Liebchen. You are thinking of Hugh.'

She did not answer for a while, then told him that she wanted to make Hugh her lover. He had been prepared for this, perhaps from the day Hugh had come to the house, and had made a bargain with himself that he would share her. She was amazed of course. It wasn't an everyday reaction, but even as they spoke he knew it was true that he only needed her to love him some of the time, whereas he could love her without condition. She asked him why she was doing it, and that touched him. It didn't matter if she was deferring to him to compensate by making him feel important, or if she was so driven by instinct that she could not fathom her motive. He told her why, with a calmness and tenderness which surprised him. If she did not know why she was seducing the younger man, then also, he did not know why he was making it easier for her. She told him she loved him, and that was his reward, but he could not help but wonder where love ended and gratitude began.

'What? You talk such nonsense, sometimes,' she chided him.

They kissed, and to his surprise, he felt pleasure. Ludicrously, their conspiracy had brought them closer, if only for a while. He almost laughed.

She sat into his lap and was still.

'Come to bed with me,' she said, her voice muffled against his chest.

'When are you going to seduce him?' His hands were on her waist, his fingers touching her rear, and making that slow journey upwards that he loved.

'Seduce him? Yes . . . I suppose so. Tonight, I think. But I want you before him. To make me secure, Karl.'

His hand rested on her left breast. He too needed security, an armour against the protesting voices in his head.

'Can we stay like this, for just a few moments?' he asked her quietly.

'For as long as you like.'

'Are you afraid?'

'No. I was.'

Yes. That was how he felt also.

He was determined to lose himself in her as they made love. This was as it should always be, with nothing dragging them down. A great romance of bodies which had been through much together. He could not be like this with any other woman. With Elizabeth, there were no questions to be

answered, she knew him perfectly. She was pulling his body
into her, actively wanting him. To be wanted, that was the
most erotic of all, and, his pleasure reaching towards agony
as his heart and head pounded, he lost himself to her writhing
body, to her wonderful moans. Then she arched into him and
cried out weirdly as he continued, unable to stop. And then,
all his life flowed into her, everything, and he plunged ecstat-
ically into death. He stayed on top of her as he recovered, and
could feel her heart still beating heavily, not quite in time
with his. That this might never happen again was unbearable.
Even as he thought it, he was grateful that he could feel, and
he let his tears flow. She worked her fingers through his hair,
protesting softly that it wasn't just gratitude she felt, but love.

'You are much stronger than I,' he said. He knew at once
that he had ruined these precious moments by saying that –
by saying anything at all. It was an old story with him. How
could it be, he thought as she babbled on, that in ordinary
moments he could be strong, thoughtful, almost a dependable
man; but as soon as he made love to her he was like a needful
child, unable to hold his tongue? And then it was an opportunity for her to justify herself, by praising him, what he had
done for her, and there was nothing he could tolerate less
than justification of either of them at the present time. So they
ended their brief intimacy in resentful silence, as more than
once before.

Over dinner, Hugh made a vacuous remark about priests
and hell. It was his chance to strike at Elizabeth, and Hugh
also, to spew some nonsense about living in hell every day.
But he didn't have to utter a word. Elizabeth knew what he
was thinking, he could see that, and he enjoyed her anger. Yet
as soon as he had left them alone, he wondered why he was
hurting her, when it was the last thing he wanted to do. Or
was that the truth? He did not know what he felt, and the
battle to know wearied him.

In his room he took down his astronomy book and forced
himself to read. Hugh came upstairs to his room. So. It seemed
Elizabeth had delayed her seduction, had perhaps lost her

nerve. Maybe she was still too angry. Anger was not the ideal emotion with which to begin an affair, that was clear.

Elizabeth closed her bedroom door beneath him, and despite himself he listened hard. This was not like him. He had always respected her privacy. Nothing. No opening or closing of drawers, no audible weeping, or swearing, and no awful music from her radio. Nothing.

He went back to his book. Was the universe finite or infinite? He closed the book. His own feeling was that it was infinite and unknowable, unlike hell. It was immaterial to him what they did. It was crazy. It was madness, but he had said it all. He belonged in hell.

Hugh left. What was going on? Despite himself, his heart jumped in hope. He read on. It was immaterial, completely immaterial to him what they did. He was alone at last, his natural state.

It was a while before Hugh returned, and this time he knocked on Elizabeth's door. Karl's heart pounded. He tried not to, but as if hypnotized, he went to his door and opened it, listening intently. He could not hear what they were saying, but they were in her room. He grabbed his jacket and noisily descended the stairs. He closed the door normally, and left, blanking out the thoughts which drove him on. Only one thing mattered to him now.

He reached the bombsite, and struggled through the darkness, stumbling and cutting his hand against something sharp, probably a jagged brick, but he blundered on. He found what he thought of as his bed as easily as if it had been daylight and lay down, suddenly exhausted. The glow of the city cast a pale reflection on the sky, but when he closed his eyes all was mercifully dark.

When he opened them again he was beside the inner Alster and the bombers had gone. He walked along the tree-lined Junfernstieg and a car passed at a leisurely speed. There were fires everywhere but nobody he could see was running or shouting; they just stood on the promenade, hands in pockets, gazing at the fires in silence. He recognized one building. The Alster Pavilion, even at this distance, burnt like a sun, so that it seemed its roof was suspended in flames. To the left, another large building, probably a church, was consumed. He could not remember what it was. There was so much he could not remember. The spectators did not move, as if they were exhausted yet still transfixed. It was terrible, yet beautiful. Water lapped against the pier. Another unhurried car passed. He recalled the Pavilion from his youth, with its balconies and flag turret, on the leafy avenue, relaxed people taking the sun at the pavement tables. He had often wondered what meandered through their minds as they sat there, talking and laughing, or arguing; what lust or sorrow these poor bodies supported as they raised a glass to their lips. How many of them were dead, beyond all that forever? He was so tired, and lay down under a tree and slept.

When he woke, it was dawn and the shells of buildings were in silhouette. He was cold and stiff, but once he had walked a distance he felt good. He let himself in quietly, and checked the clock by his bed. 6.05. That was alright, then. He went to the bathroom and shaved. He had cut his hand somehow, and he examined the congealed blood mixed through the shaving soap before washing it. It was an irritation, no more. Then he remembered the Pavilion inferno. He washed and dried his face, and towel in hand, he looked into the mirror. It was true. He had been there. He had done it. It was no dream; he had been there, and at last he could relax. Whether it was a time for joy or peace, he did not know. Peace, certainly, because although he had not yet found them, he was on his way. Were Elizabeth and Hugh on their way? he wondered. A drama had occurred in his absence. A certain place, in a certain passage of time, a particular, unique drama, pregnant with consequence, unfolded. He smiled, wanting to play Mahler, his beloved Mahler, who seemed to know all about hell, and now by some miracle, the same music spoke of heaven, too. But instead he dressed and called Hugh for work.

Blánaid McKinney

The Outfielder, the Indian-Giver

A s they touched down at O'Hare, Fergal wondered how he'd gotten himself into this. Okay, Martin was charming and clever, and as persuasive as an upper-class rat with a gold tooth, but Fergal had only known him a month and now he was going to be spending the next week covering swathes of a country Fergal knew nothing about with this middle-aged man who was completely drunk two hours after take-off, and whose seduction technique involved roaring at a stewardess that 'Kafka was in fact, sweetheart, a fucking *comedian!*'

They had met at a dinner party in Dublin. Martin was a sportswriter for the *Telegraph*. Cricket commentator mainly. Fergal was a research assistant to the Politics professor at Trinity College. He knew nothing about cricket, so when, in the middle of Martin's unintelligible gabble about front foot and middle stumps, cover point and deep mid-wicket, he quietly mentioned that he was going to America for a week or so, he didn't expect him to be interested. He was wrong. Martin pounced, grabbing his hand and spilling gin on his lapel.

'America! *Really?* Why?'

'Well, ah, I'm just going to have a look at the original homelands of the, um, the Choctaw . . . in Mississippi . . .'

'The what?'

'The Choctaw.' Fergal felt a little embarrassed. He wasn't sure if that was the real reason he was going, but he needed an excuse to get away, and if he could do some research on the relocation of native Americans in the 1830s, then that was as good an excuse as any. Research, hell – he just wanted to find himself driving through somewhere different. Martin was bewildered.

'So what's the Choctaw, then?' he demanded.

Fergal sighed, then sat him down and explained all about the Choctaw tribe and their $710.

In 1847, sixteen years after their forcible removal to Oklahoma, their Trail of Tears, news reached the Choctaw of Skullyville about the Irish Famine. So they took up a collection. And in the midst of their own poverty and the memory of their fourteen thousand dead, they raised $710. A fortune. Two years later, six hundred people died as they struggled across the Mayo mountains from Doolough to Louisburgh in search of food. The parallels made Fergal shiver, so he'd taken it upon himself to find out a little more about the Choctaw and the other Mid-West tribes, about where and how they lived before they were squeezed out west of the Mississippi River. He was planning to start in Chicago and work his way south to New Orleans.

'Chicago!' spluttered Martin. 'That's where they're sending me! Well, to start with anyway . . . they're sending me to cover the first couple of weeks of the baseball season. My editor thinks it's a cute idea.'

He spat out the word 'baseball' as if it were the most vulgar concept he'd ever encountered.

'The first game is on the first of April. Chicago Cubs versus the Anaheim Angels. If I screw this up, that's it – I'm out on my arse. This is my last chance, I think,' he said mournfully, staring at his gin.

Fergal looked at him for a while. He was pretty drunk. And he seemed to be in trouble, lost somehow. Then he suddenly clapped a heavy hand on Fergal's shoulder and almost shouted, 'Come with me! Really! I can cover games anywhere along your route. We can travel together – and the paper will pay,' he added conspiratorially. 'The car hire, the expenses – the lot! Come on – it'll be great!'

When he thought about it afterwards, Fergal didn't remember actually agreeing to anything, but he didn't remember saying no with any great conviction either. And Martin was a great talker. Before the evening was out he'd had the whole thing organized. Fergal remembered vaguely thinking, 'This is insane. I don't even know this guy. This is insane.' But he was pretty skint. And he had to get away. So he let Martin talk, and plan, and nodded dumbly in all the right places. When Martin showed up on his doorstep a week later with a plane ticket and an itinerary, he didn't even bother to argue. What the hell, he thought, it might be good. It might be fun. Besides, this clown needed looking after.

As the plane taxied to a halt, Fergal glanced at Martin's sleeping form, and thought about Siofradh. If this trip stopped him from thinking about the past, about her, then that would be something, and maybe he wouldn't feel like a bully any more. Maybe he could discover something new and breezy, a small thing to make him feel lightweight and glamorous once again. As they left the airport to pick up their hired Pontiac, Fergal noticed a *Sun-Times* headline outside the newspaper stall – '*Appeal Rejected: La Salle to Die.*' After half an hour Fergal gradually got the hang of driving the Pontiac and headed, very slowly, into town.

In their hotel Fergal tried to phone home. Martin cleaned out the mini-bar and then started on his duty-free. He hated America and made no secret of it. He knew little about baseball and this assignment scared the hell out of him. He would much rather have been at home, covering the cricket, and the drunker he became, the more sour his rant.

'Multi-ethnicity, my arse! These people can't stand the thought that they're surrounded by shite, so they call it something else. Their theatre is vaudeville, their psychiatry is babble, their art is self-conscious tat and their whole fucking culture consists of giving enormous amounts of money to manicured gits who tell them it's okay to have the attention span of a fucking gnat!'

On his sixth whiskey, he was getting into his stride.

'Huxley was right,' he growled. 'We won't be corralled off and marched into oblivion – we will quite cheerfully dream and *dance* our way into it. Silence is mistaken for profundity, incompetent nonsense becomes "artful" kitsch and *Mr Ed* is hailed as seminal television!' He ranted on, becoming drunker all the while, not caring if Fergal was listening or not.

This guy's off his rocker, thought Fergal, as he tried Siofradh's number again. And again there was no answer. She'd told him not to call her. Ever. But somehow, he thought that the novelty of his calling her from another continent would make a difference. After a while he gave it up, and persuaded Martin to get some sleep. He was still rambling angrily to himself when Fergal climbed into his own bed and turned out the light.

'And they're all so fucking cheerful too . . . my God, you could probably get arrested for having a depressing thought . . . they wouldn't recognize a thing of wit or grace if it jumped up screaming and bit them in the arse . . . well, I don't care what the revisionists say – *The Beverly Hillbillies* was talentless shite then, and it's talentless shite now . . . baseball . . . Jesus H. Christ on a crutch.'

He fell asleep on his bed, still fully clothed.

In the dark, Fergal cursed silently. This was going to be a long trip. He knew little of America, but he liked the idea of it. And he'd come to be fascinated by its first inhabitants, the first true Americans. He thought about Sears Tower, built by the Mohawks, the Genawoggi to be specific, the legendary tribe with absolutely no fear of heights and therefore a talent for building skyscrapers, who would dance and shimmy on its steel skeleton at 1,400 feet, and do two hundred sit-ups before breakfast, their torsos dangling over the abyss. As he drifted off to sleep, it occurred to Fergal that if a thing *belonged* to the man who worked on it, who built it, then London belonged to the Irish, America's railways belonged to the Chinese, and all the grand, soaring towers belonged to the Mohawk.

'How long will the noblest of God's creatures, honest men,
be doomed to want food and to famish in the midst of plenty
in their own nature-blessed but misruled country?'

The Waterford Freeman, 9 June 1846

'You ask me to plough the ground. Shall I take a knife and
tear my mother's breast? Then when I die, she will not take
me to her bosom to rest. You ask me to cut grass and make
hay and sell it and be rich like a white man. But how shall
I dare cut off my mother's hair?'

Smohalla, of the Sokulk (Nez Perce) tribe, 1850

The next morning, Martin awoke, groaning and clutching his head.

'Oh, Christ. I feel like a pigeon caught in a badminton match – what the hell did I drink last night?'

Fergal laughed and pointed at the empty bottles on the floor.

'C'mon, kid – you've got copy to file – up and at 'em!'

Martin's first game coverage was over at Wrigley Field, home of the Cubs, and he had to e-mail his report from his laptop to London by 8 o'clock at the very latest. Still groaning, he headed for the bathroom while Fergal called Reception and asked them to arrange a hire car for him, just for the day. Preferably European. He was going for a drive. He just hoped Martin's expenses weren't going to be examined too closely when they got home. He was poring over a map of Illinois when Martin emerged from the bathroom.

Fergal said, 'So, Theresa's Lounge, nine o'clock, okay? It's on the south side, near the—'

'Hey!' Martin threw him a withering look. 'I've never failed to find a pub in my life, and I'm not about to start now,' he said. 'See you later.'

Fergal tooled the Volkswagen down East Wacker Drive into Adams Street, then left into Franklin. The traffic was surprisingly civilized. He drove slowly out of town in what he hoped was a vaguely west/north-westerly direction, found Highway 20, and headed for what two hundred years ago was the Peoria homeland. He wasn't sightseeing, he was just driving through. He drove for a couple of hours through Elgin, Cherry Valley, Pecatonica, before hitting Dubuque, almost on the Wisconsin border. There was no real countryside, just flat expanses dotted with gas stations, motels, diners and suburbia's identikit presence, again and again. There was nothing much to look at, but Fergal enjoyed the simple fact that he was moving through it, simply travelling.

He turned north on to Highway 151, past Cuba City, on to Platteville and east on to Highway 18. He was enjoying himself. He loved the bizarre names – Mt Horeb, Verona, New Glarus – but after two hundred miles of driving in a wide circle, he decided to head back to town. He was in another State, for God's sake, and the sheer hugeness of the place was beginning to scare him. He skirted Madison and, as the light began to fade, headed south on I-51 towards Chicago. He enjoyed his jaunt and was feeling quite brave at having negotiated these alien roads. But there was no trace left of what the Peoria had been, nor of their lives before the whites came. He hadn't expected any. He just found it interesting to wonder, to guess about the intricacies of their daily existence in this giant parish where once had been only prairie, timber, buffalo, and greenness as far as the eye could see. This part of Illinois had been home not just to the Peorias but also the Kickapoos, the Cahokia, the Sauk and Fox, the Kas-Kas-Ki-As, the Illinois themselves. Sophisticated farmers and vintners, they also cultivated square miles of plum trees, gooseberries, wild currants, prickly pears and, for the love of it, wild roses. Whiskey and smallpox did for the Kickapoos and the Kas-Kas-Ki-As, and by 1830 the kind and inoffensive Peorias were down to two hundred civilized members, under contract to move west of the Mississippi. Just like everybody else.

*

He dropped the keys at Reception and, outside, hailed a cab. When he got to Theresa's, Martin was already there. He'd filed his copy an hour ago and was sitting in a dim booth at the back, rewarding himself with a bottle of Black Bush.

'So, how was the game?' said Fergal as he sat down.

'Three hours of boredom, topped off with fifteen minutes of mild excitement, I'd say. What did you do, anyway?'

'Oh, I just went for a spin around the county.'

He knew that Martin wasn't remotely interested in either the landscape or the Indians.

'Really, though – tell me about the game.'

If I can keep him talking, thought Fergal, he might not get completely rat-arsed.

Martin looked at him for a moment. He smiled slightly.

'Well, the Cubs have got Brant Brown, a fine defensive first baseman, who hits for a high average but without much power. Against that is the Angels' Rob Jennings, the front runner in what is, admittedly, a pretty crowded left field. Okay, he doesn't have the highest ceiling of his group, but he's a .293 hitter over his career, a utility player and heir apparent to second base. Now, the first six innings were low scoring. The Cubs kept trying to steal second base before the pitcher got to the plate, and Doug Abbott just picked 'em off one by one. Sloppy running as well, I noticed – too many fade-away slides; okay, it's effective because it gives the fielder nothing to tag, but not very interesting to watch, you know? Now in the bottom of the ninth, it actually became quite exciting. Two bases were loaded, the score was close, Castillo batted to the infield after a couple of sacrifice bunks, Garvie the catcher bounced up as first baseman, and shortstop Pemberton covered second. Cameron on third didn't stand a chance. Ball came back in from fair territory, he broke too early, catcher tagged his arse. Castillo should've bunted, given him a sacrifice fly. But there were less than two outs, and it was a classic suicide squeeze. Hajek's split-finger knuckleball, that's some asset, believe me . . .'

Martin winked at him and sipped from his glass, pinky in the air.

Fergal stared at him. He'd barely understood a word.

'So who won?' he said through gritted teeth.

'The Cubs,' replied Martin, smiling sweetly.

'How did you get to be so knowledgeable about baseball?'

'I didn't. I lifted it straight from this afternoon's radio coverage. Why do you think I bought a tape recorder?'

And then he began to laugh.

'You think my editor knows the first damn thing about baseball? You think he's going to know the difference? Of course not. All he wants is jargon, a spiel, something that makes everybody feel as if they know what they're talking about. When they don't. To tell you the truth, it's not so different from my early cricket days. All I have to do is walk the walk, talk the talk, throw in some fancy verbiage and spell the fucking players' names correctly! Besides, when I get home, he's probably going to fire me anyway. Bastard. The man is not a writer. He doesn't know good coverage when he sees it, so how's he going to recognize a straight lift? Good writing? That swine couldn't write the word "FUCK" on a dusty Venetian blind. So why should I bother . . .? Hey! Just call me the Bubonic Plagiarist.'

He laughed again and drained his glass. This is not a happy man, thought Fergal. But even so, it was pretty funny.

'Fair play to you,' he said, smiling. 'Why not? It's a good plot.'

He wanted to talk about the Peorias, but he knew there was no point. As he went to the bar for another bottle of Bush, he glanced up at the television. The news report was about James La Salle, the convicted killer on Death Row in Jackson, Georgia. He was due to go to the chair in six days. Behind him, Martin was staring intently at the screen. La Salle was convicted eight years ago of murdering a gas station cashier. He had been as high as a kite. But he did it. No question. The location TV reporter, a pretty brunette, was standing outside

Georgia's Diagnostic and Classification Center, where La Salle and a hundred other Death Row inmates were being kept, most of them in H–5 block. The camera panned across the dozens of pro-capital punishment groupies as they waved banners and drank from their thermos flasks and hollered for blood in the chilly night. Further along was a small group of La Salle's supporters, with candles and prayerful songs and no banners. They looked pretty pathetic. When it was announced that La Salle's latest application for a stay of execution had been turned down, there was a low murmur of approval from the other patrons, but apart from that no one was really interested. Except Martin. As the night wore on, he became increasingly vocal in his disapproval.

'Fucking savages,' he snarled loudly.

'Please, Martin, shut up,' pleaded Fergal.

A few people looked around.

'No, I won't shut up! It's barbaric and it makes me sick. And they call themselves civilized? Fucking Americans . . .'

At this, a large man stepped out of the next booth and looming over their table, said, 'Well, I think the scumbag should fry, and the sooner the better. I ain't got no problem with that, not one bit.'

He stared menacingly at Martin, who merely arched one snobby eyebrow.

'Well, sir,' he said pompously, 'as a guest in your fine country, my position does not permit me to argue with you. However,' he hissed, narrowing his eyes, 'if it ever did come to a choice of weapons, mine would be *grammar*.'

For a long moment there was silence.

He didn't even see the punch coming and he was probably too drunk to feel it. Fergal spent the next ten minutes apologizing for his friend's rudeness and, when Martin had managed to haul himself off the floor and was steady enough to walk, they headed outside for a taxi. Fergal was furious.

'What's the matter with you? Why are you always looking for a fight? Jesus Christ, man – you want to get yourself killed – fine, but just don't drag me into it, okay?'

'I'm sorry,' Martin said thickly, holding a hanky to his nose. 'I'm just fed up with people dying all over the shop. Ah, fuck it, I need some kip. Let's go back to the hotel.'

This time, despite another whisky, he actually managed to get his jacket and shoes off, before collapsing face down on his bed, mumbling to himself about fat comedians.

'What's that all about then, eh?' he drawled, his voice muffled. 'Oliver Hardy, Jackie Gleason, Zero Mostel, Jonathan Winters—'

'Martin, please be quiet. Go to sleep.'

'Alexei Sayle, Fatty Arbuckle, George Wendt, Mike Mc-Shane – what is it about big blokes and jokes? And why is it—'

'Martin, *please.*'

' – why is it that we got the best tragedy when times were good, y'know, like ancient Greece and Elizabethan England, and the best comedy—'

'I'm going to kill you in a minute.'

' – and the best comedy when times were tough – the thirties, y'know, the Marx Brothers and that, eh? I wonder if Shakespeare could've come up with a decent comedy if he'd been writing in the 1980s, eh?'

Yeah, thought Fergal, he'd have written a blistering comedy about sleep deprivation and dead sportswriters . . .

'And another thing—'

'Martin, SHUT UP!'

People dying all over the shop. What had he meant by that? Something was eating this guy up, but Fergal was too tired to figure it out.

In the dark he wondered if she would ever speak to him again. God. Siofradh was so lovely. A placid, delicate woman with a breezy intelligence who was too nice to deny his anxiety, his fears for the future, a woman who had caved in so quietly he'd barely noticed. His decorative common sense had been too much for her; when she found she was pregnant, the whiplash dynamic of his logic, his financial nous, simply left her with nowhere to go, no space to stroll.

The fresh, scrappy enchantment she'd felt in those first few days didn't stand a chance against him and his list of effortlessly worrying formulae, and gradually he whittled her precarious joy into a gloomy little problem that had to be solved. With his pessimistically steely chatter, he just wore her down until he had turned it into little more than a day trip without privileges. He never knew he could do that. He had never realized that fear could turn a good man into a kindly and nerveless lout. In the dark Martin's phrase made a little more vile sense, and Fergal forced himself to think of other things.

> *'Fellow countrymen – surely God is angry with this land. The potatoes would not have rotted unless He sent the rot into them; God can never be taken unawares; nothing can happen but as He orders it. God is good, and because He is, He never sends a scourge upon His creatures unless they deserve it – but He is so good that He often punishes people in mercy . . .'*
>
> Rev. Edward Nagle, Achill Island, *Missionary Herald*, 24 February 1847

> *'When he first came over the wide waters, he was but a little man, very little . . . But when the white man had warmed himself at the Indians' fire, he became very large. With a step he bestrode the mountains and his feet covered the plains and the valleys. His hand grasped the eastern and western sea, and his head rested on the moon. Then he became our Great Father. He loved his red children, and he said, "Get a little further, lest I tread on thee . . ." Brothers, I have listened to a great many talks from our Great Father. But they always began and ended in this – "Get a little further; you are too near me . . ."'*
>
> Speckled Snake, Creek Indian, 1829

They paid up and set off very early the following morning for Indianapolis. And despite feeling about as lively as a galvanized corpse, Martin actually volunteered to do some of the driving. After a couple of hours and 150 miles, they stopped off in Peoria, Illinois. In a shiny café that seemed to be constructed from plastic, Martin sucked on a beer and studied his new-found bible, USA TODAY's *Baseball Weekly*. The Seattle Mariners were taking on the Milwaukee Brewers. In Peoria. Peoria, Arizona, that is. He sighed and looked at Fergal across the table.

'God knows how many Peorias there are. Jesus, sometimes the *size* of this place just does my head in.'

He went back to his paper, concentrating hard. He looked like a one-man slum. Talk about a fish out of water, thought Fergal. He studied Martin's furrowed brow.

'"Ken Cameron",' said Martin, reading from the paper, '"the best, and most underrated five-tool prospect around", it says here.'

He looked up and winked at Fergal, smiling evilly.

'"This right-fielder's prospect ceiling is sky high; he flirted with a 30–30 season at Double-A Birmingham, falling two short in the homer department, but still leading the Southern League with 39 steals, a great vertical leap and a good, solid work ethic."'

Fergal laughed gently.

'So a few more paragraphs nicked and that's today's copy sorted, is it?'

'Pretty much, yeah,' said Martin. 'Mind you,' he said, his nose still buried in the paper, 'this game's beginning to make a bit more sense . . .'

He read in silence for an hour, while Fergal stared out the window at the people going by in the town plaza. Everything outside shone in the bright early afternoon sun. Over to the left of the square there was a space in the throng, a gap around the edges of which shoppers veered, as if quietly avoiding something, and yet not avoiding, just subconsciously veering, smoothly. And in the middle was a man, a preacher of sorts. Fergal shielded his eyes against the sun to have a better look at his livid mime. The man wore an ill-fitting suit and thrashed in circles, pointing accusingly at passers-by. Some smiled nervously, but most shied away from his mad eyes and windmill arms and his yawning threnody, a silent rant of doom and condemnation. Fergal was mesmerized. The man was actually frothing, his pet faith, whatever it was, insanity's party line. On-lookers were scared and yet not scared, veering yet laughing, and shaking their heads at this duff casualty. And the longer he sloshed around in his well-defined circle, the surer Fergal became that what he was screaming about was retribution and death and days to come. He watched that mad, miserable flamenco until he realized that Martin was watching it too, and that he also was dumbly hypnotized. His cigarette had burned through his bible's 'White Sox Spring Training Review', and he had noticed neither the smell of scorched paper nor his own trembling fingers.

Fergal took over the driving, south then east on to Interstate 36 through Normal, Bloomington, Decature and Tuscola. At last, he thought, some of the open space he'd read about. Out here, at last, there existed a fine, big sky with ball-point streaks of dirty cloud, and all around a montage of sheet, spring fields, growing little yet, but green and promising. An immense and orbiting version of home. He gathered speed, enjoying the Pontiac's power and the space he found himself in, and aimed the wheel at the goalposts of the road's distant horizon. Whatever had happened in the past, at that moment he felt better than he had in two years, and neither this place's metallic cities nor Martin's sulphuric, cavalier piffle could drag him down. He was tired of being held a twitching hostage to thoughts that mugged him in the night. He was just bloody fed up with it.

After 250 miles, Martin hadn't said a word. In Indianapolis they checked into the Regal 8 Inn around 7 o'clock. Martin headed for the nearest pub and Fergal settled on his bed with his books. This could get to be a routine.

*

Indiana. Shawnee territory. This once powerful tribe had occupied grand tracts of Pennsylvania and New Jersey, and the Delaware and Chesapeake Bays, before being shunted west into Ohio and Indiana on a long and disastrous pilgrimage which reduced them to 1,200 in number, poor, miserably dependent, and without the nerve either to work or hunt. Even Tecumseh, Shooting Star, their greatest orator and celebrated war chief, could not rescind the 1809 Treaty whereby the Shawnee ceded most of the land others regarded as theirs to the government. They sold it because quite possibly they had never regarded themselves as its owners. Whatever prospects Tecumseh's great Indian Confederacy ever had, died with him. There would be no Red uprising from Mexico to the Great Lakes, no mystery fire nor schemes of sacredness, nor battle frenzy to drive back the Whites. Placid agriculturists, raising corn and beans, potatoes and hogs. A small piece of land in promised perpetuity was, by 1850, all that remained.

Fergal threw the book aside, irritated. He was getting tired of sad stories about loss and plunder, true or otherwise. His earlier, buoyant mood had disappeared and offensive sorrow was crowding in on him. This trip was to have taken him out of himself, to banish the past, yet that was all he could think about. Whole peoples shrinking and shivering into nothingness, his own vicious heart, and a fellow traveller whose dedicated mockery spoke of something Fergal could not read. Christ, he needed a drink.

When Martin said 'the nearest pub' he'd obviously meant just that. Twenty yards from the hotel, Fergal found him perched precariously on a bar stool in a place called Gerry's. Unsurprisingly he was pissed, but that didn't stop him talking. As Fergal approached, he was expounding to a recently acquired coterie of bemused locals his theory on Heaven and Hell. His accent had acquired an almost cartoonish Englishness. He sounded like Prince Charles stoned. The locals loved it. Nothing better than a drunk, talkative tourist. Cheaper than the juke box. Fergal parked himself with a lager at the far end of the bar, head down.

'You think Heaven is some out-of-body experience, where everybody finds their own little psychic niche?' shouted Martin. 'Where everybody's happy and redeemed, and floats about like a fart in a blizzard in a place of great and infinite height? The ethereal, vaulted abode of God? Well, that's bullshit, okay?' Oh, this was going down well. A couple of drunk girls asked to check his wallet, just to see if he was for real; Martin handed it over. He didn't give a shit. Fergal swerved quietly into the noise and the giggles and, smiling the smile of the apologetic friend, retrieved the wallet, while Martin just carried right on. People were starting to laugh at him, but kindly so. He kept swigging and he kept blathering.

'The Heaven we imagine, right? It's shite. The true Heaven is the Heaven we were taught when we were six years old. Heaven really *is* the pearly gates, choirs of angels, gleaming spires and an old, white-haired bloke who's been in a bad mood *forever*. Except his son's a cripple. And it's the most boring place imaginable. Marginally worse than Hell, which, I might add, is also *exactly* how you remember it – fire, brimstone, screaming souls, guys with horns and pitchforks. The works.

'Great stuff,' he added happily, and polished off another drink.

One of the girls draped an arm across his shoulder and said, 'Guys with horns, eh?'

Martin cocked a baleful eyebrow at her.

'You can buy me a drink if you like, sweetheart,' she cooed.

'Madam,' snapped Martin, recoiling. 'I strongly suspect that if *you* were in Hell, Dante himself wouldn't piss on you.'

Her smile slipped.

'But being American, I imagine you already know what Hell is like,' he added spitefully.

That did it. After she'd slapped him across the face and kicked him in the kneecaps a couple of times, Fergal was obliged to bundle him out the door before her burly friends did it for him, probably breaking a few bones in the process.

You just don't go around insulting women, that's all. Or America, for that matter. As Fergal dragged him outside, Martin was still shouting over his shoulder.

'And if this place is so fucking great, how come the bald eagle, your national symbol for God's sake, is practically fucking *extinct*, eh? Answer that and stay fashionable, you bastards!'

I should've let them have his bloody wallet, thought Fergal, as he dragged Martin down the street by the scruff, still mouthing to himself. He suddenly pulled up short and looked blearily at Fergal.

'I did it again, didn't I?' he said miserably.

'Yep. Martin – what exactly is your problem? These people haven't done you any harm. This place is okay. Why are you always trying to get yourself hurt?'

'That's what my wife used to ask. All the time,' Martin said, looking at the ground.

'Your wife? You never mentioned a wife.' Fergal was surprised.

'Ex-wife.'

'Ah.' Hardly surprising, really.

'Can't blame the girl, I must admit. When she found out what I was like, she went through with the divorce faster than a dose of salts through a short grandmother.

'Nice girl,' he added sadly, swaying and rubbing his eyes. 'A very, very nice girl. Mind you, when she was annoyed about something, she could have a tongue on her like a bee's bum . . . Poor cow.'

Fergal looked at him for a moment. He was too tired to be angry for long.

'Come on,' he sighed, 'bedtime,' and took him by the elbow.

Martin fell asleep sprawled on his bed, so Fergal took off his shoes and tie and made an effort to cover him up and tuck him in. Those guys would've killed him if I hadn't been there, he thought, and that thought made him, in an odd way, feel good.

At some point during the night he heard Martin's voice in the dark, a small child's voice, saying his name and asking him a question. Fergal struggled to waken properly.

'What?'

'I said, do you know how many US soldiers died in Vietnam?'

'For God's sake – no. I don't know. I don't know. How many?' he asked wearily, blinking into the blackness.

'Just under sixty thousand.'

'So?' This was ridiculous.

'Almost eighty thousand veterans have committed suicide since then.'

'Martin,' Fergal hissed, 'it's the middle of the night. Is there a point to this?'

'No. I'm sorry. It's just that some figures stick in the mind, that's all. Sorry.' His voice was barely more than a thin, grieving whisper.

'Sorry. Go back to sleep . . .'

'The Public Works have been a costly failure . . . the tide of Irish distress appears now to have completely overflowed the barriers we opposed to it. This is a real famine in which thousands and thousands of people are likely to die; none the less, if the Irish once find out there are any circumstances in which they can get free Government grants . . . we shall have a system of mendicancy such as the world never saw.'

Lord Trevelyan, 1 February 1847

'I can remember when the bison were so many that they could not be counted, but more and more Wasichus came to kill them until there was only heaps of bones scattered where they used to be. The Wasichus did not kill them to eat; they killed them for the metal that makes them crazy, and they took only the hides to sell. Sometimes they did not even take the hides, only the tongues . . . Sometimes they did not take the tongues; they just killed and killed because

*they liked to do that. When we hunted bison, we killed only
what we needed.'*

Hehaka Sapa (Black Elk), Sioux Chief, 1890

In the morning Fergal agreed to detour to St Louis so that
Martin could take in the game between the Cardinals and the
Minnesota Twins. Martin found it strange that a lot of teams
weren't even based in their home town. The Cardinals lived
in Phoenix, Arizona; this was just a visit home.

'And the Atlanta Braves are based in Palm Beach, for
God's sake – next year, they're moving to Walt Disney World!
And some of the best players are Cuban, or Puerto Rican or,
these days, Japanese. It's strange,' he murmured, as he looked
out the car window. 'It doesn't seem to matter where they call
home.'

He'd been reading more about the game. That morning
before they set off he'd nipped out and bought a couple of
books about the history and strategy of baseball, and buried
his nose in them as Fergal eventually found Interstate 40 and
headed south-west. They passed through a couple of medium-
sized, compact towns – Brazil, Casey, Vandalia – before it
started to rain. Sure, they all had the iconic pinnacles of
McDonald arches and out-of-town small malls, but Fergal
loved each of them. He had trouble keeping his eyes on the
road, he was so busy watching the kids and the late-afternoon
matrons, the shops and the generally flat, two-storey, unam-
bitious skylines. He'd seen this populated, concrete landscape
a million times on TV and in the movies. It was ordinary and
familiar to him and yet, because he was now in it, screamingly
different. The rain kept up until they reached town, then
lightened and stopped. The 630-ft steel Gateway Arch
gleamed in the sudden early afternoon sunshine; Martin
swapped his books for a city map and they headed for the
stadium. Flicking around the radio stations, Fergal alighted
on a brief news report. La Salle had been granted a stay of
execution. Martin stopped wrestling with the map for a
moment and glanced at the radio, but he didn't say anything.

In the car park outside the stadium they agreed to meet back at the Ramada after the game. The Pontiac could stay there all night and to hell with the expense.

'Why don't you come on in and watch the game?' said Martin suddenly. A dull cheer went up from inside the grounds.

'No thanks,' said Fergal, 'I'm not really interested. I think I'll just go for a wander, have a beer, do some reading . . .'

'Well, okay, but to be honest, I could get quite fond of baseball. Once you understand the rules, it's pretty interesting . . . well, anyway. See you later.' Martin looked disappointed.

'Yeah.'

A thought occurred to Fergal as he walked away.

'The Choctaw played ball, you know,' he called. 'A hundred years ago. Great ball players. Nothing like baseball. Or cricket, either. But they played a massive, big bloody game of ball.'

Martin looked at him, baffled.

Fergal laughed. 'I'll tell you about it another time.'

He walked around the city for a couple of hours, poking around in second-hand bookshops and coffee houses, visiting the Old Cathedral Museum, learning about the fur trade and the tobacco trade and the cotton trade, the selling and the buying, the loading and the shifting and the unloading, the slaves and the free men, the lives lost and the fortunes won. He learned a lot in one afternoon but, after a while, his head began to spin and he needed to sit down somewhere quiet with a cold beer and no one for company. In a small, graceful bar on Chestnut Street he flicked through the books he'd bought – local history mainly – and sipped his Miller. He hadn't attempted to phone her in two days. There was no point. And there was no point in wittering on internally about the possibility of getting her back. At the bar no one bothered him. No one spoke to him. Fergal had always liked that. In public places he had a knack for creating around him an impenetrable shield which, while not making him appear remotely unfriendly or odd, simply put people off. But if he did feel like talking, he just had to smile or raise an eyebrow, the invisible barrier dissolved, and after ten minutes most people thought he was a pretty nice guy. Maybe it wasn't a knack. Maybe it was dumb strategy. But he had never done that with Siofradh. No, she had marched right in like some fearsome pixie and nibbled on his heart until he felt bright and chuffed and madly in love. He could not understand why he had been so afraid, so anxious, why this announced little snippet, barely a life, had sent him into the bullying freefall. She went to the clinic by herself and, after that, he wasn't brilliant any more. After that he was a care-beaten chicken who'd won his argument. He was the clever, steroidal boy whose touch she could no longer bear. He was the man with all the wrong jokes. A month later she'd packed and moved out, crying and empty still.

Martin showed up in the Ramada bar around 10 o'clock, looking flushed and pleased with himself. He'd finished his report earlier in another bar; the owner, an ex-pat Brummie, had let him plug in his laptop and send it there and then.

'And it's good stuff too – you missed a really good game! Wanna hear about it?'

'Oh sure,' said Fergal drily. 'Do I have time to run out and get hit by a bus first?'

Martin laughed and talked enthusiastically for ten minutes about the outfielders' balleticism, about Mark Wellington's miraculous south-paw hitting (in spite of a shoulder injury), about how the Cardinals' second and third base runners almost accidentally flattened each other, about the Twins' three homers from Hideki Hirasatu, about how the crowd went crazy, and did the cleanest Mexican wave ever ... Martin stopped and looked at Fergal. He laughed, almost sheepishly.

'I think it's that thing about the rules. Once you understand the rules, everything else just automatically makes sense. Sort of. And I didn't even swipe the copy. Wrote it myself.'

'I understand that, I think,' said Fergal.

They talked for a while about St Louis and tried to ignore the TV report on La Salle. The flickering background candles, people in thick jackets, the pseudo-urgency of the reporter's voice, mike in hand – it was becoming as familiar as *Panorama*. La Salle's stay of execution had been withdrawn and a few banner-waving rednecks were having a satisfying whoop. Martin poured himself another Scotch, downed it in one and covered his ears with his hands. This case was getting on his nerves. Fergal didn't mind it so much. He patted him briefly on the head. Poor Martin. It was sad, but what can you do? Why, scientists in Moscow and Atlanta were currently arguing the toss about whether or not to kill off the world's last two remaining stocks of the smallpox virus, kept in secure laboratories. Kill it and keep us all safe in our beds, or let it live and study it? Fergal didn't fancy the idea of a life without risk, or even the desire for a life without risk; otherwise we'd all end up like the moron who got half-fried in Yellowstone Park and sued the authorities for not advising her on where lightning was likely to strike. And won. As for risk – well, thought Fergal, if Martin was too tired to start another fight, then he'd be happy enough with that particular result. Martin had uncovered his ears and was listening to the news. The way they mangled the English language seemed to hold for him a kind of horrified fascination.

'My God,' he said at last, 'it's like watching a monkey with a Ming vase . . . Christ, I need some kip.'

As he drifted off he was mumbling about TV shows and their 'chickenshit 5–5–5. You don't get that at home, I'll tell you. I bet our lot give out *real* phone numbers. I'll bet we've got thousands of little old ladies being tormented twenty-four hours a day, up and down the country . . .'

There was no real venom in it though; he was simply talking for the quiet joy of hearing the sound of his own voice.

It was his own sweet personal lullaby, a thing to keep a man company when nothing else seemed to work any more.

In the dark Fergal found his thoughts drawn to La Salle and his three days of life left. What a thing that must be. To know. I'd rather be sitting in a Chinese restaurant with my friends, he thought, after a good meal, plenty of wine and beer, and just have some total stranger sneak up behind me with a double-barrelled shotgun. I wouldn't know a thing. Perfect. The chair. Jesus, that must be like some modern equivalent of being burnt at the stake. Fergal had read stories of prisoners' eyeballs popping out and their hair catching fire, of how the brain reaches 60°C, about how, when the autopsy is performed, the liver is still so hot it cannot be touched by human hands, about how one guy took six jolts and forty minutes to finally die, whimpering for his life most of the way.

Fergal shuddered and turned over in his bed. He didn't want to feel sympathy for La Salle. What he did feel wasn't sympathy, exactly. It was more like what a soft, shrinking child feels when scolded. The feeling that rebounds, antiquely, saying 'You should have known better'. La Salle should've known better. Fergal should've known better. Better than to have trusted the interior colony of his own scared common sense. Martin's distressingly quiet snoring drifted across the room, a trademark of wincing bliss. Wondrous affliction.

'The general feeling is one of despair. The subjection of the masses in Westport is extraordinary. A large crowd marched to Westport House and asked to see Lord Sligo. When his lordship appeared, someone cried "kneel, kneel," and the crowd dropped on its knees before him.'

Commissariat Officer, Westport, October 1846

'In the life of the Indian there was only one inevitable duty – the duty of prayer – the daily recognition of the Unseen

*and Eternal . . . His mate may precede him or follow him in
his devotions, but never accompanies him. Each soul must
meet the morning sun, the new sweet earth and the Great
Silence, alone . . . He sees no need for setting apart one day
in seven as a holy day, since to him all days are God's.'*

Ohiyesa, Santee Dakota physician, 1911

Martin, despite his hangover, drove most of the three hundred
miles from St Louis to Memphis, where he wanted to drop in
on a small game between the Knoxville Smokies and the
Memphis Chicks. Neither team was major league, but that was
okay. Besides, Fergal wanted to be able to say he'd at least
driven past Graceland. In filthy hail, they caught Highway 45,
east through Cairo, Clinton and Greenfield. After stopping off
for a quick beer in Milan – Martin wanted to commemorate the
fact that he'd just driven through a town called Martin, and
Fergal had just about persuaded him that pissing on the town's
namepost was neither a grand nor a wise gesture – they headed
south-west on 70 through Humboldt and Bells. Flicking
through his reference books, Fergal realized vaguely that this
had once been Chickasaw country, along with the Quapaw
slightly to the north-west, and their eastern neighbours, the
Koasati. The Chickasaws and Choctaws were amiable enough
neighbours, sharing cultural idiosyncrasies such as head-
flattening, which they seemed to have borrowed from the
Chinooks. According to Fergal's reference book, from which he
read aloud, 'This process was done in earliest infancy, with an
inclined piece of wood strapped against the child's forehead,
and drawn down a little more tightly each day. Whilst seemingly cruel, it probably caused little pain since, at that age,
the bones of the skull are soft and cartilaginous, and easily
pressed into that distorted shape. By this process, the brain
was changed from its natural dimensions, but not in the least
diminished or injured in its natural functions.'

'They probably ended up looking like some of the guys I
went to public school with,' snorted Martin. 'Flatheads, to a
man.'

Despite the dirty noon weather, Martin was determined to catch at least some of the game. He dropped Fergal off near Elvis Presley Boulevard, agreeing to meet at the same spot at 5 o'clock. They had to get to Atlanta, over four hundred miles away, before their hotel gave the room away. Fergal thought he might go for a wander around town, see a few things.

In the end he saw nothing of Memphis and nothing of Graceland. He spent all afternoon in the gift shop. It was the most mind-boggling shop he'd ever been in, and he wasn't even a fan. He pored over the velveteen paintings of the King in Heaven, the mugs, embossed with the lyrics to 'Love Me Tender', in the shape of Elvis's head, the 24-piece dinner sets emblazoned with images of the mansion. He was mesmerized by the sheer imagination required to come up with something like a white jump-suit teacosy. Who drank tea, anyway? Eventually, he caved in and, for $4.50, bought himself a small pouch of dirt in a special folder, officially certified to be taken from Graceland's flowerbeds. It even came with a stamped gold seal of authenticity. A snip.

It was almost dark when Martin rolled up. He'd filled the tank so they made straight for I-78, and south-east. Just after New Albany, Fergal took over the driving.

'So, what was the game like?' he said.

'Oh, the Chicks got hammered, but it was good. Lots of families. Lots of kids. Guess what I did?'

'Punched a linesman?'

'Sod off. No. I had a hotdog. And a Coke.'

'Oh Jesus,' said Fergal, 'that's it. There's no hope for you now. You've gone the Way of all Flesh.'

'With mustard and onions.'

'Well, I might as well just take you out and shoot you right now, eh?'

Martin smiled to himself and got out his copy of *Baseball Weekly*.

They drove through the evening gloom for a couple of hours in a silence that was almost comradely. Forty minutes after crossing the Alabama State Line, Martin shouted.

'Stop! I've got to see this!'

'What? Jesus . . .' said Fergal anxiously.

'Turn left here.'

'We can by-pass Birmingham.'

'No, I want to see it. It'll only take a minute.'

'See what?'

'The Stadium. Rickwood Field. It's the oldest baseball stadium in America, according to this,' Martin said, jabbing a finger at his paper. 'Come on, please. I want to see it.'

'Well, gee whiz . . .' muttered Fergal sarcastically as he found the next exit.

Outside the stadium Martin produced a bottle from his pocket, took a swig, replaced it, and began to climb over the fence. He rolled over the top and landed with an audible thump.

'Martin, this is fucking insane! We're gonna get arrested!'

'By whom, pray tell?' came Martin's voice, grunting, from the other side.

He had a point. There was no one around. It was dark.

Oh, fuck it, thought Fergal, and climbed over. Sitting smack in the centre of the pitcher's mound, in complete and frosty darkness, Martin took out his pen-torch and his bottle, and offered it to Fergal.

Fergal took it and sat down. This was surreal.

'Eighteenth August 1910,' said Martin, shining the light in Fergal's face.

'Don't do that.' Fergal took a large swig.

'Sorry. Ty Cobb, Babe Ruth, Satchel Paige, Josh Gibson, Frank Thomas, Walt Dropo, Cool Papa Bell. They say Papa Bell was so fast he could turn off the light switch and be in bed before it got dark.'

Martin laughed. He flopped on to his back and laughed gently to himself. Then he stopped laughing, grabbed the bottle and finished it off.

'The White Sox shouldn't have been crucified for taking the easy option,' he drawled. 'That wasn't right. Nobody should be crucified for doing the only thing they can do. For just looking after themselves. Everybody would go crazy otherwise, wouldn't they? That's why I left. I left and *then* she divorced me. And I don't blame her one bit. No sirree Boy – hey, I'm even picking up the language!'

And he started to laugh again, and a crusty, bitter sound it was. Fergal shone the torch at him for a long time.

'Why did you leave?'

The Stadium seemed to him like a giant grave. The blackness and the deserted space were tangible things, swallowing up Martin's cracked laughter, dissolving blackly the torchlight, the feel of cold grass sucking their very breathing into funky silence. They lay on their backs for a while, freezing and thinking about people who leave and people who are driven away, freezing and staring at the stars, the only light, cold and considering their options.

Martin didn't answer.

Eventually, Fergal decided he was still sober enough to drive, so he hauled Martin off the grass and they searched blindly for an exit. With the thin torch, they found a tunnel leading out on to the street. The place wasn't even locked . . .

Fergal drove through the chilly night, through Leeds and Bremen and Tallapoosa, while Martin slept on the back seat, and he remembered that this was Cherokee country. He couldn't get out his books, but he remembered, as cars thundered past him in the dark, that in the 1830s they comprised about 22,000 members. Skilled agriculturists and well advanced in the arts. Their chief, John Ross, was a man known for the 'rigid temperance of his habits and the purity of his language', a man who opposed the treaty obliging the Cherokee to move. Again, west of the Mississippi. The river seemed to be a totemic benchmark, the watery line of banishment. Even Ross couldn't fight it, and they moved. West of the Mississippi. Fergal looked out the side window into the dark and the orange, distant chimera of towns he had no wish to visit, and tried to imagine their obliteration and a green ancient daylight, filled with quiet colour and underpopulated industry, without exotic Whites, shorn of grimly flashy incomers. They never stood a chance. Neither the Cherokee nor their good North Carolina neighbours, the gentle Yuchi, nor any of the rest ever stood a chance. To move west was the ultimate, unbeatable virtue. For Fergal, to try to imagine a flipside history, with eternal stasis and no one having to leave, simply made his head hurt. And besides, the notorious Atlanta By-pass was coming up. He had to concentrate on what he was doing if he wasn't going to get blown away by the Indy-500 boy racers. Even at 10.30 p.m. it was packed and furious. Once in town, Fergal stopped dead in a sidestreet and asked for directions to the Red Roof Inn. In the back Martin began to talk softly to himself.

In the hotel room neither of them wanted to turn on the radio. Martin laid his clothes out neatly. He didn't touch the mini-bar. He sat silently for an hour, typing out his copy on the small, unimportant game between the Chicks and the Smokies. It was going to be late, but he wanted to take his time with it. He wanted it to be good. He wanted it to be poetic. Fergal swiped a min-gin, read his book and said nothing. Just after they turned out the light, Martin slotted a tape into his cassette, pressed 'play' and turned the volume almost completely down. Fergal could just barely hear it, a sweet, forlorn horn, so familiar yet now a strange, fine sound. He smiled to himself as he drifted off. The tune played all night on a soft and low continuous loop. It was the theme from *Coronation Street*.

'I often think of betaking myself to some other country, rather than see with my eyes and hear with my ears the melancholy spectacle and dismal wailing of the gaunt spectres that persecute and crowd about me from morning until night, imploring for some assistance.'

Archdeacon John O'Sullivan, Kenmore, Co. Kerry,
January 1847

'Had our forefathers spurned you when the French were thundering . . . to drive you into the sea, whatever has been

> *the fate of other Indians, the Iroquois might still have been*
> *a nation; and I – instead of pleading for the privilege of*
> *living within your borders – I might have had a country!'*
> Wa-owo-wa-no-onk, Cayuga Chief, May 1847

In the late morning, Martin sat in the lobby, boning up on the
Braves who that afternoon were making an infrequent trip
home to take on the New York Yankees. He was actually
pretty excited about this game. He'd learned a lot in less than
a week.

Fergal took himself off for a wander and some lunch. He
mooched around the art gallery, or rather the High Museum
of Art, on Peachtree, with its great Le Witt and Stella rooms,
and then decided to try out some southern cooking in a nearby
restaurant. After an astonishing plateful of fried chicken,
baked squash, turnip greens and corn muffins, he settled back
in his chair with his books. The waitress didn't seem to mind.
The sun streamed in the window. There were only three other
diners. It was very quiet. He skimmed over the pages and
wondered if Martin was okay. In the last five days Fergal had
spoken to virtually no one else; he wasn't a great one for
getting in with the locals. Hotel receptionists, gas station
attendants, waiters, dog-walkers – with fingers pointing
vaguely and garbled directions – that was it. That suited him.
His books spoke of authentic tongues, of Mak-pi-ha Lu-ta, and
of Tatanka Yotanka – Red Cloud and Sitting Bull – but Fergal
felt too full and sleepy and warmed by the sunshine to think
about anything very deeply. He knew he wasn't adventurous
or a great and good talker. He could do it, but he preferred to
watch and to indulge himself in the wisdom of idleness and
observation. Well, that's how he liked to think of it. If he was
honest, it was probably laziness as much as anything. He
leaned further back in his chair and closed his eyes and hoped
Martin was getting a good take on the game. He kept his eyes
closed and allowed the sun to warm his face and decided that
he might make a phone call home. And then he decided
that he wouldn't. He could not compete with the ferocious

niceties of justified hatred. And that's what it was. No getting away from it. She hated him. It was a hatred so tangible, distantly, it felt like reassurance. He could hang on to that. There were to be neither sophisticated pleas, nor hot sympathy, only a taut acceptance. His stomach heaved every time he thought about it. He couldn't help it, but no amount of haywire, hurtful gut-rumbling was going to make him pick up a phone. No point in being a sheer fool about it. Sometimes he wished for Martin's syncretic blather, a small turn at being aloof, at playing the bristling fancyman who could advise earnestly and with real love. Instead of leaning with a cool and heavy kindness, and a fear that spoke of no love at all, a fear that spoke of solutions, of cares and of a grieving commonwealth. Fergal leaned further back in his chair, knowing, even with his eyes closed, that the waitress was watching him and waiting for him to fall over backwards. No chance. He teetered in the sun's rays for a long while, head back and filled with nothing very much.

'Let's go to Jackson!'

Fergal opened his eyes. It was Martin. The sun had begun to set.

'How did you know I was here?'

'I didn't,' said Martin. 'I was just looking for a drink. I walk in and here you are. Amazing eh? Anyway c'mon, let's go to Jackson.'

'Isn't that a song?'

'Yes. No. I don't know. Never mind. I want to go to the Centre.'

'La Salle?'

'Yeah. C'mon, let's go.'

'Why? I mean, *why*? Martin, you hate all this La Salle stuff. You *hate* it.'

'I know. That's why I have to go.'

Martin swiped him over the head with his *Baseball Weekly*.

'It's only thirty or forty miles south of here. I just want to see it. Please. I'm half-pissed. I can't drive. I have to see it. Come on, Fergal, be a good boy and do the driving. C'mon,

Fergal, we have to at least see it. To just stand outside for a while.'

That was the first time in a month and a week that Martin had used his name.

'What was the game like?' asked Fergal, trying to calm him down.

'Never mind that. It was wonderful. It was sublime. It was fantastic. Never mind. I'll tell you later. Never mind that now. C'mon. Now!'

The man seemed to be raving. But he wasn't. He wasn't even that drunk. Fergal decided – what the hell. They might as well. But if Martin started anything, Fergal was going to throttle him.

They found the prison easily. It glowed from a mile away in the late dusk, and the approaching roads were jammed with TV vans and parked cars and pedestrians all heading in the same direction. Fergal parked on the side of the road several hundred yards from the prison walls and walked towards the gathered crowd. It was like a quiet circus. On one side the eerie, almost blinding glow of the high prison lights picked up every shiny surface, reflecting them back until it seemed almost like daylight. Outside the walls, dozens of TV crews had rigged up their own lightshows; the place was a metallic jungle of cameras, cables, aerials, sound booms, and of the tinny, continuous babbling from the reporters, each more sincerely urgent than the next. The anti-death penalty protesters numbered a couple of dozen at most, separated from the other lot by a line of policemen. They stamped their feet and hugged themselves against the cold and tried in vain to keep candles lit against the slight, nippy breeze. There was no shouting from either side. It was all very placid. There were to be no more appeals. La Salle would fry either tomorrow or the day after. Fergal and Martin backed off a hundred yards or so, and sat down on a grassy patch, observing the scene. Martin produced a half-bottle and took a long, mean swig, never once taking his eyes off the prison walls.

'Martin, what are we doing here?'

'Same as everyone else,' replied Martin quietly. 'Nothing. We're just here to watch. We're just here for the sake of being here.'

Fergal studied the quiet, milling, glare-lit crowd outside the walls, all bundled up in their thick jackets, trailing wires around, pointing, patting their dogs, smoking. He felt strange. He scanned the building, wondering where La Salle was within, what he might be doing, thinking, eating. His dull, mean-featured face popped up periodically on the TV crews' monitors, an ugly cathode poltergeist, accompanied by the familiar drone of his crime recounted. Oh, he was a brutal bastard all right, a plundering, vicious life-grabber. The steam from thermos flasks rose through the cold air like a sugar-spun, thin textile. Fergal couldn't take his eyes off it. He felt as if he would not be able to haul himself off the grass, to turn away, to stop looking at what was in front of him. He felt calm and transfixed at the same time. Marooned in the strangest place, with a man whose inexplicable and drunken concern made no sense. He looked at Martin. He had finished the bottle, still staring beyond, then dropped his head into his hands. He sighed a hard, jittery sigh.

'It was such a beautiful game today,' he said softly. 'All that energy. All that skill. The Braves were so good. It was almost like being at Headingley. Lopez pitched like some kind of lovely, short-arsed android. The Yankees couldn't touch him. The last time I saw a thrower as saucy as that was Patterson in the '86 One-Day International in Jamaica.'

Martin kept his eyes closed tightly and his head bowed, as if he was praying for a miracle, or a refuge from disaster.

'Martin, are you okay?' Fergal was beginning to feel a little worried.

'And Jones, my God, that youngster's a bloody marvel. He hit three homers in twenty minutes. Big, soaring bastards, too. He still needs to work on his switch-hitting, but maybe he should forget that and concentrate on his fastball – he can hit the low nineties on a good day, y'know, and today could've been a good day. Today could've been such a good day. Now Perry, he could've shown us the shiftiest, most subterranean pitches you've ever seen; I know all about *his* plays. After *that* trade, the Braves couldn't find room for him on the forty-man roster. So they've gotta trade or release, trade or release—'

Martin's eyes were still screwed shut and he was balling his fists spasmodically.

'Martin, come on, let's go.' This babble was beginning to unnerve Fergal.

' – trade or release, or send to the Minors. Trade or release. Trade or release . . .'

'Martin. Stop it. Come on. Let's go back.'

Suddenly Martin opened his eyes and looked at the crowd. He could barely focus. He was breathing in soft ragged gulps.

'It was so beautiful.'

Fergal laid a tentative hand on his shoulder.

'Come on. Let's go.' He couldn't think of anything else to say.

Martin stood up, wobbling slightly.

'I'm just fed up with bastards dying everywhere,' he said, and weaved away towards the car.

Fergal stared after him. He suddenly felt very tired. The candle-wavers had started to sing an anthemic song, but softly so, marred by a yelping dog and the damn lights. Fergal looked at the ruined skyline, at the devout cameras and the steamy, well-behaved people, and for a moment he felt that he might never be able to walk away. The sound of Martin falling over in the dark twenty yards away brought him up short. He turned his back and walked.

In the middle of the night a noise wakened him. It was a near-inaudible crying, the kind of shuddering, silent-type crying that tears out your heart and against which you must, for the sake of decency, turn your back.

'There should be no question of supporting a government that will not fling its wretched blighted theories to the

611

*winds when the people are starving – open the ports,
establish depots for the sale of food to the poor at moderate
prices, and employ the destitute.'*

Father Bernard Duncan, Kilconduff, Co. Mayo,
December 1846

*'We did not think of the great open plains, the beautiful
rolling hills and winding streams with tangled growth as
"wild". Only to the white man was nature a wilderness . . .
To us it was tame. When the hairy man from the east came
and . . . the very animals of the forest began fleeing from
his approach – then it was that for us the "Wild West"
began.'*

Chief Luther Standing Bear, Ogala Sioux

In the morning, Martin was listless and quiet.

'Where are we going now?' he asked, sitting on the edge of his bed like an obedient, debauched child. 'I've forgotten.'

'Jackson,' said Fergal, putting on his coat. It was 6 a.m. They had ground to cover.

'We've *been* to Jackson.'

'Jackson, Mississippi, you clown. It's almost five hundred miles west. We'd better get going.'

'And what's in Jackson, *Mississippi*, then?' He was still barely awake.

'My Choctaw turf. Your baseball game. Whatever. Let's go.'

He wasn't drinking but, nevertheless, Martin slept the sleep of the dead in the back seat as they headed south-west on I-29 through La Grange and into Alabama. He woke up briefly, struggled upright and stared gloomily out of the window at the dainty, tidy towns of Opelika and Auburn, before falling asleep again just as they reached Montgomery. Fergal pitched an almost perfectly western route through Uniontown and Demopolis, then after getting briefly lost looking for I-80 made pretty good time across the Mississippi

State Line, through Meridian, Forest and Pelahatchie. He was dog-tired, and the lowish, springtime, sidelong sun was baking the right side of his face and making one eye water.

They got to Jackson around 2 o'clock in the afternoon. After badgering a sleepy Martin out of the car, Fergal booked them both into the Friendship Inn International. Budget, but at least it was clean. Martin collapsed on to his bed and Fergal freshened up, as best he could. His back was beginning to ache continuously from all this driving.

'Aren't you going to cover the game?' he said, emerging from the bathroom.

Martin sat up slowly, rubbing his chin. He needed a shave.

'A *college* game? What's the point? Memphis State versus South Alabama University? Jesus Christ, I doubt if either team could pour piss out of a shoe if the instructions were written on the heel. I've seen footage of this college crap. They're babies. They're fat. And they're lazy. Lazy, lazy, *lazy*! Give 'em a cocktail mixer and most of these fuckers would stand around and wait for an earthquake. I don't want to see that game. I've already seen the best game. I saw the best game I've ever seen in my *life* and I'm too tired and too fucked up to describe it. I couldn't type one word. Not a word. I'm not even going to try. Because I'm fired already. He's got it in for me. I know it.'

He put his head in his hands.

'I'm dead meat. Where am I going to get another job? I'm dead meat. I'm dead. She's dead. I'm dead.'

Fergal stared at him.

'What do you mean "She's dead"?' he said, as softly as he could.

Martin's head snapped back. He smiled warmly.

'Nothing. Nobody. Figure of speech,' he said and, without even taking off his coat, reclined gracefully back on his bed. Within a minute he was snoring.

*

Fergal sat by the window, looking out at a delirious sunset. He was 160 miles from New Orleans. Everything that happened to him seemed to be happening at dusk. That's early spring for you, he thought. At home everything would be growing, a fête of greasy particles and green things whose names he didn't even know. He looked at Martin's prone form, twisted up in his glossy overcoat. He was just hanging around for contrast's fun, a baseball tyro whose wet arrogance hid very little these days. If he doesn't watch himself, thought Fergal, this bossy dazzle-dragon is going to plug himself into the mains. He's going to skedaddle from one crisis to another until he's hobbled for good. And Fergal wasn't entirely certain what those crises were. Suddenly, and without knowing why, he was almost overwhelmed by a protective tenderness for this dodgy messer, this mournful jackass who genuinely needed looking after.

He stood up, walked over and kicked him on the shin.

'Come on, get up. If you're not going to the game, then we're going for a drive. I want to show you something.'

Martin snorted, grunted almost angelically, and pulled himself off his cot.

'What? Show me what?' he demanded querulously, eyes still closed against the light.

'Nothing very much. In fact nothing at all, really. But let's go for a spin anyway. Better than sitting around here.'

They drove south for about thirty miles. There was still a good deal of light in the sky. Fergal wasn't looking for anywhere. He was looking for nowhere; or more specifically, the middle of nowhere. Just past Crystal Springs he found it. An out-of-town, mall-free, open and empty field. Grass and nothing else. Some farmer's big fallow patch. He parked by the road, got out and looked around at the landscape. This had been Choctaw territory. Sainted Mississippi, virtually a third of it, had been their home since God knows when. Not because they owned it, but because they moved through it, up and down, following the food, north and south. Of course, he knew that two hundred years ago there had probably been forests and scabrous beasts, but just being in that place, looking at a modern, clean patch of grass, made it easier for him to close his eyes and grab some vicarious memory.

'Fergal, why am I standing in the middle of a field, in the middle of the night, in the middle of fucking Mississippi?' said Martin politely.

Fergal looked at him and laughed aloud, spreading his arms wide.

'I don't know. I just wanted to show you where the Choctaw used to live. Anyway, there's a little light left yet. It's not dark yet. Remember their ball game I told you about? Remember the $710?'

Martin leaned against the car, extracted his bottle, took a civilized nip, folded his arms and said, 'Yes, I remember. Carry on. Show me.'

Fergal should have felt self-conscious but he didn't. He wanted to teach Martin *something* about the Choctaw. He marched into the middle of the field and whirled around, arms outstretched. The light was fading fast.

'Well, for a start there would be two narrow goals and one ball. And anywhere between six hundred and a thousand players.'

Martin almost choked on his whisky.

'Yeah! And the whole tribe would gather and there would be five or six thousand people watching.'

Fergal's voice grew louder in the gloom.

'And the players were all naked, except for a breech-cloth with a beaded belt, and mane of dyed horsehair on their heads!'

'And then what happened?' called Martin across the field, as he leaned in and switched on the car's headlights. Fergal found himself bathed in light, centre-stage, and he felt like shouting and hollering.

'These games started at sunrise and ended at sundown, Martin! A thousand guys, all going *mad*!' He gesticulated wildly, trying to describe the beribboned, thronged sticks every player carried, the throw-up, the instant scrambles, the insane dust and the kicking, the jokes and the water-breaks, the tripping and throwing and howling, and the women gambling on the sidelines, gambling with pots and kettles, dogs and knives, blankets and guns.

'Can you imagine the noise, the *commotion*?' shouted Fergal. 'A thousand players, all going after one ball on a pitch the size of two acres? Mad! And when their ball-sticks were all broken, they used their hands, their feet, their heads, *anything* to keep the game going until new ones were brought on. And this went on for twelve hours without a break! Can you imagine it, Martin? Can you imagine it?'

He was getting hoarse and the headlights blinded him, but he didn't care. He whirled and whooped and ranted on about the Choctaw, imagining hysterically, until it felt as real as remembering.

'Sometimes, when the ball got to the ground, a hundred guys would pounce and for fifteen minutes there would be nothing but a man-high cloud of dust, with no one even able to *see* the damn ball! Sometimes it would be two hundred yards away, and these guys would still be whacking and scuffling and barking and eating dust like madmen! God, it must have been something to see . . . And when the game was over, ten thousand people had a party, danced the Eagle Dance in their finery and drank for two days. Christ, it must have been something to see. A game of a thousand players . . .'

His voice trailed off. He put his hands on top of his head and walked around in small circles, trying to imagine, in this quiet carlamp-lit field, a scene of such nourishing chaos. Such fun. He looked over at Martin's silhouette, black against the headlights. And he still wasn't embarrassed.

'Better than baseball any day, eh?' he called. His voice now seemed unbearably loud in the near-dark.

'Better than cricket, too.' Martin's voice was barely audible. The bombast seemed to have leaked out of his throat, and in Fergal's beam-wounded sights Martin's outline suddenly looked hunched and smallish.

'And on 27 September 1830, it all ended,' Martin whispered, and his words zoomed the distance between them. Fergal stared at his outline.

'The Treaty of Dancing Rabbit Creek. The Choctaw gave up their last acre in Mississippi, and twenty thousand of them moved west, in steamboats and wagons. The government paid for it. Sixteenth Article. The government pays. I've been reading some of your books.'

Fergal just stared at him. He couldn't even see his face, but when he looked up at the starry sky because he didn't know what else to do, Martin's voice carried on floating across to where Fergal stood and, against the washing cascade of stars, it was a shy and playpen sound, a sound of hardness abandoned and efforts made. His voice was that of a holy academic.

'But the Choctaw believed that spirits of the dead lived in a future state, that they had a great distance to travel after death, across a dreadful, high river. And that while they crossed, those spirits who had gone before separated the good from the bad by throwing rocks at them as they crossed over a slippery pine-log bridge. The bad people succumbed and drowned. But the good people walked on safely, to the good hunting grounds, where there is one continual day, where the trees are always green, where there are fine breezes and the sky has no clouds, where food is plentiful for ever, and where there is no pain or trouble and people never grow old but live, young, for ever, where . . .'

Martin's voice cracked in the dark. His silhouette shrank from the shoulders down and, as Fergal ran towards him, he sank to his knees and began to weep. Fergal grabbed him and looked directly into his eyes.

'What was her name?'

'Hannah. Her name is Hannah,' Martin croaked, head bent.

'You said she was dead. You said "She's dead". I heard you.'

'She's not dead yet. She will be. Three or four months.

Tops. Cancer. Breast cancer. I have to go and see her. I have to. But I can't. I'm afraid. I haven't spoken to her in four years, for God's sake.' Martin covered his face and sobbed silently, his whole frame shuddering.

'All I ever did was hurt her,' he whispered wetly. 'When I found out, all I wanted to do was run. That's why I didn't tell them to stuff this bloody assignment.'

Fergal sat down heavily beside him in the dirt and leaned against a tyre, eyes closed. He patted Martin on the shoulder, and gently on the back of his clenched hand until he'd stopped crying and sniffing, and his breathing became more stable.

'Ah, Christ,' sighed Martin.

'Martin. Why did you leave? It wasn't just the booze, was it?'

Fergal was terrified of asking, but he had to.

'No, it wasn't just the booze. The booze was the least of it,' Martin said quietly. 'Let's just say I turned out not to be the man she married.'

There was a sardonic condescension in his voice that was not entirely unkind. And with that, he took Fergal's hand and looked into his eyes with the look of a man who was no longer scared of being crucified one more time, a man who had travelled the scant distance between fear and fearful fun, a man who had once tried to be brave and gotten it half-right.

He patted Fergal's frozen hand and said, 'Hell's teeth, pet, precisely how thick *are* you?'

Fergal stared at him. He didn't exactly recoil. He remembered how Martin's flinching disdain had exquisitely clobbered that poor cow in Indianapolis, and he felt like the stupidest man on the planet. Oh Christ, he thought, withdrawing his hand and covering his eyes – I've been *stripping* in front of this guy for a week ... And for some reason the thought made him smile, and then laugh to himself. He was only embarrassed, and if he was honest about it, he wasn't really that surprised. He was just embarrassed and sorry.

'Don't panic,' said Martin almost brightly. 'And stop flattering yourself, for God's sake – you're not my type.

Besides, haven't you heard? Celibacy is the new rock'n'roll . . . and I should know, believe me.'

Fergal stared at the ground and felt insulted. Almost. He was too tired to care, really. Slightly sheepish and couldn't-care-less. He felt just like that. And more.

'Nothing more tiresome than a cowardly old queen, eh kid?'

'You should go and see her,' said Fergal quietly. 'You really should. Listen. I know it's none of my business, but it would be . . . the gentlemanly thing to do.'

'I know. Oh God, I know. But that's me – every other inch a gentleman. Oh Christ, I hate hospitals . . .'

They sat on the grass at the field's edge for a while. The wind picked up a little and the cold began to set in. But neither of them felt like moving just yet. Martin blew his nose loudly, took a comforting swig and sighed a sigh that lasted for a frosty age. Fergal took the bottle and finished it in two swallows. The damp of the grass was beginning to soak the arse of his trousers. The night darkness was complete now and the blackish sky a hand-tinted thing so huge it could have been a terror. A few cars passed by on the main road, a hundred yards away, their noise and light scared into needle-thin redundancy by the darkness. Fergal thought of Siofradh and felt his gorge rise. But he knew for a fact that it was the whisky. He knew for a fact. Whatever twists of distress were going on in his gut were no longer for himself but for this poor, bereft bastard beside him, whose loss had happened once, and would happen soon again.

He looked out over the black field, whereof only a sliver existed in the narrow, jealous headlight. It was so quiet. Martin sat beside him, still with his head in his hands. So anxious. So quiet. Whatever hybrid sympathy Fergal felt was for him. Fergal needed someone to take care of. He was filled with a need to rummage through the debris and find a one that he could look after, a one whom he could drag, priceless, from the mire and look after. He'd had his chance once. And he blew it. He had worn his common sense like a girdle of chastity and he had lost her because of it. The thought of his own foolishness made him clench his fists and fling away the bottle, and feel dressed in violence, but then Martin, head still down, coughed and sniffled like a sick baby, so Fergal again patted his head in the dark and made a soothing sound and thought, again, about the Choctaw and their $710. What a thing that was. What a thing that was. Wherever loss and the pain of banishment existed, he could still hang on to that. He leaned his head back against the car's cold metal and comforted himself with the ringing focus of that particular piece of generosity. The rest of us could fashionably slum, but there was no subtracting from that $710.

It was getting really cold now and he could feel Martin begin to shiver. Troublesome, muddy swine that he was, a dim and pained poor sod. Well, Siofradh was gone and Fergal didn't know where to put himself any more, so he stood up and took off his coat, and wrapped it around Martin's shoulders. He didn't get as much as a thank-you, but that was okay. He looked around this now ridiculous patch of blacked-out green and wondered what the farmer grew in this place. Not spuds, anyway, that's for sure. Behind him Martin very slowly keeled over and curled up on the ground, drawing Fergal's coat around him with a polished smoothness that spoke of many, many nights on other people's sofas. Fergal looked up again at the sky. He couldn't help it. It was a fine and mesmerizing sky. The kind of sky he could only see at home with no light pollution, no streetlights to get in his way, no delta of spots or the becurtained, sneaky blue of TV sets. There was nothing out here, just one dilapidated set of head-lights, his famished heart and a gently purring heap who called himself a sportswriter. Fergal sat down again and wished he had another bottle, even though he felt pretty drunk already. He thought of hunger, although he was not himself hungry. He was very cold. He was beginning to freeze. But the thought of hunger hit him in his gut like some rebel, historical strand of DNA kicking in, and for a nanosec-ond he felt starving and perished in the night, with pictures of gleaming and bony stretched skin thieving and shifting around his head, and for a longer moment he felt the archivist's malice creep upon him.

Fergal leaned across and, just the once, stroked Martin's head. He was dead to the world and snoring still. Whatever dented skill in denying the past Fergal had left dribbled away from him just then; he kept patting Martin's sleeping head and, looking upwards at the sheen and stranded sky, he was stunned by a tiny vision of scrawny, needful hordes and a killer killed, and a nice girl's hatred, and if he hadn't been flattering himself on being tougher than that, he would've laid his head down next to Martin's and wept. He was freezing and he wanted to go home. He was hungry and he wanted to go home, and in this difficult place he could find no compensation. No compensation at all. He was tired and sick of being touched by memory and by Martin's ailing warmth. He wanted some cool distance and he knew that, if only he were selfish enough, he might, someday, get it before he died. Even if she didn't take him back, and he knew she wouldn't, he still might get that thing before he died. So he hauled himself up, again in the frosty air, and struggled with a limp and annoying Martin. And he bundled him exhausted into the car because he wanted to feel responsible, and to feel good, and to feel like a man who had once known how to be kind without thinking about it first.

> 'We are told that we have a large number of our own poor and destitute to take care of, that the charity we dispense should be bestowed in this quarter, that the peculiar position of ourselves and our co-religionists demands it at our hands, that justice is a higher virtue than generosity, that self-preservation is a law and principle of our nature ... It is true that there is not one connecting link between us and the sufferers ... That link is humanity.'
>
> Rabbi Jacques Judah Lyons, Famine Relief fund-raiser,
> New York, February 1847

'Brother, my voice is become weak – you can scarcely hear me. It is not the shout of a warrior but the wail of an infant. I have lost it in mourning over the desolation and injuries of my people ... Our warriors are nearly all gone to the West, but here are our dead. Will you compel us to go too, and give their bones to the wolves? Our people's tears fell like drops of rain, their lamentations were borne away by the passing winds. The palefaces heeded them not and our land was taken from us. Brother! You speak the words of a mighty nation. I am a shadow ... my people are scattered and gone. When I shout, I hear my voice in the depths of the forest, but no answering voice comes back to me – all is silent around me. My words therefore must be few. I can now say no more.'

Colonel Cobb, Choctaw Chief, 1831

It was their last day. Their flight home from New Orleans airport was due to take off at 9.15 p.m. Fergal and Martin were sitting in a bar on Decatur Street, on the river front. They'd delivered the Pontiac to Hertz as soon as they'd arrived in the early afternoon and Martin, between beers, was sorting out his expenses. The table was covered with invoices, receipts and a hundred other scraps of paper rescued from various trouser pockets. When he'd totted it all up, after much head-scratching and mumbling, he winced.

'Jesus,' he said, 'if they believe this figure, I'll be getting away with it by the skin of my rosy, red, royal, English arse. Luckily they never check. Well, hardly ever. To tell you the truth, I'm past caring. I don't care what they do to me.'

He looked pretty rough. But to Fergal he seemed calmer, as if he'd made a decision. Fergal decided not to bring up the subject; it would only upset him. And since he had never mentioned Siofradh, he wasn't going to bring up that subject either. He didn't really feel like talking much, so the pair of them just sleepily sat and looked out over the Mississippi. It was such a beautiful day, warm and comforting. Even the steamboat chugging along looked, not like something for the tourists, but like a real working craft, a boat with a heavy purpose and crucial cargo. The bar's background nattering was a nice watery sound, a quiet buzzsaw, and the waitress was under instructions just to keep the beers coming. Fergal reached into his pocket and took out an A4 page, ragged and crumpled. He'd been carrying it around for months.

'Martin. *Sa-ga-nosh.*'

Martin opened his eyes.

'I want to show you something. I made it myself. I'm thinking of getting it printed up and framed.' Now he felt embarrassed. Martin held out his hand, puzzled, and studied it. It was a calendar. A Lakota Moon Calendar, in which every fourteen days of all our months Fergal had translated into an Indian Moon. Martin stared at it.

'Where are we now?' he whispered.

'7 April.'

'7 April – "Big Leaf Moon".' He read out others – 'Silk Corn Moon, Flying Ants Moon, Moon of the Deer Pawing the Earth, Geese Going Moon, Moon of Popping Trees, Moon of the Snowblind, Moon when Wolves Run Together, Moon of Making Fat . . .' He looked up.

'How long did this take you?'

'Oh – months of research!' laughed Fergal. It was closer to two years. 'I dunno – I kept reading all this stuff and it just struck me as a nice idea. Something to do.'

Martin trailed his finger along those Moons which represented June, and July, and August, and was struck by the optimism and beauty of how they sounded. July or August. Tops. No chance for her beyond that. Not seriously. Strawberry Moon, Ripe Cherries Moon, Moon of the Red Blooming Lilies, Hot Weather Begins Moon. He was miserable but he smiled to himself anyway, and Fergal studiously looked out the window. To Martin this made it seem a tiny bit less painful somehow, as if by stepping outside our own notions of time, we could make the history to come bounce off us in a different way.

'What does *Sa-ga-nosh* mean, by the way?'

' "Englishman". Sounds like "*Sassenach*", doesn't it . . .?'

'Oh – I thought it might have meant "faggot".' He smiled before Fergal could protest.

Behind the bar someone turned on the TV.

'Fergal?' said Martin.

Fergal turned to look at him. Martin had tears in his eyes, but looked less of a mess now. Stronger, more nailed down somehow.

'I just want to thank you for letting me tag along. It's been . . . interesting. And I'm sorry for being a pain in the arse sometimes.'

He really meant it.

Fergal smiled warmly. You silly sod, he thought.

'Hey – don't worry about it. Thanks for the car hire. And listen – when we get home, I'll come with you.'

Martin flinched slightly.

'I'll come with you. You won't have to go to the hospital by yourself. It'll be okay. It really will. I'll come with you. That kind of thing doesn't bother me at all.'

Martin looked at him seriously.

'Thank you. I'd like that.' He reached out his hand. Fergal took it and as they grasped each other's palms, the TV reporter's astringent voice pierced the cool and placid air.

'*James La Salle, convicted killer, died today at fourteen minutes past two, in the electric chair at Georgia's Diagnostic and Classification Center. Officials at the Center report that it was a clean and standard execution. About twenty anti-death penalty advocates remained outside the prison right up to the end. At this stage, we do not yet know if La Salle had any last words, but it is rumored that —*'

Behind the bar someone turned off the TV. A disinterested murmur moved around the lounge.

Fergal and Martin gripped each other's hands still, and stared into each other's eyes. Martin was trembling. Fergal tried to transmit calmness through his pores. Martin looked quietly transfixed for a moment, and Fergal's knuckles were beginning to hurt. After a long moment, Martin took a deep breath, very slowly let go of Fergal's hand and sat back in his chair, staring at the table. Then he looked up and smiled the saddest smile Fergal ever saw.

'It's okay. Really.'

And then he poured himself another beer, got out his paper and began to read. It wasn't okay. But it might be. Good enough to be going on with.

Fergal gazed out again at the river. He felt calm. Misplaced tenderness. That was okay. Nourishment for the guilty. A slap on the wrist for the despairing. A little plundering mirth for the hungry. He glanced at the phone and glanced away again. Had La Salle asked for forgiveness in his last moments?

The sun began to go down west of the Mississippi and a piece of sweet and anxious blues leaked from the jukebox, like some eighth harmony of the rainbow. He lazily watched the bar staff moving around and the waitresses, the essence of caution, with their trays balanced, and balancing themselves over tables like shy apprentices. He watched Martin put down his paper and pick up a pen and take a piece of blank paper from his inside pocket and begin to write in careful longhand. He was writing his last piece of copy. He didn't even know if he had a job any more, but he was going to get the Braves down on paper if it killed him. Without asking, Fergal knew what he was writing, and he knew that it would be good. He was writing and oblivious, brow furrowed, tongue protruding, and it would be a wonderful story of guts and skill and the broken hearts of some players who have to lose because they are scared of winning. Fergal settled back in his chair. He had never felt so sleepily comfortable in his life. He looked again at the phone. He would go with him, and perhaps look after him a little, and he would try to be an impeccable friend. There was always hope. There must be. Because if there wasn't, then he and others would lie down and simply die. So there was always hope. It was common sense. He hoped that La Salle had asked for forgiveness. That would be a good and clean thing, if he had. A clean moment for all our charlatans' hearts. Charity from a wounded and disappearing wife, from a stunning and reasonable girl, forgiveness from a small life barely started. It was not a possibility. It was a necessity.

The sun went down and the bar filled up and Fergal spent the late, lazy afternoon simply watching. Watching, and glancing now and again at the phone, and listening to the jukebox and the muffled crinkle of pen on paper.

> *'What is life? It is the flash of a firefly in the night. It is the breath of a buffalo in the winter time. It is the little shadow which runs across the grass and loses itself in the sunset.'*
>
> Crowfoot, Spokesman for the Blackfoot Confederacy,
> April 1890

Mike McCormack

Thomas Crumlesh 1960–1992: A Retrospective

M Y FIRST CONTACT with Thomas Crumlesh was in 1984 when he exhibited with a small artists' collective in the Temple Bar area of the city. His was one of the many fringe exhibitions hoping to draw the attention of the international buyers who were in Dublin for the official Rosc Exhibition at the Guinness Hops Store. It was July, just four months after Thomas had been expelled from the National College of Art and Design for persevering with work that, in the opinion of his tutors, dealt obscenely and obsessively with themes of gratuitous violence.

His exhibition, *Notes Towards an Autobiography*, had been hanging less than three days and already word had got out and excited quite a bit of outraged comment. It consisted of four box frames with black silk backgrounds on which were mounted his left lung, the thumb of his left hand, his right ear and the middle toe of his left foot. Crumlesh was present also and easily recognizable – he was standing by the invigilator's desk with his head and left hand swathed in white and not-too-clean bandages. He was deathly pale and carrying himself delicately; like most young bohemians he was badly in need of a shave. After I got over my initial shock I ventured a few words of congratulations, more by way of curiosity than from any heartfelt belief in his work's merit. He surprised me with a lavish smile and a resolute handshake, contradicting completely his frail appearance. This was my first experience of the central paradox in his personality – the palpably gruesome nature of his work set against his unfailing good spirits and optimism. He surprised me further by telling me in conspiratorial tones that he planned to leave the country that very evening. Some criticism of his work had found its way into the national press and already a few people with placards had picketed the exhibition. He had even heard word that the police were pressing for warrants to arrest him under the obscenity laws. He confided further that what really worried him was that he might fall foul of Ireland's notoriously lax committal laws; he quoted an impressive array of statistics on secondary committals in the Republic.

I ended that encounter by buying his lung. His enthusiasm and verve convinced me of its worth and his whole appearance told me that he was in need of the money. Before I left he outlined the programme of work he had laid out for himself – a programme that would take him up to 1992, the year he hoped to retire. I offered to check his wounds – his bandages looked like they had not been changed in a few days. He declined the offer saying that he did not have the time, he needed to cash the cheque and he was afraid of missing the ferry to Holyhead. We shook hands before parting and I did not expect to see him ever again.

Our paths crossed again two years later. I was in London, attending a symposium on trauma and phantom pains in amputees at the Royal College of Surgeons. By chance, in a Crouch End pub, I picked up a flyer advertising the upcoming festival of Irish culture and music in Finsbury Park. Near the bottom of a list of rock bands and comedians was mention of a small exhibition of avant-garde work to be shown at a tiny gallery in Birchington Road. Thomas' name was mentioned second from the bottom. When I eventually found the gallery it was nothing more than two rooms knocked together on the third floor over a Chinese restaurant. Among the second-rate paintings and sculptures Thomas' work was not difficult to recognize. It stood in the middle of the floor, mounted on a black, metal stand, a single human arm stripped of skin and musculature leaning at an obtuse angle to the floor. The bleached bones of the hand were closed in a half fist and the whole thing looked like the arm of some nightmare robot. As I approached it the arm jerked into life, the fingers contracted completely and the thumb bone stood vertical. It looked eerily like a ghost hitching a lift from some passing phantom car. It was untitled but carried a price of two thousand pounds.

Thomas entered the room and recognized me instantly. I attempted to shake hands – an embarrassing blunder since I had to withdraw my right hand when I saw the stump near his shoulder. As before, he was in good spirits and he entered quickly into a detailed explanation of what he called his 'technique'. He had bleached the bone in an acid formula of his own devising to give it its luminous whiteness and then wired it to electrical switches concealed beneath the carpet which would be unwittingly activated by the viewer whenever he got within a certain radius – he admitted borrowing this subterfuge from the work of Jean Tinguely. He then circled the arm and put it through its motions, four in all. Firstly, a snake pose that turned the palm downwards from the elbow and extended the fingers fearsomely, then the hitching gesture, then a foppish, disowning gesture that swivelled the forearm at the elbow and threw the hand forward, palm upwards, and lastly and most comically an 'up yours' middle finger gesture that faced the viewer head on. He grinned like a child when I expressed my genuine admiration. I had no doubt but that I was looking at a postmodern masterpiece. I little suspected at the time that this piece would enter into the popular imagery of the late twentieth century, reaching iconic status through exposure on album covers, T-shirts and posters. I only regretted at the time that I had not the means to acquire it.

But Thomas was not without worries. He confided that he had found it extremely difficult to find a surgeon who would carry out the amputations, he had to be extremely careful to whom he even voiced the idea – the terror of committal again. It had taken him three months to track down an ex-army medic with shellshock who had been discharged from the parachute regiment after the Falklands War to where he ran a covert abortion clinic in Holloway. In a fugue of anaesthesia and marijuana Thomas had undergone his operation, a traumatic affair that had left him so pained and unnerved he doubted he would be able to undergo the experience again. This fright had put his life's work in jeopardy, he pointed out. He was looking me straight in the eye as he said this; I sensed that he was putting me on the spot. Then he came out straight with his request. What I need is a skilled surgeon I can rely on, not some strung-out psycho. He spoke evenly, without the least hint of hysteria in his voice. He will of course be paid, he added coyly. I told him that I needed time to think on it – it was an unusual request. He nodded his agreement, he understood fully the difficulties of his request and he would not blame me if I refused him outright. We shook hands before we parted and I promised to contact him the following day after I had given his request some thought.

In fact I had little to think about. I very quickly resolved my fundamental dilemma: the healing ethic of my craft set against the demands of Thomas' talents. One parting glance at the arm convinced me that I had encountered a fiercely committed genius who it seemed to me had already made a crucial contribution to the imagery of the late twentieth century. It was obvious to me that I had an obligation to put my skills at his disposal; the century could not be denied his singular vision on grounds of arbitrary scruples. My problem was how exactly I was to make my skills available. That evening in my hotel room I gave the problem much thought and I returned the following day with my plans.

I found Thomas in high spirits. The lead singer of a famous heavy metal band had just bought the arm and Thomas was celebrating with champagne, drinking it from a mug, trying to get the feel of his new-found wealth, as he laconically put it. He poured me a similar mug when I declared my intention to help him. I explained my plan quickly. Before every operation he should forward to me exact details of what he needed, then give me two weeks to put in place the necessary logistics and paperwork at the clinic where I worked. I believed I would be able to perform two operations a year without arousing suspicion. He thanked me profusely, pumping my left hand with his, telling me he could rest easy now that his future was secure. In a magniloquent moment that was not without truth he assured me that I had made a friend for life.

He contacted me for the first time in November of that year telling me that he planned to exhibit a piece during the Paris Biennale. He needed six ribs removed: when would be the most convenient time for me? I wrote in reply that I had pencilled in the operation for Christmas Eve and that he could stay with me over the festive season and into the New Year while he recovered. The operation itself, an elaborate thoracotomy carried out in the witching hour of Christmas Eve, was a complete success and when, on New Year's Day, I presented him with the bundle of curved, washed bones he was thrilled; it was good to be back at work, he said.

It was during these days of convalescence that our relationship moved onto a more intimate footing. Mostly they were days of silence, days spent reading or listening to music in the conservatory that looked out over Howth to the sea beyond. Sometimes a whole day would go by without any word passing between us. Neither of us was awkward in this. The looming, inexorable conclusion of his art ridiculed any attempts at a deeper enquiry into each other's past. He simply gave me his trust and I gave him his bones and internal organs. That was enough for both of us.

On the third of January he returned to London, he wanted to get to work as quickly as possible. Five months later he sent me a photograph from a gallery in Paris, a black and white close-up of a piece called *The Bonemobile*, an abstract, lantern-shaped structure suspended by wire. His letter informed me that although the piece had excited the inevitable outrage among the more hide-bound critics it had also generated some appreciative but furtive praise. Nevertheless, he doubted that any buyer would rise to the fifty thousand franc price tag he had placed upon it. He understood the fear of a buyer ruining his reputation by buying into what some were already calling apocalyptic voyeurism. Still, he lived in hope.

That was the first of twelve operations I performed on Thomas between 1986 and 1992. In all I removed twenty-three bones and four internal organs, eighteen inches of his digestive tract, seven teeth, four toes, his left eye and his right leg. He exhibited work on the fringe of most major European art festivals, narrowly escaping arrest in several countries and jumping bail in four. In his lifetime he sold eight pieces worth a total of fifty thousand pounds, by no means riches, but enough to fund his spartan existence.

Inevitably, by 1989 his work had taken a toll on his body. After the removal of a section of digestive tract in 1988 his body slumped badly and following the amputation of his right leg in 1989 he spent his remaining years in a wheelchair. Despite this his spirits never sank nor did his courage fail him; he was undoubtedly sustained by the tentative acclaim that greeted his work in avant-garde circles. For the first time also he was being sought out for interviews. He declined them all, pointing out simply that the spoken word was not his medium.

His deterioration could not go on indefinitely. In March 1992 he wrote telling me he planned to exhibit his final piece at the Kassel Documenta. He travelled to Dublin the following month and spent a week at my house where he outlined the procedure I was to follow after the operation. On the night of the tenth, after shaking hands with appropriate solemnity for the last time, I administered him a massive dose of morphine, a euthanasia injection. He died painlessly within four minutes. Then, following his instructions, I removed his remaining left arm and head – messy, dispiriting work. I then boiled the flesh from the arm and skull in a huge bath and using a solution of bleach and furniture polish brought the bone to a luminous whiteness. I fixed the skull in the hand and set the whole thing on a wall mount; *Alas, Poor Thomas* he had told me to call it. Then I sent it to Kassel at the end of the month, Thomas already having informed the gallery as to the kind of work they were to expect. In critical terms it was his most successful piece and when Kiefer singled him out as the genius specific to the jaded tenor of this brutal and fantastic century his reputation was cemented. This last piece sold for twenty-five thousand Deutschmarks.

When, as executor of the Thomas Crumlesh Estate, I was approached with the idea of this retrospective I welcomed it on two accounts. Firstly, it is past time that a major exhibition of his work be held in his native country, a country that does not own a single piece of work by her only artist to have made a contribution to the popular imagery of the late twentieth century – a prophet in his own land indeed. Secondly, I welcomed the opportunity to assemble together for the first time his entire oeuvre. My belief is that the cumulative effect of its technical brilliance, its humour and undeniable beauty will dispel the comfortable notion that Thomas was nothing more than a mental deviant with a classy suicide plan. The rigour and terminal logic of his art leaves no room for such easy platitudes.

Several people have speculated that I would use this introduction to the catalogue to justify my activities or, worse, as an opportunity to bewail the consequences. Some have gone so far as to hope that I would repent. I propose to do neither of these. Yet a debt of gratitude is outstanding. It falls to very few of us to be able to put our skills at the disposal of genius: most of us are doomed to ply our trades within the horizons of the blind, the realm of drones. But I was one of the few, one of the rescued. Sheer chance allowed me to have a hand in the works of art that proceeded from the body of my friend, works of art that in the last years of this century draw down the curtain on an entire tradition. His work is before us now and we should see it as an end.

All that remains for me to say is, Thomas, dear friend, it was my privilege.

Dr Frank Caulfield

Arbour Hill Prison
Dublin

Ronan Bennett

from *The Catastrophist*

LÉOPOLDVILLE

I AM STILL here, though I will leave soon. We share even less than before. Stipe advised me to hang on, but being around her and receiving nothing has discouraged me. It has worn me down. It has overthrown my self-esteem, sapped my pride. She is indifferent to my presence. I can take no more.

She has not been well. Out of habit, I suppose, I badger her about not eating properly. When she goes out on her tours with Smail and Auguste – who now seems to drive for her as much as for Stipe – she makes do with *fufu*, plantain and cassava. What's good enough for the people is good enough for her. She is so thin and worn. Her big blue eyes seem bigger now; there are black-brown smudges beneath them and they are disturbingly bright.

There is a funny side to this. Though she would deny it, Inès has a competitive sense – not about esteem or earnings or proficiency with languages or anything like that, but about health and stamina. During our first winter in London I came down with a bad cold. She brought me endless hot whiskies and whispered comforts, and informed me – a little boastfully – that she never got colds. When a few days later she took to her bed *dying* of one I teased her, but she of course could not remember having said anything of the sort. She doesn't play fair: she gives you pieces of the jigsaw and snatches them away again. Little details, the things that make up the whole.

I do not tease her now. I am too worried. When Lumumba

was unexpectedly freed to attend the Brussels conference – something she is convinced her campaign in *L'Unità* was instrumental in bringing about – she could not find the strength to get out of the apartment. She insisted she would be fine and was adamant about not seeing a doctor. Doctors are panickers, she says. But the truth is she does not want to be reminded of London, of what the doctors told her there. There are days when she is fine, and days when she is not.

I am writing at the table when I first hear it. The noise is low, indistinct, faintly like the air being sliced, a sound you think you have heard, then decide is inside your head. Inès is in the bedroom, reading, dozing. Today is one of the bad days.

'Can you hear that?' she calls out weakly.

The sound is louder now. I become conscious of something odd, something missing. I look at my watch. It is just after four. There should be traffic and there isn't any. Not a single car.

'Can you hear that?' Inès calls again from the bedroom.

'Yes.'

'What is it?'

I get up and look out the window.

'What's happening?'

Inès comes into the living room pulling a dress over her head. I glimpse her white stomach and breasts and feel a sudden sharp pang of loss. The beautiful things that were mine and are no longer. This proximity is killing me. I have to go, if I am to survive. I have to go, but I don't want to.

The phone rings.

'I can't see anything,' I say to her. 'But have you noticed? There's no traffic.'

She comes to the window and stands beside me. Her skin smells of sleep and milk and sweat. I go to answer the phone.

'Heard the news?'

It is Stipe.

'No.'

'You must be the only man in Leo who hasn't. What the hell do you writers do all day?'

'Write.'

'Try to get out a little more. Or at least listen to the radio.'

'What is the news?'

'Remember your article – six months?'

'And?'

'You weren't out by much. June 30th. It's just been announced from the round-table conference. Congratulations. Let's have a drink at the Colibri soon to celebrate.'

He hangs up. Inès is looking at me.

'Well?'

'Stipe.'

She makes a noise of disapproval and turns back to the window. Nothing Stipe has to say could possibly be of interest.

'The Belgians have set the date for independence – June 30th.'

She turns back at once.

'Jesus,' she says quietly. 'Is he joking?'

'I don't think so.'

I have never seen her look so astonished. She hurries into the bedroom to finish dressing.

I check the date: February 27th.

'Four months,' I say to myself. 'Four months to independence.'

Only now do I realize that I hadn't believed Stipe when I'd written the article. I'd been a proxy floating something speculative and provocative. I had claimed – the way journalists do – to be painting the picture I had seen before me. Inès has no time for this defence. What colours do you use? How do you mix them? Where do you stand? What factors influence your choice of perspective? But in this case the defence was especially spurious. I had painted a picture I hadn't even seen. It was Stipe's picture.

637

She re-emerges clutching a pair of scuffed old shoes and leans against me as she slips them on.

A middle-aged Belgian woman in a pale blue floral dress tugs at my arm. She clutches a white handbag to her breast. She has a desperate look.

'Nous nous trouvons devant l'inconnu complet,' she mutters. 'L'inconnu complet, l'inconnu complet.'

She wanders off with the distracted air and unseeing eye of someone who has just been told that their child has been killed in an accident. She is not alone. Every white face betrays loss, and utter bewilderment. At the corner of Lambermont a small group of white office workers have come out to confirm with their own eyes what they have been told on the radio. They are speechless, blank, horrified.

'Come on,' Inès says urgently and she starts down Avenue des Aviateurs, where the blacks are marching. I follow, pushing past the benumbed white spectators.

'Where is the army? Why are they letting this happen?' I hear a man say to his companion as I pass.

Something about this jars. Not the words. Not that. Something else. It is not until I have gone another ten or twenty paces that it hits me: the man was whispering, he was speaking under his breath. I have often heard whites being defensive and wary, but this is the first time I have ever heard a *colon* keep his voice down. In that instant I grasp the extent of what we are witnessing. I stop to look back at the speaker. I have to see him, I have to fix the image of this moment. He notices me, and so do his companions; they see me and unite against me in paranoia and aggression.

I hurry after Inès. All around is suppression and silence. There is only the steady, foreboding swish.

Towards the bottom of the avenue, near Place de la Poste, we come upon the marchers. They are in their thousands. They walk at a deliberate step, their eyes straight and implacably ahead, expressions set with a confidence I have not seen before on black faces: it is mixed with ostentation, borders on hostility. They whip the air with palm fronds to make the violent hiss I first heard in the apartment. The sound sends shivers down my spine.

A frightened white woman at the post office gathers up her daughter, an infant too big to carry, and hastens away, staggering bow-legged under her load like some comic female impersonator. The gendarmes stand around, resentful, frustrated, humiliated, leaderless.

Inès and I follow the marchers as they turn up towards the boulevard, where we bump into Grant among the growing crowd of onlookers. He puts a hand to his floppy brown fringe and brushes it from his forehead. As far as I can tell from the snatched conversation I have overheard at the Colibri or the Regina he is a man entirely devoid of enthusiasm. Inès says it was trained out of him at whatever public school or university he was educated. Today is no exception. The news to him is nothing special. He casts a languid eye over us and from his much superior height – he is at least six foot four – condescends to speak to me.

'Congratulations,' he says with a politeness so tight it conveys no congratulations at all. 'Your piece turns out to have been rather prophetic in the end.'

'Thank you,' I reply.

Inès walks ahead. Her dislike is for the type as much as the man.

'Did you know this was coming?' he asks.

'I had no idea,' I say.

'I thought your CIA chum might have told you.'

'I really had no idea,' I repeat.

He seems to read this as a competitor's rebuff. Part of me tingles with the satisfaction of the outside chance who has won the race against a stronger and more fancied opponent, and without even trying. Some of the other correspondents gravitate over. They gaze at me expectantly. One of them is trying to catch my eye. When, out of mere politeness, I nod at him he smiles as though favoured.

'You'll be in demand now,' Grant says.

Further down the boulevard one of the marchers has broken from the demonstration and run up to Inès.

'Auguste!' Inès cries out in delight.

They rush to embrace.

'It is coming,' Auguste says, his voice high and thrilled. 'Freedom is coming. Just like Patrice said.'

I hadn't realized Auguste was so ardent a Lumumbist and wonder if Stipe knows. Inès hugs him again.

'I am so happy,' I hear her say.

I watch as, arm-in-arm, gabbling excitedly, they fall in with the demonstrators. Their friendship has grown steadily over the weeks since I introduced them. Neither notices how shocking their display is to the white crowd. Grant is going on to me about the inevitable offers of work that will come from the London papers, about word-rates and expenses. I hardly hear him. My gaze is fixed on a thick-armed, stocky man who has started after Inès and Auguste. I cannot see his face, but the outrage and anger building up in him are clear from the way he moves.

'Perhaps you'd like a drink later?' Grant says.

'Excuse me,' I reply quickly and start after Inès and Auguste.

It is too late. The stocky man has exploded. He lunges from behind, throwing them apart with a violent shove.

'You like black cock, is that it, you fucking bald whore? You stinking whore! You have to get it from niggers because no real man would touch you.'

Inès shouts something back in Italian, too fast for me to understand. The white crowd hovers, tense and unpredictable. The stocky man spins round and pushes his face into Auguste's.

'Get out of here, you ugly monkey, or I'll kill you now with my bare hands. Go on, you dirty black monkey.'

Inès shouts at their antagonist, but Auguste glances warily around him. He does not want to leave Inès, but the anger of the other whites, the men and the women, is getting up. He takes a cautious step backwards. Someone lunges from the crowd and punches him in the chest.

Auguste stumbles. The whites close in. How big his eyes are now, how manifest his fear. He is like a silent movie nigger, a joke to those who cannot know the reach of his terrors. Someone kicks at his legs. He knows he must not go down. He begins to retreat, backing off carefully, trying to find a way back to the safety of the march. The demonstrators are becoming aware of what is going on but seem uncertain about what to do.

'Leave him alone!' Inès shouts.

I try to push through the clotting crowd. They are shouting insults at Inès – *Salop, salop!*

'Let me through,' I shout. 'Let me through.'

Hearing my accent they eye me suspiciously and become slow to budge. I am not one of them; they have associated me with Inès and Auguste.

'Get out of my way!'

Someone smacks the back of my head. A glob of spit lands on my nose. I push ahead, someone grabs my arm.

The stocky man is confronting Inès. She is not intimidated and gives as good as she gets.

'Shut up, you filthy whore!'

He bumps her with his fat chest, pushing her off the pavement on to the road. She pushes back. The man raises his hand and slaps her across the face. She is taken by surprise but rallies immediately, fire in her eyes, and throws a tiny fist back at him.

I am in the grip of someone who will not let go. I lash out and, without knowing who I have hit, find myself released. I think I have just seen a face I know. Smail? I turn back. It is Smail. The diamond trader is fighting with the crowd, pushing them off me, swearing and challenging them. Our eyes meet briefly, just long enough for us to confirm the presence of the other; then I turn and struggle my way through to Inès. I manage to get between her and the stocky man. I am not a fighter. I cannot remember the last time I threw a punch – a very long time ago, at school probably – but there is blood on Inès's mouth.

'Don't touch her,' I tell the stocky man.

I am not shouting, my voice is quiet. I can hear the menace in it myself. Some way behind us I am aware of the scuffle still going on around Auguste.

'You filthy racist!' Inès shouts at the stocky man.

'Be quiet!' I tell her.

I can see that the stocky man is thinking about taking me on. If he does he will beat me. I have to concentrate on not letting him see that. He pauses. There is such contempt in his eyes.

'Keep your fucking woman under control,' he says.

He spits in my face, then turns away. The crowd stares at us but no one seems to want to make the first move.

I take Inès's hand and start to lead her away.

'Auguste!' she cries.

Twenty yards further up the avenue Auguste is on his knees, encircled by the mob. Smail is doing his best to defend him. Someone kicks Auguste savagely in the chest.

It is the signal for the start of the fight proper. The marchers are already breaking ranks and, throwing aside their palm fronds and placards, they dash headlong into the enemy to rescue their comrade. Some of the whites scatter, others run to take them on. Gendarmes rush over.

'Auguste!' Inès shouts.

He staggers to his feet, helped by Smail. The marchers, the crowd and the police join in a fighting swirl.

'Auguste's all right,' I say. 'Smail's with him. He's all right.'

Auguste is not all right. But I have to get her away.

I lead her down the boulevard, back the way we have come. There is fighting all around us. The streets, normally so well kept, have a sudden air of shabbiness, of discouragement: there is a pair of man's underpants lying sodden and grey next to a storm drain (what happened that they should be there?); there are discarded palm fronds and placards; and strewn everywhere is the diamond glass of smashed car windows. An armoured car cruises up behind us, its machine-gun turret swivelling with robotic dispassion. Rioters scatter as it advances.

'Stop,' she shouts suddenly, her voice urgent and weak at the same time.

She bends over and puts her hands on her knees to try to rally her forces. I hold her from behind by the waist. She is a feather.

'Are you all right?'

She does not say anything.

'Inès?'

She makes a little groan. From behind on the boulevard there is a pop. Tear gas.

'I can't move,' she says and tries to sit down on the pavement.

I will not let her free.

'We're going home,' I say.

As I pull her gently up I notice Grant and one of the correspondents looking at us. Grant nods to me and I give him a stiff smile in return. I see a smirk cross his face. He turns to say something to his colleague. I doubt that it's kind. It must please him to see his competitor embroiled in so undignified a situation. I doubt Grant has ever been in the middle of something like this – with temper, anger, passion flaring, with someone's spit trickling from nose to chin. I doubt he has been with a woman like this, a woman who causes fights and flails with her fists. No, Grant would never put himself in such a ridiculous position.

I can see myself and Inès now, the state we're in, from where he's standing.

Frank Ronan

from *Lovely*

T HE PARTY SHOULD have been held the night before. The jungle was painted and the speakers stacked at the edge of the paddy. Chai ladies had carpeted the surrounding fields with their matting. The acid punch was brewed and the police had been given their baksheesh, or so everyone thought. But that was the year that the Goan Press decided to become more than usually hysterical with bourgeois indignation. It was time, the editor decreed, to put a stop to hippies and drug fiends, who corrupted the unsullied minds of Indian Youth and gave the state a bad reputation. That the more acceptable kind of tourists, with their golf courses and swimming pools, were wrecking the agricultural economy, was not a point which the editor, whose friends were hoteliers rather than farm labourers, was likely to raise. The result of the outburst was that the police who, by and large, had paid heavy bribes for Goan postings so that they could become rich by harassing the hippies and drug fiends, took this unprecedented spate of indignation as their cue to demand even more money from the party organizers. So a thousand ravers spent the night sitting on the chai ladies' mats, waiting for the music to begin, while acrimonious negotiations were being conducted elsewhere.

Some went home and some took their drugs anyway and wandered down to the beach where they stared, open-mouthed, at the stars. Some had taken so many drugs that they remained pinned to the paddy all night and were able to imagine the music. A deal was struck between the police and the organizers at noon on New Year's Day, and the party became, effectively, a two-day event, and the best party that anyone who had not lost the faculty of memory could remember.

Nick and Cathy were among those who stayed for the duration. That was the party at which they found a little bag of goodies which some dealer must have dropped. They experimented recklessly with the contents, dragging those thirty-six hours out into a lifetime of holiday. Because of the disarrangement and confusion of time they couldn't say exactly when it was that they first noticed the tall man, but it must have been during the second night. He was dancing near the speakers, like an otter, more cadence than rhythm, seeming incongruous with his height, and a precision to him among the sliding ravers in their cloven footwear. Nick and Cathy were themselves trying to dance, but were so far gone that they could only clutch at each other in fits of unwarranted laughter. They lost the plot just after that, and the next thing they could remember was coming away from the dancers and dropping, cross-legged, onto the matting of their chai lady. While Cathy closed her eyes, as a way of retreating into a world she could control more easily, Nick focused on a raw corrugation of muscle that still twitched in his shoulder, keeping time with the sinuous high hat, which seemed to come separately from the rest of the music, threading through the mango trees. He was devastatingly amused. It was during that distraction that the light changed; night ended and the morning began.

It was while he was sitting like that, grinning like an idiot as he grappled with the last hours of the party, that Aaron first saw him, and began to be fascinated.

So many party rumours had been washing over Baga on New Year's Day, and so many strangers had asked Aaron whether he had been to the party and whether he was going, and whether he knew what the truth was, that he had decided, in the cause of disinterested scholarship, to go and see what the fuss was about. Once there, he had swallowed a tab of something mild and dancy and enjoyed the spectacle while he waited for it to kick in.

Though he danced and exchanged mindless smiles with other dancers and gave himself all the evidence that he was having a good time, he became conscious of his isolation. He began to think of the end of his travels, when he would return home, alone, to the perfect universe he had created for himself. He had to remind himself that his life was a happy one, was the life he had chosen; but the acid in his brain would not allow the usual arguments for self-satisfaction. That word, *alone*, kept repeating in his mind. Like someone who has failed his driving test and is watching all the cars on a busy road, wondering what is wrong with him that he cannot accomplish such a simple and everyday skill, he saw couples everywhere he looked and felt himself to be a failure. It occurred to him that he was already in love, and that he had been in love all his life, but without finding the object of his love. If he didn't find it soon he might become a selfish old bachelor, too fussy about his petty and ordered life to allow another to infringe upon it.

Having thought all this, in the syncopated meter of dancing, and having reached what had the semblance of a decision, he had been overtaken by a calmness and walked away from the music. That was when he saw Cathy and Nick.

The sky was paling indigo and the light at ground level was intense and greenish from the lamps of the chai ladies. Nick was minding his own business, tripping his tits off and smiling the width of an ache, with Cathy beside him in a lesser stupor. On seeing them, the first thing Aaron thought was that this couple were the perfect illustration of what he had just been wanting, that they had some knowledge which was denied to him. He had never seen a creature so evidently, unashamedly and completely happy as Nick. It was not Nick that first attracted him, but Nick's happiness. From the way they sat together, it could be assumed that Nick and Cathy were lovers; that Nick was not available. Aaron watched the smiling man and something changed; something was signified. He could not tell what or how, but he knew that he would have to find out; that he would have to find a way of talking to this person. He had a feeling that his failure was about to be overturned.

The chai lady nearest to him was holding out a glass of coffee and asking, in an insistent voice, whether he wanted it. He folded his legs beneath him and took the glass. Through the dawn and the morning he watched the pair, making guesses as to who they were and what their relationship was. They seemed to know everyone who passed or, if they didn't, to be ready to know anyone. Aaron couldn't make out anything they said, but he could read their gestures. From the way that one of them would point out a good-looking man to the other, and the smutty look they would exchange in consequence, it soon became obvious that they were no more than friends. By this time Aaron was too involved in romantic fantasy to notice that this realization had overturned the original motivation for his interest in them. It took a very small leap of the imagination for Aaron to think that he was falling in love.

Towards the end of the party the midday sun seemed devastating. There had been stretches of time when the morning had given the impression of running on for eternity. The dawn had been diverting, followed by the appearance of thick clouds of dust between the dancers and the light. Palm trees changed from kitsch silhouettes to vegetation. Then a trick of the drug would scatter time and hours would be lost to memory, as though the noon was grafted onto the night and nothing at all had happened in between, and all the debris on the paddy fields had come from nowhere.

As the hottest part of the day began and the light became searing on his dilated pupils, Nick began to worry. He had reached the stage where it seemed that the trip would never end, trapping him forever in this condition of helplessness. He wondered if he had overdone it this time. Goa was stuffed with acid casualties, those who had taken one trip too many and never come back. He tried to think of normality, and to remember how his mind had functioned before the party. The distance covered in the previous thirty hours seemed so preposterous that he laughed out loud. Then the question of whether he had permanently lost his mind was overtaken by a ringing in his teeth, and nothing mattered but a desperate search for chewing gum.

As Aaron watched and fell in love, every detail became clear in the harshness of the light. Nick, unconscious that anyone was taking so much notice, had his arms crossed, stroking his cleavage as though he were cold, his jaw working at a rhythmic speed and his gaping pupils focusing on one point and another in logicless succession. If it had been in his power to choose a state in which to be described, or seen, for the first time, almost any other condition might have been preferable. Sweat had run and dried on him, holding a fresco of red dust over his skin and clothing. Beneath these layers was the frame of a man who had been skinny in his youth, gone to the gym in his twenties, and suffered the creeping tide of flesh that had spread from his middle in the four years since he had turned thirty. His hair would have been a sort of blond colour had it not been cut down to an eighth of an inch to mitigate a receding line, his eyebrows were white and his lashes invisible. Supporting all these was a face of a standard handsomeness, of the kind that looks good in photographs and is otherwise dependent on the expression it bears. Smiling, as it was now, it was undeniably attractive. A large hand, holding a joint, was positioned delicately, as if that joint had an irreplaceable significance. Without it, the prospect of walking two hundred yards of jungle path to find a rickshaw was unthinkable.

The remains of the party were thinning by the minute. Soon there would be no music and it was important to get away before then. It was awful to leave a dead party, and not hear the thump of the speakers ebb as you got further away, never fading completely because your overworking imagination would dub sound into the silence, and your bones would twitch as though it were sound you had in your bloodstream and not acid.

Nick glanced at the spliff between his fingers, expelled all the air that was in him, and found himself standing on his feet, wishing that he had someone to talk to.

'Are we going then?'

Cathy's voice had come from somewhere near his knees. He remembered, first, that she had been there all the time and, second, that it was she who had skinned up and handed him the joint.

He began to laugh, not because it was hilarious to have momentarily forgotten Cathy's existence, but as a result of another thing that was happening at the same time. For the previous ten minutes he'd been staring at a television set, amazed that there could be such a thing in the middle of the jungle. Then the television began to move towards him, which was even more astonishing. He was still trying to work out what programme was being shown when he realized that he had, in fact, been watching the design on a tall man's T-shirt.

'I've lost it, sweetie,' he said. 'I'm so off my face that I thought that man was a telly.'

Cathy looked in Aaron's direction while Nick helped her to her feet.

'Babysweets,' he said.

She nailed him with a look so cynical that he wondered whether she had taken any drugs at all. 'Stop that,' she growled. 'Any more slush like that and I'm going to bed with a valium when we get home. You can come down on your own for the day.'

While Nick tended to get sentimental on drugs Cathy remained so much herself that you wondered why she bothered. She knew that he was afraid of coming down and that he needed to be accompanied back to reality. The threat of her taking valium could prevent him from uttering sickening endearments for several minutes at a time. In practice though, they had known each other for so many years, and been on so many trips together, that there was no question of them not chilling out together.

Cathy was a woman whose proportions were all squares and cubes, like a diagram from one of those textbooks on how to draw the human figure. Her nose and her chin were boxes and her shoulders formed a straight line, as if they had been shaped with pegs and string. When she turned to look at you she swivelled like a Rubick's Puzzle. Over the years, at various times, she and Nick had lived together and worked together and taken holidays together and seen each other through a frightening accumulation of disastrous relationships. If they had never had a serious fight it was owing, largely, to her fierceness. He would never have dared argue with her on a vital issue. She was the sort of person who liked or hated you on sight, and if you were liked you were made to stay liked. If you were hated you might as well shoot yourself in the head and call it an economy measure.

Nick asked, 'Shouldn't we be looking for Fergus and Andrew?' He could remember that they had all arrived at the same time.

'Fuckwit,' she said. 'They went home at three this morning. You spent an hour saying goodbye to them.'

'I forgot. Sorry. Don't be cross, it isn't my fault.' Then, in an ironic tone intended, but failing, to disguise the seriousness of his question, he said, 'But you love me really, don't you?'

'No,' she said, gathering up their possessions from the mats with a disturbing efficiency. 'Only when you're not so bloody irritating. And that's hardly ever.'

He had the feeling that they had been standing for a long time, as though they had forgotten the reason for getting to their feet. Nick muttered something about vestibule paralysis, but Cathy either failed to understand or thought the expression unremarkable, and then Nick failed to see its relevance himself. Their eyes wandered the paddies, resting on each of the remaining chai ladies and their entourages of half-dressed and tattooed Europeans. There were jugglers here and there in silly hats, but they were to be ignored, because there was something immodest about them and the way they practised their trivial craft so publicly. They claimed it was a form of meditation, but it looked more like showing-off.

Nick began to say goodbye to Anya, the chai lady they

came back to at every party. She sat, placid and competent, amidst her web of kettles and basins of water, guarding the basket which contained her customers' coats and bags, behind the plates of cakes and biscuits that no one, however hungry, would buy and which were alleged to be years old, kept in a rusty tin through the rainy season.

In an unlikely moment of clarity, Nick asked Cathy if they had paid yet.

'Ages ago.' Cathy was counting the bracelets on her wrist before setting off.

'Did we give her loads?'

'Masses. Tons. A hundred rupees more than she asked for.'

They liked to be extravagant with Anya. A hundred rupees might not seem like a lot but it would have been a fortune to her. Nick sometimes thought that she should show more gratitude, but she'd only smile slightly at the corner of her mouth. That, apparently, was the way things were done in India. Someone who'd been reading a guidebook had told someone else Nick knew that there was no word in Hindi for 'thank you'. Cathy said that Anya, who was an astute businesswoman in other respects, might have done a bit more research into Western requirements, good manners costing nothing and all that.

As far as Anya was concerned, the finer feelings of her jelly-brained clients were the least of her worries. She was saving for a dowry. Having her sights set on the best sort of husband that money could buy, she had turned down three suitors already. She was gambling on a sliding scale of gold and fecundity and would go on selling oversweetened coffee to narco-tourists until the last possible moment of her eligibility, when she would pass her kettles and her cream horns on to the next of her unmarried sisters. Privately, she had little sympathy for young people who would travel halfway round the world to spend their nights staring into blank space.

They seemed to be on the verge of moving. 'Next time, no other lady,' Anya warned, by way of leavetaking. At the same time she was scanning the field for potential new clients, calling out to them. There were fewer people now, and most of the other chai ladies were packing up to go home. Anya was usually the last to leave. When the right man came along she wanted to have the price of him in her choli.

Nick followed close behind Cathy and held her fingers loosely, as though he were in danger of losing her. He had a suspicion that he might be on the verge of thinking something important, but then he shook his head and tripped a little instead, watching a boy who was dancing alone on a mound behind the speakers. His arms were writhing, describing letters against the sky, or so it seemed, but Nick was never a great one for reading.

Cathy said, without turning or looking at him, 'So where was Mr Right, then?'

He couldn't tell, from the back of her head, whether she was joking or not.

'Cathy?' he said. 'Are you happy?'

She made a noise like a horse whose face is half buried in feed.

He heard himself telling her that he was happy. He was glad to hear himself say that.

'Cathy?' he added. 'Don't take valium when we get back, please. I'm going to need you. You know what it's like when you come down and have to face all that stuff littered around in your brain.'

'I am blessed,' she said, 'with a tiny mind.'

'And if we get desperate we could have a bhang lassi, or if we get the munchies we could go to the Two Sisters' for muesli, and I'll rub your back if you like.'

'You are babbling now.'

He pulled on her hand. 'Can we stop? I'm just having a bit of a moment.'

He bent his head to her and she put her arms about his waist. 'Your hair,' she said, 'looks red. It must be the dust.'

'So long as I'm not turning ginger.'

'No,' she said. 'Can you walk now?' She stood back a little

and considered his legs as if she had doubts about their design.

Looking down it, the fifty yards of jungle path that remained seemed an impossible distance. The roar of motorbikes was louder now than the music. There was a bullock nearby, with painted horns, grazing on cigarette butts and roaches. Fear of the animal gave Nick the courage he needed to go on.

'Do you think,' he asked, 'that I am the only European in Goa without a tattoo?'

'Shall we just concentrate on walking?'

A tall man brushed past them as she spoke. Nick saw the back of his head.

At the end of the path there was only one auto-rickshaw left among the rows of hundreds of motorbikes, and the tall man was already standing beside that, in conversation with the driver. That was when Nick became conscious of the man's face for the first time. He was the one whose T-shirt had been mistaken for a television; the one who had been dancing alone in the night. Apart from that, there was something strongly familiar about him, in the angle of his shoulder and the incline of his head, as though he were someone whom Nick had known a long time before, whose appearance had changed but whose essence had remained.

Aaron turned and looked at Nick directly. It may have been narcotic delusion, but he was under the impression that Aaron had been aware of his presence before turning. Caught in that line of vision, Nick stopped breathing, only realizing that he had done so when he found himself gasping for air.

He seemed unforgivably tall, and he had a way of leaning back from his height as though he needed to view the world from even further away. His face was long and his eyes were long and he looked as though he had come from another dimension, to pass judgement. He made Nick feel naked and ashamed, made him think that here was a man he would never be able to hide anything from. Nick thought him beautiful – the most attractive man he had ever come across – but his looks were so unusual that he could just as easily have called him ugly. His mouth made you think of the word orifice.

His clothes were a little too clean for someone who had spent the night at a party. Nick assumed that he was one of those creatures who turn up at the edge of the dancefloor in the morning, shaven and pure and not there to dance but for the sake of superciliousness. Yet he knew, at the same time, that he had felt the presence of this man the whole night. There's no accounting for the ideas that drugs will put in your mind.

Nick had his back to a wall, for which he was grateful, and he leaned against it. He had a sensation that he was being pushed into the stone by the way the man was looking at him. He closed his eyes as a method of evasion, and concerned himself with the problem of whether or not he should spit out the gum, which had turned to wet blanket but was, as far as he knew, the last piece. Under the darkness of his eyelids he began to trip in colours, smiling at the sight and worried, at the same time, that the man by the rickshaw might think the smile was for him.

Cathy was speaking, but he lost several seconds before working out that he would have to open his eyes to see who it was she was talking to.

Afterwards he could only remember that he had said to her, 'Sorry, sweetie, but I've lost it completely.' At the time it seemed important to supply her with that information, as if she couldn't have guessed it for herself.

The ride home might have been dreamt. He could not, in retrospect, distinguish what had happened from what he had imagined. He knew that they took a track across a field, bouncing and speeding, and that he was slumped and wedged between Cathy and the strange man. Now and then he could open his eyes and focus on the driver's rear-view mirror and see the eyes of Aaron Gunn. They were pale brown, with a rim of violet on the circumferences of the pupils, and they appeared to be always fixed on Nick. He heard conversation, but he could make no sound himself. He may have imagined the moment when he glanced into the man's lap and saw the outline of an erection in the green cotton.

Emma Donoghue

from *Hood*

QUITE A CROWD, edging in the side door of the parish church of St Cecilia. Few of them could have known Cara; it must have been respect for Mr Wall that brought them, as well as pity for his broken home. A strange kind of neighbourliness, in this suburb of detached hedged-off residences; they wouldn't pass the time of day with you, but once you died they'd don heavy jackets in a heatwave to nod to your coffin.

Speaking of which, there it was up near the altar on the brass trolley. Weighted down with circles of roses and crosses of gladioli, despite the notice in the paper. Perhaps people forgot; perhaps trekking off to buy wreaths for that poor Wall girl relieved their feelings more than obeying her wishes would. Cara never could bear the idea of cut flowers; if you thought something was beautiful, she asked me once, why would you want to pay for its execution? Discussing our hypothetical deaths, that evening when we sat up giggling over a baking tray of ginger snaps, I seemed to remember suggesting pot-plants instead of wreaths, so that mourners could take them home afterwards and tend them in one's memory. Cara had liked that idea, but fretted over just how many pot-plants you could fit on the top of a coffin before one might slip off, scattering soil and brown plastic all over the altar carpet.

As we neared the coffin – Kate walking at, but not on, her father's elbow, myself a few feet behind – I thanked the Lord that the top had not been left off. Here was nothing to wrench at the eyes. Rich red-brown wood and, beyond the massed flowers, a tiny plaque just as I had ordered, with the vital statistics: *Cara Wall, 1963–1992.* Such a tiny span of years, from mini-skirts through to the revival of flared trousers, from Kennedy to Clinton.

I looked away, scanning the crowd for a familiar face. Like a theatre audience at a doom-laden preview, the mourners were sitting as far from each other as possible. Elderly neighbours were sprinkled in the back aisles, and the black jackets near the front had to be relations because some of them were nodding soberly to Mr Wall as he led us into the third pew. When these people looked at me they could have no idea that I was anything to their missing relative; that I had let her dip her biscuits in my tea, on and off, for thirteen years; that sometimes, in the middle of a conversation on inflation or groceries, she would look down at my hand in sudden wonder and would tell me, her voice hushed as if in church, 'Oh, I want your hand inside me.'

My mind was hurdling memories, jumping high so as not to trip. My shirt was sticking to the straps on my back. Strange how it was more respectable to show the distinct outline of a bra than the smooth surface of a back. Presumably true feminists all had small breasts and so could afford to burn them. The bras, I meant, not the breasts. That theory about 'Amazon' meaning one-breasted, the burning off of one breast in case it would impede archery, being an etymological red herring meant to convince us that along with obedience we would also have to cast off the sweet unnecessary flesh. Last summer when Cara went to the Michigan Womyn's Music Festival – I was invited to go along, but didn't think it my kind of thing – she came back singing the praises of breasts. The sheer difference of them: the nipples that simply shaded in, the ones like raspberries perched on top, the fiercely pointy ones, on all the long and flat and globelike bosoms. Watching thousands of women walk round naked in the woods, what had struck her was not the naturalness of breasts in the human body shape, but the opposite; how, after the logical lines of hips and ribcages and limbs, breasts seemed completely gratuitous.

Cara's breasts – I saw them for a moment, pale birds startled from sleep – were nesting now behind wood and brass and dying flowers. I bent my neck to the side for a look, quickly, so that no one would see me staring at the coffin and pity me. Most of the flowers were white. Traditional, I supposed, for a young woman, who is still presumed to be somehow innocent and virginal, no matter how she spent her cluster of decades.

I knotted my hands and leaned them on the back of the pew in front. No one was sitting in the first row, though whether from a reluctance to claim the status of primary mourners or the need for a kneeler I was not sure. The organ was persuading the choir into a particularly bleating rendition of 'Jesus Remember Me'. As soon as the Monsignor began to call us to attention, I allowed my forehead to sink down on to my hands, the thumb knuckles denting my skin. I always liked to pray in this position; it was both uncomfortable and unbecoming, forcing humility.

It was not private enough in this church to have a really good conversation with the Lord – or rather, one of my satisfying monologues – but I did thank him for certain things, the lack of certain expected agonies, and I did ask for some of the strengths I thought I would need to get me to the end of the week. This unreal week, not part of the weave of my life, this set of days in which I was running round thinking and feeling and remembering with all the vivacity of a headless chicken, the bloom of a cut flower. What I dreaded and demanded help with was not so much this week – which had a certain adrenalin, an Amn't I Doing Well air to it – as the following weeks, months, years, the causeway of low times. I decided not to think about those times. I leaned my head on my hands until the thumb knuckles were digging two neat pits of pain.

A sniff to my right; I glanced at Mr Wall but he was only wiping his nose with his voluminous handkerchief. I sat back, letting the bar of coat-shined mahogany take the weight of my hot flesh. The bench plaque was to my left, its brass corner under Kate's elbow. *Pray for the parents, relatives and friends of*, it began. It was as if we were sitting on the bones of the dead, and this whole building a memorial. If I were to put up a seat to Cara it would not be a pew. (What would the plaque say – best wishes to my beloved housemate, friend, schoolmate, pal? Which words would I be allowed?) Nor would it be one of those rustic benches by a canal on which old folk rest their bones in the spring evenings. I decided it would be a plank across two forks of a tree, so high that only leggy dryads like Cara could climb it. The earthbound, like myself, could stand at the bottom, craning through broken sunlight, ready to catch any fruit thrown down.

A particularly fast group gabble of the liturgy brought me back to my body. I decided that I did not want to be here. Of course mourning rituals were psychologically useful, I remembered that from the first year of teacher training. But I could not see the relevance of mass to Cara, who, in the middle of a sermon on sexual morality back in the early eighties, had got up from her seat – I thought at first that she was just adjusting her tight jeans – and strode down the aisle, her runners squeaking in outrage. It had occurred to me to join her. We had roughly the same opinions. But by the time the thought reached my feet, Cara had burst through the doors into merciful silence, and I could not bear to start up the noise again. Besides, I would not have left Mr Wall alone there. I seemed to remember that we had bent our heads over the pew, avoiding the stares, and said nothing about it to each other, then or ever. So here was Cara, back in this very church a decade later, because it had not occurred to me or Mr Wall that there was any other option. And this, after all, was the place where the whole business had begun, water from the granite font streaming over her shock of red hair and screaming new face in the summer of '63.

The Monsignor was sermonizing now. Little he knew about Cara Wall. He was making her sound like the most respectable of young women, and even if he didn't know the important fact of her being what in lighter moments she called a pussyeater, someone should have told him about her walking out of mass all those years ago.

I think she missed the church; she was always keeping an eye out for a replacement. I remembered her running home after a New Age Fair to say she was thinking of becoming a Bahá'í. (When I challenged her to spell it, she got the accents wrong, and I felt mean.) She said they promised lack of dogma, the equality of the sexes, world harmony and peace through unity in diversity. I took a quick browse through the leaflet and read aloud the bit about being 'completely chaste before marriage and totally faithful within it'.

'Bugger that,' said Cara disappointedly, and went off to grill some rashers.

The priest's clichés were turning my stomach; listen out for it, yes, 'cut off in the bloom of her youth'. Under cover of the heavy drape of hair, I buried my chin in my palms and crammed my fingers into my ears. I used to spend the greater part of each mass in this pious position when I was a youngster, face closed over the most lurid of sexual fantasies. Mass brought out the worst in me that way, especially when I used to try giving up masturbation for Lent, or at least Lenten Sundays. Somehow the attempt always threw me into a frenzy of eroticism, as when someone tells you not to think of a certain word, 'pineapple' for instance, and your sentences become haunted by that word, and all you can see for hours is that fruit, prickling across your retinas. Not that I tried those givings-up in order to enhance my solitary sex life; the attempt to quash my lust was genuine, if hopeless. It was just that the church was the perfect environment for what they still called impure thoughts in those days. Perhaps because the body was so limited in its movements, so dulled and contained, that the mind ran riot. Besides, I had always found the most effective fantasy was not to imagine one thing and do something similar, but to imagine one thing while doing something totally different. This did require some mental gymnastics; I had to practise quite a bit before I was able to lie on my back in bed and imagine I was standing against a wall in a dark nightclub, or face-down in a field of daisies. But the effects were wonderful. The body was bewildered, tricked into letting go. On my own or with Cara, I found that a demanding hand could metamorphose into an angelic tongue, or vice versa, and I could float free of the literal. Though always at the last minute Cara managed to hook me back, anchoring my swell to the here and now.

The Monsignor's regretful homily was over at last, praise be. We all struggled to our feet and chanted our way through the creed. I used to take this very seriously indeed, trying to comprehend and wholly believe each item on the list in the second or two it took to say it. I had them all in hand by the time of my confirmation at the age of eleven, I remembered, except for the resurrection of the body, which was just too silly to believe. At least, until I discovered the big O a few years later. Such rapture made me believe anything of the human body, even that it could rot away to nothing and then be revived in the playing-fields of heaven.

When it came to the sign of peace, the man in front of me with the roll of shaved red neck turned and took my hand in both of his, very gently. I gave him a startled smile. Mr Wall's papery fingers were next. I hesitated before reaching out to Kate, as did she; then we shook hands too heartily, to compensate. Her palm was startlingly warm. I tried to remember if I had ever touched her skin before.

'He Is Lord', the choir were moaning. Of course God wasn't really a he; I couldn't imagine that there were testicles in heaven. But pronouns were handy things, and that was the one I had been brought up with; 'it' was horribly inanimate, and 'she' a nice idea, but too self-conscious for me. I had to work with what I'd got, the childhood patterns of helpless prayer. It should be said that I had little interest in God the Father; he seemed to be the chief executive, rarely glimpsed in the corridors, with his own fan club of those Christians who could really only respect a middle-aged man. No, the one I worshipped, in my low-key chatty way, was Jesus, because though I called him Lord as I had been taught, he was not by any stretch of the imagination a patriarch. I saw him as a nice young guy with five o'clock shadow, the kind who might turn up on your doorstep, clearing his throat deferentially, and you would say, hey, come in, there's spaghetti in the pot. To be really fair, I supposed, I should have worshipped the widely neglected Holy Spirit, but I only know it as a flame or a dove, and doves were basically pigeons, and pigeons outside museums were irritating to the point of deserving a kick. Once I tried to imagine the HS as a woman, but the result kept flapping her Victorian lace sleeves and coughing and saying 'Don't mind me'. So I talked to the Lord instead. He was a better listener than most men I knew; he never butted in with 'I think what you're trying to say is . . .'

Mr Wall was plucking at my sleeve; I followed him into the queue for communion. Kate sat with her eyes set forward, one of the outsiders. Though, paradoxically enough, as a lapsed member, she was actually more worthy of the sacred host than was I, a practising Catholic wading through mortal sin with – how the catechism phrases rang on in my head – 'clear knowledge and full consent'. But then again, I was not alone; all the smug married women on the Pill in this queue were as guilty as I was. Besides, what I was taking into my mouth was not the church but the Lord, nourishing as bread, and he had never judged me harshly.

Despite all the contradictions and annoyances of this church, it still gave me such relief: wood, brass, the calm disc melting on the roof of my mouth. Coming down from the altar, I saw Kate staring forward, her nose and lips sculpted like the figurehead of a ship. I wondered whether she missed him, the Lord in her mouth. What did she take in that gave her equivalent relief? I knew so little about this woman whose half-grown image had haunted the margins of my thoughts for fifteen years, and I had the weary sensation that if she stayed here another year I would not know her much better.

I slid into the pew. Kate's leg was warm against mine for a fraction of a second till I balanced myself and moved away. I studied the prayer leaflet for inspiration. All I recognized was that old heroic one we used to chant at Girl Guide meetings while we practised out knots and polished our brass badges. 'Dearest Jesus teach me to be generous,' we chorused:

> *to love and serve you as you deserve*
> *to give and not to count the cost*
> *to fight and not to heed the wounds*
> *to toil and not to seek for rest*
> *to labour and to look for no reward*
> *save that of knowing that I do your holy will.*

What stirring iambic metre, and what dangerously masochistic sentiments. Reading it again, hunched in my seat as the communion queue thinned to a trickle, I smiled to remember how much I used to like this prayer. In the early days with Cara my strongest motive had been to help, to keep her alive and halfway sane.

What a big barrack of a building this was. The stations of the cross seemed to have been painted in watery coffee, egg, and blackberry jam; these drab humiliations of the Lord's life and times would not be likely to prompt the congregation to repentance so much as to embarrassment. Of course, it was hard to encapsulate any life in fourteen pictures. I tried to visualize my own in a set of snapshots. How many should I save for the rest of my life, which might turn out to be action-packed or entirely uneventful? Definite choices so far were: (1) that picture of me at three days old, upright in my father's hand like an outraged ice-cream cone; (2) at six, waltzing with Zizzy, my rag doll, who was taller than me by several inches; and (3) the one of Cara and me leaning against some brick wall, laughing ourselves sick.

Well, at least I was used to doing without her at mass; I hadn't shared a roll of the eyes with Cara during a sermon since that day she walked out. The first time I came to this church was for midnight mass the Christmas of our first year together. It had to be carefully set up; I dragged my mother and brother all the way over here on the pretext of having

heard there was a great choir. Cara caught my eye at the door
and waved us over to introduce us to her father. I stood
beside her, shaking with the excitement of having got away
with it, so that we could stand together, our first Christmas
Eve, and carol our thanks for this body magic we had discovered between us. The choir that year turned out to be
appalling, from the saccharine hush of 'Away in a Manger' to
the cracked descants of 'Hark the Herald Angels Sing'. Gavin
was forthright, and on the way home – we had to walk, there
were no late buses in those days – I said rather feebly that it
must have been the other choir, the folk one, that had such a
good reputation. Mammy made no comment, but squeezed
my fingers and said, 'Look at the stars.' The back of my hand
was still burning from brushing against Cara's as our voices
peaked in the final hosanna.

I looked up now at the wooden box under the flowers,
and told myself that Cara was inside. But I didn't believe a bit
of it. I could grant credence to the story up to the point where
the front of the car behind smashed into the bumper of the
taxi in front. I could see Cara thrown by the impact, flying
free, but not beyond that. Not the landing. She wouldn't dare.
Last time she came back she promised she'd never go away
for good without asking or at least warning me, giving me
something to hold on to. And she'd always said she wouldn't
be seen dead in a church again, those were her exact words, I
remembered with an awful gulp of laughter that I turned into
a cough.

Instead of a final hymn, the Monsignor asked us to join in
reading 'St Patrick's Breastplate', which I always thought of
as the 'Christ be'. I began obediently, my voice blending into
the muted clamour of voices, but found I had slipped into
'Cara be with me'. If I said the first word of the phrase low, I
discovered, no one would notice.

Cara within me
Cara behind me
Cara before me

And in a sense it was true and not blasphemous, I thought frantically between the lines, because if God was in us then all the titles meant the same thing.

> *Cara beside me*
> *Cara to win me*
> *Cara to comfort*
> *   and restore me*

And even if I was being blasphemous, I was sure he wouldn't mind. The Lord had so many millions chanting his multiple names, surely he wouldn't resent my clinging to the name I knew best?

> *Cara beneath me*

(I could see her now, her face crushed into the pillow, the long notched bow of her spine under my thighs.)

> *Cara above me*

Instead of a final hymn, the Monsignor asked us to join in (her ever-young nipples dancing over my eyelids).

> *Cara in quiet*
> *Cara in danger*
> *Cara in hearts of all that love me*
> *Cara in mouths of friend and stranger*

But my voice faded at that line, paralysed by my imagination. I wanted her to be in nobody's mouth but mine.

Keith Ridgway

from *The Long Falling*

M AKING LOVE. For Martin it was loaded. It was heavy
with a weight that he thought peculiar to himself. He
suspected that it did not mean as much to other people. That
no one but he felt defined by it. It was what he was. The
circumstances of his life had flowed from the way he wished
to make love. From that clumsy declaration. I am what I want.
I am this.

They left themselves no space. It was as if they rushed
together down a narrow corridor with nothing at the end
but a white light that wrestled through them and left them
weak.

In the bedroom Martin kissed him first, then worked at
his clothes like a thief. Henry allowed himself to be stripped
bare, as if he was helpless, a passenger. Martin marvelled at
it, thought it generosity, and just as he began to feel that
maybe it was not that, but something else, something cold, he
was thrown backwards – Henry's hands going at buttons and
buckles with useless fingers, laughing a little, before they fell
together on the bed with a crash, all limbs and quick eyes
with the laughter stopped.

Martin looked. He stared with a kind of disbelief at
Henry's neat waist and at the dark line that led from his navel
to the thick shock of pubic hair, distinct, like a patch of burnt
ground.

Then he continued, and he felt the progress of things
mostly in his heart, which was strange. His body was discon-
nected, distant. It raced to catch up with him; it could not
quite manage what Martin asked of it; at times it misunder-

stood, and did something that was all right, but was not what he wanted, was too superficial, too quick, too instant. He wanted to stand on the bed over Henry's body and execute a dive of some kind that would take him beneath the skin into the dark warmth where he would be covered and included and could not escape. But he could not do that.

Henry too. He gripped Martin and left marks in his skin. He kissed him, and Martin felt as if bruises were forming – small pools of sensation all over him as if he was out in the rain. Their mouths met again when the lengths of their bodies were pressed against each other as close as two hands praying, and their mouths could not open far enough, and the only sounds they made were close and silent and formed from colours and Martin told himself that it was the sound of one heart speaking to another. It was what he thought of.

Then as all this gathered, and narrowed, it became a calmer kind of lovemaking. Sentimental. That was the word that came to Martin. Sentimental. He didn't quite know what it was he meant. It was strange the way he watched himself, and watched Henry, the way he held his head and considered it all. It was not cold. It was not that kind of distance. But it was distance nonetheless, a space in which Martin measured what was happening and found himself in two places at once – in the pleasure of his body, the warm mix of senses that stretched his skin and blinded him; and in the calm concentration of his mind, the quiet, watchful space from where he considered all of this – all of this – and called it love, and weighed it then and decided in its favour, as if it was a picture of the future or the past, and not now, not real, not available to him but offered only – his if he was careful, his if he was good, his if he did it right. He closed his eyes and let the silence in him melt away into the noise that they made. There was nothing more for him to think about. It was all contained in that sound, in that rising pulse of sound that built itself around them like a cage, a house of cards, a pyramid of sticks, a height of half-words, becoming taller and taller and harder to hear, a structure that they could not see, so that they did not know it was there until the second before it collapsed, until the instant when its height towered over them and wavered at its smallest point, high in the distance, and then tumbled towards them and from them and through them and left them covered by the parts of it, panting out the evidence of a distance travelled, like two birds crashed upon a beach, the sea behind them, and the echo of the sea still ringing, clarion, crossed.

The silence moved back slowly into the space it had cleared.

They lay for a long time together. Then Martin laughed, and Henry laughed also, and they looked at each other and laughed again.

'I think we needed that,' said Henry. 'Both of us.'

After a while he slid from the bed and tiptoed through the scattered clothes to the door. Martin watched him go, smiling to himself, gently rolling his head on a cold pillow, happy, still, for the first time in days.

He listened to the breath of the city as it came back to him. Distant traffic, a low hum like fast water. Through the window he saw that it had clouded over again. He could see the bright edges of rain clouds race past chimney tops and slates that shared their colour. He felt his body cool and began to feel the air against his skin. He enjoyed the sensation, running his hand over the taut chill of his chest and his stomach.

From downstairs suddenly he heard a tiny gasp from Henry, a short exclamation of surprise. Then he heard him say something. Then Henry's feet were on the stairs, noisily racing back to the bedroom.

'Martin,' he hissed, bouncing into the room and immediately reaching for his clothes. 'Your mother is here.'

Martin sat up slowly, staring at Henry carefully, checking him for a joke. It was not there.

'Are you serious?'

'She's in the front room. I thought I heard something and looked in and she was just sitting there.'

'Christ.' Martin got off the bed and joined Henry in the scramble. They hit against each other.

'Did she see you?'

'Of course she saw me. I said hello. She must think I'm mad. I just ran.'

'Did she see all of you?'

Henry paused with his jeans halfway up his legs and looked at Martin and frowned.

'She saw my head. I don't think she saw anything else. She smiled at me. She must have come in while we were . . . Christ, Martin, this is too embarrassing.'

Martin flushed red. His T-shirt was inside out, rolled into a rope as if he had been peeled out of it. He thought of Pat Bolton, the cracked light in the shed, the hurry.

He had forgotten. She had slipped out of his present while he and Henry had made love, and she had disappeared into his past. And afterwards he had lain there for a moment and he had been in a new place. He had forgotten. And now this. As if she had waited in the street for the right moment. As if she knew. There was a speeding up in his brain. He saw Henry's ribs disappear behind the buttons of his shirt. He could not find first his sock and then his shoe. All the time he saw in his mind the shape of his mother, sitting primly downstairs, a look on her. This was not her house.

Henry found his shoe for him and stood by the door smoothing his hair and waiting.

'What'll we say?'

'About what?'

'This. What we were doing.'

'We'll say nothing,' Martin said, louder than he had intended.

He fumbled with his shoelaces, putting a knot in one that he knew he would be unable to untie. He stood up and looked at the bed, at the tossed covers and the creases in the sheets.

'Are you right?'

He couldn't fix her face in his mind. It came to him as it had been, raw in the open places. Not in city rooms.

'Yes.'

He did not look at Henry as he walked past him and started down the stairs. A silence met him that he did not like and he filled it with the sound of his feet and his hands on the bannisters and a cough that he summoned from a dry throat. He could feel Henry behind him and he wanted him gone, but could not say it. At the door to the sitting room he thought about pausing, but he did not, knowing that it would change him. He walked straight in and stood where he found himself and stared down at his mother. Her eyes met his. All wrong. Eyes from elsewhere. All wrong. The silence filled out. The doors had all been open. She would have heard them. Their racket. He set his face against the thought of that.

'Why did you kill my father?'

His voice came out in a rasp and startled him, and startled Henry too, who stood at his shoulder and turned and looked at the side of his face.

'Martin!' he said, quietly.

But Martin kept his eyes on his mother, and she held his gaze for a moment before looking down at her hands and turning them over slowly as if examining them.

'You know why.'

He did not think on that. He hardly let her finish saying it.

'Why did you come back here?'

Again Henry hissed his name at him, louder this time. His mother looked up.

'To get my things. I won't stay.'

'Dead right you won't.'

'For God's sake, Martin,' said Henry, taking a step towards him and putting out a hand which Martin shook off. He kept looking at his mother's face, waiting for a change to appear. But she did not change her expression or her colour or the line of her mouth.

'Are you not going to say anything, then? Not going to tell me how thick I am to have missed it? How stupid?' She didn't move. She was like a point, the claw of a hammer on the lip of the chair. 'What's wrong with you? Are you meno-pausal? Is that it?'

'Jesus, Martin.' Henry heaved his head to one side.

His mother seemed to half-smile. Her eyes shifted slightly, then back again, her face back to still, nothing in it, just a look, a stare.

'Like some women go shoplifting and you decide to run your husband over in the fucking car. Then forget about it. As if it's a thing you barely thought of. Laughing at Philip like that. That wasn't funny.'

She nodded.

'What?' he said.

She looked away. Shrugged.

'What did you say?'

She did not move.

'That wasn't funny,' Martin repeated.

'No.' Hollow voice.

She stood up. She took a step towards him. Her mouth opened. Martin thought she was going to say something and he made a noise, like a dismissal, a grunt to cut her off, his head going sideways away from her, and he looked back then and her mouth had closed and he wondered what she might have said. She stared at him. She glanced at Henry.

'I'll go upstairs and get my things so. I won't be long. Then I'll leave. You must be Henry. I'm sorry that we couldn't have met at a better time, but there you are.'

She walked towards them slowly and Henry stood back to let her pass. Martin hesitated. She would go now and he would be left with what he had said to her. But he could say nothing more. He moved aside. She stopped next to him and before he could back away she gripped his arms tight enough to cause him pain and she leaned forward and stretched upwards and kissed him with hard lips on his cheek.

'You have not hurt me.'

She let go and he wiped at his cheek where the kiss had hit him.

'You have not hurt me.'

He wanted to say something. Nothing came. She disappeared out the door and started up the stairs.

Henry had his eyes on him now. 'Fuck's sake,' he said, quietly, and turned away. He followed her. He went upstairs. Henry went upstairs.

'Tell her she can go stay with Sean. He'll make a story of it. Get her off. Everybody loves a battered wife.' He shouted. 'That's all you have to tell them. He hit me. So I murdered him. If, that's all right, missus, on your way now, there's a good woman.' He paced and turned and came back. His hand gripped the bannister. 'He was my father. He was my fucking father.'

Without any warning Martin began to cry. The shouting stopped and he pushed himself away from the stairs as if he was burned, and he stormed into the kitchen, filling the air with a flurry of arms and angles of his head and weird little noises that he tried to understand, as if they came from someone else. He cried like a child. He could not stop. He sat down and rocked back and forth and it occurred to him that he had seen people do it, rock back and forth like that, and he wondered whether it was learned or natural and he muttered a debate and his hands were wet.

Henry came and sat by him and put his arms around him and whispered, and Martin could not hear what he was saying. He heard only the sound of his own sobbing, and his mother's footsteps overhead, and his voice not talking, but making a noise like talking, and the footsteps on the stairs, and the small pause then, and the front door closing. He did not hear it opening. Just closing. And then he heard the howl that came out of him and he made it louder to try and cover up the thought that brushed through him like barbed wire – that Henry would stay with him now. That at least there was that.

At some point the radio came on. He heard its muffled voice announce the news as if from under water. They would not let her go. The girl. The fourteen-year-old. They would not let her go.

Henry made coffee, but Martin could not drink it. The smell of it was like sweat. He sat in the kitchen, wearing two jumpers, sniffing, dazed. He found it impossible to talk. He refused to move to the living room or upstairs. In the end Henry gave up trying to communicate and went off somewhere and Martin could hear him moving about. He thought that he might be unpacking. When he reappeared he stood in the doorway and Martin could feel him looking down at him.

'I have to eat, Martin. I've had nothing since this morning.'

Martin nodded. He stared at his hands.

'Do you want something?'

He shook his head and formed two loose fists and pushed them together and saw how the knuckles interlocked like the cogs of soft wheels. He ran his chin over them and felt the smoothness and remembered that this was the same day as it had been that morning.

'Do you think I was wrong?' he asked.

Henry stayed where he was and sighed. He did not answer.

Martin laid his hands out in front of him and looked up. 'You didn't believe it, sure you didn't?'

'Believe what?'

'That she'd killed him.'

Henry sighed again.

'No, I suppose not. I'd hoped that Sean had got it wrong, or had made it up or something. He does that kind of thing.'

There was the rustle of tin foil, a chill from the open door of the fridge. A sound started like a roll. It was the kettle. Martin began to drum his fingers on the table top and slowly shook his head.

'She would have had to drive really fast. To be sure of killing him. She would have had to pick him out in the darkness and drive at him, go for him, and keep on going. She would have had to stop then and get out of the car and check that he was dead. Can you imagine that? Can you imagine lying on a road in the dark – dying – and this face looks down at you, pokes you with a foot to see if you're still breathing. Can you imagine knowing who it was that had killed you? Then she would have had to get back into the car and drive home. I can't understand that. How she could just leave him there and head off home and go to bed like nothing had happened. Then she would have rung me later on, and told me that my father was dead. "He's dead," she said, just like that. And she watched him buried. Actually, she didn't. She stood by his grave and she was bored. Bored silly. Then she comes up here and she laughs about it and forgets. She forgets the sight of him dying on the road. How do you forget doing something like that?'

'I'm sure you don't.'

Martin looked up at him. He was pulling rashers from an opened foil wrapper and holding them up to the light. Sniffing.

'She did. It's not like she broke down and confessed. She was caught. That's what it took. Someone to catch her out. If Sean hadn't seen that cop then we'd be none the wiser.'

'You don't know that.'

'You're taking her side.'

He was quiet for a moment, and then said, very calmly, 'I wasn't aware there were sides.'

'She murdered my father.'

'You didn't love him.'

'He was my father.'

'You hated him. You loved her. You knew stuff.'

'What stuff?'

He didn't answer. Martin looked at his hands. He bit on a nail. He wondered whether he had called out words, when they made love. Whether it had just been noise, or whether there had been words there too. He felt tired and disabled, heavy in his chair, breathing with a small pain somewhere in his chest.

'I'm going upstairs for a while, okay?'

'What's wrong?'

'I just want to sleep for an hour or so. Wake me up. Wake me up later. We'll talk then. I can't think straight now.'

Henry went upstairs with him and tidied the bed and closed the curtains and sat beside him as he settled. He kissed his forehead and stroked his hair and Martin was glad when he stopped and left. That kind of thing reminded him of his mother.

Micheál Ó Conghaile

Father

How was I supposed to know what to do – once I'd told him? I'd never seen my da crying before. Even when Mum died nine months ago in the accident, he never cried as far as I know. I'm sure of it because it was me brought him the bad news. And I was around the whole time, up to and after the funeral. It was my job to stay with him. His brothers and my mother's brothers – my uncles – made all the arrangements, shouldered the coffin. And it was the neighbours, instructed by my sisters, who kept the house in some order. There was a sort of an understanding – unspoken, mind you – that it was best I stay with Dad since I was the youngest, the only one still at home all year round.

That's how I'm nearly sure he didn't shed a tear. Not in the daylight hours anyway. He didn't need his hanky even. Sure, he was all over the place, you could hardly get a word out of him. Long silences would go by and he just stared into the fire or out the kitchen window. But no tears. Maybe it was the shock. The terrible shock to his system. But then again, you wouldn't really associate tears or crying with my father.

That's why I was so taken aback. Mortified. Not just the crying. But the way he cried. In fact, you couldn't really call it crying – it was more like something between a groan and a sob stuck in his throat. Yes, a muffled, pained sigh of revulsion a few seconds long. You'd've thought he choked on it like one of those horrible pills the doctor gives you. And he didn't even look at me, except for a stray watery glance that skirred by when I told him; afterwards, it was like he was trying to hide his face from me, half of it anyway. It should've been easier for him in a way; but not for me, there was no way I could look him in the face, for all my curiosity. So, while he dithered about, I sat there like a statue – only for my body-heat. The breath was knocked out of him; and me. Then I realized that even his smothered cry – if it could be let out – was better than this silence. Maybe you could do something about the cry, if it happened. A deadly silence was unwork-able, impossible, as long drawn-out and painful as a judg-ment. I felt all the time that he wasn't looking anywhere near me, even when he got his breath back and some speech.

'And you . . .' he said, as if the word stuck or swelled up in his throat until he didn't know if it was safe to release it or rather he hoped, perhaps, that I would say it – the word that had popped in his ears just now, a word he was never likely to form in his rural throat unless it was spat out in some smutty joke for the lads down the pub. A word there wasn't even a word for in Irish, not easy to find anyway . . . I forgot I hadn't answered him, carried away trying to read his mind when suddenly he repeated:

'Are you telling me you're . . .'

'Yes,' I said, half-consciously interrupting him with the same reticence, unsure whether he was going to finish his sentence this time, or not.

'I am,' I said again quickly, uncontrollably, trying for a moment to make up for the empty silence.

'God save us,' he said. 'God *save* us,' he said again as if he had to drag the words individually all the way from Mexico. It seemed to me he wanted to say more, anything, an answer or just some ready-made platitude, a string of words to pluck from the silence.

'Do you see that now?' he complained, taking a deep sniff of the kitchen air and blowing it out again with force. 'Do you see that now?'

He grabbed the coal-bucket and opened the range to top up the fire. Then he lifted a couple of bits of turf out of the 10–10–20 plastic bag beside the range and – breaking the last two bits in half over his knee to build up his corner of the crammed space of the open range – shoved it on top. The coal was too hot – and too dear, he'd say – plus it was hard to burn the turf sometimes, or get much heat out of it, especially if it was still a bit soggy after a bad summer . . . He took the handbrush off the hook and swept any powdery bits of turf on the range into the fire. He slid the curly iron frame back into place with a clatter and took another deep breath, focusing on the range.

'And have you told your sisters about this?'

'Yes. When they were home this summer; the night before they went back to England.'

He stopped a moment, still half-stooped over the range. He opened his mouth, then closed it again, making no sound, like a goldfish in a bowl. He tried again and, still choked with emotion, managed a broken sentence:

'And your mother – did she know?'

'Dunno,' I said. 'Mothers know a lot more than they get told.'

'They do, they do. God rest them.' He blessed himself awkwardly. 'But fathers know nothing. Nothing until it's spelt out for them.'

He was standing at the table filling an already full kettle with well-water from the bucket. He placed it on the range again as if he was making tea the way he did after milking time. He always made tea with well-water, boiling it in the old kettle instead of using tap-water and the electric kettle unless it was early in the morning when he'd no time. It would save on the electric, he said. Even Mum couldn't get him to change. She wanted rid of the range altogether since the electric cooker was more consistent, more dependable for everything – dinners, cooking, boiling, baking, heating milk for the calves . . . There's always the chance of a power-cut, he'd say whenever there was a storm or thunder. If the electric runs out, it'll come in handy. And any time it happened, he'd turn to us, delighted, and say: 'Aren't you glad now of the old range?'

He lifted the poker. Opened the top door of the range.

Plunged it in to stir up the fire, trying to draw some flames from the depths. When the embers didn't respond very well, he turned the knob at the top of the range somewhat clumsily, making the chimney suck up the flame. He poked the fire another couple of times, a bit deeper, trying to let the air through. Soon there were flames dancing, blue and red, licking the dark sods and fizzing and flitting over the hard coal, shyly at first but growing in courage and strength. He closed the door with a deep thud, turning the knob firmly with his left hand, and put the poker back in the corner.

'And what about Síle Jimí Beag?' he asked suddenly, as if surprised he hadn't asked about her earlier. 'Weren't you going out with her a few years ago?' he said, a hint of hope rising in his voice.

'Yes ... in a way,' I stammered. I knew that was no answer but it was the best I could do just then.

'In a way,' he repeated. 'What do you mean? You were or you weren't. Wasn't she coming here for a year and God knows how long before that? Didn't she leave Tomáisín Tom Mhary for you?' He stared at the bars over the range.

'But I was only ... only eighteen back then,' I said, changing my mind. 'Nobody knows what they want at that age, or where they're going,' I added.

'But they do at twenty-two, it seems! They think they know it all at twenty-two.'

'It's not that simple, really,' I said, surprising myself at going so far.

'Oh, sure, it's not simple. It's anything but!'

He pushed the kettle aside and opened the top of the range again as if he was checking to see the fire was still lit. It was.

'I went out with her, because I didn't know – I didn't know what to do, because all the other lads had a girl ...'

'Oh, you were ...'

'I asked her in the first place because I had to take somebody to the school formal. Everyone was taking some girl or other. I couldn't go alone. And it would've been odd to take Máirín or Eilín. They wouldn't have gone anyway. I couldn't stay at home because I'd've been the only one in my class not there. What else could I do?' I said, amazed I'd managed to get that much out.

'How do I know what you should've done? Couldn't you just be like everyone else . . . that, that or stay home?' There was something about the way he said 'home'.

'I couldn't,' I said, 'not forever . . . It's not that I didn't try . . .' I thought it best to go no further, afraid he wouldn't understand.

'So that's what brings you up to Dublin so much,' he said, glad to have worked that much out for himself.

'Yes. Yes, I suppose.' What else could I say, I thought.

'And we were all convinced you had a woman up there. People asking me if we'd met her yet . . . or when we'd get to see her. Aunty Nóra asking just the other day when we'd have the next wedding . . . thinking a year after your mother's death would be OK.'

'Aunty Nóra doesn't have to worry about me. It's as well she didn't get married herself anyway,' I said, scunnered as soon as I'd said it at the suggestion I was making.

'Up to Dublin! Huh.' He spoke to himself. 'Dublin's quare and dangerous,' he added, in a way that didn't require an answer.

He turned around, his back to the range. Clambered over to the kitchen table. Tilted the milk-cooler with his two hands to pour a drop of it into the jug till it was near overflowing. I was glad he never spilt any on the table, ready to clean it up if I had to. I felt awkward and ashamed sitting there watching him do this – my job usually. He poured the extra milk that wouldn't fit in the jug into the saucepan the calves used and set it on the side of the range to heat it up until the cows were milked; after that he'd see to the calves. He lifted the enamel milk-bucket that was always set on the table-rails once it was cleaned every morning after the milking. Then he gave it a good scalding with hot water from the kettle – water boiled stupid that had the kettle singing earlier. He set down the kettle, with its mouth turned in, back on the side of the range so that it wouldn't boil over with the heat. He swirled the scalding water around the bottom of the bucket and then emptied it in one go into the calves' saucepan. He stretched over a bit to grab the dishcloth off the rack above the range. Dried the bucket. Hung it up again rather carelessly, watching to see it didn't roll down on top of the range. It didn't.

All at once, he straightened up as if a thought had suddenly struck him. He turned round to me. Looked for a second as our eyes met and went over each other. The look he gave was different from the first – that soft sudden glance he gave me when I first told him. I noticed the wrinkles across his forehead, some curled, some squared off, the short grey hair pulled down in a fringe, the eyebrows: the eyes. What eyes! It was those eyes drove out of me whatever dream was going through my head just then. Those eyes caught me out all right. Those eyes that could say so much without him even having to open his mouth. I understood then that the only way to look at a man was right in the eyes, even if it was a casual side-glance, on the sly . . . I looked away, couldn't take any more, grateful that he took it upon himself to speak. He had the bucket tucked up under his armpit the way he did when he was going out milking.

'And what about your health?' he managed to say, nervously. 'Is your health OK?'

'Oh, I'm fine, just fine,' I replied quick as I could, more than glad to be able to give such a clear answer. I started tapping my fingers. Then it struck me just what he was asking.

'God preserve us from the like of that,' he said over his shoulder to me, on his way to the door. You could tell he was relieved.

'You don't have to worry,' I said, trying to build his trust, having got that far. 'I'm careful. Very careful. Always.'

'Can you be a hundred per cent careful?' he added curiously, his voice more normal. 'I mean if half what's in the Sunday papers and the week's TV is true.'

I let him talk away, realizing he probably knew much

more than I thought. Wasn't the TV always turned towards him, with all sorts of talk going on in some of the programmes while he sat there in the big chair with his eyes closed, dozing by the fire it seemed but probably taking it all in.

He took his coat down off the back of the door, set it over the chair.

'And did you have to tell me all this at my age?'

'Yes and no.' I'd said it before I realized, but I continued: 'Well, I'm not saying I had to, but I was afraid you'd hear it from someone else, afraid someone'd say something about me with you there.' I thought I was getting through. 'I thought you should know anyway; I thought you were ready.'

'Ready! I'm ready now all right . . . And are you telling me people round here know?' he said, disgusted.

'Yes, as it happens. You can't hide anything . . . especially in a remote place like this.'

'And you think you can stay around here?' he exclaimed in what sounded to me like horror. His words hit home so quick I didn't know whether they were meant as a statement or a question. Did they require an answer: from me or himself?, I wondered. Sure, I was intending to stay, or I should say, happy to stay. He was my father. I was the youngest, the only son. My two sisters had emigrated. It was down to me. Although my sisters had convinced me the night before they went away that there was always a place for me in London if I needed it.

Surely, he should've known I would want to stay. Who else would look out for him? Help with the few animals we had, look after the house, keep an eye on our wee bit of a farm, see he was all right, take him to mass on Sunday, keep him company . . . 'And you think you can stay around here,' I wondered, none the wiser, still trying to work out whether I was to take it as a question or a statement; if he expected an answer or not.

He'd dragged his wellingtons over between the chair and the head of the table and was bent down struggling to undo the laces of his hobnailed boots. He looked different that way.

If I had to go, I said to myself . . . If he threw me out and told
me he didn't want to see or have anything more to do with
me . . .

Right away, I recalled some of my mates and acquain-
tances in Dublin. The ones that were kicked out by their
families when they found out: Mark whose father called him
a dirty bastard and told him not to come near the house again
as long as he lived; Keith whose da gave him a bad beating
when he discovered he'd a lover, and who kept him locked
up at home for a month even though he was near twenty;
Philip who was under so much stress he'd a nervous breakdown, who'd no option but to leave his teaching job after one
of his worst pupils saw him leaving a particular Sunday-night
venue and the news spread by lunch-time the following
Monday. The boys called him disgusting names right to his
face, never mind the unconcealed whispers behind his back.
Who could blame him for leaving, even if it meant the dole
and finding a new flat across town? The dole didn't even
come into it for Robin . . . Twenty-four hours his parents gave
him to clear out of the house and take all he had with him,
telling him he wasn't their son, that he'd brought all this on
himself, that they never wanted to see him again as long as he
lived. Which they didn't. Coming home that night to find his
body laid out on the bed in their room, empty pillboxes on
his chest, half a glass of water under the mirror on the
dressing-table, a short crumpled note telling them that his
only wish was to die where he was born, that he loved them,
and was sorry he hurt them but saw no other way.

The slow-rolling chimes of the clock interrupted my litany. He was still opposite me, working away trying to pull on
his boots with great difficulty, his trousers tucked down his
thick woollen socks. If I had to go, I thought, I'd never see my
father like this again. Never. The next time I'd see him, he'd
be stone-cold dead in his coffin, the three of us back together
on the first plane from London after getting an urgent phone
call from home telling us he was found slumped in the garden,
or that they weren't sure if he fell in the fire or was dead

before the fire burnt the house to the ground overnight, or maybe they'd find him half-dressed in the bedroom after some of the neighbours forced in the door, trying to work out when was the last time they saw him, no one able to work out exactly the time of death . . .

He'd got into his wellingtons and stood there wrapped up in his great coat holding his cap, about to put it on, the enamel milk-bucket under his arm.

He moved slowly, tottered, almost, over to the front door. My eyes followed his face, his side, his back, his awkward steps away from me as his last words of a moment ago went round and round in my head like an eel scooped out of a well on a hot summer day and set on a warm stone.

He paused at the door the way he always did on his way out and dunked his finger in the holy-water font hung up on the door-jamb. It was an old wooden font with the Sacred Heart on it my mother brought back from a pilgrimage to Knock the time the Pope was over. I could see him trying to bless himself, not even sure if it was the finger or thumb he'd dipped in the holy water he was using.

He placed his hand on the latch. Opened it and pulled it towards him.

He turned round and looked at me, head-first, his body following slowly. He was staring right at me which stopped my mind racing and swept my thoughts back to their dark corners.

'Will you stand by the braddy* cow for me?' he asked, 'while I'm milking . . . she's always had a sore teat . . .'

Translated by Frank Sewell

---

* Irish *bradach*: thieving, trespassing

Anne Haverty

from *One Day as a Tiger*

I SET THE alarm and arrived up at the house in good time, as arranged, for the fried breakfast. This too had been Nancy and Robert's custom on a day out, the big breakfast. To sustain one for the arduous stresses ahead of being abroad in the world. They seemed to me to be sitting there at table with us, invisibly approving. They seemed to me to be often there. I used to wonder if Pierce sensed them there as well. I never got round to asking him.

Pierce was busy at the grill turning sausages, Etti ironing a smart yellow summery dress for her day in the city. The archetypal homey atmosphere of laundered clothes and fry, domestic harmony, a proper family again. To all appearances. But of the three of us, only Pierce fitted the bill. Husband, farmer, frater . . . He had picked the wrong brother, however, and the wrong girl for a wife. That was Pierce's flaw. In my case, at least, he had no choice. He was landed with me as a burden on his birthright. But he did pick out Etti, out of all the girls he could have picked. Maybe she represented the hidden wrong-headedness in him, an obscure tendency to self-destruction.

I was anxious for Etti. I feared she would be cold in her light butter-coloured dress. The wind had shifted to the north. With the icy glare of Arctic winds, it brought the harsh clarity of sunlight with it, refracted through scudding dusky clouds, revealing the coarse grain of the stone of the sheds, the life-thrust of the weeds sprouting with their vulgar, random eagerness.

Pierce went out for a last-minute check-in with Raffles.

'You'll need a coat, Etti,' I suggested diffidently. It was not my place, to remind her of her coat. But I knew Etti could not be depended on to think of practical matters.

'I'm not an eejit, Marty,' she said.

I remember the smile she flashed me.

In the jeep, I sat in the back, watching the landscape I had thrown up my life for rush past. The Gillespies' new bungalow, McCarthy's neo-Edwardian monstrosity that's the envy of the neighbours. Luttrell's, falling in. No change there, at least. It's always changing, this place. Even since I first went up to Trinity with Robert at the wheel, old landmarks have gone, new ones sprung up. Old Mick Allen who still drove the horse and cart then replaced by a goer of a nephew who came back from the States and drives two tractors. Allen's sheep were munching turnips in a few acres of brown field.

I was born into change. Old houses falling down beside new ones, brash concrete structures rising up in farmyards, new machines appearing daily on the roads. Loads of money one year, little of it the next. In the country, nothing stays the same.

I sat in the back, keeping an eye on the trailer careering along behind. Even with a trailer, Pierce wouldn't modify his violent style of driving one bit. With his slow movements and his size 38 waist, you might not think it, but Pierce was a man of action. And his shyness, the way he would blink shyly behind the golden lock that hung over his left eye. The lock creeping seductively down his forehead that Nancy was so fond of. But it was his stature Etti fell for, his country stature, not his yellow ringlet. She's a town girl, from the wrongish side of town. Pierce must have seemed so solid to Etti, so comfortable and safe.

His posture in the front, heavy and slack but attentive; hers upright and slight but dreamy. They might have been Nancy and Robert and I their boy. I had after all delivered myself into their hands.

When I travelled with Etti and Pierce, there was not the same conjugal murmur of voices from the front as from Ma and Da. They did not talk much, as far as I could see, Etti and Pierce. I took a furtive satisfaction in that. But Nancy and Robert were of a generation that talked incessantly. Or they just had more to say to each other, those two. Choosing the soothing out-of-time hours in the car to talk about the past, they discussed friends and relations. Whose son had got the good Leaving; would Paddy or Mick ever marry now; whose hair was turning grey.

'Philly has got very grey,' Nancy would remark. Complacently, because her own hair was fair and lustrous as always. Who was expecting their seventh . . . 'Hmm, a bit Catholic of them,' Nancy would say, ironically, and Robert would look sideways at her appreciatively and laugh. Who had taken to the drink, whose face had a strong tint of red, showing the signs . . . Mythical figures to me, people they knew long before they knew me, whom I had never met or had met once and forgotten.

Robert drove the red Peugeot then. The farmer's car, that, disconcertingly for the kind of boy I was, showed up its patina of farmyard muck in the city and reeked humbly of cows. Their voices drifting in and out of our consciousnesses, my brother's and mine. Older I see us then, oddly, looking back, and more competent, than we were later as adults and orphans, noting with the luxurious look of inheritors without responsibilities the movement of clouds across the sky, the stout brown cows of the midlands, the familiar names of the villages we passed through in our stately way. Robert, unlike his elder son, was a cautious driver. Easily shaken by men working on the road, any unexpected hazard, a woman on a bicycle tending to veer into his path . . . The slightest element of the unexpected would bring us to an abrupt halt and drivers hooting angrily behind.

All those lost conversations, those lost people. All gone now if I were to count them up. The Hawkinses are a short-lived family.

The customary stop at Kildare for us all to pee. The woman-figure, Etti-Nancy, returning from the ladies' room wearing fresh lipstick and a look of renewed comfort and composure . . .

Etti and Pierce and I, we resorted to talk about money. There were so many subjects we preferred to avoid. It's a safe subject, money. Of course we spend more money than Nancy and Robert did and we put down more time spending it so maybe it's normal to talk about it more. Nancy and Robert now would not have gone to the Clarence for lunch. To Robert, restaurants were daylight robbery and Nancy went cheerfully along with this economy as she went along with all his little foibles. No, the picnic was Robert's choice of repast when abroad in the world. On windy beaches, on chilly benches in Stephen's Green, on a dusty roadside where the grass margin was perilously accommodating, we were given sweet stewed tea from flasks and damp tomato sandwiches out of fading biscuit-tins kept from some old Christmas. I remember the scalding taste of the tea and the grit in my apple. And my child's shame as strangers looked at us, I was certain, with pity and condescension.

That day, we went, Pierce and Etti and myself, to the smart dining-room in the Clarence for our lunch. Like Robert, Pierce had an essentially frugal nature but he was happy to bow to Etti's wishes and try the Clarence. U2's place, I told them. They were impressed. 'Bono will get the price of a haircut anyway out of that,' remarked Pierce with a hearty laugh when he was paying the bill.

We drove down Dame Street with Trinity standing up at the end of it, its reproach somehow agreeably muted. At College Green, a short stroll from Grafton Street, Etti left us. Etti liked shopping and trying on clothes and planning outfits for the Races. That day she was sure she wanted to go to race-meetings all summer, and she crossed at the lights with a jaunty step without looking back for a final wave, her long afternoon of browsing and decision ahead.

As she walked away from us, I already felt some of the light go out of the day and a vague anxiety. I was liable to worry that she would turn up early at the Clarence and panic because we weren't there. She was a country girl, after all. Or late so I would be convinced she was lost. Or be unable to find the Clarence or forget it was there we were meant to meet up. I was liable in my obsession to worry like this once she was out of my sight. I was not yet fully admitting it to myself at this time but already I missed her. I suppose all I really wanted by then was to be by her side.

We left the granite bulk of Trinity on our right, more or less unaffecting as a bad tooth when the nerve is dead, heading northside up the brash length of O'Connell Street, over-bright in the hard new light. White-complexioned women struggled with over-laden carriers and buggies, young chaps were loafing and old characters with eyes screwed up against the fitful sun were ambling up and down the prom-enade under the grimy burgeoning trees.

It was as it always was, but I had a sensation of remote-ness, of the freedom from attachment I have had in foreign cities. And also, I knew briefly, coolly, before I put it out of my mind, that I had chosen illusion in place of reality. Fansha, Etti, the sheep; they were Pierce's reality, not mine. Mine was here but I had discarded it.

The Institute was well known to Pierce. An industrial-looking place, but neat and peaceful, out on the County Louth border. In the foreground, a small Georgian farmhouse used for administration standing with an unconvincing serenity, dwarfed as it was by the high flat-roofed constructions around it of corrugated iron in harsh Arctic colours, magenta, mauve, petrol-green. These housed the animals reared with intensive and experimental methods. Beyond them there was what looked like a mile of hi-tech pens, some containing mêlées of species, emitting the odd subdued bleat or bellow or moo; others empty with hosed-down concrete steaming faintly in the afternoon sun.

This was Missy's birthplace. Progressive, tidy, scientific, more attractive to humans than to animals. Devoted to life certainly, rather than death, in the short term at least, still it reminded me of a progressive concentration camp in some pastoral spot, like Poland. The only honest-to-God agricultural thing about it was the smell of silage.

We did not meet any of the scientists whom you could call, in a sense, her progenitors. They were, I suppose, busy in the Lab working out the recipe for some other scientific freak. It was a hearty good-looking farmhand who led us out to the covered pens where the new breed of lamb was kept.

I had had no particular expectations but all the same I was vaguely disappointed. They were the usual woolly little beasts I knew so well. Though with a fine conformation certainly, well shaped, well grown for their age, healthy as snipes. Pierce was impressed. I could tell when Pierce was impressed. Hands in his pockets, head cocked critically for the assistant's benefit, he strolled up and down, looking them over with a barely controlled admiration. Deferentially, I kept my distance.

'Explain to me,' he said at last to our host, his survey completed, and flattering the man in his inimitable manner, 'what's so different about these little fellas. Genetically engineered. Is that it?'

Pronouncing 'genetically engineered' with a halting deliberation as if it was a foreign notion to himself as an amateur but which the Institute man, as an expert, could be replied upon to explicate. The fact was that Pierce needed little about the concept explained to him. He would have read it all up beforehand and been on the phone several times to the Lab. It was just Pierce's way of making friends with the chap.

Drawing himself up to his full height, the chap explained.

'You have it there, Mr Hawkins. Genetically engineered is right. You see, what we're at here is experimenting with the genetic makeup . . .'

There followed then a longish discourse on the genes as the building-blocks of life and DNA and all the rest of it. And about the radical developments in the science, where the genes of one species were being incorporated into another at an early stage of foetal growth. This far, I was listening only with half an ear because I was always a bit of a duffer at science

and anyway the fellow wasn't especially erudite on the subject. But the next thing I heard him say gave me a bit of a
shock.

'They're very troublesome to manage, sheep are, Mr Hawkins, as you know yourself. But these human genes make
them resistant to a lot of the usual ovine infections. Make
them that bit less sheeplike, if you follow me. These little
fellas here now are a fantastic improvement. They're close
enough to what you could nearly call a trouble-free sheep, Mr
Hawkins.'

'Very nice,' Pierce was saying, squatting on his hunkers in
the pen. 'Very nice,' running his hands expertly over their
small compact bodies, in his blinkered farmer's way. I stared
around me at the milling flock, meeting their stupid ovine
gaze. Sheep that were not sheep. Human sheep. But they did
not look any different.

The Institute chap's genuine pride in them was mixed
with the professional fondness of the good husbandman.

'You know, I'm sorry to see them go,' he said. 'I get
attached to them. I reared a few of them myself on the bottle.
And I'll tell you, there's some of them would nearly talk to
you.'

'The mothers died?' Pierce jerked his head up in enquiry.

'Not that. No. They were just young ewes who couldn't
be bothered. Two-year-olds. That young, they're inclined to
reject them. Don't know what they're meant to be doing with
them. Only young ones themselves.'

He laughed. Uncomfortably, I thought later, looking back.

Pierce noticed nothing. He made one of his culchie
remarks, that the sheepman would expect, about the steep
price the Institute was charging. Your man countered that
with one of those 'they're-well-worth-it-believe-me' protests.
The honest salesman.

He gave us our pick of the flock. This I left to Pierce. They
were his, after all. What was I but the kid brother, the ne'er-
do-well, there on sufferance, brought along for the outing?
He burrowed among them, examining them with his firm,

experienced, gentle hand, and making frequent murmured noises of appreciation.

It was then, waiting for Pierce to make his selection, staring about me with a new alertness, that my eye caught Missy's. She was not yet Missy to me but it was very soon after that I gave her that name, inspired by some absurd but touching quality of pride and hauteur in her bearing.

She was standing at a distance of a few yards from me, slightly apart from the rest of the flock. Her eyes were fixed on me, glittering and unfathomable, but with a look full of hope and pathos. It was a look I had seen in no lamb's eyes before. Certainly, she was as mean a specimen of a lamb as you could find. Scrawny, as if her mother had been dry as a bone, one ear floppy, and a freakish bluish tinge in those eyes of hers. But almost at once, I knew I had to have her. Not for any farmer's purpose, not for meat or to breed from, but to watch and understand. Impulsively, I called out to Pierce.

'I want this one, Pierce.'

Over he came, glad doubtless of my fit of interest. After a cursory glance at my chosen lamb, he stared at me in disbelief.

'Marty. You know as well as I do she's a dud. All you have to do is give her the once-over.'

'I don't care. I want her.'

'Will you look at her, man. The legs on her. And she's sickly. A sure sign of a bad suck. Sure she's not fit to be in with this lot at all.'

At this juncture, the Institute man interjected apologetically.

'You're right there, Mr Hawkins. She's not up to standard at all. The trouble with this one now is that she was rejected by the mother. It was touch and go for a few days. But once she got the hang of the bottle she was grand. She'd come running up to me and look into my eyes all the time I was feeding her, like a baby. I only put her in with the rest of them to see how she'd get on.'

I could see he thought I was an eejit. Any fellow who knew anything about sheep would see this one was a dud. He had quickly sized up Pierce and treated him with the respect he always commanded. Myself he treated as a child, that is, he ignored me. I didn't care. I was determined to stick to my guns. I was taking the dud home.

Pierce tried to distract me, to draw my attention to a sturdy blunt-nosed specimen with fine-boned legs and a stupid eye. As if I were a sulky kid that you could wheedle with a compensatory lollipop.

'What about that fella, Marty? If you want a lamb, now he's the lad for you.'

'It's this one I want.'

As always in his dealings with me, Pierce relented. But as a gesture of his disapproval, he made her an extra, going for thirteen instead of the twelve he had intended. Making a joke about a baker's dozen, the Institute man threw her in for half-price. I knew he was glad to be rid of her, this embarrassment to the Institute's husbandry, the run of the flock. He tried to cover up his relief with optimistic chat.

'Ah, she'll thrive all right. All she wants is a bit of time. The breeding will stand to her. She has the personality anyway, I'll tell you that.'

Whatever affection he had conceived for her personality he had overcome. When we were loading the lambs into the trailer, she was last to go in. Pierce would have nothing to do with her and sat into the driver's seat, revving the engine to express his impatience. Struggling in my arms, she made heart-rending panic-stricken little cries, twisting her head around to catch what I could tell was a last glimpse of her mother-figure. The same man had bid a heartily false farewell to me, as if I was a girl who had to be humoured, and was already walking off towards the house. My lamb's cries took on a falsetto note. He did not turn around. By the time I had fastened the hasp on the trailer, they had subsided to a despairing whimper. Then she was quiet.

In the Clarence, we found Etti sipping a vodka, several glossy carrier-bags heaped on chairs around her. She was bright-eyed and happy. Her enquiries about the new lambs were transparently disengaged. When Pierce slagged me off about the freakish specimen I had set my heart on, she laughed without quite knowing why. We had a quick pint. The lambs were packed tight in the small trailer and Pierce wanted to get them settled.

All the way home to Fansha, my brother, conscientious about the welfare of our cargo, went at a slow and careful pace so that the trailer rolled in our wake like a boat on a tranquil tide. Near Kildare, Etti dropped her head on to his hefty shoulder and drew her legs up under her in a curve on the seat. She was soon asleep.

The light was still holding as we drove west with a metallic glow in the sky above the grey. There was a storm forecast. I forced my gaze away from Etti's dark head and watched the strange light fade into night. It had an unnerving lurid look to it as it died, like in some baroque painting depicting the day of the Apocalypse.

At the start, to see how Missy would get on, I put her out with the others in the field, making my getaway without a backward look, my fingers pressed in my ears to deaden her anguished cries. That strange strangled cry so different from the imperious bleats of Pierce's healthy young sheep. Creeping back later by another route for a covert look, I found her lying awkwardly against the gate through which I had disappeared, her head, as if it was too heavy to hold upright, between her limp outstretched forelegs like a dog. Gazing in an attitude of forlorn hope in the direction of the house. Whatever attempts she had made to eat, she had abandoned. I took her into the lodge then to try her on the bottle.

Pierce was a farmer, he took pride in being an able and ambitious farmer. Why should he care whether Missy lived or died? An animal that has no hope of thriving could hold no interest for him. He could see nothing in her. I understood that.

But he was patient with me. When he wandered down to

the lodge for a visit and found me trying to feed her from a bottle while she slithered around unwillingly from my grasp, he leaned against the dresser and laughed.

'Would that bottle be too hot, Marty? You wouldn't want to burn the little tongue.'

Then he took her from me and got her to take the milk. His authority even Missy recognized. Appealing to me, she appealed to the wrong man.

I used to suspect in those frustrating feeding-sessions that she knew exactly what to do to draw out the milk but had made a decision not to. Then it came to me that she was pining to the point of despair for the fellow at the Institute. Once I saw that, I resolved to make myself his substitute and win her love.

Pierce was patient because my obsession with Missy he regarded as a nostalgic attempt to recreate the past. He imagined I was reliving the old days when we were children and Nancy would sit in the same armchair covered in faded cretonne that I now sat in, with a couple of lambs who had lost their mothers butting at her for their bottles. He was good enough to let me at it, with brotherly indulgence to encourage me.

He always did indulge my little oddnesses. Maybe he was calculating that after a plunge into nostalgia, I might come to my senses with the passing of time and return to my proper billet in Trinity. I don't know. I'm not sure that Pierce was capable even of such rudimentary calculations where I was concerned.

My awareness of Missy's despair made me anxious in the early days that she might have died in the night. In the mornings I went out first thing to her pen which I had made for her after she cowered with such distaste or fear when I put her in with the others. As I approached among the deep morning shadows, I would see hers, humped, still, her short stubby legs elongated comically. She would be waiting for me, her nose pressed between the boards, as if she had been alerted by the creak of the bed as I climbed out or the click of the door-latch when I lifted it. I would carry her in to the warmth of the house then for her breakfast.

The memory of those warm, unguilty mornings of early summer are very painful to me. Still only half-dressed and half-asleep, not being constitutionally an early riser, I stumbled, Missy under my arm, from the cooker to the table preparing her bottle. Collapsing into the armchair as she scrabbled for a footing on my lap, half in fright, half eagerness.

The kitchen would be glowing in the mellow post-dawn when I came downstairs, the oblique beam of the sun shining through the south-facing window. By the time I had coaxed her through her bottle, the full blare of its light would be streaming whitely in, showing up the cracks and burnmarks in the old appliances and the dust on the empty shelves and the shoddiness of Raffles' makeshift arrangements that I had never bothered to improve.

Pierce's exasperation with me was understandable. Missy was too mature for a bottle. Lambs her age were long out on pasture, tugging keenly at the fresh grass like their mothers. Missy wouldn't touch a blade of grass. She had no knack of eating it. When I attempted to feed her some, her nose wrinkled up and she let it hang loosely out of her mouth like an idiot.

However, on the bottle her body was losing the pitiable limpness of the half-starved and was achieving something of the solidity of the well-fed lamb. Soon she learned to trust me, to depend on me. When I put her down after a reasonably successful feed, hungry myself and wanting my own breakfast, she no longer shambled from corner to corner of the room in search of the Institute man or perhaps something unnameable to solace her yearning, but nestled against my knee companionably as I ate my cornflakes or stood at the cooker frying a couple of rashers.

All the time I talked to her, as you would talk to a young child. My favourite refrain then, and you would have had to agree it was hers too if you saw us together, was the nursery rhyme 'Mary Had a Little Lamb'. I changed it to 'Martin Had a Little Lamb', and would be composing new verses suitable to our situation as I walked about the kitchen or smoked a cigarette with my final cup of tea. She would follow me or stand at my knee, her head cocked and her glistening eyes gazing into mine, their look not anguished then but considering, alight, the look of an intelligent child.

It was not only grass, however lush and sweet, that she refused to eat. When I tempted her with mangels, nicely wilted cabbage, delicacies her kind eagerly laid into, I was convinced I heard her sigh as she wanly pecked and nibbled at them, to please me.

With the good secateurs I went out very early and cut fresh leafy branches from the young elm sapling springing up by the avenue, fresh elm being counselled in an old book on sheep-management that I found, as a food for a convalescent or finicky sheep. This act Pierce would have regarded as vandalism. He was delighted with the resurgence of an elm at last after the blight of Dutch elm disease. Missy welcomed this wantonly hacked offering no more than she welcomed the hoariest mangel with the pocks of the spade in it.

It nearly makes me laugh now. When I think of those efforts I made in my persistent attempts to induce in Missy a credible sheepiness. The misery I put her through. To prove to myself something I knew very well to be false.

At last one morning on a whim and out of desperation at her half-starved appearance, I placed in front of her my bowl of half-eaten porridge, drenched in sugar and milk, still warm. Voraciously she lapped it up and then looked at me beseechingly for more. With the look I interpreted as beseeching, the look she fixed on me when I approached her pen during the day and passed by, steeling my heart. I prepared another cupful, Missy warm at my knee as I stirred the pot. She lapped it up. This was her first decent meal. Human-food. Baby-food, even puppy-food. But not sheep-food.

Maeve Brennan

The Springs of Affection

DELIA BAGOT DIED suddenly and quietly, alone in her bed, with the door shut, and six years later, after eight months of being bedridden, Martin, her husband, died, attended by a nursing nun and his eighty-seven-year-old twin sister, Min. And at last Min was released from the duty she had imposed on herself, to remain with him as long as he needed her. She could go home now, back to her flat in Wexford, and settle into the peace and quiet she had enjoyed before Delia's death summoned her to the suburbs of Dublin. To the suburbs of Dublin and the freedom of that house where she had wandered so often in her fancy. For fifty years she had wandered in their private lives, ever since Delia appeared out of the blue and fascinated Martin, the born bachelor, into marrying her. Min wasn't likely to forget that wedding day, the misery of it, the anguish of it, the abomination of depriva- tion as she and her mother stood together and looked at him, the happy bridegroom, standing there grinning his head off as though he had ascended into Heaven. She and her mother and her two sisters, all three of them gone now, and Martin, too, gone. Min thought of the neat graves, one by one – a sister's grave, a sister's grave, a mother's grave, a brother's grave – all gone, all present, like medals on the earth. And she thought it was fitting that she should be the one to remain alive, because out of them all she was the one who was always faithful to the family. She was the only one of the lot of them who hadn't gone off and got married. She had never wanted to assert herself like that, never needed to. She had wondered at their lack of shame as they exhibited themselves, Clare and

Polly with their husbands, and Martin with poor Delia, the poor thing. They didn't seem to care what anybody thought of them when they got caught up in that excitement, like animals. It was disgusting, and they seemed to know it, the way they pretended their only concern was with the new clothes they'd have and the flowers they'd grow in their very own gardens. And now it was over for them, and they might just as well have controlled themselves, for all the good they had of it. And she, standing alone as always, had lived to sum them all up. It was a great satisfaction to see finality rising up like the sun. Min thought not many people knew that satisfaction. To watch the end of all was not much different from watching the beginning of things, and if you weren't ever going to take part anyway, then to watch the end was far and away better. You could be jealous of people who were starting out, but you could hardly be jealous of the dead.

Not that I was ever jealous, Min thought. God forbid that I should encourage small thoughts in myself, but I couldn't help but despise Delia that day, the way she stood looking up at Martin as though she was ready to fall down on her knees before him. She made a show of herself that day. We were late getting out for the wedding. We were late getting started, and then we were all late getting there and they were all waiting for us. And after it was over and they were married and we were all in the garden, she came running up to my mother and she said, 'Oh, I was afraid you weren't coming. I began to imagine Martin had changed his mind about me. I thought I would burst with impatience and longing. I had such a longing to see his face, and then, when I saw you driving up, I still had a great fear something might come between us. I'll never forget how impatient I was – I see it would be easy to go mad with love.' She said that to my mother. 'Mad with love,' she said. My mother just looked at her, and when she flew off, all full of herself as she was that day, my mother turned and looked at me, and said to me, 'Min, I am an old woman, but never in my life have I spoken like that. Never in my life have I said the like of that. All the years I've lived, and I've never, never allowed myself to feel like that about anybody, let alone be that open about it. That girl has something the matter with her. My heart goes out to Martin, I can tell you. There's something lacking in her.'

Min remembered that Martin's wedding day was a very long day, with many different views and scenes, country roads, country lanes, gardens and orchards and fields and streams, and a house with rooms that multiplied in recollection, because she visited them only that one time, and they attracted her very much – dim, old rooms that maintained an air of simple, implacable formality. She envied the way the rooms were able to remain unknown even when you were standing in them. It was the same with the people out there in the country – even when they were most friendly and open they kept a lot of themselves hidden. Min thought they were like a strange tribe that only shows up in force on festival days.

The days before the wedding were a great strain, and Min always said she never understood how they got themselves out of the house the morning of the wedding. If it had not been that Markey was standing outside with the horse and car they had hired, they might all have stayed in the house and let Martin find his way out to Oylegate as best he could. He might have changed his mind then, and remained at home where he belonged. Driving out of the town of Wexford, they crossed the bridge at Ferrycarrig, and there was the Slaney pouring away under them, flowing straight for the harbour as unconcernedly as though it were any old day. And then the long drive out to Oylegate. And when they got to Oylegate the chapel yard was waiting for them, looking more like an arena than a religious place. And the chapel itself, all solemn and hedged in with flowers so full in bloom that they seemed to be overflowing their petals, colour flowing freely through the air. Min drew deep breaths, filling her lungs with fright. The fright built up inside her chest – she could feel it beginning to smother her. There was no air in the place. She said to her mother later, 'I nearly got a headache in the chapel. I thought I might have to walk outside. It was too close in there. I began to feel weak. I thought we'd never get away out of the place.' Polly was listening. Polly always seemed to be listening in time to turn your own words against you.

Polly said, 'You always tell everybody you never had a headache in your life. You always say you never had time to have a headache. You leave the headaches to the rest of us. Clare and Polly have time for all that kind of nonsense, imagining themselves to be delicate – that's what you always say. And then in the next breath, every time anything goes against you, you tell us you *almost* got a headache. If you almost got a headache it would show on your face. You're overcome by your own bad humour – that's all that's the matter with you.'

'In the name of God,' their mother said, 'this is not the time for the two of you to start fighting. Do you want to make a show of us all, have them all laughing at us more than they're laughing already?'

They were walking through the chapel yard after the wedding, and Min went ahead, looking hurried, as though she had left something outside in the road and wanted to look for it. In Polly's voice she heard the enmity that had been oppressing her all day, enmity that came at her out of the streets of the town as they started to drive out here, distant, incomprehensible enmity that rose up at her from the bridge at Ferrycarrig, and from the road itself, and from the fields and trees and cottages they passed, and even from the sky itself, blue and white and summery though it was. Even the faraway sky looked satisfied to see her in the condition she was in. Min didn't know what condition she was in. She knew that she couldn't say a word without being misunderstood. She knew that something had happened that deprived her of an approbation so natural that she had always taken it for granted. She only noticed it now that she missed it – it was as though the whole world had turned against her. Polly must have rehearsed that speech – Polly was very spiteful. But where had Polly found that tone of voice, so hard and condescending? She's very sure of herself all of a sudden, Min thought. I must have given myself away, somehow. But what was there to give away – Min knew she had done nothing to earn that tone of contempt from a younger sister. She had an awful feeling of being in disgrace with somebody she had never seen and who had never liked her very much, never, not even when she was a little mite trying to help her mother with the younger children. No, wherever it came from, this impersonal dislike had been lying in wait for her all her life. And it was clear from the way people were looking at her that everybody knew about it. She couldn't even say a word to her mother about a headache without being attacked as though she were a scoundrel. All the good marks she had won at school were forgotten. Nothing was known about her now except that she had presumed to a place far above her station in life. She had believed she could fly sky-high, with her brains for wings. Nobody notices me as I am, Min thought; all they can see is the failure. I was done out of my right, but they'd rather say, She got too big for her boots, and Pride must have a fall. She had to face up to it. There was nothing she could say in her own defence, and she condemned herself if she remained silent. It is impossible to prove you are not a disappointed old maid.

Min remembered Martin's wedding day as the day when everything changed in their lives at home. My mother was never the same after Martin married, she thought, and it was then, too, that Clare and Polly became restless and hard to get along with, and stopped joining in the conversation we always had about the family fortunes and talked instead about what they were going to do with their own lives. *Their* lives – and what about sticking together as a family, as we had been brought up to do? They got very selfish all of a sudden, and the house seemed very empty, as though Martin had died. After the wedding he never came back again except as a visitor. They lived only around the corner, but it wasn't the same, knowing he was not sleeping in his own bed.

There was eight years between Delia and Martin, and

then, since he lived six years after her, there was fourteen years between them, and now that they were both gone, none of it mattered at all. They might have been born hundreds of years apart, Min thought with satisfaction. But it was not likely that Martin would ever have belonged to any family except his own, or that he would ever have had sisters who were not Min and Clare and Polly, or that he would ever have had another woman for his mother than their own mother, who had sacrificed everything for them and asked in return only that they stick together as a family, and build themselves up, and make a wall around themselves that nobody could see through, let alone climb. What she had in mind was a fort, a fortress, where they could build themselves up in private and strengthen their hold on the earth, because in the long run that is what matters – a firm foothold and a roof over your head. But all that hope ended and all their hard work was mocked when Delia Kelly walked into their lives. She smashed us up, Min thought, and got us all out into the open where blood didn't count anymore, and where blood wasn't thicker than water, and where the only mystery was, what did he see in her. It was like the end of the world, knowing he was at the mercy of somebody outside the family. A farmer's daughter is all she was, even if she had attended the Loreto convent and owned certificates to show what a good education she had.

Min sat beside her own gas fire in her own flat in Wexford and considered life and crime and punishment according to the laws of arithmetic. She counted up and down the years, and added and subtracted the questions and answers, and found that she came out with a very tidy balance in her favour. She glanced over to the old brown chest that now held those certificates, still in the big brown paper envelope that Delia had kept them in. Min intended to do away with the certificates, but not yet. She liked looking at them – especially at the one given for violin playing. It was strange that in spite of her good memory she had quite forgotten that Delia had a little reputation as a musician when she first met Martin. A very little reputation, and she had come by it easily, because she had been given every chance. All the chances in Min's own family had gone to Martin, because he was the boy, and he took all their chances with him when he left. And spoiled his own chances for good, because he did nothing for the rest of his life, tied down as he was, slaving to support a wife and children, turning himself into a nobody. After all that promise and all that talk and all those plans, he made nothing of himself. A few pounds in the bank, a few sticks of furniture, a few books, and a garden that still bloomed although it had gone untended for six years – that was the sum of his life, all he had to show for himself. He would have done better to think of his mother, and stay at home, and benefit from the encouragement of his own family, all of them pushing for him in everything he did. With his ability and his brains and the nice way he had about him, he could have done anything. He could have risen to any height, a natural leader like him, able to be at ease anywhere with anybody. As it was, he died friendless. How could he have friends when he was ashamed to invite anybody to the house? He was ashamed of Delia and ashamed of the house, and more than anything else, he was unwilling to let people know of his unhappiness. He was like all of us in that, Min thought, proud and sensitive and fond of our privacy. Delia came from another class of people altogether. They were a different breed, more coarse-grained than we are, country people, accustomed to being out in all weathers, ploughing, and gathering in the hay, and dealing with animals. They had no thoughts in their heads beyond saving the corn. They tried to be friendly; Min gave them that much. She wanted to be fair. But she didn't trust them, and in any case they were rejoicing over herself and her mother, because Martin made himself such an easy catch. Min didn't like to see her mother being made a fool of, and Martin too being made a fool of, because he didn't know what he was doing when he turned around and got married. He went out of his head about that girl, mad with longing, all decency gone. He was like somebody in a delirium. Min couldn't help feeling a bit contemptuous of him, to see him so helpless. And then the same thing overcame Clare and Polly, Clare marrying a dirty shabby fellow nearly old enough to be her father, and Polly marrying a commercial traveller and having one child after another until she nearly had her mother and Min out in the street with the expense she put on them. But Martin started it all, vanishing out of their lives as casually as though he had never been more than a lodger in the house.

It was a shame, what happened, all their plans gone for nothing. By that time they were all out working – Polly in the knitting factory, Clare in the newsagent's, Martin in the county surveyor's office, and Min in the dressmaking business. She was a dressmaker from the beginning, through no choice of her own, and she made a good job of it. Everybody said she was very reliable and that she had good style. As soon as she could manage it she moved the sewing machine out of her mother's front parlour and into the rooms on the Main Street, where she now lived. One way and another, she had had a title to these rooms for almost sixty years. The house changed owners, but Min remained on. She had no intention of giving up her flat, especially since her rent included the three little atticky rooms on the third floor, the top floor of the house. She showed great foresight when she had those top-floor rooms included in her original arrangement, all those many years ago. Now she had made the top floor into a little flat, makeshift but very nice. She found young couples liked it for the first years or so of their married lives. And she still had the lease of the little house at the corner of Georges Street and Oliver Plunkett Street, where her mother had taken them all to live when they were still babies. That little house Min had turned, in her informal way, into two flats, and she had the rent from them. And she had her old-age pension, and something in the bank – nobody knew how much, although there were many guesses. Some said she was too clever, too sharp altogether. The butcher downstairs under her flat hated her. She didn't care. She had the last laugh. He could stand in the doorway of his shop and watch her coming up the street, and give her all the black looks he liked – she didn't care. She couldn't help laughing when she thought of how sure he was when he bought the house that he would be able to get rid of her simply by telling her she wasn't wanted, and that he needed the whole house for his growing family. She wasn't going to die to suit him and she didn't care whether he wanted her or not. It was presumptuous of him to imagine she would care whether he wanted her there or didn't want her there. He even had the impertinence to tell her that he and his wife had the greatest respect for her. Min didn't know the wife but she knew the people the wife came from. No need to see people of that class to know what they were, and what their 'respect' was worth. She told the butcher to his face that he might as well leave her alone. She wasn't going to budge. Of course, it would be very nice and convenient for him only to have to walk upstairs to his tea at night after he shut up the shop, but he was going to have to wait for his convenience. A narrow gate alongside his shop entrance led into a covered passage, and there was her downstairs front door at the side of the house, as private as you please. She was very well off there. The place was nicely fixed up. She liked being there in the flat alone, with the downstairs door locked and the door of her flat locked and the fire going and the electric reading lamp at her shoulder and an interesting book to read and the day's paper to hand, in case she felt like going over it again. And she had Delia's little footstool to keep her feet off the floor. She thought it was like a miracle the way things had evened out in the end. She had gone around and around and up and down for all those years, doing her duty and observing the rules of life as far as she knew them, and her feet had stopped walking on the exact spot where her road ended – here in this room, with everything gathered around her, and everything in its right place. Her mother had always said that Min was the one who would keep the flag flying no matter what. Min had never in her life been content to sit down and do nothing, but now she was quite content to sit idle. What she saw about her in the room was a job well done. She had not known until now that a job well done creates an eminence that you can rest on.

The room where she sat beside the fire, and where she spent nearly all of her time, had been her workroom in the old days. It was the front room, running the whole width of the narrow old house, and it had a high ceiling and three tall windows. The windows were curtained in thin blue stuff that showed gaps of darkness outside when she pulled them together at night. Min didn't care. Often she didn't bother to pull them but just left them open. The house opposite was all given over to offices, dead at night and in any case, she told herself, she had nothing to hide ... It was only a manner of speaking with her, that she had nothing to hide: she meant that she wasn't afraid to be alone at night with the windows wide open to the night.

There were three doors in the wall that faced the three windows. Two of the doors led into the two smaller rooms of the flat, and the middle door led out into the hall. One of the smaller rooms used to be her fitting room, and the tall gilt mirror was still attached to the wall there. It was Min's bedroom now, although more and more she slept on the narrow studio couch against the wall in her big room. The gas fire was on so much, the big room was always warm. She craved the warmth. She believed the climate in Wexford to be warmer than in Dublin, and she blamed the six years she had spent living with her brother for the colds that plagued her life now. She wore two cardigans and sometimes a shawl as well, over her woollen pullover. She buttoned only the top button of the outer cardigan. The inner cardigan she buttoned from top to bottom. Her pullover had long sleeves, and so she appeared with thick stuffed arms that ended at the wrist in three worn edges – green of the pullover, beige of the inner cardigan, and mottled brown of the outer cardigan, which was of very heavy wool, an Aran knit, Min called it. Her hands were mottled too, brown on pink, and she had very

small yellow nails that were always cut short. She was very
small and thin, and only a little stooped, and in the street she
walked quickly, with no hesitation. She went out every day to
buy a newspaper, and she bought food. Bread, milk, sometimes a slice of cooked ham or a tomato. She liked hard-boiled
eggs. She nodded to very few people as she went along, and
very few people spoke to her. She was a tiny old woman,
dressed in black, wearing a scrap of a hat that she had made
herself and decorated with an eye veil.

She read a good deal, leaning attentively back towards
the weak light given by the lamp she had taken from Delia's
bedside table. Before getting the lamp she had relied on a
naked bulb screwed into a socket in the middle of the ceiling.
She was very saving in her ways – she had never lost the
habit of rigid economy, and in fact she enjoyed pinching her
pennies. She hadn't amassed a great fortune, but it was the
amassing she enjoyed as she watched her wealth grow. She
looked at people with calculation not for what she might get
from them but for what they might rake from her if she gave
them their chance. She wasn't inclined to gossip. She admitted
to disliking or hating people only to the degree in which they
reminded her of a certain type or class. 'Oh, I *hate* that class of
person,' she would say, or 'Oh, that's not a nice class of person
at all.' Grimaces, winks, nods, and gestures indicating mock
alarm, mock shyness, mock anger, and mock piety were her
repertoire, together with a collection of sarcastic or humorous
phrases she had found useful in her youth. But she saw few
people.

In the days when this was her workroom, the furniture
had been sewing machines, ironing boards, storage shelves,
and, down the centre of the room, the huge cutting table that
was always having to be cleared of its litter of fashion books
and paper patterns, and cups of tea, and scissors, and scraps
and ribbons of cloth. Underfoot there was always a field of
thread and straight pins. Mountains of colour and acres of
texture were submerged in that room under the flat, tideless
peace of Min's old age. The gas fire glowed red and orange –

it was her only extravagance. On the floor was a flowered carpet that had once been the pride of Delia's front sitting room in Dublin, and the room was furnished with Min's souvenirs – Delia's books, Martin's books, Delia's low chair, Martin's armchair. She had Delia's sewing basket and Martin's framed map of Dublin. On the fourth finger of her left hand she wore Martin's wedding ring. She had slipped it from his dead hand. She told herself she wanted to save it from grave robbers.

If she lifted her eyes from her book she could see, down a length of narrow side street, the sky over the harbour, and if she stood up and walked to the window she could see the water. Below her windows there was the Main Street. The streets in Wexford are very narrow, and crooked rather than winding. At some points the Main Street is only wide enough to allow one car to pass, and the side path for pedestrians shrinks to the width of a plank. There are always children bobbing along with one foot in the street and one on the path, and children dodging and running, making intricacies among the slowly moving bicycles and cars. It is a small, worn, angular town with plain unmatched houses that are dried into colour by the sun and washed into colour by the rain. There is nothing dark about Wexford. The sun comes up very close to the town and sometimes seems to be rising from among the houses. The wind scatters seeds against the walls and along the edges of the roofs, so that you can look up and see marigolds blooming between you and the sky.

Min's father had been a good deal older than her mother, Bridget, and he could neither read nor write. He was silent with his vivacious, quick-tempered wife, who read Dickens and Scott and Maria Edgeworth with her children, and he worked at odd jobs, when he could get them. It was the dream of his life to make money exporting pigs to the English market, and to everyone's surprise he succeeded on one occasion in getting hold of enough money to buy a few pigs and rent a pen to keep them in. He discovered at once that possession of the pigs brought him automatically into the company of a little crowd of amateurs like himself, who gathered together in serious discussion of their animals, their ambitions, their hopes, and their chances. The pigs were young and trim and pink and healthy, and they were very greedy. He found he very much enjoyed giving them their food and that he didn't mind cleaning up after them. He began talking about how clean they were, and how well mannered, and how friendly. He marvelled at the way they opened and shut their mouths, and he thought their big round nostrils were very natural-looking, not piglike at all. He liked to see them lift their heads and look up at him with their tiny, blind-looking eyes. He said a lot of lies had been told about pigs. He interpreted their grunts and squeals as words of affection for him, and after a day or two Bridget told the children their father had gone off to live with the pigs. 'He likes the pigs better than he likes his own children,' she said. He did like the pigs. He liked having a place of his own to go to, outside the house. He liked being a man of affairs. He began smiling around at his children, as though he were keeping a little secret from them. Martin kept his accounts for him, writing down the number of pigs, the price he had paid for them, and the price he expected to get for them. Once Martin visited the pen and saw the pigs. He was forbidden to go a second time. Bridget said that one lunatic in the family was enough. Martin cried and said he wanted a dog of his own. He knew better than that. There was never a dog or a cat in that house. Bridget said she had enough to do, keeping their own mouths fed.

The great day dawned when the pigs were to be sold. Their father was gone before any of them were awake, and he didn't come home until long after the hour when they were supposed to be in bed. They weren't in bed. They all waited up for him. When he came in they were all sitting around the stove in the kitchen waiting for him. They heard him coming along the passage from the door at the Georges Street side of the house and, as their mother had instructed them to do, they remained very quiet, so that he thought there was nobody up. At the doorway he saw them all, and he looked surprised and not very pleased. Then he put his hand in his top pocket and took out the money, which he had wrapped in brown paper, and he walked over to the kitchen table and put it down.

'There's the money,' he said to Bridget. 'Blood money.'

He looked very cold, but instead of getting near the stove to warm himself he sat down at the table and put his elbows on the table and his head in his hands.

'What sort of acting is this?' Bridget asked. 'What ails you now, talking about blood money in front of the children. Will you answer me?'

'I'm no better than a murderer,' he said. 'I'll never forget the look in their eyes till the day I die. I shouldn't have sold them. I lay awake all last night thinking of ways to keep them, and all day today after I sold them I kept thinking of ways I could have kept them in hiding someplace where nobody would know about them – I got that fond of them. They knew me when they saw me.'

Bridget stood up and walked to the table and picked up the money and put it into her apron pocket. She was a very small, stout, vigorous woman with round blue eyes and straight black hair, and she was proud of the reputation she had for speaking her mind. She was proud, cunning, suspicious, and resourceful, and where her slow, stumbling husband was concerned she was pitiless. She didn't want the children to grow up to be like him. She didn't want them to be seen with him. She told them she didn't want them dragging around after him. She had long ago grown tired of trying to understand what it was that was holding him back, and so impeding them all. But tonight, for once, it was clear to her that he was going to make an excuse of the pigs for doing nothing at all about anything for weeks or even months to come. It would be laughable if it weren't for the bad effect his laziness might have on the children. But he was useful to her around the house, as a bad example. The children were half afraid of him, because they were afraid of being drawn into his bad luck. They were ashamed of him. Min thought anybody could tell by the way her father spoke that he couldn't read or write. Maybe that was the great attraction between him and the pigs. He always seemed to be begging for time until his speech could catch up with his memory, and he never seemed to have come to any kind of an understanding with himself. He always seemed to be looking around as though somebody might arrange that understanding for him, and tell him about it.

On the night he came back so late after having sold the pigs, he was so distressed that he forgot to take off his hat. It was a hat he had worn as long as any of the children could remember, and Bridget told them he had been wearing it the first time she ever set eyes on him. She said she was so impressed by the hat that she hardly noticed him at first. It was a big, wide-brimmed black hat, a very distinguished-looking hat, although it was conspicuous now for its shabbiness. It was green with age, and the greenness showed up very much in the lamplight that night as he sat by the table with his face in his hands, grieving for his pigs. He never went out without first putting his hat on. He was never without it. He depended on it, and the children depended on being able to spot it in time to avoid meeting him outside on the street someplace. When the money was safe in Bridget's deep pocket she reached out and snatched the hat off her husband's head. 'Haven't I told you never to wear that hat in the house?' she said.

He looked up at her in bewilderment and then he stood up and reached out his hand for the hat. 'Give me back my hat,' he said, looking at her as though he were ready to smile.

Min hated her father's weak, foolish smile. Sometimes Martin smiled like that, when he was trying to prove he understood something he couldn't understand. She thought Martin and her father were both like cowards alongside her mother. She wished her mother would throw the hat in her father's face and make him go away. She wished everything could be different – no pigs, no old hat, no struggling and scheming. She wished her mother hadn't snatched the hat off her father's head. She didn't like it when her mother started fighting, and sometimes it seemed she was always fighting. She even went out of the house sometimes and went into the house of somebody who had annoyed her and started fighting there. Then she would come home and tell the children what she'd said and what had been said to her.

One time Bridget's sister Mary came storming into the house. Bridget and Mary hated each other. They began fighting, and then they began hitting each other. Bridget hit the hardest, and Mary ran out of the house with her children screaming at her heels. Martin and Min saw it all, and they told their mother she was very brave, but they were frightened. Afterwards, when Bridget told the story of the battle, she always ended by saying, 'And there was my sister Mary with her precious blood running down her face.' Min despised her father, but she hoped her mother wouldn't hit him. She didn't want to see his precious blood running down his face. She began to cry, and when Clare and Polly saw their formidable older sister crying they began crying along with her. Martin stood up and begged, 'Give him the hat, Mam, give him his hat!' And then he began crying and lifting his feet up and down as though he was getting ready to run a race.

'You'll frighten the wits out of the children,' their father said, and for once in his life he sounded as though he knew what he was saying. 'Give me that hat this minute. I'm going out. I'm getting out of here.' And he made a grab for the hat, which Bridget was holding behind her back.

She struck out at him. 'Don't defy me, I'm warning you!' she screamed. But he dodged her hand and reached behind her to snatch the hat away, and then he hurried out of the kitchen, and they heard the Georges Street door bang after him.

He didn't come home again that night but he was there in the morning, sitting at the kitchen table, and Bridget gave him his tea as usual. The children looked around for the hat. It was in its usual place, where he always left it, on top of a cupboard that stood to one side of the door that led out into the yard. He used to lift the hat from his head and toss it up on top of the cupboard in one gesture. Always, when he walked in from outside, he threw the hat up, as though he were saluting the wall of the house. And when he was going out, in one gesture he lifted his arm to reach the hat and put it on his head, often without even looking at it. One afternoon, when they were all in the kitchen after school, Bridget decided to play a little trick on their father, a joke. She said he needed a new hat anyway, and that a cap would suit him better. A cap would be better for keeping out the rain – a nice dark blue or dark grey cap. He looked a sketch in the old hat, and it was time he got rid of it. Once he was rid of it, he would be glad, and he would thank them all, but there was no use trying to persuade him to get rid of it himself – he would only say no. He could feel loyalty for anything, even an old hat. Look at the way he had gone on about those pigs. He wasn't able to deal with his own feelings, that was his weakness. There are only certain things a person can be true to, but he didn't know that. Once the hat was gone he'd soon forget about it, and it was a shame to see him going around with that monstrosity on his head. She had an idea. They would take the hat down and cut the crown away from the brim and then put the whole hat back on the top of the cupboard and see what happened when he lifted it down the next time he was going out. They got the hat down and Bridget cut the brim away, but she left a thin strip of the velours – hardly more than a thread – to hold the two parts of the hat together when their father lifted it down onto his head. It all happened just as they expected – the brim tumbled down around their father's face and hung around his neck. He put his hands up and felt around his face and neck to see what had happened, and then he took the hat off and looked at it.

'Which of you did this?' he said.

'We all did it,' Bridget said.

He held the hat up and looked at it. 'It's done for,' he said, but he didn't seem angry – just puzzled. Then he went out, carrying the hat in his hand, and they heard no more about it.

Not long after that, Bridget went to see a man she knew who worked in Vernon's on the Main Street, and he arranged for her to buy a sewing machine on the instalment plan, and she set about teaching herself to make dresses. Min was the one who helped her mother, so Min was sentenced to a lifetime of sewing, when she had her heart set on going to a college and becoming a teacher. Min wanted to teach. She wanted to have a dignified position in the town, to be appointed secretary to different committees, to meet important people who came to Wexford, and to have numbers of mothers and fathers deferring to her because she had their children under her thumb. But she learned to cut a pattern and run a sewing machine, and the only committee she ever sat on was the Committee of One she established in her own place on the Main Street. She always thought if her father had gone ahead with the pigs, and learned to control his feelings, and if he had cared anything about her, she would have had a better chance. But all the chances in the family had to go to Martin, because he was the only boy, and because he had the best brains, and because he was the only hope they had of struggling up out of the poverty they lived in. He was doing very well and turning out to have a good business head when he threw it all away to get married. The best part of their lives ended the day Martin met Delia. Min remembered the nights they all used to sit around talking, sometimes till past midnight. They were happy in those years, when they were all out working, and at night they had so much to talk about that they didn't know where to start or when to stop. Clare used to bring all the new books and papers and weeklies home from the newsagent's on the sly for them to read. Polly and Martin had joined the Amateur Dramatics, and they were always off at

rehearsals and recitations, and they began to talk knowledgeably about scenery and costumes and dialogue and backgrounds. They talked about nothing but plays and acting, and
they knew everything that was going to happen – they had all
the information about concerts and performances and compe-
titions that were coming off, not merely in Wexford but in
Dublin. Min thought the future was much more interesting
when you knew at least a few of the things that were going to
happen. There was something going on every minute, and it
was really very nice being in the swim. People went out of
their way to say hello to the Bagots in the street. They had a
piano now, secondhand but very good. It was the same shape
as their tiny parlour and it took up half the space there. They
took turns picking out tunes, but Clare had the advantage
over all, because she had had a few lessons from the daughter
of a German family that lived in the street for a short time.
The Germans knew their music – you had to admit that. Clare
felt that with a few more lessons she might have made a good
accompanist. They all liked to sing – they got that from
Bridget. Martin went off by himself to Dublin once in a while,
just for the night, and he always brought back something new
– a song sheet, or a book. He always went to a concert, or a
play, or to hear a lecture.

Martin and Polly liked to act out scenes, and Min used to
get behind them and imitate their gestures until her mother
said that she'd rather watch Min than the real thing any day.
Min was glad she had found a way to join in the fun. She
hadn't as much voice as the others, and serious acting was
beyond her.

In one way it was a pity their father wasn't there to
witness their prosperity, but in another way it was just as
well, because he would have done something to spoil things –
not meaning any harm but because he couldn't help himself.
Min remembered how irritating it used to be to have him
hanging around, like a skeleton at the feast. And he got on
their mother's nerves, because they all knew he didn't understand a word of what they talked about. And he had a

peaceful death. He must have been glad to go. He was never more than a burden to himself and to everybody else.

Min always remembered how stalwart and kind Martin was, comforting her mother after their father's death, and she never could understand how he could be so thoughtful, and make the promises he made, and pretend the way he did, and then run off and leave them all the first chance he got. She always said, 'I can get along without the menfolk. They are more trouble and annoyance than they're worth.' But she had liked very much having Martin in her life. She liked it very much when he crept upstairs to her workroom in the Main Street and stood outside the door and called out, 'There's a man in the house. Will you let me in, Min?' And he would stand outside making jokes while all the women scurried about pretending to be alarmed and making themselves decent. The women used to tease her about having such a handsome brother, and ask her if she wasn't afraid some girl would steal him away. And Min always replied that Martin thought far too much of his mother ever to leave home.

'He's devoted to my mother,' she always said, lowering her eyes to her work in a way that showed Martin's devotion to be of such magnitude that it was almost sacred, so that the mere mention of it made her want silence in the room. Silence or an end to that kind of careless meddlesome talk.

'Martin has no time to spend gadding around,' she said to a customer who teased her too pointedly.

'Oh, Min, you're a real old maid,' the customer said. 'Martin's going to surprise you all one of these days. Some girl will come along and sweep him off his feet. Wait and see.'

Min told her mother about that remark. 'Pay no attention to her, Min,' Bridget said. 'Martin's no fool. He knows when he's well off. He's too comfortable ever to want to leave home. He's as set in his ways as a man of forty. Martin's a born bachelor.'

And of course, the next thing they knew, Martin was married and gone. And then Polly ran off with the commercial traveller, a Protestant, and it turned out he was tired of travelling and wanted to settle down. Being settled didn't suit him either; he was never able to make a go of anything. And Clare married another Protestant, an old fellow who made a sort of living catching rabbits, and he used to walk into the house as if he owned it, with the rabbits hanging from his hand, dripping blood all over Bridget's clean floor.

Min never understood how things could come to an end so fast and so quietly. It was as though a bad trick had been played on them all. There was an end to order and thrift and books and singing, and the house seemed to fill up with detestable confusion and noise. Everywhere you turned, there was Clare's husband or Polly's children, he with his dead rabbits and his smelly pipe and the children always wanting a bag of sweets or wanting to go to the lavatory or falling down and having to be picked up screaming. She couldn't stick any of them, couldn't stand the sight of them. And then Martin moved off to Dublin in anger, telling them that his mother wouldn't let Delia have a minute's peace, that Delia had no life at all in this place, and that there was no future in Wexford anyway. Bridget always said that Delia had ruined Martin's life, and Min agreed with her, except that Min said Delia ruined all their lives. They were a good team before Delia arrived on the scene. The saying was that when a couple got married they went off by themselves and closed the door on the world, but Min thought that in her family what they did was to get married and let the whole world into the house so that there wasn't a quiet minute or a sensible thought left in this life for anybody. Such a din those marriages made, such racket and confusion and expense and quarrelling. She thought it was awful that brothers and sisters could shape your whole life with doings that had nothing at all to do with you. She felt they were all tugging at her, and that her mother was on their side.

When Min got back to Wexford after Martin's death, and got her flat all cleared out and arranged with her new acquisitions

– Delia's things, Martin's things, their set of wedding furniture, and their books and pictures and lamps – she suddenly realized that she was at home for good. There was nobody left who mattered to her, nobody to disturb her. The family circle was closed. She was the only one left of them. She could only think of them as the crowd in the kitchen at home long ago, and she felt it was they who had finally died, not the men and the women they had turned into, who had been such an aggravation to her. She dismissed Delia. Delia was just a long interlude that had separated Martin from his twin, but the twins were joined at the end as they had been at the beginning. Min was Martin's family now.

It was hard to believe that only nine years had elapsed between her father's death and Martin's marriage. Those were the best years. She remembered the day her father died, giving them all a great fright. None of them really missed him. It was a relief not to have to worry about him – an old man not able to write his name, going around looking for work, or pretending to look for work. He couldn't stay in the house. He was gone before any of them got up in the morning, but he was always there to spoil their dinnertime, and to spoil their teatime. And often in the evening he was there listening to them, although they all knew he couldn't understand a word they said. What was most annoying to Min was that he took it for granted he had a right to come in and join them and sit down in the corner and settle himself as though he had something to offer. He had nothing to offer except his restlessness. He always seemed to be on the point of leaving. He even interrupted their conversations to describe long journeys he might take, but he never went anywhere in particular. He just wandered. The restlessness that brought him to Wexford afflicted him till the day he died.

Maybe if he'd learned to read he would have been more content. He could have learned if he'd wanted to. Bridget would have taught him to read when they were first married, but he said no, he'd wait till the children were big enough and then learn when they were learning. But the children weren't pleased to have him sit down with them when they were doing their homework, and he said himself that he felt in the way. Bridget felt that he was indeed in the way, and that he was depriving the children of a part of something they needed a good deal more than he needed it. Bridget was surprised at how strongly she felt that he should not look into their books. She was afraid he might hold the children back. She despised him, the way he went on talking about his dream of being a sailor, when everybody knew he was afraid of water. Oh, he was a great trial to them all, and towards the end of his life people got to be a bit fearful of him, and even the children seemed to know there was something not quite right about him.

It was probably the same restlessness that made their father queer that drove Martin to go off and get married on impulse the way he did. He made up his mind in two seconds, and there was no arguing with him. Min would never forget that wedding day, the struggle they had to get Bridget dressed. She was dressed in black from head to toe, as though she were going to a funeral. She generally wore black, very suitable for a middle-aged woman who was a widow, but that day the black seemed blacker than usual. Min made her a new bonnet for the wedding, of black satin with jet beads, and a shoulder cape of black satin, with jet beads around the neck. It made a very fetching outfit, but Bridget spoiled the effect by carrying her old prayer book stuffed with holy pictures and leaflets and memory cards, and she wound her black rosary beads around the prayer book so that the big metal crucifix dangled free. She looked very smart, quite the Parisienne, until she got the prayer book in her hand. Her iron grey hair was pulled up into a tight knot on top of her head, the same as every day, and the bonnet, skewered with long hatpins, crowned the knot and gave her a few more inches extra height. Min and her sisters wore stiff-brimmed white hats and white blouses with their grey costumes, and Min felt they gave the country wedding a cosmopolitan touch. But of course Clare had to spoil it all by saying to anybody who would listen to her, 'We're Martin's sisters. We have the name of being short on beauty but long on brains.' Clare always said the wrong thing at the wrong time. It was her way of trying to get on the right side of people. It didn't matter whether she liked a person or not, Clare had to curry favour. She couldn't help herself. You could trust her to make a fool not only of herself but of you. And Polly got fed up and said, 'Oh, it's well known that Martin's the beauty of the family.' And naturally there was no one at the wedding but friends and relatives of Delia and her family; Bridget invited nobody, because it wasn't at all certain, she said, that Martin would go through with it.

It was true that Martin, with his glossy black curls and his bright blue eyes, was the beauty of the family. On him the features that were angular in Clare and lumpy in Polly and pinched in Min became regular and harmonious. Before he got married, when they all used to go around together, the three girls took lustre from Martin's face, and that was fair enough, because their faces reflected his so faithfully that one could say, 'He shows what they really look like.' But after he left them, the likeness between them became one they did not want attention for. Instead of being reflections of Martin they became copies of one another, or three not very fortunate copies of a face that was gone. It was as though Martin was the family silver. They all went down in value when he went out of their lives.

Martin's wedding day always opened up in Min's memory as though it had started as an explosion. It was because they had been so full of dread driving out in the car they'd hired, and then, when they arrived in Oylegate, there was everybody ready and waiting, the priests and all the strangers, and candles and flowers, and the terrible sense of being caught up in the ceremony and of having to go on and on and on, knowing all the time that you had no voice in the matter and that it didn't matter what you did now. That was a terrible drive out to Oylegate that day. When they finally succeeded in getting their mother out of the house and into the car, she closed her eyes and kept them closed until she got out at the chapel gates. Up to the last minute she had been hoping Martin would change his mind.

'Martin, I'm asking you for your own good,' she said. 'Couldn't you put it off till tomorrow? I'll never get used to losing my little son, but I might feel stronger tomorrow.' She even offered Martin the fare to go to Dublin and start up on his own, away from all of them, at least until any fuss there was blew over.

'Ah, what's the use of this, Mother?' Min said. 'Come on now, and we'll all go out together with big smiles on our faces, not to let everybody in the town know how cut up you are.'

Min was angling for a grateful look from Martin, and she got it. She thought how easily swayed he was, for all his brains. Oh, she could have kept him and given me his chances, she thought. But Min could not really have been accused of holding a grudge against Martin. She could be angry with him, but she couldn't hate him or even dislike him. He was her twin. There should have been only one of us, she thought, in despair, and saw Delia Kelly making free with a part of Min Bagot, who had known more about hard work when she was ten years old than Delia Kelly could ever know. She wondered what Delia really saw when she looked at Martin. She wondered what Delia saw and how much she noticed with those queer, cloud green eyes. All the Bagots had bright blue eyes, very keen eyes, and they all had coal black hair, but only Martin's was curly. The Kellys were much fairer in colouring; they didn't look Irish at all, Bridget said. And except for Delia they were all bigger than the Bagots, big and strong-looking, country people. Min felt defeated by them, and she didn't know why. She felt that what mattered to her could never matter a bit to them, and she didn't know what mattered to them. They were friendly enough, and why wouldn't they be, with Martin taking one of the girls off their hands. They're not our sort at all, she thought. East is East and West is West. In a way, it was worse than if Martin had married a girl from a foreign country.

On the way out to the wedding Bridget made Markey go slow. They jogged along, and they were late already; they were late leaving the house. The horse kept flicking his tail as though he were impatient with them. Markey was irritated, because he'd had such a long wait outside the house, but he tried to put a good face on it with philosophical chat about weddings and marriages and young men, and on and on. Bridget lost patience with him and asked him whether he charged extra for the conversational accompaniment. Markey was so insulted he started to stand up, which shook the car and made the horse try to turn his head to look back at them, and Polly squealed with fear and asked her mother if she was out to have them all killed with a runaway horse. Bridget replied, 'I wouldn't mind.'

It was an inside car, and they sat three on each seat, Markey and Clare on one side with Min in between, and, facing them, Bridget and Polly with Martin in the middle. Markey looked at Polly when she spoke, and then he winked at her and sat down without saying a word, and they continued on at the same slow rate until they got to the chapel gate.

Entering Oylegate, they passed the top of the lane that led with ups and downs and various curves to the house where Delia lived. The lane was on their left, and on their right there was a prosperous-looking grocery with a public house attached to it. There was a gap between the grocery and a row of whitewashed cottages with thatched roofs. Outside one of these an old white-haired woman sat crouched on a short wooden bench. The narrow door of her cottage stood open behind her, showing how much darkness can gather in a small room on a bright day in June. She had a piece of sacking tied around her waist for an apron, and on her head she wore a man's cloth cap. She smoked a clay pipe and regarded the carful of Bagots with an amusement that was as empty of malice as it was of innocence. Markey touched his hat to her and said, 'Fine day, Ma'am.' The others didn't notice her – their eyes were ahead to the little knot of people at the chapel gate. Min knew Delia must be waiting, and she thought, One good thing, we've given her a few anxious minutes. Martin looked as if he had felt a twinge of doubt about what he was doing. He said, 'I feel like a great stranger all of a sudden.'

'There's time yet, Martin,' Min said. 'We can hurry the horse and go on past them all and go to Enniscorthy and take the train back to Wexford and never see any of them again.'

Bridget turned her head and opened her eyes and looked at Martin. 'Come on home with us, darling,' she said, 'and you'll never hear another word about it.'

Markey pulled the horse up and said to Martin, 'Here you are, now.'

Martin stood up, making the little car suddenly flimsy, and he pushed his way between their skirts and jumped out onto the road. It was at that moment, when she heard his feet land on the ground, that the day began whirling in Min's memory. She had known perfectly well that the day would be hateful, but she had not known that it would all be so unnatural, or that she herself would feel worn and dry and unable to manage, because the only thing she wanted was to escape from it all, and she couldn't leave her mother's side. Min had never felt trapped before that day. She felt like a prisoner. She longed to be back in her workroom, where she was monarch of all she surveyed. She didn't like the voices of the people out here in the country. They were hard to understand. She knew they were discussing her behind her back, and she tried to let them know she was on to them by the knowing way she looked at them. Martin behaved as though he had forgotten she was alive. She thought it was strange that the world lit up in moments of joy, but that everything remained exactly the same when disaster struck. Martin turned into a different person when he jumped out of the car at the chapel gate. From now on there would be nothing more

between her and him than running into each other in the
street once in a while.

After the wedding ceremony was over, they all drove out
a very long way along the road to Enniscorthy, and then off
that road onto a rough country road that took them to the
Slaney River. Delia's mother's family, her old brother and her
three old sisters, lived by the Slaney in a very big farmhouse,
whitewashed, with a towering thatched roof. The size of the
house and the prosperous appearance of the place impressed
Min. Delia's aunts and her uncle were all unmarried, and
they had all been born here. Min heard the house was very
old, and that the family had been in this lovely spot beside
the Slaney for centuries. She and her mother were amazed
by the furniture they saw in the parlour and in the rooms
beyond the parlour. It was grandeur to have furniture like this.

'This house must have a great upstairs,' Bridget whispered
to Min, and Min felt very sorry for her mother. The best her
mother had been able to do was to struggle out of a district
where the people were down and out and into a street where
the poor lived – self-respecting people, but poor. And here
they were, at Martin's wedding, surrounded by women who
were mistresses of possession of so many acres, and even the
least of them with a firm hold on the house she lived in, even
if it was only a cottage, or even a half acre.

Min glanced about. These people out here in the country
all belonged to one another, and they were related to one
another from the distant past. These families went a long way
back in time, and they remembered marriages that had taken
place a hundred years before. They didn't talk, as Min understood talk. Here in the country they wove webs with names
and dates and places. The dead were mentioned in the same
voice with the living, so that fathers and sisters and cousins
who had been gone for decades could have trooped through
the house and through the orchards and gardens and found
themselves at home, the same as always, and they could even
have counted on finding their own names and their own faces

registered faithfully somewhere among the generations that had succeeded them. Min thought of all the dead who had been familiar here, and she wished her name could have been woven into talk somehow. She noticed there were no children in sight – they must have been sent off to play by themselves. There was plenty of room for children here – the farm was big, a hundred acres.

She thought many acres seemed to have been given to the orchard – there was no end to it, and from where she stood, the view was more like a forest than like a field of fruit trees, which is what she understood an orchard to be. The ground was uneven, for one thing, slanting this way and that. In her reading, she had always imagined an orchard to be a geometrical place, square or oblong, with the trees spaced evenly. This orchard was wild and looked unknown, as though it had been laid out and cultivated long ago and then forgotten until this wedding day. Min thought of the town of Wexford, of the trees and houses and shops, and she thought of the harbour. Even in the dead of night when people were asleep, the town remained alive and occupied, waiting to be reclaimed in the morning, and the harbour was always restless. The town was always the same, very old and always on the go, with people around every corner, and no matter who they were, you knew you had as much right there as they had. Min knew every inch of Wexford and every lift of the water in the harbour, and she thought that even if everybody belonging to her was dead and gone she would never feel lost or out of place as long as she could walk about in the streets she had known all her life. Out here in the country, things were different. You had to own your place – not merely the house but some of the land. And the houses were miles apart from one another, and the families lived according to laws of succession that were known only to them, and people had to depend for recognition on a loose web of relationships, a complicated genealogy that they kept in their heads and reinforced by repetition on days like today when they were all gathered together. Min thought it would be pleasant to walk around the orchard once in a while when the weather was fine, but for a nice interesting walk she would take the streets of Wexford any time.

Min stood on a narrow path that led from the orchard's entrance to nowhere – it seemed to pause and fade under grass somewhere among the trees. There were rounded grassy banks on either side of the path, but they disappeared into high ground beyond the point where the path gave out. Near the edge of the bank, which was not very high, Min's mother sat talking with two of Delia's aunts – Aunt Mag and Aunt Annie. Some of the lads had carried out three kitchen chairs so that the ladies could rest themselves while they looked at the orchard. The ladies talked comfortably, all of them glad to have something to divert them from the marriage that had brought them together. Bridget lost something of her edginess and made complimentary remarks about the house, and said it was a treat to get out into the country on a day like this. The day grew in beauty, coming in like the tide, minute by minute. There were a lot of butterflies. Min saw a bronze-and-gold one she would have liked for a dress, except that she was not likely to have occasion to wear such colours, and it would be hard to find a design like that anyway, even in the best silk.

'Oh, Min has good sense. She is a born old maid. I can always depend on Min,' she heard her mother say, but she kept her eyes on the ground as though she were deep in thought. She didn't care what they said, and she wasn't going to be drawn into their talk. She thought of wandering off towards the garden. Most of the younger people were there, and she supposed Martin was there too, with Delia at his side. She wondered when Martin and Delia would be leaving for the station. They were taking the train to Dublin. They were going to a hotel there. Well, she wasn't going to the station to see them off. She would get out of that little demonstration, even if it meant she had to walk back to Wexford. She would go on towards the garden now, not to have to listen to her mother talking nonsense to these strangers. There were times when her mother was as bad as Clare.

There was a stone wall around the garden, and inside the wall a rich green box hedge that grew very tall and was clipped into a round arch over the narrow gate at the garden entrance. A similar green box arch showed the way into the orchard, but the orchard had no gate. When Min and her mother walked into the orchard earlier, Min had the impression, just for a second, that she was coming out of a dark tunnel, the green box was so thick at her sides and over her head – so dense, you might say – and that they were walking into an unfamiliar, brilliantly illuminated place full of shadows and green caves and a floor of broken sunlight that seemed to undulate before their dazzled eyes. The boys who carried the chairs out from the kitchen were going to put them in an open space where the ground dipped – a very suitable-looking grassy sward, Min thought it. But Delia's Aunt Mag wanted to sit close to a particular tree she said was her favourite, and that is where the chair was placed, with the two other chairs nearby. The boys couldn't get the chair close enough to the tree to suit Delia's Aunt Mag, and when she sat down she moved her body sideways in a very adroit quick way, and then she put her arm around the tree and her face up against the trunk as though she were cuddling it. 'I love my old tree,' she said. She looked up into the tree, stretching her head back, and she began laughing. 'The best parts of the sky show through this tree. Now you know my secret.' Min thought she was a bit queer.

She told them the tree bore cooking apples that were as big as your head and too sour to eat. Delia's Aunt Mag and her three sisters, including Delia's mother, all wore long-sleeved, high-necked black dresses cut to show the rigidity of their busts and waists, and the straightness of their backs. They were big women, and the sweeping motion of their long heavy skirts gave them the appearance of nuns. Yes, they looked like women belonging to a religious order. Min thought them very forbidding, all four of them, and she was surprised at the change in Aunt Mag once she got her arm around the tree. Her face got much younger and she looked a bit mischievous. She was a strange, wayward old woman, and Min wondered if Delia took after her. There was something dreamy about Delia that Min didn't really trust.

Thirty years later, when Min was obliged to have Clare locked up in the Enniscorthy lunatic asylum, she remembered Delia's Aunt Mag, and she wondered how many people were abroad in the world who should by rights be locked up out of harm's way. By then, of course, Bridget was dead. Bridget had always said that their father would have ended up in the poorhouse if he had been left to himself. Min thought he might have been very well off in the poorhouse. Maybe that was where his place was. There were people who couldn't manage in the world. But Bridget would never have let Clare go into the lunatic asylum. She always said, 'Poor Clare, she takes after her father.' Min couldn't see that at all. Their father had been very silent. But Clare never shut up, and all she did was pray for them all. It got on Min's nerves to hear the rosary going day and night. Clare's rabbit-chasing husband was no help at all. He just laughed, probably pleased in his heart to hear the prayers mocked. Min finally lost patience when she found out that Clare had given away every piece but one of the blue-and-white German china their mother had treasured. Only the soup tureen remained, with its heavy lid. Min never got over the loss of that china. She would have gone and demanded it back, but Clare wouldn't tell her who had it. It was gone for good, no hope of ever seeing it again. Clare claimed the china was hers, and that where it went was none of Min's business. Min knew otherwise. Clare didn't live many years after being shut up, and Min brought her body back to Wexford and buried her there where they would all be buried. All but Martin. Martin and Delia were buried together in St Jerome's in Dublin.

During the years she lived with him after Delia died, Min found Martin very changed. Fifty years with Delia had left their mark on him. He wasn't the brother she remembered.

She had seen other men like that – so buried in habit that their lives were worth nothing to them when the wife was gone. Martin would begin to read, and then his hand would sink down, with the book in it, and he would stare over to the side of his chair, as though he were trying to remember something. More likely he was trying to understand something, Min thought. He had had a habit like that when he was young, of staring away at the wall, or at nothing, when things were going against him. He didn't want her in the house with him – that was obvious – but he had to put up with her. She didn't care. She was being loyal to their mother, that was the main thing. He continued to take his walk every day till his legs gave out. He never went out in the garden, never, but every once in a while he would go to the big window that looked out on the garden and he would stand there staring and always turn away saying, 'The garden misses her.'

Min got tired of that, and one day she burst out, 'Oh, she was a good gardener. That is what she had a talent for. She was good at gardening.' He turned from the window and he said to her, 'What did you say? What was that you said?' She repeated what she had said. She wasn't afraid of him. 'I said she was a good gardener. That is what she was good at, I said.' Min was shocked at what he said to her then. 'And what were you ever good at, may we ask?' he said. Martin of all people ought to know she had always been good at anything she chose to put her hand to. All the times she came here to visit them, he used to hold her up as an example to Delia. He used to tell Delia that Min could have done wonders if she hadn't been tied to the sewing machine. Martin ought to be ashamed of himself, but she said nothing to defend herself now. He was an old man, wandering in his mind like their father.

Martin was restless too, and the more feeble he became, the less he wanted to stay in the house. He said he wanted to see the water again. He wanted to go to the sea. He wanted to walk on the strand. He even talked about paying a last visit to the west of Ireland. He wanted to walk by the Atlantic

Ocean once again. He said the air there would put new life into him. Once he began talking about Connemara and Kerry, there was no stopping him. He liked to recall the adventures he'd had on the holidays he used to take by himself in Connemara and Kerry long ago. He used to go on long walking tours by himself. He'd stay away for a week at a time. He liked to recall those days when he was on his own. He seemed proud of having gone off on his own, away from this house and from Delia and the children, away from all he knew. He sounded like a conjuror describing some magical rope trick when he talked about how he left the house at such and such an hour, and what So-and-So had said to him on the train, and how he carried nothing with him but his knapsack and his blackthorn stick. Min didn't like hearing about it. She knew his adventures, and she had no sympathy with him. If he was all that anxious to have a change from Delia – and nobody could blame him for that – why hadn't he come to Wexford to see his mother, and to see his sisters, and to go about the town and have a word with all the old crowd? Most of them were still there at that time.

He could have taken a walk about the town with me, Min thought. It would have set me up, in those days, to be seen with him, show off a bit. Many a time he could have come down to see us, but no, he was off to Connemara, or to Kerry, to enjoy another holiday by himself with the Atlantic Ocean. The Irish Sea wasn't good enough for him anymore and Wexford Harbour was nothing compared with the beauties of Galway Bay. He talked about the wild Mayo coast as though wildness were a sort of virtue, and one you didn't find in the scenery in Wexford. She reminded him that he had once been in love with their own strand at Rosslare, and she described to him how he used to spend half his life out there, riding out on his bicycle every chance he got. Every free minute he could get he spent at Rosslare. He listened to her, but as though he was being patient with her. 'I'd be very glad to see Rosslare again,' he said when she had finished talking.

Then he gave up talking about Connemara and Kerry,

and he began to wish for a day out at Dun Laoghaire. And he said he'd like to have a day at Greystones. And he wanted to go out to Killiney for a day. Which would Min like best? Maybe they could manage it. Min didn't see how they were going to manage it. A whole day out of the house, and no guarantee of what the weather might be like. They might not be able to find shelter so easily in case of a sudden shower. If he got his feet wet there'd be the devil to pay. They had no car, even if they could drive, and it was an awful drag out to Killiney and back on the bus, or on the train, if they took the train. It would be foolish to go to the expense of hiring a car. She didn't see how they were going to do it.

He seemed to let go of the idea, and then one day he said, 'Min, do you remember the lovely view of the Slaney from the garden that day? Do you remember how the Slaney looked that day, flowing past us into Wexford? And we all stood looking at it? I thought of the passage of time. I stood there, and I thought for a minute that the garden was moving along with the river. And then later on when Delia and I were at Edermine station waiting for the train to Dublin, there were all the flowers in the station, and the stationmaster laughing at us and talking to us, and the white stones spelling out the name of the station. Delia said an expert gardener must have planted the bed of flowers beside the station house, and the stationmaster said he'd done it all himself, getting the place ready for her. But the garden they had there by the Slaney – that was magnificent. Wasn't it, Min?'

Min remembered standing in the garden, surrounded by roses with big heavy heads, and hearing her mother say that she would like very much to have a bunch of flowers to take back to Wexford with her. They all got bunches of flowers to take home. And there was a bunch of flowers for Markey to take to his wife. The car was filled with flowers, and still the garden looked as though it hadn't been touched.

'That was a grand place they had there,' Min said, and she was glad to know that the garden was in ruins now, and that the house stood empty with the roof falling in and the door there stood open to display the vacant rooms and the cold hearth in the kitchen. 'It's all gone now,' she said.

'It was a marvellous day,' Martin said. 'I never forgot what Delia's Aunt Mag said to me. Do you remember – she said the air was like mother o' pearl. Wasn't that a funny thing for an old country woman to say? I wonder what put a thought like that in her head. "The air is like mother o' pearl today," she said looking at me as though we were the same age and had known each other all our lives.'

'She didn't look at me that way,' Min said. 'But I remember her saying that. She was a bit affected, I think – inclined to talk above herself. I didn't care for her. Something about her made me very uneasy.'

'Ah, no,' Martin said. 'Delia was very fond of her.'

'Oh, Delia,' Min said impatiently. 'Delia said the first thing that came into her head. You told her so often enough, to her face, with me sitting here in this room listening to you barging at her. She couldn't open her mouth to suit you. There was no harm in Delia, but she never knew what she said. Half the time she made no sense. There was nothing to Delia.'

The minute she finished speaking, she was sorry. She didn't want to start a row. But Martin was silent, and then he said, 'Nothing to Delia. That's true. I never thought that. But as Shakespeare says, It's true. It's true, it's a pity, and pity 'tis it's true. Nothing to Delia. Shakespeare was right that time.'

'Shakespeare didn't say it. I said it,' Min cried furiously.

'You or Shakespeare, what matter now. It's true, there was nothing to Delia. Wasn't she a lovely girl, though.'

'Are you going to make a song out of it?' Min said. 'What's got into you, Martin?'

She looked at him sitting across the hearth from her. His snow white curls floated on his head. His narrow face was the same shape as her own face. His blue eyes watched her through his rimless spectacles, and he smiled easily, as though they were discussing something pleasant from the past. She thought of Clare singing 'You stick to the boats, lads . . .' that morning when she was being driven off in the car that took her to the asylum. They told Min later that Clare stopped singing quick enough when she saw where she was going. Min wondered if the queer strain that was in Clare had touched Martin, and she was glad that she herself was free of it. Martin seemed to follow her thoughts.

'You put poor Clare into the asylum,' he said gently.

'She was off her head, driving us all to distraction, trying to give the house away!' Min said indignantly. 'What help were you, up here in Dublin, away from all the unpleasantness?'

'Clare was mad,' Martin said. 'There was nothing to Delia. That's a weight off my mind. I know where I am now. I always knew where I was with her, even though I didn't know what she was, and now I still don't know what she was, and God knows I don't know where I am without her. But there was nothing to her.'

'My mother said Delia didn't amount to much,' Min said spitefully. 'Right from the beginning she said that.'

'Nothing to her. You said it yourself,' Martin said. 'I'll show you a picture of her, taken when she was sixteen years old.'

He pulled himself slowly to his feet, and made his way across the room to the cupboard, which had glass doors on top and solid wooden doors underneath. Behind the glass doors Delia's Waterford glass bowls and her Waterford glass jug shimmered dimly. They had a shelf to themselves. Another shelf held her good Arklow china. Martin bent painfully to open the lower doors, and when they were open wide he reached in and took out a large brown envelope. He pushed the doors shut and made his way back to where Min sat in Delia's chair on Delia's side of the fire. He unfastened the envelope and slid the photograph out carefully, holding it as though it were thin glass. His hands are trembling more these days, Min thought. When the photograph was free, he held it up for Min to see.

'There she is,' he said. 'That's what she looked like. Look at the hair she had. Who ever had hair like that, that colour?

Nobody else in that family had hair like that. They said she took after her father. He died young. Look at that, Min.'

'That photograph glorifies her,' Min said.

'She was very good,' Martin said. 'I remember that day we got married, I was standing off to myself, looking at the Slaney. I was lost in admiration. I was looking through a gap in the hedge – one of the children had pulled open a place there, to look through. The river seemed very close up to the garden, under my feet. It was very close. Even then the water was eating in under the garden, and the little strand they told me they had there at one time was gone, or nearly gone. I remember I was there by myself – the water was dazzling. I didn't know where I was. I was inside a dream, and every-thing was safe, I know. The Slaney was very broad that day, and powerful, sure and strong – you know the way it used to be. An Irish river of great importance, the inspector said the day he visited the school. But I felt grand, looking at the Slaney that day. To know it was my own native river and was so, long before I was born. I was standing there like that, when Delia's Aunt Mag came up alongside me. "I was looking for you," she said. My God, how well I remember her voice, as if it was five minutes ago. We might still be there. "I was looking for you," she said. She saw the break in the hedge. "Ah, you found a spy hole," she said. And do you know what she did? She put her arm around my shoulders. She was taller than me – they were big women in that family – and she stuck her face out past me so that she could see what I was looking at. I started to move to the side, to give her room, but she held on to me. "Stay where you are," she said. I said, "I'm in your way." "You're not in my way, child," she said. "Haven't you more right to stand here than anybody? I only want to have a little look before Willie comes along and finds this hole and starts to patch it up. 'The lads have been up to mischief again' – that's what Willie will say. He says they're tearing down the hedge, helping the garden into the river. The river is eating up the garden, you know – if it wasn't for Willie always on guard, we'd be swallowed up." I said, "It's great to see the Slaney like this." "I have a great fondness for the water," she said. "I couldn't be content any place but here where I was born and brought up. I've never spent a night away from this house in my life, do you know that? It's a blessing the day turned out so grand. And nobody was sick or anything. Everybody was able to come see Delia married. The Slaney is in full flood, and the springs of affection are rising around us." She spoke the truth. The Slaney was in full flood that day.'

'That's sheer nonsense,' Min said. 'How could the Slaney be in full flood on a fine day in June? The Slaney was the same as any other day.'

Martin went to his own chair and sat down. 'My legs aren't getting any better,' he said. 'I can't stand on my own feet these days.'

'You've tired yourself out making speeches,' Min said.

Martin still held the photograph of Delia. He lifted it to see it better. He's trembling too much, Min thought. She wondered if she could get him to go to his room and lie down. 'You're wearing yourself out,' she said.

Martin gazed at the shaking photograph. 'It's very like her,' he said. Then he fitted it back into its envelope, pressing his lips together and frowning, like a foolish old man making an effort to do something that was beyond him.

'I'll do that for you,' she said, getting ready to stand up and go over to him.

'You stay where you are,' he said, and when he had the photograph safe he placed the envelope on the low shelf under his table. 'I shouldn't have stood up so long,' he said, and then he took his book from the table and began reading, but after a minute he got up and went out of the room, carrying the book with him. 'I'm going to my room,' he said without looking at her. 'I might lie down for a bit.'

Min was glad to see him go. There would be peace now, for a while. She didn't like to see him getting into these states where he talked so much. All that raking up of the past was a bad sign. She would have asked the priest to come in and talk to him, but she knew Martin would fight the priest's coming until he could fight no more. Martin didn't want the priest in the house. His mind was made up to that, and there was no use arguing with him. Min only hoped she would be able to get the priest in time, when the time came. She didn't want her brother dying without the Last Sacraments. She didn't understand Martin's bitter attitude towards the Church. Polly went very much the same way, of course. Min would never forget Polly's blasphemous language when the third-eldest child died, the little one they called Mary. Min was trying to comfort Polly by telling her the baby would be well taken care of in Heaven, when Polly burst out laughing and crying and saying she could take care of her own child better than God and His Blessed Mother and all the saints and angels put together. 'They might have left poor little Mary with her own Mammy!' Polly said. 'They must have seen the way she was holding on to my hand, wanting to stay with me. They have very hard hearts up there, if you ask me.' Martin had never gone that far in his talk against the Church. At least, as far as Min knew he'd never gone that far, but she knew she was going to have to do a bit of scheming to get the priest into the house. 'The springs of affection are rising.' She didn't like to hear him talking like that. What Min remembered of that day in the garden by the Slaney was that she felt worn out and dried up, and trapped, crushed in by people who were determined to see only the bright surface of the occasion. They could call it a wedding or anything they liked, but she knew it was a holocaust and that she was the victim, although nobody would ever admit that.

She thought they were all very clumsy. It wasn't that she wanted to be noticed. But she knew that any notice she got was pity, or derision. Nothing she could say was right. She was out of it, and nothing could convince those people that she wanted to be out of it. She would ten times rather have been back in Wexford working as usual, but she had to go to the wedding or cause a scandal. Now here they were. Bridget was giving every evidence of enjoying herself, and so were

Polly and Clare, and in Min's opinion they were letting the side down. She had been dragged out here like a victim of war at the back of a chariot, and all to bolster Martin up, and he didn't need bolstering up.

She stood outside the garden gate. The children had all vanished, and she imagined they had gone to play somewhere by themselves, but suddenly the place was full of children running around, and she thought they must have been having their dinner. Children always had to be fed, no matter what. These children were a healthy-looking lot, fair-haired or red-headed, most of them. Min remembered how black she and Martin had been as children, Martin with his black curls and she with her straight black plait. They were a skinny pair, very different from these children. A little boy ran up to her so suddenly that she thought he was going to crash into her, but he stopped just in time and stared up at her. He was about five years old, a very solid-looking little fellow. His eyes were so blue that it was like two flowers looking at you, and he had a very short nose, and there was sweat on his forehead. His hair was nearly white. He wore a little suit of clothes, a little coat and trousers and a white shirt, and black stockings pulled up on his legs under the trousers. He opened his mouth, but he said nothing, just stared at her. Min gave him no encouragement. She didn't dislike children, but she had no great fondness for them, and she didn't want a whole crowd of them trooping along after him and asking her questions and making her conspicuous. He turned red, and he threw his arm up over his eyes, and peered up at her from under his sleeve, and began to smile. She smiled at him. He was a nice little fellow. She ought to say something to him.

'Are you a good boy?' she asked him. He turned and ran off, flapping his arms at his sides like a farmyard bird, and when he was a little distance away he turned and looked back to see if she was watching him. Then he ran off out of the garden. She didn't see him again.

The next thing she remembered was a moment of terrible unhappiness – it gave her a shock. What happened was that

Martin and one of Delia's brothers and a woman she didn't even know came up to her and began talking about the train. They kept saying that it wouldn't do for Delia and Martin to miss the train. Min never knew the woman's name but she remembered that she made a great fuss, as though she imagined that the day depended on her. There were always people like that everywhere, trying to boss things. She wanted to tell that woman to mind her own business. All these strangers were taking Martin over. They thought they owned him now.

'The springs of affection are rising.' It would be those people who would say a thing like that, including everybody in their inspirations, everybody, even people who didn't want to be included. Min thought of that garden. She thought of the green box hedge and the monkey-puzzle tree and the pink and white roses and all the big dark and white star-shaped flowers, and she thought of Delia's Aunt Mag on the kitchen chair under the cooking-apple tree, and she remembered Delia's brothers and sisters and Delia's mother, and the white-haired child. She had forgotten nothing of that glittering day, and she saw it all enclosed in a radiant fountain that rushed up through a rain of sunlight to meet with and rejoice with whatever was up there – Heaven, God the Father, the Good Shepherd, everything everybody ever wanted, wonderful prizes, happiness.

Min knew it was only the transfiguration of memory. She was no fool, and she was not likely to mistake herself for a visionary. The lovely fountain was like a mirage, except that in a mirage people saw what they wanted and were starving for, and in the fountain Min saw what she did not want and never had wanted. Why was it nobody ever believed her when she told them she wanted nothing to do with all that hullabaloo? The fortunes of war condemned her to a silence that misrepresented her as thoroughly as the words she was too proud to speak would have done, and she knew all that. Martin's lightmindedness had changed the course of her life, and there wasn't one single thing she could do about it. He turned all their lives around. He cared no more about his mother and sisters and what happened to them than if he had been a stranger passing through the house on his way to a far better place, where the people were more interesting.

He made his mother cry. For a wedding present, Bridget wanted to give Martin the good dining-room set that she had paid for penny by penny at a time when she couldn't afford it. A big round mahogany table and four matching chairs that must have had pride of place in some great house at one time. She kept that furniture up to the nines, polished and waxed till you could see to do your hair in it. But Martin turned up his nose at it. No secondhand stuff for him and Delia, and the mahogany was too big and heavy anyway. He didn't want it. He and Delia went and ordered furniture made just for them; new furniture, all walnut – a bed, a chest of drawers, a wardrobe, a washstand, and two sitting-room chairs so that Delia could hold court in style when they had visitors. Those were Martin's very words. 'Now Delia can hold court in style,' he said, and never noticed the look on his mother's face. Min noticed the bed had vanished out of the house in Dublin, and she was never able to find out what happened to it. But the other things were still there. Above all, the two sitting-room chairs were still there – Martin sat in his own, and she sat in Delia's. She would take the whole lot back to Wexford when the time came. She would bring the furniture back where it belonged. It was never too late to make things right.

In Wexford, in her own flat, she sat in Delia's chair and sometimes for a change sat propped up with pillows in Martin's big chair, his armchair. It was nice to have the two chairs. The wardrobe and the chest of drawers went into her bedroom, and the washstand into the room she used for a kitchen. Delia's old sitting-room carpet was threadbare, but the colours held up well, and it looked nice on the floor, almost like an antique carpet. And the hearthrug from the house in Dublin looked very suitable in front of Min's old fireplace, where so many girls and ladies had warmed themselves when they came to be measured for a dress, or to have a fitting.

Against the end wall, facing down the room to the fire-place, Delia's bookshelves were ranged along, filled with Delia's books, and with some of Martin's books. Some of Martin's books Min wouldn't have in the house, and she had sold them. She was glad now that she had never spent money on books; these had been waiting for her. The room looked very distinguished, very literary. It was what she should always have had. She wished they could all see it. There was room for them, and a welcome. There was even a deep, dim corner there between the end wall and the far window where her father could steal in and sit down and listen to them with his silence, as he used to do. There was a place here for all of them – a place for Polly, a place for poor Clare. A place in the middle for Bridget. A place for Martin in his own chair. They could come in anytime and feel right at home although the room was warmer and the furniture a bit better than anything they had been used to in the old days.

Eamonn Sweeney

from *Waiting for the Healer*

Eddie Clyne wasn't drinking. He was sitting at a table where you could see occasional glimpses of the wood through a forest of pint glasses. A half-full glass of flat Ballygowan was sitting in front of him and a half-empty bottle of the stuff beside him.

—You're sure you won't have a drink, Eddie?

—No. No. I'm grand. If I went back on the beer, I'd be scared I'd go on a mad batter.

—You're sure now?

—Oh, yeah. This stuff does me grand. I'll be driving home anyways. One of us has to be sober in my house.

Dalton Dunbar came over.

—Hit that cunt a box if he's bothering you. It's the only language he understands. Are you on for going up to the Dandy Diner, Mary Colreavy's hen party is on but we're all invited.

I was going to say I couldn't because it was the night of my brother's funeral but I didn't. I didn't have any place else I wanted to go and I couldn't face going back to the house. Not yet at least. So I went and left 0800 and Francie at the bar together.

A squad slowed down and drove along beside us for a few yards when we left Donoghue's. It was pulling away when Beetlejuice let a wolf-whistle at it. The car reversed and Cosgrave stuck his head out the window.

—Does someone have a problem?

—You what?

—You'll whistle soon enough if you're brought down to the barracks. You'd need to watch yourselves.

—You must be fucking hearing things, guard. First sign of madness, that.

The cop slammed the door. A dozen whistles in different keys started up the second it closed. A couple of cans clattered against the back of the squad as it sped away.

The Dandy Diner must have been cursed at one stage by someone who knew how to curse. A Nevin or a McDonagh. Whoever owned it always put a ridiculous name on it. Once it had been the Nashville Rooms. Another time Kades Kounty. At one stage it was even Nijinsky's Nite Spot. That name would have delighted the Gay Swimming Club who came into the King William every Thursday night for a few pints after leaving the Lido.

A space opened up in front of us when we walked in. It developed into a funnel which fed us straight through to the bar even though the joint was wedged. Two of a Kind were playing. I got jammed against a pillar. A poster threatened to fall on my head.

OKEY DOKEY KARAOKE. EVERY MONDAY NIGHT WITH P. J. AND MARGARET. SUBSTANTIAL CASH PRIZES.

The hen party sat in one corner of the pub with their chairs drawn round in a circle. Mary Colreavy in the middle had a party hat on her head and streamers waterfalling from her shoulders. I wondered if Lydia's hen had been like this. It struck me I'd never asked her about it.

Clinger arrived and hovered over my shoulder. He reached to shake hands with me.

—All right.

—All right. I'll buy you a pint. I reckoned you must be broke when you didn't show up in Donoghue's.

He winked at me and extended his leg so it touched the pillar. Then he reached towards his shoes.

—I have a few pound put away, see. And if we'd gone to Donoghue's the quare one would have known I had it and I'd have to give her some.

Clinger took off his shoe and reached into a blue sock that covered all of his left foot except for the big toe that poked out of a frayed hole and wriggled around frantically like it was trying to dig into sand as the tide went out. A black circle covered the top end of the nail.

—The oul sock, you see, it's the only safe place in the end.

He took out two tenners and brushed some flakes of skin off their surface. I still bought the first round. We talked about football.

I bought the next round as well. And put on a chaser for myself. Beetlejuice was there when I got back from the bar. His hands shook a lot. He lifted his pint to his mouth and left it down a couple of times without taking more than a sup. When he spoke his lips shook too.

—I'm nervous, Paul, I just am. I have this feeling and it's the same feeling I had the night Johnny was killed. I know something's going happening.

Beetlejuice stuttered through most of the words. He reached his hand out for his pint and pulled it back before it got there.

—That fuck. That fuck, him he's up to something.

An old man loitered at the bottom of the stairs. He was hopping a thick brown walking stick off the floor. The pub was at basting temperature but he was rigged out in a thick pair of specs, a tweed cap and a long coat buttoned to the top.

—He's at something. I'll skull him.

—He's a fucking oul man. What could he be at?

—I'm going to fucking skull him.

Beetlejuice got to within a couple of yards of the old geezer before Richie Fee caught him. They had a few words. Beetlejuice had stopped shaking when he came back.

Richie told me the score, boys. It's all copacetic. Jesus, such crack, wait till you see it.

A couple of the hens walked up to the stage. Two of a Kind launched straight away into an instrumental. The one they play on telly at the end of the World Snooker Championship when they show the funny shots.

A big movement from our side of the pub over to the chair where Mary Colreavy was. Beetlejuice pulled my arm.

—Come over. The crack is going starting.

The band started to run through the tune a second time. People were standing on chairs now and looking into the circle of hens. It reminded me of the time in the Horse and Groom a squaddie bet he'd be able to drink a pint of sick.

—Wait till you see this for crack.

Beetlejuice was happy. The band looked down the pub like they were waiting for some sort of signal. The pub went silent as the old man dondered towards Mary Colreavy. He leaned heavily on his stick. I half expected him to drop before he got to her. He peered at her through his double-glazed glasses.

—Are you the girleen who's getting married? Sure you'll give us a biteen of an oul kiss.

His lips puckered out about half a mile in front of his face. Mary looked around for some assistance but there wasn't any. Belinda Greer was breaking her heart laughing. Beetlejuice snickered. The old guy put his arm around Mary's neck and planted a big slimy kiss on her lips before jumping into the air and clicking his heels together. He threw the tweed cap on the floor.

Hasta la vista, baby.

The glasses, the coat, the cap and the stick were all on the floor within ten seconds of that spake and the old geezer was now a young guy with muscles on him that looked like they were going to burst. All he had on was a deep suntan and a pair of boxer shorts. A noise sprinted round the pub.

—Woooo.

Even the barmen stopped what they were doing and looked over at the ex-old man sitting on Mary's knee. Belinda bent double with laughing. Mary looked terrified. Her new pal planted another kiss on her lips and got a roar from the hens as he flexed the muscles on his arm. They shone under the lights. He looked like a chicken covered in cooking oil.

—A lot of them bucks is queer, said someone a couple of yards behind me.

It was a man's voice. Not one of the women had touched

a drink since bucko shed his coat and fifty years. Missus Fee looked like one of those Charismatics who have just been possessed by the Spirit of the Lord. But she wasn't speaking in tongues.

—You're lovely, you're lovely. Go on and show us what you've got.

The stripper jumped off Mary's lap and gave a little bow before pulling a string which disintegrated his boxers into a heap on the floor. For a second everyone thought he didn't have anything at all on. His arse was bare. But there was a little string running around the front and an orange pouch for him to cram his tackle into. He bent down to his coat and took out a piece of paper. The chest muscles got another flex before he started declaiming:

> Hello Mary here I am
> Your saucy sexy stripogram
> Please be good you know you should
> Let's get on this could be good
> I've got a present I thought would suit
> Now I want you to suck my . . .

He paused. A couple of people bellowed:

—Flute.

He waited a couple more seconds before he took the banana out of his coat.

—Fruit.

—You've some fucking body on you.

A woman shouts from the balcony. I held my breath and tried to hold in my stomach. I wouldn't say I was the only one imagining what I'd look like in front of a pub of women with my kit off. You could jog, I suppose. And there's American exercises that get you in shape in just ten minutes a day and you end up only having to do them three times a week. You could go on the Scarsdale Diet. Fuck it. He probably wasn't happy in his life.

Belinda got hold of him by the pouch. His lad popped out

but he just grinned and flicked it expertly back in with his left hand. All the men were disappointed it was a good size. He arranged the banana as it protruded from his pouch.

—Suction. It must be, said a voice full of awe.

The women clattered the tables. The stripper pushed Mary's head towards his groin. She shied her head away at first. The buck she was marrying was in the army with 0800. He'd been going out with Mary for six years and he bursted anyone who looked crooked at her. I was fierce sorry he wasn't in the Dandy Diner. Someone should have asked him to come along.

A drum-roll from Two of a Kind. Snap. Mary's head came up. She had the top half of the banana in her mouth. A dozen flashes went off at once and the stripper threw on his coat and got the fuck out of there. He was just past the table when Missus Fee got him a pinch on the arse you could nearly feel just from seeing it. Another woman grabbed him by the kecks and tried to yank them off. He bolted for the door with a gang of women after him. Screaming. I'd never heard screaming like it. He nearly knocked down the barman who was bringing down a cake in the shape of a muscle-man.

Someone grabbed me around the waist and the next thing I knew I was in a circle twirling around the floor with Two of a Kind playing the can-can and of course there's always one header who levers himself up on his neighbour's shoulders and does a wild kick with both of his feet up in the air and falls down then and nearly brings everyone else with them and it was Beetlejuice naturally enough. He was gone fucking hyper.

Mary opened a package. Belinda helped her. They removed the wrapping and took out a pair of big Y-fronty knickers about the size of two wigwams.

—Woooo.

The Jordan woman who used be a midwife crammed a big slice of the muscle-man cake into her mouth. Oozy black cherries dangled from it. She picked them off and put them into the ashtray. A few of Mary's buddies stood her up and put her legs into the knickers. Belinda planted a kiss that left a ruby smear of lipstick on Mary's face.

The can-can stopped and myself and Missus Fee were left leaning awkwardly against each other and trying to remember what the weather had been like so we could talk about it.

Two of a Kind played a country song about honky-tonks and broken hearts. Beetlejuice hugged Mary Colreavy. He was enjoying himself like . . . No. Like nothing. You think of these things later. More significance. More Columbo. He stuck his legs into the giant underpants. First the left. Then the right. He put his arms around Mary and they danced.

Suspended in their giant nappy with green balloons flying over their heads. Myself, Clinger and Dalton stood in a circle and headed a balloon to each other. Each determined not to be the first to let it hit the ground or float away.

—Fuck's sake. Another one of these lads, they're gone mad on them altogether.

Clinger controlled the balloon with his shoulder.

—Handball.

Myself and Dalton at the same time. The guitarist in Two of a Kind did one of those long, twiddly-bit, Jesus I'm Eddie Van Halen can't you nearly see the smoke rising off me fingers solos. I couldn't make out what the song was because he was gone so much to town on it.

—What's that song, boys?

—Jesus. It's a bit much now all the same, a second lad, it nearly knocks the good out of it.

—What? I didn't catch you right.

—One of those stripogram bucks again.

—What's the name of that song?

A tall man in a long black coat, wearing a plastic gorilla false face topped by a baseball cap, pushed his way through the crowd. A dancing arm clipped the side of his head and knocked his cap skew-ways. He stopped and straightened it very deliberately with his left hand. Then he patted the cap down on his nut to make sure it was properly balanced. With his left hand again. He held his right arm under his coat like it was broken and suspended in a sling. The cap was a Utah Jazz one. You had to laugh at this grinning gorilla face making its way across the pub. People smiled and stood back to let him through.

—Beetlejuice. Beetlejuice Reilly. Noelie Reilly.

The voice came from underneath the mask. Beetlejuice and Mary were still jumping up and down.

—Beetlejuice Reilly. Is that you?

Beetlejuice tried to turn round. The upper half of his body swivelled but his legs stayed facing Mary Colreavy.

—Away we go, said the false face.

A revolver came out from under the coat. Beetlejuice's gob was fixed in a toothy smile when the gun blew it away. He staggered and the man stepped forward and shot him in the back of the head. A tiny burst of flame seemed to jump from the gun. The gorilla's hand was rock-steady.

Mary Colreavy's face was covered in blood and goo. She screeched as Beetlejuice fell and dragged her to the floor. Both of them were still trapped in those monster Y-fronts. Nothing was left of Beetlejuice's head only a sight of blood. Mary was in hysterics. Two of a Kind stopped playing. The singer crouched down behind one of the amps. People knocked over tables and chairs as they tried to get out of the pub.

Beetlejuice wasn't moving. Mary kicked like mad to try and disentangle herself from him. Belinda shoved through the crowd and bent down to her. The gunman aimed carefully and put a third shot through Beetlejuice's head. I heard the sound of something soggy falling on a concrete path from a great height. Beetlejuice's body jerked. Mary's body had to make the same movement. She was gone pure white in the face. She looked past Belinda who had pulled her head off the floor and was cradling her.

Mary's face and neck and the front of her little black dress were all covered with whatever comes out when someone's head explodes. She slipped out of Belinda's arms and lay on the floor again. Blood seeped out of what used to be Beetlejuice.

—What's my name, what's my name.

The gunman's words were all muffled by the plastic mask. He turned and walked towards the door like he didn't give a breeze. I tried to shrink back into one of the alcoves. I had a feeling he'd want to shoot me if he knew I was in the pub. Clinger and Dalton started after him.

—Get the cunt. Stop him.

Have-a-go heroes. He turned and fired a couple of shots at them. They seemed like noisier shots. The Dandy Diner filled up with the sound of firecrackers let off in a small space. Clinger was on the ground with blood soaking through his shirt. Dalton was plugged in the arm. The gunman did a little dance.

—How you like me now, motherfuckers. How you like me now.

It was a fake American accent but it wouldn't have fooled anyone except maybe for one of those women who refused to believe that Big Tex and the Rangers were a gang of lads from Sheepwalk who worked in the abattoir. He let off a couple more shots but his hand was jumping around now. A hole appeared in one of the windows. Glasses tinkled. He walked out the side door of the Dandy Diner.

A car revved up and took off. It left two perky blasts of a horn behind it in the night air. The killer had been wearing those Converse basketball boots with the star at the side of them. It's funny what you think of. I couldn't take in much else.

Mary lay stock-still in a corner with a gang of her friends screaming at everybody to do something. Clinger had dragged himself up on to a chair. He leaned back with his shirt open and blood slowly trickling down in different streams. Richie Fee walked Dalton out of the door. Dalton's arm hung down like it wasn't really attached to him.

Blood all over the gaff. Little specks in the ashtrays. Splotches on the walls. Long streaks on the glass of the alcoves. Spots of it soaked through the cheap paper Dandy Diner beer mats. The late Noel Reilly lay face down in a big pool of the stuff with the woman of the Jordans who'd been a midwife hunkered down beside him. She shook her head.

I was left on my own in my alcove when everyone else moved on to the street. There I was, looking at what was left of Beetlejuice lying there like an old Guy Fawkes fucked into an estate lift in the middle of November. Rag and bone. Stupid bastard. Friend of my brother. The late John Kelly. Whatever the fuck the story was, someone had it in for them big time.

The light show outside. Ambulances and squads and the streetlamps. And the noise of the sirens adding to it. Except you couldn't hardly hear them. You could hear the crying in the street a bit better. But what you could hear most was the screaming of the women. It kept at the same pitch and level until they sounded like they were going hoarse and then it'd stop for an instant and start again. Back at the same level and pitch.

The husband-to-be had arrived by the time they got Mary Colreavy to her feet. He hammered his way through the cops at the door and put his arms out to her. I don't know did she see him. She just screamed. I never heard screaming like it.

The cops brought me into the street and asked did I want a lift home. I didn't answer them. I just pretended to myself I was a knight of the road in the middle of a journey. And kept thinking if it hadn't been for me going to a party on the night of my brother's funeral none of this would have happened and everyone would have been safe. You couldn't have luck.

Claire Keegan

The Ginger Rogers Sermon

Don't ASK ME why we called him Slapper Jim. My mother stamped his image in my head, and I was at an age when pictures of a man precede the man himself. The posters verify: Thin Lizzie with a V of chest exposed, Pat Spillane's legs racing across my bedroom wall, the ball poised. I was the girl with the sweet tooth and a taste for men.

And pictures. I have a photographic memory. I can see every tacky page of my cousin's wedding album, the horse-shoe on the cake with the man slightly taller than the woman and their feet stuck in the frosting. I parcel out my life in images the way other people let the calendar draw a line around them every month. That time of Slapper Jim was the time of the strangest pictures.

We killed pigs around then, ate pork cracked in its own fat with a pulpy sauce. Plasticine grey and apple green, those were the colours of my home. Ma held my dinner plate with the tail of her skirt and talked through her day while I tucked in:

'You should see the new lumberjack your da hired. Slapper Jim, they call him. A great big fella he is! Walked in here and I'll tell ya nothing but the truth, he leaned up against the partition there and I thought the whole yoke was going to cave in.'

My brother, Eugene, quacks his hand behind her back. I spear a slice of pork and in my mind I see a giant, the earth tremoring where he walks. A man who doesn't know his own strength. That can be dangerous. I've seen my father crack a cow's ribs with his fist, just trying to slide her over in the stall.

'I gave him his bit of dinner and he was able to reach over for the handle on the saucepan without getting up. Ate eleven spuds. Eleven spuds if ya don't mind! Yer lucky there's aer a one left.'

Ma rummages in the cutlery drawer for a spoon. Tapioca and stewed apples, I suppose. I hope for sherry trifle, gooey caramel, dollops of ice-cream.

'What's for afters?'

They leave me alone here on Saturday nights. Eugene goes too, even though he doesn't dance. Him staying home with me is a sissy thing to do because he's so much older. Seven years older. I was made out of the last of my father's sperm. I found that out just recently. My mother says I am The Accident in the family. My father tells people I am The Shakings of the Bag, which I suppose is much the same thing.

Dance-mad, my parents. Ma says a man who can't dance is half a man. She's taught me the harvest jig and the waltz, the quick-step and the Siege of Ennis in the parlour. She says dancing is good therapy, makes her feel like she's in time with the world. Mostly we move where we're put, stooping under the rain and such, but dancing frees her up, oils her joints, she says. Everyone should know how to move in their own time. She puts the record on, I shake Lux across the lino, and we whirl around the parlour floor like two loonies. I am the man loony. I pretend I don't see her watching her reflection in the mirror of the sideboard as we pass. 'The Walls of Limerick' requires two-facing-two, so we hold our hands out to imaginary partners and move them into the places they should go. I like this, knowing what Ma will do, where she'll go before she does, not having to think about it.

Saturdays smell of girls; wet wool, nail-polish and camomile shampoo. In the kitchen, Ma sets her hair. We call it The Salon. I hold the pins between my lips and roll her hair around the spiky curlers, stiffen them with setting lotion. Her head goes into the net and she sits in under the hood of the dryer we bought down at the auction when the His 'n' Hers went out of business. I hand her an old *Woman's Weekly* and imagine it's *Vogue*. The last page is ripped out so Da can't read about women's problems.

'Do you want a coffee!' I shout above the noise.

There was never any coffee in that house. She stays under there, deaf and talking loud like an old person and I hand her a cup of frothy Ovaltine and an hour later she's out, relieved and pink. Then the daubs of shoe-cream, the shush of the steam iron smoothing out the creases. The shuffle of the entertainment pages and Da working a lather for his face, sticking the headlines on his chin to stop the blood. Ma wriggling into her flesh-coloured roll-on, big elastic knickers to keep her belly in. Pot Belly, I call her:

'Are ya going dancing now, Pot Belly?'

'Where's the beauty contest, Pot Belly?'

'Where did yer pot-belly go, Pot Belly?'

She calls me The Terror: 'Shut up, ya terror.' She dots Lily of the Valley behind her ears with the glass stopper and slides her tapping feet into her dancing shoes, ready to take off.

'You won't fall into the fire, now, will ya?' Da always having the last word, jingling his keys like they belong to the only car in the parish.

'No, Da.'

Eugene pulling on his corduroy jacket, giving me a look like I shouldn't be alive.

The film comes on after the 9 o'clock news. I change into my pyjamas and find the biscuits. She hides them in the washing machine or the accordion case or the churn. Once Eugene ate them all and left a note that said 'Find a better hiding place next time', but Pot Belly went mad, so now we leave nothing and she says nothing. That's the way it is in our house, everybody knowing things but pretending they don't.

I turn off all the lights and sit with my feet up and play with myself in the dark and hope the actors take off every stitch and go skinny-dipping in close-up. *The Birds* is the name of tonight's film. Birds line up on the wires, watching the children with their glassy eyes. Ready to swoop. Even the teachers can't offer them protection. I think of the grey crows picking out our ewes' eyes. I hear a noise but it's only the milk strainer hammering the glass in the wind. Looked like a metal claw, a wiry hand. I slide the bolt across the door and let the setter up on the couch. I squeeze my eyes shut when the birds dive on the town.

It's after midnight when the headlights cross the room. Ma wobbles in, opens the fridge, its light shining pink on her cheeks. Da slides the kettle over on the hot-plate and warms his hands, ready for a feed. 'Saw the Slapper down in Shillelagh. He was out on the floor with a one.'

'And the size of her,' Ma chips in. 'No bigger than a bantam hen she is, sitting up beside him. And neather one of 'em has a step in their foot. Fecking useless.' She bites into a tomato with a vengeance and Eugene heads for the stairs before she starts her Ginger Rogers sermon.

'How's the bantam?' is the first thing I say when I meet Slapper Jim. He laughs a big red laugh that sounds like the beginning of something. He has plump lips and blond hair and standing beside him is like standing in the shade. He's as big as a wardrobe. I want to open all his shirt buttons and look inside. 'Haw' is the word he uses all the time.

'Who's this bantam now, haw?' Sounds like he's talking down a well.

My father sits at the head of the table and rubs a wedge of tobacco between his palms and packs his pipe. He has no teeth to distract the smile away from his eyes.

'Ma says your one is like a bantam,' I say.

'Haw?'

'Do ya leave her sitting on the nest all week?'

'Maybe she's not nesting at all.'

'Pluck her.'

The bantam jokes went on until the end. The hatching, plucking, sideways-looking, gawky jokes carried us through summer and beyond.

Slapper doesn't wear a belt. Even when he pulls his trousers up, the hems don't reach his ankles. On real wet days, the men stay home and do odd jobs around the yard. They fence, pare sheep's feet, weld bits and pieces. On Saturdays Eugene watches *Sports Stadium* and bites his nails. I help Slapper split the sticks. I am a girl who knows one end of a block from the other, know to place it on the chopping block the way it grows, make it easier for Slapper. But I don't suppose it would make any difference. That axe comes down and splits that wood open every time, knots or no knots. Even the holly, which my father calls 'a bitch of a stick to split', breaks open under his easy strike. We have a rhythm going: I put them up, he splits them open. With other people, I take my hand away fast, but not with the Slapper Jim. He and I are like two parts of the same machine, fast and smooth. We trust each other. And always he gives his waistband a little tug when I'm putting them up, and that waistband slides down with the swing of the axe and the crack of his arse shows every time.

I too am a lumberjack in summer. Pot Belly says it is no job for a girl. Girls should flute the pastry-edge or wash the car at best is what she thinks. I should wallpaper my room, practise walking around with a book flat on my head to help my posture. Anything to keep me home.

'Keep her away from the saws. If that girl comes home from that wood with no feet, don't come home here.'

We've all seen such things. Toes sawed off, an arm mangled in a winch, and once, a mare gone mad with the sting of a gad-fly, pulling the slig out onto the road and scrapping the car. But when morning comes I'm up and ready, watching for Slapper's Escort on the lane.

Following the mare is the job for me. A grey Clydesdale with a white face, she's seventeen hands if she's an inch. And the smell of her, the warm, earth smell like the inside of a

damp flowerpot. I put my nose on her neck and breathe in.
And she's smart too, knows to stop when she snags and bikes
up without putting out your shoulder. No dirt in her, but still
she'll lash your face with that tail if you're not quick. We're
clear-falling every second line on the slopes. Slapper and Da
fall and trim, sitka spruce mostly, and larch, the trimmer's
dream. I hook the chain around the slig and follow the mare
down the lines onto the car-road, drawing the timber as close
together as I can, keeping the butts even. I unhook the slig
and lift the swing back up on the hames and then my favourite
part – holding onto the mare's tail and letting her pull me
back up the line. Slapper says I have brains to burn, thinking
of that. Da says I should give some to Eugene because he does
nothing only sit around on his arse with his nose in a book all
day.

We drink mugs of tea from a flask at nosh-up, milk from
an old Corcoran's lemonade bottle. Soda-bread soggy with
tomatoes and sardines in red sauce. The tea tastes bitter
towards the end of the day. Slapper dents the bumper where
he sits, talks with his mouth full.

''Uckin 'lies,' he says when he swats the flies. They light
on the horse-dung and the bread. They chase me up and
down the lines and drive the mare cuckoo. I sit on the mare
backwards with my feet up on her flanks while she grazes the
bank, and wait for somebody to open the biscuits. Slapper
lifts me up there. Peaches, he calls me but I am nothing like a
peach. My father says I'm more like a stalk of rhubarb, long
and sour.

'Ya have a way with that baste, Peaches. She bites the arse
off me.'

'It's always hanging out anyway, Slapper. Here,' Da says,
handing over a wad of bailing twine, 'until ya buy yerself a
belt.'

'Haw?' Slapper smiles but he doesn't tie his trousers up.
He just looks at the twine in a way that makes Da put it back
into his pocket, and gives his waistband a tug the way another
man might push his glasses up on his nose.

Slapper teaches me the tricks of the trade. He holds his big finger up but doesn't stoop when he says these things: 'Don't open the slig until you've unhooked her, if she takes off, yer fingers will be dogmeat. Don't stand in front of the saw; if there's a loose link and the chain breaks, you're fucked.' He opens up that forbidden world of adult language and invites me in. Then he leaves me alone to be capable.

We stay at it until dusk. Foresters come around with their kettles in the evenings and paint the stumps with the pink poison. We hide the saws and the oil and petrol cans under the tops up the line and let the mare loose in the field down the road. Each week, the lorries drive up with their robot claws and load up the lengths. Twenty-five tons is a load for them, a cheque for us, and a pound of wine gums and a *Bunty* and *Judy* after mass and two choc-ices and gobstoppers for me.

'What do they learn ya in school?' Slapper asks as we're driving the mare down to the field.

I know trigonometry. 'I know that the square of the hypotenuse is equal to the sum of the square on the other two sides.'

'What's a highpotinuze?' Jim pushes back the passenger seat to make room for his legs, but his knees are snug against the dashboard. He holds the mare's reins out through the open window as she trots next to the car. 'Go on, ya lazy cunt ya! Whup! Whup! Yas hairy, farting fucker ya. Go on!' He claps the outside of the door with his left hand.

'The child, Slapper. The child!' Da admonishes.

Slapper looks back at me. My father's eyes watch me in the rear-view mirror. I pretend I haven't heard a bad word.

'What's a highpotinuze?'

Those are the pictures from that time. Three dirty lumber-jacks sligging out timber, the wood slick and white beneath the bark. Eating packets of Coconut Creams, spitting, listening to Radio 1 in the car when it rained, sharpening chain, files grinding on the rakers, the cutters shining all round like some deadly necklace. Slapper asking what they learned me in school, his file sharpening smack-on with the slant of the

cutters every time. Da says Slapper's a great man with a saw.
The last fella Da had working with him slid a matchstick in
between the spark-plug and the petrol tank so she wouldn't
start but Da found out and gave him his walking papers. I tell
Slapper Jim the things I learn in school. I know that Oliver
Cromwell told the poor people 'To hell or to Connaught' (I
can see him on his black horse, pointing West), that Jesus lost
his temper. I can recite William Blake: *Tyger, tyger, burning
bright in the forests of the night, what immortal hand or eye could
frame thy fearful symmetry?* I can see it on the page, the curve
of the question mark at the end. Slapper holds my hand and
stands me up on the bonnet of the car in the rain, telling me
to say the poems. I read them off my memory. He asks
me what 'immortal' means but I don't know. He says I am the
morbidest child in Ireland.

'Get that child in out of the rain!' Da putting a damper on
it from the driver's seat. 'Do ya hear me, Slapper? She'll catch
her end and you can be the one to bring her home!'

But Slapper just smiles. 'Say the poems, Peaches.'

I shoot up like the rhubarb stalk Da says I am and the
transformation begins. I take an interest in my cousin's old
dresses. Flowery things with thin patent belts and matching
pointy shoes that pinch my toes. I limp home from school and
make the announcement. Ma says 'Shussssh!' and gives me
the elastic belt and towels. I think it's the equivalent of Da's
newspaper for his chin.

'Don't let yer father see them,' she says. Her always hiding
women away, like we're forbidden.

Now that I am thirteen, I am sectioned off from men. It
happens in school too, in gym class. I play basketball and
jump over hurdles and come back all red-faced and sweaty
and talk non-stop in class. Nobody sits beside me because I
smell like an afterbirth. I wear the pads and Lily of the Valley
and go dancing down the pub. Slapper Jim is always there
with the bantam. I waltz around in the cigarette smoke with

old men my father knows. Watch Sam Collins prancing across the floor in his patent shoes, swinging Pot Belly around, and him with his left hand up so high, she can barely reach it. Foxy, we call him, with his head of slicked-back silver hair, his horse's eye. The men's hands grip me by the waist and swing me round, same as I'm a bucket of water. They hold me close as an excuse not to let me go. The backs of their shirts are wet. I drink Babycham out of long-stemmed glasses. They taste like ice-cream and soften the pictures. Eugene sits with his elbows on the bar, watching the dancers, his shoe tapping in perfect time on the rung of his stool but he won't get out on the floor.

Slapper cannot dance. If his feet move on the beat, it's an accident. He just doesn't catch the rhythm. He takes me out onto the floor and puts his arms around me and shifts his weight from one leg to the other, taking huge strides for the waltz. My head comes up to the fourth button on his shirt. I could almost see past him if I stood on my toes. I can smell him, get the whiff of the sticks on his chest as if he sweats out resin. Reminds me of the mare, the hair and the warmth under his shirt, the big feet moving over the floor. I try to lead him into the rhythm, exaggerating my sways, but he does not feel the music, and I wind up stepping on his toes.

'Should have worn me steel toe-caps,' he says.

His bantam isn't even as tall as me, a dark, plump woman with a mouth like his. She wears a royal blue blouse with gold sequins blown across the bust. He could scrape her sequins with the buckle on his trousers, if he had a buckle. That's how funny-looking they are.

At closing time, the couples stand against the gable wall; women with their backs against the wall, the men leaning against them, both hands against the bricks, kissing. Snogging, we call it at school. I want to see Slapper snogging the bantam, I don't know why but I want to see what that looks like. I think he'd have to stand her on a beer barrel. I look for them, but they're never there at the gable wall. I wonder what it would be like to kiss Slapper, to have the tough, hard hands inside my dress and his mouth on my mouth. Ma puts her arm around my shoulders and leads me to the car, shielding out that world of romance and men and women touching.

The winters are dark here. I shiver from the chill behind the curtains, squat without touching the toilet seat. Downstairs, the paraffin oil heater throws shapes like tears onto the kitchen ceiling. Ma turns up the wick, making the shapes dance when Slapper comes in. I think of the way she turns up the oven when she puts the second loaf in. She braids my hair in two long plaits while I eat spaghetti hoops and a fried sausage. She wets her thumbs on her tongue, catching up the stray hairs. I listen to the suck of Slapper's pink mouth slurping tea, the cast-iron pot swinging on its hinge outside the window. I don't want to go to school.

I crack wafer ice on the puddles in the lane and smoke twigs until the bus comes, blow my breath out white. I bring home nits from school. Da holds me down with his farmer's grip while Ma douses my head with turpentine-smelling lotion. She pulls the comb along my scalp and catches the nits between the teeth and crushes them with a crunch beneath her thumbnail on the kitchen table saying, 'There, we've got him.'

The snow has come this Saturday. I have taken everything but the blinkers off the mare, left the men to pack the gear. I am riding her the whole way home to keep her in the stable until the weather improves. When the car passes me on the road, the mare whinnies and trots on after them, but soon we are left behind. Slapper's hand waves from the passenger window. Sometimes you'd think he was the Pope or somebody. The road is quiet, but the mare's ears are up. Then further on, I see three yearling colts leaning up against a field gate, waiting. I try to pull the mare to the far side of the road, but there's no bit in her mouth and it's impossible. She puts her nose to theirs, and squeals. I dismount. The colts have their willies out, the pink and black hoses almost reaching their girth lines. They snort and push the gate until I think it will fall over onto me. The mare kicks out with her hind leg and squats to piss on the road. I pull the reins down hard but she is oblivious to me now. Her snorts deepen and the colts bite each other, their mouths fast and open. They scrape the bars with their hooves. I throw stones at them and eventually they launch into a farting gallop down the field and back again, trotting inside the ditch beside the mare as I pull her home. I am afraid to mount her until I get well away from the colts, knowing she will canter back given the slightest chance.

When I reach home, Slapper's grey Escort is still parked in the yard. He comes out of the barn and reaches up and pulls me down into his arms.

'Are ya frozen, Peaches?' he says.

'She's horsing, Slapper!' My teeth chatter and my hands are stiff.

'Haw?'

'I'm not joking ya. Them colts nearly climbed over the gate to get at her.'

Slapper says nothing but smiles as he empties oats into her trough. We walk across the frozen mud towards the house. Pot Belly has made beef stew with the bone from the round steak sitting in the soup. Dumplings bobbing on the surface. Eugene's reading a book called *Seven Deadly Nights at the Edge of the Universe*. His eyebrows have grown together since the last time I looked at him. Pot Belly gives out and tells Slapper he's not to be going home in this weather. He is to stay the night and she'll not hear otherwise.

Upstairs, we make up the extra bed.

'I hope the shagger doesn't snore and keep me and Eugene up all night,' I say to put her off the track.

'Your mouth's getting worse, young lady. I'll have to have a word with Slapper about that.'

But she never would. She, like the rest of us, thought the sun shone out of Slapper's arse.

*

He doesn't know I'm watching. He stands where the slant of
blue light partitions the room. I am glad of the snow. Slapper
closes the door behind him and doesn't bother to open the
buttons on his shirt. Instead, he holds the back of his collar
and pulls it over his head. Unlike Eugene, he doesn't wear a
vest. There's hair all over his chest and more on his back. His
stomach is a plank of muscle. He slides the zip down, exposes
his legs, sits down, pulls the waistband down over his feet. I
imitate Eugene's breathing in the far bed. Slapper comes over
to my bed in his navy-blue underwear. He bends down and I
close my eye. His breath fans my face. I am just about to let
him kiss me when I hear the creak of the other bed.

His feet hang over the end of the mattress. I know by the
quiet that the snow is still coming down outside. The light
gets whiter. We are safe inside the drifts. Snowed in. Tucked
up. Perhaps the drifts will come and he will have to stay
another night.

'Are ya asleep, Slapper?'

'Haw?' For a long time he says nothing. 'It's a cold fucking
house.'

I go to him, wrapped in my blankets. I pull his bedclothes
down and get in, compounding our warmth. I lie up against
his back and breathe on the blond down of his neck. My hand
slides around his waist, feels his hard belly, wanders shyly
down through the curls of his pubic hair. I feel him stiffen. I
think of the colts. He moves to the edge of the mattress but
I follow him. When he turns over, his hands are cold. Big and
gentle and precise. 'Jesus, Peaches,' I hear him whisper as his
will subsides. Eugene's breathing is steady in the far bed and
I am thankful the bed does not creak.

Three feet of snow has fallen over Ireland, the wireless
says. I find a bonnet from an old Volkswagen and Slapper
and I spend the afternoon sliding down the top field, right
over the ditch, across the lane and into a nice curve in the
field below. The tracks gets a little longer every time, but
when we get off at the bottom and look back up, I cannot
resist doing it again. Slapper pulls the bonnet in one hand and

mine in the other and hardly says a word. Suddenly, I am somebody no one is supposed to know about.

I saddle the mare and take her the full circuit through the snow, down the lane and up past the bog-field. The moon brightens the dark sky like a fake sun, but the land is white. The world's turned upside-down. The evening is edged in blue like TV light. All the chainsaws have stopped. I listen to the puff of the mare's breath and her hooves compressing tracks along the snow. The smell of the pines is everywhere for the snow has bedded down all else. We have just eased into a canter along the car-road when she shies. A pheasant flutters out over the trees. Horses frighten easily at night. Especially when there's wind. I pull her up and listen. It may be deer. I dismount and lead the mare down between the trees. The ground is dry, the moss smooth underfoot, and the mare stumbles. It's black beneath the branches. And then I get the smell. The mare pulls on the reins. I stop and listen. The wind *pheews* through the treetops, like someone learning to whistle. We walk towards the smell and then I see the source. Slapper's boots are at eye-level. They are resting on nothing. As I draw closer, I see his face, his face is black and Christ, the smell. The wind spins him gently on the rope. I can't even cut him down. I leave him there, hanging in his own dung, and gallop home.

That was the hardest part, taking the others up there, letting them see him like that. The way they stood and looked and cursed and said Jaysus and Holy Mother of Divine Jaysus and What in the name of Jaysus would a fine fella like him go and do a thing like that for? and took their caps off and carried him down the hill on the bonnet of the Volkswagen we had used as a sled, my father's coat draped over his body. Eugene standing there looking at me like I did it. I was sorry I hadn't stayed longer with him there among the trees.

We come home from the wake and sit in the parlour. The room is like a second-hand furniture shop, the walls painted lime green, a border of faded roses creeping below the ceiling. Pot Belly produces a bottle of Bristol Cream from the sideboard and fills four glasses to the brim. The padlock on the yard gate beats its clasp, hammering down the silence of the room. My father watches the sparks lifting into the soot. Eugene has no nails to bite; they are bloody at the quick. When his eyes meet mine, they are full of accusation and blame. I am aware of my own breathing.

Pot Belly brings candles down out of the kitchen, white, blessed candles she got at Easter and lights them from my father's match. She stands them upright in their own grease and places them about the room. She takes a record from its sleeve and turns the light off. The room is lit by flame. On the mantelpiece stand trophies, silver-plated couples frozen in mid-swirl. They quiver in the firelight. The music starts. Pot Belly catches Eugene's hand and pulls him upright. He does not want to dance, but her tug is steady. I know what she is doing, and from my father's evasive eyes, that look he has when Ma is changing her dress, I know that something's going on, know my parents have spoken of this. They have it planned. Ma has always thought a man should know how to dance. The only flaw she could see in Slapper Jim was his leggy, graceless motion on the floor. She is teaching Eugene, as a precaution, as if him knowing these steps will carry him through, prevent him from tying a noose around his neck later on.

She begins the slow waltz and reluctantly he follows her, shifting his weight, his body stiff, his feet imitating hers. My father keeps his eyes on the fire. Pot Belly takes Eugene around the furniture whispering one-two-three, one-two-three until the music stops. The stylus crackles in the groove and the rhythm changes to a quick-step. Da stands up and pulls off his overcoat and takes my hand. The steel of his suspender digs into my side. The voice of a travelling woman clear and stern, pushes us together. Pot Belly counts the beats into Eugene's ear. One, one-two, one. We dance around each other, cautious of the space we're taking up. And then the song changes to a reel and there is nothing but the primitive *da-rum* of the bodhrán, the sound of wood pounding skin. *Da-rum. Da-rum.* The near screech of a fiddle, the pull of hair on string, the melodeon, the wheeze of bellows catching up, and the slight imprecision of the live instruments playing. We lift the furniture to the edge of the room, and I shake the Lux across the floor. We swig our drinks and exchange our partners. Eugene starts moving with the beat, throwing himself in time. Ma removes her shoes. A V of sweat darkens the back of my father's shirt. The music is raucous, ornamented. Our shadows are larger than we are, doubling our statures, bending us up onto the ceiling. It is two-facing-two. We face each other. Eugene jumps up and down like a highland dancer and although he does not know the moves, he has found the rhythm. We move him into the places he should go. First the ladies exchange places, then the men. We take the man facing us and go right for seven and back again. We swing our partners and begin over. The fire heats the room and I peel off my cardigan when the tune ends. Eugene and I gulp sherry. Ma gets the stand from the hair-drier and sings into it like it's a microphone. Eugene puts his hand up very high, imitating Foxy, sticks his belly out and we move around in circles.

'Do ya come here often?' he says.

'I do when the ewes aren't lambing.'

'Do ya live in a disadvantaged area?' He belches.

'Yeah, I get the subsidy.'

'God, you're lovely. There's nothing like the smell of a hogget ewe.'

He breathes me in with his sherry breath. We move with the squeal and squeeze of the uileann pipes, we are pulled in with the bellows. The quavering lilt and sway of a tin whistle curls through the darkness. The long swath of hair that covers Da's bald patch falls down and almost touches his shoulder. Ma pulls off her roll-on and swings it like a hula hoop on her index finger, keeping her left hand at her waist. The last picture I remember is the roll-on flying across the room with the snap of elastic and Eugene asking, 'Can I interest you in a snog at the gable wall?' as he swings me in a perfect twist.

Niall Williams

from *Four Letters of Love*

I SABEL WAS BORN on an island in the west.

When I thought of it later, adding the fragments she told to the ones I imagined, I would see her childhood like some fine cloth spun of sealight and sand, frayed and ribboned with beauty and grief. Hers was the place my boyhood eyes had pictured my father painting, hers the great expensive skies, the little stonewalled fields trapping the runaround summer breeze, the endlessly felt presence of the hushed or crashing sea. Looking up from running or skipping or chasing on the little white hoop of sand that was the eastern shore, Isabel would see the grey hulk of the edge of the country and wonder at the world that awaited her.

The island was small and quiet; it had no cars. From a little rough pier in the early mornings, fishing boats sailing on the slapping waters, dancing round the island and off into the sea of loneliness and rain, disappearing to the west towards the unseeable horizon of America where in the rising, falling waves the fish were netted and brought home.

With her brother she would cross the island sometimes after school. Their father was the Master and while he tidied the schoolroom or stopped in at Coman's for two short glasses of Irish whiskey, they would leave their schoolbags over a low place in a wall and walk off over the hill at the back of the houses. She was eleven, he was ten. Down the labyrinth of rough gravelled pathways where even bicycles would hardly travel, they made their way, across the cragged stretch of grey limestone to the western shore of rock and foaming sea. They walked to the island's edge, a sharp jut of high stone with a sudden drop to shiny black rocks the tide made vanish under the tumbling waters. The shoreline itself appeared and disappeared like magic below them as the waves crashed. There, they had a favourite place to play, a little sea-gallery of stone steps, levels, platforms. They were the King and Queen there. In the majestic hush and beauty of the land's end they could imagine themselves ruling a fabled kingdom of fiddlers and poets. Men like their father, women like their mother. They spoke in Irish, and in the spoken phrases of their game a little Gaelic world took life. Playing numerous parts for each other, they were now chieftains, now bards, now blacksmiths and bakers. Isabel danced on the high slab of rock to Sean's imaginary fiddle. They issued commands, and turned around to obey them. Sometimes, in the afternoons of early spring when sudden bounds of new life seemed to come at them across the surface of the sea, they would pretend they were invader and defender of their island, one grappling the other in mock fight, crying out to unseen armies of men and plundering the riches of the kingdom. Seabirds screamed in choruses overhead, and the fabulous light of the spring skies made a tapestry above them. Clouds white and fast were the sails of ships come to visit.

When Isabel danced on the rock's edge she felt the wind dance with her; she felt it touch her legs and run the danger through her. Her cheeks burned, her eyes fixed on the far sea and her hands down by her sides. In his squat position behind her, Sean sawed the pretend fiddle in perfect jigtime. He knew the tune well, had played it and dozens of others for gathered crowds in Coman's pub on Saturday nights. For he was one of those children, an ordinary-looking, freckled, round-nosed boy with ears like cup handles stuck to the sides of his head, by whose hands God seemed to play music. He played whatever he picked up, fiddle, whistle, flute, bodhran, banjo, spoons, and played each effortlessly well as he released the notes in the dead instrument and looked around him in mild bemusement at the dancing or gaping adults ringed around. For his sister, Isabel, he was happy to pretend and made himself giddy by changing the instruments he played as she was dancing. Now he was fiddling, next whistling, and so on through all the instruments without his losing the tune or Isabel the steps.

'Sean!' she shouted in mock annoyance, crossing the rock in her jig steps without looking at him. How she loved to dance, she thought, leaping on the grey edge of the Atlantic.

They played the game for an hour or so on those rocks above the sea. For a time Sean teased her. She was dancing farther back from the edge, he said.

'Is meatachan tusa,' he said, calling her a coward. The next tune he jigged he hurried the music out of time, going faster and faster, letting a little laugh break into the notes, shaking his head.

'Sean!' Isabel called as the music sped on and she tried to dance with it, crossing the edge of the bare rock back and forth like a tormented puppet, dancing as fast as he could play, on and on, back and forth, faster and faster until suddenly he stopped. She sighed, exhausted. What wonderful dancing! God, how she loved it. The silence swept up the cliffs over them and when she turned around she saw that he had taken a fit. His face was a sticky white, his eyes were gone back into his head and his whole body shook stiffly on the stone. At first she thought he was pretending, that it was some further facility he had developed, this wild horror, the stuff that was drooling from him. But when she reached her hand to touch his forehead her fingers knew; the illness came off on them, the filmy sweat of his disorder that she brought to her lips, then cried out.

It seemed forever, but was over in minutes. In minutes Sean's body had slumped back on the rock, limp and slimy as fish. His eyes had come back, returned from another world with a glassy expression. He gasped. He tried to talk and couldn't, and when at last he managed her name, it was a thick mumble, as if stuffed in his mouth was the useless lump of someone else's tongue.

Isabel lifted him. He was light and weak, the wind might

have carried him into the sea. Gulls had landed on the platform above them, watching, waiting for the rain that was about to fall. Now, as she ringed her arm around her brother and helped him make stumbling progress over the broken gravel track that led back across the island, the heavens opened. The rain came as it always came, travelling across the horizon in swift soft veils of water, joining the sea and sky in a seamless grey and curtaining the island from the world. It poured down on them. Sean walked shakily at his sister's side, making slow steps as if each was a separate new creation. They made their way home across the quiet of the island. They left their schoolbags in the puddled place by the wall and carried on to the house where their mother and father had begun to worry for them.

Off Isabel's arm, Sean flopped onto the flags of the kitchen floor. Margaret Gore cried out. She bent to help but her husband was there before her, picking up the boy and carrying him quickly from the kitchen to the bed. For a moment Isabel sat there, slumped and wet on the floor, the long mass of her dark hair tangling down across her face as her mother rushed over. What had happened? What in God's name had happened?

She was out of her clothes, wrapped in towels shivering before the fire. Her father had gone out into the rain to the post office to telephone the next island for the doctor. Her mother was sitting across from her at the fire, getting up and sitting down, going in and out of the boy's room where he lay lifeless in a stupor beneath the blankets. The rain lashed down. *What had happened? What had happened?* At eleven years of age, Isabel Gore had no idea. She stared into the fire as the boat bearing the doctor thrashed across the angry sea. She kept her face close to the flames until the heat began to burn her and she felt the pain, saying nothing at all, staring into the orange glow of the turf and thinking: I caused this. I've hurt my brother.

*

On the island of quietness, Isabel began to feel a prisoner of what she had done. Somehow, she felt, her dancing had been the cause of her brother's illness, and after each day's school she came home to his bedside. In the small damp bedroom Sean lay motionless beneath a great layering of woollen blankets, looking up into the clear white aftermath of his fit as if the world had suddenly been laid bare for him. The music was gone and he was as stilled and useless as an instrument laid aside, God gone to play on someone else. He took food with difficulty, dribbled watery mashed-up meals on to a baby's linen nappy about his chest, then lay back again into his deep drift of quiet, not noticing the little clusters of sorrow-faced men and women in wet coats and headscarfs who leaned in the bedroom door to look. Rumblings of rosaries and other players hovered over him.

Alone next to his bed, Isabel whispered in his ear. At first it was only: get well, Sean, feel better, or the words of her sorrow, 'Sean, ta aifeala orm.' But as the first weeks stretched into months, and it began to seem as if he would never recover himself again, she tried to offer him as recompense the whispered words of her secrets.

On a still blue September day, Muiris Gore took her by boat to the mainland to enrol in a boarding secondary school in Galway. Isabel had always known she would be leaving, and yet as the little ferry bounced across the water and the small walled fields of the island became a featureless grey hump in the distance, she felt banished. She sat on the bench at the side of the boat beside her father with the soft spray washing over them and a flock of gulls screaming in a trail behind. She clutched the handle of her bag, and wondered if she fell overboard would it float. After three sips from the flask in his coat pocket, her father warned her about the nuns. He spoke in English and told her to do the same.

'Issy,' he said, 'you'll be good, won't you? You'll show them up, you'll show them we know a thing or two. There'll be girls from the city there, and all over, but you'll be smarter and better than all of them.' He looked to the sea behind them. 'We're not ignorant or backward or stupid, Issy, remember. You'll be better than all of them.'

She couldn't look at him. She knew the patterns and rhythms of this speed already, had with all her classmates heard a hundred versions of it in the small green schoolroom where the map of Ireland hung on the wall. It was her father's main theme, the pride of their place and the unsurrenderable conviction of who they were when they ventured forth from the small intimacy of their world. She knew, and knew too that the whiskey and the journey were adding new emphasis. In a moment he might have stood up and stammered it out for the handful of other passengers, speaking with a kind of self-conscious careful deliberation until the swaying of the boat would topple him against the railing and over, stammering on into the sea.

When he looked at her she nodded. He did not say anything about Sean. From the day of the accident he had never quite known what to think. What had happened on that shelf of rock by the sea to rob his only son of speech and movement was still one of God's mysteries to him. In the first days afterwards he had sat in the kitchen and heard Isabel tell it over and over, how she had danced as she always danced, how Sean had sped the music in fun and she had kept with it, crossing the rock in front of him, leaping into the wind until the music suddenly stopped. For Muiris some clue was absent, and in his weaker moments in Coman's he had wept openly at his grief and frustration in being unable to understand it. For a time he thought it was a judgement on his vanity, his pride in his son, the gifted musician, the prodigy now lying gaggling and drooling in the songless bedroom where the window let in the low sounds of the sea. Was there not something more, something Isabel was not saying, he wondered sometimes. He looked down the classroom at her, he watched her walking home. How different she seemed from other girls. She had something wildly beautiful about her, a quality he took for pride and independence. She would be stubborn, he thought, like her mother, a woman who combined hasty fire and brutal common sense in such proportions that he had long abandoned debate with her. He was the Master. He was a man of substance on the island. To him, he imagined, fell the awesome responsibility of kneading, rolling and moulding the raw rough stuff of the island mind. He had read more books than anyone, including the priest. He could recite poems in Irish of a hundred lines and more, and often at weddings or wakes was called upon to deliver those late-night age-old verses that would still the house and make women cry. He loved himself for it. He had tried to give his children his love of poetry and song, their game at the island's edge he had all but showed them himself. Now, sitting on the boat crossing to Galway under the September sky, he looked at his daughter and flushed with terror and pride at what he might have created. She would be beautiful, he knew. Her eyes were already extraordinary, her hair was thick and dark, and she walked, even as a young girl, with her head upright and a certain aloneness in her stride. She was polite with him. She answered him in few words. But something in her face filled him with the feeling that she was full of secrets he would never penetrate.

To his wife this was nonsense. The girl was quiet, that's all. She had had a bad fright, she would be back to herself in a short while. Besides, Galway would change her, she had told her husband. The mainland changed all the island girls. They left as children and never came back quite the same. Their childhood was left on the island, and coming back they could only visit it anymore, she said, thumping the iron to her words while he sat saying nothing by the fire. Perhaps she should stay back another year in his school, he thought, but didn't say it. He knew what his wife's response would be. Besides, Isabel was quick and clever, and, even quiet and apart in her seat, she had been among the best in the class.

The brown suitcase had been taken down and packed while she slept. In the morning before the two passengers left for the ferry, Mrs Gore gave each of them fresh scones in paper bags in their pockets. She held her daughter to her tightly, holding her there against her so that Isabel could not see her face, nor how the tears kept falling and how the mother tilted up her head so that they might drop back silently and unseen into the great grieving wells of her eyes. For a moment, the girl's father stood beside them like a useless extra. His cap on his head, the suitcase in his hand, the lump of the scone bag in his coat pocket and the whiskey flask in the other, he seemed for a moment a figure entirely adrift, cut off from the massive closed circle of emotion that locked itself between mother and daughter's arms. He swallowed thickly and stared. Neither Isabel nor her mother had spoken a hundred words together about her leaving; it was he who had sat her opposite him in the parlour to talk, he who had walked alongside her across the white arc of sand in the summertime, telling her to think of Galway. Yet now, in this locked embrace without word or sound, Muiris Gore saw with amazement the hopeless inadequacy of the human mind to fathom the miracle of love. When Isabel let go of her mother, she turned to him and seemed at once to have lived ten years in as many instants. Her face was not wet with tears, those dark and extravagant eyes were not swollen or red, but somewhere there she wore the grief of her going and it became her like a black stole. One last time she asked to see Sean, and ran in through the house to his room. She was no more than a minute. He lay on his bed and took her kiss and the squeeze of her hand with a broken little wail of sound and a sweeping roll of his eyes. Into the cup of his ear, as always, she hummed the few notes of a tune, and then hurried back to where her father was waiting.

Out the door then, down the little stone path, and pulling open the small white iron gate that her father always said he must oil, out down the slope of the island to the pier. Three of their neighbours had seen them off. Two other girls were going to the nuns also. The Master would take them too. There was a flutter of Irish, the last sounds of the island and then the roar of the engine.

As the ferry bumped in against the wall of the mainland

Muiris Gore stirred himself out of his memories. His daughter was standing beside him watching as the man threw the knotted rope and tied it to its mooring. Gathering himself up and quickly summoning an air of authority and importance, Isabel's father placed his hand on her shoulder, faltered back a step with the rushing realization that the whiskey and nostalgia had unsteadied him, and stepped onto the mainland holding onto her as his buoy.

They sat down on the pier. The two other girls were giddy and light-headed with freedom. They stood and bumped against each other and giggled. Isabel, as always with her father, said nothing. She waited for the air to bring him back; she had seen him like this before and knew it was nothing. And yet, even as at last he stood right and smiled and led them off into the city where Isabel was to spend the next six years of her life, she had fortified even stronger in herself an idea of men, pale rhapsodical creatures, figures touched by God, with weak sickening bodies and musical, immortal souls.

Biographical Notes

JOHN BANVILLE was born in Wexford in 1945. His many acclaimed novels include *Doctor Copernicus*, *Kepler*, *The Newton Letters*, *Mefisto*, *The Book of Evidence* (which was shortlisted for the Booker Prize and received the GPA Award), *Ghosts* and *The Untouchable*.

LELAND BARDWELL was born in India of Irish parents in 1928. A poet and playwright, her novels include *Girl on a Bicycle*, *That London Winter* and *The House*. Joint editor of the Dublin literary magazine *Cyphers*, her latest collection of poetry is *The White Beach*, and her plays have included a musical life of Edith Piaf.

SEBASTIAN BARRY was born in Dublin in 1955 and travelled widely in Europe before returning to live in Dublin in 1985. A poet, his plays (frequently based on aspects of his family's past) include *Boss Grady's Boys* and *The Steward of Christendom*, and his novels include the experimental *The Engine of Owl-Light* and *The Whereabouts of Eneas McNulty*, his first novel in ten years, published in 1998.

MARY BECKETT was born in Ardoyne, Belfast, in 1926 and moved to Dublin in 1956, where she stopped writing for two decades while raising her family. Her work includes collections of stories, *A Belfast Woman* and *A Literary Woman*, a novel, *Give Them Stones*, and books for children.

SAMUEL BECKETT was born in Dublin in 1906 and died in Paris (where he lived since the 1930s) in 1989. One of the most important writers of the century, his novels include the trilogy *Molloy*, *Malone Dies* and *The Unnameable*. His plays include *Waiting for Godot*, *Krapp's Last Tape* and *Happy Days*. He received the Nobel Prize for Literature.

RONAN BENNETT was born in 1956 and brought up in Belfast. The author of three novels, *The Second Prison*, *Overthrown by Strangers* and *The Catastrophist*, he has also written extensively for television and film.

SARA BERKELEY was born in Dublin in 1967. Her first two collections of poetry, *Penn* and *Home Movie Nights*, and her début collection of stories, *The Swimmer in the Deep Blue Dream*, were published in

Ireland and Canada, and her third collection of poetry, *Facts About Water* (Bloodaxe Books/New Island Books), was published in 1994. Her first novel, *Shadowing Hannah*, was published by New Island Books, Dublin, in 1999. Since graduating from Trinity College, Dublin, she has lived and worked in London and America.

DERMOT BOLGER was born in Dublin in 1959. Poet, editor and publisher, his novels incude *The Journey Home*, *The Woman's Daughter*, *Emily's Shoes*, *A Second Life*, and *Father's Music*. He also edited and co-wrote the collaborative novel *Finbar's Hotel* and edited its sequel, *Ladies Night at Finbar's Hotel*. His plays include *The Lament for Arthur Cleary*, *Blinded by the Light* and *One Last Horse*.

CLARE BOYLAN was born in Dublin in 1948. A highly successful journalist and magazine editor before turning to fiction, her novels include *Holy Pictures*, *Black Baby*, *Room for a Single Lady* and *Last Resorts* and her short stories have been widely published and filmed for television. She has edited *The Agony and Ego*, a collection of literary essays, and compiled *The Literary Companion to Cats*. Her most recent novel is *Beloved Stranger*.

MAEVE BRENNAN was born in 1916 in Dublin. She moved to the United States in the 1930s and joined the *New Yorker*, where her stories appeared until she stopped writing, following a nervous breakdown, in 1973. She published two collections in America, in 1969 and 1974, and her work was finally published in Europe in 1999, six years after her death.

PHILIP CASEY was born in London to Irish parents in 1950 and brought up in Co. Wexford. He was best known as a poet, for such books as *The Year of the Knife: Poems 1980–1990*, before publishing two novels, *The Fabulists* (1994) and *The Water Star* (1999).

SHANE CONNAUGHTON was born in 1941 in Co. Cavan, where his father was the local sergeant, and was raised in a garda barracks. He worked as, among other things, an actor in Britain before the publication of his collection of stories, *A Border Station*, and his novel, *The Run of the Country* – both of which (like his film *The Playboys*) closely reflected his childhood, and especially the figure of his father. He co-wrote the screenplay for the Oscar-winning *My Left Foot*.

SEAMUS DEANE was born in Derry in 1940. He has published various works of criticism and poetry and is the general editor of the

Field Day Anthology of Irish Writing. Reading in the Dark is his first novel.

EMMA DONOGHUE was born in Dublin in 1969. She is the author of two novels, *Stir Fry* and *Hood,* and several plays, including *Ladies & Gentlemen.* Her non-fiction works include *Passions Between Ourselves: British Lesbian Culture 1668–1801.*

MARY DORCEY was born in Dublin in 1950 and, having lived in several countries, now lives in Ireland again. Her poetry collections include *Not Everybody Sees This Night, Moving Into the Space Cleared by Our Mothers* and *The River that Carries Me.* She has published collections of stories, including *A Noise in the Woodshed,* and one novel, *Biography of Desire.* She has received the Rooney Prize.

RODDY DOYLE was born in Dublin in 1958. His hugely popular trilogy of novels, *The Commitments, The Snapper* and the Booker shortlisted *The Van* (all successfully filmed) have been collected together as *The Barrystown Trilogy.* His other novels are *Paddy Clarke Ha Ha Ha,* which received the Booker Prize, *The Woman Who Walked into Doors* and, most recently, *A Star called Henry.* His television work includes *The Family* and his plays include *Brown Bread.*

ANNE ENRIGHT was born in Dublin in 1962. She worked in fringe theatre as an actress and producer, before moving to television where her production credits include the innovative Irish series *Night Hawks.* She has published a collection of stories, *The Portable Virgin,* which received the Rooney Prize, and two novels, including *The Wig My Father Wore.*

HUGO HAMILTON was born in Dublin in 1953 of a German mother and Irish father. He lived in Germany and Austria in the late seventies before returning to Dublin where he worked in the recording and publishing business. He has published five novels, *Surrogate City, The Last Shot, The Love Test, Headbanger* and *Sad Bastard,* and a collection of stories, *Dublin Where the Palm Trees Grow.* He has received the Rooney Prize.

ANNE HAVERTY'S first book was *An Independent Life,* a biography of Constance Markievicz. Her novel *One Day As A Tiger* won the Rooney Prize, was shortlisted for the Whitbread and was Ireland's entry in 1998 for Aristeion Prize. A collection of poems, *The Beauty of the Moon,* is a PBS recommendation. She lives in Dublin.

Biographical Notes

DERMOT HEALY was born in Co. Westmeath in 1947, lived in Cavan, where he edited the innovative *Drumlin* magazine, and now lives in Co. Sligo, where he edits *Force 10*. He wrote the screenplay for Cathal Black's study of the Christian Brothers, *Our Boys*, and has written for the stage. He has written one collection of stories, *Banished Misfortune*, and three novels, *Fighting with Shadows*, *A Goat's Song* and *Sudden Times*, published in 1999. He has also had poetry and translations published, and an autobiography, *The Bend for Home*.

AIDAN HIGGINS was born in Co. Kildare in 1927. His novels, which have been translated into many languages, include the famous 1966 *Langrishe Go Down*, *Balcony of Europe* and *Bornholm Night-Ferry*. He has also published collections of stories and of travel writing, and a memoir, *Donkey's Years*. He now lives in Kinsale, Co. Cork.

DESMOND HOGAN was born in Galway in 1951 and helped found the Irish Writers Co-op. His novels, which have sometimes received a hostile reception in Ireland, include *The Ikon Maker*, *The Leaves on Grey* and *A Curious Street*, and he is the author of several collections of short stories. He has travelled extensively and is based in London where – after a long silence – he published *The Edge of the City*, a collection of travel writing.

JENNIFER JOHNSTON was born in Dublin in 1930, the daughter of distinguished author and judge Denis Johnston and the Abbey actress Sheila Richards. Her many novels, which have frequently been filmed, include *The Captains and the Kings*, *How Many Miles to Babylon*, *The Old Jest*, *The Railway Station Man* and, most recently, *Two Moons*. A playwright, she now lives in Derry.

NEIL JORDAN was born in Sligo in 1951 and grew up in Dublin, where he helped found the Irish Writers Co-op. He worked with theatre groups and briefly as a musician. Although the author of one collection of stories, *Night in Tunisia*, and three novels, *The Past*, *The Dream of a Beast* and *Sunrise with Sea Monster*, he is best known for the films he has scripted and directed, such as *Company of Wolves*, *Mona Lisa*, *The Crying Game* – for which he received an Oscar – *Michael Collins* and his adaptation of Patrick McCabe's *The Butcher Boy*.

MOLLY KEANE was born in 1905 and died in 1996. She wrote many novels and comedies for the London stage from the 1930s onwards under the pen-name M. J. Farrell – writing, it is said, being considered unsuitable for a woman of her Anglo-Irish family and class. After a silence of decades she achieved acclaim again, under her own name, with *Good Behaviour* and *Time After Time* in 1981 and 1983.

CLAIRE KEEGAN was born in 1968 and grew up in County Wicklow. Her first collection of short stories, *Antarctica*, was published by Faber & Faber in 1999.

MAEVE KELLY was born in Dundalk in 1930. She qualified as a nurse in London, farmed with her husband, and is now administrator of the Limerick Centre for Abused Women and their Children. She has published two novels, *Necessary Treasons* and *Florrie's Girls*, two collections of stories and a volume of poetry.

BENEDICT KIELY was born in Tyrone in 1919. A journalist in the 1950s and 60s, since 1947 he has been publishing novels, including *The Cards of the Gambler*, *Dogs Enjoy the Morning*, *Proxopera* and *Nothing Happens in Carmincross*. His short story collections include *A Journey to the Seven Streams*. He appears frequently on Irish radio and television.

MARY LAVIN was born in Massachusetts in 1912. Most famous for her acclaimed stories in books like *Happiness and Other Stories* and *In the Middle of the Fields*, which have been collected together in three volumes, she is also the author of several novels. Her many awards include two Guggenheim Fellowships and the Katherine Mansfield Prize. She died in 1996.

MARY LELAND was born in Cork in 1941. She is the author of one novel, *The Killeen*, and a collection of stories, *Little Galloway Girls*.

ANTONIA LOGUE was born in Co. Derry in 1972 and brought up in Brussels. *Shadow Box*, her first novel, won the 1999 *Irish Times* Irish Literature Prize.

EUGENE McCABE was born in Glasgow in 1930 and now farms outside Clones in Co. Monaghan. His plays include *The King of the Castle* (which caused great controversy both when first staged in 1964 and later when filmed for Irish television) and *Gale Day*. He followed his début novel *Victims* with a powerful collection of stories, *Heritage* (1978), many of which were also filmed for television, and in 1992, after a long silence, produced the superb novel *Death and Nightingales*.

Tales from the Poorhouse was published in 1999 by the Gallery Press in Ireland.

PATRICK MCCABE was born in Clones, Co. Monoghan, in 1955. He is the author of six novels, including most recently *Breakfast on Pluto* and *Mondo Desperado*. His novel *The Butcher Boy* was the winner of the *Irish Times*/Aer Lingus Literature Prize and was shortlisted for the 1992 Booker Prize. His stage adaptation of this work, *Frank Pig Says Hello*, was a major success in the 1992 Dublin Festival and he co-wrote the screenplay for Neil Jordan's highly acclaimed film, *The Butcher Boy*.

COLUM MCCANN was born in Dublin in 1965. His first collection of stories, *Fishing the Sloe-Black River*, was published in 1994 and was awarded the Rooney Prize. His story, *Stolen Child*, won the Hennessy Award for Best Newcomer and Best Overall Story in 1990. He has had three novels published, *Songdogs*, *This Side of Brightness* and *Underground Snow*. He now divides his time between New York City and Dublin.

MIKE MCCORMACK was born in 1965 and now lives in the west of Ireland. He has published one collection of stories, *Getting It In The Head*, which received the Rooney Prize for Irish Literature, and one novel, *Crowe's Requiem*.

JOHN MCGAHERN was born in Dublin in 1935, and now writes and farms in Leitrim. His second novel, *The Dark*, caused intense controversy (and the loss of his job as a national teacher) before being banned in 1966. His other novels include *The Barracks*, *The Pornographer* and *Amongst Women* – which enjoyed phenomenal success in 1990. His play, *The Power of Darkness*, proved his work was still capable of attracting great discussion and debate when staged by the Abbey in 1991. He is the author of three collections of stories.

TOM MAC INTYRE was born in Cavan in 1931. A novelist and poet, he has produced a series of highly experimental plays over the past decade, including *The Great Hunger* and *The Bearded Lady*. He has also published a novel, short stories, poetry and translations from the Irish.

JOHN MACKENNA was born in Castledermot, Co. Kildare, in 1952. As well as being well known for his innovative radio documentaries, he has edited two books by the Quaker diarist, Mary Leadbeater, and written a play and a novel based around the life of John Clare. His has also written two collections of stories, *The Fallen* (which received the 1993 *Irish Times* Irish Literature Prize) and *A Year of Our Lives*, and two other novels, *The Last Fine Summer* and *A Haunted Heart*.

BLÁNAID McKINNEY was born in 1961 in Enniskillen, graduated from Queen's University Belfast in 1984 and currently lives in London. Her first collection of short stories, *Big Mouth*, will be published by Phoenix House in 2000.

BERNARD MacLAVERTY was born in Belfast, Northern Ireland, but has lived for many years in Scotland. An accomplished fiction writer, he is the author of the novels *Lamb* and *Cal* (both of which he adapted for screen and which were made into successful movies), as well as several collections of short stories, including *A Time to Dance* and *The Great Profundo*. His third novel, *Grace Notes*, was shortlisted for the Booker Prize.

BRYAN MacMAHON was born in Kerry in 1909, where he lived and taught until his retirement in Listowel. He died in 1997. Best known for his short stories in collections like *The End of the World* and *The Sound of Hooves*, he enjoyed huge success with his novel *Children of the Rainbow* in 1952, and also *The Honey Spike*, his novel and play of the same name. His autobiography, *The Master*, was an Irish bestseller. Poolbeg Press in Ireland have recently published *A Final Fling*.

EOIN McNAMEE was born in Kilkeel, Co. Down, in 1961. His poetry first appeared in *Raven Introductions*, and he is the author of two short novels, *The Last of Deeds* (short-listed for the *Irish Times*/Aer Lingus Literature Prize) and *Love in History*. His first full-length novel, *Resurrection Man*, was published in 1994 and was successfully made into a film. As well as prose, he has written screenplays. He received the Macaulay Fellowship.

DEIRDRE MADDEN was born in Toomebridge, Co. Antrim, in 1960. Married to the Irish poet Harry Clifton, she has lived for some years in Italy and most recently in France. Her five novels are *Hidden Symptoms*, *The Birds of Innocent Wood*, *Remembering Light and Stone*,

One by One in the Darkness and *Nothing is Black*. She has received the Rooney Prize and the Somerset Maugham Award.

AIDAN MATHEWS was born in Dublin in 1956. The author of two collections of stories, including *Adventures in a Bathyscope,* and two novels, *Muesli at Midnight* and *Lipstick on the Host,* he is also a poet with books like *Windfalls* and *According to the Small Hours*. His third novel, *Nora's Notebooks*, will be published by Jonathan Cape. His play *Exit-Entrance* was, in part, inspired by the twin suicides of Arthur Koestler and his wife.

GERARDINE MEANEY has published short stories in a variety of Irish and US journals and anthologies. She is also the author of *(Un)Like Subjects: Women, Theory, Fiction* (Routledge, 1993) and a principal editor of the forthcoming *Field Day Anthology of Irish Women's Writing*. She is currently Director of the Centre For Film Studies at University College Dublin.

BRIAN MOORE was born in Belfast in 1921 and died in Malibu, California, in 1999. In the aftermath of World War Two he worked as a reporter around Europe, before moving to Canada where he worked in a construction camp. His first novel, *The Lonely Passion of Judith Hearne*, was a huge success and was followed by eighteen others, the most recent being *The Magician's Wife*. He wrote screenplays and many of his books, like *Black Robes*, have been made into films.

MARY MORRISSY was born in Dublin, where she still lives, in 1957. Her stories have appeared widely in magazines and anthologies and her first collection, *A Lazy Eye*, was published in 1993. She has written a novel, *Mother of Pearl*, published in 1996.

VAL MULKERNS was born in Dublin in 1925. She released early novels in 1951 and 1954 while associate editor of the famous Dublin magazine *The Bell*. She resumed her publishing career in 1978 with a series of novels like *The Summerhouse* and *Very Like a Whale*, and story collections like *Antiquities* and *A Friend of Don Juan*.

ÉILÍS NÍ DHUIBHNE was born in Dublin in 1954 and works as a keeper in the National Library of Ireland and a lecturer in folklore. She has published collections of stories, including *Blood and Water, The Inland Ice* and *Eating Women is Not Recommended*, and two novels, *The Bray House* and *The Dancers Dancing*.

Biographical Notes

EDNA O'BRIEN was born in Clare in 1932. Her fame and (in 1960s Ireland) notoriety were immediate with the publication of her first novel, *The Country Girls*, in 1960. One of Ireland's most successful writers, she has since written many novels, including *Girls in Their Married Bliss*, *Night* and *Time and Tide*, as well as collections of stories. She has most recently written a biography of Joyce, and a novel, *Wild Decembers*.

MICHEÁL Ó CONGHAILE was born in 1962 in the Connemara Gaeltecht. He has published two collections of stories in Irish, *Mac an tSagairt* and *An Fear a Phléasc* and received, among other prizes, the Butler Literary Award.

BRIDGET O'CONNOR was born in London of Irish parents in 1961. Her first collection of stories, *Here Comes John*, was published in 1993. Her most recent collection is *Tell Her You Love Her*.

JOSEPH O'CONNOR was born in Dublin in 1963 and has lived in New York and London before returning to Dublin. His novels include *Cowboys and Indians*, *Desperadoes* and *The Salesman*. His best-selling non-fiction writings include *The Secret World of the Irish Male* and *The Irish Male at Home and Abroad*. A playwright, he has also published one collection of stories, *True Believers*.

SEAN O'FAOLAIN was born in Cork in 1900 and died in Dublin in 1990. The author of four novels, he is one of the acknowledged masters of the twentieth-century short story with books like *The Heat of the Sun* and *I Remember! I Remember!* He fought on the Republican side in the Irish Civil War, and later – as editor of *The Bell* from 1940–46 – fought against censorship and stagnation.

MICHAEL O'LOUGHLIN was born in Dublin in 1958 and lived for many years in Amsterdam. He has published many collections of poetry including *Another Nation*, and a collection of stories, *The Inside Story*, which has been published in Dutch translation. His first novel, *The Jewish Bride*, will be published by Picador.

DAVID PARK is the author of a volume of stories, *Oranges from Spain*, and three novels, *The Healing*, *The Rye Man* and *Stone Kingdoms*.

GLENN PATTERSON was born in Belfast in 1961. He is the author of four novels, *Burning Your Own*, *Fat Lad*, *Black Night at Big Thunder Mountain* and, most recently, *The International*.

Biographical Notes

KEITH RIDGWAY lives in Dublin. He has published two novels, *The Long Falling* and *Horses*, and his short stories have appeared in several anthologies.

FRANK RONAN was born in Co. Wexford in 1963 and has lived in France and England. His first novel, *The Man Who Loved Evelyn Cotton*, received the *Irish Times*/Aer Lingus Irish Literature Prize, and later novels include *A Picnic in Eden*, *The Better Angel*, *Dixie Chicken* and *Lovely*.

FRANCIS STUART was born in Australia in 1902. The author of more than twenty novels over a long and frequently controversial life, his most famous novel remains *Black List, Section H*, based in part on his imprisonment without charge by the French after spending the war years in Berlin lecturing and broadcasting as the citizen of a neutral country. Imprisoned for his part on the Republican side in the Irish Civil War, he briefly sprang to fame in the 1930s with his first novels *Pigeon Irish* and *The Coloured Dome*, and again immediately after the war with two novels written while a refugee, *Redemption* and *The Pillar of Cloud* (both reissued by New Island Books). After a long period of silence and neglect, *Black List, Section H* in 1971 began a late harvest of experimental novels.

EAMONN SWEENEY was born in Sligo in 1968 and has published two novels, *Waiting for the Healer* and *The Photograph*, plus a memoir of his family's lifelong support for Sligo Rovers, *There's Only One Red Army*.

COLM TÓIBÍN was born in Wexford in 1955. He proved a lively editor of *In Dublin* and *Magill* in the 1980s and his collected journalism has been published as *The Trial of the General*. His first novel, *The South*, was winner of the *Irish Times*/Aer Lingus Literature Prize in 1991 and was followed by *The Heather Blazing*, *The Story of the Night* and, most recently, *The Blackwater Lightship*. He is co-editor with Carmen Callil of *The Modern Library* and has published travel books, including *Walking Along the Border*, *Homage to Barcelona* and *The Sign of the Cross*.

WILLIAM TREVOR was born in Co. Cork in 1928. His many novels include *The Old Boys*, *Fools of Fortune*, *Reading Turgenev* and the recently published *Death in Summer*. His *Collected Stories* were published in 1992. He has written very extensively for radio and television, is the only author ever to win the Whitbread Prize twice, and has been shortlisted for the Booker Prize.

NIALL WILLIAMS was born in 1958 and lives in Co. Clare. A playwright, whose works include *The Way You Look Tonight*, he has published two novels, *Four Letters of Love* and *As it is in Heaven*.

ROBERT McLIAM WILSON was born in Belfast in 1964. A period of living rough in London provided the impetus for his award-winning début novel *Ripley Bogle*, which was followed by *Manfred's Pain*, *Eureka Street* and, recently, by *The Inflatable Citizen*. He is the co-author of a study of poverty, *The Dispossessed*, and now lives in Belfast.

Acknowledgements

Extract from *Mefisto* by John Banville, first published by Martin Secker & Warburg, 1986. Reprinted with the permission of Sheil Land Associates Ltd.

'The Hairdresser' by Leland Bardwell, from *Different Kinds of Love*, first published by Attic Press Ltd, 1987. Copyright © Leland Bardwell 1987. Reprinted with permission.

Extract from *The Engine of Owl-Light* by Sebastian Barry, first published by Carcanet, 1988. Copyright © Sebastian Barry 1988. Reprinted with the permission of Curtis Brown Ltd.

'Heaven' by Mary Beckett, from *A Literary Woman*, first published by Bloomsbury Publishing Ltd, 1990. Copyright © Mary Beckett 1990. Reprinted with the permission of Bloomsbury Publishing Ltd.

'For to End Yet Again' by Samuel Beckett from *Collected Shorter Prose 1945–1988*, published by Calder Publications Ltd, London. Copyright © this translation The Samuel Beckett Estate 1976, 1992. Reproduced by permission of The Samuel Beckett Estate and The Calder Educational Trust, London.

Extract from *The Catastrophist* by Ronan Bennett, first published by Review, 1998. Copyright © Ronan Bennett 1998. Reprinted with the permission of Headline Review.

'The Sky's Gone Out' by Sara Berkeley, from *The Swimmer in The Deep Blue Dream*, first published in Ireland by The Raven Arts Press and by Thistledown Press in Canada, 1991. Copyright © Sara Berkeley 1991. Reprinted with permission.

Extract from *The Journey Home* by Dermot Bolger, first published by Viking, 1990. Copyright © Dermot Bolger 1990. Reprinted with the permission of A. P. Watt Ltd.

'Villa Marta' by Clare Boylan, from *Concerning Virgins*, first published by Hamish Hamilton, 1989. Copyright © Clare Boylan 1989. Reprinted with permission of Rogers, Coleridge & White Ltd.

'The Springs of Affection' by Maeve Brennan, first published by Flamingo, 1999. Copyright © Maeve Brennan 1999. Reprinted with the permission of Flamingo, part of HarperCollins Publishers Ltd.

Extract from *The Water Star* by Philip Casey, first published by Picador, part of Pan Macmillan Ltd, 1999. Copyright © Philip Casey 1999. Reprinted with permission.

'Ojus' by Shane Connaughton, from *A Border Station*, first published by Hamish Hamilton 1989. Copyright © Shane Connaughton, 1989. Reprinted with permission of Penguin Books Ltd.

Acknowledgements

Extract from *Reading in the Dark* by Seamus Deane, first published by Jonathan Cape, 1966. Copyright © Seamus Deane 1996. Reprinted with the permission of Jonathan Cape Ltd.

Extract from *Hood* by Emma Donoghue, first published by Penguin, 1996. Copyright © Emma Donoghue 1966. Reprinted with the permission of Penguin Books Ltd.

'The Husband' by Mary Dorcey, from *A Noise From The Woodshed*, first published by Onlywomen Press, 1989. Copyright © Mary Dorcey 1989. Reprinted with permission.

Extract from *The Snapper* by Roddy Doyle, first published by Martin Secker & Warburg Ltd, 1990. Copyright © Roddy Doyle 1990. Reprinted with the permission of Martin Secker & Warburg Ltd.

'Men and Angels' by Anne Enright, from *The Portable Virgin*, first published by Martin Secker & Warburg. Reprinted with permission.

Extract from *Surrogate City* by Hugo Hamilton, first published by Faber & Faber, 1990. Copyright © Hugo Hamilton 1990. Reprinted with the permission of Faber & Faber Ltd.

Extract from *One Day as a Tiger* by Anne Haverty, first published by Chatto & Windus, 1996. Copyright © Anne Haverty 1996. Reprinted with the permission of Chatto & Windus Publishers.

'The Death of Matti Bonner' by Dermot Healy, from *A Goat's Song*, first published by Harvill, 1994, an imprint of HarperCollins. Copyright © Dermot Healy 1994. Reprinted with permission.

Balcony of Europe by Aidan Higgins, published by Calder & Boyars Ltd, London and Riverrun Press, New York. Copyright © Aidan Higgins 1972. Reproduced by permission of The Calder Educational Trust, London.

Extract from *A Curious Street* by Desmond Hogan, first published by Hamish Hamilton. Copyright © Desmond Hogan 1985. Reproduced by permission of Rogers, Coleridge & White Ltd, and Faber & Faber Ltd.

Extract from *The Christmas Tree* by Jennifer Johnston, first published by Hamish Hamilton. Copyright © Jennifer Johnston, 1981. Reprinted with permission.

Last Rites by Neil Jordan, first published by Co-op Books 1976, reprinted with the permission of Sheil Land Associates Ltd.

Extract from *Good Behaviour* by Molly Keane, first published by André Deutsch. Copyright © Molly Keane 1981. Reprinted with the permission of André Deutsch Ltd.

'The Ginger Rogers Sermon' by Claire Keegan, first published by Phoenix House, 1997. Copyright © Claire Keegan 1997. Reprinted with the permission of Curtis Brown Ltd.

Acknowledgements

'Orange Horses' by Maeve Kelly, from *Orange Horses*, first published in hardback in 1990 by Michael Joseph Ltd, first published in paperback by Blackstaff Press Ltd in 1991. Copyright © Maeve Kelly 1990. Reprinted with permission.

Extract from *Proxopera* by Benedict Kiely, first published by Victor Gollancz Ltd, 1977. Copyright © Benedict Kiely 1977. Reprinted with the permission of A. P. Watt Ltd.

'Happiness' by Mary Lavin, from *Happiness and Other Stories*, first published by Constable Publishers. Copyright © 1969. Reprinted with permission.

Extract from *The Killeen* by Mary Leland, first published by Hamish Hamilton, 1985. Copyright © Mary Leland 1985. Reproduced by permission of A. P. Watt Ltd on behalf of Mary Leland.

Extract from *Shadow Box* by Antonia Logue, first published by Bloomsbury, 1999. Copyright © Antonia Logue 1999. Reprinted with the permission of Bloomsbury Plc.

'Cancer' by Eugene McCabe, from *Heritage & Other Stories*, first published by Victor Gollancz Ltd, 1978. Copyright © Eugene McCabe 1978. Reprinted with permission of Victor Gollancz Ltd.

Extract from *The Butcher Boy* by Patrick McCabe, first published by Picador, part of Pan Macmillan Ltd. Copyright © Patrick McCabe 1992. Reprinted with permission.

'Through the Field' by Colum McCann, from *Fishing the Sloe-Black River*, first published by Phoenix, an imprint of Orion Publishing Group, 1994. Copyright © Colum McCann 1994. Reprinted with permission.

'Thomas Crumlesh 1960–1992: A Retrospective' by Mike McCormack, from *Getting It in the Head*, first published by Jonathan Cape, 1996. Copyright © Mike McCormack 1996. Reprinted with the permission of Jonathan Cape Ltd.

'High Ground' by John McGahern, from *High Ground & Other Stories*, first published by Faber & Faber Ltd. Copyright © 1985. Reprinted with permission.

'The Man-Keeper' from *The Word for Yes*, New and Selected Stories by Tom Mac Intyre, Copyright © Tom Mac Intyre 1991; with the permission of The Gallery Press.

'Absent Children' by John MacKenna, from *The Fallen & Other Stories*, first published by Blackstaff Press Ltd, 1992. Copyright © John MacKenna 1992. Reprinted with permission.

'The Outfielder, The Indian Giver' by Blánaid McKinney, first published by Phoenix House, 1998. Copyright © Blánaid McKinney. Reprinted with the permission of Curtis Brown Ltd.

'Between Two Shores' by Bernard MacLaverty, from *Secrets & Other Stories*, first published by Blackstaff Press Ltd, 1977. Copyright © Bernard Mac-Laverty 1977. Reprinted with permission.

Acknowledgements

'A Woman's Hair' by Bryan MacMahon, from *The Sound of Hooves*, first published by The Poolbeg Press, 1976. Copyright © Bryan MacMahon 1976. Reprinted with the permission of A. P. Watt Ltd.

'If Angels Had Wings' by Eoin McNamee, from *Raven Introductions 5*, first published by Raven Arts Press, 1988. Reprinted with the permission of Raven Arts Press.

Extract from *Remembering Light and Stone* by Deirdre Madden, first published by Faber & Faber Ltd. Reprinted with permission.

'Incident on the El Camino Real' by Aidan Mathews, from *Adventures in a Bathyscope*, first published by Martin Secker & Warburg, 1988. Copyright © Aidan Mathews 1988. Reprinted with permission.

'Counterpoints' by Gerardine Meaney, first published in *The Second Blackstaff Book of Stories*. Reprinted with the permission of Gerardine Meaney.

'The Sight' by Brian Moore, first published in *Irish Ghost Stories* edited by Joseph Hone, published by Hamish Hamilton, 1977. Reprinted with the permission of Curtis Brown Ltd.

'Divided Attention' by Mary Morrissy from *A Lazy Eye*, first published by Jonathan Cape Ltd, 1993. Copyright © Mary Morrissy 1993. Reprinted with permission.

'Memory And Desire' by Val Mulkerns, from *A Friend of Don Juan*, first published by John Murray (Publishers) Ltd, 1979. Copyright © Val Mulkerns 1979. Reprinted with the permission of John Murray (Publishers) Ltd.

'Blood And Water' by Éilís Ní Dhuibhne, from *Blood And Water & Other Stories*, first published by The Attic Press, 1988. Copyright © Éilís Ní Dhuibhne 1988. Reprinted with the permission of The Attic Press Ltd.

'What a Sky' from *Lantern Slides* by Edna O'Brien, first published by Weidenfeld & Nicolson, 1990. Reprinted with permission.

'Father' by Micheál Ó Conghaile, translated by Frank Sewell, from *An Fear a Phléasc*, first published by Cló Iar-Chonnachta, 1997, and *Fourfront*, 1988. Copyright © Micheál Ó Conghaile 1997. Copyright © translation Frank Sewell 1997. Reprinted with permission of the author and his agent Kimberley Witherspoon and Associates.

'Postcards' by Bridget O'Connor, from *Here Comes John*, published by Jonathan Cape Ltd, 1993. Reprinted with permission of Random House UK Ltd.

'Mothers Were All The Same' by Joseph O'Connor, from *True Believers*, first published by Sinclair Stevenson, 1991. Copyright © Joseph O'Connor 1991. Reprinted with permission.

'The Talking Trees' by Sean O'Faolain, from *The Talking Trees & Other Stories*, first published by Jonathan Cape Ltd, 1971. Reprinted with permission of Julia Martines.

Acknowledgements

'A Rock-'n'-Roll Death' by Michael O'Loughlin, from *The Inside Story*, first published by Raven Arts Press, 1989. Copyright © Michael O'Loughlin 1989. Reprinted with permission.

'Oranges From Spain' by David Park, from *Oranges From Spain*, first published by Jonathan Cape Ltd, 1988. Copyright © David Park 1988. Reprinted with the permission of Sheil Land Associates Ltd.

Extract from *Burning Your Own* by Glenn Patterson, first published by Chatto & Windus in 1988. Copyright © Glenn Patterson 1988. Reprinted with permission of Random House UK Ltd.

Extract from *The Long Falling* by Keith Ridgway, first published by Faber & Faber 1998. Copyright © Keith Ridgway 1998. Reprinted with the permission of Faber & Faber Ltd.

Extract from *Lovely* by Frank Ronan, first published by Sceptre, 1996. Copyright © Frank Ronan 1996. Reprinted with the permission of Sceptre.

Extract from *Black List, Section H* by Francis Stuart, first published by Southern Illinois University Press. Copyright © 1971. First published in Great Britain in 1973 by Martin Brian O'Keeffe Ltd. Reprinted with permission.

Extract from *Waiting for the Healer* by Eamonn Sweeney, first published by Picador, part of Pan Macmillan Ltd, 1998. Copyright © Eamonn Sweeney 1998. Reprinted with permission.

Extract from *The Heather Blazing* by Colm Tóibín, first published by Picador, part of Pan Macmillan Ltd, 1992. Copyright © Colm Tóibín 1992. Reprinted with permission.

'The Ballroom of Romance' by William Trevor, from *The Ballroom of Romance & Other Stories*, first published by The Bodley Head, 1972. Copyright © William Trevor 1972, and subsequently appeared in *The Collected Stories* by William Trevor, published by Viking 1992. Reprinted with the permission of John Johnson (Authors' Agents) Ltd.

Extract from *Four Letters of Love* by Niall Williams, first published by Picador, part of Pan Macmillan Ltd, 1997. Copyright © Niall Williams 1997. Reprinted with permission.

Extract from *Ripley Bogle* by Robert McLiam Wilson, first published by Blackstaff Press Ltd in Ireland and by André Deutsch Ltd in England in 1989. Copyright © Robert McLiam Wilson 1989. Reprinted with permission of André Deutsch Ltd.

Every effort has been made by the publishers to contact the copyright holders of the material published in this book but any omissions will be rectified at the earliest opportunity.

Thanks to Mr Evan Salholm, the Librarian at St Patrick's College, Drumcondra, and his staff for all their help and patience.